# THE HOS-BLETHAN AFFAIR

JOHN F. CARR
AND
WOLFGANG DIEHR

Pequod Press

**The Hos-Blethan Affair**
A Pequod Press Adventure Novel



First Edition

Manufactured in the United States of America

V 10 9 8 7 6 5 4 3 2

ISBN: 978-0-937912-63-8

On the cover: Alan Gutierrez, The Hos-Blethan Affair,
(*www.alangutierrez.com*)

Pequod Press
P.O. Box 80
Boalsburg, PA 16827
*www.PequodPress.com*

## Lord Kalvan Novels

by John F. Carr

*Great Kings' War (with Roland Green)*
*Kalvan Kingmaker*
*The Hos-Blethan Affair (with Wolfgang Diehr)*
*Siege of Tarr-Hostigos*
*The Fireseed Wars*
*Gunpowder God*

## Paratime Police Novels

by John F. Carr

*Time Crime (with H. Beam Piper)*

# DRAMATIS PERSONAE

## HOS-HOSTIGOS & ALLIES

**Aglos**—Fire Master of the temple-farm set up by Skranga.

**Andros**—Former royal petty-captain who becomes part of the Hos-Blethan Operation.

**Calthros**—Former Styphon's House underpriest who becomes instrumental in helping Skranga play Highpriest Sangar.

**Democriphon**—Colonel in charge of Hos-Blethan Operation. He later takes on the role of the Orphan Prince as Valthros.

**Valthros**—the name of the Orphan Prince of Hos-Bletha.

**Gasphros**—A former Hos-Blethan. Troubadour and scout for the expedition.

**Gycules**—Petty-Captain and a giant in both size and spirit.

**Kalvan**—Former Penn. State Trooper and Great King of Hos-Hostigos.

**Karthros**—Uncle Wolf. Prince Mythros' healer.

**Mardros**—High Reece of Mallegast.

**Myklon**—Hostigi Grand-Captain who joins the expedition. In charge of the faux Hostigi Styphon's Own Guard.

**Robinos**—Ranthar Jard in disguise.

**Rylla**—Great Queen of Hos-Hostigos, Kalvan's wife and co-ruler.

**Skranga**—Chief of Hostigos Intelligence. Undercover as Highpriest Sangar.

**Syros**—Uncle Wolf and becomes one of the expedition's leaders.

**Tylla**—Slave girl rescued by Gycules.

**Tyog**—Farm Master of Skranga's phony temple-farm.

**Vanir**—Former sharper who becomes one of the conspirators and Chief of Hos-Blethan Intelligence under Duke Skranga.

**Xylon**—Hostigi spy who has infiltrated Styphon's House as a Temple Guardsman.

**Yaholo**—Ruthani scout loyal to the Hostigi conspirators.

**Zentros**—Head of sharper band.

## PARATIMERS

**Baltrov Eldra**—University Professor and gadabout. Works for the Kalvan Study Team.

**Danthor Dras**—University Professor and expert on Styphon's House Subsector.

**Hadron Dalla**—Verkan Vall's wife and Paratime Police Chief's Special Assistant.

**Hadron Tharn**—Dalla's power mad younger brother.

**Ranthar Jard**—Paratime Police Inspector who works undercover for Kalvan as First Captain Ranthar and later as Robinos.

**Tanzla Rav**—Field Agent at the Blethan Town outpost.

**Tortha Karf**—Former Paratime Police Chief.

**Verkan Vall**—Paratime Police Chief.

## STYPHON'S HOUSE

**Anaxthenes**—Archpriest and Speaker for Styphon's Own Voice.

**Cimon**—Inner Circle Archpriest called the "Peasant Priest."

**Danthor**—Danthor Dras' undercover identity as Styphon's House Archpriest.

**Dracar**—Archpriest of Inner Circle and Roxthar's puppet.

**Lesthros**—the new Highpriest of Hos-Bletha.

**Neamenestros**—Archpriest and one of Anaxthenes' allies.

**Lysandros**—Newly enthroned Great King of Hos-Harphax.

**Prythames**—Archpriest of the Inner Circle and Highpriest of Hos-Bletha.

**Prythos**—First Level underworld spy passing as an Archpriest.

**Roxthar**—Holy Investigator and Torquemada of Styphon's House.

**Sesklos**—Supreme Priest of Styphon's House.

**Soton**—Grand Master of the Order of Zarthani Knights.

**Vuklos**—Head of Styphon's Own Guard sent to Hos-Bletha to restore order.

**Yagos**—Anaxthenes' Special Deputy and spy master.

**Xenophes**—High Marshal of the Styphon's House Temple Guard.

**Zemnos**—Archpriest and one of Anaxthenes' allies.

## HOS-BLETHA

**Archimanes**—Chancellor of Hos-Bletha.

**Althaphon**—Baron and old enemy of Gasphros.

**Basilron**—Blethan Prince of Syragon.

**Carthames**—Blethan Prince of Drathor.

**Kosklos**—Blethan Prince of Artigos.

**Lykron**—Captain-General of Hos-Bletha until sent to Balph.

**Mythros**—Blethan Prince of Pytha.

**Niclophon**—Great King of Hos-Bletha.

**Phidestros**—Former mercenary and Grand Captain-General of the Grand Host of Styphon's House.

**Theodoros**—Captain-General of the Hos-Blethan Royal Army.

**Vythron**—Blethan Prince of Taurnos.

## NEUTRALS

**Cleitharses**—Great King of Hos-Ktemnos.

**Demistophon**—Great King of Hos-Agrys.

**Phaedron**—Blethan Prince of Eythros.

**Ranjar Sargos**—Var-Wannax of the Sastragath.

**Selestros**—Son of former Great King Kaiphranos of Hos-Harphax.

**Sopharar**—Great King of Hos-Zygros.

**Xandros**—Blethan Prince of Zynophon.

Hostigos Town
Tigos Mountains
1. Ptosphes' Palace
2. Yirtta's Temple
3. High Temple Of Dralm
4. Hostigos Apothecary
5. Guild Hall
6. Galazar Shrine House
7. Royal Armory
8. Fynos Mill
9. Tranth's Hall
10. The Royal Hos-Hostgos Bank
11. Lytris Shrine
12. Saturday Market
13. Gull's Nest
14. Ptosphes' Almshouse
15. Royal Foundling House
16. Royal Army Barracks
17. Tranth's Temple
18. Red Halberd Inn
19. Silver Stag
N
Great Kings Highway
Ryphos Road
Priest's Crossing
Old Tigos Road
Lyssa Street
Market Street
Bear Creek Bridge
High Street
Prince Zythanes Road
Darro Creek
Cannos St
Axyon Street
Great Kings Highway

Tarr-Hostigos
Hostigos Gap
14
Xyth Street
15
Styh Street
Ivros Road
Thal Road
Market Street
16
Malthos Road
Coopers
Tanners Way

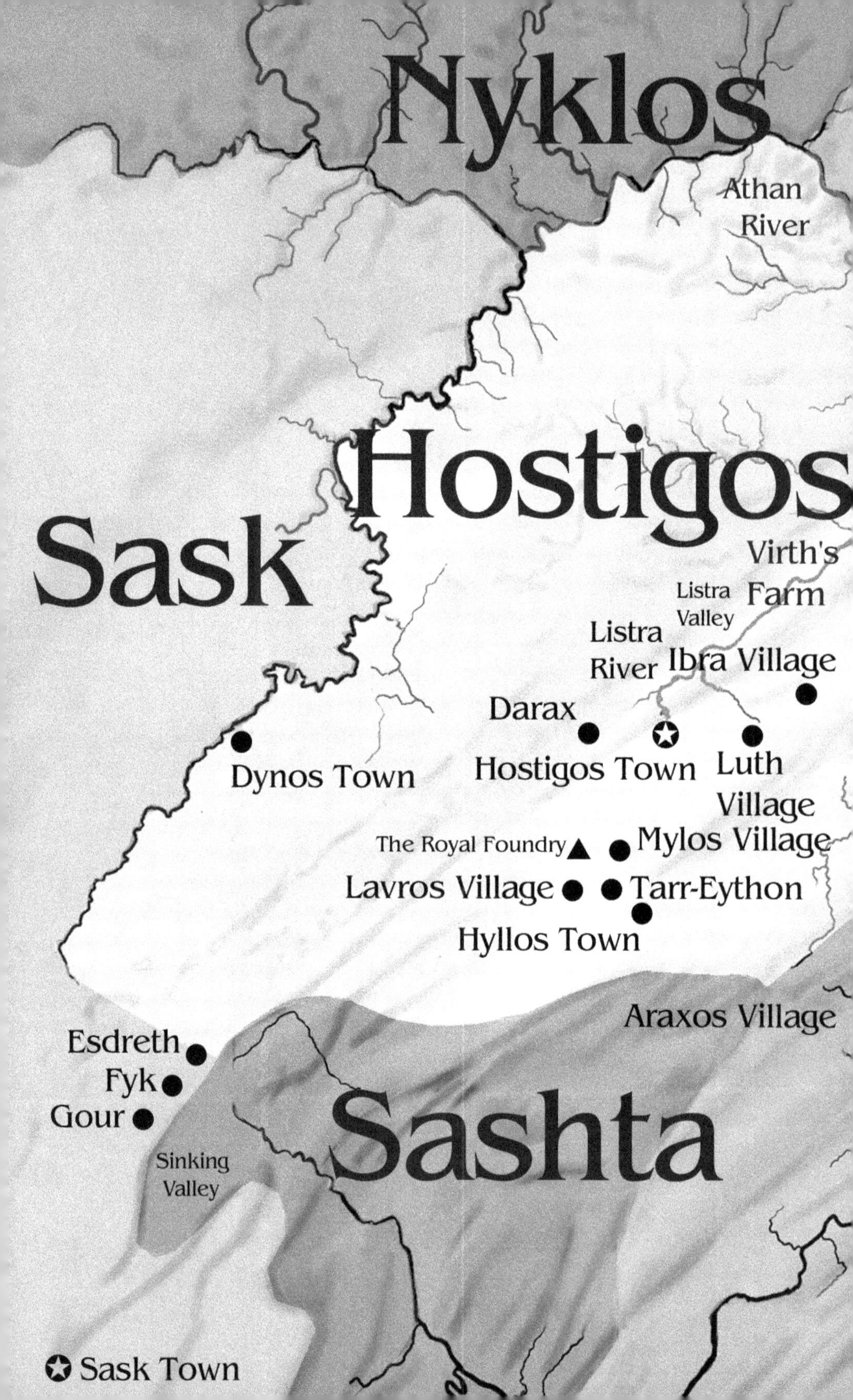
Nyklos
Athan River
Hostigos
Sask
Virth's Farm
Listra Valley
Listra River
Ibra Village
Darax
Dynos Town
Hostigos Town
Luth Village
The Royal Foundry
Mylos Village
Lavros Village
Tarr-Eython
Hyllos Town
Araxos Village
Esdreth
Fyk
Gour
Sashta
Sinking Valley
Sask Town

Nostor
Gorge River
Nirfd
Nostor Town
Narza Gap
Dyssa
Seven Hills Valley
Systos
Dombra Town
Listra Mouth
Fitra
Wolf Valley
Athan River
Ryx Village
Beshta
Harph River
N
Besh River
Hos-Harphax
Scale: 1" = 8 mi.
1" = 16 Marches

Pellor
Hassfryth Sea
Orchon Town
Orchon
Sea of Skirlos
Port Itya
Eubros Town
Varthon Town
Glarth Town
Varthon
Kryphlon
Sea of Aesklos
Alssa
Tarr Kendreth
Glarth
Eubros
Kryphlon City
H
Nyklos Town
Ulthor
Nyklos
Nostor
Nostor Town
Phaxos
Kyblos
Hostigos
Hostigos Town
Phaxos
Sask
Hos-Harphax
Greater Beshta
Thaphig
Pindar
Xanx

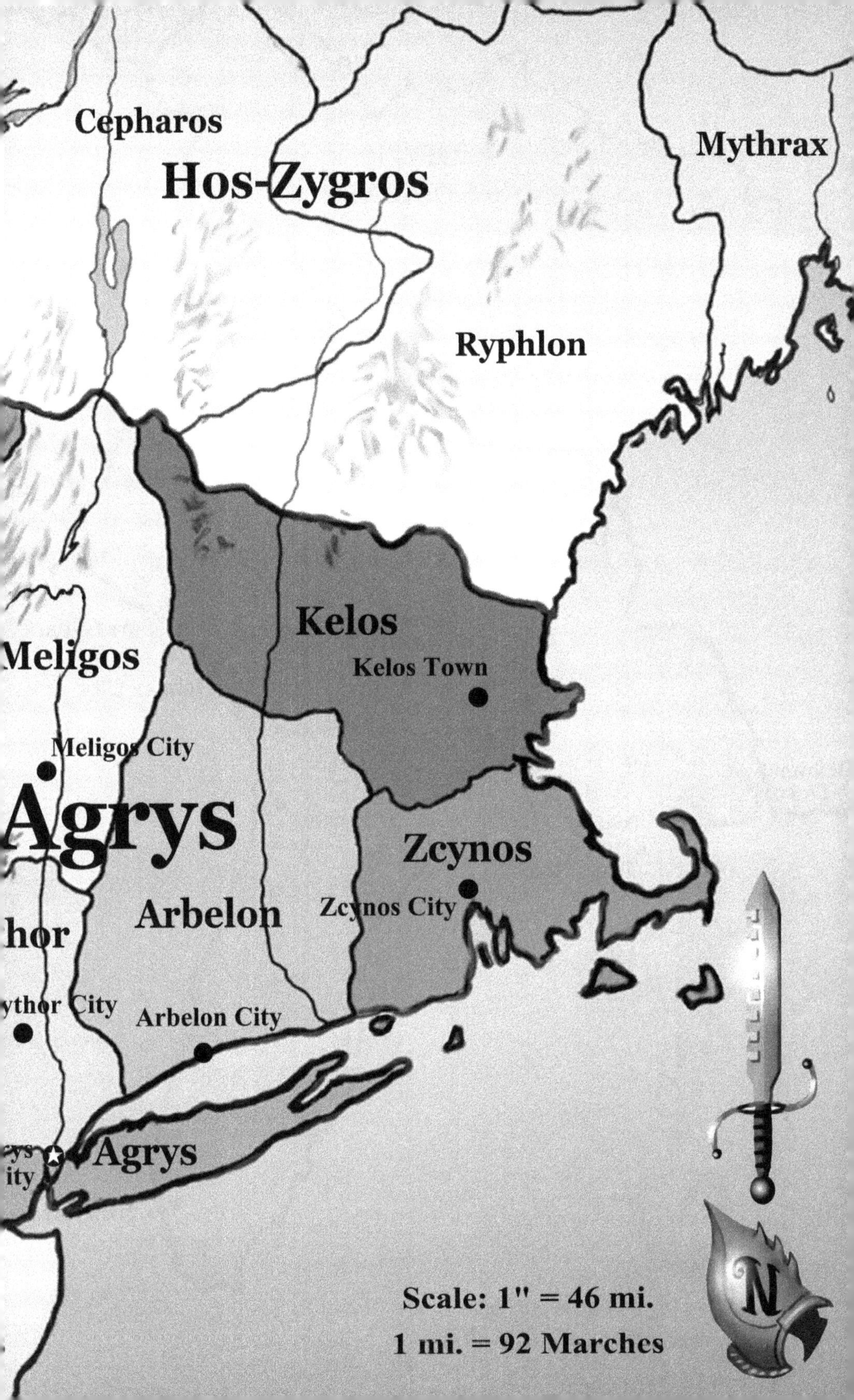

Cepharos
Hos-Zygros
Mythrax
Ryphlon
Kelos
Kelos Town
Meligos
Meligos City
Agrys
Zcynos
Zcynos City
Arbelon
hor
ythor City
Arbelon City
Agrys
Scale: 1" = 46 mi.
1 mi. = 92 Marches
N

UPPER
SASTRAGATH
Hos-Ktemn
LOWER
SASTRAGATH
Zynophon
Town
Artigos Town
ARTIGOS
Erygon
ZYNOPHON
Mathrax
Thanor
Hos-Bletha
TAURNOS
PYTHA
Bletha
Town
Port Gytha
Pytha
Town
Syragon Town
BLETHA
Dalthax City
Mallegast
SYRAGON
DRATHOR
Drathor
Town
Eythros
Town
Eryn
Town
EYTHROS
Clythros Town
N
Scale: 1" = 57 mi.
1" = 114 Marches

Hos-Zygros
Zygros City
Saltless Seas
Karphya
Vulthar City
Fryttander
Grefftscharr
Thagnor
Upper Middle Kingdoms
Morthron
Ulthor Port
Glarth City
Hos-Agrys
Hos-Hostigos
Dyssa
Lista River
Nostor Town
Hostigos Town
Hyllos Town
Beshta Town
Tarr-Beshta
Agrys City
Tenabra
Harphax City
Mrathos
Hos-Harphax
Trygath
Thebra City
Tarr-Ceros
Upper Sastragath
Hos-Ktemnos
Lower Sastragath
Hos-Ktemnos
Balph
Bletha Town
Dalthax City
Hos-Bletha
Eryn Town
Gythros Town
The Great Kingdoms
N
Scale: 1" = 200 mi.
1" = 400 Marches

# ACKNOWLEDGEMENTS

I would like to thank the following copyeditors, Victoria Alexander, Richard Oakley, Dennis Frank, Dwight Decker and David E. Williams for their proofreading and help in making this a better book.

## AUTHORS' NOTE

The *Hos-Blethan Affair* is the fourth volume in the Kalvan Saga, taking place after *Kalvan Kingmaker* and just before, as well as at the same time, as *Siege of Tarr-Hostigos*.

# PROLOGUE

Due to Investigator Roxthar's presence in Balph, Archpriest Anaxthenes and his allies were gathered at his own mansion where security could be guaranteed. Like most archpriests, Anaxthenes had formed his own private bodyguard. The Holy City was no longer secure: Supreme Priest Sesklos was losing control of the Inner Circle, while Roxthar and his teams of Investigators were roaming the city byways like wolves persecuting those thought not to be true believers of Styphon. Since there were few believers in the Holy City, Roxthar's Investigators had much to work with. Fortunately, they lacked the power to question the highpriests and archpriests, but everyone was aware that could change with Sesklos death or a reshuffling of the Inner Circle now that Archpriest Dracar and his bloc of archpriests were allied with Roxthar.

To avoid informants and agent-inquisitors, the conspirators were forced to meet in private homes in the fringes of the Holy City. The fact that they were at the pinnacle of Styphon's House's power structure was an irony that did not amuse the First Speaker.

Archpriest Zythos, newly elevated to the Inner Circle of Styphon's House, stared around the lavishly appointed Great Hall like some lackwit peasant boy.

*The thin reeds that I have to use as foundation timbers for our temple leave me in fear for the future of Styphon's House*, Anaxthenes fretted.

Zythos had bought his way into the Inner Circle with a donation of five hundred slaves and two hundred and fifty thousand ounces of gold. He had come to Balph as a Highpriest from the Princedom of Mythrax in Hos-Agrys to further his ambitions. According to the records provided to him by Highpriest Heraclestros, Zythos was the youngest son of a wealthy family who had blackmailed his oldest brother for half the patrimony when their father Duke Ryblos died. His father had owned one of the largest merchant fleets in Hos-Agrys and had been known to be as parsimonious as Balthar the Black.

Anaxthenes couldn't help but wonder about the nature of the ruinous information Zythos held over his older brother; it could be useful. For now, the real question was: could he trust him? If Anaxthenes wasn't in such desperate need of support, he would have never countenanced bringing Zythos to their most-secret conclave. However, with Roxthar clearly on the ascendancy within the Inner Circle, he needed all the allies he could find, bribe or coerce.

Neamenestros swore by his favorite concubine that the porcine Zythos was trustworthy and lived in fear of Roxthar's Investigation. Under questioning Zythos admitted he no more believed in Styphon's divinity, than he believed that Kalvan was a demi-god sent by Dralm to punish Styphon's House.

For some time, Anaxthenes' agents-inquisitory had been picking up rumors of Kalvan's supposed divinity, mostly from the lower orders, throughout the Five Kingdoms. Was that goat-faced Hostigi intelligencer, Duke Skranga, responsible for these rumors, or were they peasant inspired? *That needs checking into*, he decided.

When all the archpriests were seated at the big wooden trestle table at the center of the hall, his servant and loyal dogsbody Yagos served everyone a goblet of Ermut's Best, as the Hostigi called it. A wagonload of it had come into his hands by way of Prince Lysandros of Hos-Harphax, and he had grown fond of its taste and strong bite. It could even be said—although not outside these walls—that not everything Kalvan had brought to the Five Kingdoms was accursed, certainly not this powerful new drink.

When everyone had been served, Anaxthenes banged on the table with his dagger pommel to gain everyone's attention. There were eight of them altogether, not counting Yagos who didn't count for much.

"My fellow Archpriests, Styphon's House has never throughout its long history been as tested as it has this past winter. Not only did the Usurper defeat the Royal Army of Hos-Harphax and our other allies, but we now have Roxthar's mad dogs ravaging the Holy City."

There were nods from all the assembled archpriests.

"Styphon's Own Voice Sesklos is too weak to do anything to stop this madman and much of the Inner Circle is in his thrall."

Again heads shook in accord, although none dared mention that it was Anaxthenes' own plots and counterplots that were partly to blame for Sesklos' ineffective leadership.

"Dracar the Fearful cowers behind Roxthar's white robes in fear. Roxthar has extorted Sesklos' support for Dracar, and will attempt to elevate this milksop to the post of Supreme Priest upon Sesklos' death. We will have to hope that Supreme Priest Sesklos does not depart from this plain until after I return from Harphax City."

"Harphax City, Your Eminence, but why?" Neamenestros wheedled.

Anaxthenes had little love for the stick-like archpriest, but he was a stalwart follower and more avaricious than most and therefore firmly in his camp.

"Great King Kaiphranos—damn his eyes—is no longer of this world. And his eldest son was killed in battle, leaving only the Wastrel Selestros."

They all nodded. They were all familiar with the dynasty that had practically given Kalvan his own kingdom after providing only token opposition.

"Prince Lysandros, the only warrior in that line worthy of that accolade, has persuaded his nephew Selestros to forgo his patrimony, which never will be his since the Harphaxi Electors view the Wastrel with little more favor than they do Kalvan. I have to be in Harphax City to conduct Lysandros' enthronement and ensure that he does what we're paying him to do."

Zythos interrupted saying, "Where did you find this delectable beverage? I could use a barrel or two for my own cellar."

"Then you'll have to march to Hostigos," Anaxthenes replied. "This is Ermut's Best, a beverage made by the Usurper's vintners."

"Heresy," Lymachor whispered.

The other Archpriests laughed at his naiveté.

"Why leave now, Speaker, when Roxthar's ascendancy is growing?" Archpriest Zemnos asked. Zemnos was moon-faced but had piercingly dark eyes. He was not only one of the richest Archpriests in Balph, but among the most ambitious. His ambitions were not for power, but for more riches. He was allied with Anaxthenes because he believed that the Speaker was the only member of the Inner Circle who would ensure that outcome.

Anaxthenes nodded. Zemnos' question was one that deserved an answer. "Because, this is a battle, not only for the soul of the Temple, but for its future. We desperately need a champion in the north if we are to halt the Usurper's rise to power. Of all the contenders for the Iron Throne of Hos-Harphax, only Prince Lysandros has the military prowess and strength to oppose the Daemon Kalvan. We have aided his ascendency ever since the Usurper made his first conquests."

They all nodded. It was well-known that Styphon's House had loaned the Prince almost a million ounces of gold to solidify his candidacy as the new Great King. Most of that gold had been spent *buying* the support of several of the Princely Electors who would meet shortly in Harphax City to elect the new King. The gold had been well spent and—despite firm opposition—Lysandros appeared to have the election in hand.

"I have agreed with the expenditures," Neamenestros said. "But are you sure that he will win the Election? Many in Hos-Harphax oppose Lysandros' elevation to the Iron Throne for he is not beloved among either the commoners or the nobles."

"There is another candidate," Anaxthenes said. "Prince Soligon of Argros, former Great King Kaiphranos' cousin and brother-in-law, who is a known worshipper of Dralm and, unfortunately, is not in our debt. He has his supporters among the followers of the False God Dralm, and among those who fear we might use Lysandros to usurp the Kingdom of Hos-Harphax."

"Isn't this because many of the princes believe we are trying to purchase Lysandros' Election," Archpriest Zemnos asked rhetorically. "Therefore, it might be considered more politic, not to send one as elevated as Your Eminence to preside over Lysandros' enthronement, in the case that he is elected."

"Lysandros will be the next Great King of Hos-Harphax. We have spent enough gold to ensure his election; although this is not widely known—yet. However, Grand Master Soton and I have decided that it is more important to demonstrate to the surviving princes of Hos-Harphax that Styphon's House is willing to back the war against the Usurper Kalvan with not only our gold, but with our military might and full support of the Inner Circle. We are not going to win over our detractors so we will not even attempt to try. What we will demonstrate is our will and gold to the campaign of destroying the False Kingdom of Hos-Hostigos and killing its illicit leaders."

"But what about the Investigation?" Neamenestros squawked. "Roxthar's ambitions will know no bounds when he learns you are leaving for Hos-Harphax."

"He will not be able to increase his powers," Anaxthenes stated, "not without the full support of the Inner Circle. If you hold fast and refuse to grant him the power he seeks, he will have to curb his appetite and feast upon the underpriests. Hold firm and deny all his proclamations. The Grand Master and I will deal with him upon our return to Balph.

"However, if you fail in this, we will all suffer."

# ONE

## I

Kalvan looked down at the parchment sent to him by his Chief of Intelligence, Duke Skranga. He had spent the day with Master Ermut trying to explain the concept of a lens for the new telescopes, or farseers as Ermut called them. It was too late to return to Tarr-Hostigos, so he was running over some of the day's briefings. One of Skranga's moles at Tarr-Harphax had picked up a very interesting bit of information from a communiqué between Great King Lysandros and Great King Niclophon of Hos-Bletha. The Hos-Blethan King was promising to send five thousand regulars from the Royal Army and another six thousand irregulars, mostly light cavalry and javelin throwers, under the command of Captain-General Lykron to join the invasion of Hos-Hostigos in the spring. The troops and their mounts would be ferried by Styphon's Great Fleet directly to Port Naphros in Hos-Ktemnos and from there they would join the Grand Host.

Kalvan shook his head wearily and poured another shot of Ermut's Best into his new glass goblet, swirling the burgundy spirits around the glass before taking a draught. Suddenly the Styphon's House sponsored invasion force was beginning to live up to its billing as the Grand Host, as Great King Lysandros was calling it as he rallied his under lords. Captain-General Phidestros already had a sizeable Harphaxi force, five thousand cavalry and six thousand infantry, not counting the Harphax City Bands. If Great King Cleitharses sent the Sacred Squares and the other Princely squares, Kalvan could be facing another twelve to fifteen thousand Ktemnoi—next to the Hostigi the best man-for-man army in the Seven Kingdoms, or Eight counting the Sastragath under Wannax Sargos as a Great Kingdom, which it could become under Sargos' dynamic leadership. Kalvan could really use the sixty thousand nomads that had helped chase Grand Master Soton and his Knights back to Tarr-Ceros; unfortunately, they were all irregulars and couldn't be harnessed up and set aside for a rainy day. He had a feeling that Hos-Hostigos was going to be in the middle of a veritable manure storm come spring.

He needed a way to tie down those troops from Hos-Bletha, since there was nothing he could do short of an invasion of Hos-Ktemnos to keep the Sacred Squares out of the war. Maybe it was time to use some of the Confederate guerrilla tactics that his maternal great-grandfather, a former Confederate officer, used to tell him about as a lad. Winter was approaching and time was running short. Who could he send? Skranga had the brains; once he was given the mission he would improvise and make it work, if it could be done at all. However, he was no soldier. Kalvan needed a military advisor, but which one? Someone with leadership qualities, like Harmakros—but he needed Harmakros in Hostigos to fight the Styphoni.

If truth be known, Kalvan knew himself to be the perfect candidate to lead a popular uprising. With Verkan's help, they could have the Blethan countryside in such an uproar that it wouldn't subside for a decade! It would be fun too. A sojourn to Hos-Bletha would give him and Rylla some needed breathing room too but, sadly, without the Gods-Sent-Kalvan to depend upon, the Army of Hos-Hostigos would shrivel up and blow away. He was growing damned weary of the role of the indispensable man. Kalvan poured himself another slug of brandy.

Then it hit him like a flash: Colonel Democriphon. Democriphon was an excellent officer and tactician as long as it was an independent command, but balked at orders when part of a larger force. Yes, he would be an ideal officer for this kind of campaign, although like Custer before him, Democriphon suffered from a bad case of over-inflated ego. If he pulled this off and took some of the military pressure off Hostigos, he would be welcome to it.

It would be best to let Democriphon pick his own troops, too. Currently, the Colonel was commander of the Third Royal Regiment of Horse. However, he would be restricted to calivermen and pistoleers, no riflemen. Rifles would mark them as Hostigi right at the outset. Also, Democriphon needed some kind of cover story.

Kalvan needed more information about Hos-Bletha, but Skranga was back in Hostigos Town, and the only Blethan Kalvan knew was the troubadour Gasphros who was the University gadfly. For being untutored—although Kalvan suspected Gasphros' childhood station had been higher than the troubadour let on—he had the intuitive gift of making interesting connections and asking the right questions. Gasphros had proven to be an asset to the University—enough so that Kalvan had put him on salary as a 'roving' recruiter. Young people flocked after him like the Pied Piper.

Gasphros had also been one of Skranga's best operatives in Harphax City until the Duke's cover had been blown. He had been a fixture at Skranga's legendary soirées and had left, like Skranga, one step ahead of the local gendarmes.

Kalvan had given his man-servant Cleon permission to retire hours ago, so he went down the stairs into the kitchen where the best of the University's interdisciplinary work took place. He found Ermut in the midst of a deep discussion with Gasphros over the length of the copper condensing tubes for the new distillery that was being constructed on the outskirts of Hostigos Town. Already, the taverns and inns in town were ordering more brandy than Ermut could produce at the University's makeshift distillery. Kalvan, with a huge standing army to support, needed all the revenue he could squeeze—casks of brandy were selling for three times the price of winter wine.

Kalvan was tempted to start distilling corn mash, until he remembered the horror stories that occurred when cheap gin was distilled from grain and sold in England on the streets by the cupful—"drunk for a penny, dead drunk for two." Alcoholism had hit England's poor with the savagery of the Great Pox. Cheap distilled spirits from barley or corn would come along soon enough, with or without his help.

## II

"Gasphros, come into my study. I have some questions about Hos-Bletha I need answered."

Gasphros emptied his tankard of beer and pushed himself away from the table with his more than ample belly. "Yes, Your Majesty," he replied. It seemed that these days Kalvan was spending most of his time in the University; he had even moved into the old quarters of the former Baron who'd once owned the estate. Gasphros guessed it was warmer than the Great King's marriage bed. The chill that had swept through the Royal bedchamber had also blown through the Great Kingdom of Hos-Hostigos. It could prove fatal if unchecked since it provided "aid and comfort" to the enemy, as Kalvan would have put it in his own words.

"My information is badly out of date, but I'd be glad to share what I know with you, Your Majesty."

"Good," Kalvan said as he led the way up the staircase.

Gasphros was puffing by the time they reached the study. "I'm out of shape. It's time to go a-wandering again."

Kalvan smiled. "That's just what I had in mind."

Gasphros eyes peered out over his bearded cheeks and into Kalvan's own. Kalvan pointed to a chair, sat down behind his desk and pulled out a pouch of tobacco. Gasphros' long clay pipe was out and filled before Kalvan had time to reach for his own. They both lit up, using Kalvan's Name Day tinderbox, which was made of brass and in the shape of a cannon: a present from Rylla during better times.

Gasphros picked up the heavy tinderbox and examined it closely. “This is a remarkable piece of craftsmanship. It even has a real barrel.” Truth was he would like to have one for himself.

Kalvan pointed to the flintlock mechanism. “Reverse this and you’ve got a working pistol!” Kalvan reached over and reversed the flintlock to where it would flash into the touchhole of the tiny barrel.

“Amazing! Who was the artificer who made this?”

“Count Rogos, a friend of the family and a wonderful goldsmith. Rylla likes for me to shoot it off whenever we win a battle.” He pointed to the baseboard where there were two rows of tiny lead balls sunken into the wood. “Have to be careful of the load or it’ll put a hole in the wall.” He uncorked the stopper on the decanter of Ermut’s Best and asked, “Would you like a drink?”

“Certainly. If I didn’t take one, it would be the first one I’ve ever turned down, Your Majesty.” He wondered why the Great King was taking so long to get to the point of why he had called him in for a private consultation. *Is he going to interrogate me about Duke Skranga? I hope not; I still don’t know whether or not Skranga’s as crooked as the road leading up to Tarr-Hostigos, or just one step ahead of everyone else. I do know that he is the best agent-inquisitory I’ve ever run across.*

Kalvan nodded, then filled Gasphros’ goblet and his own. “From the intelligence reports from Harphax City, it appears that Styphon’s House is using every bit of influence it has to get all the soldiers in the Five Kingdoms into Hos-Harphax to fight against Hostigos.”

“You’ll tan their hides, Your Majesty! You always have before.” Even as the words came out of his mouth, Gasphros knew that he was just throwing bacon fat into the fire. From what he heard before leaving Harphax City, Great King Lysandros and his Styphon’s House allies were working on putting together the largest army ever seen in the Great Kingdoms. The Styphoni were even calling it the Grand Host of Styphon’s House.

The arrival of so many of Styphon’s agents-inquisitory had been one of the reasons why Duke Skranga had closed up their own shop in Harphax City and returned to Hostigos Town. The other had been the very likely election of Lysandros as Great King of Hos-Harphax. Skranga was astute enough to realize that under Lysandros rule there would be greater scrutiny of foreigners and people of questionable origins, like himself.

Kalvan bit down on his pipe stem. "This is going to be a bigger and tougher and more experienced army than anything we've faced."

"You mean the so-called Grand Host might even live up to its name?"

"Exactly. I just learned today that a sizable contingent of this army is set to arrive this spring from Hos-Bletha. Delivered to our back porch, lock, stock and barrel, by Styphon's Great Fleet. What I need to do is to pick your brain for knowledge about Hos-Bletha."

More of Skranga's work, Gasphros decided, exhaling heavily. Gasphros knew little about Bletha's current rulers, and none of their secrets. "Whew! Most of what I know is some fifteen winters past." He couldn't help but wonder what he knew that might help the King. He hadn't been back to his homeland in over five years, and that visit had been an unmitigated disaster. He had left with a broken heart and Baron Althaphon's agents on his trail.

Kalvan blew out a small cloud of smoke. "Understood."

"Your Majesty, I've spent most of my life traveling all over the Great Kingdoms, and I've learned that Hos-Bletha is completely unlike any of the other Five Kingdoms. Bletha was originally settled by colonists from Hos-Ktemnos around three hundred winters ago. Even today most of the Blethan nobility have links to the noble houses of Hos-Ktemnos. Bletha is also different in that there are large numbers of Ruthani living in the swamplands, which extend for many hundreds of marches to lands' end. We call it the Magaouisse Swamp. Only the Ruthani and a few outcast swampmen live in those lands of disease and mud.

"Even Bletha Town is not a true city like Harphax City or Agrys City, but a town the size of Hostigos Town. Because the lands are sparsely populated and the lords are accustomed to having their own way, the Great King of Bletha is a title little honored outside of the Princedom of Bletha. Several of the princes and major dukes believe they should be great king and have claims going back a century or more. These are a source of great friction and occasional rebellions. This independence also extends to the freemen themselves, many of whom consider themselves the equal of any noble."

Gasphros looked at Kalvan closely to see how he took to this notion. When he didn't react negatively to the idea, he continued. "This notion of independence among the commoners has long frustrated the Blethan nobility."

"It's an affliction that is common in the Cold Lands, as well."

Gasphros looked into his Great King's eyes. "Someday you will have to tell me more about your days in the Lands of the Gods."

Kalvan gave him a tight-lipped wry smile that told him there was very little chance of that ever happening.

Gasphros wondered why. *What is the Great King hiding? I don't believe in the gods, much less that Kalvan is one of Dralm's sons, or a demi-god, sent by the Allfather to foil Styphon's House, as the peasants believe. Yet, the Great King does carry an air of command and nobility that indicates he was someone of great importance in the Cold Lands. If so, why had he fled them, or had he been exiled? Too many questions, too few answers,* he decided. *Maybe someday another exile from the Cold Lands will arrive and be less withholding of his origins.*

"From what I hear," Kalvan continued, "Great King Niclophon is a puppet of Styphon's House. Hos-Ktemnos, at Supreme Priest Sesklos' bidding, has been importing mercenaries to enforce his rule. There have been two rebellions that I've heard about in the last ten winters."

Gasphros nodded. "From what I've heard, mostly gossip, Niclophon does not sit too firmly on the Silver Throne. There have been questions about how the former Great King Marocles and Queen Delra died. Their infant son, Prince Valthros, is still missing, but assumed to be dead. Some blame Niclophon for their deaths."

Kalvan's eyebrows rose, as though he had heard the same rumors. "Maybe we can use that," he said, thinking of Boris Godunov and the three False Dmitrys that appeared after the death of Ivan the Terrible. The First False Dmitry was supported by Polish noblemen and boyars unhappy with Godunov's reign. He not only unsettled the regime, but was made Tsar.

"How, Your Majesty?"

"By planting false rumors and using the infant's name as a cover."

Gasphros smiled "Yes, which could sow confusion among the enemy. There have long been questions about Niclophon's sudden rise to the Silver Throne."

"Good. Do you still have friends in Hos-Bletha?"

Gasphros snorted. *I wish*, he thought, thinking of a certain lady. "None that I've heard from in five years. I get my information from merchants and peddlers."

"So no one would recognize you if you were to return?"

"Not anymore." This time there was a note of sadness in his voice. *My parents are surely dead by now and my kin will have forgotten me. As far as Marisol was concerned, she was certainly married and a mother by now.* "Why, Your Majesty?"

"I want you to help head up an operation to neutralize the Hos-Blethan Army."

"ME?!"

"Yes, you're the only man in Hostigos who knows anything about Hos-Bletha or Blethan politics. Of course, you'll have plenty of help. I want to bring about an insurrection within Hos-Bletha that will force Great King Niclophon to recall his troops from the Holy Host."

"Is that all?" *Kalvan must be mad if he expects me to head up a rebellion. I know nothing of arms and armies.*

"For now, yes."

"By myself?" he asked, nervously lighting up his pipe. He drew a lungful of tobacco smoke and suddenly began coughing.

Kalvan smiled at him as if he were feeble-minded. "No, of course not. Duke Skranga will head up the Hos-Blethan Affair. You will be his guide and helpmate. He's told me that the two of you work together well." The Great King looked at him with his piercing gray eyes, as though he could read through the bone and into his mind.

Gasphros gulped. "Yes, Your Majesty. The Duke has a wonderfully complex way of viewing the world and does well when challenged—especially with the impossible. I know of no one else who could have placed several spies within Balph itself."

Kalvan nodded. "Unfortunately, they're not yet in a place to be very useful. With the gods help, this war against Styphon's House will be over before that time arrives."

"May the Allfather grant us that boon," he replied, with more fervor than he expected. *Maybe I'm just like all the rest of the fools; waiting for a gods given miracle.*

"I will also provide a military leader. I don't expect you or the Duke to plan the campaign itself."

*Praise Dralm*, Gasphros thought. "There's a small trading party in Hostigos Town from Bletha. I'll arrange to meet them tonight and see what information I can obtain."

Kalvan smiled and he felt his spirits lift. "I knew I could depend on you. Successful or not, there will be a barony waiting for you upon your return."

"Thank you, Your Majesty," he replied. *For the first time in fifteen years, I may actually have a home to call my own.* He liked the feeling that gave him. The only problem was that they would have to travel through hostile territory for two thousand marches to get to Hos-Bletha. Once there, foment a rebellion forcing Great King Niclophon to keep his troops sequestered within Hos-Bletha and, while doing this, somehow survive until the war against Styphon's House was over. *No small thing....*

# TWO

## I

Colonel Democriphon knew he had a reputation for having both a lightning-quick temper and acting rashly on the field of battle. His bad temper was both a curse and a blessing. For one, it made him a fearless warrior, but it also unnecessarily put his life in danger. Something that Great King Kalvan had reminded him about on more than one occasion. *Is that why he removed me from my command of Tarr-Veblos and put Captain-General Hestophes in change?* he wondered. *Is Kalvan afraid that I might attack the Harphaxi if provoked?*

Two winters ago he would have taken great umbrage at that thought and sulked—even given his Great King a piece of his mind. Now, he waited quietly outside Kalvan's office at the University of Hos-Hostigos. He rose up when Cleon, the Great King's personal servant, ushered him into Kalvan's office.

Upon entering, Democriphon bowed, saying, "Your Majesty, I'm here at your command."

The Great King, looking distracted,

pointed to a high-backed wooden chair. "Please, have a seat, Colonel."

He sat down and waited for Kalvan to speak.

"I've got an important mission, and I'm wondering if you're the right man for the job."

Democriphon couldn't frame an answer to that question so he locked his jaw to keep his tongue from blurting out the wrong words.

The Great King appeared satisfied with his nonresponse. "It's an independent command in a distant kingdom. Would you be interested in such a position?"

*Is Kalvan trying to shuffle me into an inferior position or is he granting me an important command?* "I would need more information before making an informed decision, Your Majesty."

"Good," Kalvan replied. "The situation is thus: one of our intelligence sources has informed us that Great King Niclophon of Hos-Bletha will be sending over ten thousand soldiers to reinforce the Hos-Harphax army and the soldiers of Styphon's House gathered at Harphax City. I would prefer that they remain in Hos-Bletha. To such an end, I am assembling a party of individuals, under the auspices of Duke Skranga, to foment a rebellion or revolt such that Great King Niclophon will find it impossible to honor his agreements with Styphon's House. Is that clear?"

"Yes, Your Majesty," Democriphon replied. *An independent command,* he pondered, *one where I do not have to answer to a higher military authority.* He knew Skranga well and while there was no one better at the intelligence business, he was not a leader of men—certainly not of soldiers. This meant Skranga would be their leader in name only. This might be the very opportunity he had been searching for his entire military career. He would never outshine Captain-General Harmakros, Captain-General Hestophes or even the Greffan, Colonel Verkan—not as long as he stayed in Hos-Hostigos.

In Hos-Bletha he just might be able to establish his place in the sun. "I am interested in this opportunity, Your Majesty. What are my orders and who will be my subordinates?"

Kalvan nodded as though pleased with his reply. He stood up, turned around, taking his pipe out of his mouth and pointed to a place near the bottom of the large deerskin map of the Six Kingdoms behind his desk. "First of all, you're going to have to go here to Hos-Bletha. That means travelling through Hos-Ktemnos, the center of Styphon's House's power.

"Duke Skranga will be in charge and the troubadour, Gasphros, will be your guide. He was born in Hos-Bletha and knows more about that kingdom than anyone else in Hostigos. I will be sending along two companies of soldiers, most of whom were former Blethan mercenaries who've sworn an oath to the Royal Army of Hos-Hostigos. I will also be providing a large chest of gold to help you purchase the help you will need after you arrive in Hos-Bletha. Once there, how the operation is mounted and carried out will be up to you and Duke Skranga."

"I am sure we will be able to work together," Democriphon declared.

"Good," Kalvan said with an air of finality. "I need you to pull this off, Colonel. Hos-Hostigos needs you to keep the Blethans out of the war. Now, I want you to meet with Skranga and Gasphros and figure out what you need to take with you and come up with some ideas of what you will do once you arrive."

## II

Duke Skranga had been lucky to get out of Harphax City with his intelligence ring just before Great King Kaiphranos died. In one fell swoop, an incompetent ruler had been replaced by a totally ruthless one, First Prince Lysandros—soon to be Great King of Hos-Harphax. If the rumors were true—and he believed them—Lysandros had poisoned his older brother with Styphon's House's backing. The Temple wanted a great king who was in their pocket and one who was not afraid to press the war against Kalvan; they had both in Prince Lysandros.

Duke Skranga was not a member of the nobility by birth. Far from it. While on a mission for Lord Kalvan in Nostor he had been elevated to a duke after sharing the secret of fireseed with Prince Gormoth. Later, after the armies of Nostor had been defeated by the Hostigi, Gormoth died under suspicious circumstances. Many thought Duke Skranga might have played a part in Gormoth's death, but he never admitted to it, nor even intimated he had knowledge of the matter.

In truth, Skranga had been born to the house of a Balph wine merchant. While far from wealthy, Skranga's family had been comfortable and wanted for little. Then Skranga's father, Perstros, agreed to fill a wine order for another merchant who was supplying libations to Styphon's House. The order had been a large one and had to be filled in advance of payment. Perstros put everything he had into meeting the order only to lose everything when the merchant he supplied died before remitting compensation.

The strain of trying to rebuild the business afterwards proved fatal to Perstros and the job of supporting the family fell to Skranga. With no money or even a good reputation in business, Skranga quickly moved outside the normal boundaries of the law to meet his obligations. He first turned to banditry then ran a small black market scheme dealing in anything he could lay his hands on. Skranga was close to reopening his father's wine shop when his mother succumbed to a stroke and passed shortly after.

With nothing left to hold him in Balph, Skranga left the city, moved to Agrys and turned to other enterprises: horse theft, loan sharking, pawn broking, con games and occasionally banditry. He was good at everything he turned his mind to and had amassed a tidy sum of gold while staying two steps ahead of the law. When he decided he had enough to tide him over, Skranga shifted his sights to more legal schemes, though he wasn't above brokering an occasional criminal venture when the price was right.

He was a horse-trader when he came to the attention of Lord Kalvan of Hostigos. Skranga had sold his entire supply of Trygathi horses in Hostigos when he learned that due to the coming war he would not be allowed to leave. Hostigos had closed its borders; anyone could enter, none could leave. Not wanting to live off of his profits until the borders reopened, he took a job at the newly created Hostigos Fireseed Works.

Normally, such manual labor was beneath his dignity, but the advantages of learning how to make fireseed was not lost on him. Skranga learned all he could about its manufacture in hopes of returning to Agrys to start his own fireseed works, making and selling fireseed on the black market. Kalvan's fireseed was far superior to Styphon's fireseed and he knew he could make a fortune.

Skranga was badly frightened when Lord Kalvan had him summoned after his shift one day, fearing that the strange Coldlander found out about his plans through sorcerous means. He had felt as if the then Lord Kalvan was somehow looking through him, as if he could see everything in his past. It made him nervous to say the least since the common belief was that Kalvan had been sent by Dralm and possessed otherworldly knowledge. Skranga was afraid that Kalvan knew of his plans and would have his head taken off until he was offered a very strange assignment: Skranga was to go to Prince Gormoth in Nostor and *give* him the secret of fireseed!

Kalvan explained that giving Gormoth the fireseed secret would make him an enemy of Styphon's House. That would cost Gormoth Styphoni support and even the playing field in the coming battle. Skranga quickly accepted and went to Nostor.

Gormoth immediately had Skranga imprisoned, for his own protection, until he could prove he knew how to make real fireseed without Styphon's House's help. That done, Skranga was instantly jumped up to a duke by the Nostori prince and given sufficient land to support his new title. Only Gormoth had been his superior in all of Nostor. Then Count Pheblon, Gormoth's cousin, had the Prince assassinated. The newly crowned Prince Pheblon had given Skranga a choice: join the conspiracy and keep his title—or die.

He still felt bad that he had lied to Kalvan about not knowing Gormoth's assassins, but it had all worked out. Especially when the Great King had made him Chief of Hos-Hostigos Intelligence. From that point on, he vowed that wherever Lord Kalvan would lead, Duke Skranga would follow. Skranga was quick to know a good thing when he saw it. Serving Lord Kalvan had already given him greater wealth and prestige than all of his previous schemes combined.

So when Great King Kalvan tasked Duke Skranga with stirring up trouble in Hos-Bletha for the sole purpose of keeping the Blethans out of the Fireseed Wars, he was at first a bit leery. Trouble was something the duke sought to avoid most of his life. Trouble was not profitable and could lead to losing one's head. Still, Kalvan had never steered him wrong and almost every mission he worked for the Great King had increased his personal holdings in one way or another.

Even this new assignment, which Great King Kalvan called the Hos-Blethan Affair, appeared to be both dangerous and somewhat futile; regardless, he would do his best. If nothing else, it might well provide numerous opportunities to enrich his holdings and wealth. *A whole Kingdom to pillage, not too bad for a former sharper and bone-raker!*

## III

Ranthar Jard waded through pools of muddy water as he made his way to the Royal Foundry. The Foundry was busy and the sound of hammers smashing steel on forges the size of huge tree stumps buffeted his ears. In a small alcove at the back of the building, he went over to the collapsed-nickel door. After making sure he wasn't being observed by any of the local workers, he entered the proper code. The door whooshed open and he walked down the stairway to the basement below.

There he found Verkan Vall sitting at his desk with his boots up, cleaning his flintlock hideaway pistol. Thanks to the collapsed-nickel ceiling it was quiet inside the basement: no banging of anvils or endless chatter of Kalvan Study Team intellectuals.

Ranthar's eyes automatically went straight to the wall visiplate which displayed a close-up of Tarr-Hostigos, from the sky-eye above Hostigos Town, showing dozens of carts and flatbed wagons full of provisions and weapons snaking their way up the hills back and forth on the switchbacks to the outer bailey. The rainy season was in full drizzle, but that hadn't stopped the stream of foodstuffs and tools of war from flowing into the castle. The Royal Foundry was working night and day to turn out more big guns. The cobblestone streets of Hostigos Town were so filled with wagons a pedestrian wasn't safe on the streets, night or day.

When he caught the Chief's eye, Verkan rose to his feet and they clasped shoulders.

Ranthar saw Verkan checking out his face. "What happened to you: A cat fight?" he asked.

Ranthar winced. "In a manner of speaking. I got between Scholar Lala and Baltrov Eldra in the middle of their argument over Kalvan's decision to teach the Ruthani orphans 'male pattern bonding and archaic aggressive male behavior patterns' and Professor Baltrov Eldra's rebuttal, which included a detailed description of Sastragathi slave laws. When Varnath Lala couldn't hold her ears tight enough to protect them from Eldra's rather colorful language, she struck out with her nails. I got in the way, only to be on the receiving end of Lala's claws and Eldra's elbow, meant—I believe—for Lala's nose! They were both most apologetic, and it did stop their interminable argument as they went looking for the unguents for my face. Unfortunately, they'll be at it again in another couple of hours."

Verkan laughed. "By then you're going to have one Dralm-blasted black eye. Do you want to use my medpak now, or after our talk?"

He shrugged. "Well, Chief, unless you've got another assignment for me—please, tell me you do—then I'm stuck. Our little contretemps was witnessed by several of the Foundry staff, who would think it Dralm's Own Miracle if I were to arrive with anything less than a bruised eye. Thanks anyway, boss."

"Well, Ranthar, this may be your lucky day indeed. I had a discussion with Kalvan this morning and he's quite impressed by your leadership abilities."

"Likewise, Chief. I think Kalvan could even run this outfit."

"Don't say that within spitting distance of the Kalvan Study Team or you will have another cat fight on your hands!"

Ranthar laughed, holding up his arms, hands spread, in the universal sign of surrender. "Please, say no more. So what's this new assignment?"

"It's a surprise to me. Things are getting bad enough in the war against Styphon's House that Kalvan is taking a few pages from one of his own Europo-American headlines. He wants to start a revolt in Hos-Bletha to force them to withdraw their forces from the Grand Host. He's got a whale of a plan—to use one of his terms—and I think it's more than plausible. Part of it involves a guerilla uprising in the southern provinces starring yourself as none other than Robin Hood—that name's from a common Europo-American myth of a bandit who robs from the rich to give to the poor. Obviously, a fairy tale for children. Kalvan remembers the story and told it to me in great detail. I had to agree that you would make a most excellent Robin Hood."

"Actually, if it will get me away from the Foundry and the Kalvan Study Team, I'd accept an assignment to break into the Caverns of Regwarn!" While Ranthar enjoyed outtime work, he hated babysitting a bunch of hothouse intellectuals who couldn't survive a day out in the field without constant supervision.

"Well, you've got it, my friend. And, that isn't all. Guess who else Kalvan wants to *borrow*?"

Ranthar shook his head, then flashed a wicked smile. "He wants to borrow Varnath Lala's head to use for one of his scarecrows!"

Verkan hooted. "Good guess, but no. He wants to have Baltrov Eldra join his merry little band."

"Baltrov Eldra! Why, Chief?"

"Think. You were at the University Founder's celebration."

"Sure—I got real plastered—left my alcodote pills at home on purpose. Had a good time."

"Do you remember seeing Eldra?"

Ranthar's brow furrowed. "Sure. She was hanging around that skinny horse-trader, Duke Skranga, and Kalvan for the first part of the evening. Then later on she was decorating Colonel Democriphon's uniform—he seemed to like it."

"Well, before she changed dance partners, she approached Kalvan and said something into his ear I'm too polite to repeat in mixed company."

"She tried to seduce Kalvan in public? Does she have a death wish? Sure Kalvan and Rylla are having problems, but Rylla would fillet any woman she saw get within kissing distance of her husband."

"Absolutely. When I heard about it, I was ready to send her packing. But it's not that simple."

"What do you mean, Chief? It looks pretty simple to me. Send Eldra home to First Level 'for her own protection' and let the University of Dhergabar figure out what to do with her. Flirting with Kalvan could be construed as Paratemporal Contamination, I don't know for sure how the Paratime Commission would view it, but I do know that it more than skirts outtime ethics. University Study Team participants are instructed to act as 'observers only.' Trying to set up a liaison with the primary agent of change on Kalvan's Time Line is bad procedure—even if she wasn't successful. Success could get her killed and who knows what else. She goes home when you give the order. I can escort her out of the Foundry and have her on an outbound conveyor in ten minutes. She'll be back on Home Time-Line so fast she'll never know what hit her!"

Verkan shook his head. "Very few people know this, but I was sharing my quarters with Eldra when that Second Level reincarnation fracas came up on Akor-Neb, which led to Dalla and me renewing our marriage contract. You've just witnessed an example of Eldra's temper—how do you think she took that? Or my asking her to leave our dwell!"

"Wow, Chief, you sure can pick them!"

Verkan looked down at his shoes.

"Why in Xerpa's Mandibles did you ever pick Eldra as our undercover operative for the Kalvan Study Team?"

Verkan was still studying the floor when he answered. "I owed her one. She could have stirred up a real firestorm for me back then, but she kept it between the two of us. Kept Dalla out of it, too. Eldra heard about the Kalvan Study Team, knew I'd be involved and asked if she could become a member. She had the right credentials so I called one of our *friends* at the University and arranged for her to be assigned to the Kalvan Study Team. It was the least I could do."

"Blackmail?" Ranthar asked with a frown.

"No. Eldra was nice about it. She just reminded me of a promise I'd made to her when she left: I'd told her I'd do her a favor if ever she needed one."

"Some favor. Does Dalla know any of this?"

Verkan shook his head.

Ranthar whistled. "Dalla has always had a temper. And jealous! I remember that time she caught you with that prole scarf dancer—"

"You were there. You know it was perfectly innocent!"

"Sure, but it didn't look that way to Dalla. It didn't help that the girl had lost all her scarves in the riot—not that it made much of a difference!"

"And, since I've never told her about Eldra..."

"Yes," Ranthar said, trying to keep a straight face. "It would look bad."

"Eldra even offered, I guess to sweeten the pot, to go undercover and spy on her own cohorts. She's the one who spotted the redhead sending up message balls to Hadron Tharn."

"She's done a good job. After that little tussle I just partook in, no one would ever accuse Eldra of being *our* agent. You should have heard some of the creative language she used on both Lala and me. Still, Verkan—"

"A stupid blunder—I've never even told Tortha! I'd never hear the end of it. I didn't even want to tell you, but someone needs to know and since you'll be Johnny-on-the-spot, well, Eldra's going to be the party's black widow spider and Skranga's spy mistress."

"And just when this was sounding like fun!"

"It's not that bad. She may not be working with your team. I haven't drawn up the assignments yet."

"Praise Dralm! And, Chief, you'd better think of telling Dalla about your history with our spy vixen. If she ever hears it from Eldra, Styphon be damned, it will be a disaster—your disaster!"

As he left the basement, Ranthar shook his head. It was amazing how someone as smart as Verkan could be so stupid when it came to the opposite sex. He better hope that some outtimer in Hos-Bletha drew a bead on Eldra and ended his problem once and for all. *I hope Eldra doesn't try to work those wiles of hers on me*, he thought. *If she does, she'll find out just what a cold shoulder means.*

# THREE

## I

As the carriage rode up the hill, Duke Skranga cursed the dust, raised by the horses' hooves, which was clogging his throat and nose. He wondered how Lady Eldra and Gasphros were doing in the carriage following theirs. Skranga sneezed and then coughed, clearing his throat. As a lord of the realm, he was expected to follow certain proprieties. Like Great King Kalvan, he much preferred riding his own horse to sitting in a wooden cage that bounced him around like a squirrel in a basket every time the carriage wheels hit a pothole or small gully. Sometimes getting your fondest wish was not all it was cracked up to be. Fortunately, he would soon be away from all obligations and expectations running a new intelligence ring, which was what he did best.

Skranga had his first look at the Locra Valley in over a winter as the clattering carriage came over the rise. Tarr-Locra was an old castle that had been expanded as part of the war against Hos-Harphax. Most of the trees in the surrounding area within four marches had been cut down.

There was now a small town where there had been a village and it was a hive of activity. Tarr-Locra now covered the entire hilltop and at the base was one of Kalvan's new star forts. Instead of a circular outer wall at the base of the hill, the Great King had Captain-General Harmakros build a large star with about a dozen points that Skranga could see from his position on the opposite ridge. There were eight and ten-pound culverins set at each point.

"What do you think, Captain Ranthar?" he asked.

"I think the Grandiose Host of Styphon's House is going to bang their toes on this place."

Skranga nodded. He liked Ranthar; he was a no-nonsense kind of soldier. Colonel Democriphon, who was riding alongside the carriage on his horse, he wasn't so sure about.

While his party was stopped at the gate by the guard, Skranga got a closer look at the walls themselves. They were about ten lances tall and about a third that in width. Tarr-Locra would be a tough nut to crack even for the entire Harphaxi Army. Skranga's estimation of Harmakros went up several notches. He hoped that Hestophes could fill his superior's shoes. Skranga mentally reviewed what he knew about Captain-General Hestophes:

First, at twenty-three winters Hestophes was the youngest general on Kalvan's mostly youthful General Staff. His father was a publican; he owned the Silver Stag. Like many other businessmen in Hostigos, his tavern had flourished under Kalvan's rule—war was *always* good for the spirits business. Hestophes had been an infantry officer in the Army of Hostigos when Kalvan had arrived.

During the war with Nostor, Hestophes had been the captain who had held the Narza Gap with little better than two companies and two old guns. Hestophes had beaten off ten times his number three times before retreating to the top of the Narza ridge and encouraging the already retiring enemy to return to Nostor. Kalvan had been impressed enough to make him one of the first generals in his new Royal Army of Hos-Hostigos.

Hestophes' record during the battles at Chothros Heights and Phyrax was such that Kalvan had elevated him to baron and awarded Hestophes a nice estate and castle at Eython. That was when his rising cloud had begun to stall; Hestophes had met the Lady Lavena, the daughter of Baron Sthentros, whose estate at Hyllos bordered the young Captain-General's. Hestophes had become besotted with Lavena, and he wasn't the first either, so Skranga had learned when he arrived undercover as an itinerant peddler in Hyllos to see if there was any truth to the rumors reaching Hostigos Town. While no lady, the baroness was a comely wench and Skranga—had he been a pup like Hestophes—might have followed her dragging his tail behind his legs, too. Still, he knew trouble when he saw it, even if it walked on two lovely legs.

After his report to Kalvan, it had been the Great King's idea to immediately reassign Hestophes to Tarr-Locra and put him in charge of the Great Kingdom's eastern frontier. And from the vigilance of his guards, Skranga would have to say Hestophes had done a bang-up job of it, too.

While Grand-Captain Myklon saw to boarding his horses and seeing to his troopers, Skranga was taken up to the fortress for an audience with the Captain-General. Hestophes was seated behind a large desk that looked as if it were modeled after Kalvan's desk at Tarr-Hostigos. When the Captain-General rose up to touch palms, Skranga realized just how truly large a man Hestophes was. While not as tall as himself, Hestophes was almost half as wide as he was tall, but without an extra ounce of weight. He was as strong-looking a man as Skranga had ever seen, bringing back to mind a comment about the Captain-General he once overheard: "The General looks like a hibernating bear."

## II

Captain-General Hestophes was pouring over his muster list; it took a lot of effort since he had only learned to read runes since Kalvan's arrival. The Great King had provided Hestophes with one of his own scribes, tasking him with the job of teaching the Captain-General to read. He had only read haltingly in the beginning, but now Hestophes' skill at deciphering the runes was equivalent to most of the lesser nobles under his command. He had also learned its importance; this afternoon he was determining which soldiers would have day or night guard duty. He found that morale was better when the schedules were changed every moon-half.

At the moment, with no enemy closer than a hundred marches, there was little need for vigilance; but come next spring, Tarr-Lorca would be the focus of the huge army that was rumored to be assembling in the outlying outskirts of Harphax City.

There was a knock at the door.

"Come in." he ordered.

"Captain-General, a carriage has been observed coming over the Varnoss Pass," his orderly reported. "It is accompanied by two companies of troops in Hostigos colors."

"Hmm," Hestophes muttered. He wasn't expecting any reinforcements and a mere company or two would make little difference to the coming hostilities.

"Send a scout to see who our visitors are and report back."

"I've already done so, sir. We should have some answers shortly."

"Good. Dismissed."

Hestophes went back to work on the muster lists. He knew a number of captains, valiant leaders of men and good fighters, who could not read and found their possibilities for advancement curtailed. Great King Kalvan has set up "schools"—as he called them—to teach these skills, but many captains were too proud to avail themselves of such an opportunity. *More fools them*, he thought.

There was another knock, only this time his orderly came right into the chamber. "Yes," he said.

"It's a party from Hostigos Town led by a Duke Skranga. He has a pass signed by Great King Kalvan."

"Good." *Skranga's an odd duck that neither quacks nor waddles*, Hestophes thought. Initially, when Kalvan had made him head of Hostigi Intelligence, he had thought the Great King had made a poor choice. But he had been wrong and it was one of the observations that caused him to change his mind about initial impressions. Skranga, a former horse-trader, had turned out to be both diligent at his work as well as loyal to king and throne.

"Show him in when he arrives."

"Yes, sir."

In less than a quarter-candle, his orderly returned followed by the tall, bandy-legged Chief of Intelligence. Skranga was wearing a blue velvet robe with fur lining and his red hair, or what was left of it, was trimmed nicely. While he didn't quite look regal, he did look respectable, which was quite an accomplishment.

"What can I do for you, Your Grace? I see you brought two companies of reinforcements which we greatly need."

"I'm sorry, Captain-General, but these troopers are but my own personal guards."

"Really!"

"Yes, I've been charged by King Kalvan to leave for Hos-Bletha on a secret mission."

Hestophes' eyebrows went up. "I think you had best tell me just what you're up to."

Skranga pulled out a scroll from his side pouch. "Read this, orders for you from Great King Kalvan."

Hestophes picked up the scroll, unwound it and began to slowly and quietly read out loud. Skranga smoked two bowls of tobacco before Hestophes read the letter twice, sighed and set down the paper scroll. "The Great King says I am to trust you and give you any aid that you require. He does not say why."

Skranga took out his pipe and began to fill it with tobacco again.

Hestophes figured that Skranga was mulling over whether or not to trust him with the nature of his mission.

Skranga removed a flask from the inside of his buff jack and presented it to Hestophes. "Some of Ermut's Best."

"Hmm." Hestophes turned to pick up two goblets and filled them with the dark liquid. He only had two small casks left out of his personal stock and appreciated the offer.

"As you may or may not know, Great King Niclophon of Hos-Bletha has been squeezing his Kingdom dry to aid Styphon's House in its war against Hos-Hostigos," opened Skranga. "The Blethans are relatively poor and, outside Bletha Town, there's little support for either their King or Styphon's House. Now that Niclophon is poised to send most of the Royal Army to Balph to aid King Lysandros, we thought this might be a good time to start a revolt within Hos-Bletha. At worst we might pin down units that would otherwise aid in the fight against Hostigos, while at best King Niclophon might have to refuse his contribution to the Styphoni war effort."

Hestophes shook his head. "You actually sold this dream story to Kalvan? I'd heard you were silver-tongued enough to sell a dog to an Uncle Wolf, but I didn't believe it until now!"

Skranga held both hands to his chest. "Truth: it was Kalvan's idea, not mine. You don't think it will work?"

Hestophes paused to give some thought to the idea. "Whether it works is of little importance right now, since it certainly isn't going to do any good before next spring. Meanwhile, you've got two companies of good troops who could be used in the defense of the realm chasing fireflies... I take it they are former Blethan mercenaries?"

"Most. Some of them are Hostigi who have worked on *special* missions with me before. All the Blethans have families they're leaving behind for this duty to ensure their loyalty. Most have been fighting with Kalvan since Fyk." For half a candle, Skranga continued to explain Kalvan's reasoning behind the operation and their intelligence information on Hos-Bletha.

Hestophes nodded slowly after he finished. "With good soldiers you could stir up serious trouble, if even half of what you say about Hos-Bletha is true! I will admit this idea isn't as harebrained as it first appeared; however, it will be your responsibility to see that these soldiers do not end up fighting for Styphon's House against us. So just how is it that you propose to arrive in Hos-Bletha from here?"

"I was planning to go by way of Syriphlon and from there down through the Pirsystros Valley and into Hos-Ktemnos. From there we were going to take a ship to Hos-Bletha."

Hestophes shook his head.

Skranga looked as if he had just taken a bite out of an onion.

"Why not?"

"Soton is hiring every mercenary in Hos-Harphax and Hos-Ktemnos. Do you really believe his agents are going to let two companies of experienced mercenaries, who can't even account for their whereabouts for the past two years, slip through their fingers? You will be up in irons before the moon is up. If you're lucky, they'll hang you—if not you'll be up before Roxthar's Investigation."

Skranga paled.

Hestophes didn't blame him. He had fought a lot of foes, but being tortured by a fanatical archpriest went beyond death by sword, lance or bullet.

"What do you suggest, Captain-General?" Skranga asked.

"First, your men need a disguise, and so do you. And a good one at that, something unexpected, yet commonplace. An alias, too. I've got it! You can be Highpriest Sangar from somewhere in Hos-Agrys or Hos-Zygros, the farther away the better, and your men will be a Temple Band of Styphon's Own Guard."

"You mean disguise ourselves as a Band of Styphon's Red Hand! By Galzar, I love it. Who is going to dare question the presence of a Temple Band escorting a Styphon's House Highpriest?"

"Down south in Hos-Ktemnos, maybe. But if you take your Band up north through Nostor and the Kratiphlon Pass into Hos-Agrys, you should be home safe. Once in Agrys City, you can probably find a sailing vessel to take you down to Hos-Bletha, even this late in the year. That is, if you have enough gold."

Skranga smiled. Besides two score of ingots that had once decorated the roof of Styphon's Temple in Phaxos town, he had his own not inconsiderable fortune. "We are adequately financed. I also have two gunsmiths and six fireseed makers."

Hestophes nodded. "It is true that our Great King sets his sights far into the distance. I am surprised Kalvan let two gunsmiths leave now, though."

"After what he did this summer, the Kingdom has more riflesmiths than even we need."

"I hadn't heard about his latest dealing with the Gunsmiths Guild. What happened?"

"When they wouldn't increase their production of rifles, King Kalvan started selling smoothbores from the Royal Armory. He sold them for half of what it cost the gunsmiths to make a musket stock! Whoa, were they unhappy. Then he told them that he would buy all the rifles they could make, but, if they still continued to defy him, he'd give away every arquebus and musket in the Armory! By Yirtta's Dugs, did that put a fire under their arses!"

Hestophes laughed at the idea of such an incongruous sight. "Maybe it *is* possible that our Great King will pull off another of his miracles and vanquish whatever army Styphon's House is putting together. I'm just glad I'm on his side."

Skranga's own opinion was that no one should be required to make miracles on demand, because it was human nature that demand for more would quickly outstrip any and all abilities....

"Now, you're going to need the proper uniforms," Hestophes said.

"That's right. The Red Hand dresses in silvered armor and fancy red capes. Do you have anything in the armory at Tarr-Locra we can use?"

"Yes. We have a lot of the armor scavenged from the Battle of Chothros Heights and a room full of Guardsman armor—that is, what hasn't been stolen by the castle staff. I'll see what we have left. You can use some of the other armor. As I recall, your Blethan mercenaries don't believe in armor heavier than boiled leather."

"A few have seen the error of their ways, but you are right. What about capes and breeches?"

"We have lots of seamstresses in Locra Town. If we put a few score of them to work, we should have speedy results. Especially, since you have coin enough to limber their fingers. We also need to have them sew you a yellow highpriest's vestments. I've got a woman here in Tarr-Lorca that can do that in secret *and* keep her mouth shut. We don't want people thinking we've taken up wearing Styphoni robes!"

Skranga nodded, then finished off the last of the brandy. Yes, there was no doubt about it; the resourceful young Captain-General was going to go a long way under Great King Kalvan. “That will work, but their job must be done in total secrecy; otherwise, if there is a single intelligencer in this town, the Styphoni will be alerted.”

“Good point, Baron,” Hestophes replied. “I will have my men pick a score of the best seamstresses and confine them to the fort until their work is done. There are other jobs that need to be done after you leave. How long should I keep them confined?”

“A half-moon should do it. If we’re not far away from Hos-Harphax by then, it won’t matter.”

Hestophes paused to refill his pipe. “You’re also going to need more men if you’re going to pass yourselves off as a Temple Band. Most Styphoni units are under-strength, but not so bad as yours will be. I’ve got about fifty Blethan mercenaries here, almost all who would jump at a chance to go home. Just one thing.”

“What’s that?” he asked.

“If I end up facing any of them next spring, Duke, I’m going to personally come after you with gelding shears.”

Skranga gulped and tried not to squirm. “It won’t happen, Hestophes. Galzar’s Oath.”

“Good. By Dralm, we’ve finished off the brandy. Let me call one of my servants and have him bring a barrel of winter wine.”

“Yes, by all means. It’s been a long and dusty ride.”

“By the way, Duke, what do you know of Styphon’s House greetings and rituals?”

Skranga felt a shiver run up and down his spine. “Very little, I fear.”

Hestophes smiled. “That’s what I thought. If you’re going to pass as a Styphon’s House upperpriest you’re going to need some instruction.”

“Dralm-damnit, if I’d of thought of this disguise earlier, I could have had Baron Zothnes help build my cover. Unfortunately, he’s still back in Hostigos Town.”

“Ah, yes, former Archpriest Zothnes… Maybe I can help,” Hestophes added.

"What do you know about Styphon's House liturgy?" Skranga asked.

"Very little, to be honest. However, about a moon ago, one of our raiding parties captured a party of Styphon's House priests who were on their way to Harphax City from Arklos Town and got lost. We took them prisoner. I beheaded the highpriests and put the underpriests to work. There was one black-robed priest who was very cooperative and pointed out one of the highpriests who had donned a black robe to escape punishment. He might be willing to aid in your deception. He's certainly got nothing to lose."

# FOUR

## I

Duke Skranga went to look for Captain Ranthar and found him in the fort's duty room talking with the other soldiers. Democriphon was holed up with Captain-General Hestophes going over some maps to find the fastest way to Agrys City.

"Captain Ranthar, I would like for you to accompany me to the dungeon," Skranga said. "I'm going to interrogate one of the Styphoni prisoners."

Ranthar nodded. "Not a bad idea to have someone with you who has a sword close at hand."

Skranga shook his head. "I don't believe this man is dangerous. He's been working as a laborer on the fort's outer works for the past moon. I think he'll be glad to escape duty for a candle-half."

They took a passageway down to the bailey and from there a stone stairway down into the dungeon. The fort's foundation was solid stone with lime-washed walls and dark timbering. Unlike most gaols or dungeons Skranga had seen, the walls were clean and free of mold and mildew. The door was a wide expanse of old oak with heavy iron hinges. Skranga knocked on the door and it was promptly opened by a soldier dressed in the maroon and green colors of Hos-Hostigos.

"Come in, Your Grace."

"Thank you."

The prisoner, a middle-aged man with a sunburned face, was standing at a small table. His brown hair had been hacked short and he wore an untrimmed goatee under his thin nose. His blue eyes flicked warily back and forth between Skranga and Captain Ranthar.

"You can sit down," Skranga told the prisoner. The man slumped wearily onto the closest chair.

"What's your name?"

"Calthros."

"He's Your Grace, to you," Ranthar snapped. "This is Duke Skranga of Nostor."

The prisoner winced as if he expected a blow. "Yes, Your Grace."

"Calthros, I understand you are a Styphon's House priest, is that correct?"

"Yes, Your Grace. I've worn the black robe of an underpriest for almost ten winters. With few rewards, if any, for my service, and now I am worked like a common drudge at your hands."

Skranga was pleased; unlike many prisoners, this Calthros still retained some spirit. Now, for the important question. "Do you believe that Styphon is the One True God."

The prisoner snickered. "True god, my arse! All the gods are frauds and Styphon is the biggest lie of all."

"So you're not a supporter of Archpriest Roxthar and his Investigation?" he asked.

"Roxthar is a madman! He will bring the Temple down around his heels. A pox on the Investigator and the Inner Circle who suckled him at its breast!"

Skranga smiled. "Then you wouldn't object to working against the Temple?"

Calthros' eyebrows furrowed. "Just what do you have in mind, sire?"

"My Great King has sent me on a mission—.

Ranthar hissed in his ear. "Do you think it's safe to tell him so much?"

Skranga nodded, then continued, "My team and I have been ordered to enter Hos-Bletha in order to subvert Styphon's House from within."

Calthros' eyes widened, then a smile slowly formed. "What are my conditions, if I to agree to help with your plot?"

Skranga had to hide his own grin; now, it was down to bargaining. "I want you to teach me all the proper liturgy and rituals of a Styphon's House highpriest. I want to know how to talk like a highpriest, walk like one and, in effect, become one. I also will want you to act as my aide and personal assistant until the mission is over. In return, once we have left those lands under Styphon's sway, I will set you free and grant you a thousand ounces of gold and a small holding should you decide to stay in Hostigos."

"You are generous, My Grace. I would have accepted your terms even for five hundred ounces of gold."

"My generosity is a spur to encourage you to become devoted to our cause. I believe in rewarding good help and your reward will be commensurate with our achievements."

Calthros frowned. "And what might that be, sire?"

"If we can bring down the Silver Throne, thereby removing Hos-Bletha from the war against Hos-Hostigos, I will see that you are made a baron of the realm."

"How can I be sure that your words are true?"

"I give you my sworn-oath that if you do as I have directed, I will see that you are elevated to the barony and given a holding commensurate with your new status. I'm sure you've heard rumors about Archpriest Zothnes."

Calthros nodded. "Yes, the Archpriest who denounced Styphon and became the Usur—, I mean Great King Kalvan's vassal."

"Right; Zothnes was a member of the Inner Circle who surrendered to the Great King and provided detailed intelligence about the Temple of Styphon's House. In return, Kalvan granted him a barony."

"Your Grace, I shall be your most ardent supporter."

Skranga turned to the guard. "See that he is dressed in proper raiment and brought to my chamber."

As they took the stairway out of the dungeon, Ranthar asked, "Don't you think that maybe you were being a little too generous with your terms, Duke?"

"No, I want Calthros solidly in our camp. With just one false misstep, my cover as a highpriest can be blown with dire consequences for me and our mission. I could have threatened him with death if such happened, but it is not unusual for men to work in their worst interest if they do not see a proper reward or believe they are being taken advantage of. Now, Calthros has something to believe in—a future as nobleman. This he will not lightly discard."

Ranthar nodded. "You might have something there. And, it is true that we know little about the inner workings of the Temple of Styphon."

"Yes, if I had known before we left that I was going to have to disguise myself as a highpriest, I would have asked the Great King to send Baron Zothnes along."

"Zothnes would have been a big help."

"Unless he was recognized by one of the Styphoni. Maybe it's better that he's aiding the Intelligence Service back in Hostigos Town."

## II

Ranthar wasn't as convinced as Duke Skranga that they could trust the Styphoni turncoat Calthros, especially now that he was decked out in his black robe of office. Still, they had little choice since none of them knew all the secret handshakes and randygazoo that were *de rigeur* in the Temple of Styphon's House and distinguished their priesthood from outsiders. He would keep an eye on Calthros and at the first opportunity put a sticky-dot receiver and mini-transceiver on his robes. That was well within the Paratime Code; the Paratime Police didn't send its investigators outtime to get killed.

Calthros was now explaining the apparel worn by Styphon's Own

Guard. It turned out there was more than enough of the Guardsman's silvered armor; the silver plate was too thin to remove economically so the discarded armor had been tossed into the Tarr-Lorca armory in piles. The red capes had all been removed by the peasants on the battlefield, so new ones were now being sewn by the local townswomen.

A small ramshackle town had sprouted around Tarr-Lorca's borders. Most of the wooden structures would be pulled down the first time a hostile force appeared. Still, wherever there were soldiers with gold in the pockets, there were those who would do their best to relieve them of that burden whether through games of chance by sharpers and bone rattlers, barkeeps with alcoholic drinks, prostitutes or simple thievery.

"Each Temple Band, as they are called, has its own grand-captain. Who among you will play that part?" Calthros asked, looking right at Ranthar.

Ranthar wanted no part of that deal; it would tie his hands to be in command of the faux guardsmen. He looked over at Colonel Democriphon. "Who do you suggest?"

"Grand-Captain Myklon has been in charge of the troopers ever since we left Hostigos. Let him lead the Band."

Myklon smiled happily. His command now comprised almost three hundred men with the addition of eighty or so former Beshtan volunteers from the Tarr-Locra garrison.

"A Styphon's House Temple Band at full strength would contain over four hundred men," Calthros mentioned. "However, since the war many Temple Bands are understrength and I don't believe that our troop will garner any attention. It will also allow us to refuse any requests for reinforcements from the Styphon's House temples we encounter at our destination."

"That's good," Democriphon noted. "The last thing we want to do is attract any attention."

Calthros shrugged. "There will be few among those we encounter who will have the stones to accost a Band of Styphon's Own Guard. The only ones we will have to be wary of are other highpriests and, much rarer, an archpriest. Fortunately, most of the archpriests spend all their days in Balph and are rarely on the road. Of course, we will want to avoid other Temple Bands. When we're in Hos-Agrys, we'll say we're from Hos-Ktemnos. When we reach Hos-Bletha, we'll say we're from Hos-Agrys. That way, if we run into another Band, it will reduce questions from fellow guardsmen in other units."

He unfurled a bright red banner, roughly the size of a big bed sheet, which displayed a white representation of Styphon's Sun-Wheel, the reversed swastika that was Styphon's device, with the rune for the number fifteen. "We will carry this proudly wherever we will go. People will move aside when they see this coming."

Ranthar looked at Calthros closely. "Isn't that numerical designation a problem? What if we run into another Band and they have the same number or know the members of that Band?"

Calthros shook his head. "The Fifteenth Band died to a man at the Battle of Chothros Heights. I doubt that they have this information yet at Janthra Town where the Guards Headquarters are located. If the unit does not have a numerical designation, it will immediately identify it as a fraud."

"Then we don't have a choice," Ranthar said.

Calthros nodded. "As Styphon's Own Guard, you will fight on foot," he continued, "but, since the guard travels by horseback, those new to the command have been provided horses by order of Captain-General Hestophes."

One of Hestophes' aides came over to where Ranthar and Democriphon were seated, saying, "The rest of your capes will be delivered by tomorrow morning. You can leave anytime thereafter, Colonel."

"Excellent," Democriphon said. "We've been here long enough. We've got mountains to cross and I'd rather do it before the rains begin in earnest."

# FIVE

## I

Due to inclement weather, the journey from Tarr-Locra to Agrys City had taken Skranga's party over a moon to reach Agrys City. Rainstorms had washed out several roads and they had been forced to wait over three days for the waters to recede enough to ferry across the swollen Agrys River. When they arrived in Agrys City, there were half a dozen other Temple Bands in the city, so no one took particular notice of one more. Skranga chose not to visit the High Temple of Styphon's House at Agrys City as he was still uncomfortable impersonating a highpriest.

At the Wharf Rat, the local tavern where captains and ship masters meet with merchants and travelers, Skranga met with a shipping agent to secure transport to Hos-Bletha.

The agent was a grizzled older man with a gray beard and wind-roughened face. "It's almost too late in the season, Your Worship, for travel on the Great Eastern Ocean. And Port Gytha is a long distance away."

Skranga sat back in his chair and

viewed the former captain as though he were an insect he was about to crush. "It is Styphon's Own Work that requires us to make this journey. You will be well compensated." Kalvan had given him several of the Styphon's House bank drafts that had been liberated from sacked temples. He rather enjoyed the irony of having the Temple paying for their journey. By the time anyone in Styphon's House bureaucracy ever realized the drafts were counterfeit, his mission would likely be long over.

The agent scowled, but Skranga could see the wheels turning behind his eyes.

"It will cost you, Your Worship. Only a few captains will go to sea this time of year."

"Price is no object," Skranga announced cavalierly. "Styphon will provide."

The agent actually smiled. "Then let's work out the details. How many people are there in your party?"

"I have three hundred and sixty-seven Temple Guardsmen and my retinue which numbers forty priests and underpriests. Plus, myself."

The agent took out a piece of lamb's hide that appeared to have been scraped so many times it was almost transparent and made some rough scribbles. "You're going to need at least ten cogs for your guardsmen and one hulk for your party. Plus, four galleys for protection. Pirates and the Caribi warships often swarm the coastal waters looking for ships to plunder this time of year since there are few galleys on patrol duty. If you assign some of your guardsmen to the galleys that will cut down on the number of cogs and reduce costs since I won't have to hire so many mercenaries."

Skranga had done his own survey and found that the sailing cogs held enough room for fifty men, twelve of those being sailors. The hulks were much larger and could hold the main party. "I can muster two hundred Temple Guardsmen for the galleys, but fifty will stay aboard the hulk with me and my party."

The agent nodded. "That can be arranged. You will only need four cogs. Captain Portos' ship will easily take your main party and the fifty guardsmen. It will not be cheap, though."

Skranga smiled. "The Temple can be generous when the need is great."

They had sold the two carriages and horses in Agrys City for enough gold to fill a small chest. No horse-trader—at least one who valued his life—would dare cheat a highpriest of Styphon's House. The sea journey had been free of really bad weather—so Captain Portos claimed—although Skranga had his own view of that. The hulk had been crowded and he had been seasick for most of the voyage.

As he stepped off the plank leading the wharf, Skranga found himself lurching as if drunk on Ermut's Best. It had taken almost a moon-quarter, what with four to five stops, for the party to reach their destination. Whenever the sea got too rough, the expedition sailed to the nearest port. As soon as his stomach would begin to settle at a stop, he would be hustled back aboard the ship and his upset would begin all over again. Nor was it helped by the cog's creaking timbers and the high swells that tossed the small boat like a leaf on a pond due to the lateness of the season.

*By the True Gods I will never travel on water again*, Skranga promised himself. *I will not even drink it!* His yellow robe was stained from both sea water and vomit. He would have to get it washed right away; the smell of it was making him nauseated all over again.

As soon as his legs became accustomed to land, Skranga motioned for Gasphros to join him. "Can you find us an inn where we can gather and discuss our mission?"

Port Gytha was a good-sized town and had several inns and wine shops along the waterfront, as well as workshops and stores. Inevitably in a town this size there would be a Styphon's House temple. He decided he would have Calthros reconnoiter the temple before he made an appearance.

Gasphros shrugged. "I will find us an inn, but the soldiers will have to find other accommodations, perhaps outside the town."

The soldiers, who were disembarking from the boats, were forming up into a column, glaives over their shoulders. Those inhabitants still on the streets quickly went indoors.

"Bah!" Skranga muttered. "I'll order the local headman or mayor to provide them shelter. I'm a Highpriest; I can do that!"

The troubadour said, "Yes, but you won't win us any friends that way."

Colonel Democriphon nodded in agreement.

"We're not here to win friends. Now, on your way."

Gasphros gave him a hard-eyed look beneath a furrowed forehead before departing.

*Maybe I'm starting to take this role too seriously*, Skranga thought. The problem was the power of a highpriest was inordinate and corruptive. If he was going to successfully play a highpriest he had to be in character at all times, or at least those times he was in public view.

Skranga noted that several notables were approaching the wharf.

The man leading the pack said, "I am Varnos, Head Selectman of the Town Council of Ten. Welcome to Port Gytha." The Selectman was a thick-bodied man with a tight doublet. Around his neck he wore a gold chain of office. "How can I serve you, Your Worship?" he asked in an oily tone of voice.

"I am Highpriest Sangar with my retinue. I have been sent here by the Styphon's Own Voice to oversee the preparations in Hos-Bletha for the war against the Usurper Kalvan."

The headman shrugged. "What preparations? The Usurper is far away; he will not bother us. Let the Harphaxi dogs, who allowed this whelp to gain ascendancy, stop him."

Grand-Captain Myklon, who had sidled up to Skranga, put his hand on his sword pommel, saying, "Headman, watch your words. This is Highpriest Sangar you are speaking to!"

The Selectman jerked back. "My apologies, Your Worship, we are all on edge. There have been bandit attacks outside of town. Maybe you and your Guardsmen can aid us, Styphon Be Blessed."

Skranga nodded graciously. "I will look into it. Why has your Prince not taken care of it?"

The headman shook his head nervously. "Prince Vythron is more concerned with his riches and concubines than our troubles."

"That is the way of overlords near and far," Skranga observed. "I will have my agents look into your complaint. Who is the Highpriest of the Gytha Temple?"

"That would be Highpriest Ptolomos," the headman replied. "The

Temple of Styphon is in the main square, next to the Great Banking House of Styphon and the Hall of Justice."

"I will meet with Ptolomos at daybreak tomorrow. I will need accommodations for my Guardsmen."

"I will find places to billet them, Your Worship," the Selectman replied, his forehead beginning to bead-up with sweat.

"Let it be done. And quickly," Skranga ordered. "You are excused."

The selectman and his advisors made a quick exit over the cobblestone street. Skranga suspected they were not happy about the arrival of several hundred of Styphon's Own Guard who needed both shelter and food. And possibly entertainment....

"See," Skranga said, turning to Democriphon. "I told you they'd find accommodations for the men."

"True, but they were not happy to do it. Still, what are they to do against the might of Styphon's House?"

Skranga snickered. "Hestophes couldn't have suggested a better disguise. This yellow robe will open any door in Hos-Bletha."

"So far," Democriphon said.

"I pray that Gasphros has found us an inn. I need to sleep without the sea tossing me around like a piece of wood!"

"Yes," Democriphon said, as he stifled a grin. "You were not cut out to be a sailor, Your Worship."

Skranga was pleased to see that the Colonel was following orders and treating him as if he were a highpriest. It was a dangerous game they were playing and one slip could be fatal for the whole party.

"Calthros, bring me my fur robe. It's getting cold."

The underpriest opened a trunk that had been taken off-ship and rooted around in it until he found Skranga's bearskin robe. On the back, the robe had Styphon's sun-wheel, a reverse swastika, emblazoned in red cloth over black fur.

By the time he slipped it over his shoulders, Gasphros was approaching the party.

"I've found rooms for us at an inn called the Rusty Harpoon," the troubadour told them.

"Good work," Skranga said. "After you've dropped off your trunks, I want you and Captain Ranthar to make the rounds of the local taverns and gather what intelligence you can about Port Gytha and these bandits the selectman mentioned."

## II

Inside the cramped room, Ranthar Jard used his radio, which was disguised as a silver wolf's-head pendant, to call the Hostigos Paratime team.

"Aldran Vanar here."

"Hi, Vanar, Ranthar Jard here. Is Chief Verkan available?"

"Yes, let me patch you through."

"Hi, Ranthar. How's the mission going?"

"Phew. We had a miserable ocean voyage from Agrys City to Port Gytha. Skranga puked his guts out. First time I've ever felt sorry for the ex-horse thief."

Verkan laughed. "Not enough to share your seasickness pills, I bet."

"No, I've stayed away from any Outtime Contamination—no matter how tempting. How are things in Hostigos Town?"

"Busy," Verkan replied. "Kalvan's trying to whip the Royal Army into shape. It looks like we'll be facing a huge Styphon's House army come spring; they're calling it the Grand Host of Styphon's House. The Styphoni have hired most of the mercenaries in the Six Kingdoms and are working on convincing Great King Cleitharses to send the Sacred Squares of Hos-Ktemnos. I think our boy may be in trouble."

"It doesn't sound good," Ranthar replied. "Our job is to pin down the Blethan forces and keep them out of the war. So far, no one has a clue as to how to perform that mission. Great King Niclophon has been bought and paid for by Styphon's House and will do whatever he can to assist in Kalvan's and Hos-Hostigos' destruction."

"I don't think Kalvan expects too much from the mission. Still, you haven't checked out the local situation yet. According to the survey team, most of the Blethan princes, with the exception of Prince Mythros and

Vythron, support their Great King. But not to the point where they'd beggar themselves to help in Styphon's war against Hos-Hostigos."

"That's good to know, Chief. Skranga, who's masquerading as Highpriest Sangar, has ordered me and Gasphros to check out the local taverns for gossip and for information on local banditry. Maybe we'll learn something that will help."

## III

It was late at night and the only private chamber large enough to hold the whole team was the Rusty Harpoon's basement. The inn's rock-walled cellar was damp and smelled of dead fish, stale beer, rotting seaweed and mildew. Duke Skranga had ordered Grand-Captain Myklon to place sentries outside the thick-plank door to keep anyone from entering. The innkeeper had been less than enthusiastic when Calthros had asked to use the space, but hadn't dared refuse.

*He probably thinks we're going to Investigate some of the local priests*, Democriphon thought, as he wiggled his bottom to get comfortable on the barrel head. *This would be the place to do it.* As far as they knew, Roxthar's Investigation had not ranged outside Hos-Ktemnos, but rumors about it had flown across all the borders of the Six Kingdoms. It was still too early to tell if those rumors would help or hinder their operation.

When everyone had come down the stairs and found seats on upturned barrels or old trunks, Skranga called the meeting to order. "Gasphros, you've had several candles to gather intelligence, so what have you learned?"

The big troubadour, his lyre strapped to his back, rose to his feet. "Like most ports, the townspeople of Gytha are more interested in trade than their great king's politics. Unlike the Princedoms of Artigos and Taurnos, which border Hos-Ktemnos, there are still temples to the old gods, Yirtta Allmother, Dralm, Galzar Wolfhead and Lytris, Goddess of Weather and Chance. In fact, Lytris may be the most important of the True Gods to the locals since many of them are sailors or fishermen.

Overall, there doesn't seem to be a large number of Styphon worshippers. The local Styphon's House Temple highpriest is not well-liked. Nor were they happy to learn that more of the 'temple rats'—their words—had arrived on the afternoon tide with a Band of Styphon's Own Guard.

"Fortunately, none of them associated me with Highpriest Sangar, and I was able to circulate freely and talk with my audience in between sets."

"I did *not* tell you to entertain them," Skranga snapped.

Gasphros looked daggers at the Duke. "You're the expert on horse trading; me, I'm good at reading audiences."

Skranga visibly restrained himself. "Go on."

"After my second set and a few rounds of the local brew, their tongues loosened up. It appears that a band of bandits has been raiding some of the small villages to the south. It's cut into the local trade and it's starting to affect their purses. No one knows much about the bandits. They've sacked four villages—that the locals know about—killing all the elderly villagers and young children. The men and women have been taken prisoner, with only a few escapees. It's generally believed they're slavers."

Democriphon had to rein in his temper. He hated slavers almost as much as Great King Kalvan. Those who dealt in the selling of human flesh were the lowest form of scum and unworthy of life.

"Well, that gives us an excuse to poke around," Skranga said. "Did you learn anything else?"

"People are still talking about the Orphan Prince."

"What's that all about?" Skranga asked.

"People have long wondered about the particulars around the death of their previous Great King," Gasphros said. "Niclophon took the throne after his brother Great King Marocles and his wife died under mysterious circumstance almost thirty winters ago. They were both in good health when they took sick and died within less than a day. Many believed they were poisoned.

"Niclophon should have simply become the Regent, but his nephew, Valthros, disappeared the same night the former king and queen died. There were numerous rumors about what happened: One had it that one of the governesses kidnapped the infant prince and fled the kingdom. Another suggested that Niclophon himself had either exiled or murdered the child. While others said that Styphon's House had taken the child to ensure that Niclophon remained in their pocket.

"I remember hearing many of these same rumors when I was a child. A score of 'Orphan Princes' have appeared through the decades; all of them discredited or murdered. Still, it might be something we can use."

There were nods of agreement among the conspirators.

"Did you learn anything else of value?" Democriphon asked.

"Only that the townspeople do not like the local Styphon's House highpriest. He's arrogant and treats the townsfolk like servants. Many are worshippers of Dralm and Lytris and resent Highpriest Ptolomos' attempts to belittle their gods. If all of the Blethan priests of Styphon are cut from the same cloth as Ptolomos, it shouldn't be difficult to fire the commoners' resentments with false rumors of atrocities and new tithes."

"Good work," Skranga said. "You've given us several directions to move in. I suggest that we leave town in the morning and see if we can hunt down those bandits."

# SIX

Duke Skranga cursed under his breath as he adjusted his sweat-soaked yellow robes to look out from his carriage to the green hills outside. It was unnaturally green for this time of year. In Hostigos most of the trees would have lost all their leaves; here in Taurnos most of the trees were green. Some were hemlocks, but most were evergreens.

Worst of all was the humidity. While he couldn't deny that he was far more comfortable than his men who were riding on horseback in the rain, he would have much preferred to join them. Unfortunately, the rains were in earnest and the road had turned into a river of mud. While the carriage air was stifling, at least it was dry. He felt sorry for the soldiers riding in full armor—a conceit of Styphon's Own Guard—during the sporadic downpours.

Additionally, he shared the carriage with Calthros, the former Styphoni underpriest, Colonel Democriphon and Ranthar of Greffa. Their combined body heat and the constant humidity made the carriage box all the hotter since there was precious little ventilation to offset the heat. The other carriage followed behind with Gasphros, Lady Eldra, her waiting woman and the rest of the party.

Of all of them, Democriphon appeared least affected by the moist air. He was perfectly groomed and sought to maintain his appearance at every opportunity. Fortunately, the local Blethan aristocracy wore their hair long so Democriphon would not have to sheer off his long locks. When he wasn't inside the carriage, the Colonel was spending a great deal of time riding on horseback with mercenaries. Skranga suspected that this was Democriphon's ploy to win the trust and loyalty of the troopers. If the men fought better that way, Skranga had no objections.

Captain Ranthar, on the other hand, was a mystery to Skranga. He was a bodyguard and comrade of Colonel Verkan's, the Greffan trader who had King Kalvan's trust and respect. But there was something off about the man. Skranga couldn't put his finger on what it was, yet something didn't seem to fit. Maybe Ranthar was an agent inquisitory of King Theovacar's. If so, why had he accompanied them to Hos-Bletha? Skranga let it go: There were enough other things to worry about without looking for problems.

Ranthar was explaining how an economy as depressed as that of Hos-Bletha's would be very vulnerable to economic disruptions. "We can do more than simply rob passing merchants. These new wolf masks that Gasphros came up with will give the impression that Galzar Wolfhead is behind our attacks."

Skranga smiled. "Yes, they will win us support among the peasants and mercenaries. The model that Gasphros displayed will strike terror in the hearts of believers." *Me, too, if I was fool enough to believe in anything I couldn't touch with my own hands.* The only god Skranga believed in was gold.

"They are surprisingly realistic," Ranthar concluded. "Gasphros is more an artist than he realizes. But we need to do more than terrorize peasants and steal from merchants and priests. Imagine if we created shortages of something everybody needs, say honey—for example. Bakeries would be the first to feel the pinch."

Democriphon paused grooming his beard long enough to contribute to the discussion. "We could also spread the word that shortages were caused by the Styphoni war effort against the Hostigi. I imagine that sort of thing is already happening."

Skranga was surprised by Democriphon's suggestion and knew he shouldn't be. Nobody rose to the rank of colonel without either a lot of powerful friends, which Democriphon didn't have until he achieved his current rank, or a sharp mind. He was smart enough, just a bit rash and overeager for glory.

"We will have to be careful not to overextend ourselves. This Robbing Hoot idea of our Great King's is a good one," Skranga said. "Why risk additional exposure?"

"Robin Hood," Ranthar corrected. "Having the remaining Blethan military chase us through the forest will cause quite a stir, but I doubt it will be enough to get the Blethan forces recalled from the Grand Host. We need to hit Hos-Bletha on multiple fronts."

Skranga snorted. "Robbing from the rich to give to the poor won't work, anyway. We need the peasantry angry and hostile to their king. Giving people money tends to make them happier with their lot."

Ranthar nodded. "We don't want to give succor to the poor. We want to finance those who are angry with the current state of affairs. People who are already angry and looking for a way to do something about it."

"People who hate Styphon's House," Democriphon added. He looked at Skranga appraisingly. "You know, with that disguise you would be welcomed into Great King Niclophon's court. I would bet a hundred gold Crowns that you could do great damage working from within in Bletha Town."

"What?" Skranga's face turned red. "It's enough that I wear these vestments in case we are discovered and need to bluff our way through enemy holdings, but to—"

"I think that is a great idea, Milord," Ranthar interrupted. "You could even suggest that additional gold is needed to win the war against the Usurper. Styphon's House does it often enough not to raise any suspicion. You would also be in a position to learn of any weaknesses we could exploit."

Skranga stopped sputtering long enough to give it some serious thought. "Do you think I can pull this charade off in Bletha Town? And what's the penalty if I am caught? Calthros?"

The former underpriest thought for a moment. Before he could speak a commotion from outside the carriage broke out. After a moment there was a firm knock on the door. Ranthar opened the door to see one of the scouts he sent out earlier. They had hired several Sastragathi scouts at Port Gytha.

"What is it, Yaholo?" Ranthar demanded.

Yaholo replied, "Styphoni party ahead, Captain."

Ranthar cursed under his breath in Greffan.

"How many?" Democriphon asked.

"Two and a half hands, maybe more."

Calthros interjected, "Too few for a traveling highpriest. Too small for anything, really."

"The war effort has everybody stretched thin," Skranga said. "Perhaps Styphon's House is starting to cut back?"

"Small parties of Styphoni are considered fair game by many, even in lands held by their allies," Calthros pointed out. "Great King Kalvan has sympathizers in many places. The Styphoni prefer to travel in larger groups for protection."

Skranga nodded. Styphon's House's dealings with the various kingdoms left a great deal to be desired. Many of Styphon's House's allies were indebted to them and found the war against Great King Kalvan a way to get from under their debt. Very few were actual believers. The farther away from Balph one traveled, the fewer worshippers of Styphon one found.

"We outnumber them considerably," Democriphon pointed out. "We could easily ambush and destroy them, take their gold and fireseed, and enjoy having that many fewer enemies running around to vex our king."

*This is that rashness for which Democriphon is so well-known*, thought Skranga. There was no way of knowing how many other foes might be lurking in the forest. A skirmish would certainly attract their attention quickly enough. Still…?

"Captain, what do you think?" he asked.

Captain Ranthar considered the situation. "I think we should follow

Colonel Democriphon's suggestion. However, I would advise we try to cut them down as quietly as possible." Ranthar turned to Yaholo. "Tell us about the terrain, activity and their weapons."

Yaholo gave a quick if clumsy account of the size, activity, location, uniforms and equipment of the Styphoni party. "Two hands or so of men, three fingers of wagons, four hands of horses. The men are armed with arquebuses and swords. No cannon, muskets, pikes or halberds. Their armor, while clean enough, is a bit worn; their cloaks threadbare. They are making camp fairly early in the day. Styphoni would keep traveling until twilight unless preparing for an engagement nearby."

Calthros shook his head. "This can't be right. The party is too small, the equipment too light and the robes in too poor a condition. Styphon's House would not allow such a poor showing in public. No highpriest would deign to sleep in a carriage or wagon if there were a town with a tavern or inn within travel distance before dark. We skirted a sizeable settlement earlier today that could easily be reached by nightfall."

Democriphon smiled. "The fact that they are on this back trail suggests that they are trying to avoid notice."

"Just as we are," Ranthar added.

Skranga let out a long breath. "It appears we will have to attack this group and take enough prisoners to find out what in the Regwarn is going on."

Democriphon nodded his accord. "I will ready the men. We will attack at first light."

Both Skranga and Ranthar were surprised.

Ranthar asked, "Why the delay?"

Democriphon smiled. "The men have been traveling all day and need their rest. I want time to plan our strategy to minimize our potential losses and take full advantage of our superior numbers."

"That is wise," Skranga agreed. Not the kind of planning he expected from the rash young man. Still, one doesn't rise to colonel without a lot of successful campaigns under one's belt. Maybe the heat of battle excited his blood? Skranga intended to keep a close eye on Democriphon during the upcoming skirmish.

After everyone had stepped out of the carriages, Skranga explained their plan to stage an attack on the phony Styphon's House party in the early morning.

Eldra spoke up. "Can we go around them? It might be better to avoid discovery, especially if Yaholo only spotted an advance guard."

"I doubt that is the case, my Lady," Skranga said. He had to admit he was smitten with Lady Eldra; a mature woman possessed of both great beauty and intelligence. "An advance guard would not have a carriage and a highpriest with them."

Calthros nodded agreement. "The advance column would be soldiers and mercenaries, nothing else. The highpriest would follow only after the way was cleared of possible hostiles or proven safe."

"We outnumber them considerably, Lady Eldra," Democriphon pointed out. "We can easily ambush and destroy them, take their gold and fireseed. We certainly don't need any more bandits running around in this area; they could easily bring unwanted attention to our party, making our job that much more difficult."

# SEVEN

## I

The only light came from the moon and stars. The caravan's guards, while awake, fought to keep their eyes open as their shift dragged on seemingly forever. Five men walked the perimeter of the camp and were replaced every four hours.

Petty-Captain Rylon, a former mercenary from Hos-Ktemnos, carefully worked his way through the high grass on his route. Much of the grass had been trampled down by the previous shift, making it easier to see where he was going, though the occasional rock or gopher hole would cause him to stumble every so often. He didn't really expect to find anyone out here in a deserted pasture in the Blethan backwoods, but experience had taught him to expect the unexpected.

Rylon whipped his head around as he heard the screeching of an owl. Cursing, he returned to his patrol when he tripped over something and fell face forward into the grass. Whatever he had tripped over was too large and soft to be a rock. Curious, he sat up and turned to examine what it was. He cursed some more when he made out Hernos' homely face in the dim moonlight.

"Dralm-damnit, Hernos!" Rylon growled in a harsh whisper. "If you get caught sleeping on duty again Balkon will cut-off your nutmeats. Get up you worthless—"

Rylon's voice stopped short as a long knife blade sliced his throat. He fell forward, gurgling as his lifeforce drained from the new opening. A Hostigi wiped his blade on the dead man's tunic then faded back into the tall grass.

It was a universal truth that veteran soldiers took every opportunity to get as much sleep as possible. Younger soldiers, not yet experienced enough to know that sleep was a rare commodity in war, often frittered away their time gambling and boasting to each other of feats real and imagined, although not loud enough to wake their senior warriors. Old soldiers took a very dim view of being awakened for no good reason.

Kaldar had just finished regaling his fellows with an improbable tale of his sexual prowess, a story involving three women, a cask of winter wine and the odd use of a rope tied to the rafters of a barn at both ends, when his boasts were interrupted by a crossbow bolt that sprang from his chest. The boiled leather armor he wore, normally proof against an arrow, provided no protection against the bolt. He fell forward, his face landing in the center of the campfire.

The remaining soldiers hesitated as they tried to make sense of what had just occurred. The two closest to Kaldar attempted to pull him away from the fire while the others quickly scrambled to their feet and fumbled for their arquebuses. The more experienced soldiers sleeping in their tents would have known better than to present such easy targets. Before anyone could shout an alarm, they were cut down in a flurry of arrows and crossbow bolts.

With everyone either dead or asleep, Democriphon led the raiding party into the camp and had them take up positions near the tents and wagons. Horses were led away from potential harm both to keep them quiet and for possible later use by Skranga's band.

Four men covered each tent; two with muskets, two with crossbows. The plan was to intimidate the sleepy soldiers with the smoothbores.

Failing that, crossbows would be used as long as possible to keep the noise from attracting anyone else that might be in the woods. The tents were carefully stripped away and soldiers prodded awake with a boot to the side. One foolhardy soul tried to scream a warning and received a knife stroke across his throat for his trouble.

In less than an eighth of a candle, all of the tents were stripped away and the sleeping occupants awakened and held at gunpoint. Their weapons were quickly confiscated and the still groggy owners bound, gagged and escorted away from the camp as quickly and quietly as circumstances allowed.

## II

Skranga, still in the yellow robes of a high priest, was escorted into the camp along with Ranthar, Eldra, Calthros and Gasphros by twelve soldiers. Skranga looked about and noticed that all of the surviving enemy soldiers were bound and under guard. There were a few dead men stretched out to the side of the campfire. None of the dead were his people as near as he could tell. It had been a clean operation.

"Excellent work, Colonel."

Democriphon sniffed in disdain. "It was much too easy. Only five men on guard spaced too far apart to keep potential enemies out. A troop of young girls could have taken these churls. It was beneath the efforts of good men like these." Democriphon waved a hand at the men he used to take the camp.

They visibly stiffened and stood straighter upon hearing his compliment.

"Where are the Styphoni priests?" Ranthar asked after looking over the prisoners.

"Still asleep inside their carriages, I assume. I thought it better to let them wake on their own and step out of their carriages to find us waiting rather than risk starting a fight that could draw unwanted attention."

Skranga looked over the prisoners. "Can you be sure that they are not disguised as one of the soldiers we're holding here?"

"If so, it has done them little good," Democriphon said with a chuckle. "I doubt they would have slept in a tent to maintain a charade without advance notice of an attack, in which case more men would have been awake and on guard. No, Your Grace, they must be either in the carriages or running for their lives through the forest. Since I had the camp surrounded before the attack, I find escape to be a most unlikely option."

Skranga nodded. "You surprise me, Colonel. In a good way."

Democriphon grimaced. "I know my reputation, Your Grace. While I think it is largely undeserved, I also think my performance here in Hos-Bletha could have a great impact on my being promoted to Captain-General someday."

*Of course he knows his reputation*, Skranga thought. *Every field commander worth his pay has his intelligencers working within as well as without. Well, if he works better that way, it's all to the good.*

"How long before the priests rouse themselves?" Ranthar asked.

"According to the prisoners, that should be any moment, now," Democriphon replied. He turned to Skranga "Your Grace, perhaps it would be better if they did not see you in those vestments when they stepped out."

Skranga looked down at his own robes. "Wouldn't it help to loosen their tongues if they thought I was a highpriest?"

"It could also make them hold those tongues," Democriphon said. "I would rather keep your appearance in reserve in case we need to threaten them with…ah…Roxthar's methods."

Skranga paled a bit at the suggestion then nodded and walked away with Eldra. It disturbed him a bit to think that Democriphon might resort to using such methods himself.

Ranthar watched Skranga and Eldra walk off then turned to Democriphon. "Will you really torture them?"

"Of course, not, Captain. If these priests fail to cooperate, I will simply have their heads chopped off. I will likely have to do that anyway since we can't let word of our presence in Hos-Bletha get around. But torture should be beneath a good soldier."

It was also unreliable, Ranthar knew, since a person in great pain will say or do anything to make it stop. Even confess to a crime that never happened. Often the threat of torture was more effective than torture itself. Not for the first time Ranthar wished he could use First Level hypnomech to extract information from reluctant sources.

"So, do we wait for them to wake on their own or do we pound on the carriage door?"

Democriphon's face went blank as he considered the question.

Ranthar knew the Colonel didn't like people being able to read his thoughts from his expressions, so he made a point of not showing any.

After some moments, Democriphon smiled. "I think the occupants of that carriage will need all the rest they can get. It is going to be a very trying day for them."

Ranthar found himself warming to the Colonel. The man had a sense of humor as well as patience. From Democriphon's reputation, Ranthar had half-expected him to set fire to the carriage to speed things along. "What shall we do in the meantime?"

"Breakfast for the men, guards on the carriage and a nice little chat with the other prisoners." Democriphon ordered four guards to watch the carriage and four more to get food for themselves and then replace the carriage guards. "The moment somebody pokes his head out send a guard to get me. Come, Ranthar. We can enjoy a leisurely meal ourselves before we interrogate the prisoners. I suppose we should feed the men as well while we are at it."

Ranthar nodded. Feeding the soldiers first was something common on the Fourth Level. It made good sense since the men did the real fighting. Eating first kept up their morale and made them more willing to fight. He wondered if Democriphon had learned this idea from his Great King.

Waiting on the interrogation was another matter altogether. It was very possible that the occupants of the carriage already knew that they had been overrun. If so, they were sweating it out waiting for their captors to come knocking. In that case, Democriphon was using a very sound tactic. The enemy would be wondering about their fate and working themselves into frenzy. By the time they were pulled from the false safety of their carriage they would likely be in a very accommodating mood. Democriphon was a lot more perceptive than he let on. He would bear a lot of watching during this mission.

By the time breakfast was finished one of the carriage guards ran up and reported that four men in the robes of Styphoni priests had surrendered to the guard and were demanding to speak with the leader.

Democriphon turned to Skranga and said, "With your permission, Your Grace?"

Duke Skranga nodded.

While Democriphon had been called impetuous, Ranthar noted, it was never said that he failed to show proper respect to his superiors.

"Calthros, could you change into your robes and join us at the carriage?"

"I will be along momentarily, Colonel," Calthros said, as he rushed off to change.

Democriphon nodded again to Skranga and headed off as well.

"Democriphon seems to be doing well," Ranthar observed after the Colonel walked away.

Skranga nodded. "That worries me, in a way. When he finally gives in to his nature it could be disastrous."

Ranthar digested that tidbit then said, "Perhaps I should join him for the interrogations."

"I would appreciate that, Captain."

Ranthar quickly caught up with Democriphon. Rather than head straight over to the carriage and interrogate the new prisoners, the Colonel detoured to visit the men under his command. He looked them over until he found a particularly large specimen, who towered over everyone else, with an impressive two-handed sword. Such men were common on the more primitive Fourth Level timelines where only the strong survived. This soldier was even bigger than Great Queen Rylla's personal guard, Xykos; he was well over two-and-a-half rods in height by local measurement, or what Kalvan would have called almost seven feet high. His girth was even more impressive; his chest the size of a barrel.

"What is your name, soldier?" Democriphon asked in a polite voice.

"Petty-Captain Gycules, sir."

"Were you born here in Hos-Bletha?"

"Yes, sir. I was born in the Princedom of Drathor."

*Aha*, Ranthar thought. *Drathor borders the Sastragath so he probably has some Urgothi blood in him, which would help explain his size.*

"What was your trade prior to becoming a soldier, Gycules?"

"Woodsman, logger and ranger, sir."

Democriphon smiled. "Are you good with that sword?"

"I like to think so." Gycules hefted the two-handed sword with the curvy blade in one great mitt and swung it about as if attacking an invisible foe. He wasted no effort on unnecessary flourishes and finished his demonstration by chopping into a nearby maple tree. The blade sunk into the wood for at least a hand's depth. Gycules pulled the blade free and started wiping it down.

"Come with me, Gycules. I think you will be very useful for what I have in mind." Democriphon pulled the large warrior aside and spoke to him in low tones beyond Ranthar's hearing. Gycules ran off and Democriphon started off toward the carriage.

Ranthar caught up and walked with the Colonel in silence. Whatever Democriphon was going to do, he must have put some thought into it beforehand. When they reached the carriage four men in the white robes of Styphoni lower priests were being held at sword point inside a circle of Hostigi soldiers.

Democriphon took a seat on a log and affected an air of disinterest in the prisoners. After a few minutes Gycules arrived with Calthros, dressed in the black robe of an underpriest. Democriphon smiled and stood then walked over to Calthros. Again he spoke in low tones that Ranthar failed to hear before standing back.

"Gentlemen, I suppose you are all wondering why I called you here, today," said Democriphon using a Fourth Level Europo-American phrase. Ranthar was surprised at the usage until he recalled that Kalvan had used that same expression in many of his meetings. *Imitation is the sincerest form of flattery.*

The false Styphoni priests barely reacted to the Colonel. Their eyes were fixed on Calthros. Calthros made a small gesture with his hand and watched the priests intently.

"We were passing through this region when we noticed your little band and became curious. Now what is a group of priests from Styphon's House doing in this remote area with such a small escort?" Democriphon asked.

Calthros again made the gesture, waited, then sighed. "These men are not of Styphon's House."

"Really?" Democriphon did not sound at all surprised. "How can you tell?"

"These men failed to respond with the correct gesture," Calthros explained. "When I did this," the former underpriest gestured, "they should have responded with this," another more intricate gesture.

"Ah. So these must be fakes?" Democriphon looked over the four with a critical eye. "Are you quite certain?"

"Yes, definitely fakes, and not very convincing ones. That one wears the yellow robes of a highpriest, but he is much too young and this escort is far too small. Also, if he were a highpriest, he would not be traveling by back trails in friendly territory. The three white-robed priests have the look of fighters, not holy men. They have deep tans and rough calloused hands."

Calthros held up his own hands and spread his fingers wide to show that there were no calluses. "Even a lower priest wearing the white robe rarely performs any strenuous labor. Styphon's House has slaves for that, and there are no slaves here at all."

Ranthar stepped over to the nearest priest and inspected his face and hands. He found minute scars on his face and heavy calluses on both hands. Calthros had a good eye to have spotted these things so quickly.

"There are a number of other glaring errors, like the lack of a proper retinue, but I think my point is made," Calthros finished and took a seat on a nearby log.

"This is a band of sharpers, I'll warrant," Democriphon said.

Ranthar blanked on the word. The Hypno-mech language program, while extensive, occasionally missed a word here and there, especially colloquial slang terms. Fortunately, his training also included drawing meaning from context. These were obviously con men or grifters of some sort. Ranthar made a mental note to submit the new word for addition to the Hypno-mech linguistic database in his next report.

"You don't sound surprised," Ranthar observed.

"I'm not." Democriphon looked the captives over then spotted one who seemed particularly unpleasant. "You." The Colonel pointed and three of his men manhandled the phony underpriest and brought him forward. "What is your name?"

In lieu of an answer, the man spat at the Colonel. Before the spittle reached the ground the sharper's head followed. Gycules wiped the blade of his great sword on the headless man's robes then returned it to its scabbard.

"I may have neglected to mention that I have no patience for difficult prisoners. You will speak, truthfully, or you will die, instantly." Democriphon pointed to another white-robed man at random. "You."

# EIGHT

Duke Skranga possessed a surprising appetite for such a bag of bones. While he waited for Democriphon, Calthros and Ranthar to return he gnawed on a turkey leg, more to keep himself occupied than anything else. He had just finished when the trio returned from questioning the prisoners.

"Ah! So, Colonel, did you learn anything useful?"

"Yes," Democriphon replied. "What we have here is a band of sharpers passing themselves off as an Investigation squad. Word of Roxthar's Investigation has spread to Hos-Bletha and the small towns and villages are frightened witless over it. These men,"—he made a sweeping gesture in the direction of the captives—"have been capitalizing on that fear and extorting gold, food and other valuables to take their Investigation elsewhere."

"Where are they from?" Captain Ranthar asked.

"Mostly from Hos-Bletha, though some are former mercenaries from all over the Five Kingdoms including a few

Sastragathi. Their leaders hatched this scam after their previous one became unworkable."

Skranga's forehead wrinkled. "Previous scam?"

"Previously, they passed one of their members off as the long lost Prince in Exile," Democriphon supplied. "That fell apart when their 'Prince' was caught with the wrong farmer's daughter. Nobody else was handsome enough to pull off the role after that, so they changed their routine."

Skranga shook his head in disgust. "We should take off the leaders' heads, at the very least."

"Most of them have already lost their heads, Your Grace," Calthros said.

Skranga turned to Democriphon. "Colonel?"

Democriphon lowered his eyes. "In the event that any of the prisoners were reluctant to answer my questions or lied, I instructed Gycules to decapitate the prisoners upon a nod of my head. The first prisoner actually spat at me. The second tried to bluff his way out by claiming that they had been separated from the Grand Host during a heavy fog."

Skranga nodded. In their current circumstances they had little choice in how they dealt with situations like this. "And the rest?"

"I…um…well, the third was being very cooperative, or so I thought. Gycules misinterpreted me when I nodded while listening to the man. His head flew off before I could do anything to stop it. With only one man left to question I instructed Gycules to strike only on my express verbal order." Democriphon shrugged. "That proved unnecessary as the last man *spilled his guts* so quickly I barely had time to ask any questions."

Skranga had to fight to suppress a smile. While he took no joy in the casual killing of these men, Democriphon's embarrassment was truly comical. "I…see. Did you chastise this Gycules?"

"I should say not! I would be a fool to punish a man who obeyed my own orders. The fault was mine, not his."

Skranga had to agree. He was not a military man and thought officers never admitted to making mistakes; at least not in front of their own men. His estimation of the Colonel went up a notch. "What do you propose we do with the rest of the prisoners?"

Democriphon answered as if he had given the matter some thought already. "Most of them are mercenaries who have fallen on hard times; too old or battle damaged to manage in a sustained war. I suggest we take their oath to Galzar and let them join us. We could use the extra men, and veteran mercenaries can train any new recruits we might acquire along the way."

"And the ones who are not mercenaries?" Skranga prompted.

"A professional sharper could be of great help to us, I think. Calthros, Vanir and I…"

"Vanir?"

"The last of the four Styphoni imposters from the carriage," Ranthar reported. "The one we didn't behead."

"I will talk with this Vanir after the meeting to determine if he can be trusted," Skranga said. From experience, he knew that men of loose virtue could be bought cheaply, but afterward they would flip sides at the first sight of a gold coin. *If the sharper can convince me that he can be trusted, his life will be saved; if not, he will fertilize next spring's garden.*

## II

Great King Niclophon paced back and forth in his private chambers. Though late in the season, the weather was still too warm for the robes of his office, so instead he wore his linen toga with the purple half cape and his ever present gold circlet that served as his crown when not presiding over royal court.

He had been expecting a contingent of Styphoni to return ever since Archpriest Heraclestros from the Inner Circle had arrived and requested a sizeable portion of his army for the war against the Usurper. Unfortunately, he was in debt to Styphon's House for more than just gold. He had been forced to promise the Archpriest an army as the Hos-Blethan contingent of the Grand Host. They were not due to leave until next spring, but winter was just over the horizon and spring would be here soon enough.

Great King Kaiphranos had lost most of his army to the Daemon Kalvan at the Battle of Chothros Heights. The loss of his eldest son had caused him so much woe he had fallen deathly ill. And the Harphaxi army had been twice the size of anything Niclophon could raise, assuming his princely levy was mustered out. Always a chancy thing with the unreliable and obstreperous princes of Hos-Bletha. His realm was too large and with too few subjects, and his princes knew all too well that there was little Niclophon could do to coerce their cooperation.

Niclophon was also worried that this so-called Grand Host of Styphon's House might very well lose to Kalvan. Who knew what demonic forces this demi-god could conjure up from the Cold Lands or possibly even Regwarn, home of the dead? If Styphon's forces were defeated, the False King of Hos-Hostigos might then turn his sights on Hos-Bletha. The idea of facing the Daemon in combat terrified Niclophon, especially since he had commanded that Kalvan's fireseed would not be permitted within the borders of his realm. It was said to be of superior quality, but that was how daemons fooled and tricked the unwary. Supreme Priest Sesklos Himself had written to him telling him that the Daemon's fireseed released invisible devils to plague the countryside.

Even worse, the troops Styphon's House was demanding would leave him with insufficient troops to defend Hos-Bletha if Kalvan invaded the Kingdom. With over five thousand of his regulars and another six thousand of his irregulars, mostly light cavalry and some javelin throwers, in Hos-Harphax, there would be only about six thousand regulars and four thousand irregulars to guard the Kingdom in case of attack. Even at full strength, the military might of Hos-Bletha was a fraction of that conjured up by the False Great King of Hos-Hostigos. Moreover, the Daemon had proved capable of fending off superior numbers on the battlefield on more than one occasion. Kalvan had to be getting help from Hadron himself to bedevil the Styphoni as he had been doing so far.

Niclophon knew he was no warrior king like Kalvan, or even First Prince Lysandros of Hos-Harphax. He had taken the throne after his brother Marocles, the previous Great King, passed away along with his wife over thirty winters ago. Actually, he should have simply become the

Regent, but his nephew, Valthros, disappeared the same night the former king and queen died. There were several different rumors about what had happened to Valthros. One had it that one of the governesses had kidnapped the infant prince and fled the princedom with him. Another suggested that Niclophon himself had either exiled or murdered the child.

Valthros was often referred to as either the Prince in Exile or the Orphan Prince. Niclophon had nearly torn the kingdom in half trying to find him, almost causing a civil war in the process.

At first Niclophon had genuinely wanted to hold the throne for his lost nephew. He believed that he could raise the boy right and turn him into a devout follower of Styphon, something his brother and his wife would never have done. Niclophon was convinced it was Styphon Himself who had struck down his brother for blasphemy.

As the years went by and Niclophon became more comfortable in his role as Great King, he found he was less and less interested in finding his nephew and restoring his throne. After all, Valthros might have been led astray by the worshippers of Dralm and Yirtta Allmother—or even Galzar the Wargod. The thought of royal blood being raised by an Uncle Wolf made him ill. Eventually, he had grown to fear the discovery of Valthros to the point where he was prepared to have him quietly dispatched should he ever turn up.

One problem with killing the Orphan Prince, as the troubadours called him, was that Niclophon had failed to provide an heir to assume the throne when he died. Niclophon had a wife, of course. He had married the daughter of Phaedron, Prince of Eythros, to secure his position as Great King, though he spent precious little time in her company. She was pleasant enough, even comely. The Queen was much younger than his fifty-three years and still of child-bearing age, and she managed the castle staff with a firm, yet gentle hand. Unfortunately, she was not to his taste. His marriage was one of political expediency, not love. In all fairness no woman was to his taste. Niclophon's interests lay elsewhere.

He stopped his pacing and plopped down onto a pile of cushions. Things had been so much simpler before the Daemon Kalvan had been spit out of Regwarn's Caverns. True, there had been petty bickering between the principalities as well as the interminable urgings from his advisers to supply an heir, not to mention the regular tempests or *huracans*, as the Arawak called them, that threatened to wash away some of the more southerly regions of the kingdom. Of course there were also the Carib and Sastragathi tribes that would harry the smaller towns, committing all of the usual atrocities plus a few of the more horrid ones, such as cannibalism. Niclophon actually felt a bit nostalgic for those times.

The Usurper was a different kind of panther altogether. Thanks to the Daemon Kalvan, fireseed could now be made by any peasant with access to sulfur, charcoal and a dung heap. Great armies were tearing through the Northern Kingdoms like swarms of locusts destroying everything in their path. Food supplies, running short in the war-torn areas, had to be brought in from the less affected areas whenever possible. Not only was he shipping beans and corn north, but endless supplies of gold and silver to feed the ever-gaping maw of the Styphoni war machine.

Niclophon's chain of thought was broken when Archimanes, his Chancellor, walked in and cleared his throat. Archimanes tended to move into a room silently and wait to be noticed. Failing that, he would make some polite noise to draw his overlord's attention.

"Yes, Archimanes?"

"Your Majesty, a message has arrived from Styphon's House requesting gold to help the war effort against the Daemon Kalvan."

"Of course. Arrange the usual tribute wagon along with a note of debt reduction. Send it off as soon as it is ready along with two cavalry troops as escorts. Provide orders, in My Name, for those cavalrymen to join the Grand Host of Styphon's House after the gold is delivered to Balph. Maybe that will forestall Grand Master Soton from demanding more of Our men."

"As you command, Your Majesty."

Archimanes started to withdraw when Niclophon had a thought. "Archimanes, order them to take the tribute wagon along a less traveled route. No point announcing to the people that more gold is going to Styphon's House, or making it an easy target for bandits."

"Very well, Your Majesty." Archimanes waited a moment in case of another command. When none was forthcoming he quietly backed out of the chamber.

## III

Duke Skranga waited until the sickle-shaped moon was overhead before having the prisoner brought before him. Skranga sat before the campfire, ringed in stones, stirring the glowing coals with an old sword. He had asked Gycules to bring the sharper to the fire ring. *How can I purchase his loyalty?* he asked himself. *Any man will swear entreaties to the gods to save his life, but renounce them as soon as he's out of your sight.*

The giant former mercenary brought the sharper to him by the scruff of his neck, much like a mastiff would bring a rat caught eating his master's table scraps. "Here's the prisoner, Your Grace."

The baldheaded man was a bag of suet held together by a torn and dirty robe that had once been white. He looked down at the glowing coals, then at the sword in Skranga's hand. His eyes widened and he looked as if his head was about to explode. "Please, Your Lordship—"

"Quiet," Gycules ordered, as he dropped the man like an unwanted bag of refuse. "Do you want I should stay, Your Grace?"

"Yes," Skranga said. He had never killed anyone with his own hands, and wasn't about to start now.

The sharper started whimpering.

Gycules turned to him, and shouted, "Shut up! Or I'll slice off your nutmeats and sew them into your cheeks."

The sharper's face turned white, except for the red blossoms on his cheeks.

*Good, he's a drunk*, Skranga observed. "What's your name?"

"My name…is Vanir, Your Lordship. What do you want—information, I'll tell you all I know. Gold, we haven't much but I'll tell you where it's buried! Mercy, please. I swear, I'll repent. May Allfather Dralm be my witness—"

"Shut your skull cave!" Skranga cracked as he used his sword to stir the coals, releasing a burst of red sparks. "I'll ask the questions and you'll give me straight answers. No begging, no pleading. If your answers are straight and true, we may have a job for you. If not"—he turned his head toward Gycules—"I'll give you to his sword."

Vanir held his hands out in supplication. "Whatever you want to know, I'll tell you. I swear by the True Gods!"

"Tell me, what do you know about the Orphan Prince?"

Vanir quickly spun out almost the same story that Gasphros had told them at the inn. Some thirty winters ago Great King Marocles and his wife had died under mysterious conditions. The next morning their son, Valthros, disappeared. "No one ever found his corpse, nor any sign of the young boy. Many townsfolk suspected that the King's brother, Niclophon, had the boy killed and his body buried. Over the winters scores of people have claimed to have seen him, and for some time imposters have popped up claiming to be Valthros. We had our own Orphan Prince racket until our 'prince' got involved with the wrong wench. That's when we turned to brigandage. I came up with the idea of impersonating a squad of Archpriest Roxthar's Investigators. It worked like magic. We would arrive at a village in our white robes and announce that we were Investigators, and we would be given anything and everything we asked for."

Skranga knew a lot about Roxthar's Investigation and believed only the most heartless of human scum would use it as an extortion racket. He felt unclean and wanted to wash his hands just hearing about it.

Vanir shrugged. "The only problem is that one day a troop of real Investigators will show up and that racket will come to a quick end. However, the right man can earn a lot of gold,"—he winked at Skranga knowingly—"claiming to be the Orphan Prince."

Skranga had to restrain himself from kicking him into the fire ring. This was the second time he heard this story and it looked like one that could be spun into gold. Colonel Democriphon, of all the mission members, looked and acted the most like a prince. It probably wouldn't be hard, with the right advance work, to sell him to the locals as the Orphan Prince. And, what could be more destabilizing to the kingdom than a *legitimate* claimant to the Silver Throne?

"We can use a man with your experience," Skranga said, although it pained him to admit. The man was a fraud and outright scoundrel, but useful.

A look of relief flooded the man's florid face. Fortunately, he was smart enough to keep his mouth shut—this time.

"My real question: can I trust you?"

"Yes, yes, milord. I will aid you in whatever flimflam you decide needs my talents." He dropped to his knees. "I swear before the Twelve True Gods that I will be a loyal and faithful servant."

Skranga suspected that the sharper's oath was only as stout as the man himself, and would be cast aside at the first available opportunity. He would have one of his men shadow him until his loyalty was proven.

"Besides, Your Lordship, I've always wanted to run with a good crew of sharpers, men that had funds and talent. I've never run across a better crew of mountebanks than the crew you have assembled here. I mean that as a compliment! You even have your own false Temple Band that looks so real it would even fool old Sesklos himself."

Skranga said, "You'll have ample opportunities to prove your loyalty, and only one to disprove it." He nodded at Gycules, whose hand went right to the pommel of his great sword.

The sharper followed his eyes and swallowed hard.

"There will be rewards, too. Gycules, bring me a jar of Ermut's Best to seal the deal."

Vanir took to Ermut's brandy like a duck to water. Wiping his chin with his sleeve, he cried out, "This is the best tipple I've ever had. Is there more?"

Gycules poured him another jar full.

"If we're successful in our cozenage with the Orphan Prince, I will personally see to it that you're presented with your own tavern stocked with Ermut's Best. This I swear, by Dralm's Staff."

From the look of sheer joy on the sharper's face, Skranga knew he had just bought the man's eternal loyalty.

# NINE

## I

As Gasphros made his way down the streets of Bletha Town, he was surprised by how small and shabby it appeared. It had seemed much grander to him on his last visit some thirty winters ago. The town was certainly provincial when contrasted with bustling Hostigos Town where merchants, soldiers and travelers of all stripes made their way through the streets and byways. Here most of the town buildings were made of wood and stood no taller than the city walls. Some of the outbuildings were made of dried mud over lathes with wattle roofs. The main thoroughfare was more impressive and led to the hos-plazos where the Great King's palace and Styphon's High Temple resided, as well as the town gallows and the slaving block. The sun was waning, but still cast a golden glow over the dome of the temple.

*There must be over a hundred thousand ounces of gold on that great dome*, he thought. Still, it would take an army to besiege this town. Not that he was here to study the town's defenses; his job was to get real information, not rumor and innuendo, about how the townspeople felt about their Great King and Styphon's House. The travelers he had talked to as he made his way along the Silos road indicated Styphon's House was not held in high esteem. At several of the inns, after he determined there were no Royal Soldiers in attendance, he sang a couple of verses of "When the Prince Comes Marching Home" to great acclaim.

Gasphros had been on the road since daybreak and had a growing thirst. He spotted a ramshackle tavern under a sign showing a ram's head, underneath were runes which read Ram's Horn Tavern. He decided this might be the place to slake his thirst, as well as a good place to play for his supper.

Inside, the tavern's lime-washed walls were slashed with blackened beams. Cressets set on every other table provided minimal light to the room and on one wall there was a gonfalon displaying a Ram's head. Against the opposite wall was a rough-plank bar behind which sat a bald-headed man with a stomach almost as large as one of the ale barrels that stood next to him.

A blowsy serving wench with two large catheads, which threatened to pop out of her bodice, asked him what he wanted to drink.

He held up his lyre. "Miss, may I play and sing for my dinner?"

She looked at him scornfully, and pulled her top up. "You'll have to talk to Vano," she said, pointing to the obese bartender.

Gasphros made a slight bow and got up. He walked over to the bartender who feigned indifference. "My good man, in exchange for dinner and a few ales, I will play and sing for your patrons."

The bartender shrugged, as he passed over a tankard of ale. "Go ahead, but don't sing that Orphan Prince song. A couple of Royals were inside yesterday and a couple fools started singing it. Almost caused a riot. Two of them got punched out by the soldiers, one left most of his teeth in the sawdust."

"I'm not familiar with that ditty," he replied, trying to hide his excitement. *Nor will I play it in Bletha Town again*, he decided. *That song is doing my job for me.*

## II

Eldra sat on a cushion next to Skranga as she finished writing something on parchment with a quill pen. Sitting beside them on the ground or on large rocks were Ranthar, Myklon, Democriphon and Calthros.

"The letter is done, Your Worship," Lady Eldra said, holding out the parchment.

Skranga accepted the document and looked it over, then sealed the pouch with wax and put his ring's imprint into the wax seal. "Good. This might save my hide later on if things get sticky. I want this sent to my agent in Balph immediately. The name of whom this missive is to go to is inside this pouch. Democriphon, please have your man take it to my agent and none other. Use your most trustworthy man to deliver it. He is not to read the contents nor ever mention the name of the agent."

Democriphon accepted the letter. "What is it?"

"Instructions to get 'Sangar' on the priestly rolls in case I arouse suspicion," Skranga said, looking smug. "We don't want somebody sending a message to Balph and finding out that no one in Balph has ever heard of me, now, do we?"

"You have a man inside…?"

"According to our Great King the first rule of spycraft is to keep your secrets close, and your spies even closer," Skranga interrupted. "What I do or do not have in that area is not to be discussed. Ever. Understood?" Everybody nodded. *Good. Xylon has sacrificed much to be my agent in Balph, and I won't have his life endangered by loose talk.*

"Now, what about this Robbing Hoot you were talking about, Ranthar?" Skranga said.

"Robin Hood," Ranthar corrected Skranga for the *nth* time. He didn't blame the duke since the name didn't translate well into Zarthani. Ranthar also made a mental note to pick up a copy of *The Adventures of Robin Hood* the next time he returned to Fifth Level Police Terminal. Chief Verkan had promised to put in a conveyor head in Bletha Town in case of an emergency. Ranthar decided he would take a quick visit to

Home Time Line as soon as it became operational. "It was one of King Kalvan's ideas based on a famous outlaw in the Cold Lands."

"Such an odd name," Skranga commented. "I can see either Ranthar or Myklon playing the part of this...rogue bandit. However, I want it very clear that there will be no raping or outright murder by any of your men, Colonel. If we're going to pass you off as the Orphan Prince, you need to have the people's support. Abusing them will work against that. Robbing rich merchants is all fine and well, but do not kill any of them if you can avoid it. You should view them as future subjects of the throne and we must act as if we will have to compensate them later."

"I agree, Your Worship," Ranthar said. Calthros had convinced everyone that they had to start using Skranga's Styphon's House honorific to ensure no one slipped up at the wrong time. It was obvious that Skranga was still uncomfortable with his new identity as a Styphon's House highpriest.

Skranga suddenly got up. "Ranthar you can play the part of Robinos. That's what we'll call you, not Robin Hood. Now, any soldiers that Niclophon sends after you are fair game. I can spare eighty men to keep these mercenaries we just captured in line. What else do you think you will need?"

Captain Ranthar made a show of considering the question. "If I may, Your Worship, I'd like to select the men individually. I will want at least one baker, a fletcher and bowyer, any craftsmen that we can find, an experienced ranger, blacksmiths and a tailor."

Skranga was surprised. "From where? All we have are mercenaries, Captain."

Colonel Democriphon shook his head. "Most mercenaries started out in other vocations before turning to war for their daily bread. Failed apprentices, runaways, or even men whose prior life was destroyed in a military action or poor business practices. Mercenaries, and even common soldiers, have to come from somewhere. I would hazard an ingot of gold I will find most, if not all of these craftsmen among your soldiers."

Skranga nodded. "No bet, Colonel. But, Ranthar, I am curious as to why you need such skills. We have plenty of fireseed to spare you, so I don't see the need for fletchers, for example."

"Ah, you have not spent a great deal of time living off the land, Your Grace," Ranthar replied. "*Guerilla warfare*, as our Great King calls it, is still fairly new to all of us, but Kalvan stressed the need for stealth and a tactic that he calls 'hit and run.' I want archers and crossbowmen for ambushes, as they are almost completely silent. Arrows and bolts are much quieter than arquebuses and muskets, and just as deadly in the hands of an experienced shooter, especially at close range. Picking off men from the rear of a convoy or company of soldiers could go unnoticed long enough to whittle the numbers down to manageable size.

"Rangers are experienced at living off the land and I expect we will be doing a lot of that. Trackers should be self-evident. The craftsmen and blacksmiths are to build such items as needed for the men's comfort and replacement arms since we have no way of knowing either how long we will be out on a mission or away from any place for resupply. We will be using swords as much as bows and need somebody to maintain them. We may also have to trade with the locals at some point. A healer would also be a good idea as well as an Uncle Wolf. Unfortunately, we neglected to bring either of these with us."

Skranga considered Ranthar's words, then nodded. "Take your pick of the men, Captain. I'll provide you with enough gold to send men into the local towns to stock up on provisions in advance. I suppose you will need a baker's oven and blacksmithing tools as well as other supplies. Where do you propose to set up camp?"

Ranthar shrugged. "I'm not sure, but Vanir knows the territory and several bolt-holes unknown to the locals. We'll set up in one of those and have a couple others readied in case we have to move fast."

*Finding the band of sharpers was a stroke of luck*, Skranga decided. *Dralm knows we were due for some.*

## III

It took over a moon-half, but Gasphros and a few of the more trusted Blethan mercenaries returned with the supplies needed to set up a working mini-village in the deep forest. The supplies had been gathered in Bletha Town and villages far enough away from their camp not to attract any attention. Meanwhile, Democriphon and Ranthar had overseen the clearing of rocks and brush as well as the construction of the settlement. Only the trees that were directly in the way of construction were removed, and lean-tos were built around the remaining trees. This was to allow for maximum camouflage, something Democriphon had learned from his Great King.

The horses that they had purchased in Gytha Port were put in corrals. Democriphon hoped to acquire new mounts in his raids. To that end, a stable and more corrals had been erected at the edge of the encampment near a small stream to water the horses. Tall grass had been gathered and placed in the corral to feed the horses until hay and grain could be brought in, others were haltered outside the camp and allowed to graze.

As he took in the work done in his absence, Gasphros said. "You've accomplished much while I was away, Colonel."

Democriphon smiled. "Fortunately, I was right about the mercenaries numbering artisans and former apprentices among them. Sophlos over there was an experienced carpenter until he gambled away his shop. He became a soldier of fortune hoping to earn enough to begin anew. Lathros has much the same story. Then the Fireseed Wars started and, well, you know how that is turning out."

"Indeed. A standing mercenary cannot walk down the street without being pressed into service by one side or the other. And they are making money hand over fist in the process between the hiring bonuses and battlefield looting."

Democriphon looked over at the mercenaries that had accompanied the bard. They were all unloading the three wagons Gasphros had purchased along with several small one-horse carts. "Did we get everything we needed?"

"I believe so. I found an ironmonger who assisted me in getting everything necessary for opening a small blacksmith shop, with the understanding that I would do so in another village; he didn't want any local competition. I also have the carpentry tools, tailoring equipment, and even a small oven, the type favored by military cooks for long sieges. We have beer and ale, victuals and wine enough to hold us for some time. The wine was far more expensive here than in Hostigos. We brought honey, and at a good price, but maple is all but unknown in this region."

Democriphon nodded. "Good enough. We'll add to the stores with forage and robbery. No point in just taking a passing merchant's gold and silver if they have victuals as well."

"That reminds me," Gasphros added. "I overheard a rumor that Great King Niclophon is sending two wagons of gold from Bletha Town to Balph along with eight wagons of victuals and four wagons of arms and armor. They're reinforcements and supplies for the Grand Host of Styphon's House."

That made Democriphon take notice. "When? What route and how many men will be escorting the gold?"

"A moon-quarter from now. I was unable to get the exact route. I plied a Royal captain with many tankards of ale just to get that much. I do know that it will be a little used back trail. There will also be about a company of foot and squadron of twenty cavalry escorting the wagons."

Democriphon looked as pleased at this news as a seaport madam upon hearing that a troop ship was arriving in port.

"Do you have time to return to Bletha Town and try to get more intelligence on their route? I will speak with Ranthar and discuss a proper ambush."

Gasphros shrugged. "The journey to Balph Town from here is almost a moon-quarter. That's why I left as soon as we finished getting the supplies."

Democriphon began pacing back and forth in front of the guard station. His brow was furrowed and he was pulling the ends of his mustache.

Ranthar approached Democriphon from behind and startled him.

"Dralm, Galzar and Yirtta! Ranthar, you move like a panther."

*First Level stealth training*, Ranthar realized. He hadn't even noticed that he was using it. "My apologies, Democriphon. I overheard part of your conversation with Gasphros. It doesn't sound as though he'll be able to obtain any more information on this military convoy."

"I know, Captain. Not enough time. Nevertheless, what can we do? We do not have enough men to cover every path, road and trail between Bletha Town and Balph. I am not even sure we should try. Our mission would be short indeed if we were to lose the better part of our command attacking the convoy."

Ranthar had to agree. "Well, we might be able to narrow the possibilities a bit. Let's get Duke Skranga and the rest of the crew. We'll meet at the cabin he's calling the War Room and look over some maps. I'll bring Vanir along, as he knows this country well. Gasphros, too, after he has eaten."

The buildings were crude. Ranthar could not help comparing them to Fourth Level log cabins he had seen during his assignments on Europo-American over a hundred years ago. *Has it been that long?* The cabin-like structures were built of interlocking logs cut to size. Mud was used to seal the spaces between the logs. They were rough but serviceable for the purposes for which they were intended.

# TEN

## I

There was a certain degree of universality evident in the design and décor that was particular to inns and taverns. The bar was situated strategically to allow ready access to as many patrons as possible while leaving an opening between the kitchen and dining area. The tables were arranged to allow the tavern wenches unobstructed passage and the lighting was typically dim. Some corners are almost stygian in their near total absence of light.

In one particularly dark corner slouched a man with a kitten on the table and dog at his feet. The collection of empty and overturned steins and bottles hinted at how far in his cups he had plummeted. The candle that would normally provide some slight relief from the shadows had been snuffed out long ago, allowing the table's lone occupant to become nearly invisible.

He was barely aware of the fight that had started between a mercenary and one of the king's guards. Such occurrences were common enough under normal circumstances. The cause of the fights often varied: patriotism versus money, the attentions of a particular barmaid, or even the classic "Hey, I don't like your face" after several cups of ale or flasks of wine. Even one's choice of drink could be cause for an argument.

The man ignored the fight until one of the combatants flew onto his table, scaring the kitten. The man quickly collected the frightened feline and placed it on the empty chair next to him and near the dog.

Satisfied that his furry friend was now safe, the man turned his attention to the soldier who had been so rude as to collide with the table. He grabbed the soldier by his tunic with one hand and hauled him to his feet, then threw a vicious punch into his face. The soldier fell back with blood gushing from his nose. The man then turned his attention to the mercenary who had sent the soldier flying and rushed towards him. The mercenary raised his fists then saw his new attacker clearly and lowered them. He received a powerful belt to the jaw as a result.

The others in the tavern, both mercenaries and soldiers, backed quickly away from the man. The bartender came around the bar and put up his hands in a placating gesture. "Uncle Wolf, if you wish to participate in the brawl you should not wear your vestments. No man here will raise a hand against you otherwise."

The vestments the barkeep referred to were the hauberk of fine chainmail and the wolfskin hood topped with a jewel-eyed wolf head. There was also the spiked mace and dagger on his belt.

The Uncle Wolf stared at the barkeep for a moment as if he didn't recognize him, then turned his attention to the men he had struck. "Galzar, forgive me!" he muttered under his breath. "Help me get these men on a table where I can tend their hurts."

Quarrels were forgotten as soldiers and mercenaries alike crowded over to help the fallen men onto tables where the Uncle Wolf quickly examined them. After several heartbeats he declared the men hale enough and said they would be ready for battle in half a moon-quarter, sooner if they slowed down their drinking. When the two men had recovered their senses the Uncle Wolf bought each a large ale and conferred a blessing on both to do well in battle.

When things had returned to what passes for normal in the tavern, the Uncle Wolf collected the kitten, left some coins on the table and quietly left with the dog close on his heels. The Uncle Wolf staggered a bit as he walked. He had drunk quite a bit in the last several hours, not to mention the last several moons.

The wooziness he felt added to his feelings of shame over his behavior in the tavern. An Uncle Wolf did not engage in battle with the men he ministered to. In fact, he should not even engage others in an open conflict against the enemies of whatever kingdom he resided in; at least not against foes that also worshipped the Twelve Gods. Heathens such as the Mexicotál or the cannibalistic Carib were the exception. Striking a mercenary or soldier in a bar brawl was completely unacceptable and indefensible. Even the lowest novice in training knew better.

"Ah, Syros," the Uncle Wolf muttered to himself as he slumped against a wall, "What have you come to?"

## II

"Our wandering troubadour has returned. How were your tales of the Orphan Prince received in Bletha Town?" Duke Skranga asked, as he puffed on his pipe. Also seated around the table in the improvised War Room, actually a hastily built cabin, were Grand-Captain Myklon, Colonel Democriphon, Captain Ranthar, Lady Eldra, Gasphros, Calthros and the ex-sharper Vanir.

Gasphros smiled. "Great King Niclophon is not well-regarded even in his own capital. I opened my set with the "Ballad of the Lost Prince" and it went over very well. Of course, the rulers it mentions are out of the Founding Legends, but everyone in the room seemed to know who I was referring to. Then I played a new song, "When the Orphan Prince Comes Marching Home," based on the melody of a song Great King Kalvan taught me. It's all about the Orphan Prince and how he returns with a band of great warriors, kills his uncle—the murderer of the real Great King and Queen—and for an encore, attacks Styphon's House. Everyone enjoyed it and half the troubadours and minstrels in Bletha Town had added it to their repertoire by the time I left. In fact, it started drawing attention from the local gendarmes and I had to drop it from my set."

"Good move," Skranga agreed. "You don't want to attract any attention either to you or to the mission. I'm glad to hear that it's been picked up by other minstrels. Banning it will only make it that much more popular."

Gasphros smiled. "My audiences especially enjoyed the lines about shooting Styphon's priests out of guns."

"Yes," Skranga said with a look of fond remembrance . "I can recall when Kalvan used to shoot Styphon's highpriests out of those old bombards."

"I missed that," Gasphros replied. "I don't think Styphon's Inner Circle realizes how much anger the peasants and townspeople have against the Temple, but you can really sense it in the taverns and wineshops. The patron's ears really perked up when I mentioned in passing that it was rumored the Orphan Prince had been seen in Syragon. It got everyone gossiping about other Orphan Princes who had appeared in the past and the terrible fates they had suffered: impalement, hanging, quartering, burning at the stake, and other unpleasant punishments."

Colonel Democriphon's fingers started twisting the ends of his mustache.

"Still," the troubadour continued, "the general consensus was that whoever the Orphan Prince truly is, he'd be better than Niclophon whose strings are pulled by Styphon's House and Chancellor Archimanes. Niclophon is rumored to be levying an ale and wine tax which will put most of the publicans in Bletha Town out of business. This will be the third new tax since last winter; everyone knows that he is sending gold to Balph and most resent him and Styphon's House for raising taxes and tolls."

Skranga took his pipe out of his mouth, looked into the bowl, then began hitting the butt with the palm of his hand until the dottle fell out. After blowing into the bowl to get the last remnants, he began reloading it with fresh leaf. "If the townsfolk of Bletha Town are this upset with their king, what of the subjects who live here in Taurnos or in the Princedoms of Pytha or Syragon? Do they also believe the kingdom is ready for a new ruler?"

Gasphros replied, "Since we arrived at Port Gytha I've visited over a dozen taverns in town and on the road to Bletha Town, and almost to a man the patrons were angry about taxes and the heavy hand that Styphon's House presses upon their shoulders. I believe most of Niclophon's subjects would welcome a new great king."

"This is good news, indeed," Skranga said. "Colonel, I want you to sit down with Vanir. He's run this Orphan Prince deception game before, and I want you to pluck the strings of his mind until you learn everything he knows."

Vanir nodded, "I will do my best, Your Grace."

Democriphon felt uncomfortable about this lie he would soon be living. *All my life I've only wanted to be a soldier, a renowned captain-general who orchestrated great victories. Not a Great King, or pretender…* It didn't look like the Duke was going to give him a choice; on the other hand, there was no one else in the expedition who was the right age, or had what it would take to pass himself off as the Orphan Prince. *The job is mine by default. But, if I'm going to do it, this is the time to set some ground rules.*

"Are you all right with this hoax?" Skranga asked.

Democriphon said, "Yes. However, if I'm going to be the new pretender to the Silver Throne, I'm going to need everyone's cooperation. Vanir, I'll talk to you shortly. Gasphros, see what else you can learn about the Orphan Prince on your next visit to Bletha Town. Talk to some of the older townsfolk, people who remember when he disappeared. But not so obviously that it gets you an escort into the Great King's dungeons."

Gasphros gave a weak smile, then nodded.

"I believe we need to keep this operation secret to everyone but those of us in this room," Democriphon finished. "If not, let's end it now!"

Duke Skranga tugged his chin hairs. "All right, it's your arse on the line, Colonel. Does anyone disagree?"

Everyone was silent.

"Fine, now on to other topics. Gasphros you did a very good, but quick job of reconnaissance in Bletha Town," he told the bard in between puffs on his pipe. "I think it's time for you to take another visit."

"Thank you, Your Grace," Gasphros returned. "Ah, but if I'm to return, I will need more coins..."

"Yes, of course. A man in his cups is loose with his tongue, and nobody can guzzle brew like a soldier. I will write you a chit to take to the paymaster."

Skranga issued the musician a chit for eighty silver crowns and a hundred coppers. He looked at Democriphon and asked, "Is that enough?"

Democriphon nodded. Few troubadours carried much in the way of wealth and spending gold coins might raise suspicions that he was an agent-inquisitory. Still, that was enough money for several rounds of drinks for every soldier and mercenary in a dozen Blethan Town wineshops and taverns.

"Your Grace, don't be too free with those coins," Democriphon cautioned. "While we currently have specie enough to meet our needs for several months, and expect to bring in more, we can't be too extravagant. Great King Kalvan has an adage about counting our turkeys before they hatch. And Gasphros, you don't want it known that you carry that kind of wealth on your person."

Gasphros laughed. "Men of my profession are known to sing for our supper, Colonel. It is always assumed we have little worth stealing. I will do little to disabuse them of that belief."

"Good. Take a meal with the men and rest up before you leave at sunrise. Take a few more guards with you, just to be safe. Different men. I want to keep the faces from becoming too familiar. The same with the local villages."

"I can also spread some lies about the Orphan Prince."

Gasphros nodded and started to leave, then stopped and turned. "I almost forgot; there's also a slaver caravan expected within the quarter-moon."

Democriphon started. *Slavers! I would love to get my hands on them. But how would they know in Bletha Town that a slave caravan was on its way?* Then he remembered that each Styphon's House temple had its own post station with a relay of fresh horses. In Hos-Hostigos they had what Kalvan called a "pony express," but—unlike Styphon's House—the slavers did not have permission to travel through the other five kingdoms. "Do you know what route they will take?"

"They typically take the main road from Balph to Bletha Town since sea travel has become so expensive. The war has raised the price of sea transport to ridiculous heights," Gasphros explained. "They'll get the most business and best prices for their slaves in Bletha Town, so they won't be likely to stop in the smaller villages along the way save to resupply or rest. Besides, slavers are not well received here, not even in towns that have slaveholders."

Democriphon called to Gycules. "I want you to send three men out to scout the Silos Road. If there's a slave caravan coming, then I want to know where it is and when it will get here. We are going to have what King Kalvan calls a *practice run* and maybe get ourselves some new recruits. Gasphros, take all the wagons for your next foray. Buy more victuals, but not all in Bletha Town. Buy all you can from the local villages on the way back. I expect we'll have many more mouths to feed very soon."

## III

Petty-Captain Andros filled the air with metaphors both blasphemous and biologically improbable. The captain had put Andros in charge of setting up the convoy while he relaxed at a nearby tavern. It wasn't that Andros was angry that he had the work dumped on him; petty-captains were used to that kind of treatment. It was because the captain had first tried to arrange things himself. The result was a foul-up that was taking Andros twice as long as it should have to correct.

The captain, the youngest son of a noble family who had dreams of glory on the battlefield, was too inexperienced to be trusted with setting up a convoy. To be fair, this was true of most officers. Sadly, the captain thought all he had to do was tell the men to get the wagons hitched-up to the oxen, point them in the right direction, then add the detachment of a hundred foot and twenty cavalry and start moving. What he didn't do was requisition additional victuals for the men to eat instead of the supplies being sent to the war effort up north. He failed to inspect the oxen to be sure they were all healthy and properly fed and to insure they had food enough for the journey. The same was true of the horses. Of course, there were other supplies the men would need as well; tents, replacements for damaged equipment and clothing, tinderboxes, torches, candles, arquebus' locks, blankets, fireseed…the list went on and on.

The men being sent had to be selected properly as well. The captain simply pointed at some men and told them they were going. He did not bother to check what their specialties were. Andros had to replace three cooks, two sutlers, four healers and a muster clerk with actual fighting men. Of the actual fighters that the captain selected, most of them were still in training and would not last a half-candle on the battlefield. Andros replaced them with more seasoned warriors. Not his best men, of course, as they might be needed at home, but men well-enough seasoned that they would live long enough to learn. As a bonus, Andros selected the most difficult men, men who would improve the Blethan army by their absence. If the convoy were attacked, they would either straighten up or die on the road.

Then there was the route the captain selected. *Who left this idiot in charge in the first place?* The trail he chose would have taken them right through the swamplands. Men could get through that well enough, unless they got the flux, but not oxen and wagons, especially wagons loaded with gold and silver. The rainy season was almost over, but many of the trails would still be washed out, as any fool should know.

Next, there was the security of the mission. One simply did not go blabbing to one and all that he was taking two wagons full of gold for a trip through the wilderness. Andros had spotted the Captain talking to a troubadour in a tavern while in his cups. No telling what he said while besotted. He and his men would have to be extra alert for fear that bandits might try for the gold. While he had never heard of a band of thieves large enough to threaten the convoy, it did not pay to take chances. Even if there were no bandits on the trail, there were still the Ruthani barbarians of which to be wary.

It was going to be a long trek to Balph on foot for the men. There would be blisters, sunburn, mosquitoes and other biting insects, not to mention the endless complaining and occasional fight among the men. Andros would not mind any of it if he could just leave that idiot captain behind.

"Petty-Captain Andros."

Andros fought not to grind his teeth in annoyance. He turned to face the source of his infinite displeasure. "Yes, Captain."

"How go the prep…prepree-ations?" The captain was still in his cups, slurring his words and shaky on his feet.

"Captain Nephron, I should point out again that sending these men and equipment by ship would be faster and safer, both for the men and the wagons."

"Not my…not my 'cision. Captain-General Theodoros wans 'em toughened up by da march. He doesn' want 'em gettin' soft on sum ship."

*That figured,* thought Andros. Theodoros had been elevated to captain-general as a political move by Great King Niclophon. Theodoros had never even served or trained with the army. His sole qualification was being the son of Prince Phaedron whose daughter was also the Great Queen. The Prince was rumored to have some knowledge that could embarrass his overlord. Niclophon could not simply have Phaedron assassinated without stirring up the other princes of the realm—to say nothing of his wife—so he bought off the Prince with a favorable posting for his son. Fortunately, the Captain-General was in a position where he was usually harmless. Usually.

Not for the first time, Andros considered deserting. He had never cared for Great King Niclophon and suspected he was a regicide; the Styphoni were no better. Now he and some men were being sent to fight for the Grand Host of Styphon against Great King Kalvan. *For what? Because this Kalvan released the fireseed secret that had been the sole domain of Styphon's House for centuries. Curse and blast the lot of them! Because of Styphon's House my father lost the family farm.*

"Then we should at least have a larger company. This is too small a group for this kind of journey." Andros pointed at the wagons that would be filled with gold and victuals in the morning. "All this gold is too tempting a prize. Somebody is going to try for it, and even if we beat them back, we will lose men."

"We has our orders, Petty-Captain," the Captain nodded. He seemed to have sobered a bit after hearing Andros' warning. "If it helps any…I agree with ya."

*Maybe he isn't a total idiot after all*, Andros decided.

# ELEVEN

## I

Before leaving Hostigos Town, Duke Skranga had stocked up on supplies for the mission. Among them was a deerskin map of Hos-Bletha with as much detail as was available to the Royal Cartographers. Paper was to be avoided as it might give away who they actually served. Hos-Hostigos was the only kingdom with paper, although the quality still left much to be desired. Several Blethan former mercenaries had been brought in to add their knowledge of back trails and streams that were missing from the map. At Kalvan's suggestion, they added color to the map with dyes to show where the swamps, rivers and lakes were. This was yet another innovation on the part of the Great King.

Democriphon, Ranthar, Gasphros and Vanir were going over the map trying to determine the gold convoy's possible routes. Vanir pointed out a few minor errors and added some trails the Blethan mercenaries had been unaware of. The sharper's knowledge of the back areas of the realm was truly impressive, the benefit of having to hide out from angry townsfolk looking for revenge after a fiddle or scam went sour.

Vanir pointed at the map with the point of his dirk. "From Bletha Town there are many trails and roads that will lead to Balph. Most merchants stick to the main roads to avoid bandits, for what little good it does them. The smarter ones take the little-known back trails. I would hazard that the army convoy will do the same to avoid being noticed."

"Good observation," Democriphon said. "Which paths do you think they will take?"

"That I cannot say, but I think I can narrow down the possibilities." Vanir pointed at a trail near a blue spot on the map. "This trail will be washed out this time of year."

Ranthar nodded. "I don't know how good their officers are…" In actual fact, Ranthar had a very good idea of the military situation in Hos-Bletha thanks to studies done in the nearby Styphon's House control time-lines, "…but any petty-captain worth his pay will have scouted out the trails and will try to keep from taking any that might prove too difficult to traverse."

"If that is so, then we can eliminate this, this and this trail," Gasphros pointed at lines on the map near large blue sections. "Even if they are not washed out, they will be too muddy to move through. At least with heavy wagons."

Democriphon agreed. "I wouldn't want to go that way, especially if I thought I might be attacked."

"That leaves these seven trails and two roads," Ranthar pointed out.

"I don't understand why they don't take their caravan straight to Dalthax City, load up a ship and sail up to Balph." Democriphon used a dagger to point at Bletha Town then traced the road leading to Dalthax. "It would be twice the overall distance, but only a third of it on land. Are they afraid of pirates?"

Gasphros shook his head. "Most of the pirates on the Eastern Ocean are Caribi, but they rarely come this far north except for surprise raids. Their boats are no match for Styphon's galleys, but they are smaller and faster. Ideal for quick smash and grab raids. However, the conditions are treacherous on the Eastern Ocean this close to winter; I doubt they could find a captain willing to travel north and risk his vessel."

Vanir indicated a place between the two cities. "There has been a lot of Ruthani activity in this area and the army has had little success in rooting it out. These barbarians are skilled at attacking locations where the army is not, then vanishing into the forests and swamps before any action against them can be organized."

"The Ruthani rarely attack this far north," Gasphros added pointing to the easternmost and westernmost trails between Bletha and Balph.

"If they are trying to avoid the barbarians, then they will likely choose the paths furthest from their hunting grounds," Vanir said. "I think in that case we can eliminate these three trails."

"That leaves us six possibilities." Democriphon looked over the map. "The westernmost trails run through some hilly country. A heavy wagon might prove too much for the oxen to ascend. I would avoid those if I had a choice."

Ranthar said, "That leaves three possibilities and they all look about the same. Gasphros, what do you think?"

"I agree, for the most part," Gasphros said. "Until you get to the river. Only two trails come to a ferry. This third spot is too deep to ford even without the wagons."

Democriphon slammed his fist on the rough table. "None of this makes sense. No matter what trail they take the convoy is in far greater danger than simply going to Dalthax and waiting for spring. It's not like the Grand Host is going to open its campaign against Hos-Hostigos in the dead of winter."

Ranthar scowled as he considered the situation. "I agree. If I were to run this mission, I would go straight to Dalthax and wait out the rainy season."

"Then why aren't they?" Vanir asked.

Democriphon looked over the map then swore. "They are!"

"What? My information is that…"

"You've been misled, Gasphros. Somebody in the Blethan army has studied King Kalvan and adopted some of his tricks." Democriphon sat down on a stump and took a drink of Ermut's Best from a flask. "This is a case of misinformation. The soldiers you plied with drink were told the wrong thing. Someone expected them to be questioned."

"Then you believe that they will take the road to Dalthax?" Ranthar asked.

Democriphon nodded. "Yes. But not the main path as that would give away their plan too soon. They will take whatever route will get them there the fastest without being readily observed. That is how I would do it."

"And if you are wrong," Gasphros asked.

"Then we miss an opportunity to ambush the convoy, and I will learn from my mistake. Vanir, what path will get the convoy to Dalthax City the quickest and without being noticed? A trail that the bandits are unlikely to use."

"There are two paths that parallel the main road." Vanir pointed at two points on the map. He settled the point of his dirk on the north side of the main road. "This one is more likely to be attacked by the Ruthani barbarians. However, they have few fireseed weapons and would hesitate to attack an armed convoy of regular soldiers." Vanir moved his point to the line south of the main road. "This trail tends to be the favorite of many of the local bandit gangs. They have fireseed weapons, but rarely the manpower to attack that many armed men. The bandits also move around a lot and often attack small parties on the main road as well."

"So the question is which trail would the convoy commanders be more likely to avoid?" Ranthar asked. "Bandits or the Ruthani?"

"Actually, Ranthar, I think it is more a question of which group would be more dangerous," Democriphon replied. "I would think the Ruthani, with their tendency to sell their captives to the Caribi who would eat them would be the ones to avoid." Democriphon thought for a moment. "How far along is the smith…with the wolf-helms?"

"He can only make one or two a day. The last time I spoke with him he had seven ready for the wolf hide to be attached." Ranthar appeared lost in thought for a moment. "We won't have them ready before the convoy leaves for Dalthax.

"Then we'll try something else. We can play the part of simple bandits or...yes! We'll disguise ourselves as Ruthani. We can use the fear they instill to our advantage. We'll do the same with the slaver convoy. Vanir, do you have the costumes needed for this?"

"Very little is needed. Some paint and feathers, the cast-off wolf pelts and deer hides we have collected. The Ruthani run about almost completely naked, so it won't take much. Sometimes they wear the clothes and breastplates of their victims, but not a lot of it as they are unaccustomed to the weight or the feel of armor and cloth on their skin. And those mustaches and beards will have to go; Ruthani have no facial hair and the runaway slaves that join them shave to fit in. A couple of the sharpers' company, Roaring Panther and Silent Wolf, are Ruthani. They can help us with that."

Democriphon absently touched his long flowing mustache. "Why did Roaring Panther and Silent Wolf join your band, Vanir?"

"They were exiled from their tribe, Colonel. Why, they never said, but they have behaved themselves well enough since we found them half dead near a swamp. It is sharper custom not to inquire too closely about anyone's past unless one has reason to suspect that they are spies."

"The Ruthani like the boots they find," added Gasphros returning to the original topic. "The thicker soles protect their feet better than those moccasins they make."

Ranthar looked down at his boots made in Hos-Hostigos shortly after the arrival of Calvin Morrison. He could well imagine they would be highly prized by some backwoods barbarians. Even the Blethans might find them desirable since Kalvan had introduced the concept of right and left foot specialization.

"Wait. What if we run into the real Ruthani or even local bandits?"

"Good question, Ranthar." Democriphon turned to Vanir and Gasphros. "What do you two think?"

"Fight like Galzar's legions and pray," Vanir said.

"In that order," Gasphros added.

## II

"Syros," the Uncle Wolf muttered to himself as he slumped against a wall, "what have you come to?"

For the first time in his forty-odd winters, Uncle Wolf Syros felt shame as he approached the Temple of Galzar. The granite statue with its ruby eyes towered over the entrance to the temple. As he walked between the giant legs and into the temple, the idol's red eyes appeared to be glaring down at him, almost as if the god himself were debating whether or not to smite Syros with his great iron mace.

Once inside, Uncle Wolf Syros imagined he could still smell the bear grease used to keep the mace from rusting. He hurried forward to the altar where another statue, much smaller than the huge statue that straddled the entrance, hunched forward in the stance of one bracing for attack. This statue of Galzar Wolfhead was made of brass—a metal often used in guns—instead of granite, although it had the same scintillating-red ruby eyes.

Syros took out his mace and held it out to the War God's image with both hands before tapping it gently three times on the altar. Kneeling and acts of supplication were for other gods, not the Overlord of Battle. Silently, as Galzar had no use for prayers unless they were offered up on a field of battle, Syros took out six gold crowns and placed them in the brass bowl on the altar; three ounces each for the men he attacked in the tavern a few days earlier.

His act of contrition done, Uncle Wolf Syros drew his knife and tapped it gently three times on the altar and turned to go. He was startled to find another Uncle Wolf facing him.

"Syros, how good to see you again."

"Parthros, I did not know you would be here."

The elder Uncle Wolf smiled broadly. "Then we are both blessed by chance and the Overlord of Battle this day. Come, I have some winter wine brought down from the north. Share a cup with me while we catch up."

"I am honored, Brother."

Syros followed the elder Uncle Wolf past the novices, privately called cubs by the established Uncle Wolfs. There were also the women and elder children of slain mercenaries or soldiers performing the menial tasks, such as scrubbing floors and emptying chamber pots, necessary for the temple's maintenance. In this manner the widows and orphans could feed themselves without resorting to thieving, begging or whoring. Their pay came from the collection plates such as the one Syros had just filled. Sometimes the cleaning women would find a new husband. Syros recalled that he met his own wife that way, though she was an orphan, not a widow, who had worked there for many years.

Syros followed Parthros to his cell and took a seat on the hide-covered chair. The black chair was much softer than most owning to goose down stuffing under the cowhide. Syros accepted a brass cup filled with winter wine and waited until Parthros filled his own. They both raised their cups to the small brass image of Galzar Wolfhead that dominated the mantel over the fireplace before drinking.

"Ahh, I was staying alive for days waiting for one of these," Syros said. "Winter wine is hard to come by here in Hos-Bletha. Where did you find it?"

"A trader I know used to be a mercenary I patched up after a skirmish with some Caribi. He was damned lucky I had some wine with me then; I used it to clean a wound on his leg to ward off the fester devils. Now he brings me a barrel every time he comes through and gives me a small discount. Or at least he claims he does," Parthros finished with a laugh.

"Whatever he charged, you got the best of the deal." Syros drained his cup and Parthros quickly refilled it.

Parthros sat down in another chair across from Syros and took on a serious mien. "So what disturbs you, old friend?"

"Is it that obvious?"

Parthros shrugged. "To me, it is. Six ounces of gold in the bowl is a lot for a poor Uncle Wolf like us. Will you tell me of it?"

Syros smiled ruefully. "I…I struck a soldier and a mercenary while in my cups. They never even tried to defend themselves."

"With your mace?" Parthros couldn't keep the shock from his face.

"Nay! With bare fists. Still…"

"Whew! I am not sure your mace wouldn't have been kinder. I recall you were a terror with those fists in the tourneys we held among the novices."

"They both live and are fit for duty by now."

Parthros became confused. "Then why so melancholy? No real harm has been done…"

"Because it Dralm-damned shouldn't have happened!" Syros took a few deep breaths to calm himself. "They did nothing to me other than bump my table, and I nearly killed them with my bare hands. I am supposed to heal fighting men, not inflict new wounds."

Parthros nodded. "This is because of your family." It was not a question.

"No. Yes. I don't know." Syros drained his cup and waved off the offered refill. "Yes, I still grieve the loss of my wife and daughter. Were it not for my Oath to the Order, I would hunt down those barbarians myself. Instead, I petitioned the king to send out soldiers to deal with them. He did nothing. I considered hiring a mercenary band myself, but lack the gold."

Parthros nodded in understanding. Most of Galzar's priests eschewed marriage and families in favor of their duties. There were no proscriptions against engaging in carnal pursuits, so they tended to spend time with camp followers instead. Syros was the other kind, a man who needed a family to keep him stable and satisfied. Or…"You need to get out and find a war."

Syros looked up. "What?"

"Hos-Bletha has been far too quiet of late. The princedoms have been at peace since before war broke out in the north. Peace is hard on our kind as we are all far too accustomed to the excitement of battle. You need to get out and do something. Why not go north and work with the Hostigi?"

"I have considered it. I certainly like them better than the Styphoni, though we are not supposed to take sides…"

"Styphon's House has declared that Styphon is the only true god and the rest are false. Highpriests from all over the Six Kingdoms have gathered in Hos-Agrys at Galzar's Great Hall Upon Earth to make a decision regarding Archpriest Roxthar's Holy Investigation, as he calls it. Most of us believe that Styphon's House has finally overreached itself. There's even talk of a Ban. If that comes about, we will all be free to fight with any Styphoni that we meet on the battlefield."

*An Uncle Wolf taking part in a battle*? That went against all of the rules. Yet how fair were the rules if they only applied to believers in the Twelve True Gods, but not to the corrupt priests of Styphon's House? "How did I not hear of this?"

"You have been away for a while, and this sort of news is discouraged by the Styphoni and Great King Niclophon." Parthros refilled his own cup. "Even Styphon's House's infidels are not so arrogant as to declare open warfare on the Wargod's priests."

"Indeed..." Syros said.

"However, this Investigation and their killing of innocents—have you heard the stories about the atrocities committed by the Investigation in the marches of Hos-Ktemnos?"

"No. But I've heard rumors about even Styphon's underpriests being dragged off the streets of Balph and being tortured or even murdered."

"Sadly, it is true," Parthros said, as he shook his head. "Sheer madness. This Roxthar is like a dog with the foaming-mouth disease. He needs to be put down and quickly."

Parthros again offered the wine and Syros held out his cup. "This really turns things upside-down, I guess. For too long, our Order has ignored the goings-on in Balph and the oppression spawned by Styphon's House. While it has been many winters since my own mercenary days, I'm thinking about going north and aiding the Hostigi against the godless minions of Styphon."

"Parthros!"

The elder Uncle Wolf chuckled. "I know; I am too old for that sort of thing."

"Ha!" Syros leaned forward. "We both know that isn't so. No. It is the thought of an Uncle Wolf actually attacking and killing somebody. Well, maybe Prymenos or Tharses, but not you."

"Eh, maybe not. But Styphon's House has placed itself above everyone else, including the True Gods, and that cannot be allowed to continue. Not just here in Hos-Bletha, but in all of the great kingdoms."

Syros allowed those words to sink in. An Uncle Wolf's job was to care for the soldiers and mercenaries who believed in the True Gods. The Styphoni only believed in the false god Styphon so, technically, they did not qualify. But to actually fight them, to use the mace and crush the skull of a man, even a Styphoni…it flew against the training every novitiate underwent.

"I…don't know if I could do that, Parthros."

"Oh, you had little enough trouble thrashing two mercenaries…"

"While in my cups—and I did not kill them," Syros protested. "And I still feel terrible about that. I don't even want to think about…"

"Then don't. Syros, you can still be the same old Uncle Wolf you have always been. Frankly, I don't see any real difference in how we conduct our duties. We have always been allowed to defend ourselves when attacked, as you well know. However, once the conclave in Hos-Agrys proclaims the Ban of Galzar, we will all stand a better chance of *being* attacked. The Styphoni and their allies will no longer recognize our authority as healers and arbiters. There is a solid chance that they will attack and try to kill you as they would any other fighter. When that happens, what will you do?"

Syros contemplated Parthros' words. What would he do? Like all Uncle Wolfs he had been a fighting man in his youth. A good one, in fact, which is why he had lived long enough to become an Initiate. It could be argued that the Uncle Wolfs were the elite fighters of the Five Kingdoms. Since becoming an Uncle Wolf, he had not actively fought and killed in battle, but all of his order still trained regularly. No priest of the Wargod could be allowed to let his skills atrophy.

"I will need to meditate on this, Parthros." Syros stood and turned to go. "I will be in my old cell…if it is vacant?"

"Yes, just recently."

"Thank you, my friend. I will see you at evening meal."

Syros left, presumably to find his cell. Parthros finished his wine and contemplated how he might aid his old friend. Nothing came to mind.

# TWELVE

The next several days were busy ones for Democriphon's men: training with bows and crossbows, sorting out men with leadership skills and scouting out as many of the trails and swamps in the local area as possible.

Gycules took to his role of petty-captain with vigor. It was easy to underestimate the giant's intelligence as he said very little and rarely argued. In truth, there was a keen mind in that oversized body. Gycules spent a great deal of time with the sharper Vanir. At one point he came up with a training plan to get the mercenaries who had accompanied the sharpers ready for combat; he had them role-playing a group of men seeking to become bandits after losing a war.

Colonel Democriphon watched as the mercenaries practiced on one of the wagons. He also had them on the practice field shooting with crossbows and bow and arrows. They were rusty, but improving quickly. However, they were very convincing at demanding gold and making threats. On the rare occasions he felt something needed to be changed or worked on, he addressed his concerns to Gycules and left him to handle it. That bolstered confidence in the petty-captain and his subordinates.

"How is the show coming along?" Captain Ranthar asked.

"Rather entertaining," Democriphon said. "I think it is time to do a dry run."

"What do you have in mind?" Ranthar looked over at the mercenaries who were in the middle of a mock hold-up.

"There are a few merchant caravans that come down Silos Road in groups of two and three wagons with a ten horse escort," Democriphon said. "According to Gasphros, we can expect one of these to come through tomorrow or the next day. I think we should greet them as they pass by."

"Do you believe these men are ready?" Ranthar gestured at the mercenaries. "Shouldn't we use our regulars?"

Democriphon shook his head no. "Our Hostigi regulars have proven themselves on the battlefield. We need to test the new mercenaries' mettle before we mix them in with our own soldiers. I believe this is the best way to test their battle readiness. We'll start with a small target first, then work our way up." Democriphon looked Ranthar square in the face. "If they can't manage a couple of merchants, what hope do they have against a military convoy? This will show us their weaknesses, if nothing else. If the ambush is successful, the men will gain confidence."

"Too much confidence can be as bad as too little," Ranthar warned.

"And none can be disastrous."

## II

Vanir sweated heavily under his wolf-helm as he waited on a high branch. There were not yet enough wolf-helms for everybody so only a few selected men were issued them for the ambush. The idea was that only those who would be seen by their victims would wear the helms while the rest would attack from hidden positions.

Below, Petty-Captain Gycules stood at the edge of the trail. Unlike the rest, he had no bow or crossbow. Instead, the giant bore a heavy towershield large enough to cover even his oversized frame. The shield was so heavy an ordinary man needed two hands to lift it. Gycules appeared to manage its heft without strain. In his other hand he wielded his greatsword.

Back in the trees behind heavy cover sat Democriphon and Ranthar. Democriphon wanted to take an active part in the ambush, but he was talked out of it by Ranthar. He was reminded that generals were too important to be risked on a training detail; one lucky shot and the entire mission would be imperiled.

The rest of the band hid among the trees and brush while they waited for the merchant's party to arrive. If nothing happened before nightfall, they would make camp and try again the following day.

Gycules rested against a tree with the shield down next to him. While he liked to make a great show of how easily he hefted it, after a while the weight would start to wear on him. The towershield was designed to withstand close gunfire by virtue of the exceptional thickness of the oak and the hammered metal plates covering both sides. Unfortunately, it was too heavy even for the giant to use in a pitched battle where running and dodging were necessary. In addition, prolonged or concentrated blasts of arquebus fire would eventually shred the shield into so much kindling.

The Petty-Captain was satisfied to let his burden lie until he heard the sound of hoof beats and the squeaking of wagon wheels overdue for greasing. Wordlessly, Gycules pulled down his wolf-helm, picked up the towershield and his greatsword and took his position in the middle of the trail.

Four horses with riders led the procession. After them came two ox-drawn wagons, followed by eight more horses. The lead horseman saw Gycules and called for his men to halt. If he suspected an ambush he said nothing, nor was there anything to be done about it. While the horses could easily outrace the bandits, the ox-drawn wagons would be too slow to get away.

"Throw out your gold, silver and goods and you will be allowed to pass," roared the giant.

From well back in the lead wagon, a porcine face poked out of a portal and demanded what the delay was. "A road agent," called back the lead horseman.

"Well, shoot him and let us be on our way."

Before Gycules could react, the horseman drew his pistol and shot at the giant. The bullet spannged off of the top of the helm, stunning Gycules for a brief moment. The horseman, surprised that his bullet failed to down the human roadblock, drew a second pistol and took aim. Gycules managed to recover just enough to put his shield between himself and the next oncoming bullet. The round embedded in the shield forcing the petty-captain to take a step back.

"Now you have angered me," Gycules roared. "I call on my legions to strike you down!"

From all around came the howling of wolves. The horses spooked while the riders fought to keep them under control. The lead horseman heard the wolf-headed giant roar "Now!" and the air filled with arrows and crossbow quarrels. Most of the missiles targeted the wagons until they resembled giant porcupines. The horsemen received far fewer strikes, but they landed with great accuracy. Arms and legs seemed to be the targets of choice.

The horsemen were not idle as they came under attack. They drew their horse pistols and tried to find a target. Each rider had six pistols on his saddle, pistols that were quickly emptied as they tried to defend themselves.

Several of the riders dropped from their mounts, dead or wounded; the others were out of loaded pistols.

"Halt!" roared the giant. Instantly, the arrows and bolts stopped flying. "I can have you all killed in a heartbeat! You are brave men and I see no need to waste your lives. You are outnumbered and out-armed. Surrender your goods and treasures and you shall live to fight another day. Raise arms and none shall survive our wrath."

Back in the brush, Colonel Democriphon rolled his eyes. Gycules was being incredibly over-dramatic. Still, it seemed to have the desired effect. The horsemen threw down their swords and dismounted. The wounded helped each other to pull the bolts and arrows from each other and bind their wounds.

From out of the brush, several more wolf-helmed men surrounded the wagons. Gycules moved back to the first wagon and pulled the door from its hinges with one hand. Inside, the fat merchant cowered in his seat. Across from him was a young woman.

"It distresses me greatly that I must ask you to step out of the wagon while my men search it," Gycules said in his most reasonable tone. The two hurried to comply.

Once out of the wagon, the merchant took a protective posture in front of the young woman. "Take what you will, just do not harm my daughter."

*Daughter?* "And if I decide to take her with me as my prize?"

The merchant drew a dirk and launched himself at Gycules. So surprised was the giant that he failed to block the attack. The dirk struck the petty-captain's armor, but only pierced the leather an inch or so. Gycules backhanded the merchant and pulled the dirk out as though it were a thorn. He quickly staunched the blood flow with some dry moss from his belt pouch.

"You are braver than I expected, and ready to spend your life for your child," Gycules said. "I respect your valor if not your good sense. I would spare you half your gold if I did not fear others would follow your example. That would get too many people killed. I will spare your daughter the indignity of being searched, and no more. I give my oath to the True Gods that we will leave you some food, a few horses and your lives if there is no more resistance. Agreed?"

Having no other choice, the merchant nodded, though he still remained between the girl and the wolf-headed men.

## III

"Why didn't you kill the merchant when he stabbed you?" Democriphon asked on the way back to camp. He wasn't angry; just curious.

"I respect a man who fights for his family, even when he has no chance," Gycules replied. "I also recall your orders to kill as few people as possible. Six of the horsemen and a reinsman died in the assault. I did not wish to add to that if I could avoid it."

Democriphon nodded in accord. Gycules had followed his orders to the rune. "I commend your restraint, Petty-Captain. However, had you killed him I would not have protested the action; you are all expected to defend yourselves."

Gycules shrugged. "I was in little enough danger. The dirk was too small and the hand that wielded it too weak to seriously threaten me. We should consider using mail under our tunics, though."

"Agreed. Now let us put some of Ermut's Best on that wound," Democriphon said. "To be safe, let us apply it within and without."

"My thanks, sir. I didn't want any of the others to know, but the wound, though small, hurts like all of Regwarn."

Democriphon laughed, then slapped the big man on the back. It had been a good day. Only two of his men had been wounded, none killed, and now he knew they were ready for the next attack.

# THIRTEEN

As with any large organization, paperwork was an unavoidable evil. Documents ranging from supply requests to personnel changes were created on a daily, even hourly basis. Even in a society where the process by which paper was created was absent, something had to be used to record the organization's operations. In Styphon's House Upon Earth in Balph, where paper had yet to be introduced, parchments were used to track every action on the part of Styphon's House. Once created, the documents were never destroyed. Everything, every transaction ever committed to parchment, was filed and stored in the Archives. Hundreds of years of information and history filling shelf after shelf in the massive repository.

Within the Archives black-robed priests scurried in every direction adding to the piles of scrolls, books, and documents. Outside the Archives, underpriests struggled to get past each other as they came with new records to drop off.

Underpriest Vulthar struggled with his burden of scrolls when he collided with what seemed, to him, a living wall. Scrolls and parchments flew in every direction as the underpriest scrambled to recollect them.

Above him, the living-wall known as Xylon, dressed in the garb of Styphon's Guard, watched as Vulthar feverishly worked. Silently, Xylon bent down to assist the priest. As he did so, the giant pulled several scrolls from under his tunic and nonchalantly slipped them into the mess on the marbled floor. Vulthar gratefully accepted the assistance.

From down the wide hallway one set of eyes observed the transaction with keen, though hidden interest. First Level Scholar Danthor Dras, in his disguise as Highpriest Danthor, knew the giant was one of the Golden Temple's Guardsmen.

When the documents were finally collected and Xylon went down the hall, Highpriest Danthor followed the underpriest into the Temple Archives. Danthor was the most recent addition to the Balph Study Team and was posing as a Styphon's House highpriest from Hos-Bletha, seeking advancement and riches in the Holy City of Balph. He had seen the Archives as an ideal post; the Temple Archivist Highpriest Vyros was approaching eighty winters of age and could barely see through the thick milky cataracts that almost completely obscured his eyes. He needed a reader who was also a highpriest, due to security concerns and his own pride; it was a dead-end post disdained by the run-of-the-mill highpriests, but perfect for a researcher studying the Temple history and its hierarchy.

As the black-robed underpriest placed each scroll on the proper shelf, Danthor took note of them. When novitiate Vulthar had finally completed his task and left, Danthor checked each scroll. With his First Level recall he was able to spot the ones Xylon had slipped in by color, texture and size. Three of the scrolls matched what he was looking for.

One was a receipt of payment for fireseed by a Baron Parthenos. The name meant nothing to Danthor, suggesting he was a minor noble from a kingdom outside of Hos-Ktemnos. Any local baron would be involved in the war against Kalvan and getting his fireseed at no charge.

The second was a parchment ordering a highpriest named Sangar to tour the temples of Hos-Bletha, inspect them, and determine if Styphon's Own Guard at each was fit to join in the war against the Usurper Kalvan.

Danthor did not recognize the name although that was not surprising; there were hundreds, even thousands, of highpriests, underpriests and novices spread over the Five Kingdoms. No member of the Inner Circle knew, let alone ever met, even a tenth of them. The only odd thing was the date on the parchment, making the document several months older than the others being filed that day. It could have been lost in the bureaucracy, or something else could be at work.

The final manuscript was a report on the increase of banditry in Hos-Bletha by forces unknown. The document was signed by an underpriest called Calthros, assistant to His Worship Sangar. This name was more familiar to Danthor if only because it was similar to Calthor, a common name, like Karf on First Level or Joseph on Fourth Level Europo-American.

Danthor committed the three manuscripts to memory before returning them to their proper shelves. All three documents seemed legitimate enough; all had the proper writing style favored by Styphon's House clerks and all had the proper seals, yet all three had been surreptitiously slipped into the pile by the giant guard for a reason. Danthor decided to keep his suspicions to himself until he knew more. *Anaxthenes or one of the other members of the Inner Circle could be engaged in one of their intrigues. By Great Blaxthakka's Beard, it could even be some subterfuge on the part of King Kalvan.*

## II

Barlon took in the land on both sides of the trail and smiled. It was a long, sometimes dusty, often wet, journey from Balph to Bletha Town; he did not mind it a bit. Anything was better than the rocking of the ship and the overpowering stench of too many unwashed bodies in the hold.

As the master of the slave caravan, Barlon was entitled to a private carriage for the journey. Instead, he spent most of his time on the back of his horse where he could watch over his men and his human cargo. It was a fair-sized lot, although he had run in to much larger coffles in the past. Two hundred men, women and children would be sold at auction in Bletha Town. Many of the men were Hostigi soldiers captured during the Fireseed Wars and would bring in good prices; upwards of a hundred silver crowns. Some of the women, also Hostigi, would bring that price in gold at the Blethan brothels. So would some of the children at the less reputable Houses. Those who were not sold at auction would be purchased by agents of Styphon's House. Even Barlon felt sorry for those unfortunates, but not enough to keep from making the sale. In his mind, he was already spending the thousands of silver crowns he would get for this lot.

He signaled for one of the overseers. The man prodded his horse forward next to the caravan master.

"Yes, Master Barlon?"

"Send one of the scouts up ahead to see if the usual rest stop is clear. We'll take a meal there and rest the stock for a candle. We will also swap some of the walkers with the wagon riders. We don't want any limpers when we arrive in Bletha Town, it could lower their price at auction. Keep the whipping to a minimum as well. Otherwise, the buyers will suspect the slaves are unruly. These Dralm-damned Hostigi have a bad enough reputation for slaves as it is!"

The overseer nodded and spurred his horse into a gallop. Barlon watched him shrink into the distance and turned his thoughts to what he would do when the caravan came to a halt. One of the younger slave girls had caught his eye the day before. Maybe he would try her out before selling her at auction. He might even decide to keep her for himself.

## III

Democriphon fidgeted as though his doublet had kittens crawling under it. Hiding back behind the tree line with Ranthar and the men, he watched silently while the slaver guard scouted out the clearing. The guard glanced at the tree line then around the clearing. He never even dismounted. Democriphon would have shaken his head in disgust if he were not afraid the movement might attract attention. It would be unfortunate to kill the guard before the caravan arrived.

The guard rode off without a glance backward. Democriphon waited for a moment then swore. He then turned to his men and said, "If any of you ever do that sloppy a job when scouting for me I will hang you by your privy parts and leave you for the crows to peck at."

His spleen vented, the Colonel ordered the men to spread out and take up their position. Some climbed up into trees while others simply crouched down or stood behind trees on both sides of the trail. Democriphon considered using crossbows, then decided they would be too dangerous for the slaves. Accuracy was too important. He wished they could have brought rifles with them as they were the most accurate and powerful small arms in the world. Unfortunately, they were also the sole domain of the Royal Army of Hos-Hostigos and would have betrayed the mission if any of Democriphon's men were caught with one.

"Ranthar, take charge of the other side," Democriphon said. "I need somebody I know who is, uh, *levelheaded*. Where is Gasphros?"

"Right here, Colonel," the Bard said.

*Another one that moves like a panther, Dralm-damnit.* "This isn't your kind of fight, so I want you to scout ahead with Vanir and make sure we do not get any unexpected company."

"Actually, Colonel, I was a mercenary and a, um, well, a thief before I became a troubadour." Gasphros looked a bit abashed at his confession.

"Really?" Democriphon digested the information, and then shrugged. "Well, we're all thieves for the duration of this mission, and it is nice to have another professional with us. Still, I would rather you and Vanir watched the riverside. You two are too important to risk in a fight like this."

"I have to agree with Democriphon," Ranthar added. "The information you two carry is far too valuable to risk losing. Just try to spot any traffic coming our way if you can."

## IV

Uncle Wolf Syros bent down and scratched the head of his dog as he walked down the trail toward the east. The kitten scrambled to keep its footing on the Uncle Wolf's shoulder, digging his tiny claws into the wolf-pelt hood. Uncle Wolf Syros did not notice the kitten's plight until he righted himself then helped his furry passenger to get settled, stroking the kitten's head until it became calm again.

It had almost been a moon-half since his fight in the tavern, and two days since he left the temple. He had wrestled with his demons and prayed for guidance. Finally it came to him that he should start north and take part in the war.

An Uncle Wolf was not supposed to care what side he was on in a battle provided they believed in Dralm, Galzar and the rest of the True Gods. An Uncle Wolf's job was to tend to the wounded, act as heralds and help mediate when one side or the other sued for peace. Yet, even before the arrival of Lord Kalvan, the idea of working with the allies of Styphon's House rubbed him the wrong way. The Styphoni were too arrogant by half, for starters, and most had no respect for the True Gods.

When the Styphoni came into a princedom, they raised temples, built temple-farms and made slaves of everyone living on the former farmlands. Even worse, they often enslaved ex-soldiers and refugees, whipping them with iron-barbed cords. They taxed the prince, and made him tax his subjects for their coffers. They also kept slave-farms where men and women labored from early in the morning until late at night. They even made the peasants cart their manure to the temple-farms till they had none left for their own fields. No outsider knew what they did with it until Kalvan came along and revealed the truth behind the Fireseed Trinity.

After a great deal of soul-searching and meditation, Syros had decided to join the Hostigi in their war against Styphon's House. The Hostigi worshipped the True Gods and treated prisoners with the proper respect. Besides, he might even get to see old Uncle Wolf Tharses again.

Up ahead he saw two men walking toward him. This was hardly

surprising as it was a well-traveled trail. One had the look of a troubadour even though he had no musical instrument that Syros could see. The other was a mystery though he had the look of one unaccustomed to doing a solid day's work.

The oddest thing was that the two men were walking instead of riding yet did not look as though they had traveled far. There were no towns or villages in easy walking distance to account for this. *Could it be they lost their horses to bandits?*

## V

"Oh, shite!" exclaimed Vanir. "Is that an Uncle Wolf?"

Gasphros nodded. "Nobody would dare to wear that wolfskin head and cape if they were not. We have to stop him without causing him any harm."

"How in Regwarn do we do that?" Vanir noticed that the Uncle Wolf was coming into hearing distance and lowered his voice. "Word among the sharpers is that no Uncle Wolf has ever been taken in by a scam. As for fighting, I doubt twice our number could subdue him physically. All Uncle Wolfs are former mercenaries and damned good at their jobs."

"That is one of the reasons they become an Uncle Wolf," Gasphros replied. "As negotiators they are trained to read people and not to be taken in by a possible double-cross. Gullible people washout very quickly. They were also great warriors in their mercenary days. Back when I still fought for pay, I saw a mercenary prisoner break his oath to Galzar and kill a guard. Our Uncle Wolf thrashed that man so badly he was almost crippled for life. Afterwards he yelled that he had no patience with oath-breakers. Nobody else joked about trying to escape after that."

Vanir became pale. "By the gods, what are we going to do?"

"Praying comes to mind. I hope Dralm is paying attention."

# FOURTEEN

## I

Master Barlon called for the slave train to stop when they arrived at the clearing. The guards automatically spread out, riding to the edges of the clearing on both sides of the trail while the slaves were forced into the center where they were allowed to sit and eat. The overseers surrounded the slaves with a lance-length between them and their stock before also sitting and taking their meal. Barlon looked over the scene and decided it was good. He called for an overseer, spoke to him in low tones then retired to his wagon. In half a candle the overseer returned with the slave girl he had been admiring earlier.

Democriphon could not believe what he was seeing. The guards remained in their saddles circling the edge of the clearing. Their attention was focused solely on the slaves within the circle and not on any possible outside attackers. Every four candles a guard would be replaced to go eat then he would return to replace the next guard. *Guards should not be that predictable.*

After waiting half a candle, Democriphon decided that it was time to attack. He raised his horse pistol into the air and fired. From all around the clearing men disguised as Ruthani surged out of the tree line and attacked the guards with spears, swords, bows and crossbows. It happened so quickly that the overseers and wagon drivers didn't even have the chance to get to their feet. They were cut down with arrows and crossbow bolts from above.

A few bolts went into the crowd of slaves causing them to panic. Only the chains strung from the shackles on their ankles kept them from breaking away in every direction. Still, they screamed and pulled on the chains in an attempt to flee the red-skinned barbarians they had heard so many terrible tales about.

## II

Master Barlon staggered out of his wagon simultaneously pulling up his breeches and drawing a sword. He never succeeded in either endeavor. A knife blade from behind slit his throat and he fell forward into the dirt. There his blood soaked into the earth as he gurgled out his last breath. Above him, the slave girl he had taken a fancy to held a bloodied knife. She looked around and saw the Ruthani attacking the guards and overseers, then dove back into the wagon in panic.

Colonel Democriphon watched over the battle with mixed feelings. The fighting was decidedly one-sided, which was good by any measure, but it was going *too* well. His men were not being challenged. Back before King Kalvan entered the scene, Democriphon would simply have enjoyed the easy victory. Now he understood new concepts, to him, like his men becoming overconfident. The next battle might not go so well and some cocky troopers would end up dead as a result.

Across the clearing, he could see Captain Ranthar's team mopping up and directing his men to secure the victuals wagon. Ranthar, in Democriphon's estimation, would make a great captain-general someday. The Greffan knew how to handle the men like a well-seasoned petty-captain, a skill most officers never developed, and followed orders without argument or complaint. Moreover, he knew when and how to make suggestions to his superiors that would shore up weaknesses in a plan of action without causing offence.

The battle was over in less than half a candle. All of the guards, overseers and wagon drivers were dead. Horses were gathered together and tethered to trees and the wagon oxen were being calmed to keep them from bolting. The slaves were proving to be the most difficult.

Captain Ranthar ran over to Democriphon shouting orders at the men along the way. "Colonel, we need to assure the slaves that they won't be killed and eaten. They seem to think that we are Caribi, not Ruthani."

Democriphon looked over the slaves straining against their chains trying to go in every direction at once.

"Coming from the north, I doubt they think that there is any difference between Caribi and Ruthani. How many are there?"

"Rough count is around two hundred. We'll have a hard time keeping that many under control."

"Dralm, Galzar and Yirtta," Democriphon grumbled. "All right, we'll have to keep them chained for now. After we get them back to camp and remove our disguises they should calm down enough so that we can unchain them." Democriphon glanced at the bodies of the slavers and got an idea. "Have the bodies lined up so the slaves can kick them on the way out. It should give them some pleasure, at least for the moment."

Ranthar nodded once then ran off to carry out the orders. As the slaves were being lined up, Gasphros and Vanir approached with a guest. Democriphon checked his impulse to draw his sword when he saw who it was. No follower of Galzar Wolfhead would ever take up arms against an Uncle Wolf.

As the trio drew closer, Democriphon could see that Gasphros and Vanir looked nervous. At first he couldn't understand why until he recalled his orders to stop anyone from approaching the clearing. Democriphon snorted; they had a better chance of stopping Grand Master Soton and a Lance of Zarthani Knights than a single Uncle Wolf determined to pass. Vanir was not a fighting man and Gasphros, as a former mercenary, could no more act against an Uncle Wolf than he could against the sun.

The Uncle Wolf quickly took in the scene, spotted the commanding officer and marched in Democriphon's direction. "You! Are you in charge here?"

*How in Regwarn did he figure that out so quickly? Did Vanir or Gasphros tell him?* "I am the commander, Uncle Wolf."

"Well, if you are going to dress up as a Ruthani, you should do something about that hair." Uncle Wolf glanced at the slaves being lined up and the bodies being laid in their path. "What do you intend to do with these slaves?"

Democriphon considered his options and decided on the truth. Lying to an Uncle Wolf brought bad luck and things were precarious enough already. "Once I have them away from here, and can calm them down, I will free them. Those who wish to can join my company. The rest will be free to go."

Uncle Wolf Syros nodded. "Looking for more recruits to aid Great King Kalvan, eh?"

"What? How did you..." He turned and glared at Vanir and Gasphros.

The Uncle Wolf shook his head. "They said nothing. Your accent, however, is pure Harphaxi, son. It's as telling as that golden hair of yours. I assume you are here to find men to fight against the Styphoni. I understand Styphon's House has gathered a truly massive army, but isn't this a little far from Hos-Hostigos to be recruiting?"

*In for a copper, in for a crown.* "Actually, Uncle Wolf, I am here to keep Hos-Bletha from joining Styphon's House war against Great King Kalvan. I like the idea of sending recruits to Hos-Hostigos, but I fear that is unworkable at present. Killing slavers and freeing these slaves is just a *bonus*."

The Uncle Wolf nodded, as though he had heard of Kalvan's new style of making war. "How exactly does this keep Hos-Bletha out of the war? Freeing slaves might be upsetting to certain cartels, but they do not have the Great King's ear."

Democriphon considered his options. He could lie to the Uncle Wolf, which no soldier did lightly for fear of provoking Galzar's wrath. He could tell the Uncle Wolf everything, and trust in his oath to not reveal anything. Actually, the second route was best, as no Uncle Wolf would ever betray a confidence.

"Uncle Wolf, would you come with us and join us in a meal? All will be explained when we return to camp."

Syros noticed that the slaves, still in chains, were being led over the bodies of the fallen overseers. Several slaves kicked or stomped on the bodies as they went. "I suppose I could spare the time to join you. You might want to collect the young maiden over in that wagon, though. She might run away and tell others of your plans."

Democriphon looked in the direction indicated by the Uncle Wolf. Sure enough, a young woman, scarcely in her teens, was looking out through the side of the wagon. At the bottom of the steps was the body of a large man bleeding from a neck wound. *Did the girl kill him in the confusion?*

"Uncle Wolf, would you be kind enough to ask the young lady to join us? I fear she might be frightened by any of my men until conditions here are explained."

"Can I assure her that she will not be molested?"

Democriphon smiled wide. "Any of my men who try to harm any of the slaves will have their unmentionables fed to themselves raw. I have no tolerance for those who would abuse anyone under my protection."

The Uncle Wolf's face relaxed as though he had come to the conclusion that Colonel Democriphon was sincere. "Very well, you may call me Syros. No need to wear our titles when we speak among ourselves. Vanir? Gasphros? Please help me with the poor lass. She may be too frightened to realize that I am an Uncle Wolf and not a Ruthani dressed in wolfskins."

## III

The trek back to the camp was long and slow. The party had to move through the forests and swamps to avoid detection while the rearguard with Silent Wolf and Roaring Panther erased signs of their passage. The slaves, accustomed by now to obeying their masters, stayed silent the entire trek. Only the clanking of their chains could be heard as they followed the lead.

At the front, on the horses that had been liberated from the dead guards, rode Democriphon, Ranthar, Uncle Wolf Syros and a few mercenaries. The wagons were traveling a better trail, wide enough for both the teams and wagons, and would join the rest later at the encampment.

"Do you really believe you will find any suitable recruits among these slaves," Syros asked. "They look to be a thin, haggard lot."

"Indeed. Still, I suspect many may have been soldiers captured in battle and sold on the auction block," Democriphon explained. "If not, well, these are people with little love for their former masters and may want to vent their spleens on any enemy we can provide."

"Styphon's House has a particularly unpleasant reputation in their treatment of slaves and would be a welcome target to the poor buggers once they're freed," Ranthar added.

"You will still have to house, feed and clothe these people," Syros pointed out. "Have you the resources?"

"If not, we will get them," Democriphon said airily. He wanted to give the impression of a man who was confident and resourceful.

"Does your Great King send you gold to meet your needs? How would he get it here?"

Democriphon held up a restraining hand. "I came here with gold and enough supplies to last for several moons, but I don't intend to live off my Great King's bounty. I prefer to support my people through other means."

Syros laughed. "I think I just saw an example of those 'other means' you spoke of. Banditry, judiciously applied, could take you far. Provided you don't end up on the gibbet, of course."

"The Colonel plans our forays well, Uncle Wolf," Ranthar said.

"Colonel? What is a *colonel*, Captain Ranthar?"

Ranthar mentally slapped his head. Of course the Uncle Wolf had no idea what rank a colonel represented. Kalvan had instituted the rank as a means of clearing up some of the confusion regarding all the various kinds of captains in the Zarthani military forces. "It is a rank in between grand-captain and captain-general used in the Royal Army of Hos-Hostigos."

"Then I suggest you call yourself a grand-captain or captain-general.

You don't want to drop hints that you're from Hostigos, do you?"

Democriphon had to agree, even though he liked the new rank bestowed upon him by his Great King. "Captain-General it is. Ranthar, you will be First Captain as I expect we will be needing more of them, and I don't want anyone arguing over who is in charge when I am busy elsewhere."

Ranthar nodded and made a mental note to pass that information on to the Study Team. If a grand-captain was the here-and-now equivalent to a major, then first captain would have to be a lieutenant colonel. *Maybe I should put in for a promotion next time I'm back on First Level.*

# FIFTEEN

## I

It was almost nightfall by the time they reached the encampment. Uncle Wolf Syros looked it over with a critical eye. As a temporary settlement for a few hundred men it was adequate. For over five hundred it would be far too small. He glanced over at Democriphon and guessed the same thoughts were going through his head.

Democriphon dismounted and called some men over. "Gycules, organize the men and try to make some accommodations for our new guests. We'll need another latrine dug, sleeping space and some food distributed. Gasphros, take some men into town and get as many sackcloth tunics as you can. Spread out the purchases..."

"Petty-Captain Gycules oversaw the latrines yesterday, while Captain Ranthar had previously ordered me get the tunics, only they are cotton," Gasphros explained. "You were busy planning the attack, so I addressed the details of the expected aftermath," he added. "I hope I didn't overstep my authority, sir." *Or as he had heard Kalvan say, it's easier to beg forgiveness than ask permission.*

"Great leaders are made by even better followers," Syros said quoting from the Book of Galzar. He appeared impressed by what he saw.

Democriphon said. "Indeed. Well done, Gasphros. Gather the slaves into a circle and I shall address them in a candle-half. Make sure everybody sheds their Ruthani garb and attires themselves as warriors. No Styphoni armor is to be displayed. We don't want to frighten our new guests. Uncle Wolf Syros?"

"Yes, Captain-General?"

"Captain-General, for formal address. However, Democriphon will do in private, Uncle Wolf." He paused to take out his tobacco pouch and fill his pipe.

"A promotion. Good choice, your command has grown far beyond the auspices of a grand-captain," Gasphros noted.

Democriphon smiled. "That's not my only promotion. I will take this opportunity to inform them that I am the true Orphan Prince, First Prince Valthros."

Uncle Wolf Syros looked askance. "Ha! You wouldn't be the first."

Gasphros added, "But he will be the last."

Syros took out his tinderbox and used it to light a thick splinter. While lighting his pipe, he considered Democriphon's latest bolt from the Skypalace of the gods. *Could this Hostigi general really be the lost prince? No, impossible. Well, not impossible, but highly unlikely. Unless it's a Dralm-sent miracle, like Great King Kalvan. Why else would Kalvan entrust such an operation to him otherwise? The man was clearly from the ranks of the nobility; he spoke well, marked his runes and carried himself with grace and nobility. Why couldn't he be Valthros?*

*Well, there were a hundred reasons why this man had to be an imposter. The real Prince Valthros was most likely a bundle of bones buried underneath some culvert on the main road out of Bletha Town. Yet, Democriphon's demeanor was right and he even had a slight resemblance to the former Great King. Who am I to say? Whether he is or not, he could easily become the symbol to ignite Hos-Bletha against Styphon's House and the regicide who sat falsely upon the Silver Throne.* "But why would the Orphan Prince speak with a northern accent?"

"I was spirited away from the place by a pair of my father's faithful retainers. They took me out of the palace, hid me in their hut and left during the confusion after my parents were murdered. When I was older, I was sent to stay with a family in Harphax City, which is where I picked up my accent. Niclophon—who I will not honor with the title Great King—is a regicide and I mean to overthrow him and the corrupt priests of Styphon who prop up his corrupt regime."

Syros smiled. "You have the proper words, and I can see a slight resemblance to Great King Marocles."

Democriphon nodded. "Perhaps you can be persuaded to speak with the slaves and assure them that they are not in any danger while in our camp?"

"I shall be pleased to do so," the Uncle Wolf said. "However, I think you should address them, as well. I also suggest that you keep your true mission a secret. There will be turncoats among the former slaves that would sell you out for a purse of silver."

## II

Half a candle later, the slaves were sitting in a wide semi-circle before Democriphon, Uncle Wolf Syros and Gasphros. Gasphros was playing a tune on his lyre he had heard Kalvan humming once. The meaning of the tune was lost on him, though he managed a reasonably faithful rendition of "Little Brown Jug" that had some of the slaves clapping in time.

Democriphon nodded at Gasphros and the bard stopped playing. "Former slaves, I am Captain-General Democriphon," he began. There was some murmuring among them and he patiently waited until it died down. "Yes, I said *former* slaves. You have my apologies for not removing your shackles earlier, but I feared that some of you would panic and flee."

Democriphon nodded to Gycules and several who had been blacksmiths. At once, they began to remove their shackles. They were followed by Vanir and a few of the former sharper mercenaries who passed out food and tunics. "As you can see, we are not Ruthani or Caribi or—worst of all, Styphoni. We are soldiers who seek to place the true king of Hos-Bletha on the throne. For those of you who do not know me, I go by many names. I will now give you my true name. I am Valthros, also called the Orphan Prince and the Prince in Exile."

As he paused to let that sink in, he got a very suspicious glare from Uncle Wolf Syros. He ignored it, continuing: "I seek to remove my uncle, Niclophon, from my throne and take my rightful place as great king of Hos-Bletha. To do this I need to build an army. I ask that every man jack of you who is willing to fight injustice, to join me in removing this traitor and murderer from the Silver Throne. But I will need more than just soldiers. I need men and women who know how to sew, cook and build. I need carpenters, stone masons, furriers, ironmongers, healers and many other skilled artisans and craftsmen."

Democriphon paused for a moment. He had seen Great King Kalvan do such things for dramatic effect. It also allowed his words to sink in.

"Soon we will be moving to a better, larger location where we will all have space enough to be comfortable. There we will build up a village with homes for us all."

Somewhere among the slaves, a voice called out. "What if we should wish to return home?"

Democriphon had anticipated that question. "Then you will be escorted to the border of this realm and allowed to do so. However, the war still rages on in the north. You will have to pass through enemy territory to reach Hos-Hostigos or Hos-Harphax. Furthermore, you could be killed by either side before explaining who you are. That is if you are not recaptured and again sold as slaves. On the other hand, you could be pressed into military service by whichever side finds you first. There is even the possibility that you would be robbed and killed by bandits or other refugees. Most of you have been weakened during your captivity. With us you have a chance to rebuild you strength and maybe even take revenge on those who wronged you so grievously.

"We will be attacking other slave caravans and freeing the men and women they seek to sell as chattel. I offer you the opportunity to join us in freeing others. And when I am restored to my rightful place as Great King of Hos-Bletha, you will all be well compensated for your efforts. Even in the dark event that I fail, and a wise man anticipates failure in the hopes of avoiding it, you will receive wages for your work while among us, giving you a stake on which to build your future. What say you?"

From the back of the crowd came a voice that yelled out, "Long Live Great King Valthros!"

The shout was repeated as more voices joined in. By the fifth repetition, all of the freed slaves were joining in.

"Long Live Great King Valthros! Long Live Great King Valthros! Long Live Great King Valthros!"

## III

"That went much better than I had expected," Democriphon said as he collapsed onto a pile of hides. "If not for that first shout, I doubt things would have gone so well."

Uncle Wolf Syros chuckled. "I thought you had arranged for that yourself."

"Actually," Ranthar said, "That was Vanir's doing. He had one of his men dressed in one of those slave tunics to get the charge started."

"Really?" Democriphon turned his gaze to the former sharper. "I'll have to find a suitable rank for you."

"I've got a rank for you," Duke Skranga announced. "From now on you're the Chief of Hos-Blethan Intelligence. You will work under me and we will work on building you a network of spies, or what you call agents-inquisitory or intelligencers."

"I am honored, Your Worship," Vanir said, with probably more sincerity than he had shown since his Name Day. "I will do my best to repay this great honor."

"What do we do next," Uncle Wolf Syros asked. "I assume you have something in the works."

"We? Then you are with us?"

“Indeed. I had intended to join up with the Hostigi in the north. This is more convenient. What would you have done had I decided to move on? I know a great deal about your, uh, *operation*.”

“Nothing beyond accepting your Oath to Galzar that you would not reveal that which you had seen,” Democriphon said with a yawn. “If I can’t trust an Uncle Wolf then there is little left in this world that I *can* trust.”

# SIXTEEN

## I

Petty-Captain Andros inspected the men, the wagons, the horses, oxen and equipment. It took nearly the entire morning, but all appeared to be ready. While he waited for the captain, he ordered the men to fall into formation. It took some doing, but he enjoyed considerable success, not that the higher-ups ever noticed.

He looked up at the sun and decided it was past time to get started. *Where in the Caverns of Regwarn is that Dralm-damned captain?* As if summoned by his thoughts Captain Nephron marched over to him.

The Captain looked over the men and wagons already lined up for departure. "Petty-Captain Andros, are the men prepared?"

"Yes, Captain." Andros noticed that Nephron was completely sober and didn't even seem to be suffering from the previous day's excesses. Andros could respect that, if little else about the man. He was also out of his armor, though that was common for officers while in garrison.

"Good. The destination has changed."

Nephron pulled a parchment map from his tunic and unrolled it. “We will be taking this trail to Dalthax City where we will load the men and wagons onto a ship. The ship will transport us all to Balph.”

Andros fought to keep from rolling his eyes in exasperation. *That was my plan all along, you idiot!* Aloud he said, “What about the weather, Captain? Isn’t it too late in the year for a sea journey?”

Nephron nodded. “If there’s a break in the weather, we can still make our way to Balph. Otherwise, we’ll be billeted there until spring.”

“But why the circuitous route, sir?”

“My orders were to keep the mission secret. That was why you and the men were given false information until now. My superiors believed the men might talk and give away the route. Now, nobody but you and I know where we are going and how. The men will simply follow us.”

*Oh, Great Galzar, save us from fools!* “Captain, the scouts will need to know the route as well, elsewise they won’t be able to clear the path for us.”

“Ah, yes, quite right, Petty-Captain. Inform such men as you see fit, and we will begin once you are satisfied we are ready.”

*Sometimes I don’t know whether to kiss or kill this man. One moment he acts completely clueless, the next he trusts me to do the job right.* Andros gave a curt nod and said, “We’ll be ready in half a candle, Captain. As soon as the scouts have been briefed we can go.”

The caravan moved at the usual slow pace set by the oxen pulling the wagons. In good weather on a smooth and even road oxen could pull a wagon roughly thirty marches a day. With a heavy load, like a wagon full of gold, the pace was considerably less, even with double teams of the beasts. The men, initially pleased with the slow pace in the heat and humidity, were beginning to grumble.

Andros considered letting the men remove their back-and-breast armor to allow them some degree of comfort, then dismissed the idea. Better protected and uncomfortable. Bandits or Ruthani could be about; even the Caribi occasionally crept inland when things became difficult near the Great Eastern Ocean. The petty-captain had no intention of letting the men be caught with their armor off.

Andros looked up at the canopy of green that blocked out most of the sunlight. *Thank Dralm for small favors!* The heat would be even worse under direct sunlight, heating up armor and burning exposed skin. *Thank the gods it's almost winter and not summer.* The oxen were less inclined to complain the way the troops could, but they were the better for the shade as well. One stubborn beast could hold up the entire convoy, especially if it was on the gold wagon team.

At least the captain was holding up well enough at the front of the procession. That was good; the men typically followed the officer's example until they became jaded by overexposure. Then they turned to the petty-captains for leadership and survival.

*Now if we can just get to Dalthax without running into trouble.*

II

"Looks like you were right, Captain-General," Gycules said.

"Keep your voice down," Democriphon cautioned the larger man. He had used his scouts to keep watch on the obvious back trails leading to Dalthax City, but had stationed the men at the route he suspected the Blethans might take.

"Remember to aim for the arms and legs. We want to keep the deaths to a minimum. We need frightened men to run back to Bletha Town screaming about the horrible Ruthani that fell upon them."

Gycules nodded. "The men know what to do, sir."

On both sides of the trail men dressed in loin cloths, random pieces of clothing and armor and war paint waited in the trees with longbows and crossbows. The longbows were somewhat problematic with the tree branches forming an impenetrable mat in many places. The trees here were much lusher than the hardwood trees back in Hostigos.

Great care had been taken to choose the locations where their missile weapons could be used effectively. The crossbows, while smaller, presented a problem with reloading; one had to stand the nose between his legs in order to lever back the prod before loading a fresh quarrel. That was difficult to do while standing on a branch. One man had already fallen and broken an arm while arming his crossbow.

Fireseed weapons were to be held in reserve. Democriphon wanted the attack to be authentic-looking, but not at the cost of his men's lives. If things got too rough, the smoothbores would be brought out.

The convoy moved slowly into the position Democriphon wanted. The scouts had been allowed to pass under them unmolested and the main force trudged on without any idea of what was above them. Democriphon nodded at Gycules who nodded back then let out a good approximation of a wolf howl. That was the signal to fire arrows and crossbow bolts.

The first volley was aimed at the lead oxen of each wagon, the second the horses and the third at the soldiers moving at the front and in the rear. The oxen proved harder to kill than anticipated while the horses fell, usually after bucking off their riders and on occasion rolling over them.

Captain Nephron was killed when his horse threw him and another crushed his skull with its hooves. Nephron was the first to die, but not the last.

## III

Petty-Captain Andros barked orders in an attempt to rally his men. At this point he realized the decision to leave the most seasoned soldiers behind might cost him and his men their lives. He looked about for a place where the men could take cover without success. Hiding behind the downed animals did no good as the arrows and bolts were raining down from high up in the trees.

He had been caught before in these ambushes and lived to tell the tale. Fortunately, he didn't have Captain Nephron to countermand his orders. He knew that staying on the road was suicide. Andros lifted his arm to rally his men, then pointed to the wood line at the right of the trail, crying, "Charge!"

Most of the men followed him, except for a few who were trying to hide underneath the wagons or behind dead horses. If their counterattack failed, those men would die pinned down while the Ruthani picked them off at their leisure.

His soldiers charged into the woods, taking shots from above. Andros pointed his arquebus at a figure in one of the trees and fired. The man tumbled out of the tree and landed in some brush. Moments later he was fighting with his sword against two opponents, one he slashed across the face while using his arquebus to fend off the other opponent's slashing sword. One of his men clubbed the attacker from behind.

"Well done," he cried.

Their enemies were hard to discern hidden as they were among the tree branches and ground cover. The Ruthani often painted themselves to blend in with the foliage. Andros took a moment to remove his ramrod and reload his arquebus. He spotted some movements that could have been a bird for all he knew and fired at it. Nothing happened as far as he could see.

"We can't hold this position, Dralm-damnit! Retreat back the way we came. Drag any wounded that can walk with you." Andros ran past the wagons until he slipped on a pool of blood and entrails. On his way down his head struck a wagon wheel and darkness took him. There he lay as his remaining soldiers ran away down the road.

## IV

Democriphon watched in satisfaction as the last of the Blethan soldiers ran off the way they had come. He nodded at Gycules who roared like a panther. That was the signal to descend from the branches and surround the remaining Blethans. Some eighty to a hundred men lay wounded or dead strewn about the trail.

"Clear the dead animals out of the way and bring in more oxen to haul the wagons," Democriphon ordered Gycules. While the giant mercenary rounded up the necessary men, Democriphon turned to Ranthar. "What are our casualties?"

"Surprisingly light," First Captain Ranthar said. "Minor wounds, mostly. Only a few fatalities." Ranthar pointed up to a tree where one of the former sharper mercenaries lay on a branch. The top of his head was missing. "That petty-captain over there got him, I think. Galzar knows how."

Democriphon went over to where Andros lay. "What makes you so certain this man killed him? There was a lot of shot peppering the trees."

"I noticed he was shouting orders at his men. He stopped, aimed and shot while I was taking aim at him. Before I let fly, he ran and fell. He may still be alive."

"I hope so," Democriphon said. "I would like to meet the man who is handy enough with a smoothbore that he can kill a man in camouflage behind the cover of leaves."

"We can take him with us for questioning," Ranthar suggested. "We could use some more immediate information on the state of affairs in Hos-Bletha. That is, if we can get him to talk."

The Captain-General nodded. "We would have to kill him afterwards, though. I hate to do that to a prisoner, but we can't simply take his oath to Galzar and release him afterwards. He could endanger our mission."

Ranthar agreed. "Maybe we should just leave him with these wounded men. Or do we kill them as well?"

"No. Leave the wounded here. Their own people will be back for them soon enough, I think. Strip them of arms, armor and any valuables as the Swamp Ruthani would. Recover the bolts and arrows we used as well. We'll just leave the dead bodies here. They can take their petty-captain with them if he awakens in time."

Captain Ranthar looked over the Blethan soldiers who lay about the trail. "The Ruthani wouldn't leave these men alive."

Democriphon looked about him. At least five score or more lay dead or wounded. The usual Sastragathi or Ruthani practice in such a situation was to cut the men's throats and leave the bodies. Democriphon had overseen such actions himself in the past. Yet, something was wrong about this.

"I have another idea. Send me the Ruthani from the sharper band."

## V

The wounded had been pulled away from the dead and their wounds were wrapped with leaves and cloth from the dead men's tunics. Roaring Panther and Silent Wolf walked among the wounded, glaring at the Blethan soldiers. The idea was to keep them confused and nervous. The plan was working well.

When Roaring Panther finally spoke, he dumbed down his speech so as to sound more like a Swamp Ruthani who was largely unfamiliar with the Zarthani tongue.

"You! All you. We maybe kill you all. But maybe not kill. You not worth trouble. You hear? You go. Tell great chief this Ruthani place. Tell everybody. No come back! Come back, you die! All who come die. This Ruthani land, now. Go!"

The wounded soldiers who could get to their feet rose up and hastened to obey; stripped of arms and armor, and surrounded by armed hostiles, sapped whatever little courage that remained. Sticks and branches were provided to allow those with leg wounds to hobble away. A few arrows sprouted at their feet to speed them on.

Democriphon waved Gycules over. "Petty-Captain, order the men to butcher the dead oxen for their meat. When they're done, I want the ox carcasses, dead men and horse's bodies thrown into the swamp for the river dragons to feast on."

Gycules gave a curt nod and rushed away to carry out his orders.

Ranthar watched as the Blethans limped off then turned to Democriphon. "It would have been easier to simply slit their throats."

"It would," the Captain-General said. "This, however, sends a better message. When they get back to Bletha Town, all they'll talk about are the savage Ruthani and the disdain they showed for the power of the Blethan Royal Army."

Ranthar had to agree. "Still, I am surprised you went to so much trouble. Why bother?"

Democriphon leaned on one of the wagons waiting to be hauled away. "Our mission is to stir things up and keep the Blethans from supporting the Styphoni. I liked that plan and I'm pleased to take part in it. I also have no problem with killing men I have faced in open warfare, even the wounded when the battle is done."

"So why the change?"

Democriphon let out a long sigh. "There is much about King Kalvan's new way of making war that I like. I have heard him speak of treating prisoners, even the wounded, well back in the Cold Lands. They tend to the wounded enemies and imprison them until war is over. Something he called a *Gin-ee-vah* Rules of War. I admit that that sounds a bit strange to me. These men, however,"—he swung an arm to indicate the dead Blethans on the trail—"had no idea that they were in a war. We came down on them and attacked without warning or declaration of hostilities. And I don't like it. I will do what is necessary for Hos-Hostigos and my king no matter what my personal feelings are, but I do not like attacking soldiers who are not yet our enemies. That is why I wanted as many of them spared as possible. Were they in a declared war with Hos-Hostigos, I would have slit every one of their throats myself. Or at least accepted their oath to Galzar and taken them prisoner. That was not an option, so I did what I felt was right and proper. It still serves the mission and will allow me to sleep well tonight. Besides, I think Uncle Wolf Syros will approve."

"I understand what you're saying," Ranthar said. "However, don't forget that these soldiers were on their way to Hos-Ktemnos to join the Grand Host to fight against Hos-Hostigos. That makes them declared enemies. Still, I agree with the way you handled this." Ranthar jerked a thumb at Andros who still lay where he fell. "What about that unconscious petty-captain? The wounded neglected to take him."

"Damn. I forgot about him. Tie him up and put a bag over his head. We'll take him with us." Democriphon turned and went to oversee the harnessing of the fresh oxen to the wagons.

Ranthar watched the Captain-General with puzzlement. *Democriphon is acting differently from what I recall. Maybe he has been manipulated in some way?* The thought made him uneasy when he considered the most likely source of such personality-altering methods.

# SEVENTEEN

## I

Petty-Captain Andros awoke to a pounding headache and a sense of embarrassment. He could recall shooting into the trees then tripping over something. He didn't recall what he tripped over or what he struck his head on, only that he had been as clumsy as a new recruit and set a poor example to his men.

As Andros stirred he found that his arms and legs were bound. At least he was lying on an animal hide and not on the ground. That showed some consideration for his comfort rarely shown to an enemy—especially by Ruthani. To be left alive and still be drawing breath was a surprise.

He looked around as best he could and decided he was in a small log building about large enough to hold two horses. For a Zarthani it would be a storage shed. He had no idea what Ruthani would use it for. Few outsiders had ever seen a Ruthani village and lived to tell of it.

"Well, they must be waiting for me to wake up," Andros said aloud. He waited a second and when nobody ran in he raised his voice and called out, "If you are waiting for me to wake up before torturing me, then it is time to get busy, you murdering bastards!"

Nothing.

"Not in a hurry to cut on me, I guess." Andros rolled over to a more comfortable position. In the process of adjusting himself, he was able to see through a crack between the logs. *Somebody did a sloppy job with the pitch.* On the other side of the crack he could see feet moving back and forth. Mostly boots, a few sandals and the occasional bare foot.

It took a few minutes before Andros realized what was wrong with the scene; there wasn't a moccasin in the lot. Ruthani were known for taking the boots from their victims, true, yet all of the footgear he saw was in good repair and in some cases almost new. The sandals made no sense until Andros recalled that escaped slaves were rumored to join up with Ruthani tribes. Still, where were the moccasins? There was also something odd about the boots beyond their good repair.

Andros heard a noise behind him and rolled over to see what it was. Two Ruthani were standing before him. From the skin tone and tribal accessories the petty-captain had no doubt these were the genuine item. One of them even wore the moccasins he had been wondering about. The other wore the strange boots he had seen through the crack. Now, he could see what was odd about them; they were designed to fit by the foot. One boot was specifically made for the right foot and the other for the left. Andros had only seen boots like that from one place.

"Gentlemen, you can spare me the act. Bring me your true leaders. The ones from up north."

Roaring Panther and Silent Wolf looked at each other, then back at Andros. They turned and left without saying a word.

## II

"No point in bluffing him," Captain-General Democriphon said. "He took one look at Silent Wolf's boots and had us pegged. I should have known better."

"Boots?" Uncle Wolf Syros asked.

Captain Ranthar shrugged. "We have all been wearing these new boots for so long we forgot it was King Kalvan who designed them. I first started wearing them when I came down from Greffa. Now it seems like I've never worn anything else." He stretched one leg then the other out for Syros to look at.

"I know what you mean," Democriphon agreed. "You can't beat them for comfort, and marching in them is far easier on the feet. What I want to know is how a Blethan petty-captain spotted them and knew where they came from?"

"Well, there is one easy way to find out," Ranthar said.

"So there is, sir. Let us get to it."

"Say," Syros said as the two moved away. "Where can I get a pair of boots like that?"

## III

Petty-Captain Andros watched with interest as the two men entered through the door. Both were dressed like woodsmen with green and brown clothing, swords and the specialized boots that could only have come from Hos-Hostigos. The man on the left had shoulder length blond hair, a wing-shaped mustache and a young handsome face. *This one must do well with the ladies*. The one on the right wore a thin mustache under a beak-shaped nose and short chestnut hair. Both men had the bearing of one accustomed to leading men.

"You must be the leaders of this band," Andros said. "Will you torture me soon, or just kill me?"

The one with the golden hair laughed. "Neither, I should think."

"Why would we torture you?" the older and crueler-looking one asked. "It would be noisy and messy, and I doubt it would reveal much."

"No?" Andros sounded disappointed. "Why not?"

"We do not kill people unnecessarily," the blond said. Although the younger of the two, he appeared to be in charge. "Captain Ranthar watched you back at the ambush. You kept your head, managed to kill one of us, and tried to rally your troops. To kill a soldier of your caliber would be a tragic waste."

"Tell me, how you feel about Styphon's House and Great King Niclophon?" the older leader asked.

"What? Don't you want to take revenge for the men I killed?"

The blond man shook his head. "We attacked you. We knew the risks and didn't expect any of you not to fight back. In fact, you were the only one of your troop to kill any of us, although a few of us were wounded. Please answer my question: How do you feel about Styphon's House and Great King Niclophon?"

Andros looked into the blond's blue eyes, then the other man's brown eyes. There was no malice in them. "Humph. Styphon's House is a blight on every kingdom. They took my family's farm with Niclophon's help."

Democriphon and Ranthar noticed that Andros omitted 'Great King'. "How would you like to get some revenge on both of them?"

"What do you mean? I am no traitor to my homeland. If you want a new recruit look elsewhere."

Democriphon glanced at Ranthar. "I like this man. Brave, loyal… maybe not as smart as I thought."

"Look, either kill me or take my Oath to Galzar and let me go. I don't know where we are so I can't lead anybody back to you. The most I can reveal is what you look like and that you are not Ruthani. Well, most of you. Those first two you sent in here were Ruthani or I'm a Balph pleasure girl."

"Would it be treason if Niclophon were a regicide" Ranthar asked. "Isn't it a bit convenient that Great King Marocles and Great Queen Delra died and their son Valthros disappeared along with his wet-nurse?"

"Niclophon becomes the new great king and Styphon's House starts getting preferential treatment," Democriphon added. "Sounds very convenient indeed…for Styphon's House and Niclophon both, doesn't it?"

Andros listened. The two men weren't telling him anything he hadn't thought for himself many times. "Well, convenient or not, Niclophon is the lawful king of Hos-Bletha and there is nothing to be done for it."

"Isn't there," the older one asked.

"What about the Orphan Prince?" the blond prodded.

"What about him? He has been gone nearly thirty winters," Andros countered.

"Well, I am back now," declared the blond-haired leader.

"Oh, By Styphon's Own Bollocks!" Andros snorted. "Could you at least untie me so I can laugh in your face on my feet?"

"What makes you so certain that I am not?"

Andros let out a long breath. "Look, this sharpers' game has been played before. I have personally assisted in the hanging of one Orphan Prince and observed a couple more. I'll grant that you look the part. And you have the right amount of arrogance in your demeanor, but I can't make myself believe for a heartbeat that you are who you claim to be."

The blond-haired one shook his head. "I don't know if I am or not. I was a foundling in Hos-Harphax, or what is now Hos-Hostigos. I was found by some peasants and sold to a wealthy couple who raised me. I know I am the right age and coloring, but beyond that I have no proof of who my family might be. And yes, I very much doubt I am your lost prince."

Andros adjusted himself into a sitting position. "Okay, you are telling me the truth or you would try to sell me on the Orphan Prince story. So what do you want with me?"

The older leader drew his knife and approached him. Andros steeled himself to have his throat cut. Instead the man cut the ropes from his feet and hands.

"We just want to talk," the self-pronounced Prince declared. "We won't force you to break any oaths or betray any confidences. You impressed Captain Ranthar back at the ambush. He doesn't impress easily, and that impresses me."

"By getting captured through my own clumsiness?" Andros shook his head. At least now he knew one of their names. "You are impressed by strange things."

"By not losing your head and taking charge when your captain was felled," supplied Ranthar. "Tripping over a body on the battlefield happens to everybody sooner or later."

"At least you didn't land face down in horse manure," Democriphon added.

Ranthar looked at him with wide eyes. "Did that ever happen to…?"

"No. I'm just saying he was lucky."

Ranthar made a mental note to see if any of the mercenaries might have been with Democriphon in battle, and if they ever saw him trip. It would make a nice footnote in a study team report.

## IV

Andros watched the byplay between the two commanders and didn't know what to think. When he first recovered his senses he had expected to be tortured and killed by Ruthani. Then he figured he would be tortured and killed by bandits *dressed* as Ruthani. Now he had no idea what was going on. The two men before him didn't appear to want him to come to harm, but that was no guarantee of anything—it could be Lyklos, the god of mischief, at play.

Another thing hit the petty-captain; the self-proclaimed prince spoke with a foreign accent. Harphaxi, if he was any judge. The older one spoke like a Blethan native, yet his skin was too fair to be from anywhere this far south. He watched as they signaled a man wearing a wolfskin hood and the usual accoutrements of an Uncle Wolf to join them

"What do you want to talk about?" he asked.

"We want you to join us," the Orphan Prince stated. "You and Uncle Wolf Syros could train the men, mostly former slaves—"

"You have an Uncle Wolf?" he asked interrupting the Prince. "I thought his dress was another disguise. I've never heard of one working with bandits."

"That is because we are not bandits. We are rebels," the Prince explained as though his patience were coming to an end. "We rob merchants to finance the rebellion."

"And free the slaves," Captain Ranthar added. "The Great King Kalvan of Hos-Hostigos freed his slaves and we like that idea, so we intend to do the same when Niclophon is ousted."

Andros laughed. "Then you are a fool. The principalities will rise up against you. And what would we do with our criminals if you free them?"

"He makes a good point," the Uncle Wolf joined in. "Our facilities for holding transgressors are small, just enough to hold the worst of them before they are hanged."

The so-called Prince Valthros appeared to think about it. "Hmm. I don't consider that to be true slavery. That is punishment against men who deserve it. I understand they are eventually freed. Is that not true?"

The Uncle Wolf nodded. "Yes, they are, provided they do not try to escape and add additional time to their sentence."

"Then I see no point in changing that," Valthros said. "But bringing in outsiders to be sold on the auction block will end. That includes local villagers and townsfolk being enslaved without committing a crime."

Andros shrugged. "That will win you some support from the common people, but don't count on the nobility or merchant class. Except Prince Mythros, maybe."

"Mythros?" the man they called the Prince glanced cover at the Uncle Wolf.

"Mythros was the Great Queen's brother," the Uncle Wolf said. "He has never held slaves of any kind and often speaks out against the practice. He is unusual in that respect. It is rumored that he harbors ill will against Niclophon, also."

"Really?" Valthros appeared surprised by that piece of news. "Maybe we can make an ally of him."

"I wouldn't count on that, sire," Andros said. "He takes a dim view of those who try to profit from the memory of his lost nephew. One of those hangings I saw; it was Prince Mythros who ordered it."

The Uncle Wolf nodded. "Your Highness, it is commonly agreed among all sharpers not to run the Orphan Prince game in Mythros' realm. The petty-captain is not exaggerating the prince's ill-tolerance."

"That," Andros interjected, "would be a problem. If you really want to bring down Niclophon, you will need as many of the princes on your side as you can get."

The Prince appeared to be mulling over his words. "Actually, our mission is to keep Hos-Bletha from taking part in the war. Ousting Niclophon would do that, but it is not our primary goal. We just need to keep things, uh, *hopping* down here until the dust settles up north." Democriphon turned to Andros. "What would *you* like us to do?"

Andros started in surprise, as he was not used to being asked for his opinion. "If Niclophon is the regicide we think he is, then he is unworthy to rule. If he is merely a dupe of Styphon's House, then he is likewise unworthy. Though it be treason, I think he needs to be brought down. Prince Mythros would be your best ally in removing him from the Silver Throne."

Democriphon took in a deep breath and let it out slowly. "Very well. Let us see if we can make a compromise of things. We will stay out of Mythros' realm, for now. The same with the banditry. If we can make an ally of him, we shall. If not, then perhaps he will not take offence as long as we don't sully his realm with our actions. First, however, I think we should take care of some business with Styphon's minions."

Andros shrugged. "I am with you in this, though I do not think highly of our chances at survival."

The Prince looked him in the eye. "Will you give your sworn oath, in Galzar's Name, to be loyal to me and my cause? If so, I will have you released and you will be given back your rank."

Andros paused to mull this over for a bit. *What do I owe Great King Niclophon? I am an oath-sworn officer in the Royal Army of Hos-Bletha, but does that oath hold for a king who has committed regicide? No, it doesn't.*

"Prince, I will give you my sworn-oath on one condition."

"Yes, and what is that?" the Prince asked.

"Before the true gods, I will follow all your orders and will fight all your enemies with all my might, with one exception. I will not fight against my former cohorts with the Royal Army. Is that acceptable?"

The Prince paused as he thought over the proposal. Then he smiled, "It is agreeable and an honorable decision."

# EIGHTEEN

## I

The journey had been a wet one and everybody was in a foul mood. Even First Captain Ranthar was having difficulty retaining his aplomb. The rain had soaked them all to the bone and he was beginning to envy Duke Skranga, who was back at their base overseeing training the new recruits and reconnaissance. At least the Duke had a hut to keep the weather at bay and his clothes dry.

Their goal was to go deep into the Princedom of Artigos to a town near the Hos-Ktemnos border and raid a Styphoni temple, something none of his men had ever done. Ranthar, at least, had the benefit of having visited one such temple in Sask Town after Lord Kalvan had it stripped of gold and priests. Calthros had assured him that every temple was built much along the same lines.

The only difference was in a matter of scale. The major towns and seaports had the largest temples. The smaller but still important towns had smaller temples with fewer sleeping cells and smaller holding pens for slaves. The village temples were simple affairs that did not bother with the gold-covered domes.

Initially, Ranthar had wanted to dress up as Styphon's Own Guard to bluff his way inside. But Duke Skranga had overruled him. He believed it was too soon to use the Temple Guardsmen. This operation was more to scout out the enemy, see what their normal precautions were and explore the local temple layouts.

So, instead of bluffing their way inside the temple, they would try to scale the rear walls of the temple, then don the wolf-faced helms hoping to inspire terror in their victims. Only the more uncivilized sectors of the Fourth Level, like Aryan-Transpacific would fall prey to such an artifice. More civilized Fourth Level civilizations, with their Halloween traditions and horror movies, wouldn't even blink twice at the wolf-helms. In fact, the primary reaction, especially in Europo-American, would be, "Hey, where can I get one of those?"

Ranthar's mind was brought back from his musings when a scout rode up gesticulating madly.

"Sir, there is a Styphoni caravan three marches up the road. They are coming our way."

"Tell me everything you can about them," Ranthar ordered.

"Um, there are at least a hundred of them, mostly Styphon's Own Guard, and maybe twenty slaves. They are escorting some horse-drawn wagons."

"And?" Ranthar waited for more information, but none was forthcoming. He mentally cursed the rules of the Paratime Code that prevented him from training these men in more advanced scouting disciplines. In the military of most Europo-American subsectors there was an acronym that covered virtually everything a scout should look for. It was called S.A.L.U.T.E.: size, activity, location, uniform, time and equipment. "What were they doing?"

"Marching this way, sir."

"What kind of equipment were they carrying?"

"Oh, glaives, musketoons, swords. I think I saw some horse-pistols. No cannons."

Better. "How many wagons?"

"Six, sir."

Now what would so few men need with that many wagons? "Gasphros, any ideas what they might be carrying?"

The bard thought it over for a moment, then a sly look crossed his face. "I think it is a transfer train between banking houses."

This was a new phrase not covered in the Hypno-mech. "Transfer train? Transferring what?"

"Gold, silver, slaves, equipment. From what Calthros tells me, the Styphoni run gold between banking houses when one either gets too full, which is often, or too low, which is almost never." Gasphros looked back and forth as though considering the direction of the road and where the caravan was headed. "My guess is that this one is headed to the Artigos Town Banking House to deposit gold. The extra wagons would be for victuals and supplies, but the rest will be filled almost to the top with gold and silver, maybe even precious gems."

Ranthar's eyes widened. "That would be millions of ounces of gold and silver! You could run a war on that much."

"A small one, to be sure," the bard agreed. "Too bad it would be impossible to take."

"What? Why?"

"Because the escort is Styphon's Own Guard, the best of the best, trained to deal with robbers and bandits and all sorts of subterfuge. Eighty men are not enough to deal with a hundred Guardsmen."

"Maybe not in a straight up confrontation." Ranthar looked over the landscape the road cut through. Trees and low hills. "This will not be as hard as you might think."

## II

Minos, a former mercenary, grunted as he was pulled by his chains behind the hindmost wagon. Off to his side rode the Slave Master whose function was to keep the slaves from getting out of hand. The rest of Styphon's Own Guard rode well ahead of the caravan; they did not care for the stink of sweating unwashed bodies, especially those with fester devils on their backs where the iron-barbed whips had been applied.

From the corner of his eye he saw something moving in the brush. He hoped it was either a tribe of Ruthani come to kill everybody, himself included, or at least a band of bandits with the same goals in mind. He could just make out the chestnut colored hair of a man peeking from behind a tree. Not Ruthani, since their hair was almost universally black. Bandits after the gold, then. Minos did not care as long as he was either killed or set free. He suspected the former rather than the latter was to be his fate.

"What are you looking at, slave?" The slave master brought his whip down on Minos' back, tearing flesh and reopening old wounds.

The slave master brought his arm back for another swing. As he jerked his arm forward, something held the whip tight. As he turned to see if the lash became caught on a tree limb, he was pulled from his horse. He tried to cry out in vain. The dagger that protruded from his throat was an effective means of keeping him quiet.

The attacker pulled the body back into the trees and quickly stripped it. After donning the Guardsman's armor, he ran back to the horse and mounted it. Minos watched as the man gestured him to silence and winked at him.

The other slaves began to whisper among themselves. Minos quickly shushed them. Whatever was going to happen, good or ill for the slaves, at least they would see their Styphoni captors die first.

The mounted man pulled alongside and whispered to Minos, "You can be Dralm-damned sure we're going to kill these godless swine. Here are the keys. Unchain yourself and your friends, but stay with the caravan until I give you the signal to go. Understood?"

"Oath to Galzar, master."

The man did a double take. "Were you a mercenary?"

"Yes. I fell on hard times after I was mustered out, then I was enslaved for failure to pay Styphon's House money I owed while in Balph."

"In that case, take this knife. You may have as much revenge as you can take when I give the signal. Mind you, be careful on whom you use it," the man said as he passed over a lengthy blade. "My name is…

unimportant. Just watch what happens and choose your targets carefully."

Minos nodded and watched ahead. He had an idea what to expect after seeing the nameless man kill the slave master. As he watched, two men moved past him on either side of the marching line. They silently ran forward and leapt onto the backs of the horses that bracketed the rearmost wagon and slit the throats of the riders before they could shout a warning. Two more men came out of the woods and received the bodies, dragging them behind the tree line. Moments later, they returned dressed as Styphon's Own Guard and replaced the men on the horses.

Ahead, one foot guard looked back and spoke to the other guard on the opposite side of the next wagon. They broke ranks and turned back to investigate.

"Did you see something moving in the brush?" the Guardsman asked the newly mounted man.

"Nah," answered the mounted man. "Take six men with you and investigate."

The guard nodded and obeyed. Moments later seven new men returned from the tree line dressed in Styphoni armor. They took over the marching positions abandoned by the previous soldiers. Two more started out for the tree line when a halt was called to the caravan. They barely returned to cover before being discovered.

"What are we stopping for?" the mounted man asked Minos.

"Mid-day meal. We will be rested for two candles, maybe even fed some bread and cheese, while the horses and oxen are watered and fed. This is when the soldiers will also relieve themselves. They tend to spread out a bit as most are still shy about their circumcisions."

The mounted man acted surprised. "Styphon's Own Guard are circumcised? I thought that was only for the priests."

Minos shook his head. "It is a sign of devotion to their god. Maybe Styphon eats the leavings or something. This is a new squad. Fighting men are more sensitive about it than the priests, and it takes a while before they become comfortable with their loss."

"Interesting. I think we can take advantage of that." The man dismounted. "Stay here. I will return after I have…relieved myself."

The man entered the wood line and disappeared. After the usual amount of time allotted for such a mission, he returned. "I have a job for you. If you do well, then you will be welcome to join us. If you choose not to, then you and your fellows are free to leave with enough gold to make your way to wherever you wish. What say you?"

"Down Styphon!" Minos answered.

## III

Captain Anexros waited for his men to return from the brush. His standing rule was that no more than eight men at a time could leave to attend to their personal needs. The rest stayed with the wagons until their turn in the rotation. It was a system that had always served him well. The only drawback was that he had to wait until every single man had returned before he could address his own needs.

More than half of his men had returned when he heard a shout from the rear of the caravan. It was from one of the guards. Slaves were running away. *How in Regwarn did they get out of their chains?*

Anexros pointed to the mounted men closest to him. "Get some men and go after the slaves. Try not to kill any as we need them to transfer the gold from the wagons to the vault…unless you want to do that job yourselves."

The two petty-captains gave a quick salute before turning their horses and racing back to the end of the caravan. Anexros shook his head in disgust. Now he would have to wait until the slaves were rounded up before he could empty his bladder.

"To Regwarn with it," he said as he dismounted. He had a full bladder from too much winter wine that morning and he couldn't wait any longer. Nodding to a soldier near him, he handed over the reins and walked off behind the tree line. Not for the first time he complained about the difficulty of relieving himself while in full armor.

After completing his task, Anexros drew a contented sigh then turned to start back to the caravan. His journey was cut short by the nearly naked man standing before him with a knife. Before he could reach for his sword the other man's blade found its way into his throat. He gurgled his surprise before falling dead.

## IV

Ranthar took his place at the lead of the caravan. The operation had gone more smoothly than he could have hoped. When the real Styphoni went after the escaped slaves, his replacements caught them by surprise. He only lost eleven men in total; five dead and six severely wounded. The wounded were put to sleep by the Uncle Wolf, and then given a mercy stroke across the throat. The friendly dead were buried behind the tree line while the Styphoni were dumped into a swamp hole.

The less severely wounded were treated by Gasphros as were the slaves. Armor was collected, cleaned, and quickly appropriated by Ranthar's men. The first slave he released cursed prolifically at the idea of wearing such hated colors until Ranthar pointed out the advantages of doing so.

"What advantages?"

"We will be raiding the Styphoni Banking House in Syragon Town," Ranthar explained. "You will act as the Slave Master because the other slaves know and trust you. Ah, they do trust you, do they not?"

"Better than you," Minos admitted. "Fine. After that are we free to go as we choose?"

"With more gold than you could earn in a lifetime as a mercenary."

"Humph. Kill Styphoni and get paid handsomely for it, or just run away and hope I don't get caught again." Minos smiled, from ear to ear. "By Galzar, just try to stop me from coming along!"

# NINETEEN

Minos proved to be an invaluable source of information in Ranthar's estimation. After months of slavery, being used to carry gold in and out of several of Styphon's House banking and money lending institutions, he knew everything about their layout and protocols. He was easily as good as any "inside man."

First Captain Ranthar had been prepared to simply take the wagons to the front of the banking house where many a Fourth Level Europo-American robbery movie would have the guards shot and the bags of money taken before a high-speed chase. Styphon's House had obviously never seen any of those movies.

Instead, they used a guarded gate behind the banking house where the transfer train marched in and settled within the protected enclosure. This was very clever on the part of Styphon's House; it disguised the purpose of the caravan as there was no percentage in showing off their wealth, and protected them while they made the transfer. That made them head and shoulders smarter than Europo-American filmmakers.

"Are you Captain Anexros?

Ranthar turned to see a black-robed priest with a gold chain belt about his ample midriff. He had been warned about the recognition protocol by Minos.

"Nay, I be Styphon's Own Money Changer."

They shared a laugh and Ranthar produced the document Gasphros had made for him. Forgery, as it turned out, was among the bard's many gifts.

The priest looked over the document in confusion. "I do not understand. We were expecting a large deposit of funds from Taurnos Town. This is a request for almost everything we have in our vault. I will have to consult Highpriest Lophlos."

"Now see here, I have a schedule to keep…"

While Ranthar kept the priest busy with double-talk, Gasphros, disguised as a petty-captain, led a group of ersatz Styphoni guardsmen into the building. There, the bard and his compatriots looked over the security and number of guards. Once satisfied, they returned to the wagons.

Ranthar, running out of objections for the priest, was relieved to see Gasphros return. "Fine. Go see Highpriest Lophlos. I suspect he will have you whipped for wasting his time."

The priest, mollified to be able to get away from the argumentative captain, rushed back into the banking house. As he left, Gasphros walked over to give his report.

"Ten guards inside watching the lobby," stated the bard, "a dozen underpriests behind counters with wire mesh screens they can close if they think they need to, four guards at the entrance to the vault room. I cannot speak to what may be down the hall or in the upper level."

"How do you know where the vault is?"

"Bah. In the time it takes for that oversized-sausage to turn around I saw four underpriests go in and out of the room. Two came out with gold or silver, the other two took gold in, then came out empty-handed. The guards watched them like hawks in either case."

Ranthar nodded. "Good. Have the men clear all the Styphoni out of this courtyard before this Lophlos comes out. Once we have him, we go inside and engage in some serious larceny."

Gasphros started to smile, then quickly suppressed it. What was to come next would be no laughing matter. He walked over to the men and whispered their instructions. The faux Guardsmen paired off and went to speak with the bank house guards in the courtyard. It was over in moments. One man would strike up a conversation with a guard, then his partner would slice the man's throat from behind. The bodies were quickly dragged to one of the wagons and thrown inside and then Ranthar's men would assume their posts.

Ranthar watched as the bodies were stacked like so much cordwood, while Minos threw dirt over the ground where blood spatters could be seen. When the priest returned with Lophlos, there remained no sign that anything amiss had occurred.

"What is the meaning of this?" Highpriest Lophlos shouted. "I know of no Sangar in Hos-Bletha, nor will I open my vault to just anyone!"

"Your Worship, Sangar has been sent to Hos-Bletha by the Inner Circle on an inspection tour and to gather funds for the war against the Daemon Kalvan," Ranthar said. "The war is not going well and we need to hire many more mercenaries if we are to bring the Usurper down. Highpriest Sangar has tasked me to hire these mercenaries and that document authorizes me to seize the funds necessary to do so. I understand His Worship Sangar is close friends with Archpriest Roxthar. Or would you rather address your objections to the Holy Investigator himself?"

Lophlos' face, normally ashen, turned even whiter. The mere mention of Roxthar had that effect. He turned and whispered something to the underpriest who immediately ran back to the building, then returned his attention to Ranthar.

"Very well, Grand-Captain Anexros. Send your men in to collect the allotted sum. Leave the slaves outside as I do not want their stink to befoul my lobby."

"Yes, Your Worship." Ranthar watched the highpriest waddle back into the building.

"He means to betray you."

Ranthar spun about to find Gasphros. He had come up upon Ranthar so quietly that even his First Level hearing failed to detect his approach.

"By Galzar, you move like a wildcat!"

"A survival trait," Gasphros said lightly. "Another is reading lips. Lophlos instructed that underpriest to lay a trap for you inside. That was why he didn't want the slaves going in; he would need them afterwards to remove your bodies."

"What? Why?"

"He did not say, but I suspect he has been embezzling gold and silver from the banking house and does not have the funds your document demands. Instead, he will have you—us—all killed, then claim we never arrived."

*Was anybody in Styphon's House on the up and up?* he wondered. "Fine, we will turn the tables on them. We just need a distraction."

"I can take care of that." Gasphros said with a grin.

Before Ranthar could ask what he meant, the bard walked off, removing his armor as he went. *Whatever he is up to, it should be interesting.*

"Minos. Get the men ready for an assault. No gunfire unless they shoot at us first. I do not want the locals getting curious about what is going on in here."

Minos nodded once, then went to ready the men for what was to come. Ranthar looked for Gasphros, only to discover the bard had vanished. A moment later he could hear screaming from inside the banking house.

"What the hell?" Ranthar looked in the direction of the screams and saw smoke billowing out through windows and doors. "All right, that is our distraction. Let's go!"

Ranthar led the men in through the main door with sword drawn. He almost stopped when he found himself engulfed in a foul smelling smoke that obscured anything more than an arms-length away. The knowledge that other men with drawn swords were right on his heels kept him moving.

*This is a fine distraction, Gasphros, but how do I find anybody in this fog?* Almost as fast as he thought it the smoke thinned and started to settle. Without thinking, Ranthar struck at the first priest he saw, nearly beheading the man, his sword catching on the neck vertebrae. By the time the smoke had completely cleared, Minos had led the others into the banking house. From there it was short work to put down the interior guard and the remaining priests.

Ranthar looked around. Gasphros and Lophlos were still missing. "Look everywhere for the fat highpriest and Gasphros. We do not leave until both are found and one is dead."

"I hope that one is not me."

Ranthar spun around to find Gasphros with Highpriest Lophlos in tow. "Would you please stop doing that! Where did that smoke come from?"

"My apologies, Grand-Captain Anexros," Gasphros said with a flourish. "The smoke was a little thing I learned with a traveling entertainment troupe. A little fireseed, some of this and some of that." The Bard pushed the highpriest forward. "Would you like the honors?"

"No, please! I am far more valuable alive." Lophlos went to his knees to beg only to be jerked back up by Gasphros. "You can ransom me back to Styphon's House for a handsome sum!"

Ranthar sighed. He disliked killing an unarmed man, though in the course of his years as a Paratime cop he had done so on more than one occasion. He was about to strike when something occurred to him. "Minos. You have more right than any to take your revenge…."

Minos did not hesitate. Before Ranthar finished speaking he thrust his sword into Lophlos expansive abdomen and twisted the blade. He took a full candle to expire, and did so in great agony.

With the fighting over and the highpriest dying, Ranthar turned back to the mission at hand. "Take everything of value that is not nailed down and put it in the wagons. Minos, please supervise the men and be sure they pack things right."

"Where is the vault," Minos inquired.

Ranthar cursed. "Is it open is a better question."

"Oh, very much so," Gasphros said. "Highpriest Lophlos expected you to head straight for the vault, so he left it unsecured to distract you. Not that it mattered." Gasphros bent down and pulled something from under the highpriest's robes, then held it out for Ranthar and Minos to see. "We have the key."

# TWENTY

"...and then told us to leave, Your Majesty."

Great King Niclophon had listened to three separate accounts of what had happened to the company of men and their supplies, not to mention the gold, and could still barely credit his ears. True, the Ruthani had been known to harass travelers and small villages, but never anything on this scale. Even more surprising was the mercy they had shown the wounded. Normally their victims were killed and the bodies dumped in the swamps for the river dragons to feast on. What had changed?

Niclophon looked over at his Chancellor Archimanes and nodded slightly.

"His Majesty thanks you for your report, soldier," the Chancellor stated. "You may now report back to your company."

"My thanks, Your Majesty," the soldier said, as he bowed low and backed out of the presence chamber. The soldier narrowly avoided a collision with Captain-General Theodoros. The young soldier turned and tried to apologize. All that came out of his mouth was a strangled squeak. Theodoros smiled and waved him on.

Niclophon observed the incident with mild amusement. After the frightened soldier rushed off, he gestured the captain-general forward. "I am surprised you didn't have him sent to the stockade, Theodoros."

"For not having eyes on his arse? I can hardly fault him for showing you the proper respect and not seeing me as he backed out, Your Majesty."

Theodoros was correct, of course, but discipline was maintained by holding the men accountable for everything, or so Niclophon's more experienced captain-generals would have him believe. Theodoros was a little too lax with the soldiers under his command in their opinion. Having never been personally involved in military matters of any real significance, Niclophon had no idea one way or the other.

"You missed hearing his report, Theodoros. I was curious and circumvented the chain of command and had him brought to me."

"Actually, Your Majesty, I was at the infirmary questioning the wounded that came in after him. Normally I would simply have taken the report from the captain or petty-captain. Unfortunately, my understanding is that the captain was killed and the petty-captain is either dead or wounded and left behind. That is a pity; petty-captains like Andros are very difficult to come by."

Niclophon was impressed. For a captain-general to take notice of a mere petty-captain, let alone know his name, this Andros must have been an exceptional soldier. That said something about Theodoros as well. Then again, Theodoros wasn't highly regarded by Captain-General Lykron and the other top officers since his appointment was a political favor. The fact that most captain-generals acquired their positions due to their noble rank and not through expertise in combat was ignored by all.

Theodoros acted as if he didn't care what the others thought of him. Instead he tried to cultivate a favorable impression from those in his command. He also studied the tactics of other military leaders, both living and dead. Among these, to Niclophon's chagrin, was the Daemon Kalvan of Hostigos. The wisdom of studying a potential enemy was lost on the Great King of Hos-Bletha.

"What have you learned?"

"If the soldiers' accounts are to be credited, the Ruthani have become bolder," Theodoros replied. "By attacking a military caravan they are telling us they have no fear of reprisal. Furthermore, letting the wounded return instead of simply killing them is also significant."

"Significant in what way?" Niclophon prodded.

"It tells us that they think we are not even worth killing. Oddly, to us, this is an insult to their way of thinking. Something has changed; they may have created an alliance between their tribes, or even joined with the Caribi. For that matter, it is even possible that they are being aided by the Urgothi clans or even the Mexicotál."

"What! How can this be? The Zarthani Knights keep those barbarians away from our lands."

Theodoros nodded. "Yes. But too many of the Knights have been diverted to the wars in the north. The Order no longer possesses the strength it once owned. Tarr-Ceros barely survived a major attack by the nomads and the Usurper Kalvan last summer. It's quite likely that small bands of Urgothi and western Ruthani have been slipping through and joining the local Ruthani."

Niclophon fell backward into the deep cushions of the Silver Throne. A Ruthani/Urgothi alliance was a nightmare. "Are you certain?"

"Nay. I have only supposition. It may not be any of those things or all of them. It could even be that escaped slaves have been welcomed into the Ruthani tribes bolstering their numbers. The slaves would have little love for their former masters, especially those that fled the tender mercies of Styphon's House, and would be most happy to bedevil us all."

"Escaped slaves?"

"According to the men I questioned many of the Ruthani attackers had pale skin, even paler than our own. Either they came down from the north, which I can hardly credit, or they are escaped slaves who rarely had the opportunity to walk in the sunlight, such as those who labor in the Styphon's House temples."

Niclophon digested what he heard. He had to agree that the slave theory made the most sense. It was also the least frightening possibility.

"Theodoros, I want you to arrange an inspection tour of all of the major slave owners. See if any of them claim to have lost some of their property."

"I will do as Your Majesty requests. However, it might be more productive if Your Majesty questioned Archpriest Prythames."

Niclophon made a wry smile, but said nothing in reply.

Theodoros bowed low and backed out in much the same way as the frightened soldier had earlier. Once he cleared the chamber he straightened up and headed out of the palace. He finally had the opportunity to prove he was more than a political peace offering to the other captain-generals. He also had another theory as to where the Ruthani might have acquired new allies and intended to investigate the matter.

## II

First Captain Ranthar returned to camp and made his report to Democriphon about hijacking the gold shipments. However, Ranthar's real interest in talking with the Captain-General was to learn whether or not someone from Home Time Line was performing unauthorized Hypno-mech programming on him. It was possible that someone who wanted to hurt Chief Verkan might be meddling with prominent Hostigi figures, like Democriphon. The information he had relayed about Democriphon had been collected by a First Level observation team in Bletha Town while he did his own research. He was worried because so far he hadn't learned a single thing for all of his efforts.

Before making a report on this matter to Chief Verkan, Ranthar decided to first have a talk with Democriphon. Maybe there was a more pedestrian explanation for his behavior. The only question was how to approach the man.

Democriphon shook his head in disbelief. "I sent you out to rob a temple or gold shipment, and here you come back with almost three hundred thousand ounces of gold! Not to mention the over twenty wagon loads of silver. It's too bad that there are so few mercenaries available for hire in the Six Kingdoms; otherwise, we would hire ourselves an army with this bounty."

"Yes, I was surprised at how much gold we recovered. But we would have never been so successful without Minos' help."

After finishing his report and celebrating with goblets of winter wine, Ranthar decided the direct approach would work best.

"Captain-General, I have been wondering something and was hoping I could ask you a direct question without causing offence."

Democriphon actually laughed. "First of all, in private or with the other leaders, please use my name—not my title. I suspect you are wondering why I am acting in a more cautious manner, yes? Unlike my reputation on the battlefield?"

Ranthar was surprised. Democriphon was doing that more and more often as of late. "Well, to be quite honest, yes."

Democriphon sat down on a log, and while taking out his tobacco pouch, indicated that Ranthar, too, should have a seat. "As you may know, I was not King Kalvan's first choice to go on this mission. I was called into his chambers for a private discussion about it. He believes that I am prone to make decisions based on my desire for glory rather than the needs of the kingdom. He also pointed out that I had the highest casualties of any commander in his army. I insisted that I would do well on this mission and Duke Skranga supported me."

"He did? Why?"

Democriphon shrugged. "You will have to ask him about that. The Great King decided to tell me a story about a captain-general in the Cold Lands called Custer. It seemed that this Custer was the youngest captain-general to ever command an army there. He was brave and clever but a little too full of himself. He ended up leading all of his men into a slaughter from which none survived. Kalvan stressed that he had no need of leaders who got their own people killed uselessly.

"There was another captain-general called Patton who said, 'No bastard ever won a war by dying for his kingdom. He won it by making the other poor dumb bastard die for his kingdom.' I have been worrying over those words ever since. Kalvan also said something else that has run through my mind like a frightened stallion. There was this great duke in the Cold Lands. In fact, he was so highly regarded he was always called *The Duke*, as if he were the only one. This Duke once said, 'Life is hard. It's even harder when you are foolish.'"

Democriphon nodded to himself. "The Great King wasn't actually calling me a fool, I realize that now, but at the time I was angered. While I held my tongue, I imagine King Kalvan could read it in my eyes. That is when he called in a peasant family. The man who should be providing for his wife and children was unable to do so because of the wounds he received at the Battle of Fyk. Then he called in a woman who had lost her husband. He gave both a few gold crowns, then had them escorted out. I asked King Kalvan why he had shown me these people."

Ranthar waited for Democriphon to continue. When nothing was forthcoming, he asked him why.

Democriphon put his pipe aside, took a deep breath and slowly let it out. "The King wanted me to understand that the soldiers who fight under my command were men with lives and often families of their own. Men who fought and died to protect those families. The men from both families had been under my command; I was responsible for one man's death and the other's injuries. I took the meaning to heart; leaders should not spend the lives of those they command needlessly. It is a lesson I was long overdue to learn."

Ranthar weighed the words he heard against his suspicions. Everything Democriphon said could have been the result of hypno-mech conditioning, but it rang too true. The quotes, the presentation—all sounded very much like Calvin Morrison. He would still send his suspicions up to Chief Verkan, but he would add his conclusions as well.

He turned when he heard someone entering the cabin, and relaxed when he realized it was Duke Skranga with Gasphros.

"Phew, I was hoping to catch you two together," the Duke said, as he took out his tobacco pouch and began filling his pipe bowl. "We have a couple of big problems."

Democriphon looked up questioningly. "Hmm. So far our raids and attacks on the enemy have been successful. Maybe too successful…"

Ranthar nodded his head. "True, but our success here has had a lot to do with the Temple's dominance of this kingdom. For over two hundred winters Styphon's House has lorded over the Blethan great kings and princes. They've become complacent and arrogant, to the point where even the Temple Guardsmen here are time-wasters and rejects from the northern kingdoms. Eventually we'll wake up the sleeping giant, but until then I believe we'll continue to do quite well here."

Skranga let out a big breath. "I pray to Galzar you are right. Still, I keep waiting for 'the other boot to drop,' as our Great King puts it."

"It's good you brought this up," Democriphon said. "We need to watch out that our troops don't become complacent or jaded by these cheap victories. Eventually, Styphon's House will realize there's a real problem here in Hos-Bletha and things will get serious in a hurry. We want to be prepared for that moment, not lulled into a false sense of security. Until then, we need to capitalize on our early victories. I've come up with a plan to raid a couple of Styphoni temples that I was just about to share with Captain Ranthar."

Skranga sighed. "That's the other thing we need to talk about. Our success is quickly turning into a major liability. Right now we're holding way too much gold and silver in the camp. Most of which is locked up in two heavily-guarded sheds. Still, we need to find a place away from camp to store it safely before some of our former mercenaries get to thinking, or one of our men says something to an outsider; all our work and treasure will go to Regwarn!"

Ranthar clenched his teeth. "Good point, sire." Then inspiration struck! He had been looking for a good excuse to make his way to the Blethan headquarters and Skranga had just handed it to him on a silver platter. "I was about to take a small party to Bletha Town with Gasphros to find more supplies. Maybe I can use this journey to find a place we can use to act as our treasury."

"What do you mean, First Captain?" Skranga asked, looking at him as if he had just announced he was going to steal the gold for himself.

"As you pointed out, Duke, we cannot leave the gold in camp. Nor can we take it with us on our raids. The new camp may be safer, but all that specie in one spot will still be too much temptation for some of our soldiers, especially when we're out raiding temples or waylaying merchants and slave traders. And it's a lure for bandits and outlaws. You both know how difficult it will be to keep the knowledge of its existence within the walls of our camp."

Skranga and Democriphon both glumly nodded their accord.

"So what is your plan?" Democriphon asked.

"We need to find an old castle or manor house, one that's been deserted for many winters. One with a dungeon. Once we find a promising place, I will purchase it if need be. Otherwise, we'll just occupy it if it's abandoned. We can use the castle both as a fort and treasury." Ranthar paused to aim his pipe stem at the bard Gasphros. "You know this area better than any of us. What do you think?"

Gasphros tugged at his curly beard before replying. "There are some old border forts between the Taurnos/Artigos border that have been abandoned for many winters. Maybe if we went to Artigos Town for supplies, rather than Bletha Town, we could scout out the best possible locations."

"An excellent suggestion," Ranthar replied. "The sooner we establish a permanent treasury the better."

"How do we keep it secure?" Duke Skranga asked, his forehead wrinkled like a washboard.

"We'll need a good cover story," Gasphros suggested.

"How about that of a Beshtan noble who's in tax trouble with Niclophon?" Democriphon offered.

"I don't think so," Gasphros said. "The local villagers and townspeople are very nosy about new arrivals. Somebody might check it out, or one of the locals might turn us in to Prince Kosklos."

Skranga smiled. "I've got an idea. What about a Styphon's House temple-farm? No one is going to check that out—not even the nosiest local. With the war against Hostigos heating up, it makes perfect sense that the Temple is looking to make more fireseed."

"Very good, Duke!" Democriphon exclaimed. "Plus, we can use the temple-farm to provide us with fireseed since we're using up our stockpiles."

"And," Ranthar added, "we've got all these slaves with whip scars and we need a place to keep them safe and out of our hair. However, we'll have to be careful about which formula we use."

Democriphon slumped. "More of Styphon's Best, Dralm-damnit! It's crap fireseed, but it's better than nothing. It's too dangerous to use Kalvan's formula here in Bletha."

"Duke, I think you've solved our problem," Ranthar declared. "The last thing anyone will suspect is that we're using a Styphon's House temple-farm as a place to store our gold and silver. Plus, no one will be surprised by the continual comings and goings of wagons and supplies."

"True, but that will mean using some of our most loyal men as guards and overseers for the temple-farm," Democriphon noted unhappily.

"I know," Ranthar replied. "But I don't see that we have any other choice. We'll need about fifty Hostigi soldiers and two to three hundred former slaves."

"We'll have to make do," Democriphon said. "We cannot leave all this gold and silver in our camp for much longer. Ranthar, you can take Calthros with you as the Styphon's House representative. He'll have no problem setting the locals straight. From what I've seen, no one wants to see the inside of a temple-farm for fear they may not be allowed to leave."

Ranthar nodded. *One of the advantages of a fear-based theocracy is that it keeps the lower orders in their place. The disadvantage is that knowledgeable outsiders can use that very fear and ignorance as a cover for their own nefarious purposes. He had to hand it to the old horse thief.*

"Oh, I like this idea," Skranga said, rubbing his hands together. "We'll store our gold and silver in fireseed magazines in a treasury that looks like one of our enemy's temple-farms. No one will ever look for it there. Positively brilliant!"

"There is one problem," Ranthar said. He needed to report in to Chief Verkan, not take off on some expedition to Artigos.

"What's that?" Democriphon asked.

"If we're going to establish a fireseed temple-farm, we're going to need a highpriest to run the operation," Ranthar said, his eyes going straight to Duke Skranga.

Skranga groaned. "So this is my reward for a good idea? Unfortunately, I fear you're right, First Captain. Let me talk with Calthros and we can start putting together a team to run this temple-farm."

Democriphon smiled. "This is going to work out very well, Duke. It will give you a chance to work on your highpriest impersonation and test it out on the locals. Better in Erygon or Taurnos Town than Bletha Town."

"You've got me there. I'll meet with Calthros and work up an operation plan."

# TWENTY-ONE

## I

Calthros and Vanir were teaching some of the new recruits, who would shortly be passing themselves off as Styphon's House underpriests, the Temple rituals and standard greetings. They were seated at a large table under a big evergreen tree. The rains had stopped in the morning and the sky was a dazzling blue. Calthros was beginning to enjoy the southern climate. Fall in Hos-Harphax was bone-chilling with too much wind, rain and sleet.

One of the recruits pointed to a bandy-legged figure heading their way. "Isn't that Highpriest Sangar?"

Calthros said, "Correct, Tyog. Good job of staying in character, too." *I only wish Duke Skranga shared your dedication,* he thought to himself. "Staying in character, as upperpriest Vanir has so often pointed out, may be the difference between a successful impersonation or death by quartering or auto-da-fé."

*This one will do well,* Calthros thought. *Skranga will do likewise once he is forced to play his role in the pageant we are about to play in Bletha Town*. He studied the bandy-legged Duke as he made his way over to the table. Skranga had one of the most devious minds he had ever encountered outside of Styphon's House. He was a natural Styphon's House priest. If Skranga had joined the Temple as a youth, by now he would have been a member of the Inner Circle wrangling for the post of Supreme Priest the moment Sesklos' body was interred in the catacombs underneath Styphon's Great Temple in Balph.

When Skranga was within hailing distance, he called out. "Calthros, we need to talk. Come with me to my quarters."

Another nice thing about working with Skranga, he decided, was he didn't have to worry about a brow-beating or a lashing whenever the Duke demanded his presence, unlike the years he had spent as a Styphon's House underpriest.

Calthros caught up with Skranga and walked over to his quarters together, an unpretentious cabin with no gold ornaments, statuary, hangings or other ostentatious ornamentation. The Duke was going to have to change his ways when they left for Bletha Town. No self-respecting Styphon's House highpriest would ever live in anything less than a manor fit for a prince.

"Have a seat, Calthros," Skranga said, as he took two goblets off a shelf and filled them both with wine. He then proceeded to fill Calthros in on the temple-farm plan he had worked out with Democriphon and Captain Ranthar. When he was finished, he asked, "What do you think?"

Another thing he liked about the Duke was that he was willing to entertain his inferiors' suggestions—and even more amazing—act upon them. A strange man, this Hostigi intelligencer. "I think at heart it is a sound plan, Your Worship. Temple-farms are run like small baronies with little direction from the outside and almost no accountability—as long as they produce the required amount of fireseed. Some have even been known to sell their stocks privately to local lords and barons."

"Will we have any trouble setting one up in Artigos without official Temple oversight?" Skranga asked.

Calthros shook his head. "I don't believe so. Before the Fireseed Wars, I would have said differently. But now the Temple is in disarray and things are not always done in the old manner. There is great need in both Hos-Ktemnos and Hos-Harphax for fireseed and stocks are starting to run low, even in Balph. New temple-farms are sprouting up throughout the Five Kingdoms. I don't think the local Artigi priests will pay much attention to another one. However, I do recommend we make a short stop at Artigos Town to establish your credentials as an overseer from Balph. That will quell any questions that might otherwise arise."

"What do you think of my idea to store the expedition's gold and silver in the fireseed magazines?"

"An excellent idea, Your Worship. Especially, considering how fast the treasury is growing. Only the temple master and his assistants will have access to the magazines. In truth, no one will enter them without orders. In the past, magazines have exploded with dire results. Only an imbecile would ever think to search for a treasure within their walls."

"That's what I thought. I remember how our Great King personally handpicked the men for the Royal Arsenals, and was particularly concerned about the fireseed works. Now, once we set up the temple-farm neither of us will be in a position to run it. Who do you suggest as a candidate for highpriest?"

Calthros didn't have to think twice. "Tyog, Your Worship. He's a fast learner; he's already learned all the liturgy and doctrine that I can teach him. Also, most importantly, he's a leader whom the other men will follow."

Skranga leaned back in his chair, puffing on his pipe. "I remember him. He was a Blethan foundry owner who became too successful. Well, successful enough to draw the attention of a local baron who wanted his property. The baron paid off Prince Balthar and Tyog was imprisoned on false charges, whereupon he was sold to the Styphoni. He was released only after Great King Kalvan invested Tarr-Beshta. He has a deep hatred for both the Black Prince and Styphon's House. Yes, he'll do. What will his Styphon's House rank be?"

*Tyog would know,* he thought. Skranga was not always the best student, but was a fast learner when he needed to be. "The title would be farm master. It's lower than temple master and highpriest. Like myself, as your advisor, he would wear a black robe with a yellow border which will signify his rank as an upperpriest, but well below that of highpriest. His rank would be similar to that of a lord, while a highpriest's rank is more like that of a Duke."

## II

It took them five days to load up the wagons and organize the temple-farm crew. The former sharper Vanir would be coming along as one of the upperpriests; he had helped Calthros and Skranga organize and train a score of phony black-robed underpriests and white-robed novices to run the operation. All of them were former Hostigi and to a man they were disgusted with their new roles, but determined to do them to the best of their ability, regardless. Democriphon had convinced them of the importance of their task and its importance to the war against Styphon's House and Hos-Harphax.

Calthros gave them a crash course in Styphoni rituals and practices.

"What if a real Styphon's House priest shows up?" Tyog asked. He was a barrel-chested man who had been handpicked by Skranga to act as the temple-farm upperpriest.

"It's rare for an upperpriest to make an unscheduled visit to a temple-farm; it's too much like work," Skranga answered

That brought a laugh from the crew.

"Calthros," Skranga said, "tell them how the temple-farms work."

The former Styphon's House priest rose up from the stump he was sitting on. "A typical temple-farm has a farm master, which in our case will be Tyog's role. To help out there will be six to eight black-robed middle priests who will take over the day to day operation, including the post of overseer. They will also be in charge of fifteen to twenty white-robed underpriests, or novices. They will do all the cooking, cleaning and scut work inside the temple that no black-robed priest would ever deign to do—"

"What about slave labor?" Tyog asked.

"Good question," Calthros responded. "Most of the slaves are kept outside and do the dangerous work of making fireseed, gathering the ingredients, mixing them and corning the dried paste. Sometimes slave work parties are brought into the rectory to swamp the floors or move heavy objects. But they are dressed in filthy rags and stink so badly they're not used much within the priests' quarters. Of course, if they're women, they're often kept inside as scullery maids and bed-warmers. We will be bringing along some former slave women and children, but just for a disguise. We'll find proper work for them and they will be treated as free-women, not slaves or wenches."

"As Calthros has pointed out, our 'slaves' will be treated much better than the typical Styphon's House slaves," Skranga said, "because they're not slaves; they're freemen. Unfortunately, they will have to play that role for as long as we need the temple-farm."

"Who will play their part?" one of the trainees asked.

"None of you, if that's what you're worried about," Skranga replied to a round of relieved laughs and guffaws. "The former slaves we've rescued will take on that role. However, they will only be 'mistreated' when observed by outsiders. Of course, this 'mistreatment' will be carefully orchestrated. Is that understood?"

The group answered with a collective aye ayes.

"Good, because at some point you may have to depend upon them to save your lives."

Calthros added, "What His Worship means is that when they're not 'playing' slaves for the benefit of observers or outsiders, they will be practicing the use of arms and weapons. In that sense, they are your guardians and protectors. Otherwise, they will be treated as full members of our expedition."

"Don't the typical temple-farms also have a squad of Styphon's Own Guard to protect them?" Tyog asked.

"Yes," Calthros said, smiling. "You have learned your lessons well, Farm Master. We will leave you a squad of twenty Guardsmen; they will be the ones training your 'slaves' in combat drills. The plan is to make this temple-farm as typical of their type as possible."

"But why do we need our own temple-farm?" one of the recruits asked.

*Good question*, Calthros thought. Only the inner council knew the real reason so he dissembled, being sure to add a kernel of truth for verisimilitude. "Those of you who are former soldiers or mercenaries might have noticed that our stocks of fireseed are running low."

There were murmurs of agreement from the assembled men.

"This temple-farm is an experiment to see if we can create a reliable source of fireseed outside of robbing Styphon's Temples and stores. Eventually, the Temple will catch on to what we are doing and we might find our stocks running out. With our own temple-farm, we will have an independent source of fireseed. Does that answer your question, Aglos?"

"Yes, Your Grace."

"Good. Now, has anyone ever worked with fireseed before?"

Aglos stood up. "I have, Your Grace. I worked at the Royal Fireseed Works in Sask. I know the Great King's formula well."

"Well, forget it," Skranga said. "We will not be using Kalvan's formula here. We will be using the standard formula for Styphon's Best."

There were groans all around.

"Your lives may depend upon it," Skranga added, getting their full attention. "Aglos, I will appoint you Fire Master. Upperpriest Calthros will teach you the proper portions and procedures in making Styphon's Own Fireseed. Is that understood?"

"Yes, Your Worship," Aglos replied.

"Good. Nothing could give us away faster than producing Hostigos quality fireseed. For one, I don't even know if the formula has reached this far south. But, if it has, it has the touch of heresy about it. Who knows when some outside highpriest may request a few barrels of our product or want to test it himself in some oversight capacity. We must always be prepared for the worst case or we will surely fail at some point. And we can't afford failure. The survival of Hos-Hostigos is in part dependent upon our success.

"Is that understood?"

"Yes, sir," came a round of replies, followed by a chorus of "Down Styphon!"

# TWENTY-TWO

## I

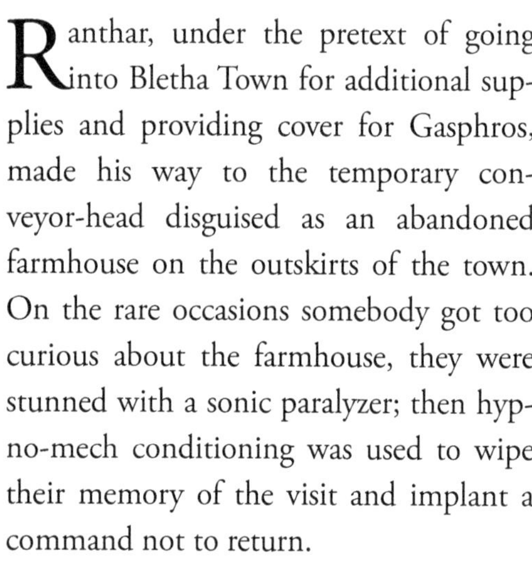

Ranthar, under the pretext of going into Bletha Town for additional supplies and providing cover for Gasphros, made his way to the temporary conveyor-head disguised as an abandoned farmhouse on the outskirts of the town. On the rare occasions somebody got too curious about the farmhouse, they were stunned with a sonic paralyzer; then hypno-mech conditioning was used to wipe their memory of the visit and implant a command not to return.

Field Agent Tanzla Rav escorted Ranthar Jard past a security wall disguised as a storage closet. "How goes the Blethan mission, Inspector?"

Inside the conveyor-head, Ranthar visibly relaxed, taking off his morion helmet. "It's still too early to tell, but we've had some successes." He turned to the other operative, "Could you see if you can get the Chief for me."

"Sure, Inspector."

Tanzla said, "My briefing said you're on some secret mission of Great King Kalvan's to infiltrate the Hos-Blethan and foment a rebellion."

Ranthar shrugged. "Yes, Kalvan was hoping we might cause enough internal disruption to pull Hos-Bletha out of the war."

Tanzla shook his head. "That sounds like a fever dream."

Ranthar splayed his hands. "It's a longshot, as Kalvan might put it. But, on the other hand, it hasn't cost him much, either. Just a couple of companies of men and Duke Skranga, his Chief of Intelligence. And, so far, the team has been surprisingly effective."

There was a beep from the visiscreen console. The communications tech said, "Inspector Ranthar, the Chief is on the line."

The screen showed Paratime Police Chief Verkan Vall still dressed in three-quarter blackened armor, but without his burgonet helmet.

"Hi, Chief," Ranthar said. "It looks like you've been out in the field."

"Just some training exercises with the Mounted Rifles. Any success so far in disrupting Hos-Bletha's entry into the war against Hostigos?"

"Yes, we've had a couple of successful actions, hitting Styphon's House where it hurts."

Verkan laughed. "In the purse, right?"

"Yes, we just made a big raid against Styphon's Banking House and Colonel—well, I should say 'Prince'—Democriphon is planning several raids against various Styphon's House temples throughout the kingdom. We also hijacked a shipment of gold from Bletha Town headed for Balph."

"Impressive. But, Prince Democriphon! Whose idea was that?"

"Well, after Duke Skranga became Highpriest Sangar and Democriphon was elevated to Captain-General and persuaded to play the part of the Orphan Prince—"

"Orphan Prince?" Verkan interrupted. "This is the first I've heard about it. What's that all about?"

"It turns out that Great King Niclophon's brother, Marocles, and his wife were murdered, and their son, Valthros disappeared. Probably dead, would be my guess. Well, as those things go, the Great King's enemies have encouraged stories about the missing prince and how he will return one day to save the realm. You know the routine, Chief."

"Yeah, those kinds of legends pop up throughout monarchical

time-lines all over Fourth Level Europo-American, whenever a popular prince or king dies mysteriously or disappears. Like the one about Holy Roman Emperor Frederic Barbarossa who died crossing the Saleph River in Anatolia on his way to retake Jerusalem from Saladin during the Third Crusade. His body was recovered and an attempt was made to preserve it vinegar, but it was unsuccessful.

"However, it was widely believed that his body was never recovered and his return was rumored for hundreds of years after his death. According to the legend, Barbarossa was not in fact dead, but asleep in a hidden chamber underneath the Kyffhäuser hills, sitting at a stone table. It was believed that his beard grew so long over the centuries that it pushed its way through the table. As in the legend of King Arthur, Barbarossa sleeps peacefully awaiting Germany's greatest hour of need when he will once again emerge from deep in the bowels of the mountain. The continuing presence of ravens circling the Kyffhäuser summit is said to be a sign of Barbarossa's continuing slumber."

"Exactly, Chief. It doesn't help Niclophon's case that many of his nobles believe that Styphon's House was behind the murders and since the Great King is deeply in debt to the Temple...."

"It sounds like this Niclophon could use some good PR. So, I take it, that Democriphon is taking up the mantle of the 'Orphan Prince.'"

"Correct," Ranthar replied. "I've gotten a promotion, too. I'm now First Captain of the Army of Conquest, well it's not much of an army—yet."

Verkan laughed. "It's good to see that you're having fun. What do you think of the operation's chances of success?"

"At first, I'd have said thin to none. But our little army is growing and we've had a surprising number of successful strikes against Styphon House's temples and Niclophon troops."

"Yes, but the goal of the mission was not to replace Great King Niclophon with Democriphon, but to keep his troops from reinforcing the Grand Host of Styphon's House. How's that coming along?"

Ranthar shrugged. "Too early to tell, Chief. But I wouldn't count this little team out. Skranga's always coming up with diabolical ideas, while

Democriphon is proving to be an inspired leader. Why? Is Kalvan in trouble?"

Verkan nodded in the affirmative. "He doesn't know it yet, but the Grand Host of Styphon's House is growing like the proverbial snowball. By spring it will be a veritable avalanche. Plus, it looks like Grand Master Soton's working behind the scenes to ensure that the mercenary Phidestros will be in charge, instead of Lysandros. Phidestros has proven to be a thorn in Kalvan's boot on several occasions; who knows what he's capable of given enough support and troops to command—and that he has, my friend! Kalvan may be facing the biggest army ever assembled on any Aryan-Transpacific, Styphon's House Subsector time-line."

"So, even keeping ten or twelve thousands effectives out of the upcoming fray might well make a big difference come next spring?"

"Exactly," Verkan replied.

"How about the other big problem Hostigos is facing?"

"What's that?"

"The Phaxos fiasco. After the successful invasion of Phaxos, Rylla had most of the reigning prince's family killed, and it created a rift between Kalvan and Rylla. The last time I saw those two together sparks were flying."

"Oh, you don't know," Verkan said. "Shortly after you left Hostigos, Harmakros and Prince Ptosphes worked out a scheme to get the two of them together for a ceremony making Kalvan godfather of Aspasthar—Harmakros' bastard son."

"Did it work?" Ranthar asked.

"Kind of. They're sharing the same bed again and they're talking. Little Demia's helped, too. There still some tension between them, but nothing like what there was before you left."

"Good. They've got enough enemies already, what with Styphon's House and most of the Great Kings against them. We'll do what we can here in Bletha."

"Good luck, Ranthar. I've got to go; more problems with the Kalvan Study Team…"

"I don't miss those days, Chief," he said with a laugh.

After signing off, Ranthar looked about the room. "Tanzla, do you have the updated logs on the hypno-mech records?"

"As of this morning. An update comes in every evening. Need to check something?"

"Oh, not really. Just curious. It never hurts to stay up-to-date on things like that."

Tanzla chuckled and nodded. "You sound just like Chief Verkan. Is that all you're here for?"

"Yes…wait, no. Do we have a copy of *Robin Hood* on hand?"

"Hmm. Couldn't say off the top of my head. If not in hard copy, I can do a data pool search and run off a copy for you. Which time-line's version are you after?"

"Something close to Calvin Morrison's time-line. His own time-line, if one's available."

## II

Highpriest Xiphnos snuffed out the candles and lay down on his cot. As the temple master of the Styphon's House temple of Marthrax Town little was demanded of him physically. Still, at the end of the day he grew weary of the mental stress of overseeing temple operations. It fell to him to inspect the fireseed works, see that saltpeter production was meeting quotas at the temple-farms, deal with the local merchants, farmers, politicians and army captains and oversee the purchase of new slaves. Slaves who tended to wear out and die quickly.

Little time was left for private meditation and relaxation save those few candles a day when he pretended to pray in private to Styphon. Like most of the high-ranking priests, he didn't believe in Styphon or any other god. Despite their pretense of piety, he suspected that most of the priests of Dralm, Tranth and Galzar felt the same way. Gods were just a convenient way to extract money and loyalty from the superstitious fools who believed in them. Xiphnos used his prayer time to take a short mid-day nap.

After some restless movements the priest settled into a comfortable position and waited for sleep to take him. He had just started to doze when a sudden pounding at his chamber door roused him. He cursed under his breath and threw his blanket off.

"What is it?" he called out irritably.

"Your Worship, we have a visitor," called back the voice of Kylog, his personal aide.

"At this time of night? Tell him to return tomorrow. Preferably at a respectable hour."

"Your Worship, it is an underpriest from Erygon Town. He is injured and looks to have been ill-used."

*Ill-used?* Kylog always did use polite euphemisms. Annoyingly so.

"Make him comfortable, and I will be there shortly." Xiphnos stood up, relit the candle by his cot from the tinderbox he kept next to it, put on his yellow robe and hurried out of the prayer chamber. An injured priest, even an underpriest could herald dire tidings. The lessons of Hos-Hostigos were still fresh in his mind.

Styphon's House was once dedicated to the healing arts long before the discovery of fireseed. While the priests made the bulk of their wealth selling fireseed to the various kingdoms, a small group still pursued the healing arts if only for their own benefit.

He found the injured underpriest in the remedial chamber. He was bruised and had a number of cuts that were being bandaged. The wounds seemed superficial to him; however, he doubted the poor underpriest would agree. Injuries were always worse when they were on your own body.

"Who or what has done this to you," he demanded.

"Rebels, Your Worship," the black-robed underpriest replied. "The minions of the Orphan Prince. They disguised themselves as Styphon's Own Guard and sacked the Erygon temple after killing everyone within. Though attacked, I fought them off and escaped, but before I escaped I learned that they would be taking their ill-gained gold and fireseed to their hiding place in Dratha Forest."

*Fought? More likely he ran and hid like a frightened child. Well, underpriests were not trained for battle.* "How did you learn of their plans?"

"Your Worship, after I escaped I hid behind a tapestry and overheard them. They plan to use the gold to finance a rebellion against Great King Niclophon."

Xiphnos had to admit the story was plausible enough. Ever since the Daemon Kalvan released the fireseed formula many temples have been sacked, although this was the first time he had heard of such a thing happening in Hos-Bletha. Such desecration could not be permitted to continue.

"Call up Grand-Captain Baltos and have him ready his men," Highpriest Xiphnos ordered Kylog. "They will march on Dratha Forest tonight, before the infidels have the chance to flee." He turned to the underpriest. "What is your name, my son?"

"Vanir, Your Worship."

# TWENTY-THREE

## I

Grand-Captain Baltos cursed under his breath as he trudged through the foliage of Dratha Forest in the dead of night dodging brush and tree limbs. He would have much rather been back in his quarters in the Marthrax Temple with a willing slave girl and a flask of wine. "Hold that damn torch higher, soldier! Or I'll fall on you like a mountain wall."

Nor did he enjoy being wakened from a sound sleep only to gather his men and ride hard into the night. Not having time to form a plan of attack he liked even less. Like any soldier, he preferred to have as much information on the enemy as possible then plan accordingly. That option had been denied him this time. Refusing direct orders from a highpriest, no matter how mistaken, was career suicide in the Guard.

The horses had to be left at the edge of the tree line. It was too dangerous to take them into the woods where men could be unhorsed by low branches, or their position betrayed by an ill-timed whicker. He couldn't even spare any men to guard the mounts as he had no idea how many foes he would be facing; every man he had could be needed for battle.

The moon was full, which helped a little, but it was already sinking low in the sky, taking what little light that filtered down through the canopy of leaves with it.

Like most of Styphon's Own Guard, he was a true believer in Styphon. So, if the enemies of Styphon reared their godless heads, it fell to him and his brethren to send them straight to Regwarn, even at the cost of a good night's sleep.

One of the guardsmen behind him stumbled and cursed. There had been a lot of that. Sadly, there was nothing to be done about it; even torches had a hard time penetrating the well of darkness as well as that engendered by the thick brush and tree limbs. He was mildly worried that the torches would make them targets for the rebels, if not simply warn them of the impending attack. However, without some light the rebels could simply vanish into the night, and he would lose his chance to recover the treasure they had stolen from the Erygon Temple. That would not be allowed, not by him. *I mean to have my share—*

Baltos heard a branch break somewhere ahead. *That has to be the rebels. Why weren't they using torches?* He signaled his men to stop. It took a while for everybody to get the message as his orders had to be whispered back and forth.

"That must be them ahead," Baltos whispered to the men closest to him. "Be careful, they might be expecting us. That would explain why they're not using torches." After the whisper had been relayed back, he added, "At my command, run forward and engage the enemy. No quarter for these infidel hawbucks!"

As quietly as possible the guard moved forward. It was many slow heartbeats before Baltos could see the enemy in the flickering torch light. It was as the underpriest had claimed; the rebel scum were wearing the sacred arms and colors of Styphon's Own Guard. He felt his blood boil at the sight of this blasphemy.

"Attack!"

At their Grand-Captain's shouted command, his party rushed forward and ran into the enemy's position.

"Charge!" was the enemy's reply.

In the darkness it wasn't safe to use fireseed weapons. Instead, both sides elected to use their swords, or glaives—when possible—in close combat. The fighting was fierce and bloody. Men fell like wheat from a scythe. There was much cursing and screaming among the combatants as they killed and were killed in turn. It was a melee like nothing Baltos had ever seen, not even during his ten winters in Hos-Harphax as a mercenary.

The ground became slippery with the blood that mixed with the earth below them as the sky grew lighter. Baltos and his opponent slipped on the muddy ground, fell and grappled, each trying to get the upper hand. By chance they fell into a section where the light was better and saw, for the first time, each other's faces.

He was about to trust a dagger into his opponent's face, then hesitated. The face was familiar. "Captain Zentros?"

"Baltos! What treachery is this?"

Baltos instantly grasped the situation. He and his men had been deceived, as had Zentros and his men. "Stop fighting! Stop fighting! We have been de—"

"Fire!" a new voice cried out.

Baltos never finished his statement. A crossbow bolt found its way through his eye socket and into his brain. A volley of bolts and arrows rained down on the other fighters before they could react. In moments half a dozen guardsmen had fallen and were dead or dying. Disordered and trying to retreat, the rest were quickly cut down by swords and halberds.

## II

From one side of the battleground sixty men in brown and green clothing emerged from the trees where they had been hiding. Captain-General Democriphon looked over the carnage and nodded. The plan had worked even better than expected. Vanir had played his part to perfection. They had made a feint at the Erygon Temple and led the Styphon's

Guardsmen in a merry chase for three days, ending at the Dratha Forest. He suspected the Erygon force had lost half their number in these woods; they would return to their temple in ignominious defeat.

"Captain, what would you have us do with the dead and wounded?"

Ranthar let out a sigh. "Kill anyone still alive, wounded or not, then strip the bodies of armor, weapons, clothes, everything that we can use. Dump the bodies into the swamp. Let the river dragons feast well tonight. Move quickly, this job is only half done."

Ranthar looked over the bodies at his feet. He found the one he was looking for, the guard-captain. He pulled the bolt out of the eye socket and looked over the face. This one might work. "Phebros, come here."

Petty-Captain Phebros, a big man with a bald pate, hastened to obey. Ranthar looked him over, then again at Baltos body. "You'll do. Strip this body and don his armor. You get to play a grand-captain of Styphon's Own Guard for a while. Everybody find some armor that you can fit into and put it on." There was some grumbling and cursing from the men; nobody wanted to wear the colors of the hated enemy again. Still, they quickly obeyed. "Gycules, I doubt they will have anything that will fit you, so I want you to take the horses and remaining armor we won't be using to our campsite. Take ten men with you."

Gycules looked disappointed but hastened to obey.

## III

Highpriest Xiphnos was tired and in a foul mood. He couldn't get back to sleep after Baltos and his men rode off to meet with the rebels. He considered sending a messenger to all of the nearby temples asking for help, and then decided against it. It would elevate him in the eyes of the Inner Circle if he could say he handled things by himself. Like most of Styphon's priests, advancement in the hierarchy was always foremost on his mind.

The elderly priest stood up from his bench and donned his early-morning prayer vestments and walked down to the worship hall. It was a chore to hold services for the novices and underpriests. As hard as it was to believe, some of the lower echelons actually believed in Styphon! He thought it best to encourage them in that belief; it helped keep them in line.

By the time Xiphnos entered the worship hall the black-robed middle priests and white-robed novices and underpriests were already kneeling on their mats waiting for him. The Highpriest stifled a sigh and took his position on the dais at the front of the hall. As always, he raised his arms to the gold plated idol and intoned some nonsensical syllables in a semblance of prayer. The idea was to convince the lower orders that he spoke a holy language unknown to them, understandable only to their god.

When finished, Xiphnos turned to the congregation. He had just started when the sound of horses clattering on the cobblestones outside the temple could be faintly heard. He nodded to Kylog. The priest hastened out of the room. Moments later Styphon's Own Guard filtered into the back of the hall.

The guard was a bedraggled bloody lot. Their armor was dented and smeared with gore, red capes torn and tattered, the faces covered in mud and blood. It must have been a terrible battle. Xiphnos could only see about a score of men. *The rest must either be dead or severely wounded*, he thought. Still, they must have been successful or they would not have returned at all.

"Behold the returning heroes," Xiphnos shouted mid-prayer. "They have met the heretics in battle and returned triumphant. Praise Styphon, Lord of the Gods. Please give our valiant warriors thanks, one and all."

The congregation stood and turned to applaud Styphon's Own Guard only to be met with steel. The guard drew their glaives and scattered about the room hacking away at anything that moved. In less than an eighth of a candle, all were dead save the guardsmen and Xiphnos.

"What…what is this blasphemy?" he shouted, backing away from the carnage until his back came to rest against the gold idol of Styphon. "Get out! Get out or Styphon will strike you all down!"

Captain-General Democriphon stepped up to the dais and sheathed his sword and drew out his poignard. Just before he thrust it into Xiphnos' throat, he cried out: "Down Styphon!"

Xiphnos fell slowly to the floor, his back trailing a line of blood down the front of idol's golden robes, gurgling out his final breath all the way down.

"Search the temple from top to bottom and make sure there are no priests or novices in hiding. I want two men at each door; nobody escapes. Kill any priest you find. Explore every room and seize anything of use or value. Free any slaves of their chains and let them eat all they can, but they stay here with us until we move out. The slaves will have to go with us, so clean them up as much as possible. They may want to join up with us. Those who do not will be freed and given ten ounces of silver. Get their sworn oaths to reveal nothing of what has happened here, first. If they refuse to give it, kill them.

"I want this place stripped of everything of value, gold, silver, fireseed, victuals, tapestries, candlesticks, works of art. Have the slaves help out; they know this building better than any of us.

"We'll leave tomorrow night, after the temple's dome has been stripped of gold. It's too late to do it tonight. These manure eaters have wagons and oxen enough that we should be able to take it all. What we can't take we will burn with the rest of the temple when we depart. Is that understood?"

Everyone nodded. It had been explained to the men earlier not to shout or raise their voices. The idea was to make it look like business as usual to anybody outside of the temple. If anybody came to call, for whatever reason, they would be turned away, unless it was more of Styphon's priests or soldiers. Those would be invited in, seized, questioned and then executed. The wagons full of treasure could be sent out during the day since such comings and goings were commonplace at the temples. Their booty would be taken to a remote location in the forest, transferred to other wagons, then return for another load. Once darkness fell, the remaining fireseed would be poured out in every room and hall, then fired, destroying the temple and anything they could not take with them. It would send a loud and clear message to Styphon's House Upon Earth and Great King Niclophon.

## IV

Grand-Captain Myklon leaned back on the bench and rested his back on the wall next to Zalthar, one of Skranga's phony Styphon's House priests, in the Erygon Town temple. Duke Skranga's plan had worked perfectly. Zalthar had performed the same trick, as Democriphon had at the Marthrax Temple, sending Styphon's Own Guard out with news of a phony rebellion. The light beating the priest had taken had been just enough to be convincing. Certainly, the Styphoni had bought it.

Myklon watched as the slaves his men had freed dragged the bodies of the Styphon's House priests out of the prayer hall, kicking and spitting on them the whole way. His soldiers were gathering up everything of value in the Erygon Temple that wasn't nailed down, and a few things that were, out to the waiting wagons.

Another crew was on the roof using daggers and roofing tools to strip the gold off the temple dome. *Another twenty-five thousand ounces here and the same at Erygon. If that doesn't hit Styphon's House where it hurts, I don't know what will.*

Like Democriphon's crew, Myklon's band had donned the armor and capes of the slain Guards that Gycules had salvaged after the massacre in Dratha Forest. Democriphon and Myklon had agreed that it would imperil the mission to risk both commanders at the battle. They flipped a gold crown to determine who would have the honor of hunting down the surviving Temple Guard, and Myklon had won.

Myklon had made one change from the plan when returning to the temple; he brought the big man Gycules in as a rebel prisoner. This was to distract attention away from the phony Styphon's Own Guard. It worked well enough since Gycules could be very distracting indeed, especially when he broke the weakened chains and appeared to fly into a rage. Several black-robed priests were "accidentally" killed while trying to subdue the giant rebel. Afterwards it was just a matter of mopping up.

Myklon poured some wine into a golden chalice he found in the upperpriest's personal chambers. It was an excellent white imported from Hos-Ktemnos. He was about to drain the chalice when Gycules approached.

"Grand Captain Myklon, I have news."

"Yes, Petty-Captain?"

"The slaves, sire. Many of them are Hostigi."

"What?" Myklon dropped the golden chalice to the floor, and took to his feet. "Take me to them."

Gycules led the way. In the back of the temple, there was a long wooden building where saltpeter was separated from manure. The slaves had been forced to work, eat and sleep on the floor next to the mounds of excrement. One of their men, still in his guise as a Temple Guardsman, had tried key after key in an attempt to unchain the remaining slaves.

Gycules pointed out a group of slaves that had been severely abused. There were red welts, dark scabs and deep scars on their backs and ribs that poked through pale emaciated flesh. *Roxthar's kind of work*, Myklon thought in disgust. He had helped release the temple-farm slaves at the Sevenhills Valley temple-farm. It looked as if they had been worked over with iron barbed whips and starved, then worked nearly to death. He suspected many had died from their ill treatment. There were no women among the slaves in this room. The Styphoni had other uses for the women. Temple financed brothels were common throughout most of the Five Kingdoms.

"Get the prisoners out of this room as quickly as possible. I want these men fed and cleaned up. Afterwards, drag those Dralm-damned dung-eaters' bodies in here and throw them into the manure piles. I only wish we could bring the priests back to life and kill them again in a more painful manner."

# TWENTY-FOUR

## I

Captain-General Democriphon and Grand-Captain Myklon returned to the encampment within half a candle of each other two days later. Each took a circuitous route designed to prevent being followed. Both were surprised at the activity going on about the camp. The wagons had been arranged in a circle at the outer perimeter of the settlement. The oxen and horses were set in separate corrals near the stream and new lean-tos had been set up at the far end.

"Our new recruits have been busy, it seems," Democriphon observed.

"We've been keeping them busy," said Ranthar, who had returned to camp in their absence.

"Good thing, too," Democriphon noted. "With these newly freed slaves we brought with us, those lean-tos are the only place to house them."

"We are going to run out of space very quickly," Ranthar said. Looking out over the camp filled with newcomers, he added, "By the gods, we already have."

Democriphon sighed. "With the new

slaves, we've got almost two thousand men and women to house, not counting the two hundred Duke Skranga took with him. What we need is a full sized village. Something out of the way, yet accessible."

"You're right," Ranthar said. "We've completely outgrown this camp. Besides, it's too close to Port Gytha to remain private. Two days ago we actually had visitors, peddlers trying to sell us ironware!"

Democriphon shook his head. "That's not good at all. It won't be long before Styphon's House comes around to build us a temple! We need an out-of-the-way village all our own."

"We have the gold to buy one," Ranthar offered. "The problem is where? We need an out-of the way spot, yet near enough to major roads that it won't hamper our raids."

"And we need a place that won't attract any attention," Myklon added. "And it should be far away from here, maybe even in another princedom."

Democriphon nodded. "That's a good idea, Captain. We can keep this camp as an auxiliary hideout. It'll allow us to attack in multiple places at the same time, yet far enough away to appear to our enemies as though it's a general uprising."

"We've already been doing that with raids in Artigos and Taurnos," Ranthar said. "But it wouldn't hurt to extend our reach southward, into the Princedoms of Pytha and even Bletha and Syragon."

"Let's talk to Gasphros about it." Democriphon looked back at the poor wretches they had just saved from the cursed priests' not so tender care. "But first, let's get these people fed, clothed and settled. Uncle Wolf Syros and his healers should see to their injuries as well."

Ranthar looked over the refugees in disgust; not the freed slaves themselves, but for the treatment they had suffered through. No matter how many times he saw man's inhumanity to his fellow man outtime from one time-line to another it never ceased to turn his stomach. It was a Dralm-damned shame that the Paratime regs regarding outtime contamination prevented him from doing more about it.

## II

Andros, formerly a petty-captain in the Royal Army of Hos-Bletha before being taken prisoner, had given his Oath to Galzar that he would not try to escape or cause trouble while among the...*rebels*...*bandits*... *infiltrators*? He still wasn't sure who or what they were, but he would die before he broke his oath. He still was unable to classify his captors. *Was it possible that the captain-general was truly Prince Valthros? Or is he another in a long line of pretenders? Or, in the end, did it matter?*

They were Hostigi, more or less, that much was certain, and they were surprisingly open about their mission. That alone engendered either trust or concern. Trust was good; it meant they didn't intend to break their word and he was safe. Concern was bad; the Hostigi might be free with their information because they might decide to kill him later. For the sake of his sanity and good appetite, Andros chose to believe it was the former.

He walked around the camp appraising it. *These people know what they are doing.* Latrines were well away from the living areas, food was prepared on the opposite side of the camp reducing the possibility of spreading disease and the animals were kept well away from both.

Then he came to the...slaves? Refugees? Andros was unsure how to classify them. They were no longer slaves according to Democriphon, or Valthros as he styled himself among them. He called them freemen. They weren't really refugees in the classical sense since they had been brought here as prisoners of war and were subject to persecution and slavery if recaptured. *Why worry about labels? These are people who were rescued from a bad situation. A situation my Great King has allowed to fester.*

Seeing the people, still thin and haggard in their new tunics, made him angry. He had never liked slavery himself, other than as a deterrent to criminal behavior. It was one thing to punish somebody for a crime and a whole different thing to buy and sell people as if they were livestock.

Andros was so lost in his thoughts that it took a few moments for him to realize that the former slaves were staring at him. Their expressions were that of fear and many of them were moving away from him. He stepped forward to ask what was wrong only to find the people were getting even more excited. Children started to cry and the mothers, if those were really the mothers, took the children and scampered behind the men.

"Is something wrong," Andros asked. "Can I help you?" Four men moved to block his progress. Andros looked into their faces and found fear, determination and anger. "What is it? What is wrong? I only want to help."

One of the men stepped forward. "Help? From you? Where were you when we needed help?" He waved his hand in the direction of the others. "These people have had more than enough of that kind of help. When we were chained and dragged into this land, our *masters*,"—he spit when he said 'masters'—"had to make concessions to the border guards. What do you think those concessions were? Women, mostly. The masters would give them the use of our women, and even our children.

"Not just the border patrol, but any soldiers we chanced upon along the way. Once, even a baron who had chanced upon the caravan wanted to 'sample the wares' before the auction. They were not gentle, either. Not all of the scars on them are from the whips."

"What? I…I never took part…"

"But you know others who have, I wager," said another of the four. "I suppose there are even laws against it. Have you ever seen a fellow soldier punished for it?"

Andros was unable to frame a reply. While he had never taken part in such a thing or even seen it personally, he had heard barracks stories of such things. In his youth he had even made-up such stories simply to fit in with the older, more experienced soldiers.

"The armor you wear so proudly is offensive to us," said a third man.

Andros turned and walked away. He went back to the shack where he had awakened in the morning and removed the armor he had worn for so long. He felt sick at heart just looking at it.

## III

Ranthar walked through the camp looking for Gasphros. Usually the troubadour was easy to find: just listen for the sound of his lyre and voice raised in song or look for where the camp's children, or dogs, were gathered. He loved to tell stories almost as much as he enjoyed music. *Kalvan knew what he was doing when he sent Gasphros along*, he decided.

Then he heard his tenor voice. He was too far away to make out the words, but as he drew closer Ranthar recognized the melody. It took him back almost a hundred years. As he drew closer he could make out the words.

*When the Orphan Prince comes marching home,*
*Hurrah! Hurrah!*
*We'll give him a hearty welcome then,*
*Hurrah! Hurrah!*
*We'll hoist Old Nic upon a stick,*
*Then use our swords to cut him quick,*
*And we'll all be dancing when the Prince comes marching home!*

*Niclophon will lose his crown,*
*Hurrah! Hurrah!*
*And Styphon's House will tumble down,*
*Hurrah! Hurrah!*
*Rejoicing we will light our fires,*
*While drowning in our own desires,*
*And we'll all be dancing when the Prince comes marching home!*

As Ranthar drew closer to the campfire, he could hear more voices joining in. *This is the kind of thing that will draw these poor people together. And wait 'til Great King Niclophon gets an earful.*

*King Marocles' son and heir,*
*Hurrah! Hurrah!*
*Will restore justice ev'rywhere,*
*Hurrah! Hurrah!*
*Let's drink a jar and sing a song,*
*We'll all get drunk and get along,*
*And we'll all be dancing when the Prince comes marching home!*

*He'll take the crown and buy a round,*
*Hurrah! Hurrah!*
*Now that the true king has been found,*
*Hurrah! Hurrah!*
*Not only will he bring us peace,*
*But we will also be released,*
*And we'll all be dancing when the Prince comes marching home!*

*The Styphon's House priests will all die.*
*Hurrah! Hurrah!*
*From giant cannon they will fly,*
*Hurrah! Hurrah!*
*Sparks and embers will abound,*
*And bloody parts lay on the ground,*
*And we'll all be dancing when the Prince comes marching home!*

*The regicide will be denied,*
*Hurrah! Hurrah!*
*Down in Regwarn he'll abide,*
*Hurrah! Hurrah!*
*He'll beg and plead upon his knees,*
*His carcass burns while we hear his screams,*
*And we'll all be dancing when the Prince comes marching home!*

Ranthar smiled. *Now that's going to cause one whale of a commotion when Styphon's House wraps its ear around those lyrics.*

# TWENTY-FIVE

## I

After spending the last six days in a coach, Skranga was enjoying riding on horseback. Normally, it was not seemly for a Styphon's House highpriest to actually ride a horse; however, since they were in the hinterlands of the Taurnos/Artigos border it was probably acceptable. The path—it was too overgrown to call a road anymore—to the deserted tarr they were visiting was over a dozen marches from the nearest village and at the top of a small rise. He hoped this ruined fortification would serve as the new temple-farm as he was getting tired of riding through the border wilderness that separated the two Blethan princedoms.

His visit to Taurnos Town to meet with the local Styphon's House leadership had been a roaring success. The Styphon's House yokels in Taurnos were pretty much ignored by the Inner Circle and the Balph hierarchy. They had welcomed him with open arms, hoping to hear the latest gossip about Archpriests Roxthar, Anaxthenes and Dracar. They had all been properly horrified by his tales about the

Holy Investigation and how priests suspected of being non-believers, had been dragged off the streets of Balph to be Investigated. Skranga had heard a number of these tales while running the Hostigi spy ring in Harphax City, before leaving town one step ahead of the local provosts, along with a few he made up on the spot.

They were scandalized about the new One God movement that was sweeping through the Temple. Everyone knew that Supreme Priest Sesklos was at death's door and were terrified that Roxthar's puppet, Archpriest Dracar, would become the new Styphon's Voice when Sesklos died. Skranga suspected that by now several of them were already proclaiming their belief in Styphon's divinity, hoping that would keep their necks off the chopping block.

The most interested in what he had to say had been the lower priests who had the most to gain by Roxthar's ascendancy. Everyone knew that the road to the top of Styphon's House hierarchy was a long and treacherous journey which few survived. However, joining the Investigation could turn out to be a worthwhile shortcut to advancement for young and ambitious underpriests.

The trip had been worthwhile as he had gotten good practice at playing highpriest and high marks from Calthros for his impersonation. Now, they needed to find a good place for their temple-farm so they would have a safe place to store all the gold and silver the team was quickly accumulating. He had heard about the successful attacks on the Thanor and Erygon temples and knew there was a lot more treasure that needed to be safely cached.

Up ahead Skranga could see the ramparts of the ruined castle. It was a big one at the top of a small rise. There were few real hills in the tidelands. As they drew closer, he saw that the tarr had mostly fallen in upon itself; the keep was badly damaged and would need substantial rebuilding. The good news was that most of the stones had not been carted away; the old castle was far enough from the nearest villages that it hadn't been economical to move the stones for new buildings, unlike the last place they had visited. All that had been left of that abandoned manor house had been the foundation.

As they drew closer, Calthros pointed out the lumps of trash overgrown with weeds and small trees that had once been the local villagers daub and wattle huts. “This place is ideal, Your Worship,” Calthros pronounced.

Skranga was inclined to agree. “I hope so. We need to return to camp; there’s much work to be done there.”

“True.”

He motioned over Tyog the new Farm Master. “What do you think?”

Tyog smiled. “I think we’ve found our temple-farm, Your Worship.”

“I’m glad we agree.” Skranga had visited several temple-farms and most of them had been laid out like small forts, since one of their primary duties was to protect the secret of fireseed production. “You’ll need to rebuild the keep. That will serve as your headquarters and a place to keep your guardsmen. In addition, you’ll need stone walls around the entire farm.”

“We’ll need a lot more rocks than I see here, Your Worship,” Tyog said.

“Agreed. In fact, that’s something we can use to our advantage. I’ll have more stone shipped by wagon from Dalthax City, which will allow us to ship more treasure wagons without attracting undue attention. We want the locals to become used to a lot of traffic coming and going from this temple-farm. In fact, as soon as your men get the huts built, I suggest you have the road cleared and stabilized.”

“We can do both, Your Worship. I’ll have work gangs sent out to clear the road of brush and small trees as soon as the mid-day meal is done.”

Skranga was pleased that Farm Master Tyog was thinking about the welfare of his men as well as the job.

Already the first wagons were rumbling over the poor road and men were jumping off them like fleas off a wet dog.

“I’ll stay here for another two days, then we’ll be off. I’m sure you’ll do a good job for your Great King. ”

“Yes, Your Worship,” Tyog said, showing visible relief, as though looking forward to being in charge without someone overseeing him and getting in the way.

## II

Archpriest Prythames waited impatiently for the Chancellor to announce him to the king. He went through the pockets of his robe for his pipe and tobacco and when they didn't turn up realized he had left them at the temple in his anxiety to speak to Niclophon. The kingdom was suddenly full of bandits and blackguards intent on robbing every Styphon's House temple they could reach, even going to the extent of skinning their domes of the gold that gave them their majesty! All the Chancellor had done in response to his pronouncements was shrug his shoulders. *Another unbeliever*, he thought, dismissing the man. In a civilized kingdom, the man would be gallows' fruit; here in this backwoods bumpkin realm he was the Great King's closest advisor.

Not that Great King Niclophon was much better. It was true that Niclophon was a believer in Styphon; all that proved was that he was mentally deficient and a poor judge of character. Any man with even a half-candle of wit knew that the gods were pure hokum. Why would any deities care about the comings and goings of the humans that covered the land with ant hives they called towns and cities? And who created the gods in the first place? In truth, every man was his own deity and it was up to him to create the wealth and stature he deserved by himself.

It was also true that the Temple had pushed Niclophon onto the Silver Throne after dispatching the previous Great King and his witch of a wife. If only the infant hadn't escaped their hands. Still, Valthros was most certainly moldering in an unmarked grave. Unfortunately, not having his body for burial gave every charlatan and sharper in the kingdom the opportunity to play pretender.

At long last, the Chancellor returned to the presence chamber. "His Majesty will see you now, Your Sanctity."

"Yes, Your Excellency."

He followed the tall Chancellor to Niclophon's private audience chamber, where it was rumored the Great King seduced pages and handpicked guardsmen. As he entered, Niclophon, dressed in a white linen tunic, looked up from a scroll he was reading. It was not a document of state, as he expected, but finely etched drawings of a lewd and lascivious nature, featuring men doing unthinkable things to other men. He felt his flesh crawl…

"Have a seat, Your Sanctity."

Prythames looked at the divan and shook his head. Just the thought of what unspeakable acts had been performed on its purple linen surface dissuaded him from sitting down.

"What new demand do you have for Us this day?" Niclophon asked, with a barely concealed scowl.

"Another temple, this one in Marthrax Town, has been raided, Your Majesty. The temple was looted, its priests murdered and our slaves stolen. This is unacceptable! Something must be done."

"I'll send out more patrols," Niclophon stated in a voice that approached boredom. "Hos-Bletha is a very large kingdom and many areas are poorly settled. These bandits could be hiding almost anywhere. Eventually, they will be caught and beheaded for their crimes."

"This will not do, Your Majesty." Prythames knew whose shoulders the blame would fall upon when word reached Balph about all the temples being pillaged and priests desecrated. He suspected that even if Niclophon was determined to stop the brigands, there was truth in his words and little that he could do. Therefore, it was up to him to bring these atrocities to the Inner Circle's attention and let them deal with it. Let them send more of Styphon's Own Guard, or even Grand Master Soton himself.

"It is all I can do, Your Sanctity. Why don't you ask Styphon Himself for help? Surely, he could reach down from his Skypalace and end these depredations."

Prythames frowned. *Surely the Great King is not that stupid?* he asked himself. *To believe that Styphon will reach down out of the sky. Or is he playing with me?* He didn't like where that last thought was going. *I'd better play along or….*

"I will have all the priests in the High Temple pray for Styphon's Deliverance."

"Good," Niclophon smiled. "Until then I will send out more patrols and some of my Guard to find out what's going on."

## III

The setting sun cast long and deep shadows when Grand-Captain Myklon and Petty-Captain Gycules crossed into Zenophon from Taurnos. Behind them marched eighty Hostigi soldiers and trusted mercenaries. All were sweating from the rigors of traveling through the forest where there were no ready-made trails. This was to avoid notice from the locals, civilian and especially military. This also meant leaving their horses and guard uniforms behind as the animals could not maneuver well through the heavy growth with riders on their backs.

At the edge of the tree line Myklon called for a halt. Ahead lay the town of Plyn. Like most small towns, this one had a large two-story inn, a bakery, two taverns, an open market in the plazos with dozens of stalls, a stable, a score of shops, and some rough-hewn wooden houses, outlying farms and a Styphon's House temple. Because of the nearby farms, the temple processed saltpeter mucked from manure piles throughout the district. This incurred the enmity of the farmers who wanted to use the manure for fertilizer.

Petty-Captain Gycules looked over the landscape. In the fading light of the sun the temple's golden dome still shined brightly.

"There is the temple, or I am a Ruthani slave," Gycules pronounced. "How do you propose we gain access?"

Captain Myklon looked at the temple walls. They stood at least two rods high, about twice the height of a tall man, which was low for a Styphoni temple. "I have an idea though I suspect you will not like it."

Two candles after the sun had set and darkness fallen, Grand-Captain Myklon and Gycules led their company to the rear wall of the temple. Gycules jumped up and found he could lay a hand on top of the wall, but not well enough that he could hold himself there.

"What is this plan that I will not like," Gycules demanded.

"You will stand against the wall." Myklon looked about and spotted a sturdy-looking trooper. "You."

"Sir?"

"I want you to get on all fours in front of Petty-Captain Gycules… no, not like that! You are a stair step, not a farm animal awaiting the advances of a lonely shepherd. Two more, you and you. Stand at Gycules' sides. Good." Andros looked for two more men, the tallest of those that remained. "You…and…you! Come here. Now, stand on…"

"Styr, sir."

"Really? Okay, use Trooper Styr as a stair step to get up on Gycules' shoulders. They are wide enough for both of you, but go one at a time. When you get to the top, make sure nobody is there! Then the both of you will sit on the wall to help the rest up and over."

Myklon turned to the rest. "Hand up your swords and arquebuses before you ascend. I pity the man who strikes Gycules in the face with a hanging weapon! Now, you," he pointed to the man closest to him, "up and over."

After a few minor mishaps, the men got the idea and quickly ascended the wall and dropped down on the other side. Myklon was the last to go before helping Gycules make the ascent. It took him and the two wall top assistants to bring the giant over.

Once down on the other side, Gycules asked, "could we not have stolen a wagon and placed it next to the wall and used it to scale the obstacle?"

Myklon admitted to himself that he did not think of it. To Gycules he whispered, "We did not have a wagon on this side to use. Better the men learn how to scale the wall without one in case we have to leave the same way we entered."

Gycules smiled and pointed to some wagons situated near the back of the temple. From the smell, they had been used for transporting manure. "You did not think of it, did you? Fear not, your secret is safe with me."

"Thank you. Now let's kill some gods-forsaken Styphoni."

Myklon tasked four sets of men to scout out the outside of the temple.

They were to look for ways to enter and make sure nobody was outside to catch them within the walls. When the men returned he learned there were two guards at the gate, a quartet playing dice near the stables and an access point in the back with a crossbar on the outside.

"No roving guards?"

"You there! What are you up to?"

Myklon turned to see two men dressed as Styphon's Own Guard approaching him and his scouts. The rest of the men were hiding in the shadows and as yet unnoticed.

"I seem to have misplaced my tinderbox," Myklon said casually. "Would you give me a light?"

One of the guardsmen was about to point out that he did not have a pipe when a huge hand grasped the side of his head and forced it sideways. His partner found himself in the same predicament only moving in the opposite direction. For the first time in the history of the two men working together, they had a true meeting of the minds. In fact, their heads came together with such force that both men dropped to the ground unconscious.

Gycules dragged the bodies into the shadows.

"And that is a solid example of what happens when scouts do a poor job," Myklon said in a matter of fact voice.

The scouts appeared uncertain as if he was referring to being discovered, or if it meant Gycules would knock their heads together.

"Now that we have dealt with the roving guard, the gate guards and gamblers are next. You two, go get that armor that Gycules has so thoughtfully supplied and put it on. The rest of you, keep a sharp eye out. I would hate for another surprise like that last one...and so would you."

## IV

In any army there are unpopular jobs that everyone below the rank of petty-captain has to perform at some time or another. Among them is guard duty. Sthenir and Mothros had drawn that duty for the third time in the last moon-half as punishment for not maintaining their armor in gleaming perfection. Captain Veriphon was incredibly particular about such things.

"I swear to Styphon, if I ever get off guard duty I will polish my breastplate until Veriphon can count his teeth in the reflection," Sthenir grumbled.

"As will I," Mothros agreed. "Do you think the rumors are true?"

"Which rumors? That Kalvan is really a Daemon from Regwarn, that Anaxthenes is secretly poisoning Styphon's Voice Sesklos and that Veriphon has questionable relations with livestock…"

"That only the dregs of Styphon's Own Guard are sent to this posting," Mothros finished. "I was sent here after accidentally bumping into Soton while in my cups. You were sent here after returning to post late after curfew. Captain Veriphon lost a skirmish against the Sastragathi Barbarians, Temple Master Bellos was sent here after he—"

"What difference does it make?" Sthenir interrupted. "Here we are and here is where we will stay for the foreseeable future."

"Maybe if we did better work, we could secure a better posting."

Sthenir snorted. "And end up fighting the Daemon Kalvan? How many of our brothers have died that way? This assignment is good enough for me. At least here we are unlikely to end up as stripped corpses dumped into a mass grave."

Mothros sighed. Sthenir was correct, though Mothros wanted to advance in the Guard and make something of himself.

"Stand tall," Sthenir hissed. "The Night Watch is coming."

Mothros quickly assumed the position of attention as the two Night Watch guards approached. He noticed that the cloak of one of the roving guards was stained with something. If Captain Veriphon saw him!

"Good evening. How goes the watch," asked the man with the dirty cloak.

"Nothing to report, sir!" Sthenir replied.

"Good. Good. Did you happen to notice the eighty odd men that jumped the wall about a half-candle ago?"

"Sir?" Mothros and Sthenir said in unison.

"Jumped over the wall, killed two Guardsmen and stole their armor and capes. You really did not see that?"

Sthenir and his partner began to wonder what game the Night Watch was playing with them.

"Oh, look! There they go!" The one with a clean cloak said and pointed behind the gate guards. Sthenir and Mothros turned to see what it was. It was their last act on the mortal plane. "My error," said one as he used his knife to slit Sthenir's throat, "they are right behind you." The two guards died without making a sound.

Grand-Captain Myklon, Gycules and two soldiers stepped out of the shadows. "Good job. Now let us get these corpses stripped and out of sight. You two take over as the gate guards. And clean the blood off of the armor."

"What will we do with all the bodies, sir," Gycules asked.

Myklon thought for a moment. A pyre would draw too much attention. It would be better if there were no bodies to find at all. "We will have to dump them in a mass grave after they are all stripped. There should be a trash pit or cesspool we can dump them in and cover over. First, we should make sure it is their bodies being buried and not our own hides."

# TWENTY-SIX

## I

"Your luck is just a little too good, Manar."

"Maybe Styphon likes me better than you, Luklos," Manar replied.

"Stop griping and roll them bones," Deimos said irritably. The dice had not been going his way all evening. The eight-sided dice had been brought in from Balph with Manar, and Deimos was beginning to wonder if Luklos was right about Manar's luck.

"Whose turn is it to throw," Stanos asked.

"Mine." Deimos picked up the five dice and shook them before tossing them into the circle etched into the ground. Two dice showed the rune for one, two showed the rune for eight, and the fifth rolled off outside of the circle into the shadows. "Damnit, where did it go?"

"Here you are."

A large hand held out the die. The four gamblers turned to see the hand's owner. They never made it. Several men with swords and knives fell among them, splashing red arterial blood and entrails over tiles. Again the bodies were stripped and carted away. Gycules collected the rest of the dice. One had a drop of blood on it.

"I would not use those if I were you," Myklon warned. "They were not very lucky for the last owner."

## II

Satisfied that the courtyard and grounds surrounding the temple had been cleared of Styphoni, Grand-Captain Myklon led his men to the back door. "Why would they bar it from the outside, sir," one of the troopers asked. "Normally, you only see that sort of thing when you cage an animal."

"We will soon find out." Myklon tried to lift the heavy oaken crossbar and failed to raise it. Wordlessly, Petty-Captain Gycules assisted him and the bar came away. "Swords at the ready, sir. We don't know what may be on the other side of this door."

Myklon started to push the door open only to stop when Gycules pulled him back. "Captain, you're the leader, but this is something for a follower to do. We need you to keep the mission on track."

He was tempted to argue the point with the giant, then realized he would have done the same thing back when he was still in the Blethan Royal Army. "Very well, Petty-Captain. Who goes in first?"

"Me." Gycules shoved the door in and ran into the room ready for battle. Instead, he lowered his sword and stared at the occupants of the room.

Outside, Myklon could smell the stench of unwashed bodies and squalor. "Gods! A slave pen. Remove those chains."

Gycules used his two-handed sword and struck off the chains of the man closest to him. Behind him, several others attempted the same with their swords.

"Stop that, you idiots," Myklon hissed. "You will ruin good steel on those chains. Find the keys." Gycules looked back at him with a slightly sheepish expression. He added, "Not everybody can swing a sword like yours."

The keys were on a hook out of reach of the slaves. The slave master had put them in plain sight, where his charges would see them, to add to their misery. With the shackles removed, the slaves stood together in clumps waiting to be told what to do.

"Curse and Blast it, look at them, Gycules. They've had their manhood stripped from them along with the flesh on their backs."

The giant nodded silently, a sickly smile on his lips.

"Get these people out of here," Grand-Captain Myklon ordered. "No matter what happens to us, they are going to escape."

Gycules selected six men to help the slaves over the back wall. Before they departed, he said, "Wait for us in the forest. If we do not return by morning, make your way as best you can."

After the men filed out, Gycules turned to Myklon. "I am through with sneaking around. Let us have done with these bastards."

"Agreed." Myklon said.

This time Myklon took the lead and tried the door leading from the slave pens to the main temple after putting an ear on the wood. It would not open. "Damn! It must be locked from the outside." Myklon bodily threw himself into the door. That only threatened to break his bones. "By Galzar's gonads! Gycules?"

The giant stepped forward and knocked on the door, then sniffed the wood. "Oak. Not new or even treated properly. Still, if there are crossbars on the other side, I will not be able to break through it. I might even break a couple bones trying."

"Shite!" Myklon exclaimed. "No point risking your health. We will go around and enter the temple from another location…"

"Sir?"

Gycules turned and saw Crytos, a small man with a face reminiscent of a large rodent. "Yes, Crytos?"

"May I try the door?"

*Whaaaat*? "You think you can get through that?" The rat-faced man nodded. He decided there was no harm in humoring the man. "By all means."

Crytos went to the door, pulled something from his tunic and went to work on the lock. In seconds the sound of a metal click issued from the lock. Crytos gave the door a small shove and it flew open. Everybody stared at the small man in surprise.

"I was a thief back in Balph before I was caught and sold as a slave. Locks, while not my specialty, are within my skills."

Gycules recalled that Crytos was among the first slaves Democriphon rescued.

"Crytos, I want you to stay in the back. Your skills may come in handy again and I do not want to risk you being injured on this mission." Myklon turned to the rest. "Does everybody agree?"

Every head nodded.

"Good. Now, let us go slay some Styphoni."

Myklon peered around the door before Gycules could stop him, then proceeded into the hall where the giant quickly caught up with him. "Gycules, is it just me or has this been far too simple? Where is everybody? I would think the halls would be filled with people going back and forth."

Gycules shrugged. "Wise soldiers sleep at every opportunity. Perhaps Styphon's Own Guard takes their slumber early."

"So soon after sunset? I think not. Those four gamblers outside suggest otherwise."

"I think they were roving guards in dereliction of their duties," Gycules offered.

Myklon nodded. "But why roll bones in a shadowy courtyard when there were comfortable rooms within the temple. Do the Styphoni disapprove of games of chance?"

The big man shrugged.

"Maybe you are correct. Well, I dislike murdering a man in his sleep, but I like being killed a great deal less." The Grand-Captain stopped at a pair of high double doors. He pressed an ear to one and heard nothing. "Maybe they are out on a patrol or some mission?"

"Or, they could be off in the village assaulting tavern wenches like any other fighting man," the giant suggested.

"Or maybe…" Myklon said as he pushed open the door. The doors opened into a chapel. The chapel was filled with guards and priests alike. "Or maybe they are at prayer services."

Sixty-odd pairs of eyes turned at the sound of Myklon's voice. For a moment nobody moved. Then the room exploded with movement on both sides of the door.

"I knew this was too easy," Myklon muttered, as he aimed his pistol and shot a Guardsman in the face. He shot a second soldier with his other pistol, threw the empty gun at a third, then charged the nearest foe rapier in hand.

The battle raged back and forth for almost a quarter-candle. Styphon's Own Guard proved to be capable fighters who could hold their own against most fighters one-on-one. Fortunately, their party had caught the Guard in service to their god and none of them had any firearms, or their fearsome polearms, although all wore swords.

Myklon thanked Galzar, Dralm and any other god he could think of that he had more men and Gycules on his side. It took all of his skill to bring down his opponent, then he moved in between other fights putting his sword to work aiding his comrades.

Gycules, enjoying greater reach with arm and sword, hewed a swath through the middle of the battle in an effort to reach the priests before they could escape. Though successful in reaching the altar in one piece, with no small thanks to the mercenary that covered his back, it proved unnecessary. Crytos, the thief, had somehow weaved his way through the fighting unnoticed and dispatched the priests before the giant could get to them.

"How in Regwarn did you do that," Gycules demanded as he back-handed a Styphoni, breaking the man's neck and sending his helmet flying.

"I was a cutpurse by trade," Crytos said lightly. He threw a knife that went just past Gycules shoulder into the eye of the man harassing the mercenary at his back. "Getting in and out of crowds unnoticed was a professional requirement."

## III

Petty-Captain Gycules leaned on his greatsword in order to stay standing. The battle had been a hard one for everybody. Even the Captain looked exhausted. A third of their men lay dead or dying on the floor along with all of Styphon's Own Guard and the temple priests. Many of the rest were badly wounded; the butcher's price for today's battle was high.

"Where is the Temple Master?" Grand-Captain Myklon yelled. "The Highpriest?"

Gycules' head shot up. The dead priests were all wearing black or white robes. "You're right. These are all underpriests."

"Search the temple and warn the gate guards," Myklon shouted. "If he gets out and alerts the village, we may be in for another battle."

Those still capable of movement rushed to obey. Gycules stepped over the bodies of the dead, avoiding the pools of drying blood, to find his way out of the chapel and into the narthex. From there he raced up the stairs taking the steps three at a time. By the time he reached the apex of the stairs, his strength was almost depleted. At a slower pace he went from door to door pushing it in and checking for stray priests or anyone else not in the chapel.

At the last door the giant could hear the sounds of a struggle. Before trying the door, he listened carefully. There were the sounds of a woman in distress. He tried the door and found it locked.

"Dralm-damnit!" Gycules kicked the door as hard as his tired muscles allowed. The wood shattered and the door broke away from the hinges.

Within the chamber a tiny woman with hair like the setting sun was fending off a fat priest with a small knife. *The Temple Master at play.* Without a word the giant rushed in and grabbed the highpriest by the neck and threw him against the wall with one hand, then skewered him with the sword in the other.

"Lady, are you…?"

Gycules turned to find the knife at his throat. "Ah…if I mistook the situation, you have my apologies."

"The only thing you took was my right to kill this bloated pig myself," shouted the redheaded woman. She was short, slight of build, and completely naked, though seemingly unaware of that fact. "Who are you?'

"Oh. I am Gycules. A mercenary by trade. I am here to rescue you… if indeed that is what you need."

"Rescue me? How sweet! I was brought here today to be this pig's slave doxy. Lucky for me he was careless with his cutlery and I was able to fend him off. I think he enjoyed it, too!" The woman spit on the corpse. "Well, if you are my rescuer, let us be away."

"Might I suggest you find something to wear, first?" Gycules nodded, and the woman looked down at herself.

"Turn around, you lout, while I dress myself!"

"Not until you give me that knife."

She relinquished the eating knife then dove into the temple master's wardrobe. There was nothing but priestly vestments, there, but she made do.

"Now, let us go. My name is Tylla, if you are interested."

Gycules was very interested; and not just in her name.

## IV

Great King Niclophon looked around at the scores of supplicants lolling around his presence chamber and wished he could just disappear. Sometimes the weight of office was more than he could bear. Nor was it helped by the tune that ran unbidden through his mind making it almost impossible to concentrate on the tedious cases he was called upon to adjudicate.

Everywhere in Bletha town he heard the cursed melody of "When the Orphan Prince Comes Marching Home" coming from each tavern or inn he passed. The worst of the blasted song were the words, damning him as a regicide and threatening his life.

He tried ordering the troubadours not to sing it. They still continued.

Then he gave them fines and, when that hadn't worked, had them arrested. Now his dungeon was filled with drunks, minstrels and troubadours. And still the townsfolk hummed the cursed song and the melody filled the town—and his mind! *If I order them not to hum it, they will laugh in my face and call me mad.*

His attention was brought back to the case he was settling. A freeman and his baron, were arguing over a pasture and grazing rights. The baron claimed the freeman's lands were part of the village commons and wanted to graze his cattle on the pasture. The nobleman was abrasive and talked too loudly; he wanted to club him with his ceremonial scepter until the baron shut his yapping maw.

He nodded to his Chancellor. Archimanes cried out: "All rise. His Majesty, Great King Niclophon will make his judgment."

The chamber went as silent as one of the vacant temples of Dralm.

"We grant the Landowner, Freeman Urthog, ownership of the disputed lands—"

"How could you—" interrupted the Baron.

"Because, I am your Great King!" he shouted. "Baron Jostran will also pay Freeman Urthog twenty ounces of silver within a moon-quarter."

The Baron was about to object, but then thought better of it.

His scribe was already writing up the judgment.

*Smart man*, Niclophon decided. *One more word and I'd have sentenced him to spend a moon in the dungeon on half-rations.*

As the next pair of petitioners came forward, he saw Archpriest Prythames burst into the chamber, followed by a pack of black-robed priests.

The other supplicants backed away from the archpriest as though he were a plague carrier.

"Your Majesty," the Archpriest said, his voice strained. "I must talk with you in private. The outrage—"

The Great King looked over at his Chancellor and made a cutting motion with the right hand across his throat.

"This audience is closed, at His Majesty's request. Please leave the presence chamber at once."

As the supplicants and petitioners filed out of the chamber, the Great King made way to his private audience chamber with the Archpriest close behind.

Even before he could reach his chair, the priest went off like a madman. "Do you know that these…these…bandits, dressed in Styphon's regalia, have robbed three more of our temples in less than a moon-quarter! It's an abomination. Heresy. A travesty against the Temple and One True God!"

Niclophon almost had to bite his cheek to keep himself from laughing. It was nice to see someone else suffer for a change. "We too have experienced losses from the bandits. They looted and destroyed our tribute wagon on its way to Balph. These are not typical robbers, they know too much. They pass themselves off as Ruthani in one attack, then Styphon's Own Guard in another. Maybe there's a rogue upperpriest among your ranks."

"Impossible, Your Majesty. No priest would act in such a base manner, nor consort with common brigands."

Once again he fought to keep a smile off his face. As far as he was concerned, the entire temple was filled to the rafters with thieves and cutthroats. Only they killed with tithes, forced donations, tribute, interest, and loan premiums. And he was one of their biggest debtors so he had to suffer fools and bores like Prythames. *Maybe I should take a page from the Usurper Kalvan's book and kill them all and rob their temples before these bandits take everything. Yes, and a moon later have Grand Master Soton and his Knights knocking over my castles and forts. If the Temple suffers another big loss or Soton is killed in battle against Kalvan, that will be the time to strike.*

"I have already sent out patrols to discover where these bandits are hiding," Niclophon said, "but there's little more I can do until I learn more about them. "Please keep me apprised of what your people learn, Your Sanctity."

"Of course, Your Majesty. However, you will have to work with Highpriest Wythros. "I will be leaving posthaste for Balph. I need to inform the Inner Circle of recent events."

*Sure*, Niclophon thought, *now that the Temple has lost half a million ounces of gold, the Inner Circle will be real interested. As for helpful, not much. They're like a murder of crows waiting for old Sesklos to finally die so they can appoint his successor*. "Go with Syphon's Blessing." *And don't come back*.

WINTER

# TWENTY-SEVEN

It was fortunate that the Hos-Blethan winter was as mild as late summer in Hostigos, otherwise they would have been forced to stay at their new camp and hunker down for bad weather. Duke Skranga knew that the candle was burning down if they were to stop Great King Niclophon from sending a contingent of his troops to the Grand Host. It was time for a Council of War, as Kalvan called them. He waited until evening and invited his inner band of conspirators into the cabin to plan their strategy for the next six moons.

After conferring with Chief Captain Ranthar, Lady Eldra, Chief Vanir, Calthros, Grand-Captain Myklon and two new members, Uncle Wolf Syros and Petty-Captain Andros, Skranga said, "I believe it's time to induct Uncle Wolf Syros into our inner council."

Ranthar agreed. "Syros has already figured out what we're up to and knows the military capabilities of the Hos-Bletha rulers better than anyone else in camp. I say we add him to our council."

"Anyone opposed?" Skranga asked.

When no one objected, Skranga turned to Ranthar and said, "Where's our peripatetic troubadour?"

"He went back to Bletha Town."

"Why?"

"I think he feels personally responsible that Niclophon has arrested most of the musicians in town because they were singing his song."

"You mean 'The Orphan Prince Goes Marching Home'?" Eldra asked.

"Yes, it became so popular that almost everyone, including some of the king's supporters, were either singing or humming that damn tune. I can't get it out of my head, either. So he decided to stay and help raise money for the families of those languishing in the dungeon of Tarr-Bletha."

"Maybe that's a sign that we should move the Orphan Prince operation to the top of our list," Ranthar said.

Skranga shook his head. "While the Orphan Prince deception has a lot of potential for destabilizing the kingdom, it's an operation that will take time and coordination. We'll have to work out the details later. Right now, it's already winter and the Blethan troops will be on their way to Hos-Harphax to join the Grand Host as soon as the weather and sea conditions permit, probably in three or four moons. So, we need to focus on our main objective, keeping the Blethan army from joining up with the Grand Host of Styphon's House."

"I agree," Captain-General Democriphon said. "Great King Kalvan told me it would take a lightning campaign, one that strikes fast and hits hard, to pull this off. A series of raids so potentially threatening that Niclophon can ignore them only at his peril."

"The problem is we just don't have enough time to besiege any of the major castles or towns," Skranga noted.

"True," Democriphon agreed. "So we'll have to depend on smaller attacks against caravans, Styphon's temples and small bands of soldiers. What we've already been doing, but on a larger scale."

"Good point," Ranthar said. "We have almost two thousand men, including the three hundred fake Hostigi temple guards we brought with us and the sixty odd mercenaries that were with the sharpers. The problem is that more than half of our force is comprised of former slaves and they won't be in condition to fight again until spring."

"The only thing we can do," Democriphon said, "is break our force into three groups. Each band would have better than a company's worth of soldiers. The new recruits will be sufficient for the Duke's protection and he can put them to work building more permanent structures, which leaves us with enough soldiers for at least three bands. I can lead one band, First Captain Ranthar can lead another one, while Grand-Captain Myklon can lead the third."

Skranga stood up and used his sword to push the glowing red embers around. "I like it. We've got three top commanders and three companies of veteran soldiers. If we use them wisely and stir up enough trouble, the princes will run screaming to Bletha Town for Niclophon's help, while the highpriests of Styphon's House scream for help from Balph. Not only will the princes refuse to release their levy, but will make demands upon their great kings' troops as well. In addition, it's possible that our actions against Styphon's House will force Grand Master Soton to send more Temple Guardsmen to Bletha."

"We're going to need another encampment," Vanir brought up. "This place is too close to Port Gytha, and there are several villages in the area. It makes a fine place to initiate local attacks, but we're going to need a permanent base of operations while these attacks are taking place. Great King Niclophon already has a lot of men out searching for us."

"That makes a lot of sense, Vanir," Skranga said. "Let's break out the maps. Regardless of whether or not we accomplish our original mission, we're stuck here for the duration of the war. So we are going to need a more permanent place of refuge where we can be relatively safe."

Inside their temporary headquarters everyone gathered about the rough-hewn table, while the deerskin map of Hos-Bletha was unrolled and weighted down with silver ingots to keep it in place. More color had been added: green was used to indicate wooded areas, blue for lakes and swamps, red for the cities and towns.

Democriphon used his sword, a rapier of Kalvan's design, to point at a large area shaded in blue and green. "There don't appear to be any towns or cities in this area. We could build a sizeable village there and go unnoticed by anything other than river dragons."

The Uncle Wolf and Vanir looked at the map, then each other, then to Democriphon.

"That isn't really true, My Prince," Vanir said.

"There are some small dwellings belonging to backwoodsmen," Syros added. "There are also sharper camps and bandit camps."

"Sharper camps? Oh, like hideouts when things get too sticky," Ranthar said. "Well, it would be easy enough to take over one of those…"

"No!" Vanir almost yelled. "I am oath-bound to keep those camp locations secret. Even under torture."

Democriphon looked angry for a moment, then settled down and even smiled. "We will not force you to break your oath, Vanir. Actually, I am pleased to find that you choose not to break your word. It gives me more confidence in the oath you gave to me when you joined us. Perhaps you can point out an area where we will be able to expand without interfering with your brethren."

Vanir and Syros pored over the map. As they pointed to different areas, they spoke in a language even Ranthar didn't understand. It had to be some polyglot of Ruthani and Zarthani. He made a mental note to get a sharper picked up and hypno-mech the language out of him.

After considerable pointing and jabbering, Vanir and Syros seemed to come to an agreement.

Uncle Wolf Syros pointed to a spot close to a lake with his knife. "This spot here is fairly close to clean water and several back trails. It used to be a bandit hideout and support village until they were burned out. The village was called Mallegast."

"Burned out?" prompted Duke Skranga.

"It was discovered by a patrol that got lost in the woods and chanced upon it," Vanir explained. "Once a depot or hideout is discovered, it is never used again."

"It sounds like the right place for our permanent camp," Ranthar said, "but we will need to look it over before making any plans."

"I am not so sure this is a desirable location," Uncle Wolf Syros said. "Take note of whose realm this site is located in."

Everybody looked. Petty-Captain Andros was first to say it out loud. "Prince Mythros. Getting caught in Pytha by the prince's troops would be as good as suicide."

"Hmm, actually, that might make it the best location," Democriphon said. "I imagine Prince Mythros' attitude towards sharpers that use the Orphan Prince dodge is known far and wide. Well, no band thinking of running that scam would dare use the prince's own realm to hide out in, so nobody will consider looking for us there."

Vanir laughed. "We'll make a sharper out of you yet, My Prince."

"That is a frightening thought," Democriphon said. "If we decide to move there, we should keep this hideout."

Skranga agreed. "We'll keep this camp we're using now as a backup and,"—he groped for the term he had heard King Kalvan use—"staging area. If the Blethan army ever comes after us, we can lead them here."

"We can also set up some traps for them," Ranthar added. "Panther traps and such."

"Those holes with, um…sharp stakes?" Uncle Wolf Syros asked.

Democriphon shook his head. "Such devices lack honor. No panther pits. Hmm…"

"What are you thinking about, My Prince?" Syros asked.

"Maybe the panther pits wouldn't be a bad idea after all. Only, instead of stakes at the bottom, we fill it knee-deep with honey. It would take weeks to clean it all out of the boots and armor."

After a brief laugh, Ranthar asked where the honey would come from. "That is another thing I have been thinking about for a while now. First we should set up the new camp."

"Before or after we take on two more temples?"

"Oh, definitely before, Ranthar. We'll need the extra space to accommodate our guests."

"I would advise against using the same trick twice, Your Majesty," Andros said.

Democriphon feigned surprise. In truth, he had been thinking much the same. "What do you think we should do?"

Andros didn't have to feign surprise. It was a rare thing for an officer, let alone a prince, to ask his opinion on anything. Petty-captains were rarely consulted in the Blethan army.

"Well, uh, sire, I would dress up your men in the armor of Styphon's Own Guard and demand entrance at the temple. Explain that you were ambushed by hostile forces and that you need time to recover and gather your strength. You could then ask that the Temple Guard go out to scout an area where you can have another ambush set up in advance. While they are gone, you can deal with the priests and whatever Guard that are left behind. Word of what happened at the other two temples will have circulated by now, so your story will be plausible."

Ranthar and Democriphon shared a meaningful look at each other. "Do bandits in Hos-Bletha practice this kind of strategy often?"

"No. Too many would think it dishonorable. It is a plan I have played with in my mind ever since my father's farm was taken and turned over to the Styphoni. Taxes, the Questors claimed. I joined the army when I was sixteen winters to support the family."

"Who are these 'questors,'" Ranthar inquired, although his language imprint told him that a questor was a tax assessor.

"The King's Questors collect taxes on the King's subjects and Styphon's House's tithes," Andros explained. "Our property was near to where Styphon's House wanted to build a shrine, so the king made sure they could get it. I knew I would never be able to get up an army to take my revenge with, but a small force seemed feasible. Someday."

Ranthar hadn't realized that Styphon's House had so much power that it could force the Great King of Hos-Bletha to collect their tithes. From Andros' words, it didn't appear to have helped their public image.

"If a Northern Kingdom ruler attempted to collect the Temple's tithes, he would find his kingdom in open rebellion," Skranga noted.

"That may be true," Andros said shaking his head. "But not in Hos-Bletha. Great King Niclophon is a devotee of Styphon's House, and indebted to them all the way up to his chin. What the rest of his subjects think means little as long as the king follows where the Styphoni lead. As a result, only Galzar of all the other gods has any standing in Hos-Bletha. Even Styphon's House treads lightly with the god of war lest they alienate the mercenaries. The other True Gods are only worshipped in the

Princedoms of Mythros and Artigos, where there is freedom of worship. In the other princedoms, the other gods are only worshipped in secret for fear of retaliation by the Great King or Styphon's House."

Democriphon slapped a hand down on the table. "By Galzar, Andros, you shall have your day. In fact, you shall lead the next temple raid."

"I will? When do we go?"

"Soon, within a moon-half. But first, we need to establish our permanent camp. This will provide time to fatten up our new freemen and let them join in. You will have to train them."

Andros stood a little straighter. "With pleasure, sire. But, may I ask an extra moon-quarter."

"Oh? I thought you'd be in more of a hurry than that."

"I am, but the slaves are in poor shape. I want as many of them to join me as possible. Two moon-quarters is too short a time to prepare such men."

Democriphon recalled the skeletal figures he had freed from the Styphoni temple. They hadn't had a decent meal since their imprisonment, and had been worked and whipped nearly to death. "The slaves we just rescued will not be in shape to fight for several moons. You can take the ones we freed earlier."

Democriphon ended the meeting and everybody filed out save for him and Ranthar.

The Prince gave Ranthar the once over. "Problem, Captain?"

Ranthar let out a sigh. "Yes. Even those slaves we freed a couple of moons ago will need a lot more time to get their strength up than a few moon-quarters. The best of the lot were sent to that new temple-farm. It'll take another two or three moons of training to turn that lot into soldiers."

"I agree."

"What! Then why did you ask for them?"

Democriphon held up a hand to forestall further questions. "The slaves Petty-Captain Andros will be using are healthy enough to deal with pampered temple priests, especially with experienced soldiers at their side. The real fighting will be between Styphon's Own Guard and our men at the ambush site."

"Assuming they fall for our ruse."

Democriphon shrugged. "True. There is always a risk. The same risk we all take every time we go out on a raid. But these poor bastards need this in a way you and I will never fully understand. They have been ripped away from their homes and homeland, separated from their families, tortured, starved and worked nearly to death. Many of them have watched friends and family members die. Every last one of them needs to get back some of his own, even if it's only his dignity.

"If we wait too long, many of them might slip away seeking revenge against the Styphoni as soon they feel strong enough. Our captains can only keep them distracted with the training for so long. They want revenge and they want it yesterday! That fire will give them strength when the time arrives for fighting."

Ranthar was impressed with Democriphon's plan. By here-and-now standards, it was sound enough. "Many will die."

"Many more have already died. We'll just have to do the best we can and hope this one skirmish will keep the former slaves from doing something rash later on."

"Rash?" Ranthar couldn't help thinking that if Democriphon was worried about somebody else doing something rash, there was something to it.

"Like going off on their own, seeking revenge and putting the rest of us in danger in the process. Or even just trying to return home. Most of them would be recaptured and questioned, possibly giving us away."

Ranthar had to admit that Democriphon had a point. "When you first started selecting the men for this mission, you wanted mercenaries with other skills. Might we not find those same skills among the men and women we freed?"

"Indeed, Ranthar. I hadn't thought of that. We can encourage them to return to their former crafts and professions while we rebuild the village of Mallegast. That should keep them out of trouble for a while. And setting up the village will keep many of them occupied until their strength and endurance returns."

"I will arrange for a scouting party to survey the location," Ranthar said. "I will also ask Gasphros to speak with the former slaves—"

"Freemen."

"Pardon?"

"We will henceforth refer to all of the former people we've rescued as freemen. That will underscore the fact they are no longer slaves," Democriphon explained. "We will use the term freemen to build up what Great King Kalvan calls their *self-image*."

Ranthar nodded his head in agreement, a little surprised at how thoroughly Democriphon had picked up many of Kalvan's ideas. *I think our boy has influenced this time-line a lot more than Chief Verkan ever anticipated.*

# TWENTY-EIGHT

## I

It took the party five days to reach the spot that Petty-Captain Andros had suggested for their permanent encampment. They traveled lesser-used trails and back roads, often retracing their steps and going backwards, to avoid patrols and the swamps that dotted the area. The land was lush with growth and Democriphon saw his first palm tree. The area was heavily populated with deer, elk, bison, beavers and even river dragons. Since there were few inhabitants, the animals were easy to bag and they had no problem finding fresh meat.

It was their Ruthani scout Yaholo who discovered the deserted village of Mallegast.

After dismounting and massaging his aching thigh muscles, Democriphon looked over the burned-out camp with a critical eye. Most of the former buildings, really just slapdash huts, had burned to the ground. Green plants and small trees had already pushed their way through the piles of charcoal and burnt timbers. There was space enough to build a small town, and raise crops and cattle pens around it. There was ready access to water at a nearby stream, plenty of trees to use for lumber and even hills around it to provide some cover on two sides.

"Why has this area not been settled already? I can't think of a better location for a village in this region."

Vanir nodded. "It has been tried a few times. Once it was wiped out by Ruthani raiders, another time by a flood. That was before some of the swamps were drained to create more farmland. During that project many of the workers became ill with a sickness even the Uncle Wolfs could not treat and several died. The last attempt to settle here was made by a band of sharpers who were burned out by the prince's troopers. Now it is considered a cursed land and everybody avoids it."

"That explains why there are no significant roads or trails nearby," Ranthar observed. "Do you think there might really be a curse on this place?"

"Pfft!" Democriphon spat. "I'll wager curses are as prolific as fireseed devils. And just as insubstantial."

He spotted Gycules running towards them. As big and strong as the petty-captain was, he was no kind of runner, especially while wearing his back-and-breast and lugging around his oversized two-handed sword. "Curse and blast it. Maybe there is some sort of curse after all. Gycules doesn't run like that without a damned good reason."

The two men waited for the petty-captain as he lumbered down the overgrown pathway. When he finally arrived it took a while before he recovered his breath enough to speak intelligibly. "My…Prince," panted Gycules, "Five of the slav—I mean…freeman. Escaped…during the… march here."

"Ran away," Democriphon corrected. "Slaves escape, freemen come and go as they please. Do you know when they departed our company?"

"My best guess is…eight or ten marches back…sire."

Democriphon considered the situation. The freemen had never been told exactly where the new encampment would be or given its name, so there was little danger of their giving away their position. While he was furious over the matter, he affected an air of outward calm; leaders who were seen to lose control of themselves soon found they could lose control of those they led.

"As much as I would like to recover them I suspect even our best trackers would find it impossible to follow their trail through the swamps and brush. That assumes they even stayed together. And even if we did find them and bring them back what kind of message does that send to the rest of the freemen?"

Ranthar nodded. "We told them that they were free. That means they have the right to leave if they wish. Now, what do you suggest we do?"

Democriphon thought on the matter, then had an idea. "Nothing as far as they are concerned. The rest of the party is still several marches to the rear. I'll go address them and let them know we will arrange for an escort if anybody else wishes to leave and leave it at that. Those who elect to remain will have to stay. If they leave our camp after my speech, we'll set the dogs on them."

Since they only had a couple of strays following the expedition, they would have to purchase some mastiffs for guard duty, he decided. The war dogs were also useful on the field of battle, although Great King Kalvan had forbidden their use. During his years as a mercenary, Democriphon had even seen them draped in chain mail on the battlefield.

"Captain Ranthar, most importantly, we need to consider the safety of our people and the security of our plan. I want you to take Uncle Wolf Syros and a small escort into the nearest town, Haltha, and purchase as much of this parcel of land and the surrounding area as you can. I suspect the current landowner will be happy with even ten ounces of silver per acre. Also, see if you can purchase any mastiffs; we can use them to guard the village against both intruders and runaways.

"Since we are planning to build a village anyway, let us do so, openly and legally. Nobody will suspect us of harboring slaves or being bandits if we buy the land and pay the appropriate tribute to Prince Mythros."

Ranthar mulled it over and agreed. "What will our cover story be? Hundreds of people do not just appear out of the air."

"We are Harphaxi refugees escaping the fighting in the north," Democriphon said. "We do not recognize Great King Lysandros as our true ruler, but we refuse to fight against our homeland. I think that is plausible enough to be accepted."

"Hmm…I think that will work. Skranga's intelligencers have brought word that many in Harphax City believe that Great King Kaiphranos was poisoned by his brother so that he could assume the Iron Throne. So it's a believable story. The silver we pay for the land will make it acceptable to the Prince and to his local subjects. But, there's no way to hide the former slaves Hostigi accents. Someone is sure to notice the whip marks on the freemen's backs, what do we do about them?"

"I hardly think we will be subjected to a strip search," Democriphon said. "Still…ah! I've got it. It is common knowledge that Kalvan freed the slaves, but some of them feared what would happen if he lost the war and fled east into Hos-Harphax. Once there they joined up with the others who wanted to flee the war, as well as those of their betters who believe that their new Great King is a regicide."

Ranthar nodded a smile slowly dawning on his face. "A very good plan, My Prince. Duke Skranga, if he were here, would be impressed."

Skranga had elected to stay back at their original encampment until the new one was fully established.

"By the gods, I hope not." Democriphon said. Skranga had been an Agrysi horse-trader—some suspected thief—back in Hostigos before being jumped up to duke by former Prince Gormoth. While he begrudgingly admired his skills as a spy-master, in no way did he want to be considered Skranga's equal. "I would prefer to impress a better class of person. Although, to be fair, Skranga is very good at what he does."

He turned to Petty-Captain Gycules. "Gather the freemen together for my speech. Lead them to someplace in the swampland they will never find again. We will provide an escort for any who wish to leave."

Ranthar added, "I suggest we will give each man and woman who chooses to go twenty-five silver crowns. After that, they're on their own. I also suggest we lay a false trail in another direction just to be on the safe side. We may have left some sign of our passing that our Ruthani scouts overlooked. Even if not, our direction was plain enough for the runaways to point out."

"Excellent advice, Captain Ranthar. I will leave it in your capable hands. Tonight we will plan our next temple raids and the beginning of the Orphan Prince project." As Democriphon got back on his mount, he fought to maintain the outward appearance of calm. Events were moving very quickly now.

II

On their way to rejoin the rest of the party, Democriphon went over and over in his mind trying to determine what he had done wrong. He should have realized that some of the former slaves might run away and tried to prevent it from happening, but happen it did. There was every chance that runaways would be caught, and then incarcerated. Once the authorities determined they were former slaves—which would be obvious once their backs were exposed—they would be heavily questioned. Even threatened with death, if they were uncooperative. Once it became known that their freedom was due to brigands, the ones causing all the trouble, they would be heavily interrogated, maybe even tortured.

The questioning was what he feared the most, and why he insisted on being called Valthros when around them. If they talked about the Orphan Prince's return, that was all fine and well; he intended to let everybody know about that soon anyway. But the fact that his men rescued slaves. Not good. Next they would be asking where they came from, which could lead to all sorts of problems.

They had been careful when leaving the first camp so it was doubtful anyone could give away that encampment. He had not told anyone, other than the scouts and his fellow conspirators, that they found the abandoned village. So that was not a problem.

Every decision Democriphon made was based on what he thought Great King Kalvan would do. Kalvan rarely lost his temper, and never without good reason. Unlike some nobles, he admitted to his mistakes, at least to the high-ranking nobles and military leaders, and acted to correct them. Democriphon tried to emulate his superior in every way since being granted this mission. It gave him a new appreciation for what Kalvan had to deal with, not to mention the sizeable headaches that came along with the job.

Things had been much easier when all he had to worry about was leading men into battle. It was straightforward, honorable work. There was no skulking about working from the shadows. What he was doing now seemed better suited to thieves and assassins. Vanir might actually have been a better choice to command the mission.

No. That was fool's talk. King Kalvan would not have sent him if he were wrong for the mission. Something about him and Skranga made them the best choice to run this operation. Skranga's credentials were obvious. The man was as crooked as a dog's hind leg; Democriphon had even heard Kalvan say so in an unguarded moment using one of his unusual turns of phrase. Skranga was at least half-sharper himself. He was made for this kind of work.

*So why was I put in charge?* Democriphon pounded on his saddle. *Ranthar is a better leader than I am, not to mention Colonel Verkan. Men followed me in the past because they respected my rank. They follow Verkan and Ranthar because they respect them as men and leaders.*

## III

"Capt—Gr—um…My Prince?"

Democriphon almost laughed at Gycules confusion over his title. From colonel to captain-general to prince. "Yes, Petty-Captain?"

"I have gathered the freemen and they are waiting for you to address them."

They were back with the main party and Democriphon mentally cursed. He hadn't intended to give any speeches until later. Unfortunately, he neglected to clarify that point to the petty-captain. "I will talk to them in a moment, Gycules. Thank you."

The giant nodded and left. Democriphon gathered himself together and tried to shake off his doubts. He had wasted the ride back worrying about what he should have done rather than rehearsing the speech he was about to give. There were a few drops of rain sprinkling down. From the look of the sky, it was going to get a great deal worse. Democriphon hated giving speeches in the rain. He tried to remember the odd phrase he had heard Kalvan use once. *Ah, yes…the show must go on.*

## IV

Prince Mythros of Pytha shifted through the parchments of the day. First there was a request for access to grazing lands for a sheep herder. Next were the repair costs for a bridge that had been washed out during the last rainstorm. Then, an offer on some land to the north, a document requiring his signature for the hanging of a deserter from his army, a request for troops from Great King Niclophon to deal with the raiders who had destroyed two Styphoni temples in Artigos and the usual demand of tribute from Styphon's House.

Mythros crumbled the last two parchments and tossed them into the fireplace. With the fireseed secret out there was no need to pay the Styphoni a bent phennig. While Mythros cared little about the war in the north, he could at least be thankful for the so-called Daemon Kalvan for revealing the fireseed mystery, and proving Styphon's House to be a complete fraud. If bandits wanted to sack and raze a few of the local Styphoni temples, good for them. Thankfully, they had stayed out of Pytha and left his own subjects alone.

Prince Mythros fancied himself a prince who cared about his people. He levied the lowest taxes on his subjects in the entire kingdom. He also protected them as much as he was able against the Ruthani, Caribi, bandits and, most importantly, Great King Niclophon's excesses. Nobody in his realm was pressed into service without a damned good reason. That included fighting foreign wars for Styphon's House.

Of course, Great King Niclophon, who was deep into Temple's pockets, would make his usual objections and Mythros would ignore them. It would look bad for the Niclophon to open hostilities with his brother-in-law. Besides, Mythros had a good-sized army, not counting his feudal levy. While it was true that the Army of Pytha could not defeat the Royal Army, they could cause no end of damage—and maybe even win a few battles. Not even the Great King dared to start a war over something so minor. It would rally most of the other princes against him and tear the kingdom apart.

Mythros signed off on the execution order, approved the grazing rights, authorized the bridge funds then stared at the last document. Who would want to buy supposedly cursed lands?

"Esmeranos," Mythros called out. In seconds, a tall slender man entered the chamber and stood in a close approximation of attention. "What can you tell me about the people who wish to purchase those lands known as Mallegast? Aren't they supposed to be cursed by the Dark Gods?"

"Sire, as I understand it they are a large group of refugees from the wars up north." Chancellor Esmeranos spoke clearly without yelling, though his voice carried well.

*Strangers*, he mulled. Since the Fireseed Wars began, there had been little movement or commerce between the northern and southern kingdoms, other than victuals and supplies for the War against the Usurper. "Who are these people?"

"These are refugees who claim they do not recognize their new great king as their legitimate ruler. They suspect Great King Lysandros of regicide. Yet, they will not take arms against their own countrymen."

Mythros waved Esmeranos to a chair while he pondered this new information. He understood the position these refugees found themselves in. He did not consider Niclophon to be the legitimate king of Hos-Bletha, but at the same time he did not want to start a civil war to remove him.

"Do these...Harphaxi know the reputation of the lands they seek to purchase?"

"They do, sire, and appear to give no credit to local superstitions."

That suggested that these were not mere peasants who saw omens in every gust of wind and flight of birds. Merchants, maybe, or lower nobility; likely a baron who lost his lands in the war and sought greener pastures. They chose an out-of-the-way section of land to avoid being noticed while still giving the reigning prince his due. It would have been easy to settle in Mallegast unnoticed, since it was shunned by locals, and thus avoid paying for the land.

"This will increase my tax base while potentially adding to my military levy," Mythros said aloud. "And they are taking a section of land nobody else will touch. Excellent. Sell them the land for half its normal value, which is more than I could expect to get otherwise. We do not want to risk scaring them off with too high a price. In addition, let us send a small envoy to welcome them to the realm. Send a messenger first since it would be rude not to give them a chance to spruce up the place." Mythros chuckled at his own joke.

"As you wish, sire," Esmeranos said, as he bowed and started backing out. He hesitated at the door. "Should we send a welcoming gift, sire?"

"Hmm. Some livestock, cows, pigs and turkeys. Since they've traveled a long distance to get here, they probably don't have much more than oxen and horses, if that. Some produce and seed as well. My new subjects should be happy in their new home and a full belly goes a long way to keeping people happy."

"Very good, sire," the Chancellor replied, as he again bowed and backed out almost running into a man who was trying to enter. Esmeranos was ready to be short with the man until he saw the other's face. Instead of rebuking the man, he simply nodded and went about his business.

"Uncle Mythros!" said the man in a voice better suited to out-of-doors. "Can we go riding, now? I saw Esmeranos leaving and that always means you are done working for the day."

"Not always, Thames, but often enough."

The prince looked over his nephew; the man was dressed in a manner below his rightful station, although the clothes were clean and in good repair. It was a necessary acknowledgement of his condition. Thames had been born with an umbilical cord wound around his neck, nearly choking the life from him. The midwives managed to save his life but not his faculties. Though in his thirties Thames would never be more than twelve winters in maturity. He tended to climb trees, wrestle with the servants and ruin his clothes almost as quickly as they were given to him. For that reason Mythros ordered that Thames' clothing be designed for sturdiness, not fashion.

The rumor around Hos-Bletha was that Thames was Mythros' bastard by a servant or harlot, depending on the charity of the person spreading the gossip. In truth this was not the case but Mythros did nothing to correct the assumption. Many highborn men took their bastards into their homes under the guise of a distant relative to save face.

Thames was handsome enough; tall, slender, gold of hair and blue of eye. Some of the wagtail serving wenches took an interest in him. More than once, he was caught in a hayloft dallying with a maiden. That, too, did not bother Mythros. Thus far, nothing came of the dalliances, although it would surely come to that eventually.

"It's too muddy for riding, Thames," Mythros said. "Maybe some sword practice?"

Disappointment briefly crossed Thames' face then passed as fast as a cloud momentarily obscuring the sun. "With you, Uncle Mythros?"

Mythros cringed internally. Thames was a competent swordsman, thanks to the tutors that he hired. Unfortunately, he tended to be a bit carried away. "Certainly. Let me put on my back-and-breast. You should put yours on as well. We must not risk any accidents, after all. Moreover, get Arthlos. He might want to play as well."

"Oh, yes, yes."

Thames ran out of the room to fetch his armor and Arthlos while Mythros let out a sigh of relief. It would not do to risk his life, let alone the boy's.

# TWENTY-NINE

## I

Democriphon listened intently as Captain Ranthar finished his report. The purchase of the land known as Mallegast had gone smoothly enough, but now they were expecting company, possibly even a company of the prince's guard.

"So they sold us the land for a ridiculously low price, threw in some livestock and seed, and now they are sending an envoy. Who do they think we are?"

Ranthar worked to keep his face straight. "I got the impression that the Chancellor thought we were exiles from a minor Harphaxi house. A displaced barony, perhaps. Prince Mythros, or rather his representative, seemed very pleased to unload this piece of land. The curse, no doubt."

"No doubt," Democriphon said with a small smile. "Should we present ourselves as a barony?"

"It depends on whether or not the Prince will be able to find out whether or not we are legitimate title holders," Ranthar said. He ran through his implanted memories on the Five Kingdoms, but couldn't find anything helpful. Hypno-mech conditioning was only as good as the available information. *Mental note: acquire information on nobility recognition between kingdoms.*

Democriphon said, "I was never a part of the noble class so I have no idea how they track each other. I purchased my estate with the booty I won as a mercenary captain. Still, the war has shaken things up quite a bit in the last few years. Baronies in Hos-Harphax have been awarded and stripped almost daily. Princes have also come, gone, and been replaced over and over. I suspect we could easily pass as new barons, but that might put our reasons for leaving Hos-Harphax into question."

"Oh, how so?" Ranthar asked.

"If we were new barons, we would have had to swear fealty to the new great king who bestowed the title," Democriphon explained. "In this case Great King Lysandros. The same goes if the title were awarded by a prince who was sworn to the new king. Since our cover story is that we left Hos-Harphax because we do not believe in Lysandros' legitimacy as Great King, that ruse will not work. If one of us was from an older noble line, and it turns out there's some sort of listing of all the nobility in the six kingdoms, then we would be quickly outed."

"Let's ask Uncle Wolf Syros about this," Ranthar suggested. "Surely he would know."

"An excellent idea."

The two men looked around the new village. Men were busy sawing boards and hammering nails. Several makeshift huts were already up. Ranthar spotted the wolf-pelt hood, then walked toward Uncle Wolf Syros who was under a lean-to. Syros was busy tending to the freemen's injuries, mostly old welts and scars on their backs.

Ranthar noticed that many of the freemen had put on some weight since being liberated.

"The scars will never completely vanish, Tomos, but they may fade a bit over time," the Uncle Wolf told the man whose back he was rubbing salve on. "Keep a tunic on when the sun is out to avoid burning. The scars won't tan like normal skin and can burn and blister badly." Noticing the newcomers, he nodded in their direction. "Take this salve and share it with the others. Rub it on once a day in the morning and do not overdo it. I don't have as much on hand as I would like."

Tomos thanked the Uncle Wolf and bowed to Democriphon and Ranthar before moving off with the other freemen.

"Now, My Prince, how may I serve thee?" Syros said after bowing low.

"You can stop bowing like that for one thing," Democriphon said. "It looks like you are mocking me."

"Heh. Maybe a little, but I think you have earned some respect by helping these poor people." Syros looked out over the former slaves. Many of the new freemen were working at felling trees, milling the lumber and building houses. Others were building furniture or skinning deer. There were a surprising number of artisans among them. "They are an industrious lot and often have to be reminded to stop working long enough to eat or sleep."

"I doubt they were given such opportunities while under the whip of their former masters," Democriphon said. "We'll have to get them on some sort of schedule to slow them down. Working themselves to death is not what I intended when we freed them."

Ranthar cut in, "Uncle Wolf, do you know if there is any kind of list of nobility that would be circulated between the kingdoms?"

"A what?" Syros thought for a moment. "Well, all of the Great Kings know of each other, of course, and their ambassadors, and the princes would typically be known far and wide, but a peer other than a duke—no. Each great king keeps a List of Peers for his kingdom, but they usually stay with his person. There's little movement of lords from one kingdom to another. Border squabbles are common enough, much like the one between Hostigos and Nostor before the wars. Mostly, anyone below the rank of duke is ignored outside of their own kingdom. Why?"

Democriphon looked about to ascertain if anyone was within hearing range. "Prince Mythros is sending an envoy to officially welcome us to his realm. We were considering using a displaced barony story to explain our presence here."

Syros shook his head. "Bad idea."

"Why is that?" Ranthar asked.

"A baron swears fealty to his prince just as the prince swears fealty to his king," Syros explained. Ranthar thought he sounded like a professor giving a lecture back at Dhergabar University. "Now, if you are a baron who fled from Hos-Harphax rather than maintaining his oath of allegiance to his prince and great king, then you are an oath-breaker and will be viewed with distrust. However, even if that is overlooked, you will be expected to give a new oath of fealty to Prince Mythros, which you will have to violate in the furtherance of the your mission. Are you prepared to become an oath-breaker, Prince Valthros?"

Democriphon looked as if he had just swallowed a crabapple whole. "No, no. Of course not. What do you suggest, Uncle Wolf?"

"You might say that you were a group of traveling Harphaxi merchants who were in Agrys City when the Daemon Kalvan arrived and all the devils in Regwarn broke loose. You were lawful guildsmen in Harphax City; however, upon returning home you learned that Great King Kaiphranos died under mysterious circumstances which you believe were instigated by his Brother, Lysandros. Rather than support a usurper you decided to leave the kingdom and eventually ended up here, because you're afraid the Fireseed Wars will soon spread north. Since you believe that if the Usurper Kalvan is successful, he will attack the Holy City of Balph, you decided not to settle in Hos-Ktemnos. I would look among the freemen for somebody experienced in trading goods and set him up as your master trader."

Democriphon nodded enthusiastically. "I have no doubt that some of these men may have been merchants or apprentices to such. Gasphros would be an ideal candidate."

Ranthar smiled. "Since merchants are not required to give oaths of fealty, we will not have to take any pledges that we may have to foreswear."

"How long do we have until the prince's envoy comes out for a visit?" Democriphon asked.

"Two moons, maybe longer," Uncle Wolf Syros said. "Things move slowly this far from Pytha Town. We can do quite a lot in that amount of time, provided we are not molested."

"Molested?" Democriphon and Ranthar spoke as one.

"There are real bandits out there, you know," Syros pointed out. "As well as Caribi, Ruthani, mercenary deserters, Styphon's House press gangs…"

"We take your meaning, Uncle Wolf." Democriphon turned and looked over the landscape. "Ranthar, have Petty-Captain Gycules put a work detail together and start work on a wall around the village. We will have to do some logging for the material. We'll need towers, a palisade and a walkway inside the wall for the guards."

"We'll have to pull men away from the housing efforts."

"I know, Ranthar, but the people will sleep better knowing they are safe. Later, when we have time, we can replace the wooden walls with stone."

Since there was little stone available locally, Ranthar thought, that meant that it would have to be imported. It appeared as though Democriphon was thinking of the village as something permanent, not just a staging ground. Was he starting to lose sight of the expedition's goal? They weren't there to make him Great King of Hos-Bletha, but to take Bletha out of the war against Hos-Hostigos.

## II

Back at the original encampment which they were now calling Camp One, Duke Skranga gathered all the remaining principals around the campfire. "While the Prince and Captain Ranthar are off establishing our new home base, we have our own work to do. I think it's time we broadened our attacks, hit some of the local barons and lords as well as the usual temples. We have to increase both the tempo and severity of our attacks if we're going to force Great King Niclophon to pull his troops out of what they are now calling the Grand Host of Styphon's House.

"Our next target is the Styphon's House temple in Labros Town. For this operation, I'd like to pair Calthros and Captain Myklon. Calthros for his knowledge of Styphon's temples and procedures. Myklon will command a company of our false Styphon's Own Guard."

"Your Worship, how do we know that this temple is worth pillaging?"

"Gasphros informed me that it is one of the wealthier towns in the Princedom of Taurnos. The townsfolk of Labros are esteemed for their weaving and spinning of wool and cotton. There's lots of cotton in Hos-Bletha and lots of gold to be made in manufacturing clothes."

"How far is the village from here, Your Worship?"

"Over two hundred marches," he replied. "You should be there in a moon-quarter. If at all possible, bring back the temple's slaves as well as the usual loot."

"It will be done," Calthros said.

"Now for some good news," Skranga reported, as he used his sword to stir the campfire embers with a flourish, releasing a scintillating cloud of sparks. "Gasphros' latest report says that Archpriest Prythames left Bletha Town over a moon ago as if he had a nest of wasps under his robe! He's gone to Balph to request additional troops to stop the despoiling of Styphon's Temples. If he screams loud enough, maybe the Inner Circle will think twice about requisitioning troops from Hos-Bletha."

His audience applauded heartily with a chorus of "Down Styphon! Down Styphon! Down Styphon!"

## III

The shavings of freshly whittled wood began to accumulate into something more than a molehill next to the stump. Sitting on the stump was Gycules. He blew on the piece of wood he was shaping then examined it closely. Satisfied, he nodded then picked up his smoothing stone. As he rubbed the stone on his craftwork, a small shadow obscured the sun.

"Making another weapon?"

Gycules glanced up then back to his work. "Hail, Tylla. How are you faring here?"

"I have been well treated since I arrived," Tylla said. "I have been given work to do, food to eat, wine to drink and a place to sleep. I would say most of my needs have been well met since you brought me here."

The giant paused in his work and looked up into Tylla's green eyes. "You are not a captive here, Tylla. You are free to leave if you so desire."

"Ha! To where? Back to the uncle who sold me to Styphon's House as a slave? I think not."

Gycules brow furrowed in ire and confusion. "I thought only criminals were enslaved here in Hos-Bletha. Oh, were you brought in by slave train?"

"Nay, I am native to this land," Tylla admitted. "But do you think Styphon's House cares a whit about the laws of this land?"

"Less than I do, I will warrant." Gycules turned his gaze back to his artifice. "Would you have any string with you?"

"String? Not unless I pull it from my hem."

The giant laughed. "I do not think that will be necessary. Some horse hair will do, if you would not mind plucking a few from one of their tails."

"Um…okay." Tylla walked to the corral as Gycules watched her go. It was pleasant to watch her move away like that. Even more so when she returned moments later. "Will these do?"

"Yes, very nicely. My thanks." Gycules threaded the hair through a hole in a small wooden ball and tied it on, then attached the other end to the cup-on-a-stick he had been making. When completed he held it up for Tylla to see.

"What in Regwarn is that?" She said. "It looks like no weapon I have ever seen. How does it work?"

The giant smiled. "Like this."

Holding the stick close to the bottom, Gycules started the ball moving back and forth on the horse hair string. After a moment he swung the ball up and deftly caught it in the cup.

"What? What will that do?"

"Watch." Gycules turned his head in the direction of some children who were sword fighting with sticks. "Timmos, Balaphon, Kendar… come over here." The three boys quickly obeyed; nobody argued with the giant! "Watch this." He repeated his demonstration with the cup-on-a-stick, then handed it to Kendar. "Now you try it."

After several attempts, Kendar succeeded in catching the ball in the cup. He then handed it to Timmos.

"You three practice with that for a while, and if you like it, I will make more."

The boys readily agreed. "Thank you, Petty-Captain Gycules."

Realization finally dawned on Tylla. "It is a toy! But why waste time with such things?"

Gycules picked up the sticks where the trio had dropped them. "These wasters are simple wooden training swords, but they could still do a lot of damage. They can wait a time before learning their use. For now, let them be children who play with childish things."

Tylla looked at the giant with some surprise. "I would have thought you were born with a sword in your hand."

"Ha! A hammer would be more accurate. I apprenticed to my father in his smithy as a child. At nine winters I was already as large as a man full grown, so my father treated me like one."

Tylla's eyes teared a little, so she turned away. "What were your parents like?"

"Hmm? Oh, well, my father was as tall as I am now, and strong enough to lift his anvil off the ground. He was a hard man, but he took time to teach me well and never laid a hand on me that I did not first deserve. He taught me his trade, how to hunt, fish, and even bare knuckle-box and wrestle.

"My mother was also tall; nearly two rods high. She taught me runes and how to dress my kills for cooking. Her father was a woodworker, which is where I learned to make these toys. They are good people and I miss them."

"Are they still alive?"

"When last I saw them. When my work here is done I will return to Drathor to see how they have fared in my absence. What of your family?"

"I…have only my uncle. My father and mother were killed in one of the great storms that come through this land. Uncle was kind at first, but when I reached my majority, he changed towards me. One night, while in his cups, he…tried to take liberties with me."

"What!" Gycules came to his feet without realizing it. "What did you…that is…"

"I hit him alongside his head with the wine jug. When he awoke the next day, he caught me, tied me up and took me to the nearest Styphoni temple. He sold me for three ounces of gold."

Gycules found himself at a loss for words. He had never heard of such a betrayal before. Finally, he said, "he was underpaid."

Tylla laughed at the statement. "That fat priest you killed might disagree." She sobered then said, "I wish I had had three gold coins to throw in his fat dead face. Thank you for that, if I forgot to mention it before."

"Believe me, it was my pleasure." Gycules sniffed the air and detected the aroma of roast venison. "Have you eaten? I feel as though I have not supped in days."

"After the shameful way you gorged yourself at breakfast?" Tylla feigned shock. "I could feed a village on the scraps that fall from your plate."

"Well, this village," Gycules slapped his midriff, "is in need of some of those scraps. Would you care to join me?"

"Only if I fill my plate first. I fear there would be nothing left after you have a go at the stewpot."

# THIRTY

Archpriest Anaxthenes was poring over the scroll containing the last quarter tithing report from Hos-Zygros. He felt the beginning of a bad headache and this one was not due to poor lighting or the tiny crabbed writing. Temple tithes were down by a third in Hos-Zygros. *It appears the Usurper Kalvan's ideas have spread through that kingdom like the pox,* he decided. The accompanying letter from Archpriest Idyol reported that several of the Zygrosi princes had joined the cursed League of Dralm, a situation that would be dealt with decisively as soon as the Grand Host of Styphon defeated the Usurper Kalvan and removed him and his spawn from the Five Kingdoms.

Since the Daemon Kalvan had first appeared, problems had sprung up like leaks on a derelict galley. Anaxthenes knew that not all of them could be laid at the Usurpers' feet. *The Temple has grown too complacent over the decades,* he concluded. *Our past success has blinded us to our weaknesses. Our allies are weak men, for the most part, a policy we have encouraged by our loans and gifts.*

He broke out of his musings when he heard a knock at the door of his private chamber. "Who is it?" he said, not bothering to conceal the irritation he felt at being disturbed.

"It's me, Your Eminence," Yagos said. "You have a visitor, Archpriest Prythames from Hos-Bletha. He says it's urgent that he speak with you."

"Come in."

Archpriest Prythames came through the door as if a brace of fireseed devils were nipping at his boots. "What's with the archpriests at the Golden Temple?" he demanded. "They're a cluster of canker-blossoms who'd rather spout spurious platitudes than make a decision."

Anaxthenes had to choke back a laugh. That was as good a description as he had heard of those witlings in some time. "In your anger, have you completely lost all civility, or forgotten who you are speaking to?"

Prythames drew back as if slapped. "Please excuse me, Your Eminence. I have just made a trip of over six hundred marches only to be met by a wall of complete indifference to my plight."

He was familiar with Prythames, the top Highpriest of Hos-Bletha, who was one of his allies and usually quite level-headed. Something or someone must have opened a bagful of devils in Hos-Bletha for him to be so rancorous. "What's the problem, Prythames? I'm all ears."

"Three of Styphon's temples have been desecrated and despoiled. And who knows how many more since I've been on the road—"

The word "despoil" caught his attention. "What do you mean: 'despoiled?'"

The Archpriest took in a deep breath before answering. "I mean that our temples were sacked, the guards and priests were slain and their corpses dumped into the streams to be devoured by river dragons..."

*River dragons?* It took Anaxthenes a few moments to remember what "river dragons" looked like. They were almost extinct in Hos-Ktemnos. The river dragons were huge lizards that lived in streams and rivers, assaulting the unwary. Some of them were more than twice the length of a man, with gapping jaws filled with sharp teeth. Not a pleasant ending… even for a corpse.

"…furthermore, the raiders stripped the temples of all silver, gold, hangings and tapestries, even food and kitchen utensils. And, the final insult; they pry off the gold from the temple roofs, just as the Hostigi do."

"Is there any reason to believe that these despoilers are Hostigi?" Anaxthenes asked, his heart beating like a drum. *If the Hostigi have infiltrated Hos-Bletha, they could be anywhere and everywhere.*

"No, Your Eminence. It would be almost impossible for a large force of Hostigi to infiltrate into Hos-Bletha; at least, not without our knowledge. These bandits are highly organized and have enough soldiers to defeat several squads of Styphon's Own Guard. I believe they are backed by one of the Blethan princes, but—if so—I have no idea as to which one. Their first attack was on a gold convoy headed to Balph with contributions and soldiers from Great King Niclophon for the Grand Host of Styphon's House."

Anaxthenes frowned. *If Niclophon is behind these raids, he wouldn't be the first ruler who'd tried to bypass his obligations to the Temple by robbing it. If so, he will suffer grievously.* "Is it possible that Great King Niclophon is secretly organizing these raids? He is in debt to Styphon's House to the sum of half a million ounces of gold. Maybe he has decided to pay us back with our own funds."

Prythames shook his head in the negative. "He might be tempted, but Niclophon is no soldier prince, nor would he sacrifice a company or two of his Royal soldiers just to gain a wagonload of gold."

*He's right.* Niclophon was a fop and a wastrel, spending most of his gold on redecorating his palace, a phalanx of pretty palace guards and an army of relations, spendthrifts all of them. "Then who do you suspect? You know the Hos-Blethan princes better than anyone here in Balph."

"Prince Xandros of Zenophon is an effete snob whose greatest interest is collecting snuff boxes and huge river dragons. He has a large pond full of them and he feeds them criminals and injured slaves. While he would love to fill his coffers with Styphon's gold, the raids are too well-executed to have been his work. Prince Basilron is an idiot and a whoremonger; he's also a bootlicker who ceaselessly tries to win Niclophon's favor, mostly by sending him his favorite concubines! If Basilron is behind these raids then we truly live at The End of Times."

They both snickered.

"So we can cross those two off our list of possible authors of these raids. What about the other princes?" he asked.

"Prince Carthames of Drathor is a worrier and an inept ruler. He's Great King Niclophon's greatest supporter because Niclophon's been great king since before the Prince put on his chain of office. Carthames lacks the imagination and gall to mount these raids. Prince Kosklos of Artigos is honor-bound to do the right thing. He would view these raids as an abomination against the established order. I don't think he likes or respects Niclophon, but he will support him to the death because he is his sworn vassal."

"Does he support the Temple?" Anaxthenes asked.

"No. Kosklos refuses to tear down the temples of the false gods and allows his subject to worship whichever god they wish—or none at all!"

"Blasphemous!" Anaxthenes cried. If all rulers felt this way, worshippers would jump away like fleas off a drowning cur.

"I have on numerous occasions tried to convince the Great King to punish him for his actions, but Niclophon has great respect for Prince Kosklos and will not move against him."

"Have you threatened him with his outstanding loans?" Anaxthenes asked.

"No, Your Eminence. That would be like using a sledgehammer to pound a nail. We need to keep that in reserve."

Anaxthenes nodded. "A well-calculated response. Once the Daemon Kalvan has been defeated, we can deal with these issues at our leisure."

"Yes, Your Eminence. Prince Phaedron of Eythros is the elder statesman of the kingdom's princes. His is the southernmost princedom and he is too busy fighting off the swamp Ruthani and the Caribi raids to raid our temples. Plus, he's a strong supporter of the Great King."

"What about the rest?"

Prythames continued, "While Prince Vythron of Taurnos is not a devout worshipper of Styphon, neither does he worship before the idols of the other gods. He is the last one I would suspect of these raids; Vythron suffers from the bleeding disease and despite this curse he is a man of honor. His greatest fault is that he often trains in the use of arms. He's quite open about his disdain of Niclophon; he finds the Great King effete and unmanly. However, if he were to rebel he would do so openly and proudly."

Anaxthenes shook his head in disbelief. *Such men would not survive long in Hos-Ktemnos where ambition was lodged in every heart.* "Isn't there one more prince?"

"Prince Mythros of the Princedom of Pytha is the most respected of the kingdom's princes," Prythames said. "Like Prince Kosklos, he is another prince who permits the worship of false gods. It is rumored that he is an ardent believer of the false-god Dralm, but he is too honorable to be behind these raids."

"Honorable!" Anaxthenes exclaimed. "The Usurper Kalvan is said to be 'honorable' by both friend and foe, and look at how much trouble he's brought down upon our heads."

"True, Your Eminence, Mythros has even gone so far as to outlaw slavery within the borders of Pytha!"

Anaxthenes shook his head in disbelief.

"However, I do not believe that Mythros is behind this attacks; he's just not in our camp. His honor would not permit him to attack our temples anonymously; he would shout it to the world. No, I do not believe he is behind these raids."

"You know him best," Anaxthenes said. "It is quite apparent that Great King Niclophon holds a very loose rein over his princes. When the false-kingdom of Hos-Hostigos is no more, we should consider his replacement. The important questions is: What is the Great King going to do to stop these raids?"

"Speaker," Prythames said, "Great King Niclophon told me that he would put out patrols and search parties to find the blackguards behind these desecrations. I believe the defeat of his own soldiers at their hands has been an embarrassment to him and to the Silver Throne. Still, these raiders move like quicksilver and will not be easily apprehended."

"Understood," Anaxthenes said. "During less unsettled times, I could send you a dozen Bands of Styphon's Own Guard to harrow these miscreants right down into their very burrow. However, due to the unsteadiness of our Harphaxi and Agrysi allies, the Guardsmen are needed to steady the troops until the fall of Hostigos. Therefore, I urge you to return to Bletha Town and continue pressing Niclophon to his greatest effort, so that he catches them without our aid."

"Yes, Your Eminence. This will not be easy. The Great King is easily distracted. Nor does he always follow through with actions, even when his intentions match our own. I was hoping that you might talk with Grand Master Soton and have him reconsider using the Blethan contingent for the war against the Usurper."

"I will speak to him. But, Soton does not dance to my tune. That is all I can offer at this time."

# THIRTY-ONE

## I

The town of Labros, normally a sleepy hamlet, became alive with the sound of men treading through the cobblestone streets. Children ignored their chores in favor of watching the company of Styphon's Own Guard march by. The Grand-Captain, who sat tall in his saddle, caught the eye of many of the young women, and occasionally nodded in the direction of a particularly comely maiden.

People whispered back and forth among themselves what it meant; change of the guard, special envoy, visiting dignitary...the small town came alive with speculation. The trading posts, normally not open for business so early, threw open their doors in the hopes of Styphoni gold coming their way. Even the brothels, which did not welcome guests until the late evening, placed their wares on display.

The company of Styphon's Own Guard did not slow or stop on their way through the village until they approached the gates of the town's Styphon's House temple. There, a lowly priest in black robes who had traveled unnoticed next to the Styphoni captain, dismounted and approached the gates.

"I am Calthros, first assistant to His Worship Sangar, many blessings upon his name, here to make ready the temple in Labros for His Worship's forthcoming inspection. Make ready to receive his envoy."

The gate guards stared mutely for a moment before whispering between themselves. After a heated discussion, one ran off into the temple.

"We must consult the Temple Master before opening the gates," the remaining guard said.

"In these dangerous times all due care must be taken," Calthros said. Then added with a smile, "We could be bandits in disguise for all you know."

## II

Temple Master Scarnos disliked being roused at so early an hour and said so, but the guard from the gate was insistent. "What in Styphon's pizzle are these idiots doing here so soon? The new detachment is not due for another—"

"This is an envoy from some worthy who calls himself Highpriest Sangar, Your Worship."

"Sangar?" Highpriest Scarnos searched his memory in vain for some mention of a Sangar back in Balph. With so many archpriests, high priests and underpriests it was impossible to keep track of them all. "How many of them are there?"

"Several squads of Styphon's Own Guard, Your Worship, plus the usual retinue."

Several squads for a simple envoy? That could only mean Sangar was *very* important. "Do not just stand there; let them in!"

The guard nodded, bowed, then hurried off. Scarnos quickly rose and threw on his best robe. Normally, he let things run themselves in a relaxed manner. An out-of-the-way town in a small realm like Taurnos did not receive much attention from the Inner Circle, so he was content to let things go. His only real concern was appearances; the temple had to be well-maintained, the grounds kept clean and the slaves productive.

Tithes, such as they were, went straight into the personal treasure chest he kept at the foot of his goose down stuffed bed.

The small detachment of Styphon's Own Guard, dregs one and all, were happy to go along with the way Scarnos ran the temple, not that they could do anything about it if they objected. The best guardsmen marched with the Grand Host under High Marshal Xenophon. Those delegated to Hos-Bletha, while well trained, were drunks, cowards or other undesirables.

Temple Master Scarnos ran down to the narthex of the temple to await his new guests. Only a black-robed priest, with a yellow band around the hem of his robe, and a guard captain entered the temple. Scarnos sized them up with a glance. The upperpriest had the look of a competent underling with the potential to rise in the hierarchy of Styphon's House. His scalp and face were cleanly shaven even after his long journey. Also, his robes were spotless and his bearing was ramrod straight. *Yes, this is a priest destined to go far.*

The guard captain was also a man to be reckoned with. Tall, straight, well built with piercing blue eyes and clean shaven face. His armor fairly gleamed! Here was someone who took his position and duties very seriously. *If only my own men were so inclined…* Word would have to be passed around the temple for everyone to be on their best behavior.

"Welcome, Calthros and…?"

"Grand-Captain Myklon, Your Worship. Commander of His Worship Sangar's personal detachment."

"Welcome. Grand-Captain Myklon. As I was not expecting you, it will take a few candles to prepare proper accommodations, but I think you will find your stay here a comfortable one."

"We require little, Your Worship," Myklon said stiffly. "We need only stay a short time. His Worship Sangar will shortly be making his own inspection tour throughout Hos-Bletha. My purpose is to give you the opportunity to place your house in order before he arrives."

Scarnos took Myklon's statement as an advisory to have certain entertainments ready. Few of Styphon's highpriests lived up to the public's perception of them. No matter, the brothels were full of comely wenches skilled in the arts of entertainment.

"Very good, Grand-Captain. If you will follow me…"

He led the way down a hall to the area designated as a barracks/dormitory. Within were pallets enough to sleep over a hundred men. Sixty appeared to have been in use very recently. "I will have the temple detachment make room for your men here, Captain. I can also have a cell cleared for you. Calthros can share a cell with one of my underpriests. I hope this will be satisfactory."

Captain Myklon ignored the question. "Where is this temple's detachment of Guardsmen?"

Scarnos was taken aback by both the question and Myklon's abrupt manner. As the temple master, he was accustomed to asking the questions, not answering. Moreover, he suspected Captain Myklon would not like his answer.

"Those not actively performing their duties are at liberty in the village," Scarnos said. "I allow such freedoms once a week to keep morale high. News from the north has not been good, after all."

Myklon nodded.

Scarnos could not be certain, but he thought he saw a brief smile flash across the captain's face. "They normally frequent the Red River Dragon tavern. I could send someone…"

"No need for that. Every fighting man needs an occasional indulgence." Myklon turned to underpriest Calthros. "I think our own men are due for some sport. Perhaps we could send half of them into the town today, and the rest tomorrow. I am certain they will have some pent-up aggressions in need of release, if you take my meaning."

Calthros nodded solemnly once, then trotted off. Scarnos watched the black robed upperpriest scamper away with wonder. *Why can't I get my own underlings to react so quickly to my orders?* Myklon went up a notch in the Temple Master's estimation.

## III

"You understand what you are to do?" Calthros asked.

"Yes," Petty-Captain Skerros replied. "No problem. "Do we have to pay for the drinks?"

Calthros nodded.

Skerros hefted his small purse. "I mean, I do not mind standing a round of drinks for fellow soldiers, but Styphon's Own Guard?"

Calthros, who not so long ago had been a real Styphoni priest, did not take insult. Instead, he tossed his own purse to Skerros and said, "Here. The first couple of rounds are on me. I expect the Styphoni to return the favor."

The men chuckled at Calthros' wit. "I think we can arrange that."

Calthros watched as half of the company broke away to find the drinking houses. There was no shortage of volunteers. However, Myklon's instructions were clear: only half the company could be relieved for the evening. Not that the rest would be idle.

"You…you…you guyz 're great…Sk'ros, ol' buddy."

Every man dressed in the armor of Styphon's Own Guard seconded that statement with much yelling and more than a little sloshing of winter wine. The Red River Dragon Inn was easily the largest drinking establishment in Labros Town. It was still early for the civilian regulars, so the guardsmen had the inn to themselves, which was fortunate as not one more person could possibly fit within its walls. One hundred twenty men, plus those who worked the drinking house, filled the inn beyond the normal capacity.

Unnoticed by the harried tavern wenches and even Styphon's Own Guard, each time a Styphoni soldier stepped out to the back alley to relieve himself, he failed to return. This continued until the early hours when even the greed of the innkeeper fell prey to exhaustion and he ordered the hall closed. Amid a great deal of grumbled complaints and drunken curses, the Styphoni, real and not, filed out into the street and set their sights on the temple. Thirty paces later one of them noticed something was awry.

"'Ey, Sk'ros…you see…my mates?" The one called Drunog asked of Skerros.

"Oh, certainly. We can take you to them if you wish."

"Yeah…dat would…be nize. Can' have 'em…stay out awl night. Temple Masser would…have 'em flogged." To emphasize the statement, Drunog let out a long belch. His remaining friends laughed loudly. "Lead away."

Skerros and the rest of his group escorted Drunog and his twenty-odd friends out of town. It took the inebriated Styphoni almost two candles to realize that they had left the confines of Labros.

"Whazz 'is?" Drunog demanded. "Whaz goin' on here?"

"Ah, therein lies the story," Skerros said somberly. "Several moons ago Great King Kalvan developed a plan to keep Hos-Bletha from aiding Styphon's House in the great war in the north. To do this, he sent many men under the leadership of a brave commander down into this hot, humid, barbarous land to stir up trouble so that Niclophon, the local king of some ill-repute, would have to keep his focus on things closer to home."

"Huh? Whazzat gotsta do wit' us?"

"I am coming to that, Drunog. I, and my fellows here, are part of the detachment that Great King Kalvan sent down here. Democriphon, that is the commander I told you about, decided that the best way to keep the Blethans from joining the war was to raid temples and kill Styphoni. That is where you come in. We are the raiders, you are the Styphoni…oh, and all these bodies in the trench…"

Skerros pointed down and Drunog's eyes followed. In the privy trench lay forty naked bodies. "…are also some Styphoni priests. Your mates, in fact. Now, we didn't want to make a big fuss, so we just bought all of you enough wine to make your sword arms weak and your minds dull. And now we come to the end of this night's revelries."

Skerros grinned as sixty sober Hostigi fell upon the last twenty Styphoni. It was over in moments. Afterwards, they stripped the bodies and heaved them into the trench.

Skerros said, "Good. Let us cover this filth over with dirt so that it will not be discovered for a while. Oh, how did we do with their purses?"

"About forty gold crowns and one hundred and sixty silvers," a trooper said. "Plus rings and other jewelry."

Skerros let out a low whistle. "Very good! I did not think Styphon's Own Guard was paid that well. Half the gold is Calthros'…now, now, he did pay for most of the drinks…the silver we divide among ourselves, and the baubles go to Captain Myklon to add to our treasury. Agreed?"

Everybody nodded.

"Good. Now hurry with the dirt and let us be away from here."

## IV

It had not been easy to sleep within the keep of the enemy. Grand-Captain Myklon knew he needed to be fresh in mind and body for the tasks to come; still, to sleep in a temple to Styphon, even with Calthros remaining awake and on watch, was difficult.

Calthros was instructed to wake him when the men returned from town, hopefully with a report of their success. Myklon was already awake and putting on his breast plate when the former priest of Styphon's House gently tapped on his door.

"You may enter," Myklon said.

Calthros walked in and saw Myklon was ready. "The men have returned, Captain."

"Sober?"

"Very. Petty-Captain Skerros handed me this to give to you." Calthros held out a bag.

Myklon inspected the contents: gold coins and men's jewelry. "No silver? Skerros must have divided that up with the rest. He was wise not to parse out the jewels; they might be noticed." Myklon stuffed the bag into his knapsack. "What of the temple guards that remained?"

"All dealt with and accounted for," Calthros said. "Our men now hold those positions."

"The bodies?"

"Stripped and dumped into a privy trench."

*A fitting end for Styphon's manure eaters*, Myklon thought. "Good. Now we finish up with the priests."

"What of the slaves?"

"Hmm...We can kill them, free them, or take them with us. I have no stomach for slaying men already ill-used by our enemy, and we cannot allow them to run free where they might be recaptured and forced to talk. They will have to go with us." Myklon wondered what Ranthar and Andros were doing with the slaves they found. Likely the same, he decided. "If any men still sleep, rouse them."

"Already done. They did not sleep any better than you, I think."

"Just as well. Have Petty-Captain Skerros and his men stand ready, just in case. It is time for the others to do their part."

# THIRTY-TWO

## I

Trooper Tranor complained all the way to the priests' sleeping cells; though silently. He did not care about losing sleep as that was a mercenary's lot, nor did he object to killing Styphoni, something he would normally do for free. It was the way he was expected to kill the priests. It seemed dishonorable; on the other hand, they were a bad lot and the Great King's enemy.

Tranor and his partner, Nolen, stood before the first cell door. All the way down the hall other teams of two followed his example. Tranor held up a fist. He raised one finger, then a second, then a third, then nodded once. At each door, one man pushed it open while the other rushed in.

Inside the cells lay two sleeping occupants on separate pallets. Tranor rushed to the one on the left while Trooper Nolen addressed the right. Two quick sword thrusts and done. Silently, they returned to the hall and waited for the rest to complete their part. In moments the other teams resumed their positions outside the doors and nodded.

Down another hall came a strangled yell, quickly cut short. Somebody was either sloppy or the priest had been awake and not taken as neatly as the rest. It mattered not. There were few left to hear the cry, and fewer still able to respond.

## II

"This is the temple master's room, Captain," Calthros whispered.

Grand-Captain Myklon placed an ear at the door. There were the sounds of a struggle within. "Did you order somebody else to attend to the temple master?"

"Nay, Captain. I reserved that pleasure for us."

"Then who…?"

Myklon's question was cut short by a shrill scream. He kicked open the door and ran in to find Highpriest Scarnos, completely naked, attacking a similarly unclothed woman. From the whip marks on her body, she was not a tavern wench enhancing her income.

"What is the meaning of this?" Highpriest Scarnos shouted. "You have no right to push your way into my private chambers. Sangar will hear of this!"

Myklon turned to Calthros. "I know I promised you this one, but I am sorely tempted."

"I understand, Captain. However, this one's mine." Calthros drew his knife and approached the temple master and slave girl. He threw a vicious punch into the priest's ponderous belly, doubling him over, then handed the blade to the woman. She looked at it without comprehension. "What would you have done before we walked in, if you had that knife then?"

Realization turned into instant action. The woman launched herself at Scarnos and thrust the blade into his back, and then his flanks, splashing blood everywhere. The priest rolled over, fell back and weakly tried to ward off the blade only to have his arms and hands carved up.

Myklon and Calthros watched dispassionately while the woman did her work. As a final act, before the light in Scarnos eyes left him, she removed the offending member that so recently had been forced upon her. The Captain and former priest both winced at the sight.

Myklon shrugged. "Well, that is that. My lady, if you would come with us…" The woman took a threatening stance and pointed the blade at Myklon. "Ah, madam, we are here as liberators, not molesters."

"My lady, please come with us," Calthros said. "We will take a robe from this butchered pig's wardrobe so you may cover yourself."

The woman did not move other than to shift the knife in Calthros' direction.

"I do not believe she trusts us," Myklon observed.

"Look at how we are attired, Captain."

Myklon had forgotten about their disguises. "My lady, we are not Styphoni. I am Grand-Captain Myklon of Hos-Hostigos. My mission is to, ah…" No point in revealing the whole mission. "…bedevil Styphon's House and seize their treasures for the war in the north."

"Am I to be part of that treasure," the woman demanded.

"While you are a vision of loveliness and would brighten any man's home, we are here only to take you away from this place until you can be set free," Calthros said smoothly. "You will be free to join the community we have created and when our mission has done, we will return you to your homeland."

"I do not believe you. How do I know you are who you say you are?"

Myklon pointed to Scarnos corpse. "Would Styphon's Own Guard have helped you with this?"

The woman wavered for a moment then hardened again. "He may have fallen into disfavor with his masters. For all I know, you are assassins from Balph."

Myklon was growing impatient. "Lady, how can I convince you that we are…?"

"Show me your member!"

"Show you…what?" The woman gestured to Scarnos' bloody groin. "If you are not circumcised, then I will believe you."

Myklon, while no prude, was not in the habit of displaying his personal 'equipment.' His first thought was to have Calthros do the honors, then recalled that he had been a true underpriest in Hos-Harphax before being turned by Duke Skranga. With an annoyed grunt, he undid his back-and-breast, raised his tunic and lowered his breaches. The woman inspected him longer than he thought was needed for the purpose at hand.

"Okay. No Styphoni, even a guardsman, would be allowed to serve unclipped. Especially one of your rank. I believe you." She lowered the knife and returned it to Calthros before ransacking the wardrobe.

"Calthros, you will not speak of this to anyone." Myklon drew his hand across his throat. "Understood?"

Calthros could barely restrain himself from laughing out loud. "Upon my honor, good Captain," he choked out.

## III

The bright morning sun did little to improve Grand-Captain Myklon's mood. Despite the fact that his men, with the help of forty newly freed slaves, managed to strip the temple of every ounce of gold over the course of the night, including the tiles covering the temple dome. However, the embarrassment he felt over being forced to display his privy parts dampened his sense of victory. Nor did it help when he saw the woman again, Gralia her name was, as they prepared to depart; she winked at him with a coquettish grin.

Fortunately, Calthros had kept his word and said nothing of the matter to the others.

Myklon inspected the ox teams and their rigging on the newly confiscated wagons which were filled to bursting with gold, silver, jewels, pieces of art and anything else that had not been too big, too heavy or too well bolted down to take. Satisfied that nothing was amiss, he ordered the gates opened and the teams to start out, caravan style.

Myklon and Calthros took their places at the lead while the former slaves, for the sake of appearance, were chained to the rearmost wagon. Some objected until Calthros handed the shackle keys to Gralia, whom they all knew and trusted. With the oxen setting the pace, they would be blessed even to achieve thirty marches a day all the way back to camp.

During that time, they would change their appearance from that of Styphon's Own Guard to simple merchants.

Something bothered Calthros as he looked ahead. "Look!"

"What is it?" Myklon asked.

"Do you see that dust cloud ahead?" Myklon admitted that he had. "Then you also saw the sparkling lights at the bottom." Myklon admitted that he had not. Calthros sighed. "I think we are in for some trouble."

"What? Why?"

"I have seen that kind of sparkling light before. It comes from highly polished silvered armor. Much like *you* are wearing. Very much like it."

Myklon squinted into the distance and saw what Calthros spoke of. "I'll be Dralm-damned! Is that a Temple Band of Styphon's Own Guard coming at us? A real one. Do you think we can talk our way past them?"

"Coming out of an empty temple with a stripped golden dome? Maybe Duke Skranga could pull it off, but not us." Calthros drew his horse pistol, checked the charge, then hid it in his robes. "What are your orders, sir?"

Myklon called Petty-Captain Skerros forward. "Get the chains off of the slaves and give them some weapons they can hide on their persons. Tell the men to prepare for an engagement with an awake and sober company of Styphon's Own Guard."

Skerros nodded and spun his horse around. Myklon turned back to Calthros. "What are the protocols for two captains meeting each other on the road."

Calthros shrugged. "I know not. I served in a temple, not a military garrison."

Myklon swore. He could not blame Calthros so he blamed himself. He should have planned for something like this. "Well, there is only one thing for it, then."

Myklon turned to see Skerros riding back to the front. "Just in time, Skerros. Tell the men we are going to charge the Styphoni as soon as we can take them by surprise. You will know the signal when it comes. Move!"

"What will the signal be, Captain?" Calthros asked.

"You'll see."

As the two groups came closer, Myklon and Calthros spurred their horses forward. The opposing grand-captain did the same and they met halfway.

"What transpires here?" the Styphoni Grand-Captain asked. "What happened to the gold on the dome of the temple?"

"There was a raid, we think," Myklon replied. "The temple is empty of men and treasure. We investigated and found only bloodstains, livestock and these wagons."

"Indeed? Who would dare?" The Styphoni Captain asked, "A Hostigi raiding team from the north, no—they're snowbound in winter. Why are you taking the wagons and livestock?"

"We are the advance envoy for His Worship Sangar on his inspection tour of the temples of Hos-Bletha," Calthros said. "We cannot stay as we have other temples to visit so there's no point in leaving the livestock to die untended, or be stolen by villagers."

*Quick thinking, Calthros*, Myklon thought, *now if he accepts your story, we can be away without further bloodshed.*

The Styphoni captain seemed to accept the story. "Yes, I see your point. However, since we are the new temple garrison, we can take charge of those wagons…wait. Since when does an underpriest ride with a special envoy? Nothing short of a yellow robe should be representing an envoy from Balph."

The shot that killed the Styphoni Grand-Captain took Myklon completely by surprise. He turned in askance to Calthros who was quickly reloading his horse-pistol.

Calthros shrugged. "He was not accepting our account. Besides, this makes up for the temple master I did not kill."

Before Myklon could respond, his mercenaries charged past screaming and shooting as they went. The captain sighed. "I guess that was the signal. Calthros, you stay back and use that horse pistol whenever you can be sure who you're shooting at."

Myklon spurred his horse forward and drew his sword. It was going to be one of those days.

The battle, while short, was incredibly brutal. Styphon's Own Guard, caught by surprise, still made a good fight of it. The Hostigi charged with their pistols, shooting both the Guardsmen and their mounts. The Guardsmen, who didn't have time to mount a countercharge, took the brunt of the galloping destriers head-on. Many were thrown from their chargers, and trampled underneath falling horses or sharp hooves. Others fought desperately with glaives and swords. When the Hostigi ran out of loaded pistols, they used their sabers and rapiers. Men on both sides hacked at each other like madmen, cleaving armor and limbs alike. The screams of dying horses and wounded men rent the air.

By the end, Myklon had lost half of his command while the Styphoni were wiped out to a man. Unable to fight on the ground with their pole-arms, the Guard were forced to fight on horseback where they were out-classed by the Hostigi, many of whom were former cavalrymen. Skerros, who Myklon had planned to promote to captain, died of his wounds shortly afterwards.

"Damn. Skerros was a good man; quick of wit, treated fairly with his fellows and knew how to follow orders and how to adjust to change. He will be hard to replace and sorely missed." Myklon picked up the body and personally tied it to the top of a wagon. "Throw Styphon's Own Bastards in a pile and douse them with turpentine. I'll not waste more time burying them. Stow Styphon's whoresons' armor in a wagon, if we have the space. Dump it in a swamp if we do not. None of our people will be left behind, be they wounded or dead!"

Myklon turned to the slaves. "You there! Get cleaned up, then find some Styphoni armor that fits. Put it on! Until we clear this area, all of you are Styphon's Own Guard. Understood?" The slaves quickly moved to obey.

Calthros asked about the women. "Put them in armor as well. Just tie their hair back and they will look like young recruits. Just do it quickly. The townsfolk will be out to investigate soon and I want to be far away from here."

By the time the first townsman summoned the courage to see what all the noise had been about, there was nothing to witness save for the blood on the road, a few broken glaives and swords and the still-smoking cremated bodies. He turned around and went back to his home. Later, when others spoke of the disturbance in the early hours of the morning, the man stayed silent. He wanted none to know he had been there.

# THIRTY-THREE

## I

"The time has come," Duke Skranga told his fellow conspirators who had all returned from Mallegast to the original encampment for a council of war, "to step up the Prince in Exile game. It's still too early to tell if our raids on the temples will stop Great King Niclophon from sending his military contribution to the Grand Host, but we have shaken Hos-Bletha to its foundations. A half-moon ago, I sent a courier off to Hostigos, by way of Drathor and Xiphlon, with a report chronicling our activities to Great King Kalvan. Right now the full might of Hos-Hostigos is being deployed to stop the Grand Host of Styphon's House."

Skranga would have liked to have sent Kalvan some gold and jewels from their swelling treasury, but the overland trails were too dangerous and rough for wagons full of gold and silver. A lone courier was much more likely to survive.

He nodded. "Let us all say a silent prayer to our god, be it Dralm, Galzar, Tranth or the Allmother, that they preserve our Great King and Queen and the realm of Hos-Hostigos."

There was a moment of silence. From what Gasphros, who had just returned from Bletha Town, told the Styphoni had gathered the greatest multitude of soldiers in the history of the Five Kingdoms. The latest report—this part of the troubadour's report had been for his ears only, otherwise morale would go belly-up—counted the Grand Host's numbers at over a hundred thousand men. More than twice the size of the combined princely and royal armies of the Kingdom of Hos-Hostigos.

He feared it would take a Dralm-damned miracle to save the Kingdom, and Skranga didn't believe in Dralm or any other gods….

*Regardless*, Skranga decided, *we have our job to do. If we prevail, a little piece of Hostigos will survive, but if we fail Hos-Hostigos and Great King Kalvan will join the other great kings and lost empires of history.*

"We have been surprisingly successful in our takeovers of Styphon's House temples," Skranga said. "I doubt that will continue. Expect the temple masters and their guardsmen to be more aware of our tactics in the future. Also, I think it's time we began making raids on more secular targets. Any ideas?"

Gasphros nodded. "Your Worship, I heard talk in Bletha Town of a big wedding in Syragon. Prince Basilron has no heirs so he is making much of his nephew's wedding. He even invited Great King Niclophon."

"Will the Great King be attending," Skranga asked.

The troubadour shook his head. "Niclophon rarely leaves his palace. And certainly not for a mere baron's wedding."

"Too bad," Skranga said. "We might have been able to waylay him. Still, if we could disrupt the wedding, it will embarrass both Prince Basilron and his Great King."

"That's exactly what I've been looking for. Who should we put in charge?" Democriphon asked.

"Ranthar is going to be busy," Gasphros replied. "I suggest Grand-Captain Myklon. He's proved himself in several temple raids. He's at Mallegast village for now; I'll have a courier sent out after the war council breaks up."

"Good," Skranga said. "Captain Ranthar, are you prepared to increase the 'Robin Hood' attacks?"

"Yes, Your Worship. The blacksmiths and furriers have put together enough of the wolf-helms that we can start the raids. From here on out no merchant, slaver or Styphon's House priest will be safe on the roads of Hos-Bletha."

"Excellent," Skranga declared.

"Meanwhile, I'll go around to the various towns and villages whipping up support for the Orphan Prince and gathering new recruits," Democriphon announced, "And gold, of course."

It was obvious they had spent a lot of time putting this plan together while they were in Mallegast and Skranga had to admit that he greatly liked what he heard so far. "Hmm…I could play the part of an old retainer of the castellan who swears to your authenticity, or some such—"

"Actually, Your Worship," Gasphros interrupted, "We came up with an entirely different plan for you."

*It's that damned Gasphros again. What kind of debacle has he set me up for now?*

Gasphros, ignoring his bent eye, continued, "Your Worship, you already wear the yellow robes of a highpriest and know all the procedural flummery of the Temple. Plus, with Calthros and a company of Styphon's Own Guard, you have the retinue to pass as a traveling highpriest of Styphon. We believe the time has arrived for you to visit Niclophon's palace and announce yourself as Highpriest Sangar, demanding more gold to wage the war against the Usurper."

Skranga could not believe what he was hearing. They had been making plans behind his back; he was sure it was Democriphon and Ranthar who'd cooked this up; Gasphros was just their spokesman. It was one thing to wear the hated colors of Styphon's House while traveling to avoid that same enemy, but to pretend he was one of their number in public, in a royal court, no less…

"I like it," Lady Eldra declared. "Sharping a king in the name of the enemy. I can't think of anything more fun."

*Fun, she says! But it's my head that is going to be on the chopping block.* Then he recalled a rumor that Eldra had tried to seduce King Kalvan. If

Queen Rylla ever caught so much as a whiff of that story, Eldra would do well to escape with so much as a thumb-joint-sized piece of her pretty skin as she was flayed from the tip of her shapely nose right down to her toenails. This Greffan lady was a little too unconcerned about her own good health for his taste.

"I do not share your views on what constitutes fun, Lady Eldra, yet I do see the value of working within Niclophon's keep." Skranga stroked his red beard in thought. "Nay. What if a true highpriest should see me? I would quickly be undone."

"There are thousands of priests in Styphon's House," Democriphon pointed out. "Those from here are unlikely to know everyone else in Hos-Bletha, let alone every highpriest from Balph or any of the other kingdoms."

Skranga gave it more thought and decided it might be worth the risk, especially if he could skim off some of the gold for himself. "Calthros will have to come with me, of course, as well as a sizeable contingent of the soldiers for appearance sake. That won't leave you much to work with, Prince."

"For guerilla actions a small band is best. Besides, with all the slaves that joined us during the fall and winter, we have over a thousand men. Plenty for what we have to do. "I do need more officers, though. Gycules has shown command abilities. He follows orders without question and is physically intimidating enough to make others do the same. He'll make Galzar's Own Captain."

Skranga stifled a chuckle. Democriphon would have to be very careful what orders he gave the big warrior. After what happened with the band of sharpers, it would be unfortunate if they left a trail of headless bodies in their wake. "You have my permission to promote him to captain."

"I hate to bring this up, Your Worship," Calthros added with an uncomfortable shrug, "but a small sacrifice on your part will be necessary."

"Oh?"

"While you were staying in the old encampment, I didn't think it was necessary to shave your beard since we were unlikely to meet any real Styphoni, but since you will be entertaining at court we will need to get you properly groomed so as to avoid discovery. Your beard is rather distinctive and I fear it might be remembered by someone who made your acquaintance in Harphax City. It should be shaved off for your own safety."

Skranga, having dealt with the Styphoni on many occasions, understood. He already had his head shaved in the style of Styphon's priests, although much of it had grown back along the sides. He tugged at his beard thoughtfully. "Hmm. Yes. I hate to do it, but I will have the barber take care of it. My beard will grow back in time…well, most of it anyway."

"There is also the matter of the circumcision—" Gasphros brought up.

Skranga stomped his foot on the ground. "Nay! I will hardly be expected to flaunt my danglies in public."

"Of course not," Calthros said softly, "but if you run into another highpriest at court and he becomes suspicious, checking your privates to see if you're circumcised is a quick way for them to prove you're a fraud."

As an intelligence officer, Skranga knew sacrifices often had to be made, but still…

"And what would Styphon's priests do if I was uncovered as an imposter? Beheading? Auto da fé?"

"If your false identity were revealed, your body would be suspended over burning coals while your intestines were slowly removed from your still living body. I have seen such a thing only once, and the imposter took hours to die." Calthros trembled for a moment at the memory as though he were hearing the man's screams all over again.

Skranga fumed as he considered Calthros' warning. Circumcision would be a painful imposition, and somewhat personally embarrassing; however, the possibility of being found out could be catastrophic: Burning coals. Spilled intestines. Lingering death. He might even be turned over to Roxthar for Investigation. Skranga broke out in a sweat. He remembered the sacrifices some of his own operatives in Harphax City and Balph had made at his request. Never in his wildest dreams had he thought that he would have to make similar sacrifices.

"Do we…is there anybody who can perform the…uh…"

"I am well versed in the procedure, Your Grace," Calthros assured the Duke, "and I know what herbs and salves will speed the healing. I suggest you first drink a great deal of wine before we start. When you are ready, that is. I advise we attend to the matter soon so you will be well-healed by the time we leave for Bletha Town."

"Gods above and below," Gasphros sputtered. "Great King Kalvan should award you a principality for such a sacrifice."

"Agreed," Skranga said testily. "Forget the wine. Bring me some of Ermut's Best. For this, I intend to be completely besotted. Ranthar, I expect you to take charge while I am indisposed. And if anybody else finds out about this I'll put Gycules and his great sword to work!"

## II

The next morning found Duke Skranga—bareheaded and clean-shaven—in a truly foul mood. Unable to walk without significant discomfort in his privy parts, he sat on a pile of pillows stripped from a former sharper's carriage. He was getting plenty of sympathy from the inner council. Unanimously, it was decided to postpone the journey to Bletha Town for a moon-quarter while Skranga was allowed time to heal and plans were made.

At Calthros' suggestion, Skranga exposed his pale cranium to the sun to develop enough of a tan in the newly shorn places that it would look as though he had been completely shaved and bald for many years. He had to be careful not to overdo it in one sitting, though, lest he burn and peel. Skranga was still finding it hard to get used to the sun all year round. *How do people living here know when the seasons change?*

"Prince, you're going to need a tailor," Skranga announced. "When the Orphan Prince, or Prince in Exile—whatever you decide to call yourself—is presented in court he should be dressed for the part. It's a shame we killed the sharper's tailor when we removed the guards."

Democriphon said, "Yes, we can send for one from Port Gytha."

"That could be a security breach," Skranga noted. "Calthros, you know the slaves better than anyone. Were any of them former tailors?"

The former underpriest said, "Yes, Melos was once a tailor for Prince Basilron of Syragon until he was caught attending a secret service for Allfather Dralm. He was whipped, stripped of his home and possessions and sold into slavery."

"Excellent. The men will also have to be well-dressed. Living in the forest has been hard on their clothing and gear; I want them presentable to the public. Plus, we will need green cloaks, hose, knee-breeches, tunics and jackets for our Robbing Hoods."

*To the public?* Then it hit him, they were working on their public face as well as striking back at the wealthy merchants and priests. "We're going to need a lot more clothing than one tailor can provide. He needs to focus his efforts on the prince's wardrobe for now. Chief Vanir, I want you to take a party to Port Gytha and buy additional clothes. Spread the purchases around so as to avoid drawing attention. It probably wouldn't hurt to also visit Dalthax. While I'm ensconced in Bletha Town, we'll need to communicate in case any difficulties arise. I suggest we use Yaholo and some of the other scouts as messengers."

When Democriphon nodded, Skranga turned his attention to the troubadour. "Gasphros, I want you to do some advance work for me. It will be at least another moon-quarter before I'm fit to ride, even by carriage." He twisted in pain.

"Are you all right?" Democriphon asked, wincing.

"Yes… I just have to be careful how I move my legs… But, back to business. Gasphros, I want you to select a few men and visit each village and town on the way to Mallegast. You will play in local inns and grog ships, spreading rumors that Roxthar might be bringing his Investigation into Hos-Bletha. Embellish as you see fit, but keep it plausible. Let's put Roxthar's atrocities to work for us." It was a good use of Gasphros' talents. He was not a fighter anymore and with his bad leg ill-suited for manual labor. "And keep singing that song of yours, "When the Orphan Prince Comes Marching Home."

"I will be happy to, Your Worship," Gasphros replied. "I would like to take a few mercenaries with me."

"As guards?" Skranga asked.

"No, Your Worship. There is something about a real fighting man, especially one who has seen action, people can sense. It will make them more believable as they relay tales about the Investigation in the inns and taverns. Especially, after I coach them a bit. I prefer battle-hardened veterans."

"Done. Select such men as you need after the Prince is done. He needs artisans for the new village; you just need veterans, and we have those in abundance. Calthros and Lady Eldra will accompany me to Bletha Town where we will try to collect intelligence and send it to the village whenever possible. I plan to make as many unreasonable demands on Niclophon in the name of Styphon's House as I can think up, bleeding him of as much treasure as possible. That should thoroughly test his devotion to Styphon's House."

Everybody laughed at that. Then Democriphon came up with something that sobered them all. "What if some genuine Styphoni come calling while you're at court?"

Skranga said, "I don't know if my cover will stand close inspection—"

"Trust me, Your Worship, your cover will pass inspection," Calthros interrupted. "I'm betting my life on it."

"Good," Skranga said, feeling more relieved than he let on. If Calthros felt that strongly, then he didn't have much to worry about. Still, the more highpriests in town, the less influence he would have over Great King Niclophon. "I'd like to keep outside interference to a minimum. Let's try to keep Styphon's House's people out of Bletha Town. Keep scouts on the main roads."

Calthros added, "Archpriest Prythames should be on his way back from Balph."

"That's a good point," Skranga noted. "Prythames is the one man who can finger me as an imposter. He's a member of the Inner Circle and certainly would have been informed if a highpriest had been sent to Hos-Bletha on an investigative mission. It's imperative that we prevent him from reaching Bletha Town."

He turned to Democriphon, "Send out a party to set up an ambush along the Silos Road. Prythames will take that road on his way to Bletha Town. When they run across the Archpriest's party, have them kill him. As for his guards and attendants, wipe them off the face of the Earth—bury the bodies and burn anything we can't use. If a large a force of Styphon's Own Guard comes in, have them send word to me through Yaholo or one of the other scouts."

# THIRTY-FOUR

## I

Grand-Captain Myklon was beginning to feel overwhelmed. Ranthar and Democriphon were at the old camp, now called Camp One, holding council with Duke Skranga. That left Captain Myklon in charge of Mallegast and running the banditry operation. He did not mind overseeing the military end since that was his stock and trade. Civilian matters, on the other hand, were less familiar and more daunting. Myklon found himself looking for an excuse to go out on a raid just to be away from the petty problems which seemed endemic to village life.

"Sir!"

Myklon jumped a little. Gycules' booming voice had that effect when not expected. "Yes, Petty-Captain?"

"Gasphros and party have arrived with news from Duke Skranga, sir."

"Oh? Please, show him in."

Myklon quickly took the seat Democriphon used when he entertained the Prince's entourage. He wanted the bard to understand that he was in charge for the nonce. Gycules escorted the troubadour into the room, then took up a position near the door. Democriphon ran a much more relaxed command than Myklon thought was wise. While he was in charge, he had taken the opportunity to tighten things up.

"Gasphros, welcome. What do you have for us?"

"Duke Skranga sent me with news. There is to be a big wedding in the Princedom of Syragon."

"Indeed? Should we send gifts?"

"The wedding is between Lord Dalthros, nephew to Prince Basilron, and Lady Krysala, a woman of some…repute in that region," he said. "Prince Basilron will be in attendance."

"A prince, a count, an assortment of nobility and all in one place." Myklon thought it over for a second. "And they neglected to invite us? This insult shall not be allowed to stand."

Gasphros smiled. "The Duke rather thought that would be your attitude. The wedding is in less than a moon. Ah, Skranga advises that we not slay the Prince."

Myklon looked scandalized. "Slay a prince? Perish the thought. That is not our mission here. Embarrass him, certainly, but not kill him. I would not want us all hunted for a princely murder! However, a moon is scant time to prepare for such a venture."

"I understand that Duke Skranga is not in good humor. He had to suffer the same fate that all of Styphon's priests do when they are ordained."

Myklon' roared with laughter. "Oh, I wish I could see him now."

"It's not pretty," Gasphros said. "I was glad to escape his ill-humor. After the incision, I made the mistake of telling him that he could leave for Bletha Town immediately if he sat side-saddle!"

They all roared with laughter.

"Everyone at Camp One is on tenterhooks," he added. "You were lucky to be left in charge of Mallegast."

Grand-Captain Myklon nodded. "I had enough of Duke Skranga on the sea journey. I was glad to be left behind for the last council meeting."

"The rest of us weren't so lucky," Gasphros replied. "However, if we're going to get there in time, we're going to have to depart quickly. The wedding will take place in Syragon and it will take more than a moon-half just to get there!"

"We'll all have to go by horseback," Myklon said. "Anything we cannot carry on the saddle packs will just have to be acquired elsewhere. We will make our plans while on the trail."

"Plans! We cannot plan a strike against an area we know nothing about," Gasphros argued.

"Look, you are the expert on Hos-Bletha and its principalities. Fine. A noble of high rank is marrying a more-or-less common lady. Where will the wedding take place?"

Gasphros thought it over. "Syragon Town. If the prince is hosting this wedding, no place else would do. Especially, in Prince Basilron's case. He's not going to travel any distance, even if it is his heir's wedding."

"Good," Myklon nodded. "Now, who would officiate?"

"An archpriest of Styphon's House or the highest ranking priest in Syragon."

Myklon smiled. "See? We know a great deal about what we are heading into. Archpriest Prythames hasn't returned yet from Balph so it will have to be the Highpriest of Syragon Town. Now, about the ceremony…"

## II

The journey from Mallegast to Syragon Town seemed to take forever. Disguised in traveling robes and riding newly purchased mounts, the old ones overworked and recovering in a stable in Bletha Town, Myklon led his band into the outskirts of town as the sun started to set. At the Captain's right was Gycules, hunched over to disguise his great height, while at his left rode Gasphros, still working on the final details of his scheme to disrupt the wedding.

Grand-Captain Myklon would have preferred to leave the giant back in the village, as his great size made him all too easy to spot in a crowd. However, when Gycules found out that the woman Tylla would be necessary to the bard's plans, Myklon knew better than to try to leave Gycules behind.

Accompanying the party was the other woman Gasphros selected. Gralia, the slave he and Calthros rescued, who winked at him every time they crossed paths. Myklon was almost certain that the bard selected her just to annoy him, but that would suggest Calthros relayed certain details of their last mission together.

That evening over the campfire they discussed Gasphros' latest ideas. "We could take out the guards the night before…" Gasphros said.

"And they would be discovered missing in the morn, replaced and security tripled," Myklon countered. "Better to remove them after the changing of the guard. They will be on high alert at first, but after a few candles they'll become bored and less vigilant."

Gasphros thought back to his mercenary days. Mercenaries were rarely counted on for guard details as they were not trusted as well as the local regulars. Often they would sneak wine into their kits, or fall asleep at their post. Occasionally, if things were tight, a few mercenaries would stand guard side by side with a regular, and yes, such guard duty became mind-numbingly dull very quickly. "I concede your point, Captain. However, I think I know how to remove them all the same."

## III

The first to arise in any castle or manor is the wait and cooking staff. Woe betides the kitchen staff that fails to have a breakfast prepared when the master of the house wakes. When a special occasion must be prepared for, more people are brought in to assist the staff.

Gralia, after several years of slavery, was no stranger to hard work and long hours. She and Tylla volunteered to insinuate themselves into the kitchen where they could do their part for Myklon's mission. Tylla, considered too small for heavy lifting, gathered the eggs needed for the feast while Gralia assisted with the cleaning and dressing of the game and fowl.

One of the benefits of working in the kitchen was the free food. Anything not up to the kitchen master's demanding standards were ordered thrown out. Rather than waste the food on the pigs, staff members not hard at work quickly consumed the rejected fare.

Gralia observed Tylla as she quickly downed a breakfast of turkey eggs and slightly overdone bacon. "Gods, girl, you can eat. Where does a wee thing like you put all of that?"

"Hopefully, up here," Tylla said around a mouthful and pointing at her chest.

Gralia guffawed. "You think you need more to keep the eye of that big man of yours?"

"Uh…" Tylla choked down her mouthful. "I…I do not know. Gycules is such a large man I fear he sees me as a child."

"Ha! I will let you in on a secret, girl," Gralia said conspiratorially. "Men see themselves as protectors. The daintier the woman, the more protective they get. That giant of yours is likely to kill any man who gives you a second look. With any other man I might tell you how to get his attention by making him jealous. I think that would get some people killed in this case. No, no games with this man. Show him respect and do not try too hard to catch his eye and I think you will do fine."

"Are you sure?"

"Oh, I am sure. I have seen how he looks at you when you are not paying attention," Gralia said with a wink. "Just be careful he doesn't split you from stem to stern if you take him for a tumble."

Tylla blushed and decided it was time to change the subject. "What about you and Myklon? Have you already…um…tumbled?"

Gralia's eyes went wide. "Myklon? What gives you a notion like that?"

"Every time you look at him you give him a wink."

This time Gralia colored a bit. "No, no tumbling for us. When he rescued me from the Styphoni, I was naked as my birth day…"

"As was I when Gycules saved me."

"Oh? Then he already knows what you have up there. Anyway, they were dressed as Styphoni so I did not trust them."

"How did they change your mind?"

Gralia smiled wryly. "I had Myklon prove he was no Styphoni."

"How did he do…oh. Oh!"

The two women laughed until the kitchen master found them.

"What are you two doing back here? Get back to work or you will be dismissed without pay."

## IV

Myklon watched from the decorative shrubbery as the guards were changed. The new men would be recently fed and alert, making them difficult to take by surprise. Normally. From his vantage point he could see Tylla bring out a tray of steins and approach each guard. He could not hear what she was saying, but had been present when Gasphros had coached her earlier before putting on his priestly robes for the wedding ceremony.

"Here is a token from Prince Basilron to his men on this joyous occasion," she would be saying. If a guard seemed reluctant to accept the stein, she would add, "Everybody is expected to drink to the health of Count Dalthros and his bride Krysala."

Every guard accepted, as Myklon knew they would. No soldier worth his sword would ever turn down a free drink, especially when offered by his lord. Moreover, none of them would expect a single stein of winter wine to have any effect on them. Of course, none of them knew that each stein had been given a powerful sleeping draught with the wine.

Myklon had been amazed to learn that Uncle Wolf Syros, not Gasphros, supplied the sleeping draught. It was normally intended for soldiers with serious wounds who could not sleep. Mixed with the wine it would be doubly effective. Syros and Gasphros had been swapping recipes to their mutual benefit.

Sure enough, within a quarter-candle of downing the contents of each stein, the men were overcome. Myklon gave the signal and his men rushed out from cover and seized the unconscious guards. Moments later, now dressed in Syragoni armor, his men returned and assumed the postings. Myklon nodded to himself, then noticed Tylla looking at him. He cursed himself for his sloppiness in not staying hidden until the tiny woman winked at him. The wink dominated his thoughts for some time to come.

## V

Prince Basilron appraised the wedding staff with a critical eye. While each of the attending maids were dressed in simple cotton gowns, each gown had to be spotless. A careless splash of winter wine would mar the perfection he wanted to achieve for his nephew's wedding. Already three gowns had been replaced after being marred by wine, a bird dropping, and in one case grass stains that covered the entire backside of the gown. Basilron made a mental note to 'talk' with the last offender later… privately.

Satisfied that all was well, the Prince dismissed the women with an admonition to be more careful, then turned his attention to the bride-to-be. Unlike Dalthros, Basilron knew Krysala's reputation and profession. Intimately.

"You look lovely, my dear," Basilron said, not without sincerity. Krysala was very fetching, which had made her very successful at her former vocation. "I suspect an heir will not be long in coming."

"I will do my best, Your Highness." Krysala almost managed to look innocent as she spoke. Then she winked. "I dare say you would know how good that is."

"Indeed, and it will not be spoken of again." Basilron's voice was firm on that point. "Never forget that the only reason I am allowing this union is that my soothsayer managed to trace noble blood in your family. However, as I am suspicious by nature, I am having the soothsayer investigated as well. I would hate to discover that he had been…coerced…into providing me with false documentation."

Krysala paled at the veiled threat. "Sire, surely you do not think that…"

"I think nothing until I have proof," Basilron said lightly. "Now, let us have a look at you. Yes, white linen suits you well, but I have a small accessory…that is what you women call these things, is it not?" Basilron extracted a gold tiara from somewhere under his cloak. "If you are to be a countess, you should look the part." He placed the tiara on Krysala's head then stepped back to look her over. "I do hope things work out. I should hate to find a new home for that bauble. Well, I leave you now to contemplate your future as my niece-in-law. Hmmm…is there such a thing? What do they call it? Well, no matter. Welcome to the family, my dear."

The Prince kissed Krysala lightly on each cheek, then forcefully on the lips. Krysala trembled as Basilron left the room. *Oh gods, what have I gotten myself into?*

## VI

Count Dalthros waited nervously at the edge of the courtyard. All around him he could see people file in and take seats at the tables arranged in a circle around the courtyard or mingle and talk among themselves. No one approached him as it was considered rude before the ceremony. The groom was expected to have weightier issues on his mind than making small talk with the guests.

There was the highly-regarded noble musician, and off at the far left, the wine merchant from Drathor whose produce was reputed to be the best in all of Hos-Bletha. It had to be for Uncle Basilron to choke down his enmity for Drathor and procure the merchant's services. Dalthros hoped the merchant had received payment in advance.

A hush fell over the courtyard. The Count turned to see if the highpriest from Styphon's House had finally arrived to officiate. He was wearing the yellow robes of office which fit snugly around his rotund figure. The Highpriest's face was obscured by a heavy hood. That mattered little to Dalthros; the priest could conduct the ceremony naked and covered in feathers, just so long as he got the job done.

The Highpriest took his place at the temporary altar that had been erected for the ceremony and held up his arms. The music stopped and the wedding guests quickly cleared the area where the ceremony would take place as four women in the cotton gowns cleared the area with ceremonial brooms and incense.

Outside of the circle children of the nobles were kept amused as they danced around a pole and wrapped it with colored ribbons. Other, older children moved among the guests and passed out leather straps.

Once the straps had been dispersed and everyone was properly seated, the music again started and Count Dalthros approached the altar alone. When he reached the edge of the cleared area, one of the women in white cotton took his hand and led him to the altar while the other three waved incense at the space through which he entered the perimeter.

Next, dressed in the simple white linen gown and the golden tiara replaced by a crown woven of soft-colored wildflowers, Krysala walked to the cleared area escorted by Prince Basilron. Normally, the father of the bride would have had that honor, but Krysala was without living relatives. They stopped at the edge of the circle.

The Highpriest asked, "Who gives this woman to be wed?"

"I, Basilron, Prince of Syragon and uncle to Count Dalthros," the Prince replied.

Four more women, known as Callers—devotees of the goddess Yirtta All-Mother, who were dressed in pink, blue, green and white—escorted Krysala to the altar while the Prince took his seat at his table.

The Highpriest turned his hooded visage on the crowd. His voice, though slightly muffled, rang out across the courtyard. "Marriage is a sacred bond; a blessed union, one that the Gods take most seriously. And so, it is not to be entered into lightly. Therefore, if any wish to contest this union let them speak up now or be forever silent."

Basilron's eyes searched out the guests. If any thought the wedding ill-advised, he kept his own counsel on the matter.

"Then let us begin!" The Callers, who had been standing behind the Highpriest, moved around to the front of the altar and, each in turn, took an implement from the altar, leaving only a jeweled dagger. The Callers then moved to positions at the perimeter of the Circle, each facing in the direction of the altar.

The Caller at North held up a lit candle and called out, "Styphon, Lord of Fire, Bringer of Warmth, we invite you to this wedding and ask that you bless this Joining!"

The Caller at South held up a chalice and called out, "Yirtta, All-Mother, Lady of Water, Bringer of Health, we invite you to this wedding and ask that you bless this Joining!"

The Caller at East held up an eagle feather and called out, "Dralm, Lord of Peace, Father to Mankind, we invite you to this wedding and ask that you bless this Joining!"

The Caller at West held up a mace and called out, "Galzar, Lord of War, Defender to All, we invite you to this wedding and ask that you bless this Joining!"

The Highpriest did not react to the invocations to the other gods. The ceremony was traditional and had been practiced for centuries before Styphon's House decided Styphon was the god of gods. The Callers remained at their posts and continually chanted, almost inaudibly, as the ceremony continued. The Highpriest asked, "Count Dalthros, do you love this woman, Lady Krysala?"

"I do," Dalthros answered.

"Do you promise to love her for the rest of your days?"

Again Dalthros said, "I do."

"Then face your bride and make your pledge," the Highpriest commanded. The bride and groom turned to face each other. Dalthros dropped to one knee, pulled his dagger from its scabbard and held it up in offering to Krysala.

"My Lady, I pledge to you my love. I pledge to you my soul. I pledge to you all that I am and all that I have, for you and you alone, for as long as my heart beats, I am yours."

The Highpriest nodded then turned to Krysala. "Lady, do you love this man?"

"I do."

"Do you promise to love him for the rest of your days?"

"I do."

The Highpriest handed Krysala a silver chalice and said, "Then face your groom and make your pledge."

Krysala looked to the still kneeling Dalthros and said, "I pledge to you my love. I pledge to you my soul. I pledge to you all that I am and all that I have, for you and you alone, for as long as my heart beats, I am yours." She then took the dagger from him and handed him the chalice.

The Highpriest said, "The wine is the blood of our Gods. Drink of it, Count Dalthros, and seal your pledge."

Dalthros sipped from the chalice and offered it back to his Lady. Absently he noted that the wine was particularly strong.

Krysala took the chalice and handed back the dagger, saying, "Rise, my husband."

As Duke Dalthros stood, he replaced his dagger into its scabbard. Krysala then dropped to one knee.

The Highpriest then said, "Sip the wine, Lady Krysala, and seal your Pledge."

Krysala sipped from the chalice and offered it back to Dalthros. He took it, then handed it to the Highpriest, who in turn set it down on the altar.

Dalthros took Krysala's hand and gently pulled her to standing, saying, "Rise, my wife."

The Highpriest said, "Give me your hands."

Dalthros offered his left hand as Krysala extended her right. The Highpriest held up a length of leather strap and said, "To symbolize their eternal bond, the couple's hands must be joined from now until night falls. To separate sooner would bring bad omens, and so their hands will be lashed together. When the ceremony is over, any who wish to bless the couple's union is welcome to add a tie of their own." He then bound the bride and groom's wrists together with the leather strap. Dalthros and Krysala's fingers intertwined without coaxing.

"In the name of the Gods, as witnessed by the Gods and with the blessing of the Prince, I now declare you husband and wife! You may kiss your bride."

As the Highpriest concluded, music began to play. The Callers ceased chanting and moved to the altar, replacing their implements and taking burning incense sticks in each hand. The four women danced about the inside of the perimeter, again waving the incense around. They circled the perimeter once, and then stopped at their compass positions where, facing out, they simultaneously dropped to their knees, heads bowed and hands, still holding the incense, thrust out to their sides.

The Highpriest moved to the space in the perimeter between East and South, laid down a sword with a richly jeweled hilt, and motioned for the couple to step over.

Once over the sword, the Highpriest turned and announced, "I present to you Count Dalthros and Countess Krysala, man and wife!"

The guests came to their feet and cheered as two women passed out ceremonial chalices filled with wine.

Prince Basilron seized a chalice and held it high. "To Dalthros and Krysala, may they have many strong children and long, happy lives!"

As everyone raised their chalices in response to the toast, Basilron accidentally spilled his wine when he bumped against his personal fanner. He quickly covered it up by drinking the remaining wine. Spilling wine during a wedding toast was seen by many as a bad omen. The Baron looked about and smiled; nobody was looking in his direction, all eyes were on the newly wedded couple.

# THIRTY-FIVE

## I

With the ceremony completed, the guests returned to their tables and took their seats. The service staff brought out the food and quickly served first the guests, then the wedded couple. The Highpriest, still obscured by his hood, took a seat at the prince's table.

At the periphery of the festivities several more men arrived, also wearing the heavy hoods that hid even the merest hint of what lay below. The hooded ones completely encircled the courtyard and its current inhabitants as the guests started eating their meals.

Prince Basilron, more observant than the rest, noticed the new arrivals and turned to the Highpriest. "Is this some new ceremonial addition?"

"You might say so, Your Highness. Oh, do try the food; it smells wonderful."

Basilron shrugged and stabbed at a piece of meat on his table. It seemed a trifle spicy. That suited the Prince well. He often enjoyed his repast with heavy spices, which was a constant source of discomfort for his food taster. Basilron smiled as he considered the discomfort his taster was no doubt feeling at that moment back in the kitchen. All around he could see people trying the food, then downing wine to douse the fire in their mouths. Around his mouthful, he asked the Highpriest, "Are you not eating?"

"That would be difficult, Your Highness."

"Oh? Are you on a fast?"

"Not at all." The Highpriest threw back his hood to reveal the head of a wolf. "I just have trouble chewing cooked food."

All around the courtyard the other hooded men threw off their robes to reveal similar features. It took a moment before anybody realized what had happened. First a woman screamed and all eyes turned to her, then to where she was pointing.

Men leapt up from their seats and reached for swords they did not have as more women screamed. Some of the guests who had already eaten the food were too busy downing their wine to quench the spicy fire on their tongues. They were the first to fall unconscious from the sleeping draught Tylla and Gralia had slipped into the drinks.

"Lords and Ladies, please remain seated as my men walk among you and collect your donations for the entertainment we are providing on this most auspicious occasion," Myklon said as he walked past the tables. One of the seated men tried to rise as if to attack the wolf-headed captain, only to fall backwards. The wine was having its effect on all who drank in toast to the newlyweds.

"That was very foolish," Myklon chided. "Brave, but foolish. By now you are all feeling the effects of the mild potion I added to the wine. It is quite harmless, and you will likely have the best sleep of your lives, but you will all be too sluggish to pose any threat. This was for your benefit as I have neither the desire nor the need to slay any of you. So please, relax, enjoy the show, and the long nap that is to follow and we will leave you much as we found you, if somewhat lighter in your purses."

The wolf-headed men quickly relieved everybody of their gold and jewelry. Vanir sniffed at one of the women as though deciding if he wanted to eat her or not. The woman fainted and he moved on to the next. Myklon suppressed a chuckle as he watched Vanir work. The sharpers are enjoying this a bit too much, he thought. He was about to say something when he noticed Tylla walking past Basilron. A very alert Basilron!

Myklon started forward too late. The prince seized the woman and held his eating knife at her throat.

"Your Highness," Myklon said, "threatening the wait staff will bring you no benefit. In fact, if you do not release that little slip of a girl, I fear you will come to a bad end."

"Only after she does," Basilron shouted. "You will all leave or she dies."

Myklon shook his head. "What makes you believe I care anything for this woman?"

"Do not test my intelligence," Basilron said in a low voice. "Only she and the other wench could have added the sleeping potion to the wine. I think she is one of yours and as such you have to care about her fate. As comely as she is, I suspect one or more of your own men will be very upset if she died." To accent his point he held the knife closer to Tylla's throat. A drop of blood emerged from her neck and trailed down to her chest.

Myklon nodded, which looked odd in his wolf-helm. "You speak the truth, which is why you want to let her go. You see, if she dies I will not be able to stop what comes next. However, if you free her, I swear by all of the True Gods we will leave you and your guests alive and whole."

"And I am to believe the word of a rogue?" Basilron sneered. "I hardly think so."

"Your Highness, I have no desire to be hunted for your murder. You should know this."

"No. I do not suppose that you would, which is why I will back out of here with this girl and you will not follow."

Basilron backed away from the table pulling Tylla with him. He managed a few steps when he felt his back strike something hard. He knew he was far from any walls so he chanced a quick glance at what was behind him. The Prince's gaze fell squarely on a massive chest a mere finger-length from his face. Looking up he saw the visage of a wolf. Even through the wolf-helm, Basilron could see the anger in the giant's eyes.

"Oh, shite," said the Prince of Syragon in a strangled voice.

The massive fist that came down on Basilron' skull dazed him and caused him to lose his grip on both woman and blade.

Gycules seized the Prince Basilron in one hand and hoisted him off of his feet. He almost failed to notice that Tylla was holding his other arm as he prepared to thrash the Prince.

"No!" Tylla yelled. "You heard Robinos! You would be branded a murderer. And you are much too big to hide, Dralm-damnit!"

Through the red haze of his rage, Gycules was more than willing to take that risk. However, Tylla was alive and pleading for the fool's life. "What would you have me do? He must be punished."

"In your hands he is little more than a child," Tylla said slyly. "Treat him as such."

Myklon, quick to take Tylla's meaning, grabbed up a great feathered fan where one of the slaves had dropped it and quickly stripped off the feathers. "I think this might serve your purpose well, mighty one."

Gycules accepted the paddle quizzically, then a sudden broad smile crossed his lips. "Ha! So it shall!"

The giant hauled Basilron over to the altar, pulled down his breeches and bent him over it. With one massive paw on the prince's neck to hold him down, Gycules used the other to bring the paddle down upon the princely posterior. The guests who had not yet succumbed to the drugged wine watched in horror as the ruler of Syragon was paddled like a naughty little boy.

Nobody, not even Gycules could have guessed how long the beating would have gone if Tylla had not declared it was enough. His ire, if not gone, had subsided enough that he relented and threw the prince to the ground. Basilron cried aloud in his pain and humiliation.

Myklon, a little sick over the spectacle, nonetheless decided to add salt to the wound. "Sire, your life has been spared. However, your freedom comes at a price. I offer you this choice: agree to pay the royal ransom of one hundred thousand silver rakmars, or be taken prisoner. Choose now."

It took Basilron a while to answer coherently through his sobs and wails. "I will…pay."

"Swear it in the name of your gods."

"I…swear in the name of Styphon and Galzar Wolfhead…that I will pay my ransom."

"And that you will take no retaliation for one moon afterwards," Myklon added. "I would be most unhappy if you were to follow the Uncle Wolf I send to pick up the ransom so that you can try to get to me or any of my men."

"Yes. I…swear, by Galzar's Mace, that I will attempt no revenge."

"Very good. I will provide you with a time and place to leave the ransom. Somewhere you will not be able to plan any unpleasant surprises for me. So, we will spare you any further indignity. I was considering leaving you hanging naked by your ankles from the ribbon pole, but that is a treatment for oath-breakers. I trust we understand each other?"

"We-e-e…do," the Prince replied, his voice shaking.

"Excellent." Myklon turned his lupine face to the remaining guests. "You will all drink a hearty toast to your host. Now!"

The wine was drunk and the remaining guests collapsed.

Then Myklon returned his attention to Basilron. "The slaves will go with us. They may stay with me, return to their homelands or even return here. It will be their choice. And now, Your Highness, I think some medicinal wine is in order to ease your mind."

Myklon walked over to the wedding table where he found Dalthros and Krysala still conscious. "Well, now, what am I to do with you?"

Dalthros stood. "Do as you will with me, but spare my wife."

*Is this man a lackwit? Surely by now he knows the ceremony was a farce! More's the pity since Gasphros performed such a beautiful service.*

"Your Grace, that was not a priest who performed your nuptials…"

A warning cry cut through the air.

Myklon spun to the side as a blade passed him. Basilron had elbowed one of his men in the face, taken his sword, and then attempted to run it through Myklon's back. A second scream snapped his attention back to the newly not-quite-wedded. Lying on the table was Dalthros, the trembling blade protruding from his chest and a sobbing Krysala, caressing his face as if to wake him.

Myklon drew his own sword and turned back toward Basilron,

prepared to sheath it in the prince's liver. Gycules stepped between them and held Myklon back. The giant shook his head.

"Remember your words to me," Gycules said.

Myklon fought for his composure before facing the Prince. "Now your ransom is doubled, only the second half goes to the Lady you have robbed of a husband." The Captain moved very close to Basilron and added, "If you fail to pay either of us that which you owe, there is no place you can go where we will not find you. A prince is a difficult mantle to conceal. You could dig a hole straight to Regwarn and pull the dirt in after you and we will still find you. And when we do, Roxthar himself will have nightmares when he hears what was done to you. I do swear by all the gods I will make this so!"

The blood drained from Basilron's face as he stared into the bandit's eyes. It was obvious he believed Myklon's every word.

"One more thing, since you clearly did not grasp the significance of the mercy we showed you earlier."

## II

It was several candles before Baron Valocles was the first of the wedding guests to awaken. All around him the guests and guards still slept. The Baron vaguely recalled that the highpriest had transformed into a wolf. *Are such dreams a bad omen?* The Baron picked up the chalice he had toasted Dalthros and his wife with and sniffed it. He could not be certain, but he suspected he and the rest of the wedding guests had been drugged.

*My best wine, too*, Valocles thought as he shook his head. A quick glance at the gift table confirmed his suspicions; the gifts were gone, including the chest filled with a thousand silver rakmars he had given the newlyweds along with the large barrel of winter wine.

*Well, nothing for it now*, Valocles thought. There would be a reckoning with the guard captain over this debacle. The Baron staggered over to the table where Dalthros and his wife sat. Only they were not sitting. Dalthros laid across the table with a sword sticking out of his chest and

Krysala, weeping, as she stroked his head softly.

"By the gods! What happened here?"

"The Prince killed him," Krysala said softly. "He meant to stick the bandit, Robinos, but he dodged and the blade struck my love."

Krysala started crying again and the Baron staggered away in search of Prince Basilron. It took almost a candle before he found the Prince of Syragon in a most compromising position.

Naked from head to toe, with a very bruised posterior branded black and blue, Basilron swung by his ankles from a tree branch. His eyes were closed but he could see the Prince's doublet was moving ever so slightly. *At least he's not dead on my grounds, Galzar be praised.*

Valocles started forward to free the Prince, then recalled Krysala's words. He decided to wait until the guards had regained consciousness. *I will feign sleep myself until after the Prince has been cut down.* After all, Basilron would not want his part in this spectacle to be remembered. The man who released him from the tree branch would find himself in a precarious position. Basilron had a bad temper and a memory as long as the road to Balph. *I must remove myself from this spectacle.* As he walked back to the courtyard he absently wondered why the ribbon pole had broken in the middle and now rested on the grass.

## III

It had been a long moon-half for the newly consecrated Highpriest Sangar, his privy parts had gotten infected and for a few days had swelled up to the size of a bloated goatskin waterbag. Calthros had administered some herbal remedies and in time the swelling had gone down, but they were still sore and Skranga was unable to ride a horse until just recently.

At last, they were preparing to leave Camp One and embark on the most dangerous phase of his deception as a Styphon's House highpriest. Plans had to be made, as well as plans within plans. Calthros pointed out that Skranga, in his guise as Sangar of Styphon's House, couldn't simply appear at Great King Niclophon's doorstep out of nowhere. He would have to take his escort, the false Styphon's Own Guard, and get to a main thoroughfare. On the journey to Bletha Town, it would be necessary to inspect some of the temples and maybe even collect some gold and fire-seed for the war effort along the way.

There was always risk no matter how good the disguise. Still, Skranga wore the robes of a priest just below the level of the Inner Circle, so he would not be challenged or questioned by temple guards or underpriests. Unfortunately within Styphon's House, the higher the rank, the greater the paranoia among the high-ranking priests and temple masters. Everyone was looking for an advantage to aid their rise within the Styphon's House hierarchy. There was always the possibility, as slight as that might be, that some priest might recognize him as Duke Skranga and raise a hue and cry. Furthermore, as a new and unknown highpriest from Balph, Sangar would be viewed with suspicion as well as reverence at each of the temples he visited.

To not visit the temples would be worse. In a war-torn area such niceties could be ignored. In peaceful Hos-Bletha it would be a very noticeable breach of etiquette.

Fortunately, one of their wolf patrols had waylaid Archpriest Prythames and his party on the Silos Road. After relieving Prythames of his gold, they had hung him from the nearest tree. Otherwise, the entire operation would have had to have been shelved. Prythames was no fool and well acquainted with the upperpriests of Balph. There was no way Sangar could have passed muster as a Styphon's House highpriest on a mission from the Inner Circle as long as the wily Archpriest was alive.

Over a first-meal of porridge and crusty day-old bread, Calthros explained that as his personal assistant he could act as a buffer between Sangar and the local temple priests. A highpriest could hardly be expected to mix with the more common lower priests of temples in backwater towns and villages.

"What do you think the ramifications of Prythames' death are going to be?" Democriphon asked.

"Hmm..." Calthros started. "That is a difficult question to answer. These days things are very chaotic and confused in the Holy City. Many of the highpriests. and even some of the archpriests, are busy squirreling gold and silver away in case Investigator Roxthar returns to Balph intent upon Investigating the upper echelons of the Temple. Others are retiring to their provincial demesnes far from Balph, hoping that the Investigation does not go far afield. Others are worried that the Grand Host might fail and Kalvan will send an army to besiege Balph.

"Furthermore, Hos-Bletha is considered the most backward of the Five Kingdoms and is poorly represented in Balph. My guess is they'll find some archpriest in disfavor and send him to replace former Archpriest Prythames. Since his replacement is a minor issue in contrast with all the political and military events going on, I suspect they'll avoid making a decision for many moons, maybe even a few winters."

"It is, of course, possible the Inner Circle might send a cadre of agents-inquisitory to find out why their archpriest was murdered, but that is a slight possibility in these tumultuous times. Even so, they should have little reason to suspect Highpriest Sangar. I received word recently that the document prepared by Lady Eldra was placed into the Temple Archives; Highpriest Sangar's credentials should be unassailable."

"Hmm…that brings us to Lady Eldra—" Calthros started.

"Hey! Just what are you implying, baldy?" Eldra snapped as she put down her eating bowl.

"Nothing, Milady, but an excuse for you to be among Sangar's entourage will need to be plausible. Unless you have changed your mind about staying with Democriphon's band in the new village."

Eldra had to admit that Democriphon wasn't hard on the eyes, and she had even considered dragging him off into the woods for some private research, but the idea of staying any longer in the forest and swamps with a bunch of coarse and sweaty former mercenaries and slaves was not to her liking. She took a quick glance at her surroundings: thatch lean-tos, a couple of makeshift wooden huts, mercenaries in formation drilling, some men splitting wood, two returning with shovels from digging the privy pit, a couple more skinning a boar and cleaning fish. She suspected things weren't much better at the new village they called Mallegast.

Out in the forest Eldra heard the scream of a panther. No, staying here was definitely not something she wanted to prolong, not in this lifetime. She had thought this was going to be a fun operation, fooling the Styphoni at their own game, not a low-intensity war in the hinterlands.

Besides, Ranthar would be keeping an eye on things here while she observed the goings-on at the palace. *A place where maybe I can get a hot bath*, she hoped.

"Okay, Calthros, you make a good point. There's nothing for me to do here and I'd like to see Bletha Town. They keep slaves here so I can be passed off as Sangar's concubine. Everybody will likely assume that I am his plaything, I suppose. Wait, do the slaves have any rights in Hos-Bletha?"

"They have very few, although most can earn back their freedom," Gasphros supplied. "Most slaves in Bletha are convicted criminals. They serve a certain number of years, depending on the crime, and are set free when they have served their term. This is to hold the cost of keeping prisoners down, and because there haven't been any prisoners of war to enslave in many years. Members of the Carib tribes, when caught, are automatically sentenced to death and the rare Mexicotál taken prisoner by the Zarthani Knights chooses suicide over enslavement. Since the Fireseed Wars started there have been slaves coming down from the north, but the trade has been slowed by the shipping problems."

"Shipping problems?" she prodded.

"The Fireseed War has brought many changes to the world," Sangar said. "Shipping has especially been affected. Entire fleets of ships have been pressed into military service to move troops and supplies for the war effort. The remaining non-military ships have more business than they can keep up with and raised their rates outrageously. Many captains refuse to allow slaves on the vessels for fear that Great King Kalvan will take revenge if he wins the war. His views on slavery are well known throughout the Five…no, make that Six Kingdoms. No captain wants to be on the end of King Kalvan's wrath when the dust settles."

"So how are slaves moved?" she asked.

"Overland," Calthros said. "They march their stock from Balph to

Bletha Town. Most of the captured Hostigi are either Investigated or put into the arenas for entertainment."

Eldra shivered. In the past she had seen arena fights and other "amusements" on Fourth Level Alexandria-Roman Sector and the Byzantine Imperial Subsector. It was not something she ever wanted to revisit.

"What about concubines?" she asked. "Are they usually slaves, or are they daughters of freemen who can't stand the idea of living in drudgery, popping out brats for some farmer or tradesman, for the rest of their lives?"

She could see Gasphros raising his hand to cover his mouth, whether in embarrassment or to hide a laugh, she was unable to tell.

Sangar, eyes bulging, looked shocked and embarrassed.

"That is something else we need to address," Gasphros said. "Whether or not Sangar here keeps a slave doxy?"

Calthros nodded. "It is rare, but not unheard of. Several archpriests of the Inner Circle are rumored to have their own harems."

"Lady Eldra is correct in that not all concubines are slaves," Gasphros noted. "Some concubines are younger daughters of tradesmen and, in a few cases, even minor nobility. We could pass her off as a baron's youngest daughter. I'll do some research and come up with the family name of some deceased baron or wealthy merchant."

"Humph. I guess I can live with this plan as long as Sangar here remembers that I am nobody's toy." Eldra threw a look at the recently frocked highpriest that left no doubt on where she stood.

"I would not dream of it, Lady Eldra," Sangar said, with a look that said he meant every word.

"I suppose it's not unheard of for women of noble birth to become attached to highpriests." She looked at Calthros for an answer.

"No, it isn't," he replied. "A Styphon's House highpriest in many ways is the secular equivalent of a prince, while an archpriest has the authority and wealth of a great king. As I'm sure a woman of your knowledge and experience realizes, wealth and power draw women much like salt licks draw deer. However, milady, I do not believe it is a good idea for you to play the part of Sangar's concubine. It's not unusual for an archpriest to become interested in a subordinate's woman, especially one with your grace and beauty. In which case, he may order his underling to have her provide him with her services. Something I suspect in your case that would not be appreciated."

Eldra cringed, despite her First Level mental control. There was no way she was going to be passed around to some slimy archpriest. She knew Archpriest Prythames was dead, but another one might be on his way from Balph shortly. "Thank you, Calthros, for bringing that to my attention. I have no desire to be anyone's plaything."

"There is another possibility," he noted, "although in this case it does stretch credibility. Often unmarried highpriests have a woman relative—usually a spinster or widow—who's in charge of their household. This not only confers status, which being a concubine does not, but would have the advantage of allowing you entrance to almost any household in Bletha Town."

*Even the idea of being related to Skranga is mildly revolting*, Eldra thought. But acceptable when contrasted with the degradation of playing Sangar's concubine. "Thank you, Calthros. I can be Highpriest Sangar's younger sister, recently widowed. My husband was a mercenary captain, killed in the war against Hos-Hostigos."

"Wonderful, milady!" Calthros all but applauded. "It also has the benefit of winning you the sympathy of almost everyone, and will make you a person of interest to all. Everyone in Hos-Bletha is fascinated by Kalvan's war against Styphon's House and will have many questions they'd love to ask you."

"What do you think, *brother?*" she asked, fighting to hold back a grin.

Sangar just shook his head wearily.

# THIRTY-SIX

## I

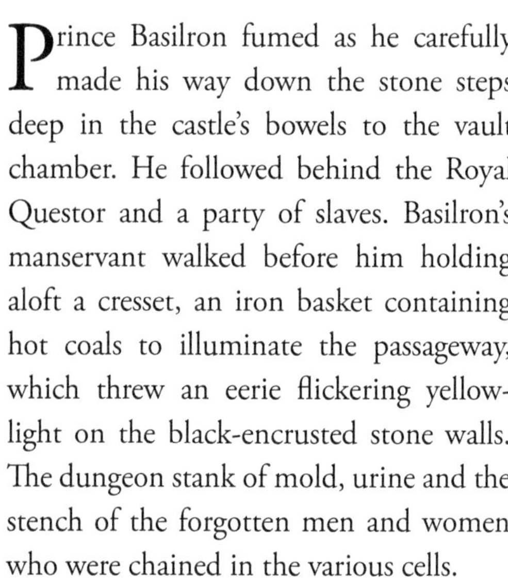

Prince Basilron fumed as he carefully made his way down the stone steps deep in the castle's bowels to the vault chamber. He followed behind the Royal Questor and a party of slaves. Basilron's manservant walked before him holding aloft a cresset, an iron basket containing hot coals to illuminate the passageway, which threw an eerie flickering yellow-light on the black-encrusted stone walls. The dungeon stank of mold, urine and the stench of the forgotten men and women who were chained in the various cells.

The vault chamber was at the bottom of the passageway below the dungeon. The door was a large expanse of ancient oak broken by iron straps and fastened to the stone walls with iron hinges. The exchequer took out his large key and opened the lock. It took the exchequer and his slaves to force open the vault door, which screeched as it was opened. Inside the large chamber were scores of huge chests bound with iron straps. The Questor used another key to open one of the chests marked with chalk runes indicating that it held silver coins.

The Questor watched intently as his Prince Basilron inspected the stacks of coins before him. Each stack represented one hundred ounces of silver and there were a thousand stacks. Basilron fumed as the stacks were placed in sturdy oaken chests and taken out of the vault. It was the second time that day he had watched a hundred thousand ounces of silver walk out of his vault.

"See to it that Krysala receives her silver in short order," Basilron commanded. "Also, post a guard at her home until she decides how to protect her newfound wealth."

The guard nodded and followed the silver out of the vault. Basilron followed him out then ordered the vault sealed. The Chancellor barely made it out before the iron and stone door slammed shut. Basilron patiently watched as the locks were secured then collected the keys.

Not for the first time he considered reneging on the payment. Not for Krysala, as she was due compensation for the death of her husband to be at his hands, accidental though it was. However, the thought of paying the bandit, Robinos as he called himself, who caused all of the trouble in the first place, galled him beyond belief. Sadly, he had to admit that he could not afford to be seen breaking his oath. Many of the guests were still conscious when he swore in the name of Styphon and Galzar that he would pay.

While the Prince only gave the gods' worship lip service, the oath was binding nonetheless. If word circulated that he was an oath-breaker, he would have trouble with any future deals he might make. Plus, he would lose face with his own soldiers. If he were to fight in another war and were captured, the enemy would know he could not be trusted to keep his word. He would be slain rather than ransomed. While another war was unlikely, bandits were now freely roaming the kingdom and it appeared that Great King Niclophon could no longer keep the peace.

On his way back to his private audience chamber, Highpriest Lythros accosted him. "Your Highness, I understand you are paying the ransom to those thieves that raided your nephew's wedding. Do you think this is wise?"

"Wiser than not paying," Basilron retorted sharply. He explained his reasons as they entered the chamber. "While I would like to blame them for the death of Count Dalthros, I cannot. My hand wielded the blade that laid him low."

"Which would never have happened had they not invaded the ceremony," Lythros argued. The Highpriest spotted a sheepskin on the table near Basilron and quickly scanned its contents.

"True. Still, they made it clear they were not interested in killing anyone at the wedding. I did that in my anger and humiliation." The Prince leaned forward. "You want revenge for having been stripped of your vestments and trussed up like a turkey for slaughter on your way to the wedding. The bandits wanted you out of the way. You should be on your knees thanking Styphon that you were not killed outright; Robinos is not known for his love of Styphon's House, as many of your temples, caravans and dead priests can attest."

Highpriest Lythros nodded absently. "So you will pay this thief without complaint."

"Pay, yes, but not without complaint to Great King Niclophon. Each princedom pays tribute to the Throne expecting certain privileges and protections. While each principality is expected to maintain order within its own borders without aid from the king, bandits such as this Robinos, who freely skip from princedom to princedom, fall under the Great King's jurisdiction.

"I am going to remind Niclophon at the next Council of Princes that we who placed him in power can also act to remove him if he is unable to execute the duties of his office. Failing to prevent Robinos from running amuck throughout the kingdom would be a good example. At the end of the moon I will be only too happy to provide my princely levy to aid the king in this matter."

Lythros nodded. "Indeed. Styphon's House has posted a reward of twenty thousand gold crowns for this bandit's head. I think between the two rewards this Robinos will find no safe quarter to hide in."

Basilron smiled wolfishly. "I hope not. Now, if you have no other business..."

"I do, but not here." Lythros bowed and left the audience chamber as quickly as dignity would allow. Having read the sheepskin he now knew the time and location of the ransom payment. Basilron was prevented from acting against Robinos by his oath, but Styphon's Own Guard operated under no such strictures.

## II

"…and now you have been well and truly thanked for my rescue from Styphon's House."

Myklon rolled over and tried to catch his breath. "I think…maybe…I rescued that…priest."

Gralia kicked Myklon's bare leg and giggled. "Trust me; he would not have enjoyed this as much as you."

Myklon leaned on one elbow and looked Gralia in the eyes. "I find that a little hard to believe."

Gralia sent a punch into his midriff with surprising strength.

"Oof. Maybe not so hard to believe after all. I would appreciate it if you did not cripple me before I went out to recover the ransom."

Gralia became serious. "Do you really think Prince Basilron will pay and not just set a trap?"

"Oh, he will pay. As for the trap, well, I intend to be wary just in case. Even if Prince Basilron keeps his word, there are other dangers to watch out for."

Myklon rolled out of the bed and started dressing. "You know, when this mission is over, I will miss this place. It is not as large as my home back in Hostigos Town, but the bed is much nicer. Not to mention the bed warmer."

Gralia threw her pillow at Myklon's head. "What kind of bed warmer did you have back in Hostigos?"

"My dog, Baltar. He could be very frisky when I wanted to sleep, though. Just like you." Myklon ducked the second pillow.

"Do you have to go?"

"Yes." Myklon pulled on his breeches and jack. "Ranthar just got back from his scouting mission. I still do not trust Andros, yet, although he would have been a good choice otherwise. No, I set this up and I should be the one to see it through."

"Will you be taking Gycules?"

"No. Gycules is preparing for a separate mission. I cannot speak of it with you."

Gralia became agitated. "Who is going with you?"

"Uhh…Vanir, who knows the landscape better than anyone else, those Ruthani scouts, Roaring Panther and Silent Wolf and Yaholo or something—those Ruthani names always confuse me. Uncle Wolf Syros to make the exchange. Oh, and about fifty trained freemen and a couple mercenaries, I forget their names."

"Freemen?" Gralia pulled the cotton sheet up as if to protect her. "They were slaves not so long ago. Beaten, half-starved, abused—"

"And with more fire for revenge than any men I have ever seen. Every last one of them would sooner die than be made slaves again. They trained hard and I trust them more than some mercenaries I have worked with. Gralia, this is just a short trip to collect the ransom; that is all."

"Dalthros was just getting married. Look at what happened to him."

"Then you should be pleased I am not going to get married. Just collect a ransom."

Gralia's eyes welled up with tears. "I am afraid something is going to happen to you."

Myklon was prepared to tell her that nothing would, but remembered that many men had died since he came to Hos-Bletha under Colonel Democriphon. "I will do my best to avoid anything unpleasant. I am not going looking for a skirmish."

"I am afraid you will not come back."

Myklon sat back down on the bed and put an arm around his woman. "I will return even if I have to drag my broken and bleeding body back by one good arm."

## III

The men stood in formation in full gear: wolf-helm, arquebus, back-and-breast over their jacks, two horse-pistols each, sword and bow with quiver. Petty-Captain Nolos stood at the front and saluted in the Zarthani style.

"Sir! The men are ready when you are," Nolos proclaimed.

"Very good, Petty-Captain. We leave as soon as First Captain Ranthar gives us leave to go."

Nolos nodded and jerked his gaze over Myklon's shoulder. Myklon turned and saluted as Ranthar approached. "Sir, the men are ready to collect the ransom."

Ranthar returned the salute. "You have my leave to go, Grand-Captain Myklon. Maybe I should go with…"

"Sir, remember what King Kalvan said about the, uh…Buddyholly Rule."

Ranthar nodded. Calvin Morrison had brought a lot of ideas with him from Fourth Level Europo-American. One of them was the Buddyholly Rule; never put more leaders in danger than necessary. It came from three entertainers from his time-line who died all in the same accident.

Myklon was correct in pointing out the rule. With Captain-General Democriphon in the field, Ranthar was the top dog in the village. As such, he did not have the option to go off on a minor adventure.

"Your point is taken, Myklon. Just be very careful out there; Basilron is not the only one who would like to see our heads on pikes."

"I shall be careful, sir."

## IV

It was hard going paddling against the current. Myklon's plan was to receive the ransom, load it onto several small boats, then let the current haul it back to the village with minimum effort. Most of the men would still have to march back, though after the number of green faces Myklon had observed, he suspected there would be no shortage of volunteers for the land route.

"We are almost there, Captain," Vanir said. "We should make land just around that bend."

"Praise Galzar!" Myklon exclaimed. He had done a fair amount of paddling himself.

Roaring Panther and Silent Wolf were the first off of the boats. Like the Caribi, Ruthani were accomplished boaters and had no trouble shifting from water to land. Most of the freemen—unaccustomed to water travel save for those who had been brought to Hos-Bletha by sea—took time to reacquaint themselves with the firmament under their feet.

The mercenaries, drawing on experience, quickly took up positions where they could keep an eye out for potential danger. There were more things to be on the watch for than just the Baron's soldiers—Ruthani, Caribi, Styphoni and even dangerous wildlife such as panthers, snakes and the river dragons.

Myklon nodded in satisfaction, then called Uncle Wolf Syros and Vanir over. "I am going to post a guard for the boats. We head out immediately afterwards. Which way from here?"

Vanir took in his surroundings, more for show than to get his bearings, and pointed off to the southwest. "Four marches that way. It will be rough country and coming back we will be hindered by the weight of the ransom. We will be distributing over three tons of silver between fifty men. That is, um…"

"A little over a hundred and twenty pounds each," Myklon finished. He had not thought of it before, but that would be a lot of weight to carry through rough country. "We will have to do it in two trips. Sixty pounds is manageable in a backpack. It is a lot more marching than I had planned for, but nothing we cannot handle."

Vanir nodded. "We should have brought Gycules."

Myklon shook his head. "The Chief Petty-Captain is not a pack mule to load up every time we have to haul something heavy. The men would lose respect for him if we used him like that. Besides, it would take twenty men of his strength to do it all in one trip."

Vanir conceded the point.

"Now, let us be on our way. I do not like the idea of walking back and forth in this forest after dark." Myklon looked around and spotted the two men he wanted. "Roaring Panther. Silent Wolf. I want you two to take the lead."

Both men nodded and took point. As silently as armed and armored men could be, the troop moved into the tree line.

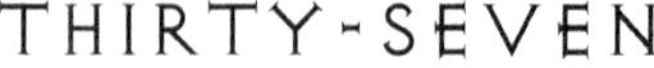


## I

It took six candles before Myklon and his men came upon the meeting place. Prince Basilron's men were already there. Silently, Myklon ordered his men to surround the small delegation.

Once his men were in position, Myklon called out: "Welcome, my friends. I see you have brought me my silver. And you had the foresight to put it in small carts for us to take it away. I appreciate that greatly."

"Our orders were to see you face-to-face before we allowed the silver to be taken," called back the Syragoni captain.

Myklon cursed. This was something else he had not counted on. "How will you know it is me you face? We all look very much alike."

The Captain frowned. "Then just let me see one of you. I doubt there are any other men in these woods with wolf faces."

"We have an Uncle Wolf with us to make the exchange. He will accompany me."

"Very well. But know this: any false

move will result in your deaths. I have over a hundred men covering you. They know what to do if you play me false." Myklon threw a wink at Syros before they stepped out of the foliage.

The Syragoni captain appeared startled, although he tried to hide it. Myklon didn't remember him from the wedding and he had probably never seen the wolf-headed men before now, though tales of them had circulated throughout the princedom. Myklon stepped forward with Uncle Wolf Syros as if he owned the forest and everything within it.

He stood back while the Uncle Wolf inspected the contents of each cart. Syros nodded. "You may go."

"Do you not wish to count it, first?" the Syragoni captain asked ironically.

The Uncle Wolf shook his head. "Time enough for that when I return to my demesne. I only needed to see that these coins are indeed silver and a great deal of it. Exactitude will come later. Know this; if there is one ounce less than the agreed sum, Galzar Himself will wreak terrible vengeance on all of Syragon, and make it known that your prince's word is meaningless."

Myklon looked at the way Syros' words shook the captain. Another thought struck him. "If any of your men extracted a personal bonus from my payment, now is the time to return it. I doubt your liege lord would appreciate his honor being tarnished by untrustworthy soldiers. I wonder what the punishment is for stealing from one's prince?"

The Syragoni captain turned a baleful eye on his men. "Here is your chance to avoid the wrath of Basilron, and worse, mine, if any of you have taken so much as a single coin. Return it now and there will be no retribution. I will turn my back so I do not see any who return what is not theirs."

The Syragoni walked closer to Myklon and steadfastly kept his gaze on the bandit. Behind him he could hear the clinking of coins. After it had been quiet for a while, he sighed.

"You have my apologies, Robinos. I hope you will not find it needful to speak of this to my prince."

Under the wolf-helm, Myklon smiled. "Have no worries, friend. I, more than most, understand the lure of silver not my own. You are free to leave though you will be watched. How far, I will not say, but we will not be caught by surprise if you choose to return for battle."

The Syragoni nodded once then turned. Almost as one the Syragoni troop vanished into the trees. Myklon let out a long breath. "I cannot believe Ranthar plays this part so easily."

"Yes, he does appear accomplished at playing Robinos," Uncle Wolf Syros noted.

"Hmm," Myklon said.

"Sir, if I may be so bold, should we not be away from here?" Vanir looked about as if expecting demons from Regwarn to jump out from behind every tree. "Quickly!"

"Agreed. We are spared two trips thanks be to the Syragoni who had the foresight to bring these hand carts. I want two men pulling and two men pushing on each cart. They may be small, but I think you will find them very heavy. Be careful to avoid any soft earth as we go."

Most of the afternoon later, after considerable sweating and cursing, the silver found its way onto the line of small boats. After a considerable internal struggle, Myklon decided to put another of his king's maxims to the test—"trust, but verify." He had little confidence in Vanir or sharpers in general. This was his chance to prove once and for all if this one, at least, could be counted on.

"Vanir, you are in charge of getting this ransom back to the village. Ranthar will be waiting with men to unload the boats. The rest of us will be back in two or three days, Galzar willing." Vanir simply nodded and boarded the boat.

After the boats started on their way, Myklon reflected on the cost of determining Vanir's loyalties. *One hundred thousand ounces of silver is a high price, but better to find out sooner rather than later.*

"You were wise to display your trust openly," Uncle Wolf Syros said. "Vanir will now try to show you that he is worthy of your trust.

"I hope you're right," Myklon said. "Otherwise, I'm going to get my arse chewed out by Democriphon!"

Syros smiled knowingly.

"All right, we have a long march through forest and swamp," Myklon said to the remaining men. "Best we get to it."

## II

As bad as rowing the small boats against the current had been, marching back seemed much worse to Myklon. After two days the uneven terrain caused men to stumble almost constantly, and the mosquitoes were so thick at times they seemed like gray clouds that flew in to attack. All of them were soaked to the bone from fording streams and wading through swamps. Myklon began to worry over the possibilities of the Yellow Fever and whether Uncle Wolf Syros would be able to treat it.

Suddenly, Roaring Panther returned from point and signaled a halt. Myklon crept up to see what might be the problem. "We are not alone."

Myklon looked around and saw nothing but trees and cattails. "What is it?"

"Listen."

The air was still. "It seems quiet to me."

"To me as well. That is bad." Roaring Panther saw the confusion on the captain's face. "No bird songs. The birds do not fear us and sing as we pass, yet now they are still."

"Large animal nearby?"

Roaring Panther shook his head. "A wolf or panther would stop the bird song for a short time. As soon as the birds realize that the wolf or panther cannot get to them they sing again. This is something more dangerous."

"More dangerous? Like what?"

"Ruthani. Too quiet for yellow hairs."

Behind him Myklon could hear weapons being brought to bear. "Will they attack?"

"I think, yes. My people do not like the yellow hairs and do not know you from them," Roaring Panther explained.

"Why haven't they already attacked?" Myklon asked.

"I do not know. It could be that they see Silent Wolf and me and are confused. That will not last long."

Sweat began to pour down Myklon's face in rivulets. "What do you suggest we do?"

"Run. Fast."

Myklon did not waste time thinking. He turned and yelled to his men, "On me, move!"

No sooner did they start running, when arrows rained down seemingly from every direction. Myklon spun and fired his first horse pistol into the trees and was surprised to see a Ruthani warrior fall. Lucky shot!

"Everybody stop, form up!" He pointed to where the majority of arrows were coming from and cried, "CHARGE!"

The mercenaries in the group were quick to follow orders. The freemen, after some confusion, followed behind. Myklon pulled out his other pistol and shot one Ruthani warrior while dodging arrows. The enemy was caught by surprise and about a dozen were shot or skewered with swords. Arrows continued to rain down as lead flew up. Men were dying on both sides.

"Roaring Panther, you know these people best. What should we do next?"

"Kill, and try not to be killed," the Ruthani said. "Firing into the leaves was wise. Keep doing that."

Myklon nodded and quickly reloaded his arquebus and fired at a shadow in one of the trees. With all three of his fireseed weapons emptied, he drew his bow and started launching arrow after arrow into the foliage. Like most of the men, he was not as proficient with the bow as he was with the arquebus. However, he was able to fire five arrows in the time it took to reload and fire his fireseed weapons. With satisfaction he saw two more Ruthani drop from the trees where he had been firing his arrows.

*Spaaang*. An arrow ricocheted off his morion helmet, knocking his head sideways. He brushed it off and aimed at a moving figure in the shadows.

Roaring Panther and Silent Wolf, the most proficient bowmen in the company, nocked, drew, fired and drew again, their hands a blur. Between them they brought down more attackers than three times their number of freemen.

One arrow caught Myklon in the left thigh. He ignored it as he fired off again in the direction the arrow had come from. He paused just long enough to break off the shaft of the arrow sticking out of his leg so that it would not interfere with his bow, then nocked another missile and fired.

When the arrows stopped flying from the trees, Myklon prayed that the fighting was done. He was sorely disappointed: Ruthani warriors came running out from behind the brush and trees. They came at him and his men from all sides. Some were armed with their traditional tomahawks made of wood and stone while others sported knives and axes no doubt seized from previous victims. Myklon wasted no time in dropping his bow and drawing his sword.

"To your swords! Close order tactics," Myklon called out. This was for the benefit of the freemen. The mercenaries needed no prompting.

"Cut these bastards into dog meat, men." Myklon caught a glimpse of Roaring Panther using a knife and hatchet against an attacker. He did not see how the contest ended as he had to concentrate on his own opponent.

## III

Captain Aralon cursed as he slogged through the muddy ground. His orders had been to follow the Syragoni soldiers at a discreet distance, then wait for them to leave before bracing the bandits. Unfortunately, 'discreet' meant getting lost in the dense foliage. He had the location as given to him by Highpriest Lythros, though it did little for him in the unfamiliar terrain.

Aralon was prepared to pack it in. His men were grumbling; the mud, the swamps and the mosquitoes were taking their toll. He would be in for a great deal of unpleasantness from the highpriest when he returned without Robinos' head, or what passed for it, yet he dared not hope to find the bandit under these conditions. If only there was a sign.

Gunfire! Aralon spun in the direction he thought it came from. More gunfire could be heard. Somebody was in a fight. He smiled. With any luck somebody else was doing his work for him.

"This way, men," Aralon signaled his half company of Styphon's Own Guard. "Move quietly. We do not want to become involved in a fight not our own."

## IV

Grand-Captain Myklon bit on a tree branch as a mercenary forced the arrow the rest of the way through the fleshy part of his thigh. It hurt like all of Regwarn. The bleeding, while bad, was not the heavy flow of an arterial rupture.

"If the fester devils fail to find you, you may live to fight another day," Uncle Wolf Syros said lightly. "I would suggest you not use that leg, but I do not know how that is possible before we return to the village. To stop the blood flow I will have to use a hot iron."

Myklon nodded weakly. The Uncle Wolf plunged his knife into the small fire and held it there until the blade glowed red hot, then seared the flesh on the entry and exit wounds on Myklon's leg. Myklon fought to keep from screaming as he bit down harder on the tree branch. Instead, he passed out from the pain. When Myklon came to a candle later, he asked for a status.

"We lost fifteen men outright," the Uncle Wolf said. "Five more are severely injured and will not make it back to camp. The rest have some cuts and bruises, but they will live…provided we do not run into more Ruthani."

Roaring Panther snorted. "Not likely. My people are very territorial. We should not meet any more between here and the village. Caribi, however…"

"Gah!" Myklon said, gnashing his teeth. "Just what we do not need. The only thing worse would be Styphon's Own Guard," Myklon grumbled. "As soon as we are patched up and have some rations, we move out.

Oh, did any Ruthani get away?"

Roaring Panther shrugged. "Yes, maybe two handfuls. Even I have trouble tracking them through the swamplands."

Myklon nodded. If Roaring Panther could not track them, then they just could not be tracked. "In that case, we eat as we march. I do not want to be here should they return with some more friends."

"They will track us if they still want to fight," Roaring Panther pointed out.

"Nothing I can do about that for the moment."

"What do we do with our dead?" the Uncle Wolf asked.

"Galzar's teeth! It pains me to say it, but we will have to strip the bodies and put them in the swamp. Bury their personal effects where we can find and dig them up later. We will hold memorial services when we get back. I will not have the living slowed down by the dead."

## V

"This is where the fighting took place, sir."

Captain Avalos looked over the dead Ruthani. Some were clearly killed with fireseed weapons while others had wounds that could only have come from arrows. The arrows had been retrieved, of course, as had most of the Ruthani missiles. The bodies had been stripped of anything remotely valuable. That would be the work of mercenaries who were experts at stripping the dead. Something else was missing.

"Where are the bodies of the people these infidels were fighting?"

The Petty-Captain shrugged. "There are none. Either they suffered no casualties, or they took the bodies with them."

Heated whispers broke out in the ranks. Avalos could not hear what was being said though he had a good idea: superstitious drivel about the wolf men being Galzar Wolfhead's avatars, immune to harm by mortal means. It would be pointless to argue with them. Instead, they would have to be shown that these bandits were mortal by cutting them down like so many corn stalks.

"We need to close the distance between us and, hopefully, take them before dark," Avalos said. "I do not want to face any Ruthani on their home ground at night."

The men hastened to form up and prepare for the march. Every eye scanned the trees and ground for signs that the Ruthani might be preparing to attack.

# THIRTY-EIGHT

## I

Myklon cursed with every step he took. His leg hurt as if every demon in Regwarn were ravaging it with red-hot talons. The staff Uncle Wolf Syros cut for him did little to ease the pain. Red tendrils snaked out from the wound in every direction. Myklon had seen enough of that on other wounded men in his time to know that he was likely to lose the leg when they got back to the village. *If I live that long.*

Uncle Wolf Syros wouldn't look him in the face when he asked if his leg could be saved.

The idea of losing an extremity did not disturb him as much as he thought it might. With the leg gone, he would be free to pursue Gralia without his military obligations interfering. Assuming Gralia would want him as half a man. That thought triggered new concerns, such as how he would earn a living without the use of the limb. *I could always take the Wargod's vows and become an Uncle Wolf....*

"Grand-Captain Myklon."

He took a moment to shift from his thoughts back to the real world. "Yes?"

Roaring Panther pointed back the way they had come. "We are being followed."

"What? More Swamp Ruthani?" Myklon was not up for another fight with the natives.

"No. Somebody new. They stomp about like great beasts with no thought for where they are. Silent Wolf is backtracking to find out who it is."

Myklon nodded. When he first met Silent Wolf, he found the man to be terse to the point of being almost mute, and assumed that was how he got the name. He was very wrong. Silent Wolf could move through the forest like a soft breeze, barely disturbing even a single blade of grass. Whatever Silent Wolf found, it was unlikely anybody would find him.

"It could be our own people coming to find us," Myklon ventured. "We were supposed to be back yesterday."

"Wrong direction," Roaring Panther countered.

"Not if they took the boats to the original landing point."

Roaring Panther nodded. It made sense. Myklon looked down at his leg to check the progress of the red lines. It was not good. When he looked back up Silent Wolf was standing next to Roaring Panther.

"Gah! Galzar's Teeth, man!" Myklon regained his composure before speaking again. "Did you find out who is following us?"

"Styphoni."

"What? What in Regwarn are they doing out here?" Myklon realized the reason before he finished speaking. "It must be that highpriest's doing. Somehow he found out the meeting place and sent some men out for a little revenge. That will teach me to leave one of those manure-eaters alive, Dralm-damnit. How many?"

"Forty-six. No horse."

Myklon began to appreciate Silent Wolf's brevity. "Forty-six to our thirty-five…"

"Thirty-three," interrupted the Uncle Wolf as he returned. "I came to tell you we lost two more. The rigors of the march, even with the slow pace, proved too much for the badly wounded. Two more have developed fester devils, and I have no wine to clean the wounds with."

"Who is carrying my equipment? I have some Ermut's Best in a flask. It will burn, but it should do the job. I should have thought of it before." *I should have thought of a lot of things*, Myklon thought, *things had been going so well I never considered how quickly things could go wrong.*

He turned back to Roaring Panther. "We cannot out-run them in our current condition. We'll have to set an ambush. Have everybody load their weapons if they have not already done so. We'll start with bows. A silent attack might allow us to whittle their numbers down a bit before they know we are here. Then we'll hit them with everything we have."

*I would give both of my legs for some of Kalvan's rifles right now.*

The two Ruthani nodded and went to work. Myklon tried to hobble around to give orders only to collapse. The pain was so bad he could scarcely think. At some point somebody was pouring Ermut's Best down his throat. It was the Uncle Wolf.

"I doubt this will help much, but it is all we have," Syros said.

Myklon sputtered. "Then do not waste it on me. Tend to the ones who can still fight. And get me my weapons, Dralm-damnit! I may be stuck on my arse, but I can still pull a trigger."

## II

Grand-Captain Avalos felt the hairs on the back of his neck rise. He could not explain why though he felt danger was present. He looked around and saw nothing sinister. His trained ear failed to detect any sound that was out of place. He could hear the slurping noise of boots rising in and out of the ubiquitous mud and the interminable buzz of mosquitos and other insects. Still, he was unable to shake the sense that something was off. He called a halt a second before he heard something. Had he not stopped the men, their own footfalls would have covered the noise.

"Everybody down! We're under attack!"

Forty-five men hit the dirt before one man in the rear noticed that the forty-sixth had an arrow protruding from his neck. "Captain! Ruthani!"

As if on cue, arrows rained down on Styphon's Own Guard. The arrows were useless against the silvery armor but were devastating on the exposed parts of the flesh. Avalos wasted no time in ordering return fire. In mere heartbeats, the forest came alive with gunfire from both sides.

## III

"Captain Myklon, we are running low on fireseed."

Myklon grunted at Uncle Wolf Syros. He had been worried about that after the battle with the Ruthani earlier. "What about the arrows?"

"A few. The freemen were somewhat enthusiastic in their assault. Sadly, their accuracy left something to be desired."

"No choice then," Myklon grunted through clenched teeth. "We go in with swords as soon as the fireseed runs out. Hopefully, the Styphoni are in the same fix we are."

"They outnumber us," the Uncle Wolf reminded the captain.

"If you have another option, I am open to suggestions."

The Uncle Wolf had no reply.

"Then we work with what we have and make the bastards pay dearly. Now help me up. I can try to use what fireseed I have left while leaning against this tree."

Syros obeyed, and then turned toward the enemy. When mercenaries fought against Styphon's Own Guard in equal numbers, almost always victory went to the Guardsmen. Against outnumbered freemen, it would be a slaughter. Still, for the first time in years, the Uncle Wolf had an enemy he could draw a sword against—Styphoni heathen. He would not turn and run. Drawing his sword and dagger, he ran to the thick of the fighting yelling, "For the Orphan Prince! Down Styphon!"

Myklon watched as Syros engaged two foes simultaneously. To his amazement, the Uncle Wolf bested both of them then moved on to the next foe. Myklon quickly lost track of the man in the mêlée.

Taking careful aim and wishing for the nth time he had one of King Kalvan's rifles, he fired off his horse pistols, then the arquebus. He quickly reloaded and again discharged his weapons. Before he could reload again, he was caught by a bullet in his shoulder.

*Damn! A finger-joint lower and my armor might have deflected that.*

A Styphoni soldier ran toward him with his sword raised high. Myklon drew his dagger and threw it. Both men were surprised when the dagger found its resting place in the man's throat.

"Thank you, Ranthar, for the knife-throwing lessons," Myklon muttered under his breath.

The battle was going badly. While the Styphoni were cut down one by one, so too were the freemen. Soon, Myklon could see, it would just be the two Ruthani scouts and Uncle Wolf Syros and a couple of former mercenaries. There was no question that the Styphoni would take no prisoners. Myklon grasped his bow and his one remaining arrow.

*If I go, I will take at least one more with me.*

Myklon drew the bow string and took aim at one soldier, then decided on a better target. He released the arrow and it flew straight into the Styphoni captain's face just below the left eye.

The captain, arrow protruding from his cheek, turned and saw Myklon leaning against the tree. Without thought to the missile embedded in his face, he started running to the source of his injury, waving his sword in the air.

Myklon, now weaponless and unable to run, awaited death. *A good death*, he concluded, *by a worthy opponent. Praise, Galzar, we shall meet again in the Wargod's Hall!*

Before Avalos could reach his target, he was cut down by a hail of lead. As his life oozed out onto the ground, he could see dozens, maybe even scores, of wolf-headed men swarming over the battle ground. They quickly overpowered and killed the remaining Styphoni.

Avalos' last sight in this life was a wolf-headed man bringing his sword down upon his face.

## IV

"How bad?" First Captain Ranthar asked.

The Uncle Wolf shook his head. "It is too late. Taking his leg now will only speed him on his way to Galzar's Hall. I am very sorry, Ranthar. There's nothing I can do."

Ranthar, for about the thousandth time since he had become a Paratime Field Agent, cursed a blue streak under his breath. He hated to see a good man die a hard death when he could save his life by using his med-kit. But it was a clear violation of the Paratime Contamination Code. And, once again, he would have to bite down and resist his better instincts.

Myklon, still in great pain, looked up. "I suspected…as much…before you arrived. What about my men?"

"All dead save Uncle Wolf Syros, Silent Wolf, who took a bullet in his side, Roaring Panther and Freeman Maral. The Styphoni were wiped out, their bodies stripped and left to rot. We recovered the armor, the dead men's possessions and wolf-helms you buried as well."

"Huh." Myklon coughed for a moment. "At least we took a lot of manure eaters with us. And some Ruthani, too, although after seeing how Panther and Wolf fought, I would recruit more of the heathen bastards. Ahh!" Myklon's body arched in pain.

Ranthar wrestled with a decision, then said to himself, "The hell with it." He filled a jar with Ermut's Best then added something Myklon could not see. "Drink this. It will not add to your life, but it could make your remaining time easier." *And mine a lot harder if anybody on First Level ever learns of this.*

Ranthar helped Myklon up into a sitting position and poured the brandy down his throat. Myklon coughed a few times, then smiled. "Thank you. That does help."

"Is there anything you want?"

Myklon thought about the request as the pain in his leg and shoulder faded away. "Two things. First, Gralia."

Ranthar nodded. “Of course. The second?”

Myklon told him and both men smiled.

## V

Gralia entered the room and saw Myklon sitting up on the cot. Tears welled up and rolled down her cheeks.

“I told you I would be back,” Myklon said in a matter of fact voice.

“Oh, Yirtta Allmother! Look at you.”

“I would rather not. I suspect I look as bad as I feel. Or felt. I have had quite a bit of very strong drink to kill the pain. I hope you will forgive me for being in my cups just now.”

“Oh! How can you jest? The healer said…said…”

“I know. I will not see the sun rise again.” Myklon held out his good arm and Gralia moved into it. “I am a soldier, and lived a soldier’s life. I have watched men die in my service as I will now die in my Prince’s service. My only regret is that I leave you.”

Gralia brushed the tears from her cheeks. “Not completely.”

“What?”

“A part of you will live on in the child you have given me.”

Myklon’s eyes went wide. “Child. I am to be a father?”

“Yes.”

“Then I die content. Do me one favor?”

“Yes. Anything.”

“If it be a boy, I would have him named after my father, Minniphon.”

“I will. And I will not wait for his third winter to do it.”

“It is good.” Myklon felt something change within. “Call Syros over.”

“Syros!” she cried.

The Uncle Wolf came over and took one of Myklon’s hands into his own.

“I’m afraid I must go now. Before the True Gods, I grant all of my possessions and holdings to you and our child.”

“It shall be done,” Uncle Wolf Syros said.

Myklon kissed Gralia gently on the lips then lay still. He closed his eyes as the breath left his body.

## VI

Highpriest Lythros paced back and forth in his chamber as he had done every free moment for the last moon. He could not understand what was taking Grand-Captain Avalos so long to return with word of his victory. The Highpriest jumped a candle's height into the air when he heard a loud knock on the door.

"Enter!"

A young white-robed novice bearing a package entered the room with his head held low. "This parcel with your name on it was found at the temple gates, Your Worship."

"Leave it on the table and go."

The novice quickly obeyed, leaving the chamber with a low bow before closing the door behind him. Lythros examined the package for a moment, then tore the linen wrap off and opened the wooden box within.

It was Captain Avalos' head.

Lythros jumped back with a strangled sound in his throat. After he recovered his courage he again approached the package. Next to the head he found a sheepskin with runes written upon it. With shaking hands he withdrew the missive.

*Highpriest Lythros, False Highpriest of the Daemon Styphon. The next head we place in a box shall be yours. Expect us soon.*

Robinos

Lythros' scream of terror could be heard throughout the temple.

# THIRTY-NINE

## I

Gasphros tried to dismiss the nervousness he felt as his party approached the Styphon's House Temple at Valos. One of the scouts had arrived from the Mallegast an eighth of a candle ago to tell him that Captain-General Democriphon had suggested that they avoid the Styphon's House temple in Spartos Town. The Captain-General was planning to raid it and would be arriving in a few days. The scout had not encountered Highpriest Sangar and his retinue on the road, finding Gasphros instead. The troubadour suspected Sangar and his band were already inside the Spartos' temple.

It might be awkward for Skranga if he and his retinue were the only survivors of Democriphon's raid on the Spartos temple. And, while Gasphros suspected that Skranga could talk the sky out of raining, there was no need to take unnecessary chances.

In truth, Gasphros had avoided Spartos Town for reasons of his own. There was a young woman he had been taken with some five winters ago. They had eloped and planned to go north. Unfortunately, her father, a baron of some influence, disapproved and sent men to bring her back. The marriage was annulled and Gasphros had been warned to stay out of Spartos Town if he wanted to live. That was when he made his way to Hos-Harphax and later followed the Hostigi Army into Hostigos and was invited to join the University of Hostigos.

Now, he would have to return to Spartos to warn Duke Skranga about the coming raid. Unfortunately, the sun was falling and soon it would be dark. Silos Road was no place to linger even with three mercenary guards. He would have to spend the night at the local temple.

He had been tempted to try and see her, but knew that after all this time she had most likely been married off to some wealthy merchant or nobleman. She probably wouldn't even remember him, for that matter. She was young with thoughts of romance in her head while he was a former mercenary, thief and finally troubadour with no place to call home after years of fighting, stealing and wandering.

When Gasphros saw his reflection in the water of a still pool, his hair, once chestnut brown, was streaked with gray, while his beard had faded to white. Where his stomach had been flat, it now showed a large paunch. The lines on his tanned face spoke of a life hard lived: one of fighting, drinking, womanizing and occasionally starving. What could a young woman see in him now?

Gasphros forced himself to put Marisol out of his mind. He had an important job to do and could not afford any distractions. If he failed to get to Skranga in time the entire mission would be compromised, not to mention the lives of Skranga, Calthros, Eldra and the men with them.

He handed Trooper Nolos, the most responsible of his three guards, two silvers and a dozen copper coins. "Stay at the white inn we passed. This should be enough for dinner, a few beers and a place to hang your helmet."

"What about you, sir?" Nolos asked.

"While we're here, I might as well reconnoiter the local temple. I'll try to meet up with you at dawn. If not, I'll send a boy with word of my plans."

The bard approached the outer gate of the Valos Temple of Styphon's House Upon Earth and was immediately challenged by one of Styphon's Own Guard. It said something about Hos-Bletha that only one guard braced him and not an entire platoon as would be the case in the other kingdoms. He wondered if they had even heard about the raids on nearby temples.

"What is your business here?" the guard demanded.

"I am a traveling minstrel and would like to share my gifts with your temple master. I would try my skills at entertaining him."

The guard grinned wryly. "Perhaps you would fare well to entertain us. His Worship Hathzar can be generous to clever minstrels. What say you?"

"Yes, that would be wonderful," he replied. "Would it be possible to take a meal as well? It is hard to sing with an empty stomach and a dry throat."

The guard laughed and winked at the bard. "You will not leave here hungry or thirsty if your skills are sharp. Highpriest Hathzar can be especially generous if you know any good ditties about the Daemon Kalvan coming to a bad end."

"I think I can scare up a tune or two in that vein." Gasphros' mind raced as he tried to decide what to do next.

The next morning found Gasphros, well fed and with a full purse, considerably more than he had expected, riding his horse through a light drizzle with his three companions. The horse managed well enough on the muddy path and made good time. Gasphros, a little the worse for wear from the previous night's revelries, fought to keep his breakfast down.

*By Phydros' Chalice, but those priests can drink! And some of the best wine I ever tasted, too. Maybe I should start a religion of my own. After the Styphoni are destroyed, of course, since they dislike competition.*

The rain steadily came down harder as Gasphros approached Spartos Town. By the time he reached the town bridge it was nearly impossible to see more than two rods ahead of him. The water was up almost to the floor of the bridge and was smashing itself against the wooden structure, which was groaning in response. The bard hopped down from the saddle and led his horse across, fearing it could break a leg with a misstep in the dismal weather.

II

Eldra had just about enough. The information she was acquiring was becoming redundant. Only the names and locations changed. Beyond that, it was all the same. Skranga would come into a new temple as Highpriest Sangar, cadge lodgings for a few nights, then leave with as much gold and silver and as many slaves as he could get away with before heading to the next temple in the next town and repeating the process.

Eldra was more than a little surprised at how easy it was for Skranga to get away with his scam. Of course, primitive organizations that ruled primarily through fear and intimidation tended to bleed the spine out of the lower members of the hierarchy. That made for many yes-men who accepted almost anything from a perceived superior. Nobody dared to challenge the boss man. Still, Skranga had a hefty set of stones on him to pull the same con repeatedly with a straight face. He even intimidated the Regwarn out of the priests. *Kalvan knew what he was doing when he assigned this mission to the old horse thief.*

After each visit Skranga sent a detail of mercenaries to escort the slaves and most of the gold back to the camp and pass on any useful information he could glean back to Democriphon and Ranthar: Styphoni temple layouts, troop strength and weaknesses in their security.

The transmission of information between Skranga and Democriphon was slow, especially compared to what Eldra and Ranthar could manage on their own using First Level technology. While the two Paratimers did converse when it was safe to do so, neither used the information they gathered by those means to aid the mission; it would have been a violation of regulations and possibly create suspicion.

Eldra pulled at the top of her dress to make sure nothing was exposed, tugged at her stays, double-checked her hair then proceeded over to Sangar's chamber for breakfast. Slaves and women, even close relations, did not take meals with the priests. Slaves, when fed at all, remained either at their workstations or in the cells where they stayed when not working, which was a rarity. Female relatives ate with their kin or in their own chambers. It was not good to let the lower priests see how the other half lived.

As Eldra was walking down the hall from their so-called private chamber—from long experience she suspected there were peep holes in the walls, although she failed to find any—there was a commotion downstairs. Eldra, out of boredom more than anything else, decided to see what it was. She went down to the main narthex where she saw two guards arguing with somebody who looked like a drenched cat.

The dripping man swept off his wide-brimmed hat and said, "You see before you Gasphros, King of Bards and Bard of Kings. I demand an audience with His Worship! I have performed for him before and he has filled my palms with gold. If you deny him the pleasure of my performance he will have your heads plucked from your neck!"

Eldra could not help laughing aloud. Gasphros stood several inches over the guards, yet his drowned demeanor robbed him of his usual dominating presence; instead, he looked like a water-logged and over-stuffed scarecrow. She found it entertaining to watch the spectacle below as he argued with the guards. Her amusement turned to indignation when one of the guards drew his sword.

"Wait!" she exclaimed. "Isn't that Gasphros the Great? How wonderful! His Worship Sangar was asking about him this morning. He was wondering when Gasphros would appear. Oh, please, King of Bards, tell me that you are here to entertain us."

Gasphros summoned all the dignity he could and bowed low to Eldra. "My Lady, I would be loath indeed to deny such a beauty any delights that I can provide." He glared meaningfully at the two guards. "However, these churls believe that I am unwelcome in this holy sanctuary."

"Unwelcome!" Eldra fairly screamed the word. "Well, I will just go tell Sangar, um, His Worship, how they are treating his favorite bard and see what he has to say about this—"

"There is no need for that, Lady Eldra," interrupted the taller of the two guards. “If you vouch for this…*person*…we will be happy to escort him to His Worship’s quarters.”

“Oh, I can do that,” Eldra said as she rushed over and took Gasphros dripping arm. “I will take him to see His Worship and allow you two to return to your duties. Thank you.” The two rushed up the stairs before the guards could voice a protest.

“What are you doing here, you idiot? Are you trying to get yourself killed?” Eldra whispered.

“I will explain when we are all together,” Gasphros whispered back. “No point in going over the same story twice.”

They quickly made their way up the stone staircase to the guest chambers. Skranga, dressed in his yellow robe, was already eating at the small writing table. He spotted Eldra at the door and waved her in. “Good morning, my child. I trust your slumber was pleasant?”

“It was, Your Worship.” Eldra had noticed that Skranga was becoming more and more comfortable in his role as Sangar. “I dreamed of a great battle between the Daemon Kalvan and the god Styphon. It shook the very Earth each time they clashed.”

“Ah! And did you see our Lord’s victory in your dream?”

“Nay, I awoke before then.” Eldra reached an arm out the doorway and brought it back with Gasphros in tow. “We have a guest for breakfast.”

“Wha—!” Skranga fought to gather his wits.

“Oh, I knew you would be pleased,” Eldra spoke up loudly. “It is Gasphros the Great! He is here to bring joy into your life with his wit, words and music.”

“Oh, I rather like that,” whispered the bard. “May I use it?”

“Knock yourself out.” Eldra noticed the confusion on Gasphros face and said, “Yes, you may.”

Gasphros nodded and turned back to Skranga. “Milor—Your Worship, you need to leave Spartos at once. Our mutual friend is expected to come calling and it might be awkward if you were to meet him under those circumstances.”

Calthros walked in before Gasphros could elaborate further. “Your Worship, our departure will be delayed.” Calthros spotted Gasphros and hesitated.

Skranga set down the flat bread he was about to eat. “Delayed? Why?”

“The bridge is washed out. It is already being repaired but that will take a few days.” Calthros continued to stare at Gasphros. It only took him a few moments to recognize the bard in his soaked state.

“Humph.” Skranga, recovering quickly, took a drink of sassafras tea then cleared his throat. “Isn’t there another route we could take?”

“Yes, but after the heavy rains the roads are covered in mud. It would be nearly impossible to travel on them until they dry. The bridge will be repaired by then.” Calthros took a seat and seized a sausage. “I don’t see any other alternative.”

“This…presents a problem,” Skranga said. “I have just learned that this temple will be receiving visitors. Very soon. We would best be away from here by then.”

“Visitors?” Calthros looked from Skranga to Gasphros and back. “Anyone we know?”

“Someone we know very well,” Skranga said, “and it would be better if we were gone before then.”

Calthros considered the options then shook his head. “To leave now would create suspicion. A priest of your ranking would just wait it out. It would look bad if you allowed yourself to become stuck in the mud like a mere peasant.”

“We need to get our phony guardsmen out of Spartos Temple before company comes,” whispered Skranga. “It would be hard enough to explain how we survived the coming attack, but what about all of our soldiers? Even I cannot fabricate a plausible explanation for that. We would have to let them leave with Democriphon, and then claim that they were slain.”

“Leaving you without your customary escort,” Eldra observed.

“Meaning the rest of the temples would have to replace your lost guardsmen from their own Temple Guard,” Gasphros added.

“Men not loyal to us or our mission,” Skranga finished. “If stay I must, then I shall, but our fighting men must be away.”

The three held silent for a while as they tried to come up with an idea.

"How about a training exercise?" Eldra suggested.

"The Spartos Temple Guardsmen would expect to go along," Calthros countered. "That would be good for the attacking raiders, initially, but then the Guard would be honor bound to hunt them down."

Skranga rubbed his forehead. "I need a target…somebody we could Investigate…"

Gasphros took a seat at the small table and used a spoon to start eating porridge. "What kind of target?" he said with his mouth full.

Skranga considered the possibilities. "Somebody big enough to be a threat, however minor, but small enough that we wouldn't provoke the Great King's ire if we, uh, *smacked him around a bit*."

*Great Blaxtha's Beard, what is Kalvan doing to the language of these people?* Eldra thought.

Gasphros face lit up with evil glee. "Oh, Your Worship, have I got the right man for you!" *He knew a baron whose demesne was just outside Spartos Town.*

# FOURTY

## I

At first light, Highpriest Sangar told the Spartos Temple Master that one of his intelligencers had informed him that a local baron was a secret worshipper of Allfather Dralm. "I am sad to be the bearer of such bad news," he ended.

The Temple Master, a thin old man with skin like dried up parchment, appeared more delighted than horrified. "Such heresy should not be allowed to flourish in our princedom. Which one of our barons is it?"

"Baron Althaphon is the man my intelligencer has identified as the heretic."

Highpriest Mnemnos smiled evilly, then rubbed his hands together with surprising gusto. "A most likely candidate. Althaphon has grown too big for breeches. This will give us the excuse we need to confiscate his lands and property."

Sangar nodded in agreement. According to Gasphros the baron was quite wealthy and not under the thumb of Styphon's House as were most of the kingdom's nobility. "I will send my aide Calthros and my personal guardsmen to investigate this charge at once."

"I can lend you some of the Spartos Temple Guard, if needed," Highpriest Mnemnos offered.

Sangar shook his head. "That would not be wise. There have been too many recent attacks upon our Temples. It would not be wise to leave your temple undermanned. It is quite possible that bandits may be lurking even here."

The old man shook with laughter. "Nay, they would not dare strike within the heart of Bletha. If they dared, Great King Niclophon would not be satisfied until all of them were rounded up and decapitated."

"If Calthros needs your help, he will send a man back to the temple," Sangar said, knowing full well that would never happen.

"Tell him, from me, to strike the infidel baron down and bring us the customary tithe of any treasure he finds. If I were a few years younger, I would fight at his side."

Sangar nodded. "When I visit the Great King in Bletha Town, I will advise him to add the barony to your temple's lands."

The old man smiled so wide that Sangar worried he would split apart like an overripe fruit.

## II

Baron Althaphon was, perhaps, the savviest businessman out of all the nobility in the Princedom of Bletha. His barony was in a lush valley just north of Spartos Town. The second eldest of the five sons of Baron Belamanes, he did not inherit the rich estate of his father until his eldest brother, Mercuron, had squandered almost all of the family fortune and drank himself to death. The only good thing Mercuron ever did was die without progeny, thus allowing Althaphon to inherit what little remained of his father's estate uncontested.

Althaphon took the reins of his position and made several changes. Much of the staff, mostly harlots, was dismissed with a small severance package. The allowance that Mercuron had given to his brothers was cut off. Althaphon made it very clear that everybody would have to labor to earn their bread, so the younger brothers were put to work in exchange for lodging, clothing and food. They grumbled about it, but had no other recourse save to find a wealthy wife, which was not possible without restoring the barony to its former glory.

Althaphon was not afraid to work hard. Even as he forced his brothers to work the fields, he stood right next to them plowing, sewing and reaping. He also started a business hunting river dragons for their meat and hides, then tanning the skins for some of the most highly prized boots in all of Hos-Bletha.

With the profits from each venture, he diversified his holdings; imported wines, cattle, and more. It took ten years to restore the family fortune, and two more to exceed it. In time he placed each of his brothers in charge of various ventures with great care. Althos was prone to excessive drinking, so he was placed in charge of the tanning operation so as not to tempt him with the wines and ales they imported and brewed. Keldar, while a savvy hunter, took unnecessary chances when chasing game, so he was placed in charge of the import and brewery ventures where he wouldn't be able to place himself in harm's way. Oliphon, a genius with numbers who was also a gambler, was allowed nowhere near the counting house. Instead, he was placed in charge of the farms and ranches as overseer where he had little opportunity to skim off profits and seek out gambling rooms.

With the restoration of the family fortune, Althaphon took every precaution to safeguard the lands, title and his life. He married the daughter of another prominent baron who had become indebted to Styphon's House. By buying up the baron's debts he won the baron's gratitude, his loyalty and his daughter. With a wife from a good family, he made every effort to sire a son. In fact, he sired two plus a daughter by his wife, and three more bastards by wenches in his employ. The wenches were paid to take the children away with the promise that they would be provided for, a promise Althaphon made good on, to insure that his bastard sons would not return seeking revenge. His legitimate children also protected him from any untimely demise at his brothers' hands since the laws of heredity favored the eldest surviving male offspring over all others.

Althaphon's fortune and estate continued to grow until war broke out between Hostigos and Styphon's House. His import business suffered the most from northern conflicts. That was when he started exporting victuals. He refused to deal directly with the Styphoni. Instead, he worked with mercenary companies and free merchants. That more than offset any losses the import business suffered.

Then the formula for making fireseed came to him through a Harphaxi mercenary wounded at the Battle of Chothros Heights. The mercenary captain had lost one of his legs, but he had learned the fireseed secret from a captured Hostigi soldier.

Great King Niclophon had forbidden the use and creation of Kalvan's unconsecrated fireseed within the borders of Hos-Bletha. Only Styphon's fireseed was permitted, and then only when purchased from Styphon's House. Althaphon decided that the decree created an opportunity he could exploit. He started his own fireseed works and only sold fireseed to mercenary companies and merchants who were leaving Hos-Bletha.

Security for his fireseed works was tight. Even his sons and brothers knew nothing of it, and he intended to keep it that way. Only slaves imported from the north were used to run the works. He was not about to risk having criminals do the work since at the end of their sentence they might tell outsiders about his fireseed production.

Baron Althaphon feared only one thing—Styphon's House. Once the Temple had one in its grip, it was a rare man who escaped with his life and property intact. Therefore, when what appeared to be a small Band of Styphon's Own Guard appeared at the gates of his fortified manor house on the outskirts of Spartos, he found himself trembling with anxiety.

Althaphon calmed himself down and rode out to the gates rather than send a servant. There was a single priest surrounded by Styphon's Own Guard waiting patiently. He knew little about the hierarchy within Styphon's House so he had no idea how high up the priest at the gate might be. Still, the black robes, with the yellow border, and the sizeable escort suggested he was an upperpriest of some power. As he approached the gate, he mentally debated how to deal with the priest. He settled on brazen.

"If it is not too much trouble, may I inquire what you are doing trespassing on my lands?" Althaphon demanded.

"We have reason to believe that you are making fireseed in violation of your own Great King's edict," Calthros replied calmly. In truth, he did not have any idea one way or the other what the Baron might be up to, nor did he care. He just needed a pretext to nose around for a few days and keep Skranga's phony temple guardsmen out of Spartos Town. "Please open the gates and allow us to look over your lands."

"What? By what right do you come here and make demands of me? I'll have none of you stomping about on my lands without an order from my Great King!"

Calthros thought quickly. Back when he was an underpriest in Styphon's House, none would have dared to defy the Temple. Kalvan changed all of that almost overnight. Still, in Hos-Bletha Styphon's House writ was still unchallenged. And, since Althaphon's barony was in Bletha, Niclophon was both Baron Althaphon's prince and his great king. Since Great King Niclophon was in Styphon's House's pocket, this meant that Calthros would eventually gain Niclophon's support in any dispute between them. *Surely, the Baron knows that?* Not that it mattered since all this was simply a ruse to get him and the guardsmen away from Spartos Town. But, he did not like the Baron's attitude. *Let him sweat it out.*

"Very well, we will wait." Calthros turned to the guardsman nearest him. "Inform the men that we will make camp here while we await word from Great King Niclophon. None are permitted to enter or leave save for the messenger the Baron will send to His Majesty." Calthros turned back to Althaphon. "It will take several days for your emissary to make the journey. I would suggest that you send him at your earliest convenience."

Althaphon started to protest then looked out at the Temple Band of Styphon's Own Guard standing at attention behind the black-robed priest. There had to be at least two or three companies worth of men, all better trained and armed than his small band of personal guards. Even with the home ground advantage he could not hope to win against such odds. He decided instead to play for time.

"I will send off a messenger to my Great King on my fastest horse.

You may camp anywhere but on my lands. I will not have my people or property molested while we wait for Great King Niclophon's reply."

"Very well," Calthros replied. In fact, the delay suited his plans very well. "You will stay within your walls until then."

Althaphon's face turned bright red and he shouted, "You have no authority to keep me or my people trapped within these walls! I am a free man and vassal only to my prince and my king. If you want to make a fight of it, so be it." A sly look covered his face as another thought took hold. "I am quite certain that the other nobles will take a dim view of having one of their own ill-used by Styphon's House and may take action. Tell me, how sure are you of your hold here? You no longer own the fireseed secret. Wouldn't it be a shame if your own unwarranted arrogance forced Hos-Bletha to side with the Daemon Kalvan, as you call him?"

Calthros was impressed by Althaphon's courage. Unfortunately, he had a job to do.

"True. Many think that Styphon's House is weakened by the Daemon, but still we still hold great power. Roxthar could easily be convinced to bring his Investigation here should I find sufficient cause…."

Calthros let the threat hang and waited for the Baron's reaction. It was not long in coming.

"I do not fear this Roxthar as others do. However, I will compromise to save time. My immediate family and I will remain on the lands. My servants and workers shall come and go as necessary to perform their duties. You will remain outside of my lands until the messenger returns."

A real priest of the Styphoni might have balked at the provisions Althaphon outlined. Calthros did not care. He only needed the excuse to be away from the Spartos Temple for the next few days. Still, he could not give in too easily.

"I will accept with one final proviso; you will provide victuals for me and my men. Our delay is at your request, so I think you could manage to provide us with food while we wait."

Althaphon was ready to object then considered the alternatives. A moon-quarter's worth of victuals would be small enough a price to keep the priests out of his business long enough to hide and disguise his fireseed works. "Very well; it is done."

The Baron turned and stormed back to his manor house forgetting that he had left his horse at the gate. Calthros mentally breathed a sigh of relief. The messenger would likely take his time getting to the king allowing, Althaphon the chance to hide whatever he did not want the Styphoni to find. Baron Althaphon would be no friend of Styphon's House from this day forward, which was another bonus.

Gasphros watched the entire exchange from the tree line where he remained hidden. Calthros had handled himself well against Baron Althaphon. He knew from personal experience how difficult the baron could be.

Unlike Calthros, Gasphros knew the baron well enough to read his manner and body language. He was definitely anxious and up to something, and feared having Styphon's House discover what it was. Of course, that could only be one thing.

*I think I can pull a sharp on the baron that will benefit the mission and me.*

The bard faded into the forest where he jumped into the saddle of his horse and spurred it for speed. He would have to act quickly for his plan to work.

## III

That evening Baron Althaphon staggered tiredly into the solar chamber where he collapsed into an overstuffed chair and set down his candle. He was too tired to light the lamps in the chamber and was content to sit in the near darkness with his thoughts.

He had all of the prepared fireseed loaded into barrels along with his stores of sulfur and saltpeter. The charcoal he could have explained away easily enough as it was a common household item used in smiths and hearths. Even the quantity he held would not rouse suspicion since he also sold charcoal to landholders in the local area. The rest had to be removed or hidden.

He considered smuggling it out with the grain on its way to market until he saw that the Styphoni were inspecting the wagons and their loads as they passed out of the gates. Hiding it was equally problematic. The only safe way to hide something that large was to bury it and the guardsmen would almost be certain to spot freshly overturned earth.

There was a chance the great king would intercede on his behalf, though not much of one. Niclophon was hip-deep in Styphon's pocket. He was a true believer and supported every Styphoni idiocy they committed.

Althaphon was on his own and knew it. "Well, old boy, looks like your goose is well and truly cooked," he said aloud to himself.

"Perhaps not."

The Baron jumped out of his chair as if he had been bitten. "Who said that?" he yelled.

From the dark shadows of the room a voice replied, "Somebody with the answers you seek."

"How did you get in here?" The owner of the voice stepped into the light. "Who are you?" The troubadour was still light on his feet enough though he had gained a belly.

"Wait—Gasphros! You dare?"

The bard smiled. "If you will recall, I am known to dare much. Marisol would tell you that if nothing else."

"This time you go too far." Althaphon opened his mouth to call for his guards only to close it again when Gasphros produced a pocket pistol.

"I would rather we not be disturbed, My Lord. Besides, it is to your benefit that I am here now."

"By Dralm, but you have nerve enough for Galzar himself. Fine, the advantage is yours. Speak your piece."

Gasphros kept the pistol leveled at the baron as he used his other hand to move a chair. He took his seat with one leg dangling over the arm. To look at him one might think he was completely at his ease.

"I have friends who can help you out of your current predicament. They are no friends of the Styphoni, which could make them your friends if you are open to the idea."

"Really? Why should I trust you?"

Gasphros lost his smile as he returned his leg to the floor and leaned forward. "You can trust me not to put Marisol in danger. You can trust me to bail you out of your troubles for her benefit. I could just as easily sit back and watch Styphon's House seize your fireseed, burn down your manor and turn you, your family and your staff over to Roxthar's butchers and dance on the ashes of your little empire. Afterwards I could buy what remained of your family at the slave auctions and do as I please with the lot of you. Instead I choose to help you. Not for your sake, of course, or even mine, but for hers. *That* is why you should trust me."

Althaphon considered Gasphros' words. Whatever else he thought of the man, he knew that the bard really did love his daughter. They had even married though he was able to get it annulled. Yes, Gasphros could be counted on to act in Marisol's best interest.

"You realize she has since married and had a child from the time when last you saw her?"

A wave of sadness crossed the bard's face. "I knew it was likely. The attractive daughter of a wealthy baron was bound to attract several suitors. It matters not. I still want to see her well and happy. Now, do we work together or not?"

Althaphon was a drowning man and he knew it. Gasphros held the end of a lifeline that could save him. What else could he do? "We do. What do you propose?"

Gasphros nodded and the smile returned to his face. "I have friends who will buy up all of your fireseed—at northern market prices, mind you—as well as the sulfur, saltpeter and charcoal. They will also get it out of the manor without Styphon's Own Bastards getting wind of it. It shall fall upon you to scrub the buildings clean and disguise their original function. I would use it for storage or as a stable if I were you."

"Wait, how are your people going to do all of this? The Styphoni are all over the place."

"Please, My Lord, I cannot be expected to betray the secrets of my friends, especially when you will benefit from their efforts."

Althaphon glared silently at the bard for several heartbeats. "Fine.

What do you want of me, then?"

Gasphros feigned bewilderment. "Want?"

"Do not try to play me for a fool, Gasphros. You want something. If not Marisol, then what?"

"In truth, I haven't decided. Before you told me Marisol was married, I might have asked to be allowed to win her over again. Sadly, I will not come between a man and his wife. It is base and unhealthy. When I do decide what I want from you, I expect to have your word that you will do it." The smile returned to Gasphros lips. "And have no fears on that. I expect you will enjoy rendering me that aid when the time comes."

# FORTY-ONE

## I

"You what!"

First Captain Ranthar's voice carried for quite a ways. Gasphros began to seriously worry that he had overstepped his authority.

"I arranged for us to acquire a great deal of fireseed, plus the materials to make more, at fair market rates. All we have to do is walk in and take it. Practically."

"Practically?" Democriphon prompted.

"We just ease past our own people and take it." Gasphros related Skranga's plan to keep his false guardsmen out of the Spartos temple and his own plan to get fireseed without having to steal it. "All we have to do is arrange for a plausible distraction for our people who are acting as Styphon's Own Guard and have them be lured away while your men jump the wall and collect all of the fireseed."

Ranthar felt his head start to throb. "Most of our people will be preparing to attack the temple. We have limits on our manpower."

"You are taking, what, forty freemen with you on this raid, yes? Well, that leaves over two hundred with nothing to do. They are still in training, yes, but this is not a military operation."

Uncle Wolf Syros stepped between the two fearing they might come to blows. "Most of the freemen are back at the village logging and milling the timber for the homes we are trying to build. In addition, most of them are not yet strong enough for the heavy lifting you are asking of them. Gycules could lift a barrel up to the top of the baron's wall, I would bet, but not all of them—"

"And," interrupted Ranthar, "I want him with me on the raid."

"Normally," Syros continued, "it would take two men to lift a barrel full of fireseed, two more to receive it at the top of the wall, and another three to gently set it down on a wagon. It would take at least double that for the freemen."

"I am afraid your plan is not workable right now, Gasphros," Ranthar concluded. "Maybe in a few days after the raid…"

"I disagree," Uncle Wolf Syros interjected. "Gasphros has a good plan and I know how to see it through. One of the problems with military men is that they see everything from a battlefield perspective. That is not the case here."

"How so?" Ranthar asked.

Syros shook his head in wonderment. "Ranthar, I at least expected you to see past the problems. You do not need that many people, for one thing. The Baron will supply the work force to transport the fireseed to the wall and over. It is in his best interest, after all. Secondly, have none of you ever used planks to move goods over an obstacle? Set some long boards on each side of the wall. The Baron's men will role the barrels up; our men will receive them at the top of the wall and gently roll them down into the wagon. The only question now is how many wagons we will need."

"And I can get Baron Althaphon to supply those as well, I'll warrant," Gasphros added. "What do we do for a distraction? Styphon's Own Guard—even if they are phonies—cannot simply ignore barrels rolling over a wall. Uncle Wolf?"

"That's easy. We shoot at them."

Democriphon, Ranthar and Gasphros all looked at Syros with expressions that ranged from confusion to shock.

"Sixty men with several horse pistols each will charge their weapons with fireseed but without the balls," Syros explained. "Lots of noise without the danger."

"Hmm…I think we can manage more than sixty freemen in this case," Ranthar said. "We might as well make a show of it."

"So we have your approval?" Gasphros asked.

"Indeed," Ranthar said. "See if you can get the Baron to kick in some grain and fresh meat as well. We could use a break from salted pork and jerked beef."

## II

Baron Althaphon did his best to fight off the growing anxiety he felt as he looked out over the grounds from his balcony. Gasphros had explained his plan and what he needed to carry it out. During the day the wagons had been loaded with fireseed, sulfur, saltpeter, charcoal, grain and fresh meat; they were already positioned near a wall that was partially obscured by trees and brush on both sides. Gasphros' friends waited somewhere on the other side for the Styphoni to be lured away.

*This should be interesting even if it fails,* Althaphon thought. *Gasphros was always entertaining even when I wanted him drawn and quartered.*

The sky was already growing dark. What light there would be to see by would come from moonlight alone. Torches would give away everything. Off in the distance he could hear the sound of gunfire.

*Are Gasphros' friends attacking Styphon's Own Guard?* Althaphon watched in fascination as muzzle flashes appeared at the edge of the forest. The Styphoni were quick to respond. Almost as a single body, they came together and charged forward into the tree line. They did not even bother to fire back, which seemed odd until he realized that it was nearly impossible to take aim while charging on horseback.

Althaphon turned his gaze to where his wagons sat. In the shadows of the trees, he could just make out movement. It was impossible to discern what was happening. Instead of being annoyed, the Baron took comfort in that fact; if he could not see what was happening then maybe the Styphoni couldn't either.

In less than a quarter-candle the first wagon was moving away from the wall. *If they keep this up, they will be done in two or three candles.* Althaphon tried to divide his attention between the wagons and the Styphoni. Styphon's Own Guard, save for two men still at the gate, had been swallowed completely by the forest. The two remaining Guardsmen kept their attention on the tree line, thus missing the activity around the curve of the wall. Occasionally a volley of shots rang out.

"Enjoying the show, My Lord?"

Althaphon tried not to act surprised though he still started a bit. "By Styphon's Brass Balls, man, don't do that!"

"You have my apologies, My Lord," Gasphros said in a contrite tone. "I wanted to be certain you were satisfied with how things are progressing." The bard joined Althaphon on the balcony. "It looks like the Styphoni were caught with their breeches down."

He mentally wrestled between his irritation with having to deal with Gasphros and his admiration over the bard pulling off his plan. Admiration won out by a narrow margin.

"I have to admit that you delivered as promised. I can't stop the manure eaters from coming into my lands for much longer, but at least they won't find anything incriminating."

Gasphros smelled an opportunity. "What would it be worth to you if I could keep the Styphoni from entering your lands? Maybe even turn their attention elsewhere? This time, I mean. I have no idea what may come in the future."

"You could…no. I do not want to know. Let us just say that you would find me neither ungrateful nor parsimonious."

Gasphros had no idea what "parsimonious" meant. Still, grateful would do for now. "This will take a bit more doing… Ah, yes. I will see what miracles I can conjure before your fine manor is further violated. I shall take my leave."

Althaphon put out a restraining hand. “Hold for one moment.”

Gasphros thought he may have overplayed his hand and considered jumping from the balcony when the baron tossed a small sack at him. Without thinking, he caught it. The sack was surprisingly heavy. Gasphros looked inside; it was filled with gold and silver coins.

“For your services,” Althaphon explained. “We have had our differences, yes, still, you never fail to entertain, and tonight was very entertaining indeed.”

## III

Skranga spent the day searching the Spartos Town temple under the guise of inspecting it for damage. In fact, he was looking for places he could hide when Democriphon or Ranthar showed up for the raid. Not that he needed it; he just wanted to have a plausible explanation for how he survived should it come up later.

As he went through each room, his mind worked overtime considering alternatives. One idea after another floated through his fertile imagination.

“Is everything to your satisfaction, Your Worship?”

Skranga was startled out of his thoughts by the resident temple master. “Indeed. You have kept this temple in good repair. That reflects well upon Styphon’s House Upon Earth. Now, more than ever we need to look strong, to friend and foe alike.”

“Well, I have to admit that we do not suffer the strain of war as our brothers in the north have of late,” Highpriest Mnemnos said. “Here things are placid enough. How is the war going, Your Worship?”

“We have had more losses than victories of late,” Skranga admitted with a morose tone of voice. “The Battle of Tenabra was our greatest victory since the war began, and now it is like it never happened. Soton was nearly excommunicated over losing the Battle of Phyrax Field. Only His Worship Roxthar managed to sway the Inner Circle from such folly.”

Highpriest Mnemnos shivered. “Are the rumors of the Holy Investigation idle gossip or are they true?”

"They are true, and probably worse than you have heard. I could not leave Balph fast enough; Archpriest Roxthar was pulling underpriests off the streets to be interrogated by the Investigation. With Supreme Priest Sesklos on his deathbed, it won't be long before the Investigation begins to question highpriests as well."

Mnemnos rubbed his hands together. "We live in a time of madness. With devils, like the Daemon Kalvan, arriving from the Cold Lands and usurping their true overlord's rights. Now, it had reached the Temple, if what you say is truth."

"It is truth. If Archpriest Dracar, Roxthar's cat's-paw, is elevated to Supreme Priest we will all be damned. There will be no succor for those of us who do not believe in the True God, as the bootlickers are now calling Styphon."

"True god, pure poppycock! These sanctimonious asses are destroying our livelihoods. A pox on all of them."

"True, and if they don't bring the Temple to its knees, the Usurper might do it for them.

Mnemnos shook his head slowly. "I have heard that the Daemon Kalvan slays every Styphoni priest he encounters. He doesn't even ransom them back to Styphon's House."

Skranga hung his head in commiseration. "True. True. He…wait, what was that again?"

The Highpriest repeated himself. "I said the Daemon Kalvan doesn't even ransom our brothers back to Styphon's House."

"Yes, that's right. I thought I misheard you for a moment." *Forget pretending to hide. I have a better idea.*

# FORTY-TWO

## I

As First Captain Ranthar waited for the scout to return, tension started to wear on him a bit. He moved his head back and forth, and used a First Level conditioning exercise to relax his muscles. They had been very lucky with their temple raids so far, and he meant to see that their run of good fortune continued. They had created enough uproar in Artigos and Taurnos that the temples in those princedoms were on full alert so Captain-General Democriphon had suggested they try the same tactics in Bletha.

Unlike Marthrax and Erygon Town, the Blethan town of Spartos was much larger and there was more traffic. That meant coming in at night under the cover of darkness as before, but not putting on Styphon's Own Guard's armor until they were close to their target. It would not do for the Temple Guard to be observed marching to the temple right before it was raided, sacked and burned. So they traveled in small groups until they met up near the temple.

It was growing late and few of the

townspeople were on the streets of Spartos except for a few meandering drunks and the night watch.

Petty-Captain Andros was first to arrive at the meeting place. As in most Blethan towns, Styphon's temple was situated on the west side of the hos-plazos, the great square, where the front of the temple would receive the morning sun. For that reason, Ranthar arranged for his mercenaries to gather in an alleyway on the north side of the plazos where they could change into the Styphoni armor unobserved while still watching the temple.

"Did you have any trouble with the night watch?" Ranthar asked.

Andros shook his head. "The first two of them were already half in the bag and we just knocked them out. They'll wake up in the morning with the worst hangover of their lives. The other two were more observant and we had to kill them."

Vanir and Petty-Captain Timnos, former head of the sharpers' mercenaries, were the next to arrive. They quickly and silently changed into the black robes of Styphon's House underpriests. When finished they placed their clothes into bags and set them down in the alley. After an eighth of a candle four more men arrived. It continued in that manner for two candles. Finally, the company was complete.

Vanir and Timnos spattered some ox blood on each other while the mercenaries dressed as Styphon's Own Guard inspected each other to be sure they looked as though they had been in a battle. More ox blood was smeared on their armor and faces. Most of the armor was scavenged from Guardsmen killed in battle so it looked authentic. Ranthar and Andros silently inspected the men to be sure everyone's appearance was convincing. Once satisfied, they nodded to Vanir and Timnos.

The two former sharpers led the way across the hos-plazos with a squad of Guardsmen behind them. Vanir screamed out breathlessly, "Guards! Open the gates. We've been attacked." The gates opened and a dozen Temple Guardsmen poured through. They instantly started firing and five of Vanir's men fell to the pavement. Instantly, return fire came back from across the street. Vanir and Timnos quickly retreated under the withering counter-fire from their party.

Several Guardsmen dropped and the rest fell back, slamming the gate closed behind them.

"How did you know?" Ranthar yelled to Andros.

"The guards at the gate," he yelled, as he fired both of his horse-pistols. "They didn't hesitate to open the gates or ask any questions."

Ranthar cursed in Greffan. Having been on several such raids already, he should have noticed the same thing. Back in Marthrax the gate guards demanded an explanation before opening the gates. There was nothing for it now save to make the best of the situation and try to survive. "Any suggestions, Petty-Captain?"

Andros risked a bullet by stepping away from the temple wall to quickly survey the scene then jumped back. "There's no way to get at the windows without being cut to ribbons by the gunfire. We'll have to go for the main entrance and force the doors open."

Ranthar recalled that every temple they had ever sacked had doors made of solid oak. Gycules and Xykos together could not break through those. "How?"

Andros shrugged, looked all around the plazos until his eyes settled on a bedraggled grove of pecan trees growing out of the ruins of a former temple to Yirtta Allmother. He pointed it out to Ranthar, saying, "We can use those trunks as battering rams."

"That's going to take too long," Ranthar replied. "Besides raking fire will decimate the company."

"Do you have a better idea, Captain?"

"Yes, get me a keg of fireseed."

Andros nodded, a smile curling his lips. Then he barked out some orders to one of the troopers.

The man returned quickly, holding aloft a small keg of fireseed.

"Will this do?" Andros asked, as if he already knew the answer to his question.

Ranthar nodded. He watched as Andros removed the stopper and shook out a handful of fireseed. He used it to fill a length of cotton cloth, brought by one of his men, twisting it tightly to make a primitive fuse. He put the fuse into the keg and said, "Concentrate your fire on those windows and murder holes."

The nearby soldiers nodded and began firing while Andros raced across the cobblestone street to place the keg before the door. He paused to light the fuse while his men kept up their withering fire. The Petty-Captain was fairly well protected by the temple overhang and took his time to light the fuse with his tinderbox. Once the fuse was set on fire, he raced across the street to shelter, zig-zagging to dodge Styphoni return fire.

One bullet *whaaanged* off the rear of Andros' back-and-breast, but otherwise he made it intact only to get a tongue-lashing from Ranthar. "You motherless snot-drizzler, you should have sent one of the men to do that!"

An explosion drowned out Andros' reply.

A piece of shrapnel slammed into Ranthar's leg and he folded up.

With the doors down the mercenaries did not need to be told what to do. They raced into the temple firing at anything that breathed and a lot of things that never did as they stepped over the bodies of several guards who had the misfortune to be standing at the ready inside the narthex. Andros struggled to protect Ranthar from return fire even as he barked orders at the men.

"Spread out in groups of four. Cover each other. I want two men using swords and the other two ready with glaives or horse pistols. Save the arquebuses for long-distance. Those of you with musketoons use them. Swordsmen, be ready to let the pistoleers use your guns and reload them when you can. Watch for ambushes and each other's backs. You two and you two, cover the stairs." Off to the side Andros spotted Vanir and Timnos. "You two, find the slaves and free them. They can help Kentros and, uh, you with the yellow beard, go with them. MOVE IT!"

Petty-Captain Andros kept yelling orders even as he tied a bandage on Ranthar's leg. When he was done, he ordered, "Stay put, sir. I'll see that the temple is taken."

Ranthar nodded, trying not to groan. The moment Andros entered the temple, he groped for his field med-kit designed to look like a large snuff box. He fumbled it open and took out the hypos-spray injector, held it up to his injured leg and hit the knob; his pain vanished in less than a heartbeat.

## II

Inside the narthex Andros drew his sword and ran for the opposite staircase shooting a guardsman and slashing a priest on the way. As he raced up the stairs, he holstered the pistol and drew his knife. At the top, he hesitated as he looked down the hallway. There were several doors on either side where armed guardsmen could be waiting in ambush. He flipped his knife into a throwing position and kicked in the first door. The room was empty.

Andros kicked in the next door to find a white-robed priest cowering in a corner. “You! Come with me or die.” The priest quickly obeyed.

The Captain placed the novice in front of him and ordered that he open the next door. No sooner had the door opened than two shots rang out, killing the young priest. One of his men flung his knife and caught one black-robed priest in the chest. Andros then rushed in to cut down the second man as he fumbled with his weapon trying to reload it.

Andros continued kicking in doors to empty rooms until he reached the second to last door. This one contained a scrawny priest with a big gut in yellow robes.

“Ah, one of the high dung-eaters. I think I will take your head as a trophy.” Andros moved forward with a wide grin on his face.

“What? No, man! Don’t you know who I am?”

“Yes. A dead man.” Andros lunged forward narrowly missing the highpriest.

“No!” the priest screamed. Then in a loud whisper, “Call Ranthar or Democriphon! They will tell you not to kill me.”

*What?* “How do you know those names?” Andros demanded.

“If you take my head, you may never find out. I am unarmed and trapped. You can spare a moment to call your commander, can’t you?”

“I…” Andros never finished his sentence. Something solid and heavy collided with his skull with enough force that even his helm could not protect him from. As he sank to the floor, the last thing he saw was a woman holding a brass chamber pot with a sizeable dent in the side.

Andros awoke in a foul mood with a throbbing headache. It took him a moment to realize he was on a well-stuffed bed. He looked about and saw that Captain Ranthar, the strange woman and the yellow-robed priest were sitting at a small table drinking from golden goblets.

"By the mace of Galzar, what's going on here?" he demanded. Yelling made his head hurt even more.

First Captain Ranthar smiled and gestured at the other two. "Andros, meet Duke Skranga and Lady Eldra. They are working with us. You never met them; they were at our other camp."

"You had me very worried for a moment, there," Skranga said. He turned to Ranthar and said, "Why wasn't this man informed of my identity?"

"First rule of espionage. Only those with a need to know need to know."

Skranga grimaced. "Under the circumstances I think this man could have been brought in on our little secret. Well, no matter. Eldra handled things rather handily. Did you manage to keep at least one priest alive?"

"We did," Ranthar replied. "He is being forced to show us where everything is. Afterwards, we'll have his head cut off and torch this cesspool."

"I think not."

Ranthar, Eldra and Andros looked confused.

Skranga explained. "We need to keep the priest alive. He is going to take the demands for my ransom to the next temple. Therefore, you will take me prisoner and demand a hefty ransom for my return. This will explain why I was spared and give us a nice little bonus for the treasury."

Ranthar had to agree. "You're right. Either somebody escaped during our previous raids and told Styphon's House our methods or they simply do not trust anybody coming in after dark. Either way, this operation is no longer useful. The temple dome is being stripped of the gold tiles as we speak by our soldiers and the slaves we freed."

"No more temple raids for a while, then," Skranga said. "Moreover, when I am ransomed back I will head straight for Tarr-Bletha and seek protection. You and Democriphon need to get the Orphan Prince game started. From what you have told me, you have a fine base from which to launch the operation. Now get busy."

"Wait," Andros said. He struggled to his feet and staggered over to the table. "What do you mean 'Orphan Prince Game'? And who is this man wearing the robes of a Styphon's House highpriest?"

Ranthar winced. *Great Galzar, now we're in for it.*

"It is an expression, Captain", Skranga said. "For those of us who are intelligencers, everything is a game. I am Captain-General Democriphon's personal spy, Duke Skranga, acting as a Styphon's House highpriest under the name Highpriest Sangar."

*Dralm, but that man thinks fast,* Ranthar thought.

Andros did not look convinced but let it lie. "So you have infiltrated the Temple?"

Skranga said, "Yes, I have. Where was I…oh, yes, we have to get everything out of here tonight and be gone before sunrise. In addition to the soldiers, how many slaves are working on stripping the gold tiles?"

"Fifty or so on the dome and another twenty gathering the gold and stowing it in the wagons," Ranthar said. "I'm not sure if they'll be finished by first light."

Skranga said. "Dralm-damnit, we may have to either leave some behind or stay here all day as we did at the other temples."

Ranthar did some fast calculating and decided Skranga was right. "I guess we will have to leave it, then—"

"We stay," interrupted Andros. "Have some of the men lay out the dead guardsmen, stripped of their armor, in the courtyard. Vanir and Timnos can explain to anyone that comes looking that we were attacked and killed the invaders. The town guard will not press the issue as they know better than to involve themselves in the affairs of Styphon's House. We will tell all callers that we will not be doing business until the godless ones have been disposed of properly and we have repaired the damage to the temple."

"Not bad," Skranga said. "What if Styphon's Own Guard or priests of another temple should seek an audience?"

"We invite them in and take off their heads," Andros said. "It is not like we are squeamish about killing more of them, is it?"

"No," Ranthar agreed. "Not at all." *Andros is someone to keep an eye on, he learns fast.*

# FORTY-THREE

## I

Baron Althaphon began to wonder if Gasphros would not be able to come through on his offer. It was not as important now that his fireseed works was dismembered and returned to its original design as a stable. He doubted that even Archpriest Anaxthenes would be able to discern that the stable had recently functioned as a fireseed works.

"My Lord."

Althaphon started again. "Dralm-damnit, stop that! How do you keep getting into my home so easily?"

"Is that what you really want to ask me?' Gasphros said with a mischievous smile.

"Yes, but I would rather know what is happening with Styphon's Own Guard outside my gates. It has been three days since you claimed that you could get rid of them."

Gasphros strummed his lyre. "Ah, yes. About that." The bard moved to the window. "Take a look."

"I looked three candles ago," Althaphon said irritably.

"A lot can happen in three candles, My Lord."

Curious, Althaphon walked over and peered out the window. The Guard and all their equipment were gone. "What! How…?"

"Were I to tell you, My Lord, I fear your life would be forfeit," Gasphros said cryptically. "Let us simply say that I have some very powerful friends."

The Baron could not help but wonder if even Great King Niclophon had the clout to order a Temple Band away from his lands. "Your friends must be truly wondrous. I should like for them to be my friends as well, Gasphros."

"Their friendship must be earned, My Lord, and such a thing can be dangerous," Gasphros warned.

"Of that I have no doubt. What are their aims?"

Gasphros had to think a moment before answering. "They are in sympathy with Great King Kalvan in that they see Styphon's House Upon Earth as blight on all of the kingdoms."

"Wait. They oppose Styphon's House, yet they were able to order the Styphoni away from my lands? That makes no sense."

Gasphros smile returned. "Who said they ordered the Styphoni away? No. My friends simply gave the dung eaters something else with which to be concerned. I am quite certain that you will hear all about it in a day or so. When you do, say nothing. I would hate to see Marisol upset by your sudden disappearance."

The threat was not ignored. "No, that would be bad…for her." Althaphon walked over to a table and picked up another sack, only larger than the one he gave Gasphros three days earlier. Instead of throwing it, he hefted it with some small effort and handed it to the bard. "A token of my appreciation for your friends."

Gasphros did not have to look inside to know the sack was filled with gold. From the weight, he estimated it held at least a hundred and eighty to two hundred ounces. "My friends will be pleased with this token. You may expect to hear from me again. Nevertheless, take heed; do not try to have me followed. It would go badly for whoever you send as well as for you."

"I wouldn't dream of it." Althaphon turned and poured two goblets of wine. When he turned back to offer one to the bard he found only empty air. He smiled then drained the first glass. "As if any of my men could follow you if they tried."

## II

Great King Niclophon could scarcely credit his ears. Another of Styphon's temples had been stripped of values and despoiled; this time inside his own Princedom. "Do we know where these raiders are coming from? Could they be Hostigi looking for revenge?"

Highpriest Lesthros, the temporary temple master of the High Temple of Bletha Town, snorted, then recovered his composure.

*It doesn't take long for their arrogance to show*, Niclophon thought. Lesthros was a recent appointment by Niclophon since they didn't have time to wait for Balph to send Prythames' replacement. *As busy as the Temple is dealing with Kalvan and Archpriest Roxthar, we could wait a dozen winters for them to pick a new archpriest for the High Temple*.

"I think the Hostigi have more than enough on their plate dealing with the Grand Host of Styphon's House," Lesthros said. "Sending men into a territory not yet involved in the war would work against them, I should think. Why spare men they desperately need to come down here and add to their list of enemies? It defies reason, Your Majesty."

Niclophon considered the Highpriest's words. For a brief moment, he wished Prythames were still alive instead of decorating some anonymous tree. Lesthros made perfect sense, of course, which was why he was so useful. Still… "Don't you think it's possible that a small contingent has come south to stir up trouble, if just to keep us too busy to join in the war effort against them?"

The Highpriest barely suppressed another snort. "Such a plan could very easily backfire, Your Majesty. We would only have to capture one of them and the entire arrangement would come undone."

Niclophon nodded. Lesthros, as usual, made sense. "Then who *is* attacking the Styphoni in my kingdom?"

The Highpriest made a show of considering the question. "I believe that it is bandits, sire."

"Bandits?"

"Indeed. Of late, the robbers and outlaws have become emboldened. They attacked a military caravan and then a slave caravan. Then Styphon's House temples. That is just what we have heard about. Who knows what diabolical arrangements they may have made with the Ruthani?"

"So, you think the bandits are working hand in hand with the Ruthani rather than fighting them?" Niclophon chewed on that for a moment. "Bandit bands have never before banded together in such large numbers."

The Highpriest nodded. "True. I suspect smaller groups and bands of outlaws have joined together to form larger companies; all the better to prey on isolated temples and wayfarers. The malefactors have been emboldened by the war against the Usurper and the Temple's activity in the north, which has necessitated the transfer of a number of Blethan Temple Bands of Styphon's Own Guard to the warfront. I also suspect that they waylaid a Styphoni convoy, seized their robes and armor, and used sharpers to gain access to the temples."

"A sharper could do that?" Niclophon asked.

"A sharper could sell saltwater to a Carib, Your Majesty," Lesthros answered. "A shaved head, priestly vestments, some blood from an ox or sheep and a company of what appeared to be Styphon's Own Guard…" He shrugged. "It wouldn't take much to sell a story about being attacked by Ruthani or bandits. Once inside they would have the advantage of surprise and make quick work of the unwary priests and guards."

Niclophon stood up from the Silver Throne and paced about the chamber. "Your theory has much to support it. I almost wish it were Hostigi. They would likely be easier to root out."

The Highpriest started to reply when he was interrupted by a commotion from the hall. Annoyed, he went out to see what the ado was all about. There he found the guards arguing with an out-of-breath underpriest. "Pray tell, what is this all about?"

"I have an urgent message from Spartos!"

"Another one? We already sent a messenger back with instructions to cooperate with Styphon's Own Guard…"

"The temple has fallen!" yelled the priest. "It was sacked and burned while the High Priest Sangar was there. Now he and his widowed sister have been abducted for ransom."

"Lesthros," Niclophon's voice called from the throne room. "Bid him enter."

"As you wish, Your Majesty." Highpriest Lesthros cast a baleful eye on the messenger and gestured him in.

Chancellor Archimanes, attracted by the noise, followed behind.

No sooner had the messenger entered he fell to his knees; not out of respect but because his remaining strength had failed him. Niclophon, thinking it a sign of respect, gestured to the man to regain his feet. After a moment of struggling, he did so.

"Another temple has been desecrated?" Niclophon asked.

"Yes, Your Majesty," the priest said breathlessly. "It was put to sword and torch after a fierce battle." The priest went on at great length to explain that the bandits had come in looking like Styphon's Own Guard after a terrible battle. While the bandits failed to take Styphon's House by surprise, still they succeeded in killing everybody within the temple. The raiders had tricked everybody into thinking that the Styphoni had been victorious by laying the bodies of the fallen in the courtyard then stripped the temple of everything of value.

Niclophon looked over at Lesthros; it appeared the Highpriest was correct, although he would have liked to wipe off his smug smile.

"Were any of the invaders left behind?"

"Nay, Your Majesty. There remains naught save charred bodies, smoldering wood and a demand of ransom for the return of His Worship, Sangar."

"Who is this Highpriest Sangar," Lesthros asked.

"Your Worship, they say he was sent from Balph to do a tour of temples raising funds for the war against the Daemon Kalvan," the underpriest replied.

Archpriest Lesthros stroked his beard. *No word was sent to the Temple about Balph sending another highpriest to raise funds, not that the Inner*

*Circle typically bothers to inform us. Probably, poor dead Prythames knew about it. Roxthar has stirred up Balph like an ant's nest. Still, it may be one of Anaxthenes' schemes; if so, he'll put the gold and silver in his own money-boxes. I must find a way to rake off my own share. I'll talk to this Sangar and see if he is a reasonable man.*

"Interesting," Niclophon said. "The raiders chose a time when Sangar's Guard was occupied with Baron…?"

"Althaphon, sire," Lesthros said.

"Althaphon's lands," Niclophon finished. "That suggests either collusion by somebody in Styphon's House, which is unthinkable, or that the bandits have good intelligencers."

"They have been far too successful for bandits. I suspect that the raiders have had inside help, sire," the Highpriest said. "Probably, from one of the local lords or barons."

"Do you think this Baron Althaphon was in on the raid? He certainly had a grievance with Styphon's House."

Lesthros had not considered that possibility. He gave it some thought then decided against it. With Styphon's Own Guard watching at his gates, it was unlikely Althaphon could use a chamber pot without one of the Temple Guardsman offering him a towel to cleanse his arse. One might as well suspect that Styphon's Own Guard was in on the raid. *Ridiculous!* He said as much.

"I would have to concur, Your Worship," Niclophon said. "To the best of my knowledge the Baron has been a loyal subject." He then turned to the messenger with a look that suggested he had forgotten the man was there, which he had. "You may go. Send a messenger to Balph and tell the Temple Almoner that the royal treasury will supply half the gold demanded for the ransom."

Lesthros grimaced. *That will not go down well with the Inner Circle. I was sent here to "fix" things. I must find the source of the rebellion, or I may wind up hanging from a tree or be recalled to Balph for a session with Roxthar's Investigators.* His stomach rumbled and he made a quick departure, heading for the nearest privy.

## III

"Another temple?"

"Yes, father. I've just learned that two more temples were sacked in the Princedom of Bletha. The bandits must be gaining confidence to attack within the heart of our Great King's power."

Prince Mythros of Pytha looked out the window into the distance as if trying to see all the way to Spartos Town. "Somebody is not very enamored of Styphon's House."

"Perhaps," Kythar nodded. "It is equally possible that somebody is ill disposed to Hos-Bletha in general, or maybe our Great King."

Mythros turned to look at his son. Kythar was still young, a mere seventeen winters, though well-tutored and mature for his age. "Why do you say so, Kythar?"

"There have been attacks on more than just Styphon's House," Kythar explained. "A military convoy, several slave trains, numerous merchant caravans and parties, as well as random acts of banditry—far more than usual."

"The convoys were attacked by Ruthani."

"Or somebody who wished to be mistaken for Ruthani."

Mythros considered Kythar's words. "You believe these attacks are connected. Why?"

Kythar cleared his throat. "The two types of attacks happened suspiciously close together and both were carried out with the same degree of efficiency. Nobody was left alive in either the slave convoy or the Styphoni temples, yet in both cases the slaves were taken away. Why? They cannot expect to sell them at auction anywhere in Hos-Bletha without proper documentation. Our nearest neighbors are too embroiled in war for the bandits to risk taking them there for sale. And how could that many slaves go unnoticed traveling anywhere within our Kingdom?"

"There were survivors from the military convoy," Mythros pointed out.

"Yes, all came back with tales of the terrible Ruthani." Kythar shook his head. "I believe this was to set the stage for a diversion. Or, maybe, somebody didn't have the stomach to kill people who've done no wrong in their eyes."

"Done no wrong?" Mythros had not considered that possibility. "Do you suspect they're escaped slaves avenging themselves?"

"At first, yes, until I realized that the attacks were carried out with far too much military precision for escaped slaves. They were well-equipped, prepared, provisioned and even managed to get hold of Styphon's Own Guard's armor and weapons. Former slaves would not have the skills or resources these attackers have. I believe we are dealing with military men; experienced warriors with a brilliant captain-general leading them."

That made sense and Mythros said so. "Do you think it could also be Hostigi?"

"Hostigi?" Kythar had not considered that possibility. He did so now. "Deserters looking for wealth are a good possibility, but any leader capable of pulling off the raids we have heard about would be very valuable to the Hostigi war effort. They would certainly offer him wealth and position, a barony or even a dukedom, to keep him. Hostigi deserters I can believe, but not their leaders. The bandit's leader is a complete mystery to me."

Mythros liked that Kythar admitted when he was stumped. Others would fill the air with conjecture hoping something would stick. A good leader and tactician admitted when he did not have all of the facts then worked to ferret out the truth.

"To me as well. A thought does occur to me; might not this brilliant leader be a rogue marshal or grand-captain from Styphon's Own Guard?"

Kythar mulled that over. It did not fit. "Styphon's House is perhaps the most vindictive organization in the Five Kingdoms; six if you credit Hos-Hostigos as a kingdom. Nobody would desert unless he was already under threat of death, mutilation, or something equally unpleasant. The actions of this mystery leader would suggest he is nearly as clever as Grand Marshal Soton. Such a man is far too valuable to risk losing, I would think, although those fools in Balph are capable of almost any stupidity."

Mythros smiled at the characterization. "Your late uncle would have agreed."

Kythar took pleasure in the compliment. His father thought highly of his brother-in-law, the former Great King, before he was murdered by persons unknown. "What should we do about these raiders, father?"

"For now? Nothing. As long as they attack only the Styphoni and vultures like the slave traders, it is not our concern. And stay away from Pytha. Let Niclophon deal with it in his own inept way."

Kythar agreed up to a point. "I think we should prepare lest we become a target as well."

"I agree," Mythros said. "I'll leave it in your very capable hands."

"Thank you, father." Kythar bowed and started to leave when another thought struck him. "While I am at it, would you like me to investigate the rumors?"

"Rumors?" The Prince had not heard any rumors, though he was hardly in a position to do so. "What rumors?"

"There is some talk of a new Prince in Exile looking for men and gold to retake the kingdom from Niclophon." Kythar chuckled. "I can't believe anybody is reviving that old ploy."

Mythros snorted. The Orphan Prince con popped up every few years or so. Whenever one cropped up in his principality, he had dealt with it severely. "Is this happening in my realm?"

"Only talk, father. As yet, none have stepped forward to claim the part, at least within Pytha's borders. In fact, most of the talk is in the other princedoms. All we seem to be hearing so far are the rumors. I suspect your past actions have discouraged any sharpers from bringing the game to our doorstep."

Mythros laughed. "Well, you know how it is. When you hang a few sharpers, you end up with a bad reputation with them all. Keep abreast of the situation. However, as long as it does not enter my realm, let it be."

# FORTY-FOUR

## I

Ranthar and his party had just passed through the village gates of Mallegast, when Prince Democriphon, trailed by several bodyguards, appeared in the village center. Democriphon gave a visible look of relief until he spotted Duke Skranga and Eldra under restraint, and his eyebrows shot up. Democriphon looked as though he was about to make an inquiry when Ranthar shook his head.

Ranthar was relieved when the Prince held his tongue, rather than endanger whatever game his First Captain might be playing, He quickly spoke up. "Your Highness, I have a special prize from our work in Spartos. Meet Sangar, a Highpriest visiting from Balph."

"Release me, infidels, or Styphon's Own Vengeance shall rain down upon you all!" Sangar screamed.

*Skranga is rather convincing in his role as Highpriest Sangar*, Ranthar noted.

"Charmed, I am sure," the Prince replied, before turning to Ranthar. "Why is this vile dung-eater still alive, let alone in our camp?"

Ranthar mentally let loose with a sigh of relief. Democriphon caught on quickly. "Because he's worth more dead than alive, sire. We're going to ransom his Worthlessness back to Balph."

Democriphon looked surprised, as though he couldn't make sense out of this phony kidnapping. "I assume all went well in Spartos, Captain?"

"Yes, Your Highness. We were able to strip all the gold from the dome, kill a score of false priests and free many slaves."

"Then why was this bag of offal brought to our camp?"

"When I saw him in his yellow robe, I questioned him and learned he had been sent by the Inner Circle to collect gold for the High Temple. It struck me that we had captured a valuable personage. Why not ransom him?"

The Prince tugged at his chin whiskers. "Why not? We can use all the gold and silver we can accumulate. What is the ransom for a high priest?"

Ranthar shrugged, admitting that he had no idea. Nobody had ever tried to ransom a priest of Styphon's House before. Kalvan either turned them, as he had done with Zothnes and Calthros, or had them executed outright.

"I'm worth a hundred thousand ounces of silver, but only if returned alive and unharmed," Skranga said. Actually, Skranga had no more idea what the going rate was than Democriphon or Ranthar, but it sounded about right, since a hundred thousand silver rakmars was the ransom price for a prince. He knew that Styphon's House could well afford it. It was a risk, though. If Xylon had failed to get "Sangar" onto the priesthood rolls in Balph, Skranga's life would not be worth a bent pfennig.

"How would we go about collecting this ransom?" Democriphon demanded. "Were you a prince or lower nobleman we would have you oath-bound and release you, and trust that the money would be sent by a courier. Unfortunately, you are not a nobleman but a priest. We do not trust the Styphoni, and since we are in hiding we can't allow anybody to know where to send the gold, especially those we number among our enemies."

*Dralm-damnit, I hadn't considered any of this when I allowed myself to be taken.* Skranga took out his pipe fixings as he scrambled for an idea.

As he was about to light his pipe, one idea slowly burrowed its way into his thoughts. "Aha! We set up a neutral meeting place where I can be exchanged for the ransom price."

"And how can we be sure that Styphon's House will deal fairly and not set a trap?"

Skranga smiled. "Since you will set the time and place, we will be the ones who can set the trap if need be."

## II

Ranthar watched as Prince Democriphon looked over the plan with apparent confusion. The design was laid out on a calfskin parchment, the only hide large enough to adequately display it.

The Prince shook his head in mystification. "I'd never heard of this bamboo until we arrived in this gods-forsaken kingdom. This plan you have doesn't make sense to me."

The three artisans, a blacksmith, a carpenter, a candle-maker and their spokesman, Uncle Wolf Syros, patiently tried to explain their idea yet again.

"There have been attempts to use bamboo as a fireseed weapon before, Your Highness," Syros explained. "The hollow interior is filled with fireseed while the ends are covered in wax save for a fuse. The fuse is lit and the bamboo is then thrown at the enemy."

"Okay. Why have I never heard of this before?" Democriphon demanded. "Great King Kalvan has talked about something like this, only he said paper was used."

*Dynamite was what Kalvan was talking about; these bamboo constructs are more like crude pipe bombs*, Ranthar noted. Pipe bombs, typically made of metal, were found all over the Fourth Level Hispano-Columbian Subsector. They were unstable and very, very dangerous to handle. Dynamite was much easier and safer to handle and packed more punch than a pipe bomb, which was filled with whatever explosive mixture the builder could obtain. These bamboo contraptions would not have a fraction of the explosive power of even a crude pipe bomb.

Syros continued. “Well, they never worked right. The fireseed would just shoot flames out at the ends when touched off. It would scare the wits out of ignorant Ruthani, and burn anything nearby, but otherwise they did nothing useful. Until these three artisans worked out a new design.”

“We are all former mercenaries and know more about fireseed than most,” the blacksmith said. “For instance, if the fireseed is not packed properly it will not explode correctly, and they’re much more deadly when nails and lead shot are added to the mixture.”

“And the fireseed needs to be in a tight space to explode or it will simply burn and sputter,” the carpenter added.

“Wax isn’t strong enough to keep the fireseed compressed tight enough to do the job,” finished the candle-maker.

“Well,” Syros continued, “I had an idea that these three men might be able to work out something between them to make the bamboo, uh, *bombs*—as they say Great King Kalvan calls them—work. I thought that the blacksmith could make iron end-caps for the bamboo with the carpenter’s help. It did work some, but the candle-maker improved the yield by wrapping the bamboo *bomb* with lead foil. It improves the seal and allows for a much more impressive explosion.” Syros handed an example to Democriphon.

“The lead also protects the fireseed from getting wet,” the candle-maker added.

Democriphon shook the tube then accidently dropped it. Ranthar dived to the ground in anticipation of what would happen next. Nothing. Ranthar looked up with a sheepish look on his face.

“That one is filled with dirt,” Uncle Wolf Syros explained. “Otherwise, it might have exploded.”

“Shaking it is also ill-advised,” the blacksmith added.

Democriphon shamefacedly handed the faux *bomb* back to the smith. “It is well that you anticipated my foolishness.”

“Not foolishness, Your Highness,” Syros said diplomatically. “Inexperience.”

“Thank you for that. Now, I can see a good use for this if we can light the fuse and throw it at the enemy with enough force to get it far away..."

"Actually, Your Highness," Syros interrupted, "The blacksmith has another idea."

## III

The ground had been trampled by horses, overturned by shovels and stamped down again by the boots of men. There were signs of clear cutting and a corral at the edge of the clearing as well as a small cabin that had recently burned to the ground. Even after the recent rains much of this was obvious to the experienced eye of Grand-Captain Mentiphon. *What in are these infidels up to?* He shrugged and dragged his mind back to matters that were more important.

It had taken several days to organize the ransom party and bring them to the place designated in the note. From the outward evidence he assumed that this had been the site of a previous encampment. That made sense; no point in setting up a meeting place in unfamiliar territory, nor would the bandits want to betray their new location to an enemy.

Mentiphon ordered the guard squads to set up a perimeter around the west side of the clearing and arrange the rest of the men to stand by inside the grassy area with the wagon of silver coins. *A hundred thousand ounces of silver for one high priest—Gak! Most of these whoresons aren't worth the fireseed it would take to blow them to Regwarn.* The plan was to get back Highpriest Sangar, then see to it that the kidnappers never lived to spend a single rakmar.

He would have liked to have brought a small gun with them to use against the raiders, he had even gone so far as to suggest that the wagon could carry a six-pounder instead of the silver. That plan had been overruled; it was too likely that the wagon would be inspected before Highpriest Sangar was sent out for the exchange.

The sun reached its zenith before the first raider appeared at the far end of the clearing. There could be a handful of companies hiding in the trees for all that Mentiphon could see.

The man rode his horse forward at a leisurely gait. His mount was as big as any war charger he had ever seen. As the figure approached, Mentiphon began to make out the details of the man's strange armor. He was wearing leather with metal studs and a strange helm. The helm shortly resolved itself into a wolf's face.

"What the Hadron?!" Mentiphon looked closer at the approaching rider and saw that he looked very much like a life-sized statue of Galzar come to life! The image was enhanced by the fact that the man was a giant with muscles that looked capable of uprooting a tree. Behind him, he could hear the guardsmen whispering among themselves.

"Have you brought my tribute?" demanded the wolf-headed man, in a deep voice.

"We…have the ransom for the return of His Worship Sangar." Mentiphon tried not to appear nervous. It was simply a man in a costume of some sort. Naturally, the raiders would seek to conceal their faces lest they be tracked down later.

"I would see the tribute before releasing your false god's lackey."

Mentiphon bit down on his reply, then pointed to the wagon. The rider dismounted and went to the back of the wagon and threw open the door. Inside were several small chests. The man opened each of them and inspected the contents. A few times, he even took out his knife and cut into a coin. Which was no surprise to Mentiphon; he would have done the same thing. There were almost as many debased rakmars in circulation as pure ones.

"These will suffice." The wolf-headed man stepped back out of the wagon and raised an arm. From across the clearing another man came running over. This one also wore a wolf-helm. "Take the wagon over and prepare the lackey."

The man nodded then jumped up onto the box, took the reins and started the horses moving. Mentiphon started to stop him, then thought better of it. His guardsmen could take back the silver after Sangar was safe.

The wagon slowly crossed the clearing then disappeared into the tree line. Mentiphon grew irritable with the waiting and absently grasped the hilt of his sword. "Where is His Worship? You have your silver, now return Highpriest Sangar."

"Gladly. I will start forward back to the other side," the man explained. "Your toady will start back at the same time and we will pass each other in the middle. His doxy will return with him if she so chooses. We do not deal in whores."

"Very well. Start forward and be gone from my sight. But if His Worship has been mistreated we will chase you to Regwarn and back if need be."

The man laughed. "So be it. But have a care; there are several muskets aimed at your false god's lackey. If I am injured on the way back, the false priest will be dead before you can reach him. And just so there is no mistake of our resolve, the wagon will be unhitched and pushed into the swamp if we are followed."

Without waiting for a reply the wolf-headed giant remounted and rode forward slowly. Across the clearing two horses with riders came out of the trees. Even at a distance, Mentiphon could make out the yellow robes of a highpriest. The other rider had to be his sister, Mistress Eldra.

## IV

Skranga and Eldra tried to feign nervousness as they approached Styphon's Own Guard. In truth, neither was particularly worried. They had been playing at their roles long enough that the Styphoni colors held no fear for them. Nor did they have anything to worry about from the so-called raiders. Only the guardsmen's need for revenge might lead to problems.

The giant wolf-headed rider drew close as they passed by. "Remember, get as far back behind the Styphoni line as quickly as you can," he hissed.

Skranga almost nodded then caught himself. It would not do to be seen socializing with his former captors. Instead he leaned away as if fearing that he might be attacked by the big man. Once the two men passed each other he tried to feign relief. It was difficult to maintain the slow pace of the horses, but vital to the plan. Democriphon's men needed time to get the wagon well away in case the Styphoni charged across the field.

Once he was close to the Styphoni company, two riders came out, seized the reins of both Skranga's and Eldra's mounts and hurried them back behind the lines. He threw a look at Eldra that said, *well, it is about to begin.*

V

From the timberline, Ranthar watched as the giant returned. Once he reached the trees, Gycules spurred his horse to speed until he met up with the rest.

"All went well, Your Highness." Gycules said as he dismounted and removed his helm.

"Excellent job, Petty-Captain," Ranthar said.

Gycules nodded and stepped back to collect his gun.

"Do you think they will try for it?" Democriphon asked Ranthar.

"I can't imagine Styphon's Own Guard letting us get away with all of this silver. I think they'll be charging forward any moment now."

"I agree." Democriphon nodded to Gycules.

"Shields up," the giant said in a loud whisper. He could have yelled for all the distance his voice would have to carry before the Styphoni could hear him. All around wooden pallets were pulled up from the ground and the men crouched behind them. The wall was made of two thick pallets of wood: leather thongs instead of ropes held the wooden pallets together. There were murder loops between the shields.

Several men lit torches and waited behind the wall.

Time seemed to slow as Ranthar waited for the Styphoni captain to order the charge. *Maybe they will just take Sangar and leave hoping to catch us unaware on another day, or even have a few scouts try to follow us back to the village.* In the distance, Skranga and Eldra boarded a carriage and departed with a small escort. He was almost ready to suggest to Democriphon it was time to retreat when he saw the Styphoni dragoons start forward on horseback.

Democriphon waited until the enemy was almost two-thirds of the way across the clearing when he smiled grimly, then raised his hand and dropped it.

"Touch off the fuses and get down!" Gycules shouted. The torchbearers dropped their faggots into holes that had been dug out earlier in the moon quarter. Once in the holes, the flames touched off the lines of fireseed that trailed off underground into a network of bamboo tubes filled nearly to bursting with fireseed.

Ranthar counted the beats of his own heart as he crouched low and covered his ears.

Styphon's Own Guard approached much faster than expected. They were less than three rods away when the first explosion occurred. Then another, and another. In seconds, the clearing was erupting with noise and flames as if Galzar's Own Wrath had arrived.

Ranthar tried to count the explosions and failed. Many seemed to happen simultaneously, throwing off his count. *To Regwarn with it!* "Fire at will!"

With the closest explosions over, the men fired their smoothbores through murder loops in the shield wall. Few guardsmen were within range, but those who were still mounted rode willy-nilly as their spooked horses tried to evade the explosions and bullets. For the *nth* time Ranthar wished he could have brought some of King Kalvan's rifles; arquebuses and muskets had far less range and very little accuracy.

After the bombs had done their work, Democriphon ordered a cease fire. "Waste no more fireseed on this godless scum. Go out and kill them all. Cut the throats of the wounded."

As one, Democriphon's force surged forth to engulf the remnants of Styphon's Own Guard. Though dazed and deafened by the explosions, the surviving Styphoni fought like wounded panthers. Ranthar noted that it took two freemen to down one Styphoni; one of the reasons why Styphon's Own Guard was the most feared military force in the Six Kingdoms. However, with two-thirds of their Band wounded or dying, the Styphoni were outnumbered three to one. In less than an eighth of a candle, the battle was over—or should he say slaughter.

Democriphon, who had held back to observe the freemen in action, strode forward. "Clear the bodies and fill the blast holes with dirt. Then strip the dead of weapons, armor, purses and anything else of use and toss the bodies into the swamp.

"Once the bodies are cleared, I need the burial detail to smooth out the ground," Ranthar added. "When the Styphoni return I want no sign of what occurred here to be seen. We have a new weapon and I want it to remain *our* secret."

The men surged forward gleefully slitting throats and cutting purses while Gycules tried to count the bodies. It was a wasted effort, Ranthar noted, as many of them had been blown to pieces by the explosions. He signaled him to stop and the giant joined in on the looting.

The Prince took a seat on a log with his gun at the ready. Ranthar stood next to him watching for any sign of movement.

"That…was loud," Democriphon said.

"Indeed," Ranthar agreed. "My ears are still ringing as if every temple in Agrys City had rung their bells at the same time."

"They won't believe us back in Hos-Hostigos when we tell them about this," Democriphon mused. "Well, King Kalvan might. I suspect they had something like this in the Cold Lands."

*A minefield.* Aloud Ranthar said, "Who cares what they believe. We saw it. Dralm-damnit, we did it! Nothing can ever take that away from us. Our own losses were about a quarter of what I expected. I can see Gasphros composing a ditty about this."

Democriphon nodded. "I don't think I will bother telling others of this save for our Great King. It doesn't seem important, somehow."

*Not important?* Ranthar wondered about that all the way back to the village.

# FORTY-FIVE

The moment they crossed the clearing, Duke Skranga and Eldra were hustled into a carriage and taken away as fast as the six-horse team would go. A squad of guardsmen accompanied them, while the rest mounted their horses. Skranga could understand wanting to get a highpriest away from his abductors with all speed, yet this seemed extreme. His mind changed when a while later he heard the explosions that shook the earth and spurred the horses on to greater speed.

"Are you well, Your Worship," asked the Petty-Captain of Styphon's Own Guard. He had been tasked with escorting Sangar and his widowed sister to safety. Like all of his kind, he took his charge very seriously.

"We are well, Petty-Captain," Skranga replied. "What was that explosion? Did your captain have a surprise for my former captors?"

"I know nothing of that, Your Worship. Grand-Captain Mentiphon said nothing to me or anyone else that I know of."

Skranga relaxed. He expected the explosions. He only wanted to be certain the Styphoni hadn't sprung a surprise of their own. Or decide he was complicit with the attack.

"Where would Your Worship wish to be taken?"

Skranga had a ready answer for that. "Take us to Bletha Town. We were on our way to meet with Great King Niclophon when we were abducted. By Styphon's Will, I want to see what this so-called Great King can do to put an end to these godless attacks."

## II

Great King Niclophon was beyond annoyed. Rumors of the Orphan Prince were popping up everywhere. Eventually the sharpers running the game would either press their luck too far and be caught with a farmer's daughter or hanged by one of the princes with no sense of humor. However, it was annoying the way the kingdom seemed to hold its collective breath as though waiting for a civil war in the meantime.

Even more annoying was the fifty thousand ounces of silver he was out for the release of Sangar. He had hoped that Styphon's Own Guard could have recovered his half of the silver. However, that was not to be. They were now feasting in Styphon's Skypalace, or wherever Styphoni went when they died in battle.

The most frustrating thing was that everything seemed to be going wrong at once: banditry, Ruthani attacks, temple raids, the rumors of the Orphan Prince popping up again and, now—Highpriest Sangar. His Worship had petitioned Niclophon for sanctuary until the temple raiders had been dealt with. That meant he had the pleasure of the highpriest's company for the foreseeable future.

Under normal circumstances, Niclophon would have been honored. As a devout follower of Styphon he was only too happy to render any assistance he could provide. Highpriests came and went, usually with a token of the king's esteem from the treasury. However, with Sangar taking semi-permanent residence, everyone would have to be on his or her best behavior. That tended to fray the nerves over time. Something would have to be done about it.

## III

Skranga looked about his new chambers in the royal palace. While the accommodations he had received in the Styphoni temples had been comfortable, these were beyond lavish. Silken tapestries covered the walls of the spacious apartment, animal skins covered most of the marble floor, furniture crafted of maple and oak was sanded and stained to a smooth fine finish and padded with down cushions and covered in rich fabrics. Exotic plants in painted pots were strategically placed about the rooms for both visual aesthetics and their fragrances. Paintings showing great battles or just simple portraits adorned every wall between tapestries. Statues small and large made of marble, silver and even gold stood on the floor and on small tables or pedestals.

Perhaps the most surprising thing was the shrine to Styphon at the far end of the room. The golden statue stood on a pedestal adorned with garlands of silver mesh entwined with precious jewels and gold coins. At either side of the statue were stacked three barrels of the type normally used for storing fireseed.

"Now this is just plain asinine," Skranga said out loud. He stared at the shrine until another thought came to mind. With great care he examined the top barrels. When satisfied that they were empty he let out a long sigh of relief. *By the True Gods, I wouldn't have put it passed some idiot in this castle to actually fill these things to the top with fireseed.*"

Satisfied that he would not be violently blasted into the next world the next time he used his tinderbox, Skranga plopped down onto a couch covered with cream-colored brocade and golden threads and helped himself to some fruit that had been thoughtfully provided by his host. As he relaxed, he noticed Eldra and Calthros entering the chamber. It had been Calthros, as his assistant, who had delivered the news of his capture and they had been reunited in the High Temple of Bletha Town. Calthros' knowledge of Styphon's House and its practices was critical to the mission's success and he had been pleased to see him again.

Eldra looked annoyed. *Oh, Dralm, what did I do now?*

"Do you have any idea where they are trying to put me?" Eldra shouted. "In Great King Niclophon's *harem*!"

"What is a *harem*," Calthros asked. The word was new to him.

"A *gaggle* of pleasure girls for the king's entertainment," Eldra explained. Her tone cowed the underpriest enough that he didn't bother to ask what a *gaggle* was.

"Oh?" Skranga had heard about that. "I can talk with the king. I am certain he will not take any liberties with the, ah, sister of a high priest of Styphon..."

"That is the very least of my concerns. I have spoken with the girls there and Niclophon barely acknowledges he even *has* a harem."

Skranga became confused and it showed on his face. "Then what is the problem with..."

Eldra's voice lowered to a dangerous register. "You are not listening; Niclophon barely acknowledges he even *has* a *harem*."

"Oh? Yes, of course! Well, then, you are safe from his attentions..."

"*His* attentions, yes. Not those of his palace guard, his creepy chancellor, retainers, visiting nobility..."

Skranga finally grasped the problem. "Niclophon uses the...the *harem* for entertaining guests and turns a blind eye to what his own court does the rest of the time."

"Exactly! The girls do not seem to mind as they are well fed and pampered. *I*,"—Eldra added with emphasis—"however, am not anybody's plaything."

Skranga had been in many dangerous situations in his life; this one made the rest seem insignificant. "I will speak with His Majesty at the very first opportunity and rectify this tragic oversight," he said quickly. "I am certain it's all a misunderstanding, once he learns that you're my widowed sister, he'll allow me to place you within my own quarters where you will be quite safe and in no danger of being mistreated."

"Make it soon, Your Worship." Eldra put special emphasis on the honorific.

"Before the day is done, Lady Eldra." Skranga turned to Calthros. As planned, the underpriest had brought along Skranga's false guardsmen when he came to Bletha Town. "How are the men situated?"

"Captain-General Theodoros arranged barracks accommodations for them by clearing out some of the castle guard and housing them elsewhere. This gives them crowded but otherwise comfortable lodgings for the time being. There is another problem, however; the men are beginning to grumble that they are not pretty show ponies. It is bad enough that they have to pretend to be Styphon's Own Guard, but they have not been allowed to take part in any real battle since the mission began."

That presented a serious problem. While pretending to be Styphoni, the mercenaries could not do battle with the Blethans or Styphon's House. In fact, they could only be seen fighting bandits, raiders and threats to their host. In other words, Democriphon's own people.

The real issue was not that they wanted to fight, of course. They wanted to loot fallen foes. A mercenary, while well paid, supplemented his pay with booty. Sometimes the *loot* scavenged from fallen foes far exceeded their normal pay and bonuses. This was further exacerbated by the fact that the rest of their brothers in arms serving under Democriphon were engaging in banditry and likely gaining gold and silver by the barrelful.

"They have a legitimate complaint, I fear." Skranga considered the matter. "Is it possible to exchange some of our men for those under Democriphon's command?"

"Perhaps, Your Worship. It would be a slow rotation as many of the Captain-General's men were slaves and have not completely recovered from their mistreatment. Plus, some suffered at the hands of Styphon's House and would not be able to 'play' their role without repercussions."

Skranga hadn't even considered that element. Calthros had a point. Still, if only there was a way to transfer some of the men back to Democriphon. He said as much.

"The only way to plausibly reduce your manpower would be to lose them in a battle," Calthros said.

"Sounds like a plan to me," Eldra said.

"What?" Skranga and Calthros spoke at the same time.

"Sure. Send them out after those bandits. Niclophon would be very grateful, I think."

"But the bandits are..." Skranga stopped as realization struck. "Oh... clever, Lady Eldra, very clever."

## IV

"...and moreover, if we do not restore the true heir of the throne to power, Hos-Bletha will be dragged into the wars in the north!"

*That line hits the right note*, thought Ranthar. The people in the crowd grumbled their agreement. Democriphon was no stranger to giving inspiring speeches. He would not have done as well with his men had he not learned to rouse them for battle.

"I know others have come before me claiming to be the Orphan Prince," Democriphon continued. "They asked for money, supplies and shelter, then took advantage of your women, your wives and daughters. I do not want your money! I do not need your supplies!" That brought a cheer from the crowd. "I do not need your women, though I wouldn't mind spending time with some of them." He added a wink and smiled as the crowd laughed.

A few of the women in the audience sighed, looking as though they would not mind spending some time with the handsome *Prince*.

"What I need are men willing to fight for what is right and just in this land. Men willing to fight for their kingdom and their true king. But not just for me...FOR YOURSELVES!"

The crowd cheered while Ranthar spoke into Democriphon's ear. "Our time is up. That distraction we created to draw the town guard away won't keep them from coming to investigate the noise of this crowd."

Democriphon nodded and turned back to his audience. "I must go before my men are forced to defend themselves against the dupes propping up the current pretender to the throne. But I will send messengers among you to sign up those willing to fight for me and Hos-Bletha! And to show my sincerity, a gift from the true Prince in Exile."

Gycules reached into a bag and drew out large handfuls of silver to the cheering crowd. These he threw into the crowd until the bag was empty. The audience rushed up to scoop up as many coins as they could get.

Democriphon waved and bowed as he left the platform in the center of the market square. Under normal circumstances, the platform had been used for public announcements, slave auctions and even executions. Democriphon made a point of kicking down the poles that were used to chain slaves during auctions as he left. He had cut his speech short just in time. At the edge of the market square he could see the town watch coming to investigate.

Democriphon had suggested fighting the town watchmen to prove his strength and resolve. Uncle Wolf Syros argued against it when they were planning the Prince's address to the crowd in the small town of Uthar. "Some of them might wish to join up with the Orphan Prince later," Syros had noted. Ranthar had supported Syros' position and Democriphon had relented.

Instead, they arranged for a "Ruthani" attack at the far side of the village and took advantage of the guards' absence. As it turned out, the silver-grasping crowd created a barrier the watch was unable to make their way though.

Rather than be seen fleeing like common cutpurses, Democriphon leapt onto the back of his horse and led his procession around the corner out of sight of the still cheering crowd. Once they were unobserved, they spurred the horses into a run and made their way out of town.

Democriphon turned to Gycules. "You did a good job of weakening the slave posts, Petty-Captain. Next time try to weaken them further, though. I think I broke a toe on that last one."

Ranthar noticed as Gycules hid a small smile.

Democriphon started for a moment at the sound of pursuit and Gycules drew his horse pistol. They all relaxed when they saw it was Uncle Wolf Syros.

"Not a bad performance, Your Highness," Syros said as he rode up. "I liked the part about keeping the people out of foreign wars that did not concern them. You might want to tone down the anti-Styphon part, though. Styphon's House has as many followers as Galzar in this realm and you don't want to antagonize them."

Democriphon nodded in agreement. "You are right, I forgot about that."

"The battle to end the Styphoni will only be settled by Great King Kalvan, when he finally razes and sacks the temples in Balph. Not here, and not by us," Ranthar added.

"Of course not, Captain," Democriphon said, "but we will keep locals busy enough to stop them from joining in the marches against our Great King."

"My Prince," Gycules interrupted, "perhaps we would fare better to voice such sentiments after we have returned to camp. Even the trees may have ears."

Most subalterns would have been afraid to speak to their superiors about such things, Ranthar noted. Gycules, though, was in a class all of his own.

"Tell me, Gycules, why haven't I promoted you to captain?" Democriphon asked.

"Because I am far more valuable as a petty-captain," replied the giant. "I would not object to the same pay as a captain, though."

*He is more than worth it*, Ranthar thought.

Democriphon must have agreed because he said, "Very well, I dub thee Chief Petty-Captain. You are now the senior petty-captain and all others must defer to you. You have been acting as such anyway, so let us make it official."

"All too true," Ranthar laughed. There was a maxim in many of the Europo-American belts that stated sergeants could run a war without officers, but officers could not run a war without sergeants. Democriphon seemed to be learning that lesson here-and-now. Gycules was now the top-kick, or sergeant-major, in Democriphon's army. This could be the start of greater separation in the enlisted ranks, the same thing Calvin Morrison had been working towards in Hos-Hostigos.

"Since a change in topic is desirable," Uncle Wolf Syros said, "I would like to use some men to acquire some supplies when we get back."

"Gasphros can get you anything you need, Uncle Wolf," Democriphon said. "Just make me a list..."

"Some things cannot be bought at a trading post, My Prince."

"Oh? Such as?"

"Maggots." Syros took in the surprised looks on Democriphon's and Ranthar's faces. "For the fester devils. Live maggots will consume the infection while leaving the healthy flesh untouched. It only works on surface wounds and ear infections, but my order has been experimenting with maggots for a few years now. It has been very effective thus far."

Everyone looked sick at the suggestion. Even Ranthar who was familiar with such practices from his outtime travels struggled to keep his stomach from rebelling. "We can leave some milk out to go bad and let the flies get at it. That should provide you with a fresh crop of...maggots soon enough."

"Yes, that should do nicely, Ranthar. I will also need white vinegar, as pure as we can get, garlic, onions, iron ingots..." The list went on and became progressively stranger as it continued. Ranthar recognized the value of some, but had no earthly clue as to what much of the rest could possibly do for a sick or injured man.

Democriphon looked to Gycules. "Arrange for Uncle Wolf Syros to get everything he needs, Petty-Captain. You know the men best, just use your best judgment and select the ones most likely to properly assist the Uncle Wolf." He turned to Syros. "What is the iron ingot for?"

"For the men with thin blood or have bled a great deal. We put the iron ingot into the stewpot with the food and serve it to them."

"They are supposed to eat the iron?" Gycules blurted out.

"What? No!" Syros laughed so hard he nearly fell from his horse. "No, medicine from the iron seeps into food and helps to fortify the blood, like tempering or when we quench a blade in pig's blood. I admit I do not know how this works but my Order has had some success with this. We could just switch out the cooking pots from copper and brass to iron, but this works just as well."

Spinach would do the job, thought Ranthar, but it was never introduced to the northern lesser landmass on this time-line. However, raisins would do almost as well. *I'll suggest that the next time I'm alone with Uncle Wolf Syros.*

"As long as I do not have to eat the iron, I am satisfied with adding the ingots to the stew," Gycules said with a sigh of relief.

"Agreed," Democriphon added.

"I will also need a large stone building in the village," added Syros. "Walls, floor and even the roof made of stone."

"Are you building a temple to Galzar," Democriphon inquired.

"Nay, though that is not a bad idea. I need such a place for healing."

Democriphon glanced at Ranthar and Gycules. They looked back with blank expressions. "Why?"

"In my order we have found that men healed faster and with fewer fester devils within the temples than out in the fields or in houses built of wood and thatch," Syros explained. "While many of my brothers maintain that it is Galzar's grace that speeds the healing, others believe that most fester devils do not breed well on stone and iron. By taking the injured away from the places where fester devils thrive, we make it easier for them to recover. We also find that vinegar often kills them so we clean every surface and the wounded men with vinegar before treating their wounds...when possible."

"Do you also wash your hands with vinegar before tending the wounded?" Ranthar asked. The Study Team would be fascinated with this new knowledge into the Uncle Wolfs' healing practices.

Uncle Wolf Syros looked confused. "Why would we do that when we have no wounds of our own?"

"Neither does the stone of your buildings," Gycules said, "yet you wash them."

Syros' eyes went wide for a moment then became thoughtful. "You make an excellent point. I shall have to discuss this with my brothers."

*Dralm-damnit!* Ranthar thought. *I just committed a minor infraction of the Paratime Code. I'll have to ask Chief Verkan about how serious it is when I return to Fifth Level Police Terminal for my report in a few days.*

# FORTY-SIX

It took Inspector Ranthar Jard a moment to realize he arrived at his destination on Fifth Level, Police Terminal. He had been rereading *The Adventures of Robin Hood* all the way from the Blethan Study Team Transposition Depot. He could have easily read the book once, then reviewed it in his mind with First Level total recall techniques, but chose to review the material in his hands rather than in his mind. He wanted to be certain that every nuance of the book was indelibly imprinted in his memory.

He put the book in his bag and joined the other passengers walking out into the terminal. After his debriefing with Chief Verkan he was due some time off for rest and relaxation. His cover story back on Kalvan's Time Line involved going off on a recon mission of the surrounding towns and villages. Most of them thought he had a lady friend in Port Gytha, a story he did little to deny. Instead, he would receive a report of the recent activities of that area from the study teams using spy eyes and infiltration units. That information would then be transferred to his mind directly through hypno-mech upon his return.

Thoughts of the debriefing left him with a sense of disquiet. Chief Verkan, while fair, could be very exacting in his disciplining of those who commit Paratime infractions when he felt the need. As Ranthar stepped off the slideway, he spotted Chief Verkan and waved.

"Hi, Chief."

"How are you, Ranthar?"

No point in going into his transgressions in the busy terminal, Ranthar thought; there would be time enough for that later at the debriefing. "Great, Chief! Playing the Robin Hood, or Robinos as we call it, has been a lot of fun. Everyone on the team has been great, even that troubadour Gasphros. We've got all of Hos-Bletha spinning like a top; including sharpers, there must be four claimants to the throne now. It'll take them fifty years to sort this mess out. That 'steal from the rich, give to the poor' idea of Kalvan's is working like a charm!"

"That Robin Hood story is a common children's tale on those Europo-American subsectors where the Norman Conquest was successful," Verkan said. "Kalvan just applied it to a new situation. Otherwise, it could be interpreted as Paratemporal Contamination. I'm not sure how the Paratime Commission would view your part as Robin Hood, either."

If that were the only problem. "It was Kalvan's plan and Duke Skranga is the operative in charge," Ranthar smiled. "I'm just following orders." *Oh, Dralm, I just invoked the Nuremberg Defense.*

Verkan laughed. "As long as you don't step out of character, I don't see any problem."

"The Blethan Operation is going great, but it's still too early to see if we're going to keep Niclophon's troops from reaching Hos-Harphax. Some of us have been hijacking and ambushing Styphon's House priests and noblemen in our green jacks and green hose, while others wearing wolf masks are attacking temples. The commoners love us. I myself haven't had this much fun in a hundred years! However, Styphon's House has put a price of twenty thousand gold rakmars on my head."

"Then don't get caught."

"I don't intend to, Chief. But we sure have Styphon's House in a lather."

"That's the goal, Ranthar. If your mission is successful, you'll have tied down ten thousand soldiers or more that won't be able to join the Grand Host in their hunt for Kalvan come spring."

Ranthar was about to reply when he saw Verkan look about suddenly. Then it hit him; the room had suddenly grown quiet, a near impossibility in a terminal of this size. Ranthar followed Verkan's gaze and spotted a bald man wearing the hooded yellow robe with a red border. It was an Archpriest of Styphon's House Inner Circle. Ranthar reached for his sword before he recalled where he was. Anybody dressed as one of the Styphoni on First Level would have to be in disguise, just like Ranthar. That knowledge did not stop others in the terminal from moving away from the man as though he carried a deadly contagion. It was not until the man approached that he recognized him.

"Hello, Dras," Verkan said.

"Chief, I didn't expect to find you down here," Danthor Dras said with a welcoming smile. After clasping hands, they moved toward the antigrav lift.

Verkan jerked a thumb in Ranthar's direction. "I'm here to debrief Inspector Ranthar."

"Oh, the Man in Green, as Styphon's House calls him," Danthor said. He turned to Ranthar who had to suppress a shudder. Months of working against the Styphoni had its effect on the Inspector. "You've caused the Inner Circle no end of headaches!"

*Good!* "That's the plan," he said aloud.

Verkan and Danthor talked about Archpriest Anaxthenes and his plans for Styphon's House when the Grand Host returned.

"The Grand Host is growing like a tropical storm," Danthor noted. "There's going to be high water in Hostigos come spring."

Chief Verkan nodded. "I know, and I think Kalvan does, too."

While maintaining peripheral awareness of what was being said, Ranthar became immersed in his own thoughts: what was happening with Skranga, Democriphon, Eldra and the rest. Despite his attempts to maintain a professional distance, these people were becoming like family to him. That hadn't happened to him since he joined the Department.

"Come on, let's go to my office, Danthor. You, too, Ranthar."

Ranthar snapped back to full awareness of his surroundings and felt a bit like a boy being sent to the principal's office for sticking a girl's ponytail into an inkwell. Once in Verkan's office, Danthor expressed his amazement that he had ever been allowed into it as a free man. After a shared chuckle, Verkan produced a bottle of Ermut's Best and offered everybody a glass.

"I haven't had that in a while," Ranthar said. He had been far too busy to do much drinking and the Ermut's Best was in short supply. Even shorter since Duke Skranga took the panther's share with him on his tour of Styphoni Temples on the way to Bletha Town.

Verkan, Ranthar and Danthor talked for a while about how Kalvan could be aided within the limits of the Paratime Secret.

"By the way, have either of you ever heard of a Baron Parthenos, Highpriest Sangar or underpriest Calthros?" Danthor asked after he emptied his glass.

"I know of a Calthros, but that is a fairly common name there." Verkan turned to Ranthar. "How about you, Ranthar?"

"Sangar is the name Duke Skranga is traveling under in Hos-Bletha. That's in my forth-coming report. Calthros is a former Styphon's House underpriest who got captured by Kalvan's forces. He's assisting Skranga in his disguise as a Highpriest."

"Aha!" Danthor put on a wide grin. "Then Xylon must be one of their confederates in Styphon's House in Balph." Danthor relayed what he had seen when Xylon added his scroll to the pile headed to the Archives. "This Skranga must have collapsed-iron balls to pull off such a con."

"That and more," Verkan said. "I had him checked out when Kalvan made him an Intelligencer. Skranga is a horse thief, black marketeer and confidence man on several adjoining belts. In at least three of them, he was lynched and in another one tortured to death by Styphon's House for selling stolen fireseed. He is devious, underhanded, morally agile and has the animal cunning of a wolverine—"

"In other words," Ranthar interrupted. "The perfect spy. His only saving grace is his disdain of slavery and loyalty to Kalvan."

"Of course he's loyal," Verkan laughed, "Kalvan is making him wealthy beyond his greatest dreams."

They all shared a laugh, then Danthor had to leave to attend some university business. Verkan put away the brandy and turned to Ranthar.

"What seems to be the problem, Ranthar?"

"Problem?"

Verkan rolled his eyes, then stared at the Inspector. "Ranthar, we have worked together far too many times for you to hide anything from me. Something is on your mind?"

*Busted!* "I think I committed a mild infraction, Chief."

Verkan sat straighter and furrowed his brow. "A Paratime Code infraction? How mild?"

Ranthar explained about asking Uncle Wolf Syros if he cleaned himself with vinegar when treating wounded men. With his First Level memory enhancements, he could repeat the conversation verbatim. When he finished, he waited for Verkan's reaction. It was not what he expected.

"You call that an infraction? What do you think the University Study Teams do? They ask questions. Lots and lots of questions. Oh, sure, they often use hypno-mech to remove the more serious infractions when necessary. Still, they understand that studying a thing is, in itself, a source of contamination and have to choose their questions carefully. Even still, accidents happen. You just asked a question and Uncle Wolf Syros ran with it."

"Forget it," Verkan added. "It isn't like you unleashed a Venusian Nighthound there. No, wait, don't forget it. Keep an eye on Syros and see if he does anything new with the concept. The Hostigos Study Team would kill for a chance to do the same."

"I'll admit that I am relieved." Ranthar relaxed and gave his full verbal report, which was recorded and automatically transcribed to hardcopy. Verkan Vall listened intently until Ranthar finished.

"They made a minefield out of interconnected bamboo shafts?" Verkan shook his head and chuckled. "Even Kalvan might not have thought up something like that. It is rather clever. Are you sure you didn't help them along?"

"Chief! I didn't even meet those three men until Uncle Wolf Syros showed us what they came up with," Ranthar said in feigned shock. "Frankly, I considered the possibility that somebody else might be tampering with the Kalvan Time-Line, but their explanation of how they developed the bamboo bombs was completely plausible for that time-line's industrial development level."

Verkan nodded. "I thought as much, but the Paratime Commission might decide to grill you on the matter, so be prepared. Now, I want you to go over to medical and get checked out."

"Chief, I'm fine. I got shot once, but it wasn't serious. I used my medpak and haven't had so much as a hangnail since."

"Guntha Gand is there. He just reported in from Fourth Level, Gaelic Empire Subsector, Irish Dynasty Belt, after having what appears to be a relapse of that virus your team picked up on lower Fifth Level a few cycles back. Get checked out, then if you are cleared for duty, take some time off. I don't want to see you back at work until you have a solid smile on your face and a good story to explain why it's there."

Ranthar nodded. He recalled that Fourth Level Gaelic Empire was a few subsectors down from the Hispano-Columbian Subsector where Ireland, Wales and Scotland combined under William Wallace to defeat the English. The Irish Empire Belt had an Irish king ruling that empire, although other belts had Welsh or Scottish rulers. He would have to visit Guntha Gand and trade stories about their respective assignments before taking a holiday. In fact, he had more than a few ideas on how he could fill the time. "Yes, Chief. One ten-day of solid debauchery coming up."

"Oh, and one more thing: get your armor duplicated and replaced with plastisteel; especially that wolf-helm."

His original plastisteel armor had been left behind in Hos-Hostigos when he joined Democriphon as everybody was traveling incognito. "Will do, Chief."

# FORTY-SEVEN

## I

"...but it will be a costly operation. Bringing down a false king will take an army and mercenaries do not work for free! My men will be moving among you for any donations you can make. Remember, this is for the power and glory of the true Prince in Exile!"

The applause was less enthusiastic than before; it was hard to whip up a frenzy over opening one's purse. Zentros understood that as well as the rest of his band. People were always looking for change as long as they did not have to pay for it. Correction: the lower classes were looking for change; the nobility was satisfied, largely, with the status quo.

Claiming to be the True Orphan Prince was a dangerous game, especially with other sharper bands pulling the same swindle. Although that new ballad, "When the Orphan Prince Comes Marching Home," had loosened a lot of purse strings. But it had also energized the competition. Zentros had to send out scouts to each town to be sure that another band of sharpers had not already been through there. It never paid to work the same town twice too soon; especially if the other band was still working the town. More than one battle had been birthed when two bands of sharpers tried to work the same side of the street.

Galin signaled it was time to go. That meant the town watch was on its way, or something even worse. "I must take my leave of you now lest I fall prey to Great King Niclophon's minions. Farewell!"

Zentros rushed down from the edge of the town well and ran out of the village square followed by Galin and eight others from his band. Once out of sight, they donned hooded robes popular among travelers to protect them from dust and rain.

He looked about and counted noses. "Looks like we all made it out. How did we do?"

Galin collected the offerings from the rest and did a quick tally. "Looks to be about five ounces of silver and ten times that amount in copper, more or less."

Zentros cursed. "We would have done better had the guard not come so quickly. Ah, well, such are the fortunes of war. What's the next town?"

"Spartos," Galin replied.

"Hmmm…wasn't there some sort of battle there recently?"

"No, it was an attack on one of the Yellow Robes' temples. The rogues emptied the temple of gold, even taking the tiles off the roof! Nothing for us to worry over."

Zentros spat at the ground. Sharpers hated Styphon's House more than even Prince Mythros, who had a habit of hanging them, which was why most of the sharpers steered clear of the Princedom of Pytha. Whenever the Yellow Robes caught a sharper, they enslaved him and worked him to death. Great King Niclophon would turn captured sharpers over to Styphon's House rather than hang them himself, which did nothing to endear the Great King of Hos-Bletha to the various sharper bands. Being caught and hanged was the price of business; being worked to death in one of Styphon's House's lead mines was something else again.

"It might be best to avoid Spartos for the time being, or any other town where a temple has been attacked. Styphon's Own Guard will be tearing up the place looking for leads as to who the raiders are or where they might have gone. I would rather not be caught in their clean-up."

A voice sounded from behind the Sharpers leader, "Then you need not worry. Such concerns are behind you, now."

Zentros spun about and saw a man dressed in armor bearing the emblem of the House of Mythros on his surcoat. While he was no expert on military rank, he would guess the man was a captain or some such. From around the buildings came more men wearing the same regalia with swords drawn and faces set in determination.

"Oh, by Ormaz's Beard," Zentros squeaked out. Of all the people to run into, Mythros' men were the second worst to meet. "Wait, this isn't Prince Mythros' realm. You have no authority here in the Princedom of Bletha."

The captain smiled. "Odd you should mention that. Some of the local guard had the same opinion. Fortunately, a few ounces of gold convinced them of the value of inter-princedom cooperation. Now, then, will you come quietly or shall I order my men to cut you down one by one until you decide to cooperate?"

The band all looked to Zentros. About half the riders surrounding them held cocked crossbows and the others had drawn swords. There was no chance of escape nor did they have any possibility of fighting the guards off; they were too many and were better armed. Prince Mythros was known for his ill-temper towards those who tried to cash in on the Orphan Prince swindle and demonstrated it on the gallows. Their only chance was to surrender and try to escape before they were dragged before Mythros' court.

"You have the advantage," Zentros said with a bow and arms held wide apart. "We surrender."

## II

The journey had been long and wet. Democriphon felt as if he had been on the road for several moons. It was time to return to the new village at Mallegast and rest his soldiers. Some had family there and others were plain worn-out. It was time to rotate his troops and give the new recruits time in the field. He also wanted to see how the village was progressing in his absence before moving on to a new town.

As the party approached the village, they could see a wall of logs set upright. Democriphon looked it over and nodded in approval. The bark had been stripped and pitch applied to the cracks between the logs, and a walkway appeared to have been set up inside the wall as he could see guards moving along the top of the palisades. Two towers book-ended the section of wall before him, overseeing the entire area.

Democriphon dismounted and stepped forward to further appraise the work. Before he took another step, an arrow sprouted at his feet.

"Galzar's teeth! What in Regwarn's Caverns is going on…"

"You there," a voice called down, "state your business."

Democriphon looked up and saw a man with a bow looking down from the top of the wall. He bit off a scathing retort and considered the situation. Uncle Wolf Syros had been concerned about bandits and barbarians, so he suggested walls be built, which Democriphon immediately ordered done. Good. Nevertheless, what was this? After a moment's reflection, he realized that Petty-Captain Andros had taken his task of protecting the village very seriously and trained some of the freemen to act as his guard. Trained them well, too, if the bowman's accuracy was any indication.

"I am Dem—, Prince Valthros," Democriphon called up. "I have returned. Call for Petty-Captain Andros. He will vouch for me."

The bowman turned to speak to another person Democriphon could not see, then called down. "Stay where you are until Petty-Captain Andros arrives, Your Highness. If you are whom you say, then you will be escorted in. If not, we will give you a fine burial."

Democriphon put a hand over his mouth to hide his smile. *Andros also schooled his men in intimidation, it seems.*

Uncle Wolf Syros approached from behind. "It looks like everybody has been busy while we were away."

"Indeed. If we ever get back to Hos-Hostigos alive, I am going to advise Great King Kalvan to make Andros a captain-general. He really knows how to follow orders and exceed expectations."

"I'll add my two phennigs in support of that suggestion, Your Highness," Uncle Wolf Syros said. "But first he needs to be promoted to captain."

Democriphon nodded. "Your rebuke has been noted. It shall be done forthwith." They watched as the wooden gate was drawn open to reveal Petty-Captain Andros, Gasphros and one of the freemen.

"Welcome back, Your Highness," Andros called out. "We are pleased to see you have all returned from your journeys in good health."

"I am pleased to be back, Petty-Captain, and impressed."

Andros preened a little as he waved the newcomers' into the compound. "We have been working from dawn to dusk to erect fortifications. We have some houses and your private quarters finished, although only with the very basic amenities thus far. Everything is built from wood and thatch, sire, but I do have teams scoring the area for stone."

"Why not just buy brick and mortar from the surrounding towns?" Democriphon asked.

"I intend to, Prince, after I know what the operating budget is," Andros explained. "By the way, I should introduce Freeman Mardros." Mardros nodded. "He has been our acting mayor and is owed far more credit than myself for organizing the workforce."

Democriphon gave Mardros a quick once-over and pegged him as supervisor of some sort before being made a slave. "Where do you hail from, Mardros?"

Mardros bowed low before answering, "Balph, Your Highness. I was a failed apprentice of carpentry before being transferred to the silver mines. There I rose to supervisor."

*That explains his organizational skills,* Democriphon thought. He considered asking how Mardros became enslaved, then decided it did not matter. The scars on his hands were proof of his loyalty. To rise so high as a slave, was proof of his competence. "You have done well, Mardros. You may style yourself the Mayor of Mallegast."

Uncle Wolf Sylos whispered in his ear. "We need a code name for this village, one that no one knows."

Democriphon searched his mind for ideas, then recalled that Great King Kalvan said that the Robin Hood in the Cold Lands hailed from a place called Sure Wood. That was as good a name as any.

"We will call this place Sure Wood. What say you?"

All agreed and some of the men nearby cheered.

"We can use Sure Wood as a, uh, code name, Your Highness," Syros added. "When on a raid we can say we are from Sure Wood and sow confusion among our enemies."

*Code name? That had to be one of King Kalvan's new ways of making war. He must have picked it up from Duke Skranga.* "Very well," Democriphon said, "I like the idea of our enemies searching for a place that doesn't exist. Men, I should like to speak with you further after I have refreshed myself and put on some dry clothing. I am certain my companions feel much the same," From behind, he heard muttered agreement. "Now, if someone could guide me to my new residence…"

## III

A short while later Democriphon sat in his new home in a throne-like chair that had to have been hand-carved by a master artisan. His house was a simple three-room affair with one of the rooms designed to accommodate twenty men around a long table with a brace of candles providing light. Seated about that table were First Captain Ranthar, Uncle Wolf Syros, Petty-Captain Andros, Gasphros, Vanir, Chief Petty-Captain Gycules and Mayor Mardros.

"My first order of business will be to promote Petty-Captain Andros to Captain Andros."

He was surprised to see Andros' cheeks glow like coals. *I do not think they appreciated him in the Royal Army of Hos-Bletha, but we do.*

"Thank you, Your Highness."

Next Democriphon thanked everybody for coming, then turned to the minstrel. "Gasphros, I trust you have been diligent in your duties while I was away?"

"Indeed, sire, and I have learned some interesting things. Did you know that there are at least four current claimants to the title of Prince in Exile, counting yourself?"

"What!" Democriphon, used to making the claim and staying in character feigned outrage. "I'll have their heads!"

It took Gasphros a moment—until Democriphon winked—to realize what he was up to. Not everybody at the table was in on the deception.

"Ah, yes, of course, Your Highness," Gasphros said. "However, you may want to hold off on any head-chopping for a while. These false claimants to your rightful throne are running Niclophon's soldiers in circles. Styphon's House has been without their normal tribute, as your uncle has had to hire more soldiers, and even mercenaries, to chase after these frauds. I think that works to our benefit just now."

Democriphon looked thoughtful. "Indeed. That also frees up Captain Ranthar for other duties."

"Sire?"

"Captain Ranthar, I think you should expand the Robinos Operation"

Ranthar nodded. "I'm all for that."

Uncle Wolf Syros nodded. "Robinos' reputation has soared ever since the wedding. Grand-Captain Myklon represented him well. It's unfortunate that we lost Myklon. He is very much missed."

Democriphon said, "Let's have a few moments of silence in his memory. Would you like to say a prayer, Uncle Wolf?"

"Yes. Grand-Captain Myklon was a great warrior who died in the heat of battle, as he would have wished, protecting friends and killing foes. May Galzar grant him a seat in his Grand Hall."

"Aye," said everyone in unison.

Myklon wasn't their first casualty, but his was the first death among the members of the inner council.

"First Captain Ranthar, choose your team," Democriphon said, "but excuse Captain Andros and Mayor Mardros; they both have duties here."

Ranthar gave the matter some quick thought. Most of the candidates were obvious choices: Gycules was a perfect Little John, Gasphros would do as Allen-a-Dale, Uncle Wolf Syros was a leaner, meaner Friar Tuck. The rest could be filled from the freemen and former mercenaries.

Gycules was visibly thrilled to be chosen; he wanted to get back out into the field. Gasphros was less thrilled but willing. Uncle Wolf Syros insisted that he would have to divide his duties between the raiding party and the village of Sure Wood.

"Very good," Democriphon nodded. He hated to lose Gycules though he could see why Ranthar selected him. "Now we should talk about allocating funds for building the village. I purchased title to the land on my trip to Pytha Town. A lot of work was done during my absence, but much more has to be done. We have Prince Mythros' envoy coming and I want to make a good impression."

# FORTY-EIGHT

## I

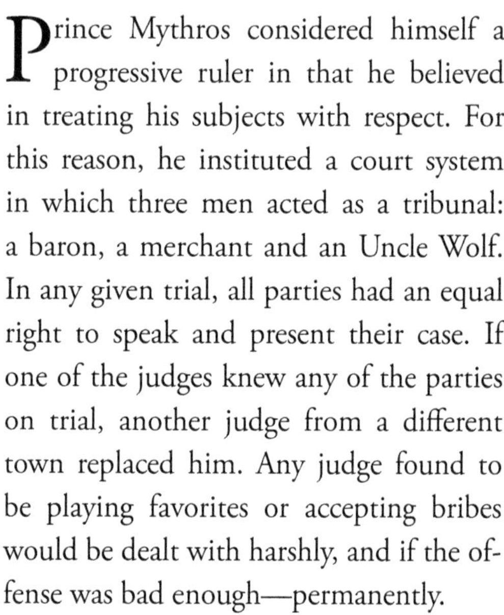

Prince Mythros considered himself a progressive ruler in that he believed in treating his subjects with respect. For this reason, he instituted a court system in which three men acted as a tribunal: a baron, a merchant and an Uncle Wolf. In any given trial, all parties had an equal right to speak and present their case. If one of the judges knew any of the parties on trial, another judge from a different town replaced him. Any judge found to be playing favorites or accepting bribes would be dealt with harshly, and if the offense was bad enough—permanently.

When Zentros and his cronies were brought before the prince, Mythros almost wished he had not been so forward-thinking in his system of criminal justice. His first impulse was to give the hangman some business. He looked at the men brought before him with a baleful glare.

"I understand that you have been masquerading as the Prince in Exile," Mythros declared. "I have to ask if it was a profitable venture."

The sharpers all looked to Zentros,

who sighed and said, "Under the circumstances, I would have to say no, Your Highness."

Mythros nodded with pursed lips. "No. I imagine not. Before I send you to the Tribunal, please tell me, why did you undertake this scheme?"

The head sharper hesitated. Then he straightened up and said, "Others had started running the game and we just decided to try and cash in as well. Unlike some of the other bands, we simply went for donations; no selling of properties or promises of titles after the revolt."

Mythros nodded again. "How commendable of you. Tell me, have you ever heard of the penalty for perpetrating this fraud in my realm?"

Zentros swallowed a sizeable lump caught in his throat. "We have. That is why none of us wanted to enter your realm. That is, until we were forcefully invited."

One of the guards fought to stifle a chuckle with very little success. Mythros ignored it. "That was very wise of you, and the only reason I am sending you before the Tribunal rather than dealing with you myself. I only deal with squabbles among the noble class and Orphan Prince frauds in my realm as a rule. This is very fortunate…for you. However, there are some things I simply must know."

Zentros sensed he and his men might yet escape with their lives, if not their freedom. "Anything you want, I will do, Your Highness."

"Typically, you sharpers try to swindle people of their gold and silver, yes?"

"Yes, Your Highness." *No point in lying now.*

"Candor. Very good. Now, I have heard tales of another band that is actually passing out silver to the peasantry and townsfolk. I admit that this is a rather novel approach, yet I fail to see how it could possibly benefit the parties involved. Is there some sort of long game expected to bring in a handsome reward associated with this tactic?"

"Sire?" Zentros said, shrugging his shoulders.

"Why is this band of sharpers giving silver away? What is the expected return?"

Zentros fought to wrap his mind around the concept and failed. "Your

Highness, this makes no sense to me. It's just plain wrong! This man, whoever he is, is giving…silver…away? What does he do afterwards?"

"He leaves and moves on to another village."

"That's insane!" Zentros shouted. "Are you playing games with me, Your Highness? No sharper ever gives away anything unless it's a bribe to a guard to let him go. What you are saying makes no sense at all!"

Zentros babbled on for a bit until Mythros lost patience. The Prince nodded to a guard and the sharpers were led out of the courtroom with Zentros screaming all the way that he did not understand why.

Mythos' Chancellor watched as the sharpers were led away with a furrowed brow. "Your Highness, I think he was being candid with you. No sharper in my experience has ever given away any form of true wealth."

"I agree, and that is what disturbs me."

His Chancellor shook his head. "Sire?"

"Whatever this group of—whoever or whatever they are?—it's obvious that they are not looking to gain wealth. These so-called sharpers must have tremendous resources to be giving away hundreds of ounces of silver in every town and village they visit. So what do they expect to gain?"

Esmeranos thought for a moment before speaking. "I would be equally curious to know how they obtained such wealth in the first place, Your Highness."

Mythros nodded. "That is another mystery I would like to see solved. Most likely, they robbed a paymaster up north or some such place. There will be a number of very angry soldiers and mercenaries looking for them if that is the case."

He thought a moment more and recalled that after Great Queen Delra had been assassinated, all of her jewelry had been taken. *No, that cannot be…*

"Sire, it occurs to me that a more local source of income is possible."

Mythros looked up. "And what would that be?"

"The raids on the Styphoni temples, perhaps, or even the banditry that has been plaguing our neighbors of late."

"Esmeranos, I have no love of bandits, even when they leave my realm alone, but these temple raiders intrigue me."

The Chancellor's head snapped up with eyes wide. "Sire, I think you have made an interesting observation."

"Such as?"

"There has been no unusual increase in banditry in your realm, nor have any of Styphon's temples been attacked within your Princedom. This new Prince in Exile band, or whatever they call themselves, have been giving your lands a wide birth, as well. I think they may all be connected."

"Hmm. Now that is an interesting possibility. It's one thing to avoid my realm due to my reputation for dealing with frauds, but now even bandits and outlaws are avoiding my realm." Mythros stood up from his throne and walked over to a window. In the courtyard, Thames was playing with his sword master, Arthlos. "I want to meet this new Prince in Exile and take his measure."

"That may prove difficult, sire."

"No doubt it will. If he were easy to catch, he would already be dead I would wager. Still, double-pay to the team that brings him to me...alive."

Chancellor Esmeranos nodded. "As you wish, sire. Uh, what about those sharpers...?"

Mythros had to think a moment, then recalled Zentros and his men. "Tell the Tribunal I have no personal interest in the fate of these criminals and they can deal with them as their own wisdom demands. They were courteous enough not to bring their games to my realm so I do not feel particularly vindictive towards them. A few years of hard labor would be punishment enough, I should think, but that will be up to the Tribunal."

"Very good, sire," Esmeranos said as he bowed and started to leave, then turned back around. "Your Highness?"

"Yes?"

"An idea just came to me. I have a plan to find this other so-proclaimed Orphan Prince."

## II

Robin Hood, Little John and Friar Tuck looked down from the trees at the passing caravan. Ranthar smiled as he fancied himself, Gycules and Uncle Wolf Syros in the roles of the legendary figures from the Europo-American Subsector.

Once Ranthar had watched the Errol Flynn movie, when it was first imported to First Level, with a woman he was involved with at that time. It was an entertaining film, although historically inaccurate. Still, the movie was fun to watch.

Now, here Ranthar was imitating Robin of Loxley in every way save for the wolf-helms they all wore. Ranthar selected some of the men for their resemblance to the literary and movie characters. Of course, no actor Ranthar had ever seen could compare with Gycules for size and strength. On the other hand, few men on Kalvan's Time-Line were a match with Basil Rathbone for swordplay.

Ranthar forced his mind back to the immediate situation. Fireseed was starting to run low. While little had been expended during normal bandit operations, the minefield and the bamboo bombs had used up a prodigious amount. The caravan below was rumored to carry a few tons worth of fireseed, and Ranthar meant to acquire it. Unfortunately, that meant using crossbows and bows instead of smoothbores and pistols; a stray shot could hit the fireseed and blow everybody to Regwarn. Everybody still carried firearms though they were ordered not to use them unless absolutely necessary.

The caravan looked like a good target. Only twenty guards to protect five wagons and the merchant's carriage. They had come down from the north, if the road they were taking was any indication, and might not be aware of the heightened banditry in the area. It was perfect.

Too perfect.

Ranthar raised a hand to signal everyone to hold his fire. It was too late. Several freemen sent a volley of arrows at the guardsmen. *We are in for it now!* Seeing no other option, he ordered the attack.

Arrows and bolts filled the air cutting into the guardsmen from every direction. Before the guards could hope to recover, wolf-headed men flew down on ropes and vines to engage them with sword and knife. Everything went well until the wagons opened and dozens of armed soldiers, wearing the yellow and blue royal uniforms of Great King Niclophon, erupted from within. Unlike Ranthar's party, these men were in no way reluctant to use firearms. A dozen bandits were cut down in seconds.

"Fireseed weapons now!" Ranthar yelled, as he drew a horse-pistol and shot a soldier in the face. With his other hand he drew his rapier and hacked at anything he could get close to.

The bandits, seeing their leader take action, quickly followed his example using their pistols and swords. Gycules used his greatsword to cut a swath through the soldiers. One managed to fire a horse-pistol directly at the giant's chest. Gycules' wolf-helm hid the pain on his face but not his anger. Moving as if unaffected by the shot, he flew into the solders and hacked away like a true minion of Galzar.

Uncle Wolf Syros stayed at the fringes of the combat and only fought when attacked. These were not Styphoni, so he could not fight without provocation. Still, his mace suffered no lack of skulls to crush.

Gasphros, who had stayed on the ground, used throwing knives whenever he could get around a tree without drawing fire. In his own mind, it was a shame that everyone was too busy to observe his skill with the projectiles. One knife entered a soldier's throat while the next entered another's eye socket, penetrating the brain.

Ranthar drew on all of his training as he danced between the soldiers hacking off arms and heads. One hand landed on the ground with a horse-pistol still in the act of firing. The discharged round went harmlessly into a tree.

The battle ended with surprising speed. Ranthar looked around and saw that several of his party had remained in the trees firing arrows and bullets at the soldiers. They had taken a big chance doing that as they would have been unable to evade effectively if the soldiers had fired back.

Ranthar, breathing hard, looked to Gycules and said, "Report."

The giant surveyed the battlefield and the copse of trees. He came back and reported, "We lost twenty-six dead, five more badly wounded, sir. The enemy lost thirty-two men and we've taken nine prisoners, three of them not expected to live through the night according to Uncle Wolf Syros."

Ranthar turned his attention to two freemen who looked healthy enough. "Check the wagons. Make sure there are no more surprises."

Gycules waited until the two returned and reported that all the soldiers in the wagon were dead before suddenly collapsing.

Uncle Wolf Syros ran over and pointed to the powder burns on the big man's chest. He called over two men and they quickly stripped off the tunic and chainmail to find boiled leather underneath.

No wonder he sweated so much, thought Ranthar.

Even with three men, it took some time to cut off the leather armor allowing Syros to inspect the wound.

"Galzar must love big louts like you, Gycules," Syros said to the unconscious man. Turning to Ranthar, he added, "That ball barely broke flesh. Not too surprising with that extra layer of armor. Still, the Wargod's luck was with him, although he won't agree for at least three or four days."

The big man's eyes popped open and he started thrashing around.

"Hold still, Petty-Captain!" the Uncle Wolf ordered. "I'm going to pour some wine on that. Um, on second thought, would you four men hold him down? This is going to hurt."

Four nearby soldiers scrambled to help the Uncle Wolf. The wine went on the wound and Gycules roared and nearly bucked the men off.

"Next time wear a back-and-breast," Syros ordered. "I know it is heavier but I doubt that will slow you down any."

"I…can't. Too hard…to get…in my size."

Syros rolled his eyes. "We have our own blacksmiths, you great hulking fool."

Ranthar came over to look over Gycules. "Will he recover?"

"Ha! It would take more than one shot to put this great oaf down. He will be fine as long as he takes it easy for a few days. I have some salves that will ease his pain and speed the healing. Now I must see to the others."

Uncle Wolf Syros went to look at the other wounded while Ranthar looked over the wagons. Empty. *This caravan was a setup, and we escaped by the skin of our teeth—and Gycules' mad charge. We'll have to be more careful in the future.*

## III

Democriphon accepted Ranthar's report dispassionately. He had been expecting something like this. He and Ranthar had discussed the fact that sooner or later they would run into something unpleasant. Now it had happened more than once; maybe it would teach the new men something about the enemy they were facing. Their men had been getting too cocky and perhaps this would help them realize that these raids were serious business.

"I accept full responsibility for the actions of my men, sir," Ranthar concluded.

"Ranthar, the fault is as much, or more, mine as anyone's," Democriphon replied. "The freemen are just not fully trained. Had they not jumped the gun, you would have retreated and not taken a single casualty. Our scouts should have studied this group better."

Democriphon noticed the pained look on Ranthar's face. "Uncle Wolf Syros gave me his account while you were organizing the burial detail. I did not ask for it, but was glad to hear it. I think you Greffans are too quick to accept the blame on behalf of your men. While I find that commendable, I believe straightening out the actual culprits will be of greater benefit to us. Talk to your men; explain again why they should not fire their weapons before you give the order. This fight and all the casualties will give your words weight. Any punishment you see fit to give is within your purview. Now, would you like some Ermut's Best? I believe you could use a few swallows."

Ranthar accepted the cup gratefully. "I think Gycules could use some, too. I could only spare a glance when I heard the shot behind me, but he tore into those soldiers like a demon! He should get some sort of award for heroism."

"I'll forward the request with the next message to Skranga. When this operation is finished, Great King Kalvan will be awarding a barrel of those medals he came up with. Dralm knows these men have earned it. Even the ones new to our service."

"I'll drink to that!" Ranthar took a healthy swallow.

# FORTY-NINE

## I

Great King Niclophon was eating his supper with his wife, about the only time—other than official events—they spent any time together. She was a pleasant woman, with a pillowy body and gray hair accented with a feather of snow at the temples. He had chosen her, the daughter of a minor prince, because he knew the instant he met her that she would accede to his every demand. Her life force was much like her bulging thighs, fleshy, malleable yet surprisingly resilient. Her only failure, although it could easily be his own, was that she had never graced him with a child. *If I had a son, there wouldn't be all this talk of an Orphan Prince.*

They tried hard at first, despite his revulsion, but after several winters with no results from their unpleasant couplings, he had withdrawn. His own family had been small, just his parents, himself and one brother—cruelly murdered. He had been blamed for Great King Marocles death by many, even though it had not been by his hand. Sadly the line would come to an end with his death. Even sadder, the man

who was most likely to follow him was his brother-in-law, that fatuous prig Prince Mythros. *Maybe I should find some way to finish him and his revoltingly large family…*

The Chamberlain approached his table, "Your Majesty, the Chancellor requests the honor of your presence."

"Bah! Tell him to leave me alone. Can't you see I'm eating dinner?"

The Chamberlain drew back as if the King had pulled his knife and made a threatening gesture.

Niclophon looked down at his plate; the half-eaten duck—its porcelain bones poking out of the half-eaten breast covered with brackish sauce—looked revolting. His stomach roiled; once again, dinner had been ruined.

"Your Majesty, he says it's important."

"Bid him enter," he said, with a swish of his hand.

Chancellor Archimanes entered the room with a flourish. "I apologize, Your Majesty, for disturbing your repast but a parcel has been found outside the gates of the palace. It is addressed to you."

"A parcel?"

"A crate, actually. Rather large."

Niclophon frequently received gifts; however, someone seeking his favor or a boon of some sort typically delivered them to the palace.

The crate shortly appeared delivered by two large sweaty men who were thoroughly intimidated by their palatial surroundings. Niclophon ordered them to open the crate and they went at it quickly. The top came off and the king waved them away so that he could view the mysterious contents.

At first, it looked like tufts of fur. Niclophon reached in and grabbed one and pulled it out for a better look. It was heavier than he had expected. When he pulled it free of the others and saw what he held, he screamed and threw it back in the crate.

"Your Majesty?"

"Look, Archimanes!" he screeched. "Look at what somebody sent me."

The Chancellor looked inside and saw the same bundle of fur that his king had thrown back into the box. It was attached to a human head. The Chancellor's face paled and he began to make noises as though his gorge was beginning to rise. As he withdrew from the crate, he spotted a parchment pinned to the inside of the lid. He picked it up and read it aloud.

"Thank you for the delightful diversion, Your Majesty. Next time, send your best. Signed, Robinos of Sure Wood."

"Get that out of here," Niclophon screamed. "Double…no, triple the patrols! I want that animal found. And I want *his* head for a centerpiece at the next feast!"

## II

The scout ran up to Ranthar and barely stopped in time to avoid a collision. It took several heartbeats for the man to control his breathing well enough to speak intelligibly.

"Master…Robinos! A caravan comes…with a Band of Styphon's Own Guard!"

"A large band, a small band—what?"

"Three hundred men, or more!" Ranthar considered his options. Even with the advantage of surprise, his men were outnumbered by far too much to expect to survive a direct confrontation. *Niclophon must have asked for some extra help after the gift we sent him.* He would have to abort the raid.

"Gycules, we will have to let this caravan pass, Dralm-damnit," Ranthar said in disgust.

"What? Why?" demanded the giant. To look at him none would guess that he had taken a chest wound a moon-quarter ago.

"We are out-gunned and out-numbered. I will not lead these men into a slaughter…"

"Why not use the, uh, bamboo bombs?"

Ranthar did a double take. *Bamboo bombs?* "We have some? How many?"

"Two hundred sticks, Master. I seized all I could carry before we left Malleg—I mean Sure Wood."

"You carried two hundred of those fireseed stuffed bamboo rods...by yourself?

He laughed. "I'm not *that* strong. No, I loaded up a couple of packhorses."

"Gycules, if you weren't so big and ugly I would kiss you full on the mouth. Distribute the *bamboo bombs* among the men, make sure they understand that they must light the fuse and throw it immediately at the enemy and that they need to take cover behind something sturdy before it explodes; ground, boulders, trees, anything available. We'll set up posts on both sides of the road, men ten paces apart. They will aim for Styphon's Own Guard, not any of the carriages or wagons. After the explosions, count to ten, then finish off any of the survivors with bow and sword. Take no chances, the bombs are unpredictable, and for the love of the True Gods warn everyone not to drop any!"

## III

Highpriest Rathocles half-dozed in his carriage while his underpriests watched the slowly passing scenery through the windows. *Trees and more trees*, he thought. The recent raids on Styphon's House's had left behind a handful of ruined temples. He had been brought from Balph for the restoration of the Marthrax Temple. Above all else, Styphon's House could not afford to look weak.

Rathocles had been provided with a Temple Band of Styphon's Own Guard for his protection. Also in the caravan were gold, silver and supplies to restore the temple to its former glory. The temple could be restored and back in operation within a couple of moons if all went well.

The highpriest roused from his slumber suddenly and violently. Outside, an earsplitting explosion rocked the carriage. Rathocles struggled to look out the window. All he could see was dust thick in the air. He drew back quickly when gunfire sounded over the ringing in his ears. His panicked underpriests threw themselves to the floor of the carriage, leaving no room for Rathocles to take cover.

The sound of what had to be a battle went on for at least half a candle before the air became quiet, again. He shoved the underpriests aside and hugged the floor of the carriage, trying not to foul himself before his inferiors. From the rising stench, he knew that some of the underpriests did not have his bladder control. He was certain that Styphon's Own Guard could handle anything mere bandits could throw at them. He maintained that belief until he saw a hand, or rather a great hairy paw, the size of a turkey platter seize the door.

The doorway filled with the largest man Rathocles had ever seen, if indeed it was a man. The creature was dressed entirely in green with light armor stained a deep brown. However, neither its size nor style of dress was the source of Rathocles' distress. In place of a man's face was the muzzle of a great wolf!

One oversized paw seized the highpriest, pulled him from the carriage as though he were an underfed child, and threw him to the ground. The priest struggled to rise until he was pinned by a booted foot. Raising his eyes slowly, he took in the green leggings, stained armor, and finally another wolf's muzzle where a man's face should be.

Superstitious fear paralyzed Rathocles. Above him, the wolf creature ordered the giant to lift him onto his feet. The priest was then seized by his shoulders and lifted onto legs that barely supported his weight. With great effort, he forced himself to speak.

"Wh-what do you want?" he cried out.

The daemon beast looked him over then came close. He started sniffing the priest. From behind, he could hear laughter. *Are these creatures going to eat me?*

A gunshot went off and something pinged off the wolf's cranium. The beast's head went back on his neck then returned to its original position. The Daemon beast remained standing. There was the sound of several more shots, then silence. He looked at the beast's wound and saw no blood. Instead, there was the sheen of iron where the fur parted.

*Wolfmen with bones of iron? Galzar's minions!* It was too much for Rathocles; he collapsed in a dead faint.

"Are there any survivors?" demanded Ranthar. He had a bad headache from the bullet that had grazed his helm.

"Just the slaves and a few of the priests," the giant replied.

Ranthar removed his wolf-helm and inspected the damage. The shot had struck the helm and rode up the flat cranium parting the fur. If his morion helmet hadn't been made of plastisteel, the ball would have simply penetrated the iron helm and, as a consequence, Ranthar's skull killing him instantly. Even if there had been somebody to take him to a First Level med unit, there would be no way to shove his brains back in his head and restore him to life. Ranthar felt a little weak and covered it by barking orders.

"Lytris, Goddess of Luck is with you today, Robinos," Gycules pronounced, as he inspected the wolf-helm.

Ranthar shook his head to clear the cobwebs slowing his thoughts. "Double-check and make sure all of the Guardsmen are dead. When in doubt, slit their throats. Free the slaves and tell them they are coming with us. Be sure to take off the wolf-helms first or they might die of fright. Kill all the Styphoni but the highpriest; he'll make the most credible witness. Make sure he never sees your true faces. Tell him Robinos has spared him to tell his tale."

Gycules nodded and returned to the carriage to fish out the remaining priests. Uncle Wolf Syros, unmasked, strode over to Ranthar.

"Great Galzar, that was one Dralm-damned big explosion," Syros said. "It was a miracle that the fireseed wagon didn't go up. How many of those, um, *bamboo bombs* did you use?"

"More than I wanted to, Uncle Wolf," Ranthar admitted. "We were prepared for a small merchant caravan, not a full Band of Styphon's Own Guard. They had us out-numbered at least two to one. I considered letting them pass until Gycules told me about the *bamboo bombs*. I am glad of it, too. We freed at least a hundred slaves. You know how Democriphon feels about slavery."

"I am in agreement with him." Uncle Wolf Syros looked out over the dead. Men and horses were strewn about the road as if they were so much bloody butcher shop cast-offs. "Though, I am not so sure I like this way of making war."

"I like me or mine dying in a futile battle a whole lot less, Uncle Wolf. Come, help me see to the slaves and then we'll see what treasures we have won."

As if on cue, Gasphros appeared. "Robinos, I checked the wagons. Gold, silver, victuals, equipment, various supplies, but no fireseed."

Ranthar unleashed every blasphemous Zarthani word in his hypnomeched vocabulary and only stopped short of using outtime curses. "We needed that damned fireseed! The bamboo bombs alone just cost us over three-hundred pounds of fireseed. Even Styphon's Best is better than nothing. Tell Gycules to have the men take extra care in stripping the bodies; gather any powder horns, or other fireseed they find. We will take it back and see if we can't do something with it. Gasphros, you can take charge of the treasure wagons."

Gasphros nodded once, then strode off at a brisk pace. Ranthar considered his options until Uncle Wolf Syros called his attention to the unconscious highpriest. "What about him?"

"Humph. I would like to string him from the highest tree limb," Ranthar said. "However, we need a witness that carries some weight. Nobody of importance in the Temple will believe an underpriest, certainly not if he babbles on about spirit wolves. He can fend for himself after we leave."

Ranthar looked up and called out several nearby men. "Relieve the highpriest of his finery and purses, then dump this trash in a ditch well away from here. However, leave the highpriest alive and whole; I want him to be able to report back to Styphon's House what has transpired here this day. As for the rest, dump their bodies in the swamp for the river dragons when you're done stripping off their armor and any valuables."

"Do you plan to make a gift of their heads to Balph?" Syros asked.

"Over three hundred heads, I think not. The highpriest will carry our message well enough."

As Ranthar watched Rathocles being dragged away, he realized that he had been very lucky this time out. Next time he would either take more men or choose smaller targets. This was twice in a row that things had not gone according to plan. He would also consult with Gycules about what equipment to bring. *I wouldn't be surprised if next time he straps a canon to his back.*

IV

Democriphon was overseeing the erection of another tower when Ranthar led his patrol in through the main gates. The First Captain eyed the newly-freed slaves and instantly grasped from the scars on their naked backs that they were former Styphoni slaves. Nobody else used metal barbed whips that left marks like that.

Ranthar spotted Democriphon, said something to Gycules then rode over. "We had a good day, My Prince, thanks to Chief Petty-Captain Gycules, though it could have gone very badly."

Democriphon shrugged. It was getting easy to expect wonders from the giant. "A man that large and strong is half an army by himself."

"Aside from that. He had the foresight to bring those bamboo bombs. They made short work of a Band of Styphon's Own Guard." Ranthar related the details of the battle. "We lost over sixty men, and another fifty are injured, half of them fatally. It would have been a lot worse without the bombs." *It would have been a lot better with hand grenades or claymore mines from Kalvan's time-line.*

"So that's what happened to the bamboo bombs," Democriphon said with relief. "I was ready to hang a few people thinking they had stolen them. Now, I'm going to chew off a chunk of Gycules' arse for not informing me! We will have to start using those…uh, those…*requisitions* that Ka—that our friend was so fond of."

Ranthar nodded. Kalvan's name could not be bandied about lightly, even in the new village. Styphon's House had a high price out for Kalvan's head and one never knew who might be listening. "I hope you didn't need them while we were gone."

"We did, but just for removing some tree stumps. Gycules left enough bamboo bombs to handle that." Democriphon's face grew sober. "Did you manage to bring back our dead?"

"Yes. Gycules is arranging a burial detail in the section you designated as a cemetery. Per your standing orders, they will be interred in full uniform. Their names are being added to the list of the honored dead. Unfortunately, we didn't find any fireseed. I think they simply planned on making it at the temple."

Democriphon shook his head in disgust. "I wager they expected their numbers to keep us from attacking them. Did you at least get any fireseed from the dead?"

"About a hundred pounds worth."

Democriphon glanced over at the shed where the fireseed was stored. "That minefield used up far too much fireseed." He shook his head in concern. "We've already used up most of the fireseed Gasphros acquired from Baron Althaphon. We'll have to find more soon. Our situation is beginning to remind me of Hostigos just before Lord Kalvan appeared."

"We should start making our own—" Ranthar started.

"From what?" Democriphon asked. "We can buy charcoal, and muck out the stables and pastures for saltpeter, but I don't know of any way to obtain sulfur without drawing a lot of suspicion. Unless you know where we can get some quietly?"

Shaking his head, Ranthar had to admit that he did not. Things were starting to look bad for the near future.

# FIFTY

## I

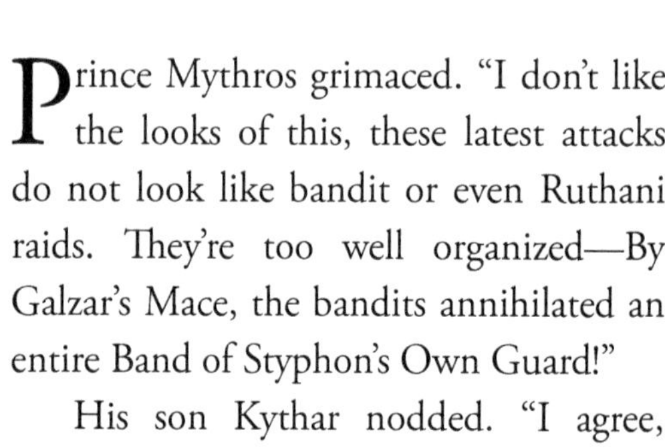

Prince Mythros grimaced. "I don't like the looks of this, these latest attacks do not look like bandit or even Ruthani raids. They're too well organized—By Galzar's Mace, the bandits annihilated an entire Band of Styphon's Own Guard!"

His son Kythar nodded. "I agree, father. This Orphan Prince, whoever's spawn he truly is, is no mere adventurer. He has powerful friends, gold and fireseed to burn."

"You are right. Furthermore, this so-called-Prince is like quicksilver; the moment you grasp him, he slips away. Have your men had any luck apprehending him?"

"No. We've sent our best trackers and agents-inquisitors into the Princedom of Taurnos, but no one knows who this man and his supporters are. There are stories about runaway slaves; we've questioned a few and they blather on about the Wolfs of Galzar, or how a Great Prince has come to deliver them from slavery. They know nothing of substance; he's as elusive as marsh gas."

Mythros paused to light his pipe. "This is bad. His men have attacked caravans, temples, convoys and small parties almost everywhere in Hos-Bletha but in my princedom. Sooner or later, Great King Niclophon will begin to look in our direction. All our plans will soon go awry." He was a patient man and knew that without any offspring, Niclophon's dynasty would die along with the Great King.

Suddenly, everything he had worked towards for the past three decades was at risk by some pox-ridden cur who claimed to be the Orphan Prince. *Ha!*

Kythar, as if reading his thoughts, said, "We have much to lose if this continues. Even a malodorous fop like Niclophon will eventually lose his patience. He does not like to act, but will if pressed hard enough. We are quickly reaching that point, father."

"I agree. Unfortunately, we do not have enough men under our banner to fight off an attack by the Great King, even though half of Niclophon's army has been promised to the Grand Host. Besides, he would not attack us directly—"

"Yes, but Xandros and Basilron would do his work for him if he promised them our lands."

"Sadly, there is much truth in your words, son. We could easily defeat either one, maybe both, but they would also have the backing of Styphon's House, which means no more fireseed."

Kythar sucked in air. "Yes, and maybe even have Styphon's arm at our rear."

The Order of Zarthani Knights was there to protect the Southern Kingdoms against the Ruthani and Sastragathi nomads, but they could just as easily turn their might against a princely foe. Fortunately, for now, most of their forces were in Hos-Harphax arrayed against the Usurper Kalvan. Those who remained were needed to protect the marches from the nomads and barbarians. "If we had more fireseed and this Kalvan supporting us…"

"Might as well wish for Galzar to leave his Great Hall and join us here in Pytha."

Mythros laughed. "From what the peasants and runaways are saying, the Wargod may already be here."

"Wolf-men! By the gods," Kythar said between laughs. "If there be gods, we are but their playthings."

"Be careful about what you say about the gods. There is an ill-wind blowing in Balph; it is called the Holy Investigator Roxthar. He is a true believer in Styphon and out to convert everyone who does not agree. And kill those who refuse. It is said that Roxthar is the most dangerous man in the Five Kingdoms, even more dangerous than Great King Kalvan."

Kythar nodded. "That reminds me. I have one of my agents freshly returned from Taurnos. He has some fresh ideas on the Orphan Prince."

"Aha. Bid him enter, by all means."

Kythar left his father's private audience chamber, still holding a goblet of wine, and returned with a thick-bodied man who looked like a former soldier.

"Father, this is Phestros. He is one of the men looking into the Orphan Prince ploy."

The man nodded, saying, "Your Highness, a pleasure."

"I understand you have some thoughts on the origins of this so-called Orphan Prince."

"That I do, sire. I do not believe that it is an accident that this pretender strikes first and mostly in Taurnos. Nor is it a coincidence that Taurnos borders the Princedom of Artigos which is claimed by Hos-Ktemnos. It is my theory that a band of Styphon's highpriests—or possibly even archpriests of the Inner Circle—have banded together and are looking for a new nest to colonize. Their destination: Hos-Bletha."

"But why?" Mythros asked. "Styphon's House already owns our king; if he was any deeper into their pockets he would disappear!"

"Yes, but since the Investigation by Archpriest Roxthar, no priest—be he underpriest, highpriest or archpriest is safe in Balph."

"I had not heard that this scabrous wretch had the power to Investigate his fellow highpriests and archpriests."

"Ah. You don't follow Temple politics, Your Highness. Styphon's Own Voice is near death and—due to pressure from Holy Investigator Roxthar—Sesklos has promised to support Archpriest Dracar as the next

Supreme Priest. Roxthar has the Inner Circle thoroughly cowed and the Investigator's cat's-paw is certain to win the election to Supreme Priest. Not even the Speaker, Archpriest Anaxthenes, will be able to stop his succession."

"This is bad news indeed," Mythros said. "But if your words hold truth: Why then the attacks on Styphon's Own Guard and their own temples?"

"Aha. This faction does not want to be seen as part of Styphon's House. These attacks and the Orphan Prince game are but a diversion. They need a new home away from the Investigation and they have chosen Hos-Bletha."

Mythros rubbed his hands together as though to warm them. "Thank you for your words, Phestros. You have given me much to mull over. I am not ready to say that you are right, but neither can I prove you wrong."

## II

Ranthar, with his small advance party of newly freed slaves, reached the village gates of Mallegast and was waved inside. Two small stone towers had been added to the palisade on either side of the gates since he had left, each containing three men armed with large-bore muskets. *They aren't Kalvan's rifles, but they'll discourage any enemies from approaching too closely.* In addition, all trees, brush and other vegetation within a half-march had been cleared from all sides of the village walls. There was a growing mountain of stone blocks piled next to the western wall. Their plan was to replace the wooden walls with stone, a section at a time.

Inside the large courtyard, Ranthar dismounted and handed the reins to one of the men still wearing a wolf-helm.

Democriphon came out of the command hut to join him. "So, Robinos, what have you brought us today?"

Ranthar shook his head. "It will be a few days before the treasures we took from Styphon's Own Fools arrive. I left Petty-Captain Gycules in charge and rode ahead to report in. There is gold and silver enough to restock a temple, plus victuals intended for the Guard. I would have been here sooner had not Gycules suggested we allow the slaves to loot the bodies of the dead before throwing them into the swamp. I wanted to make sure we wouldn't lose control of the new freemen."

"Indeed! We don't want any more deserters. We had better watch ourselves; Gycules could be after our jobs."

"Frankly, if he wasn't on our side he would scare the Styphon out of me," Ranthar joked.

Democriphon laughed briefly, then added, "He still scares me, but in a good way."

Ranthar smiled, then turned serious. "We need to send another treasure caravan to the depot. I would have sent this latest loot there, but I know we wanted to limit the number of men who know about the depot to as few as possible."

The Prince nodded. "You're right. Our vault in Mallegast is already filled to the rafters with gold and silver. With this next batch, it'll be overflowing."

Ranthar sighed. "I just wish there was some way we could send a couple of wagons of gold to Kalvan."

## III

As the new freemen were assisted, one former slave observed the goings on about the camp and took in everything: the treatment of the slaves, the dispersal of food and clothing, the construction of the wall and towers, even children, obviously also former slaves, playing with wooden swords. Those just being brought in remained fearful while others who professed to being rescued by the Orphan Prince tried to calm their fears.

Looking up at the labor force on the tower, the man could see many people working bare to the waist. Welts and scars from past injuries were apparent on most of them. None of the workers seemed resentful or fearful; in truth, they seemed happy and motivated to do good work. On an open field, men were training with swords, pikes and smoothbores.

"Excuse me," the newcomer addressed one of the men watching the arms drill. "What goes on here?"

"Huh? Oh, you must have just come in with the new batch of freemen. Yes, I can see by the marks on your back. Welcome to Mallegast. Here we are free of Styphon's House. Prince Valthros, the bright-haired man speaking with Robinos over there, is helping us and building an army to remove his uncle from the throne. He has vowed to end slavery in Hos-Bletha and force Styphon's House out. The bandit Robinos works with him to gather treasure enough to pay for all of this."

"Valthros?" The name sounded familiar, like something he had heard long ago.

"Yes, the Prince in Exile has returned. Soon, we will have strength enough to bring down the false king and place the true king on the throne."

"Many thanks, brother freeman."

The man decided he had seen and heard enough. Before the gates of the village closed, he slipped out amidst the confusion of people coming and going. Once outside of the village, he looked to the sun, gained his bearings and ran off with a vigor that belied the marks on his back.

# FIFTY-ONE

## I

Baltrov Eldra was bored beyond endurance. Despite her First Level mental abilities which allowed her to summon into memory any music, film or book she had ever heard or seen, she just couldn't concentrate on anything. The problem was her cover story: she was playing Sangar's widowed sister and as such she was expected to attend to his care. But since the palace household did everything one could ask, from making beds to removing chamber pots, she was expected to be in his quarters eating bon-bons or whatever it was female dependents did on Aryan-Transpacific when not in service to their brother.

"I've had it!" Eldra yelled at her empty chamber, "I am going to explore this castle. The study team will want to know everything I can find out down here, anyway."

Pulling on a hooded robe favored by women in Hos-Harphax, Eldra left the chamber and started down the hallway. After she took a few steps, she realized the palace guard could challenge her for moving about on her own. *When all else fails, act like you belong.*

The possibility of getting lost never entered her mind; with First Level memory training she could easily retrace her steps. Eldra decided to make a mental map of the castle one level at a time, starting with the floor on which her chamber resided. The castle proved to be deceptively large. After a candle and a half, she was ready for another level.

Capriciously, Eldra decided to go up into one of the towers. Many castles had at least four such edifices as part of their design. While the towers started out with a useful function, many tended to end up relegated for guests, prisoners, or storage, like an attic. This one was no exception. Originally designed as a lookout station, it had long been abandoned and housed only insects and other vermin.

Eldra noted the location and condition of the tower before moving down the spiral staircase to examine the next one. On the way, she passed some young men dressed in the toga-like linen favored by Niclophon. They seemed too young and soft for any kind of labor. They nodded at her politely and continued on their way. This was not the reaction she was accustomed to getting from men of any age. Eldra filed that scrap of information with the rest.

The next tower was much like the first one until Eldra reached the top; the door was locked. As an outtime study team member, locked doors were a common obstacle. In a more advanced culture, there were a number of electronic devices that could easily bypass any lock using access cards or entry codes. Aryan-Transpacific locks required a low-tech approach.

Eldra reached under the right breast support of her corset and opened a hidden pocket. Inside were lock picks. Eldra had lived over two hundred years and she had spent most of her life outtime. Often on backward time-lines like Kalvan's Time-Line. Over the years, she had become an expert marksman with everything from a flintlock rifle to a needler. She knew many different styles of hand to hand combat and her skill with a blade was legendary. Unlike most equipment used by the Study Team, her lock picks had been acquired locally from a thief in Greffa City. The thief was collected during initial studies of the timeline, hypno-meched for information, then her equipment was bought, corset and all, at a fair price. The woman's memory was adjusted to believe she was helping a talented newcomer hone her craft. While the originals had been duplicated down to the finest detail, Eldra had managed to requisition the original set and practiced with the tools until she was comfortable with them.

After double-checking to be certain she was unobserved, Eldra navigated the inner workings of the locking mechanism. It was difficult as there was a great deal of collected dust and some rust in the lock. When the door finally opened, it was with a rusty squeaking noise. The hinges had not been oiled in a very long time.

Making sure one more time that nobody was coming, Eldra went and set the door so that it would look undisturbed to the casual observer. She did not dare close it for fear it might not open again since there was no keyhole on the inside. Eldra looked about and decided the chamber had been originally used for political prisoners. There was a cot, a small table and stool, bars on the window, and a brass chamber pot. It was far more comfortable than the castle dungeon, but she wouldn't have wanted to spend a long period in the room as a prisoner.

Dust coated every surface and it appeared that no one had been inside this cell for several decades. Other than the furniture, the room was completely empty. She was about to exit the chamber when a thought struck her: *Why lock an empty room that holds nothing worth stealing?*

Her curiosity piqued, Eldra examined the room more thoroughly. Using one of her petticoats as a dust rag, she cleared the dust away from the walls of the chamber. There were scuffmarks on the floor next to the rear wall that suggested something heavy had been moved back and forth, like a door. On a number of pre-industrial time-lines, she had heard stories about kings who hid their wealth behind a wall in their dungeons.

She examined the wall carefully and found nothing until she noticed the sconce. She pulled on it and it levered down a little. With more effort, the sconce lowered until it was at a ninety-degree angle from the wall. There came a soft click and a section of wall swung out two inches. With a lot of effort, she was able use her shoulder to muscle the stone door open, which made enough noise to wake the dead. When it opened far enough to reveal a dark cavern, she went back to the cell door and opened it to see if anyone had heard the noise and come to investigate.

When no one showed up, Eldra made her way into the hidden chamber, holding a miniature flashlight which was stored inside a hidden compartment of her tinderbox. Shelves, filled with boxes, glassware and jars, lined three of the four walls. There were two trestle tables covered with large boxes, more bottles and equipment. Eldra examined the contents of each container carefully. There were several boxes of coal, several filled with sulfur, some with iron and copper, and several she couldn't recognize by sight. It was a mineralogist's playground.

On a table she found an iron-bound book filled with runes on thick linen pages. After scanning the pages, she realized that it was a scientific notebook, filled with experimental data. Most of the work involved charcoal and sulfur, and various attempts to combine it with one or more other elements.

Chemistry was not one of Eldra's strong suits. However, the use of charcoal and sulfur in most of the experiments suggested an attempt at creating fireseed. Eldra held her pendant over the pages of the book and turned the pages slowly. The pendant, disguised as a figure of Yirtta Allmother, was a product of First Level technology which recorded the data on every page through a lens designed to look like a small diamond. It also possessed the ability to compensate for the poor light in the chamber and enhance the picture when replayed on a viewscreen.

After Eldra finished with the book, she scanned the contents of the boxes and jars with the pendant, then collected samples from the boxes whose contents she was unable to identify and put them into a small pouch which she put into her pocket. The amounts she had collected were so small as to be insignificant to anyone without sophisticated spectrometers and high-resolution microscopes. Then she gathered as much dust as she could scrape together into an empty jar. Upon leaving the room and closing the hidden door, she sprinkled dust over her footprints as she backed out of the cell. Once she was back outside in the corridor, she closed and relocked the door.

"The perfect crime," Eldra said to herself, as she walked down the hallway to the staircase.

"What are you doing up here?" A voice said as she rounded the stone column at the bottom of the spiral staircase. It was one of the palace guards.

Eldra put on a frightened face. "I was just looking around. I was so bored waiting for Highpriest Sangar to come back; I thought I would take a tour of the castle. Is there a problem?"

"This tower is off limits. You will come with me." The guard took Eldra's arm in a firm grip and pulled her down the hallway.

Eldra began to become genuinely frightened. "But, I am a guest of the king! I am with Highpriest Sangar of Styphon's House."

"Then His Majesty will settle the matter, since that is where we are going."

## II

Prince Mythros listened with fascination when his Chancellor arrived with his agent-inquisitory and reported to him the results of their investigation. Chancellor Esmeranos had devised a means by which one of his guards might find this new Orphan Prince, and it had worked to perfection. He had selected a petty-captain of some renown and tasked him with infiltrating a Styphoni convoy as a slave. He had played the part of a runaway slave and the Styphoni had enthusiastically added him to their slave coffle. The hard part had been surviving the beating that followed his discovery.

To make his appearance believable, the petty-captain had needed whip marks on his back to complete his disguise. He was willing to accept five lashes per ounce of gold. Thyocles had born the pain stoically, even suggesting the last two lashes be done with greater vigor.

The petty-captain was then equipped with ragged clothing, chains with a weakened link that could easily be broken and a small knife that he could hide within his breeches. His escort took him out of Pytha under the cover of darkness, then released him at the border between Pytha and Taurnos. From there, Thyocles had been forced to make his own way. It would not be wise for one of Mythros' men to be captured in another prince's realm.

Thyocles had traveled to the edge of Taurnos and waited on the border between Hos-Bletha and Hos-Ktemnos along the Silos Road, the main road from Balph. During his wait, the petty-captain ate sparingly to reduce his already thin frame. After a moon-half of waiting where he only encountered small parties of merchants, one of which had tried to enslave him for real, he spotted a convoy of Styphon's Own Guard escorting several wagons and a large coffle of slaves. The slow pace set by the oxen, pulling heavy loads of supplies, allowed Thyocles to join the slaves.

"A sharp-eyed guard spotted me, Your Majesty, before I was able to reach the line of chained men and women. The pox-ridden cur whipped me with an iron-barbed lash. It took all of my self-control to keep from using my knife on him."

Mythros could tell by the edge in his voice that Thyocles was speaking truthfully. He made a mental note to see that he was promoted to captain and granted a small holding. *The Princedom needs more men with his mettle.*

"From there," Thyocles continued, "I stayed with the other slaves. We walked from dawn until dusk with few stops in between. They fed us stale bread and gruel and gave us only three cups of water each day, even though we passed several rivers and ponds. After four days, I began to fear that I had chosen the wrong convoy. When I considered the sheer numbers of the Temple Band, I feared they might be too strong for the bandits and there would be no attack.

"As it turned out, I had chosen well. It was mid-day when my ears were nearly destroyed by the sound of many cannons firing at once! Soldiers and horses came apart with great violence right before my eyes. However, there were no cannons. I saw a bamboo section fly through the air and erupt with great force among the Styphoni. Everything within three rods was destroyed in the blink of an eye. Horses reared up and threw their riders in panic. Their own mounts trampling some of the riders."

Prince Mythros listened in fascination as the story continued.

"When the Styphoni were out of action, dead, mutilated or just frightened, wolves with the bodies of men swarmed out of the brush, shooting and hacking away anything in armor. In a shockingly short time, none of the Styphoni I could see was left alive."

Overcome with emotion, Thyocles paused to regain his composure.

Mythros used that time to ask a question. "These men wearing wolf heads…how were they dressed?"

"The only armor I could see were the vambraces on their arms, sire. They were dressed all in green and fought like Galzar's own minions, which is what they looked like. Sire, I do not mind saying I feared for my life and my sanity. I was afraid that they would kill the slaves next and steeled myself to run.

"Before I could flee, I saw several of the wolf men come over to the slaves and strike off their chains. 'You are free, now,' said a particularly large man with arms greater in girth than my own legs. 'You may come with us or go your way, but be warned that you might be captured if you do not come with us.' Sire, he spoke with such kindness I could not believe he meant any of us harm. I followed where he led, as did all that I could see."

"Was this giant the leader?" the Prince asked.

He shook his head. "No, there were two leaders. The leader of the wolf men was called Robinos. We didn't meet the other leader until later. We were led through the woodlands and marshes while the captured wagons were taken elsewhere. I was surprised when we were brought back into Pytha through back trails and little-used roads."

"Pytha?" Mythros frowned. *Is my own realm the hiding place of these bandits? If so, I will need to make certain this information does not reach Niclophon's ears.*

"Yes, sire. I believe the lands were known as Mallegast, though I heard some call it Sure Wood."

Mallegast! The lands recently purchased by Hostigi refugees. "Are you certain of this, Thyocles?"

"Yes, Your Majesty. I can lead us back there at your pleasure." *That solves the bandit question, but what of the Orphan Prince?* "Very good. Continue."

"Well, we were taken through the gates of a log palisade erected around a new settlement. Once inside, men gave all the slaves clean cotton tunics, new hose, shoes, a blanket and food. They assigned us all a place to sleep. I observed some of the men working on the wall wearing breeches without tunics. I could clearly make out the scars of old whippings upon their backs. However, there were no overseers and the workers looked well-fed and healthy, unlike the sorry lot I had come in with. I also learned that all former slaves were called freed-men, or freemen."

Mythros nodded. "Yes, I imagine these bandits free slaves then induct them into their band."

Thyocles looked as if he were struggling to say something, but feared to correct his prince. Finally, he spat it out. "Actually, sire, I think they are building an army."

"An army?" Now this was interesting. "Why do you think so?"

"There was a tall man with long hair the color of the sun who appeared to be in charge. Everyone called him 'My Prince'."

"My Prince?" Mythros struggled to hold his temper. No man should be called 'Prince' in his realm save himself. "Did you hear anybody say his name?"

"Aye, sire. One of the wolf men called him Valthros. Oh! The wolfheads were iron helms covered in wolf fur. They took them off shortly after the battle with the Styphoni."

Mythros had stopped listening. His mind had fixed on the name 'Valthros.' This had to be the Orphan Prince who gave away silver to the masses. Few remembered the name of the true prince they believed lost so many years ago. Now Mythros also knew where the silver was coming from; Styphon's House, although they did not give it willingly.

Mythros' mind returned to the moment. "Thyocles, describe this Valthros in greater detail."

"Sire, the man was tall, about two rods in height," he replied. "Sunhaired, lean and muscular. In fact, at a short distance he could be confused with your ward, Thames, though his hair was much longer, shoulder length, and he has the look of one accustomed to leading men into battle."

Mythros nodded. Trust a petty-captain to know a fighting man and a leader at a glance. "How did he behave? What did he do or say around the others in his settlement?"

Thyocles appeared confused. "Ah, he spoke with his subordinates as equals, more or less. His commands were readily obeyed, to be sure, but none acted fearfully around him. He even spoke with some of the slaves to assure them that they would be well-treated and escorted out of Hos-Bletha if that was their wish."

"So, he takes on the role of a benevolent ruler even as he builds an army. How many people did you see?"

The Petty-Captain took his time answering. "I cannot say exactly, sire. There had to be at least five hundred men, women and children within the walls. More would have been outside the settlement farming the land and logging trees for the walls."

"Why do you say farming?"

"The food I was given was fresh. I also saw seeds being gathered for planting. Much of the food was foraged, and there were army-style victuals, no doubt taken from the Styphoni, but much appeared to have been grown locally."

Prince Mythros tried to calculate the time needed to grow crops fit for eating. In his estimation, the crops had to have been planted well before the refugees purchased the land. "Thyocles, you have done well. See the Exchequer for your pay, then go to the chief archivist and relate your report in full to him; he will write it all down. Then take two moon-quarters to recover from your wounds. As of this moment, your new rank is Captain. I will inform your superiors of this promotion. Say nothing of your mission to anyone else. Is this understood?"

Thyocles bowed low and backed out. Mythros turned to Esmeranos. "Do you think an additional one hundred ounces of gold are adequate compensation for his pains?"

"Sire, you could buy his first-born son for a fraction of that, I should think. I suspect he will have spent it all on women and drink before a moon-half has passed. Still, he accomplished his mission and well beyond my expectations. I had expected him to take far longer, if not die or be enslaved."

"My reward stands. I always pay well for results." Mythros stood up from his throne and walked to a window. In the courtyard, Thames was playing with some of the younger children of the castle staff. "Now I must decide what to do about this imposter."

"Sire, why do anything?"

Mythros turned about and faced Esmeranos. "What?"

"It seems to me that his objectives and your own line up rather nicely, and at little risk to you."

The Prince was intrigued. "Please explain."

Esmeranos stepped over to the window and spoke in low tones. "Sire, you have long desired to see Niclophon removed from the throne he does not deserve. This Valthros, the pretender, apparently seeks the same ends."

Mythros frowned. "I want the throne for the true Orphan Prince, not some outsider with his own agenda."

"Sire, we both know that it is impossible to place the true heir on the Silver Throne," Esmeranos whispered. "But, perhaps we can make this pretender our cat's-paw. From Thyocles' description he looks and acts the part well enough, and he does seem to possess a benevolent streak, much like your late brother-in-law."

"Many kings start out as benevolent rulers only to be corrupted by power," Mythros countered. "We can hardly count on this pretender to be made of a better moral fabric than Niclophon, for example."

Esmeranos nodded. "True, and some have always desired greater power. I understand the newly enthroned Great King Lysandros is one of those. I prefer the ones who at least start with the people's welfare at heart. Like yourself, sire."

If Niclophon were removed, Mythros would be the most likely candidate to replace him, save for the true Orphan Prince. "Bah! I do not want the kingdom, only justice, as well as Styphon's House and their toadies, like Niclophon, removed from Hos-Bletha. That is enough for me."

*Well, partly true*, he admitted to himself. *What I really want is the Silver Throne for the true prince's son, if he should sire one. If not, then for my son and lineage, not myself—that much is true. But I don't trust Esmeranos with the full truth.*

"Then let this pretender do that for you, sire," Esmeranos said with a sly smile. "He can rule the kingdom, while you rule him."

Mythros had to admit that Esmeranos made an excellent point. "If he can be controlled. We will need to arrange a meeting with this Valthros and his wolf's-head, Robinos."

# FIFTY-TWO

## I

Skranga's face was beet red. "Eldra, you very nearly cost us everything with your little stunt! You have no idea of the danger you were in."

Eldra sat in silence as Skranga railed at her. She had to admit she had been careless, only Skranga's fast talking had gotten her out of serious trouble.

Calthros also held his tongue.

"Fortunately, Niclophon views all women as children, or less, unable to tell right from wrong or make intelligent decisions. Plus, no one had actually forbidden you from exploring the castle. I explained you were bored and it was that time of the moon when women grow especially capricious and moody. The Great King accepted my explanation, especially when I offered to let you share his bed."

Eldra shot out of her chair. "You *what*? I'll geld you myself. How dare you—"

"Keep you alive?" Skranga interrupted. "I truly have no idea. Still, you were in little danger of his taking me up on that offer."

She nodded, but her vanity was still

stung by the idea that the king didn't want to sleep with her. "What is wrong with me?"

"As I told you before, you lack the genitalia he finds of interest," Skranga said in low tones. "I have been watching and listening to everything that happens in this castle. The queen sleeps in a separate chamber while his, uh, aides share his quarters."

Eldra recalled the two young men that did not give her a second glance when she went on her walk. Now she understood why. "What if Niclophon had taken you up on your offer?"

"Then I would have handed you over to him!" Skranga shouted. "I believed, and still do, that sharing his bed was preferable to your beheading. Besides, I daresay I have suffered no less to maintain my cover."

Eldra recalled the circumcision. She did not think it was a fair comparison, however. Still, Skranga had pulled her fat out of the fire. *I'm getting sloppy. I need to get back to Home Time Line for some retraining.*

"Since you have caused so much trouble, perhaps you would tell me if it was all worth it?"

Eldra considered her options. *Maybe he can use the truth.* "Well, yes. I think the previous Great King was trying to figure out how to make fireseed."

Skranga stared dumbly as Eldra related her discovery of the hidden chamber in the tower cell.

"Gods and monsters," Skranga whispered. "Great King Marocles was trying to make fireseed! That means Styphon's House very likely had him assassinated and placed Niclophon on the Silver Throne. We must get this information to Democriphon immediately. Calthros, I can't wait for Ranthar or Yaholo to return. You will have to go to…Mallegast, I believe it's called…and speak with Democriphon or Ranthar."

"Yes, Your Worship. Right away." Calthros appeared anxious to be on his way.

"As for you, young lady," Skranga said as he returned his attention to the source of his displeasure, "I expect you to mind yourself while we are here. I do not think I can ease your way out of another predicament like this. I advise you to keep that in mind."

"Yes, Your Worship." Eldra decided to be contrite. Skranga was right. If she had been caught inside the secret room she would have been beheaded for sure—and possibly even Skranga and Calthros might have lost their heads over it.

## II

Highpriest Rathocles finished his report and waited. It had been a lengthy interrogation and he was sweating profusely as he waited for the Inner Circle to decide his fate. Failure was not well-received in the Holy City of Balph, especially since the arrival of the Daemon Kalvan in Hostigos, and things were getting worse every day. If the Inner Circle decided the loss of the caravan and soldiers were his fault, Rathocles could be severely punished, maybe even turned over to Investigator Roxthar. Just the thought left him weak in the knees.

With him were several other highpriests who had been similarly attacked by Robinos and his wolf minions. Like him, they had been robbed, stripped and left for dead on the side of the road. Rathocles was the only one to see the wolf leader wounded, though, and his testimony did little for his credibility.

Before them at the Triangle Table were Speaker Anaxthenes, Archpriests Cimon, Dracar, Lymachor, Neamenestros, and twenty more archpriests of the Inner Circle. Styphon's Own Voice, rumored to be on his deathbed, was most noticeable by his absence. He was relieved to find Roxthar was not in attendance. The Holy Investigator was more likely than not to accuse everyone of being in collusion with the Daemon Kalvan, which would result in their Investigation. Rathocles shuddered at that thought.

"Highpriest Rathocles," Anaxthenes stated, "you claim before the Inner Circle of Styphon's House that you saw one of these wolf men shot in the head, that the shot revealed his skull, and furthermore that this skull was made of iron. Would you care to recant that statement?"

"I would change it in a heartbeat except that it would mean I was lying, Your Eminence," Rathocles replied. He suspected recanting would also call the rest of his testimony into question. "In truth, I did not have the opportunity to inspect the wound closely. It might have been zinc or silver, but it was definitely metal of some kind."

Anaxthenes nodded absently. "Very well. Do any of the rest of you have anything else to add? No? Fine. Wait outside while we discuss this."

Rathocles led the procession out of the presence room to wait in the antechamber.

"This must be the work of the Daemon Kalvan," Archpriest Timothanes said. "Somehow he has summoned Galzar's minions to do his bidding."

Speaker Anaxthenes rolled his eyes. "If Kalvan was able to summon such creatures, he would have done so long before now. Moreover, why waste them in Hos-Bletha? Thus far Great King Niclophon has done nothing more than send gold and victuals to aid us in our war effort."

"And very little of that, in fact, according to Almoner Drayton," Archpriest Neamenestros added. "To be fair, a military caravan consisting of one company of foot, twenty horses, gold and victuals was attacked by Ruthani barbarians on its way here several moons ago."

"One company and twenty cavalrymen is an insult," Anaxthenes said. "We need many times that if we are going to destroy the Daemon Kalvan and the False Kingdom of Hos-Hostigos."

"We should demand that he increase his contribution tenfold," Archpriest Dracar demanded.

For once, he agreed with his usual opponent and Roxthar's most ardent supporter. "Does anyone disagree with Dracar's demand upon Great King Niclophon?"

Everyone at the Triangle Table nodded their accord.

"Scribe, please put that in writing and see that it is dispatched to Great King Niclophon immediately.

The scribe, who was doing his best to remain unnoticed, nodded and began to scratch out the runes with his quill pen.

"Furthermore, does anybody here genuinely believe that Galzar's Minions are now stalking the land in search of prey, and that Styphon's

Own Guard is their prey of choice?" Anaxthenes demanded.

"We have been threatened with the Ban of Galzar," Cimon ventured softly. "It could be that Galzar favors—"

"Codswallops! Blasphemy," Anaxthenes cried out. He would have torn his hair out by the roots if he had any. "Fool! These minions are men in armor made to look like wolves. Iron skull, Highpriest Rathocles claimed. It was a helm covered in wolf fur! See that Rathocles is stripped of his yellow robe and returned to the ranks of the underpriests."

*That was the problem with demonizing Kalvan; everybody saw him under their bed, in their closets and even poking up out of their chamber pots. It caused them to lose sight of the fact that there are other forces at work in the world.*

"There is no Galzar," Anaxthenes continued, "Roxthar has been working day and night to prove it."

Archpriest Cimon cringed, although he tried not to show it.

Anaxthenes continued. "As for Kalvan, the Daemon has enough to worry about already with the Grand Host poised to strike in the spring. He can hardly spare soldiers or mercenaries to stir up trouble in Hos-Bletha. What would it gain him now? No, these are simple bandits made bold since Kalvan challenged our power. They no longer fear Styphon's House, nor do they believe that we will send great armies down to punish those who attack us since we are engaged in crusade against the Usurper. For the moment they are correct, but as soon as Grand Master Soton kills the Daemon Kalvan and occupies the False Kingdom of Hos-Hostigos, I will have him send the Grand Host into Hos-Bletha."

Dracar looked as if he were about to protest, then thought better of it. "Yes, Your Eminence, it is well to look ahead. But another season or two could pass before Grand Master Soton finishes the job of cleansing Hos-Hostigos. Perhaps Great King Niclophon might be encouraged to send out a few companies of his own men."

"That can be arranged," Anaxthenes replied. "But only after his contribution to the Grand Host has arrived."

"Might I suggest," Archpriest Neamenestros added, "that we place a price on this wolf-man's head? Twenty-five thousand ounces of gold might even get his own men to turn on him, Your Eminence."

*It might at that,* Anaxthenes thought. "An excellent suggestion, but let's double the reward to fifty thousand gold rakmars. That should encourage quick action. Bandits are always more loyal to themselves, than to their band." *Much like Archpriests of Styphon's House,* Anaxthenes thought wryly.

Everyone nodded in agreement. That left only one other matter to be settled.

"You've settled upon Rathocles' punishment, but what about the rest of them?" Dracar asked. "What should we do with them?"

Anaxthenes would have been happy to hand the highpriests over to Roxthar, but fortunately for everyone in Balph he was keeping Soton company and preparing his Investigation for the invasion of Hos-Hostigos. Besides, it would be bad for morale if highpriests were Investigated and executed simply for being attacked by bandits—no matter how well-deserved. It would not go over well with the other highpriests and many might decide to leave the priesthood for greener pastures. Already Roxthar had been responsible for scores of highpriests retiring to their estates and leaving the priesthood. More of that might give outsiders the impression that Styphon's House was becoming weak. Appearance was everything in Styphon's House Upon Earth.

"Strip them of their yellow robes, then reassign them to Hos-Zygros, including Rathocles. They will enjoy the cold weather. Warn them to say nothing about what happened in Hos-Bletha upon pain of death," Anaxthenes said. "Agreed?"

Everyone nodded. "Excellent. Now, on to other matters…"

## III

Paratime Police Chief Verkan Vall took the stairs down to the conveyor-head in the second cellar of the Royal Foundry of Hos-Hostigos. The blacksmiths and foundry workers were finished for the day, probably getting their dinner. During the day, their pounding could be heard even through the collapsed-nickel roof that made the conveyor-head impossible to enter.

The Grand Host was preparing for the invasion of Hos-Hostigos, with foodstuffs, weapons, armor, clothing and other essentials arriving at Harphax City daily. As soon as weather changed and the roads dried up, he suspected that Grand Master Soton would put the army into motion. There was some disagreement among the Harphax Study Team as to whether Soton was in charge of the Grand Host, or whether it was Grand Captain-General Phidestros. Not that it made much difference to Hostigos, they were both tried and tested commanders and both as good as any general he had run into in more conflicts than he would like to count.

It wouldn't be much longer than two or three moons before the Grand Host made its move, probably hitting the Princedom of Beshta first. Kalvan had decided he didn't have enough troops to defend Beshta; instead his plan was to meet the Styphoni-backed army in Sashta, rather than fight them in Hostigos. Verkan would be deploying there shortly with the Royal Mounted Rifles.

He was scheduled to do a survey in Sashta in the morning, but first he wanted to talk with Scholar Danthor Dras, the Dean of Aryan-Transpacific Studies. It was late enough that Danthor should be in his personal bedchamber in Balph. He made the call.

"Danthor here. Who is it?" His voice sounded irritable.

"It's me, Verkan." Not too long ago, they had been bitter opponents. But, once a long-standing misconception had been cleared up, they had become—well, not friends, but maybe allies. Friendship, if it came, would take time and mutual trust.

"Oh, hello. You just caught me in the middle of an interesting scroll. I hadn't realized my job as Great King Cleitharses 'voice' would allow me access to all the scrolls and books in the Royal Library." With a sigh he added, "A man could spend his lifetime—and I mean one of our long ones—and still never read half the works in the Great King's archives."

"Once the war is over," Verkan said, "you can bring in a team of scholars, have them copy everything and have it transferred to the University of

Dhergabar for future reference."

"Good idea, Vall. It's just that one likes to be the first person to document and translate these priceless documents. For example, today I ran across a scroll containing a pronouncement from Erasthames the Great, the king who organized the Chesapeake watershed into a war machine that ground down the Ruthani natives by sheer staying power when it couldn't beat them in battle. It provided a fascinating window into an earlier time and into a legendary figure.

"But time is growing short; I think Anaxthenes is working on a plan to get rid of Great King Cleitharses, now that he's starting to resist the Speaker's commands. Anaxthenes hasn't completely taken me into his confidence yet, but that time is approaching. He hinted around that if I reported all of the Great King's conversations and letters I was privy to that I might be up for elevation to the Inner Circle."

"Congratulations!" Verkan said, and meant it. "Archpriest of the Inner Circle, that would be some coup. If you weren't already a legend at the University that would cement the deal."

"Well, enough about me. Why are you calling?"

"I wanted to know if you had any new information to impart. The Grand Host is fattening up outside Harphax City preparing for the invasion of Hos-Hostigos. They'll probably strike the Princedom of Beshta first. I can't imagine them coming any other way, since their force is gathering in Hos-Harphax. I would have thought that this time they would attacked from Hos-Ktemnos and hit Hos-Hostigos through the back door, say in Sask."

"I've heard rumors to that effect," Danthor said. "Grand Master Soton discussed such a maneuver, but was told by the Inner Circle that he was to contain the war within the borders of Hos-Harphax. The archpriests fear that Kalvan might get wind of such a plan and send an expedition of his own deep into Hos-Ktemnos, possibly even to Balph itself." Danthor paused to laugh. "Those scoundrels are deathly afraid of Kalvan. Some believe he's an avatar of Dralm's, while others fear he's a demon sent to Earth to make them pay for their sins."

"Which are many, I'm sure," Verkan said, shaking his head. "What a venal bunch of hypocrites. I'm just glad I don't have to associate with them on a daily basis as you do."

Danthor sighed. "They're not any worse than some of the University tenure boards I've had the pleasure of being on. Fortunately, I'm spending most of my time with Great King Cleitharses, which is a lot easier than trying to stave off the Grand Host of Styphon's House once that juggernaut gets rolling."

"Agreed. The Grand Host is actually living up to its billing: one hundred and ten thousand men all gathering to destroy Kalvan and Hostigos."

"Nothing to be done about it, I suspect."

Verkan grinned wryly. "I'd like to bring in some outside help, but it would violate so many statutes of the Paratime Code it's not funny."

"Well, Kalvan might get some help from Hos-Bletha. The 'Orphan Prince' operation is running helter-skelter all over the Kingdom."

"Yes, Duke Skranga's people. Kalvan sent him to Hos-Bletha with a first-rate team, you remember meeting Inspector Ranthar Jard?"

"Yes, an impressive young man."

"And Lady Baltrov Eldra—"

"Lady Eldra, oh my," Danthor interrupted. "She's a one-woman demolition team all on her own!"

"You've got that right," Verkan said wryly.

"Well, I wish them luck. They've certainly got their work cut out for them.

# FIFTY-THREE

## I

The last log went into place perfectly. Pitch was then applied to the sides to fill the cracks. This was less to keep wind out than to block any potential prying eyes. Captain-General Democriphon nodded as he watched the procedure. With the completion of the wall, the village's security was reasonably assured. Over time, the wall would be replaced with stone a section at a time.

Democriphon wondered if this was the start of a new princedom. Hostigos had started much like this, centuries ago, although not with slaves and bandits. Like all realms in the original five kingdoms, Hostigos had been started by the infusion of people from the west thousands of years ago. Who knew what the future would bring for the village of Mallegast?

Thoughts of the future unsettled Democriphon. He might be recalled to aid Great King Kalvan at some point. When and if that occurred, what would become of the freemen and those that joined up with him? Most had already been trained as soldiers and might be willing to join the war in the north.

"My Lord!"

Democriphon turned to find the Mayor addressing him. "Yes, Mardros?"

Mardros took a moment to catch his breath. "An envoy from Prince Mythros is here."

That explained why Mardros addressed him as 'My Lord' instead of 'My Prince.' "Very good. I've been expecting this visit for some time. We should meet with them at the Town Hall. Have some winter wine brought over, as well as some bread and cheese. If they plan to stay overnight, have the cooks prepare something big, though simple. Roast boar or deer. Make sure no unusual victuals are used! We don't want them asking where we got them."

Mardros nodded and trotted off. Democriphon hoped he would slow down to a more dignified gait before reaching the envoy; appearances were everything. Democriphon thought about summoning Ranthar, then recalled he was out on another mission with his 'merry men' hoping to waylay rich merchants and traveling highpriests. He was not expected back for two or three moon-quarters.

The Town Hall, finally completed and properly furnished, was the largest building in the village. It also doubled as Democriphon's and Ranthar's living quarters and even boasted a few spare rooms for visiting guests.

Democriphon entered the Town Hall and took his usual seat in the great hall. He waited patiently as the envoy was escorted in. The envoy consisted of six soldiers, a flag bearer, two maidens and a tall man with unusually dark hair and beard, suggesting some Ruthani in his ancestry.

Democriphon tried to recall how one greeted a person of high standing. Prince Ptosphes rarely stood on ceremony; he greeted visiting nobles as equals regardless of their rank. Great King Kalvan could be more ceremonious, but only at Queen Rylla's urging, and even that was unusual as Rylla hadn't typically stood on ceremony until she became a queen. *To Regwarn with it, I'll just be myself.*

"Well met, gentlemen," Democriphon said as he rose from his seat. "I am Democriphon, First Citizen of Mallegast village. I bid you welcome." *Oh, Regwarn, I sound like a foppish fool.*

"Well met, First Citizen," said the dark-haired one. "I am Chancellor Esmeranos, envoy of His Highness, Prince Mythros."

Democriphon wished he had Ranthar and Uncle Wolf Syros in attendance. They, at least, seemed to know instinctively how to maneuver in these situations. "Chancellor, I am honored by your visit. Please, let us not stand on ceremony. Let us sit and enjoy some winter wine."

Esmeranos, who appeared mildly surprised at the departure from protocol, accepted the proffered seat. He turned and nodded to his retainers, who followed his example.

A body servant entered with a tray of goblets filled with winter wine and passed them around.

Democriphon noticed nobody drank. After a moment he realized he was expected to take the first drink. It had to be a local custom, he decided. "Gentlemen, to your good health."

"And to yours, First Citizen."

"Please, call me Democriphon. I hope you will not be offended at my poor understanding of the local customs. I admit I should have been learning your ways, but I have been busy setting up this village."

Esmeranos set down his wine. "You've done a lot of work in a surprisingly short time. I do not mind admitting it is pleasant to set aside protocol for a change. Tell me, is this how things are done in Hos-Hostigos?"

"In truth, I could not truly say. I was not involved in matters of court back in my homeland in what was then called Hos-Harphax. Simple merchants of common blood are not typically invited to councils with their prince." Democriphon kept reminding himself of the cover story; he and his people left Hostigos because they objected to Kalvan being elevated to great king, yet did not wish to fight their brothers in Hos-Harphax. "Prince Ptosphes was a good and noble ruler, but his recognition of Kalvan as his great king was ill-advised."

Esmeranos nodded. "Yes, ill-advised. That brings me to my mission here."

"Mission?" Democriphon didn't like the sound of that. He took a small drink just to be sociable. "Is this not simply an inspection of some sort?"

"Oh, most assuredly. Your new overlord, Prince Mythros, is very interested in what you have accomplished here. I must say your people have been very industrious. We passed crops of every sort in the land you have farmed, and I am impressed with the construction of the buildings and your village wall. Ah, are you expecting trouble of some sort?"

"We are from Hostigos, Chancellor," Democriphon said meaningfully. "We always expect trouble." Democriphon related the troubles Prince Ptosphes had, first with Styphon's House withholding fireseed, then Gormoth of Nostor's attempted invasion. There had been war every summer since. "Not to mention what I have heard of bandits, Ruthani, and the Carib stalking these realms. I could hardly sleep at night without the security of the village wall."

Esmeranos took a drink. "This wine is quite good. However, getting back to matters at hand, the Caribi keep to the sea shores, though they do occasionally travel up rivers for raids. Ruthani rarely attack a settlement as large as this. They are fierce warriors, but disorganized and few in number. Some are even civilized to the point that they work with the Zarthani Knights. My grandfather was one such."

*Now I stepped in it!* "I meant no offence to you or your family, Chancellor."

"Please, we are being informal. Call me Esmeranos, and no offence is taken. You are wise to take precautions and the more civilized Ruthani are little known outside of Hos-Bletha. I take pride in my heritage while recognizing the threat that exists. Back to your concerns, it is true that banditry has been on the rise, although, for some reason, only outside of this principality."

"Perhaps your…pardon me…*our* prince's reputation for maintaining order in this realm forces the bandits to choose less hazardous prey." *We should have had a few small raids here in Pytha, Dralm-damnit!*

"I'm sure that plays some part in it. New villages have their growing pains, and yours is coming together so much faster than any I have ever seen before. I noticed that some of the workers outside have whip marks on their backs; are they your slaves?"

"Certainly not!" Democriphon quickly took control of himself. He had not realized just how deeply Kalvan's anti-slavery beliefs had taken hold. "No, these are men freed by…the Usurper Kalvan. Many joined us on our trek from Hos-Hostigos. They were displaced by the wars and had no homes to return to, so I allowed them to join with me. Many of them were from other realms before being enslaved, I believe." *That should explain any different accents the Chancellor is likely to hear.*

"They did not attempt to return to their homes?"

"Some did. Most lost their homes in the wars and feared to return lest they be enslaved again."

The Chancellor nodded his head. "Prince Mythros tolerates slavery, but only in the case of convicted criminals, and they have the chance to earn their freedom after a set passage of time. I think you will do well under his rule. How soon can you make preparations to travel with me to Pytha Town and meet with him?"

Alarm bells sounded in Democriphon's mind. To meet with the prince was an honor, one he could not refuse without jeopardizing his cover story. Yet, all of this might be a trap. Could the prince have discovered who the bandits were, or even that he was the current Orphan Prince pretender? Still, he had no choice other than to run, which would undo all of their work.

"I can be ready on the morrow, after you and your party have rested and refreshed yourselves. This building doubles as a hostel for important visitors, so you and your men should be quite comfortable. It is not as lavish as what you may be accustomed to…"

Esmeranos smiled wide. "I daresay my men and I will be very much at home, here, and I look forward to trying some of your Harphaxi dishes."

"Excellent! How early do you prefer to rise?"

"At first light."

"Then I will see to it that tomorrow's first-meal is served before we start our journey. Evening meal will be served in about four candles, but if you would like something now…"

Esmeranos declined.

"Then let us see to your rooms."

## II

Looking out through the window, Great King Niclophon could see the courtyard and some of the town beyond. To one less well-informed all would appear to be peaceful. Niclophon knew better. The messenger from Balph, who had nearly killed two horses in his haste, had brought a missive from Styphon's House demanding that he send out at least a dozen companies of his Royal Cavalry to patrol the kingdom. Several Bands of Styphon's Own Guard would be dispatched to help.

While Niclophon was a devoted follower of Styphon, being dictated to in his own Kingdom rankled. No great king should be subject to such discourtesy. For this reason, Niclophon summoned Highpriest Sangar to his chambers. Although he had intended to hold his temper, Niclophon exploded at first sight of the Highpriest.

"What is the meaning of this?" Niclophon waved the parchment about in his hand.

Sangar, taken by surprise, managed to keep his expression neutral. "Your Majesty, I cannot answer that question without knowing the contents of that missive. May I know what has Your Highness so annoyed?"

"This…this…*demand* for my soldiers to patrol the kingdom within the moon-quarter." Niclophon crumpled the document and threw it at Highpriest Sangar, who easily plucked it from the air.

He quickly scanned the document. "Sire, while I will admit that the wording is…unfortunately phrased…the intent is to aid you in ridding your kingdom of the bandits and raiders that have recently plagued you. Surely you have no objection to taking part in this action—"

"Objections? Oh, I object a great deal to being ordered about like a commoner. Styphon's House is aiding *me*, not the other way around." Niclophon paused to regain his breath, if not his composure. He continued in a lower tone. "While I am devoted to Styphon, and happily entertain his representatives in the mortal world, I am still the ruler… nay, Great King of Hos-Bletha. I will not be ordered about like a common churl. Not by Styphon's House or any other agency. You might want to send that message back to Balph when your underling returns from his errand."

Sangar nodded. "I shall indeed make your displeasure known to the correct authorities, sire. However, you did not finish reading the document. See here: it says that Styphon's House will pay a bounty of fifty thousand ounces of gold for the head of the outlaw who calls himself Robinos."

Niclophon drew in a deep breath of air. "I didn't read that far, Your Worship. Very well. Maybe it isn't as demeaning as it first appeared."

Skranga knew what part of the problem was. Niclophon was still sensitive over the criticism he received from Prince Basilron about the wedding fiasco. His nephew had been murdered and all the wedding guests robbed. Basilron laid the lack of security on Niclophon's head. The whipping the Prince Basilron had received had turned him into the laughing stock of the Kingdom, and he did his best to share his humiliation and rage with his great king. The image of Basilron being stripped naked and whipped on the arse with a paddle would follow him to his grave. *I could almost feel sorry for the poor bugger.*

"It seems I'm being overly sensitive," Niclophon admitted. "You're right, it is a serious bounty and one that should show results. For this kind of payout, most bandits would turn over their mothers. Oh, and you shall have your companies of regulars, but make no mistake, only because I deem it a reasonable *request*—not a demand, a request. Mention that in your next packet to Balph. You may go."

Skranga walked quickly back to his chamber where Eldra sat on a cushioned bench fiddling with her necklace. She stopped as soon as he entered.

"Eldra, has Calthros returned yet?"

"Not as yet, Your Worship. Is something wrong?"

"Yes and no." Skranga detailed the meeting he had just come from. "A rift between the King and Styphon's House is good for the mission, but maybe not so good for us."

"How so?"

"What did Kalvan do when he essentially declared war on Styphon's House?"

Eldra thought back. While she had been on another time-line when Calvin Morrison first appeared in Aryan-Transpacific, she had read the reports before twisting Verkan's arm to gain his help in finding a position with the Kalvan Study Team. Lord Kalvan, as he had first been called, simply had Prince Ptosphes order the sacking of Styphoni Temples and execute all the priests. Eldra suddenly saw where he was headed. "Oh… and here *we* are the Styphoni!"

"Exactly. It may be time to continue my inspection tour of the Styphoni temples. First we have to get word to Democriphon about what is to come. A dozen companies of regulars makes for a small army, not to mention several Bands of Guardsmen."

"I'll go," Eldra said suddenly.

Skranga shook his head. "It is much too dangerous for a girl."

"I'm a *woman*, not a girl," she all but snarled. "Besides, it won't be very safe here in the palace if Niclophon decides to break with Styphon's House."

*She has a good point*, Skranga decided. "Very well, take six of our guardsmen, and for the love of Galzar, have all of them change out of their Styphoni garb as soon as you are out of Bletha Town. I don't want any of you cut down by Democriphon's people on the road." Skranga turned away, then turned back. "You will need a cover story. Here is twenty ounces of gold. Spend it on clothes, jewels, whatever you think a mistreated woman would fancy. Give the impression that you were beaten and sent on a spending spree by way of an apology."

*Not bad*, Eldra thought. By now, the entire castle would have heard of her little sight-seeing trip and how Niclophon had reacted to it. A good beating from her brother and overlord would be what they expected here-and-now. "A black eye will sell the story better."

Skranga looked shocked. "Lady Eldra, no matter what you may think of me or my past, my list of sins does not include thrashing women, free or enslaved."

"Look, we all knew certain sacrifices would have to be made on this mission," Eldra countered and pointed at Skranga's groin area. "You know that better than most. The Styphoni have a bad reputation in regards to how they treat their underlings—even family. I don't like being hit, but I like getting beheaded a whole lot less, so let us sell this story. Hit me in the eye hard enough to blacken it, but not so hard you'll break the eye socket."

Skranga sputtered as Eldra's point sunk in. He grabbed the front of her robe so that she would not fall back and hit her head on the floor tiles. "I…I am sorry to do this." It took two tries before he could bring himself to make contact.

Eldra saw bright lights as she shook off the punch. It was a good solid one and probably hurt less than a solid backhand would have. She hoped a second blow wouldn't be necessary.

After inspecting her face in the polished silver plate that took the place of a mirror on this time-line, she said," Not bad, Skrangie. That'll leave a real shiner by morning. That is when I will be ready to go. Just one more thing…" Eldra opened the heavy wooden door to the chamber then screamed out, "No! No! Your Worship, please don't—" She clapped her hands together, then screamed again. After closing the door, she turned and said, "That should sell it."

# FIFTY-FOUR

## I

Rather than sit in his horse-drawn carriage, Esmeranos elected to ride on horseback to better talk with Democriphon on the way back to Pytha Town. He had insisted on taking his own horse so that he would not have to borrow one for the return trip.

"First-meal was as impressive as last evening's dinner, Democriphon," Esmeranos said conversationally. "Peeling, cutting and frying potatoes in bacon grease is new to me. Is this a common dish in Hostigos?"

"Yes, it is now," Democriphon replied. "Kalvan introduced it to us shortly after he arrived in Hostigos Town. He called them home fries. It's filling and makes an excellent accompaniment to ham and turkey eggs."

"Indeed. I have had potatoes cut and boiled, mashed, and even baked over open flame, but these were the best potatoes I've ever had. Why didn't you have them prepared that way with the roast flamingo last night?"

"Fried potatoes are not very good with

gravy," Democriphon explained. "I also thought you might receive traditional fare more readily before offering you something more exotic. I am gratified you enjoyed your meals."

Esmeranos nodded. "Indeed. Tell me, why do you use so many of these new things brought by this Kalvan?"

Democriphon thought fast; his cover was that his people did not recognize Kalvan as a legitimate king. "Kalvan's innovations were very welcome: boots designed to fit right and left feet specifically, leaf springs on the wagons and carriages for a smoother ride, mortars, rifles and of course fireseed. It was Kalvan being declared a great king that we found objectionable. Had Kalvan been related to the true king we might have gone along with his enthronement since Great King Kaiphranos had refused to aid Hostigos in our battle against Nostor and Styphon's House—even though it was his sworn obligation to do so.

"To be ruled by a foreigner from the Cold Lands, who did not even speak our language, was unacceptable to me and many of my compatriots. After the death of his eldest son, Great King Kaiphranos hid under his bedcovers and no longer ruled. Then he died under questionable circumstances that many attributed to his brother, Lysandros. Now, the regicide Lysandros has taken his seat upon the Iron Throne. As we saw it, things in both Hos-Hostigos and Hos-Harphax were going straight to Regwarn. Therefore, we moved as far away from them and the fighting as possible, settling here in Hos-Bletha. There is no war in your princedom and we set our community far enough from any Styphoni temples so as not be bothered by their false priests."

"Ah, so you dislike the Styphoni, then." It was a statement, not a question.

"I like them less with each passing day, though I am prepared to keep quiet on that score lest I become the focus of their ire. I hope this will not be a problem for you or Prince Mythros."

Esmeranos shook his head. "The Prince allows his subjects to believe and worship as they please. He does not like to create problems where none exists. As long as people behave themselves and pay their taxes he doesn't interfere in their lives."

*Good to know.* "Then I chose the best realm to build my village in. My people eschew Styphon worship in favor of the Twelve True Gods. Speaking of taxes, when will my village be assessed?"

"Not until after the fall harvest. Prince Mythros understands that few peasants have any coins or extra produce until then."

Democriphon started to think things were going a little too well with the Chancellor. Taxes to be assessed in the fall? That was one of Kalvan's innovations. For the *nth* time he wished Ranthar had come back from his scouting mission in time to be briefed on the situation. *Well, nothing I can do about it now. I will just have to trust Andros and Uncle Wolf Syros to manage things if I do not come back.*

## II

Ranthar, refreshed from his vacation, entered Mallegast to find it a beehive of activity. He looked around and spotted Captain Andros barking orders. Ranthar walked over to the captain and asked what was going on.

"Word came two Temple Bands of Styphon's Own Guard and twelve companies of Royal Cavalry are coming to deal with the bandits who have been attacking the Styphoni caravans," Captain Andros explained.

"Good. Democriphon and I have been expecting something like this. We were hoping that Styphon's House might send more of their guardsmen south. Better here than in Hos-Harphax with the Grand Host. Unfortunately, the timing is bad."

"How so?" Andros asked.

Ranthar did the math: roughly two thousand highly trained foes versus six hundred former mercenaries and a thousand or so freemen, many of whom were untested in battle. "It may be best we suspend all banditry for a time. Niclophon is sending scouting parties out independently of the Styphoni to find us."

"Scouting parties? Then stopping the raids will earn us little time," Andros argued. "I am no expert on Styphoni military tactics, but I know how a Blethan captain-general thinks. He will order a realm by realm search of every princedom. Every home, shed and barn will be searched. People will be interrogated. Suspects will be arrested and tortured. That I am not concerned about. However, they will have every shop and tavern in every village investigated looking for unusual purchases, like the food you and Democriphon acquired before we started planting crops."

Ranthar thought about it. It would take a very long time to go through the entirety of Hos-Bletha looking for a few dozen bandits, especially if it meant going through every shop and tavern along the way. As for the supplies Gasphros bought, he was instructed to spread his purchases out among several villages and towns to avoid raising any suspicions. "I still do not see the problem, Andros. We covered our tracks well; nobody can identify us."

Captain Andros shook his head. "Ranthar, what do you think the princes of these realms will be doing while their lands are being examined as the King's army searches for us?"

"Take arms against the invaders?"

"This is not Hos-Harphax where princes refuse to cooperate with their great king. True, Niclophon has a loose enough hold on his vassals, but when the chamber pot hits the wall, they come together and support him, else he would not still be great king. The princely rulers will add their own men to the search hoping to get it over with quickly so that things will return to normal. And you can make a safe wager that the princes whose lands we have acted upon will be the most zealous in seeking us out. Moreover, some may take the opportunity to point out neighbors with whom they have a grievance. Prince Basilron, for example, would only be too happy to point a finger at Prince Carthames or Mythros."

Ranthar considered this and still did not see a problem. "So we'll hide our weapons, fireseed and treasure in the swamps."

"And what about all the freemen with the marks of the temple-farm's whips on their backs." Andros let out a long sigh. "Tell me, First Captain, what will happen when the Royal Army finally comes to Pytha and learns of a village settled by Harphaxi refugees?"

Realization hit Ranthar like an atomic bomb. Prince Mythros would likely add his men to the forces arrayed against them and send them to look into the most likely culprit, at least to the Styphoni. "Open a whole bag full of devils on us! What is Democriphon doing?"

"He has gone to Pytha Town to meet with Prince Mythros. He'd already left when the message arrived. You can speak with the Lady who delivered the warning if you think that will help. Lady Eldra is staying in the Town Hall."

"I will do that. Captain, how fast can you get the men ready for war, if it comes to that?"

"They will be as ready as I can make them in a moon-half. I, however, will not be with them."

"What?"

Andros turned his gaze to the south. "I cannot fight against men I served with. I will train these freemen to the best of my ability, but I will not fight my brothers. Should we face Styphon's Own Guard alone, I will be at your side."

Ranthar carefully considered Andros' words. If there was one thing a good Paracop understood it was loyalty. "Understood. Do what you think is right. I'll go to speak with the woman."

Ranthar turned around and started towards the Town Hall. Halfway to his destination he ran into Uncle Wolf Syros.

"Uncle Wolf. It is good to see you again."

"And you, Ranthar. Do you have a moment?"

Ranthar was anxious to speak with Eldra, but it could wait. Uncle Wolf Syros appeared worried, as though something important was on his mind. "Is there something I can help you with?"

"I do not think so. I have something you need to see. This way."

Ranthar followed Uncle Wolf to the back wall of the village. Several men were working on a tall device made of heavy timber. It took a moment for him to recognize what it was, and then pretend that he didn't recognize it. "What in Regwarn is that?"

"The ancient name is Great Far Thrower," Uncle Wolf said. "I find the name inelegant, so I am calling it Galzar's Sling."

Ranthar looked it over. It was known as a trebuchet on most Fourth

Level timelines. This one used a combination of a seesaw with a heavy load assist. Devices of this nature were typically abandoned on sectors where cannons had been invented. It was larger and heavier than any cannon on the Kalvan's Time-Line, but wouldn't have half the range of even a small bombard.

"I think I understand what it is intended to do," Ranthar said as he inspected the contraption. "How will it help? In a battle, I mean."

"Well, we do not have any mobile cannons, and I expect the King's soldiers and guardsmen won't have any, either, as they will slow them down."

As Ranthar recalled, most of the guns in Hos-Bletha were old-fashioned hooped bombards without carriages of any kind and were transported on big carts or wagons which would slow any troop of cavalry.

"After all, one doesn't haul around cannon to hunt bandits," Syros chuckled. "However, if we can lure the Styphoni to a place where we can put Galzar's Sling to use, we will have the advantage."

"That is a very big 'if,' Uncle Wolf," Ranthar noted. "Even on those wheels it will be very difficult to move something this big and heavy through the swamplands. It isn't very maneuverable and it would take at least two or three teams of oxen to move."

Uncle Wolf Syros looked over the trebuchet with a more critical eye and shrugged. "Well, better to have it and not need it than need it and not have it."

"True. What were you planning on loading it with?'

Syros smiled wide. "The bamboo bombs."

Ranthar gave that some serious thought. A single load would spread a lot of damage. Unfortunately, short of sneaking a counter-gravity lift under it, it would be too much effort to move. "If only it were not so large. Well, if anybody ever attacks the village we could certainly use it. Still it is a piece of work. If you will excuse me, I'm needed at the Town Hall."

Ranthar turned to go, noticing the look of disappointment on Uncle Wolf Syros' face as he looked at the big device.

At the Town Hall Ranthar found Lady Eldra enjoying a tankard of ale. It took him a second to recognize her with the large bruise and swelling around her eye. "Great gods, Eldra, what happened?"

Eldra set down her drink and affected an air of nonchalance. "What? This little thing? I had Skranga smack me in the eye as an excuse for leaving the palace."

"A little *thing*?"

"It looks far worse than it is. It's still tender, but no bones were broken and my vision is unimpaired." Eldra became serious. "There are two full-strength Temple Bands of Styphon's Own Guard joining up with a dozen or so companies of Blethan regulars."

"So Andros tells me. And Democriphon has gone to Pytha Town to meet with Prince Mythros. I find the timing a bit suspicious."

Eldra looked stricken. "I hadn't thought of that. Do you think Mythros knows who Democriphon, or who all of us really are?"

"There is no way of knowing. Obviously, he knows nothing of the Paratime Secret, but he might have slipped a spy into the village and gathered that this is not the simple refugee camp we have painted it to be." Ranthar took a seat across from Eldra and poured himself a tankard of ale. "What do we know about this Prince Mythros?"

"Well, in the Kalvan Control Time Lines he's considered a fair ruler. In the ones where Niclophon never rose to power, he supported the king and treated Styphon's House as an unavoidable evil. In at least three time-lines Mythros opposed Niclophon to his ruin. In one time-line he managed to rally several other princedoms to support him and took the throne in a coup."

*Eldra must have stopped off at the transposition station on the way here*, Ranthar decided. He wished he had thought to research Mythros while he was on Home Time Line.

"I find myself liking this man; at least his alternate versions," she said. "What do we know about the local edition?"

"In character, he appears to be no different than the ones you've mentioned. There is reason to think he suspects either Styphon's House, Niclophon, or both played a part in assassinating Great King Marocles and his wife, Great Queen Delra, but will not act without some sort of proof. Niclophon is his brother-in-law through his sister, Delra."

"That much I knew," she replied. "I also know that Niclophon has neither heirs nor traceable family to take the throne when he dies. That means Mythros is the closest thing to a relative Niclophon has and is the most likely successor to the crown, especially if he marries Niclophon's widow."

Ranthar digested that tidbit for a moment. Hos-Bletha's rules of succession were a bit different from the other kingdoms. They didn't use the elector system whereby the princes had a say in who would be enthroned. Instead the Blethans relied on who was closest by blood or that failing, as in this case, family. The Council of Princes vote on the Great King's ascension was merely a traditional formality.

"What about the Orphan Prince?"

"Prince Valthros is of course next in the line of secession—if he exists. Chances are he was killed with his parents. Even if he was not, we know what infant mortality is like on this time-line. What are the odds he would have lived beyond infancy?"

"Very small," Ranthar admitted. "Is Valthros alive on any of the other adjacent control time-lines?"

"A few, but he is mentally defective in the time-lines closest to this one," Eldra said sadly. Mental defective newborns were so rare on Home Time Line they seemed especially cruel. "There was a problem with his birth; the umbilical cord wrapped around his neck cutting off the air supply to the brain."

"Hmm…that would preclude him from becoming great king, no doubt. Marocles would have to sire another heir—"

"Oh, I almost forgot!" Eldra interrupted. "I found a hidden laboratory filled with all kinds of basic chemical compounds in Tarr-Bletha. There was also a book detailing various experiments. I scanned it and made a copy for you." Ranthar pulled off a small pin-on shield of the type commonly worn by devotees of Galzar. Inside was a micro scanner reader similar to Eldra's.

Ranthar looked over the materials. "Marocles, or somebody working for him, was trying to work out the formula for fireseed. Ah-ha! Then it had to be Styphon's House that had him eliminated, along with Great

Queen Delra. Did you tell Democriphon?"

"Calthros took care of that before we found out about Styphon's Own Guard coming for a visit," Eldra said. "Democriphon was gone by the time I arrived."

*So, Democriphon is visiting Mythros armed with a useful piece of information*, Ranthar thought. *If Democriphon plays his cards right, he could win the prince to his side*. "Good. Now I have to figure out what to do about the various scouting parties that are looking for me, or rather Robinos."

"I'm afraid I can't help you there, big guy," Eldra said after draining her tankard. "Just remember that whatever you come up with, do not contaminate this time-line with outtime tech or stratagems."

*As if I needed to be reminded.* "Before I do anything, I'll send Gasphros out to gather more intelligence. We can decide what to do after he returns."

# FIFTY-FIVE

## I

"Without the more colorful commentary," Gasphros said, "the scouting parties will be here in a moon quarter at least, a moon half at most."

"And you know what routes they will take?" Andros asked.

"Oh, yes. A few more ales and I would have had the key to the captain's wife's chastity belt. A look at the scouting map was easy to get." Gasphros skillfully inked a duplicate of the scouting map on a sheepskin. "I would say they could get to this point rather easily," he indicated the location with the plume of his feather pen; "however, they will have to slog through the swamp for two marches after that. That gives us plenty of time to prepare a trap."

"What kind of trap?" Andros asked.

"A simple ambush, I would imagine," Gycules replied. "We could meet them on the other side of that swampy area and simply shoot them down from—"

"Nay!" Andros stormed around the table and came face-to-face with Ranthar. "I told you when I joined that I would have no part in seeing my former brothers in arms killed by you are anyone else in the company. If you do this, it will be without me, and I shall not remain among you."

Ranthar, having taken a step back, recovered himself. "What would you have us do? We cannot wait for them to come to us. Would you have all of us stand and be slaughtered?"

"I…no. But there must be another way…"

"I am open to suggestions, Andros, but if it is a choice between them or us…"

"Robinos," Timnos interrupted, "Killing these men would only be a temporary victory. When this patrol fails to return, more will follow in larger numbers. Men looking to avenge their missing comrades."

"The reward on us would also go up," Uncle Wolf Syros added.

"I'm hearing more problems when I need solutions," Ranthar said. *What I wouldn't give for a squad of Paratime troopers!*

"First Captain, I think I have an idea," Gasphros said. "I will speak with the sharpers. If any have the skills we need, I will tell you my plan."

Ranthar shrugged and gestured for the bard to proceed.

"What do you think he has in mind?" Andros asked nobody in particular.

Uncle Wolf Syros laughed. "Who can know the mind of a bard?"

Gasphros returned half a candle later. "We have what we need, but we will have to work quickly. First…."

## II

"Half a moon, Fannar. That is how long we have been wading through muck and feeding the mosquitoes, Dralm-damnit."

"And who got lost after taking a privy break, Katan? You did!" Fannar accused. "Two days you cost us looking for your sorry arse because the petty-captain thought you might have been seized by these bandits we are looking for. Or even Ruthani. Gods, I would hate to run into them out here."

"You two will run into worse than that if you do not shut those mouths of yours," Petty-Captain Emeros hissed. "We are close to the cursed lands of Mallegast. I do not want to run into anything worse than Ruthani out here."

"Wait," Fannar said stopping. "This is Mallegast? I lost my cousin's family in a flood out here."

"No settlement was ever able to make a go of it in this place," Katan added. "If the bandits are here, Mallegast will tend to them soon enough, I say."

"It will tend to us if you fools do not keep your voices down." Emeros turned back to the rest of the squad. "That goes for the rest of you as well. There is no telling what might be hiding out here in…"

"Sir!" Katar hissed. "Listen."

Emeros raised a hand, halting the squad, then gave an ear to the surroundings. He could hear the chirping of birds, the rustling of leaves in the breeze, something splashing in the water and something else. It took him a moment to identify it as flute music. The melody, while a familiar tavern tune, was somehow different, as if there were no life in it.

"Men, we may have found our bandits celebrating. Follow me and do not make any noise you do not have to."

The soldiers dutifully followed the petty-captain's orders and lead. Emeros took great care in moving as quietly as possible and the soldiers behind him tried to emulate his example. Through the foliage they caught brief glimpses of color and movement; nothing that they could make out definitively. When finally Emeros emerged from the brush, sword in hand, he could not credit his eyes. The scene before him was like nothing he had ever witnessed before.

Crowded around a long table, easily six rods in length, were men dressed in various uniforms and armor; some wore the back-and-breast favored by the armies of the north, while some sported armor typical of the Blethan army. The faces of the men were pale, as if they had been drained of blood, and in some cases bore hideous wounds, still fresh, upon them. All were eating from the platters of fruits, vegetables and meats before them and drinking from wooden steins with silver handles.

Darting back and forth were young maidens, also pale of countenance, refilling the steins with a dark liquid that did not look like wine.

One of the maidens bore a frightful wound on her chest, though it failed to slow her in the least. Another had a blackened eye. *They look like Slain Maidens, hostesses of the dead!* The petty-captain could not help thinking of camp followers occasionally killed at the edge of the fighting.

Most of this, while noticed by Emeros and his men, failed to distract them from the most frightening thing they had ever seen; at the end of the long table, seated on a great throne of iron and brass, sat a man so large that everything else was dwarfed by his presence. Moreover, instead of a man's face, he bore the muzzle of a great wolf!

More wolf-headed men stood at the ready on either side of the giant. Those on the left held great battle-axes and those on the right wielded maces so massive no mortal man could be expected to use them in combat. It was all Emeros could do to pull his gaze away. By chance his eyes settled on a familiar face.

"Andros!"

Andros slowly turned his ashen face to meet Emeros eyes. "Emeros." He spoke flatly, without passion.

Emeros stepped forward. "What plays here? You have been gone for months."

"Has it been that long? I remember fighting the Ruthani, then arriving at this banquet." Andros voice remained flat.

As Emeros approached he saw a splash of red on Andros armor. It looked as though the petty-captain's throat had been cut open. "Gods! Andros, what happened to you?"

"I was killed by the Ruthani," Andros said simply.

"You were…what!" Emeros felt the blood rush out of his head. *Killed?*

"Have you come to join the feast?"

Emeros spun about to face empty air until he lowered his gaze. One of the maidens, the tiny one with hair like the setting sun, stood before him with a stein.

"You must have died well to arrive here, warrior. Here, drink the blood of Galzar and be welcomed." The woman held out the stein and Emeros took it without thinking.

*She said the blood of Galzar! Galzar!* Emeros again looked upon the giant. Damned if it was not the very image of the War God. Emeros lifted the stein and drank without realizing he was doing it. The drink was stronger than anything he had ever tasted. It almost instantly went to his head.

"How did you die, Emeros?" Andros asked in his flat voice.

Emeros sputtered. "What? I am not dead."

Andros nodded. "We all believe that when first we find ourselves here."

"I am not dead, I tell you," Emeros nearly shouted. He remembered the men behind him and brought himself under control. "I am on a search. There have been bandits about and—"

"So they killed you? Well, a good death is its own reward. Join us…"

"This is some kind of sham," said a voice from the back. One of the soldiers, Emeros did not recall his face, boldly marched out with his sword drawn. "That cannot be a real man, not that big, so it is some kind of stuffed effigy, I warrant." The soldier continued to walk toward the giant.

Then the giant stood up.

The soldier stopped and looked stricken, then took a step back. The giant raised a massive mace and pointed it at the frightened man. There came a bright flash from the mace and the soldier vanished in a billow of smoke.

Andros shook his head sadly. "It is always sad when a warrior is sent to Regwarn."

Behind him, Emeros heard the screams of his men as they turned and ran. Many dropped their swords and arquebuses. Emeros, no coward by any measure, knew better than to challenge the might of the gods, especially that of Galzar, the God of War. He turned and ran after his men, dropping the stein though he retained his weapons.

Two days later Emeros stood before his captain and tried to explain what had happened. Captain Mardan was not impressed. He sent a second scouting party to investigate. All they found were the weapons left in the grass and marks on the ground where something heavy had sat, like a great feasting table. They would have investigated more thoroughly but for the sudden melody that assailed their ears.

## III

Back in Mallegast the feast had not finished. The soldiers, face paint washed off and false wounds removed, enjoyed a hearty meal of roast flamingo, wild boar, rabbit, and victory.

"Gycules, you make a truly wonderful Galzar," Vanir said.

"These built-up boots added a good two hands to my height," laughed the giant, "and almost made me lose my balance! I forgot to close my eyes when I set off the mace and could not see a thing for half a candle."

Ranthar nodded knowingly to himself. Flash powder. *I will have to make a note for the study team that they have such a thing on this time-line. The hollow maces were a nice touch as well.*

"You had it easy, Petty-Captain," Timnos said. He still walked with a limp. "I twisted my ankle when I dropped through that, uh, trap door, is it called?"

"That is always a danger in theater, Timnos," Gasphros said. "You did well. Have you ever considered becoming a Sharp?"

"No, I don't think so. Though it was fun sneaking into the back of the scouting party and playing my part." Timnos thought for a second. "Won't they wonder why none of their men are missing when they return and count noses?"

"Maybe," Gasphros interjected. "If they recover their wits fast enough. However, they may decide that someone Galzar has damned is lost even to the memory of mortal man."

"Well, I hope they will not forget me," Eldra said. "Um…on second thought, they had better. I might bump into that petty-captain in Tarr-Bletha. I'll have to stay in chambers after I get back until this eye is healed. I hope Galzar appreciates my sacrifice."

"None of that, now," Ranthar said. "We do not want to annoy Uncle Wolf Syros any more than this little play already has." He handed the mercenary a fresh stein. "Here, Timnos, have some Blood of Galzar."

"Do not call it that," Uncle Wolf Syros said irritably. "I appreciate that you had no good alternatives, but Galzar should not be mocked in this manner. I advise all of you to make a sacrifice to the God of War before your next campaign."

Ranthar nodded solemnly. "We shall, Uncle Wolf, and give three ounces of silver…no, of gold, to the Temple of Galzar for each man who took part in the…uh…production! Yes, the production."

Syros eyes widened. "Uh, yes, that would be very generous. I shall ask my brothers to remember you all in their prayers."

"Good." Ranthar snatched another stein from the table. "Now, have some Ermut's Best and we will no longer call it Galzar's Blood, though I think it honors him all the same."

Gycules spotted Tylla approaching. "My fellows, a toast to our maidens! Tylla, you were especially wonderful. That Emeros fellow almost fainted when you asked how he died. Oh, where is Andros? He was the best of all of us, I think. Oof! I mean, after Tylla, of course." The giant rubbed his stomach where he had received a tiny, though well placed elbow.

"You better believe it," Tylla added.

"I will see to him," Uncle Wolf Syros said as he walked off.

Syros found Andros at the edge of the camp. "Andros, should you not be enjoying yourself. You comrades were spared and Mallegast is safe."

The Blethan released a long sigh. "I had forgotten what I left when I joined up with this bunch. Emeros was a good friend and I will miss him. I did not enjoy tricking him as I did."

Syros shrugged. "You saved his life. It was only chance that brought him to us that way. I cannot say I approved of the…production, but I am pleased nonetheless with the results."

"Uncle Wolf, we petty-captains know each other almost all across the realm. I trained many of them. If not Emeros, it would have been another I had known. I can never go back to my old life in Bletha."

Syros thought on it for a moment before speaking. "You had already made that choice when you joined with Democriphon and Ranthar. Look, you regret tricking your friend, yet you saved his life by doing so. If the charade had failed, what would have happened?"

"Ranthar would have come charging out of the brush with his men and slaughtered them all."

Uncle Wolf Syros nodded. "Just so. Take comfort in the knowledge that you saved an old comrade's life. Now come. One of those sharper women was eyeing you earlier and it would be rude of you to ignore her."

Andros smiled, though there was some sadness in it. "Not the tall horse-faced one, I pray."

"Naaaay," Syros joked. "The one that looks to be at least half Ruthani. I hear those women know things that would make even an Uncle Wolf blush."

# FIFTY-SIX

Captain-General Democriphon fought to keep his equanimity. Scarcely three rods away sat Prince Mythros, ruler of Pytha, on his Chair-of-Office, a smaller and less ornate replica of the Kingdom's Silver Throne. Democriphon had been stripped of his horse pistols but allowed to retain his rapier. He recalled that Prince Ptosphes never took the weapons from anybody in his court unless he knew in advance that there was an assassination plot against him, which was unheard of until the trouble with Nostor started. *Different rulers, different rules.*

"Welcome to Pytha Town, First Citizen Democriphon," Prince Mythros opened.

"I thank you for your welcome, Prince Mythros, and I have brought a few humble gifts."

"I look forward to seeing what you brought. I hope you had a pleasant journey."

"It was...informative, Your Highness. Chancellor Esmeranos regaled me with the history of your realm on the way here."

"I hope he didn't bore you."

"Not at all, Your Highness," Democriphon said quickly. "We passed through a Ruthani village on the way. I was surprised to learn that you allowed them to own property in your lands."

"Actually, Pytha was Ruthani land long before my most distant ancestor settled here. My great grandfather struck a treaty with a few tribes assuring mutual cooperation. I think for this reason my realm has suffered far fewer attacks from the Swamp Ruthani."

Democriphon could not help thinking that Great King Kalvan would have become good friends with Prince Mythros; they had similar views and policies. "If I may, Your Highness, I would like to present my first gift."

"You may proceed."

Democriphon turned to the Chancellor Esmeranos, who in turn nodded to a guard. Two strong men carried in a pair of wine barrels. "The first barrel of wine is from what we in Hostigos call the Winter of the Wolves. It was very cold that year and while times were harsh for the people the winter wine was the best we had ever produced in living memory." The Chancellor had informed him that all victuals and drink were served to food tasters before the Prince was served. Knowing Styphon's House's policy of poisoning rulers hostile to its hegemony, he was not surprised.

Democriphon went over to the first barrel. "I will sample it myself so that you will know it is safe, Your Highness."

Mythros smiled. "Bring chalices," he said to one retainer. A steward brought in a tray of gold chalices and presented them before Democriphon. He filled three of them from a tap in the side, another of Lord Kalvan's innovations; one for himself, one for the prince and one for Esmeranos. The steward passed them around.

Democriphon turned to Mythros and raised his chalice high. "To your continued good health, Your Highness." He downed the contents and placed the chalice on the barrel.

Esmeranos, having already dined in the Hostigi village, quickly emptied his own chalice. "This is truly an excellent vintage, My Prince."

Mythros sniffed and took a small sip, and then drank deeply. "Oh! Oh, this is very good. And quite strong. I never before had its like. Is the other barrel more of the same?"

Democriphon turned to the second barrel, pouring a little into the bottom of his chalice. "I hope Your Highness will not be displeased, but this is a new thing called *brandy*. It is another creation of Lord Kalvan's."

Democriphon took one of the empty chalices and covered the bottom, then handed it to the steward to take to Mythros. After pouring some into the Chancellor's chalice, he turned and said, "This batch was made by Master Ermut. We call this Ermut's Best and I must caution you that it is like nothing you have ever had before. It is best taken in small quantities as it is very strong and burns as it travels down to the stomach."

Democriphon took the first sip of Ermut's Best while Esmeranos, having tried it back in Mallegast, eagerly sipped his.

After a short pause, Prince Mythros tried a sip and almost choked on it. After regaining his breath, he tried again with more caution. "This is an excellent potable, Democriphon. I fear I will have to drink slowly indeed, lest its effects overcome me. Do all Hostigi drink such?"

Democriphon considered his answer carefully. "I cannot speak for everyone, but I have known many who would scarcely drink anything else."

Mythros eyed the amber fluid in his chalice. "I can't say as I blame them. I am pleased with your gifts."

"There is more, Your Highness." Again, Democriphon looked to Esmeranos. The Chancellor again nodded to a steward and several pairs of boots were brought in. "Your Highness, these boots were made here, in Mallegast, but with a new design brought from Hostigos." Democriphon grabbed a pair at random and held them up to display the soles. "Please notice how the boots are designed specifically for the right and left feet. This provides greater comfort, and reduces chafing and blisters. Also, they are measured to match the size of the wearer more closely than boots of other lands."

"This is very interesting. Why did you bring so many?"

Democriphon smiled. "My cobbler was not available to measure His Highnesses feet, so he made pairs of boots in several sizes in hopes that one pair would fit properly."

The steward took the boots over to the Mythros—after examining each pair thoroughly to be certain no venomous insect or reptile hid within, nor any other harmful artifice—was inside. Mythros tried on several pairs until he settled on one that fit as though made for him. He stood and walked about before returning to his throne. Glancing over at Esmeranos he noticed that the Chancellor had been similarly shod during his visit to Mallegast.

"These boots are amazing! A man could walk forever in such boots. Esmeranos, make a note to have the cobblers of Pytha Town go to Mallegast to learn how to make these."

Chancellor Esmeranos nodded.

Mythros eye caught something else. "Democriphon, may I see that rather interesting sword you carry? I see that the scabbard is much lighter than what my people use, so I have to believe the blade it carries is thinner."

Alarms went off in Democriphon's head. Drawing a sword in the presence of a noble, especially a king or prince, was a quick way to end up cut down by his guards, even if that noble requested it. "I would rather not provoke your guardsmen by drawing a naked blade in your presence, Your Highness, but I have no objections if Chancellor Esmeranos pulls it free." Democriphon moved his arm away to allow Esmeranos access to the sword.

Esmeranos looked to his prince. Mythros nodded and the Chancellor pulled the rapier free from the scabbard. Hilt first, he carried the sword over to the prince who accepted it.

"This blade is much lighter than any sword I have ever seen," Mythros said, rising from his Chair-of-Office, waving the sword in the air as if going through a practice exercise. "How did you come by this design?"

"Kalvan introduced it shortly after he first arrived from the Cold Lands," Democriphon explained. He tried to hide his nervousness, but being completely shorn of his weapons disconcerted him. "This is called a cavalry rapier, though there are other types. This one, while lighter than a broadsword, is still effective against an armored foe."

Mythros looked over the sword and took a few more practice swings with it. Democriphon could tell by how the prince handled the weapon that he was well-versed in swordsmanship.

"This sword is very well-balanced and comfortable to hold. I imagine a man could use such a weapon for a long time without tiring." Mythros handed the sword back to Esmeranos whom in turn returned it to Democriphon. "You claim that you reject this Kalvan as king, yet you use all of his artifices?" Mythros tapped a foot meaningfully.

Democriphon shrugged. "A good idea is a good thing. Many people hated the Styphoni yet bought their fireseed long before Lord Kalvan revealed the Fireseed Mystery. My feet are more comfortable for the boots he designed and my arm is grateful for the lighter sword. I sometimes regret my mornings after Master Ermut's product has had its way with me, though."

Mythros chuckled. "I see your point, and agree with it. I should like to speak with you less formally and more privately." He nodded at Esmeranos. The Chancellor quickly cleared the chamber of all but two very large guards and led the way to his private audience chamber.

"Now that we are effectively alone, we may speak freely. Please tell me, what is your real mission here?"

Again, alarms sounded in Democriphon's brain. "Your Highness?'

"Call me Mythros. We are all friends here, I think, and I dislike excessive ceremony. Democriphon, I know that your village is housing the bandits that have recently plagued Styphon's House in the surrounding princedoms. I suspect that you are also running the Orphan Prince game, only giving away silver instead of taking it from the people. I ask again: what is your mission here in Hos-Bletha?"

*The jig is up!* Democriphon had never really understood that strange expression he heard his great king use until this very moment. Mythros had played the child as he received his gifts, yet now he was every bit the ruler he had expected to meet. "Your Highness, I do not know how you came to your knowledge, but surely you can understand: I cannot reveal what you ask. I realize that my life is in your hands and that you will likely have me tortured. Still, I cannot tell you what you wish to know."

Mythros barely masked his surprise; it was obvious he was used to getting his way. "Then let me tell you what I believe is true. You are here to disrupt Hos-Bletha for some reason. Your Great King Kalvan, and I have no doubt that you see him as such, ordered you here. The banditry I would have guessed was a means of acquiring more gold for the war effort in the north, mostly acquired from the very enemy who has declared your king anathema. This explains the Styphoni temple and caravan raids. Even the military convoy you attacked was sent to aid Styphon's House. Yet, you started giving away that same treasure to the commoners of this Kingdom.

"The Orphan Prince game makes no sense. Why give away the treasure your great king needs in the north? That is when it occurred to me that perhaps Kalvan wants to expand his influence to the south, maybe take over Hos-Bletha. Does Great King Kalvan wish to rule over all of the Five Great Kingdoms?"

"What?" Democriphon was shocked. "Your Highness, Great King Kalvan has only ever sought to protect his people. The Fireseed Wars, which is what we now call them in Hos-Hostigos, were thrust upon our Great King by Styphon's House. They used Prince Gormoth of Nostor and Prince Sarrask of Sask to try and destroy the Princedom of Hostigos when Prince Ptosphes refused to allow Styphon's House to build their temple-farms in his lands. It was only Lord Kalvan's arrival that thwarted the Temple's plans."

"If Kalvan is not interested in seizing Hos-Bletha, then what are you doing here?" Mythros demanded.

Democriphon said nothing.

"Very well. I suspect torture would do little to persuade you, and I find the practice barbaric. Therefore, I will tell you this: explain your mission here or I will send my army down to Mallegast and raze it to the ground. Your people will be imprisoned or killed and all goods and treasure will be seized."

Democriphon remained mute.

"Finally, I will send my armies north to join with Styphon's House against your people."

"No, you cannot!" Democriphon could not be silent any longer. "Your Highness, my mission is simply to keep Hos-Bletha from joining the war against my king. We neither want nor need anything further from this realm. You can slay me, but let my people go. I will write a letter to my second in command to take the men and women of Mallegast elsewhere, even out of Hos-Bletha if that is your desire. I will even task them to turn over the panther's share of our treasury to you. I only ask that they be allowed to live and be free."

Mythros studied Democriphon's face and found no sign of dishonesty. *However, the Hostigi has been playing a sharper's game and might be skilled in the art of deception.* "Democriphon, I would like to believe you. I have no love for Styphon's House or even the wretched fools who are devoted to it; not even my own Great King. However, I cannot simply allow you and yours to run amok over the kingdom to which I have sworn fealty."

Democriphon understood Prince Mythros position. Oaths were important to all men of honor. He did not like what he was about to do. "What if you had just cause to foreswear your oath?"

Mythros eyed Democriphon evenly. "Such cause does not come easily. What do you think you know that would provide it?"

Democriphon took in a deep breath and let it out slowly. "I have reason to believe that Styphon's House was behind the assassination of Great King Marocles and Queen Delra."

Mythros came to his feet abruptly and yelled, "What!? How?"

Democriphon related the discovery of the hidden laboratory in Great King Niclophon's palace. Mythros sat down and lowered his voice. "How did you come upon such information?"

"I have agents-inquisitory within the Silver Palace. I cannot tell you who they are, of course, but I know the information is reliable. I'd stake my life on it."

Mythros digested Democriphon's words. His sister Delra, on more than one occasion, had informed him that her husband wanted to throw off the yoke of Styphon's House. The former Great King found them offensive and despised the avaricious priests who represented the Temple. The prince also recalled that his brother-in-law was a well-read and intelligent man, forward-thinking and willing to get his hands dirty. Marocles had hated Styphon's House and all they represented. It would be just like him to try to unravel the Fireseed Mystery. Still…?

"Your story is very convenient, Democriphon. How can I be certain of its veracity?"

*How indeed?* "You can have me tortured."

"As I said before, I dislike the practice. I also know a man will say anything to end his pain, even admit to a crime he never committed. Or, you might even be fanatical enough to withstand torture long enough to sell your story."

*True enough*, Democriphon thought. "You could have Ranthar, my Second, questioned independently of me to see if our stories match up. Oh…he was away when I learned of the laboratory."

"Sire," Chancellor Esmeranos spoke up, "could we not have Uncle Wolf Karthros speak with this man? Uncle Wolfs are said to be excellent judges of character and all but immune to deception."

Mythros nodded hesitantly. "Yes, send for Uncle Wolf Karthros."

Democriphon suspected that the prince shared his own doubts as to whether or not the Uncle Wolfs truly rated their reputations; yet, neither of them had any other alternative. Then inspiration struck. "Your Highness, might I suggest that we also send for Uncle Wolf Syros? He is a native Hos-Blethan and has been staying with my people for some time. If he were an imposter, your Uncle Wolf would surely see through him. Perhaps together they can arrive at the truth in my words to your satisfaction."

Mythros again appeared surprised.

From what Democriphon knew, no Uncle Wolf had ever been known to support a sharper's troupe.

"Very well. Chancellor, have a team of my fastest horses and best riders make the journey to Mallegast and request Uncle Wolf Syros' attendance. Once this matter is settled, one way or the other, I will determine my best course of action."

Esmeranos nodded and exited the audience chamber.

"Democriphon, you will be accorded the status of honored guest until this matter is resolved. However, you shall be escorted by at least two guards at all times and prevented from leaving the castle grounds.

Otherwise, you will be free to go where you wish. Do not abuse my hospitality."

"Your Highness is most generous," Democriphon said with relief. "I shall be on my best behavior."

"Excellent. Now, let us have another...*brandy*, as you called it? Let us speak of your accomplishments since your arrival in Hos-Bletha." Mythros held out his chalice. He had not even realized he had emptied it while speaking with the Hostigi.

"Personally, I hope we can verify your story. I would also like to learn more of the innovations your Great King has introduced to Hos-Hostigos."

# FIFTY-SEVEN

## I

"We need this area ready for battle in less than a moon-quarter," Ranthar shouted. With Democriphon staying in Pytha Town for the near future, it fell to him to prepare for war. More bad news: Uncle Wolf Syros had been summoned to Tarr-Pytha to assist in some matter. The message had been vague, but carried the seal of Prince Mythros. Therefore, it could not be ignored; to do so might provoke the enmity of a man they desperately needed to stay on friendly terms with. Ranthar could only hope that Democriphon and Syros made it back before hostilities began.

So far, their casualties from raiding temples and holding up caravans had been moderate, except for former Captain Myklon's party. Ranthar knew that surprise was the main reason. Next were the exotic weapons they had employed: bamboo bombs, the minefield, and the superstitious fear their wolf-helms evoked. Surprise could no longer be counted on; it was nearly impossible to surprise somebody when they were actively hunting for you. The bamboo bombs would still be useful, although Styphon's Own Guard probably had been briefed on them by now and would be taking some sort of defensive measures against them.

The minefield was still unknown since none of the enemies involved when it was employed had survived. Unfortunately, it would only be useful if the enemy could be encouraged to maneuver into a prepared position. A very difficult proposition.

The other problem was fireseed. Up until recently, a man could not swing a dead cat in Mallegast without it hitting a barrel of fireseed. Unfortunately, the bamboo bombs and minefield had used tremendous amounts of fireseed. The minefield alone had used a third of what they had on hand. More was used in target practice, training the freemen to be soldiers, and in stump removal. Since they had slowed down raids on Styphon's House temples very little had come in to replace the loss.

The Temple caravans they still raided usually carried just enough fireseed for their own use. Why waste time and effort hauling extra fireseed when the temples in Hos-Bletha produced it by the ton? Between the minefield and the bamboo bombs fireseed supplies would be running low. A protracted battle would likely wipe out their remaining supply. Not for the first time Ranthar wished he had talked Democriphon into setting up a fireseed works. Democriphon's argument had been that it was easier to steal the fireseed than the components to make it.

That was true until the Styphoni had wised up. The last raid had come up almost empty as far as fireseed was concerned. Ranthar was considering a raid on one of the temple-farms when Eldra approached. She had dressed in her traveling clothes and brought her guards with her. Ranthar also noticed that her bruised eye was almost completely healed. He hoped she was merely a fast healer and hadn't used any First Level medicine to speed her healing time.

"Heading back to the Silver Palace?"

"Right after I do a little shopping," Eldra replied lightly. "I need to look like a wronged woman given a spending spree by way of apology from her brother.

Ranthar had once visited Eldra's palatial residence on Home Time

Line and recalled the eclectic variety of outtime relics and paraphernalia scattered about the rooms. Nobody could power shop like Eldra when she got going. "Shopping on Skranga's pfennig? Try not to bust his purse."

"With a mere twenty ounces of gold?"

"Twenty ounces!" Ranthar exclaimed. "Which of Skranga's arms did you break? No matter. I have larger issues to address," Then an idea struck him. "Say, is there any way Skranga could sneak us some fireseed?"

Eldra gave it some serious thought. "I don't think so. Highpriests rarely have anything to do with anything as mundane as fireseed production or storage. It might look odd if he were suddenly to develop an interest in such matters."

Ranthar knew she was right. He found himself wishing Democriphon was back from Pytha Town. He was dancing on the edge of Paratime regulations by being in charge during the Captain-General's absence. *No worse than Chief Verkan, though.*

"Well, I guess I will have to get a fireseed works started in Mallegast… no, not there, we'll run afoul of Niclophon's prohibition. The old campsite in Taurnos, then. Although, I don't see how we'll be able to get things up and running in time to produce enough fireseed to get us through the upcoming battle."

"Well, then maybe for the next one," Eldra offered.

"Thanks," Ranthar said in exasperation.

"Look, I'll speak with Skranga when I get back to the palace and see if he can think of anything that might help." Eldra got up on her horse and joined her escorts. She stopped and turned back and, speaking in Urgothi, said, "If things get too rough, will you bug out?"

Ranthar did not take offence at the suggestion. It was standard outtime protocol to get out quick when things got too hazardous; he, like Eldra, was here as an observer and to keep outtime contamination to a minimum. Not to die in a war he didn't really belong in. However, like most men of his caliber, he wasn't about to run out on men he had come to know as friends and comrades. "No. I volunteered for this assignment, both here and…at home. I'm in until there is no hope of survival for any of us."

Eldra nodded, then made her way to the gates.

## II

The assembled princes sitting in the great hall of Tarr-Pytha muttered among themselves as they waited for their host to explain why they had been summoned. Had anyone other than Great King Niclophon or Prince Mythros called for such a gathering the turnout would have been a markedly poor one. Of the princes, only Mythros was respected enough to manage such a gathering.

Prince Carthames took a seat at the opposite end of the table from Prince Basilron. There was a lot of resentment between the two, despite the fact that five winters had passed since the border dispute between their respective realms of Drathor and Syragon. Xandros, the bloated Prince of Zynophon, swilled his winter wine as if it were water. Across from Xandros sat the painfully thin Vythron of Taurnos, in full armor, who was rumored to be in league with the Carib. Next to him was Duke Kythar, Mythros' older son. Lastly was Kosklos of Artigos, the warrior prince who made his reputation by fighting the Sastragathi and beating them so badly none had ever dared to raise arms against him again.

Among those not in attendance was Prince Phaedron, whose eldest son was a captain-general in the Hos-Blethan army. While Phaedron had no love for Great King Niclophon, he would not take part in anything that would place his son, Captain-General Theodoros, in jeopardy, and if things went as Prince Mythros hoped, that was a very real possibility.

When everyone had a drink in their hand and had quieted down, Mythros tapped the table with his signet ring. Instantly all eyes were on him. "Brothers, fellow princes and rulers, I will not dance around the reason I have asked all of you here. I have reason to believe our Great King is, at worst, a regicide, and at best a collaborator to one."

"Oh, now, really, Mythros," Xandros sputtered. "If this is a joke, it is in truly bad taste."

"On what information do you predicate such an outrageous statement?" Prince Vythron demanded.

"I have learned that Great King Marocles had been trying to learn the secret to fireseed shortly before he was assassinated," he stated clearly.

He had everyone at the table's attention.

Mythros responded softly. "Does any here doubt that, at the least, Styphon's House would order his death?"

None spoke.

"And who has benefitted most from Great King Marocles death?"

Kosklos spoke up first. "Great King Niclophon."

The princes muttered between themselves until Carthames spoke up. "What is to be done about it, if what you say is true? Niclophon has sat on the Silver Thorne for nearly thirty winters."

"Aye," added Basilron in a rare show of support for his past enemy. "Many of us were on the council that confirmed his right of succession. The rest of us are the sons of those council members."

"And what proof do we use to call for his removal from the throne?" Prince Vythron asked.

The others nodded.

"Marocles making fireseed is, perhaps, the reason for his death," Prince Carthames said, "but not proof of whose hand held the knife. We cannot challenge him with this."

Mythros nodded. "True enough. However, he is still not the legitimate king."

"Oh, no?" Xandros said loudly. "Then who is? You?"

"Me? Do not be absurd, Xandros. I speak of the son of Great King Marocles and Great Queen Delra."

"Prince Valthros?" Vythron said dubiously. "If he survived his infancy, you probably have already hanged him for a fraud. You've beheaded more self-proclaimed Orphan Princes than all of us combined."

Mythros smiled. "Yes, that is true. I would not allow my nephew's name to be used by pretenders or sharpers. However, there is something that none of you are aware of, I have been searching for the true Prince ever since the night he vanished from his crib. And, brothers, I have found him! Valthros, enter the hall and show yourself."

Behind Mythros, the drapes rustled, then a moment later a handsome man with long blond hair and a flowing moustache stepped out. He stood straight and tall, and looked each prince in the eye.

To Mythros' he had the look of a fighter and commander.

"This is ridiculous!" Prince Carthames shouted. "I'll grant he looks something like Marocles, but how do we know he is the true Orphan Prince? You've beheaded enough to know they come a pfennig a dozen."

"Again, true." Mythros nodded. "This man has something none of the others before him possessed." Mythros turned to the man and said, "Show them." The blond-haired man held up his left hand. On the first finger, a ruby ring in a gold setting glinted in the candlelight. "Brothers, this is the ring I presented my nephew three days after his birth. I placed it on a gold chain about his neck as an early name-day gift. Many of you were there on that day. Do any deny it?"

Again, there was muttering and whispers among the gathered princes until Basilron spoke up. "The ring could have been stolen, or even sold to another. A great deal of things could happen in thirty years."

Mythros had expected that. "Yes, it could. The ring alone would never sway me. Even the resemblance to my late brother-in-law means nothing. Fortunately, there is one piece of evidence that cannot be refuted. Mistress Katia, please join us."

From behind the drapes a matronly woman appeared. She was gray of hair and stooped with age. The blond man quickly pulled out a chair for her to sit in, which she accepted gratefully.

Prince Vythron examined the woman critically. She was dressed in clothing a well-treated servant in a wealthy household might wear. "Who is this woman, Mythros?"

"This is Katia, Valthros' governess and wet-nurse. Surely those of you present on Valthros' Name Day will recall this woman."

Prince Xandros nodded. "Yes, it is her."

Kosklos looked to the elder prince. "Are you certain?"

"Oh, yes," Xandros laughed, appearing to have dropped a decade off his face. "I was rather taken with you back then, Katia. Do you remember when I took you to my castle for a moon-quarter?"

"I remember you tried, Your Highness, and I refused. You, and I, were much younger and thinner back then. You have prospered since last we met."

Xandros laughed again. "In more ways than one." He turned to the others. "It is Mistress Katia back from the dead!"

"Brothers, is there anyone in this hall who doubts that this woman was the Chief Nursemaid in charge of Valthros' care all those winters ago?" Mythros asked.

"I'll not go against you and Xandros," Kosklos stated. "I was not there, so I am no judge. However, I would like to know how you found her after so many years."

Mythros nodded to Katia, saying, "Please tell your story."

Katia bowed her head. When she looked up, she looked straight into Prince Kosklos' eyes. "I was in the royal nursery when I heard the Queen screaming. She ran into the nursery and cried that Great King Marocles was dead, stabbed by persons unknown. Great Queen Delra feared that both she and the prince would be next, so she begged me to take Valthros to safety. She gave me all of the jewels she was wearing, save for her royal tiara, to sell so that we would have money enough to survive. I took Valthros in my arms and escaped through the kitchen into the buttery and out to the stables.

"It was not that difficult, really. Guards running to and fro, kitchen maids and servants screaming. Everybody running up the stairs to see what was wrong with the Queen. A common woman with a load of laundry did not attract any attention. I took a horse and buggy from the stables and hurried away. When the guards stopped me at the gates, I told them the King was dead and feared that there were assassins in the castle. One of them recognized me and let me go. The others ran to the palace."

Mythros watched as several of the princes nodded thoughtfully. Katia's words were sincere and her voice shook with remembered fear from that long ago day.

"Where have you been since then," Kosklos asked.

"I stayed in Hywal, a small village where my brother was the blacksmith. He gave us a home and protection."

They all nodded. Smiths were essential to the health of a prosperous village and were accorded the utmost of respect.

"Where did you sell the jewels?" Prince Xandros asked, with a glint of greed in his eyes.

"Oh, the jewels," Katia laughed in a sad way. "I didn't have the heart to sell them, and wouldn't have known who to sell them to if I had needed the money. Only a wealthy merchant or a noble could give me even a portion of their true worth. I knew of none whom I could trust. I mean no offence, but a common woman could hardly approach a prince."

"Prince Xandros was quite taken with you at the time: Why didn't you contact him?" Prince Vythron asked.

Mistress Katia looked Vythron right in the eye. "What Xandros was interested in was not my health. I feared for my reputation."

That brought the house down. Even Xandros' lips twisted in wry amusement.

Xandros nodded. "Still, you should have come to me for aid."

"Your realm is far away, and I feared for the young prince's safety. I had some money of my own and we lived on that for a time. Later, I took work as a housekeeper, a nursemaid, even as a serving wench after my brother died. I did whatever I could to keep Valthros safe and fed. When he became mannish, he demanded I allow him to work. I could not stop him and we needed the money. He took a job as a smith, and later as a mercenary, though I begged him not to. The work made him strong and able. You see before you the results." Katia waved a hand at the man next to her.

"Why have you finally declared Valthros' parentage to Prince Mythros, now, of all times?" Carthames demanded.

"The banditry and raids on Styphon's House, Your Highness," Katia replied. "I feared for his safety if he was forced to fight the raiders or bandits. They have killed at will and no one has been able to stop them. I am old. My life no longer matters, but someone is needed to restore order and peace to the kingdom. The time has come for Valthros to take his place on the Silver Throne as ruler of Hos-Bletha. Prince Mythros used to hang everybody who claimed to be the Orphan Prince, so I was afraid to bring him here until I learned that he had stopped executing people."

"I have recently taken a more enlightened view," Mythros added. "The last sharper I caught is still in my dungeon awaiting trial by Tribunal."

Vythron spoke up. "You say you never sold the queen's jewels. Where are they now?"

"Right here." Katia opened her purse and spilled the contents onto the table. Along with a few coins of copper and silver, and other items of womanly use that seemed strange and arcane to the men, were an assortment of tasteful, yet obviously expensive, jewelry. The pieces were of a type that no common woman could ever buy for herself, or even expect to receive from a lower-class lover.

"By Styphon's pizzle!" muttered Basilron, who was a connoisseur of precious gems. "Mythros, I swear by the gods, the jewels on your great table could buy a small barony."

The princes spoke among themselves while Mythros waited. It didn't take long.

"We are divided," Vythron said. "We agree that this must be Valthros, the Lost Prince, but not what we should do about it."

"Do? Do!" Mythros roared. "We set the true and proper king on the throne and try the usurper for treason and regicide. That is what we do!"

Xandros, Vythron and Kosklos nodded while Carthames and Basilron shook their heads.

"You forget that Niclophon has close ties to Styphon's House," Carthames argued. "If we try to remove him, Styphon's Own Guard will come down upon us like a plague of demons from Regwarn!"

"Or Grand Master Soton, himself!" Basilron interjected.

"Let them," Kosklos roared. "By Galzar, I welcome the challenge. I would like nothing better than to meet Soton on the field of battle."

"Not all of us share your love of war, Kosklos," Prince Basilron argued.

"Styphon's House is busy in the north and Soton is busy with Styphon's Grand Host," Xandros stated. "The Temple will not be able to send more troops until they have dealt with the Usurper Kalvan. That makes this the perfect time to oust the regicide Niclophon."

"This Kalvan has more lives than a black panther," Vythron joined in. "I daresay he may yet put the Styphoni out of our misery. We should do the same here at home."

Basilron and Carthames, unlikely allies that they were, shook their heads. "We cannot imperil our lands and violate our oaths of fealty to Niclophon," Basilron said. "Will we be allowed to leave unmolested?"

Mythros sighed. "Yes, if you swear on Galzar's Mace that you will not speak of what we have discussed here in this chamber, or make any mention of Prince Valthros and his claims."

Both princes gave their sworn oaths.

"Then go, but keep in mind that I have little patience for oath-breakers."

"And I have none," Kosklos added.

Basilron and Carthames left as quickly as their dignity would allow.

"Brothers, I thank you for your support, both for me and the true king of Hos-Bletha. Let us make our plans."

# FIFTY-EIGHT

## I

The meeting went long and everybody was tired. Prince Mythros arranged for accommodations for his guests, then escorted Valthros and Katia to the opposite end of his castle. Waiting for them were Uncle Wolfs Syros and Karthros. Once certain none would overhear them, Mythros plopped into a chair with a sigh of relief.

"Democriphon, you played your part well," Mythros said to the blond man. "You were wise to speak sparingly; your accent might have aroused suspicion."

"I trust the meeting went well?" Uncle Wolf Syros asked.

"Indeed," Mythros said. "Democriphon's time among the sharpers has benefited him."

"That doesn't surprise me. This boy could talk a Ruthani maiden out of her buckskins," Syros added.

"I felt as if my life depended on it," Democriphon returned. "If I failed to convince the other princes, both Mythros and I would be in a very deep midden pit. Katia, however, was brilliant. Where did you get those jewels, milady?"

"Exactly where I said I did, young man. From the Great Queen."

Democriphon was confused. "Wait, then that part of the story was true?"

"Right up until the part where I said I took work in a tavern," Katia said with a small grin.

"In truth, she brought Valthros to me shortly after she escaped from Bletha Town," Mythros explained. "I have employed her as a governess these past thirty years."

Democriphon took a second before the full impact of what he heard struck him like lightening. "The Prince in Exile is alive and here!"

Mythros nodded, with a big grin.

"Then why did you ask me to play this part…oh, you want me to be the decoy."

"Not at all," Mythros said. "Yes, Valthros is here, but he can never be great king of this kingdom, or any other."

Now Uncle Wolf Syros was the one who looked confused. "Why not?"

"Valthros is a child in a man's body," Uncle Wolf Karthros said. "He was born with the umbilical cord wrapped about his neck. He is a wonderful, kind and respectful boy, but he will never be more than that. Only Prince Mythros, Lady Katia and myself knew of this."

"Even Chancellor Esmeranos has been kept in the dark," Mythros added.

Democriphon sat down on a bench. "Wait…Thames, that's the boy—I mean man—I met earlier in the courtyard. I see your point. Then you want me to be a puppet king in his name?"

"Not a puppet," Mythros countered. "Once you are crowned I could scarcely control a man such as yourself without your cooperation. I can only hope to guide you. I would not even consider raising you up, if I did not think you would make a better monarch than Niclophon. At any rate, he has to go. I will not allow the murderer of my sister to rule my homeland."

Uncle Wolf Karthros raised his hand, counseling patience. "Sire, we have no proof that Niclophon hired the assassins who killed your brother-in-law and sister. They may just as well have been hired by Styphon's House."

Mythros shook his fist angrily. "If Niclophon wasn't directly involved in their deaths, he certainly profited by them. Nor did he demand any investigation afterwards. He may not have their blood on his hands, but he has it on his robes of state."

Karthros shrugged his shoulders.

Uncle Wolf Syros nodded. "But I think you have something more in mind than simple revenge."

Mythros smiled. "The reputation of Uncle Wolfs is not exaggerated. Here is what I want. First, once Democriphon is enthroned, he will make a treaty with Great King Kalvan. A mutual non-aggression pact that would serve both of our kingdoms."

Democriphon nodded. "All Great King Kalvan ever wanted was peace in his land and freedom from Styphon's House. I'm certain he will accommodate you in this."

"Good. Second, Valthros, while possessed of a child's mind, still has the body and inclinations of a fully-grown man. He has dallied with several maidens in the castle and the surrounding towns and villages. Thus far, there have been no offspring, as far as I know, but that is likely to happen eventually. When it does, you will take the child and make him your heir to the throne. That way the true line of succession will be in place. I hope you can refrain from producing any offspring of your own until then."

"I will do my best, Your Highness. Fortunately, I do not have any current romantic entanglements."

"Excellent. After that, when the child has reached the proper age, I want you to step down and turn the kingdom over to him."

Democriphon gave it some thought. He never really wanted to be a king, which surprised even him. Too many headaches considering everything he watched Great King Kalvan deal with: controlling princes who wanted to do things their own way, settling disputes, assassination attempts, deciding who lives and who dies and being blamed for everything including the weather. A duke, however... "How do you propose to remove me if I choose not to go?"

Mythros smiled grimly. "Democriphon, a reasonably intelligent man like yourself really doesn't need me to answer that, do you?"

"No, not at all. However, I would like a duchy for my retirement. Maybe some extra land around Mallegast?"

"I believe that is only fitting," Syros added. "Archduke, I would think."

"Fair enough," Mythros said. "I also expect you to name me as your royal advisor. I have enough influence with the other princes that they won't dispute the appointment."

Democriphon nodded. "I will need you close at hand, regardless. I know little of the politics of this realm and have much to learn."

"I am pleased to see that we are of one mind. Oh, one more thing, and I do not believe you will have a problem with it."

Democriphon eyed Mythros for a moment. "What is it? I won't betray Hos-Hostigos."

"Nothing like that. I want all of Styphon's House's temples destroyed and their priests driven from Hos-Bletha. They are directly responsible for my sister and her husband's deaths. I have heard all about what is happening in the north and fear it is only a matter of time before Styphon's House attempts to seize this and every kingdom for their own. That cannot be allowed."

"Agreed," Democriphon said. "That is something both my Great King and I want."

"The priesthood of Galzar will certainly support you in this," Uncle Wolf Karthros said.

Democriphon could not keep the smile from his face. "Prince Mythros, as what may be my final act as Democriphon, subject of Hos-Hostigos, I give you my sworn oath. I cannot imagine Great King Kalvan objecting to any of your conditions, so I will not. Shall we drink on it?"

"By all means. In fact I had some of your Ermut's Best brought in for that purpose."

Mythros distributed the brandy himself. "To Great King Valthros!"

Democriphon took a long drink and felt it burn down to his stomach.

"One thing; where does Chancellor Esmeranos come in on this? Is his greater loyalty to you or the king?"

"It is to Hos-Bletha, which is greater than any single man or king. He can always be counted on to do what is best for the Kingdom first, me second, himself third."

Democriphon nodded. He had known others like that, though rarely. If all went as planned, would he be able to find a man he could trust like that? Yes, First Captain Ranthar and Petty-Captain Gycules came to mind. "So, Mythros, when will we make our move on Bletha Town?"

Mythros looked confused. "We don't. At least, not right away. First, a declaration stating our suspicions must be circulated among the nobility and Niclophon's retainers. We will voice our suspicions and demand an accounting. Nothing will be said about the alchemical works your intelligencer found in Tarr-Bletha. We will give Niclophon the opportunity to rebut the allegations, then Xandros, Kosklos, Vythron and myself will all publically declare you, Prince Valthros, to be the true Great King of Hos-Bletha. Princes Carthames and Basilron will challenge, of course, as they made their positions clear this evening. Prince Phaedron, no doubt, would prefer to align with us, but has reasons to stay neutral. Now that Captain-General Lykron is on his way to Balph with the Hos-Bletha contribution, Phaedron's son is acting Captain-General of the Royal Army.

"The real opposition, however, will come from Styphon's House. They'll want to keep their foppish tool in power and under their thumb. They will use all the princes and noblemen who are in their debt to create a fighting force to support their puppet Great King. In addition, they can call on all the individual Temple Guardsmen to come to Niclophon's aid."

"In that case, you should shut down every Styphon's House temple in your realm," Democriphon said firmly. "Having the enemy within, as well as without, could be disastrous. Plus, each temple we sack will provide more gold, silver and fireseed to pursue the war."

"At the right time, I will," Mythros said. "However, I do not wish to tip my hand too early, which sacking Styphon's temples would do."

Democriphon gave it some thought. "Then we need to give Styphon's Own Guard a reason to leave your realm, and possibly the other realms as well."

Mythros looked intrigued. "That would be helpful, but how do we go about it?"

"Simple. My men will stage several raids in Drathor and Syragon. With the war against Hostigos about to begin, Styphon's House can scarcely spare many more men from the north. Thus, they will have to divert military resources from within Hos-Bletha."

Mythros nodded. The plan had merit. "Styphon's Own Guard were not stationed at each temple before Great King Kalvan began sacking all of the temples in Hostigos. Plus, now we have several Temple Bands and a thousand royal cavalry searching for the bandit Robinos and his confederates."

Democriphon smiled widely. "That just proves it works. How many of Styphon's Own Guard have been diverted to protecting temples instead of fighting barbarian invaders? Or the forces of Hos-Hostigos, for that matter? A lot of kings and princes would like to take down the Styphoni temples, and many did in Hos-Harphax after King Kalvan released the fireseed secret. My people have already destroyed several convoys and even a Band of Styphon's Own Guard as they came to resupply the temples we raided."

"A full Temple Band? How many people do you have?"

"In terms of fighting men, well over two thousand. However, it only took less than half a company to destroy an almost fully staffed Temple Band."

"Great Galzar's Mace," Uncle Wolf Karthros whispered. "I cannot believe it."

"Ha! I was there," Uncle Wolf Syros laughed. "It was a sight to behold though at the time it made me sick. And I even had a hand in the creation of the weapons we used."

Mythros mentally filed away the mention of new weapons for later and concentrated on Democriphon's plan. "A few thousand soldiers, even armed with the weapons you claim to have, are far too few to attack every Styphoni temple in two realms. I cannot provide my own soldiers, as I will need them here. Besides, it would break several covenants to have my own soldiers cross into another prince's realm."

"I do not want or need your soldiers, Prince Mythros. I want you to turn over the contents of your dungeons to me."

"What?"

"Great King Kalvan once spoke of something he called a Devil's Brigade. Criminals of all sorts gathered together and teamed up with some of the best fighters in the Cold Lands. These men became the fiercest warriors of a great war that makes even what the Six Kingdoms is going through now seem like an outhouse brawl. I believe we can do the same here in your Princedom."

"Do you want all the criminals in my realm?" Mythros asked, shaking his head in wonderment.

"I will have to be a little selective. Rapists might disrupt things in Mallegast, for example. However, for the most part, yes. I will likely have to lop the heads off the worst of the bunch to keep the rest in line."

The discussion went on until all were too tired to continue. Democriphon went to sleep thinking that he was doing far more to help his homeland here than he could ever have done in Hos-Hostigos.

## II

Paratime travelers, and Paracops in particular, were trained to handle stress in a variety of forms in order to keep themselves sane. A Paratime traveler needed to be equally prepared, mentally as well as physically, to deal with an attack by irate Neanderthals on Fifth Level, an interrogation by a Gestapo agent on the Fourth Level Hitler Victory Belt, a party of slave traders on Second Level Khiftan or getting lost in the endless wastelands of the First Level Abzar Sector. Stress was an unpleasant fact when traveling to other time-lines.

Ranthar had dealt with many unusual and hazardous situations on more timelines than he could count. Disease, corrupt tyrannies, foods that barely qualified as edible, violent conflicts from simple duels all the way up to full out wars and a variety of forms of imminent death. At the moment, he would have chosen any of those over what he currently faced.

"Uncle Wolf, please tell me again, slowly, what I am supposed to do with over eight hundred criminals and social malcontents that were disgorged from Pytha's prisons, dungeons and work camps?"

Syros drew a long breath and repeated himself. "You are to train these men to attack the Styphoni temples in Drathor. You have less than a moon to do so."

Ranthar stared. First at the Uncle Wolf, then at the motley dregs that had been thrust upon him. With Skranga and Democriphon away, command of the village fell to him. Ranthar made the only response that came to mind. "Andros!"

Captain Andros formed up quickly. He still reacted like a petty-captain to commands. "Yes, First Captain."

"I have about seven or eight companies of men that need to be trained in a moon. Are you up to this task?"

Captain Andros regarded the ragtag ranks of the newly released criminals and rogues. He had seen better. Much better. He had also trained worse, though not by much. "If we can refrain from engaging any enemy forces in that time, and I have the assistance of Chief Petty-Captain Gycules and others that we have already trained, I think I can make passable soldiers out of these pathetic blackguards. I will not be able to treat them gently, though, and they will need added rations to put some meat back on their bones. I gather it is too much to ask if we received any denizens from the stockade?"

Ranthar had not thought of that. Trained soldiers, even ones who had been court marshaled, would be a big help in getting the rest in line. "Uncle Wolf?"

"I am afraid I neglected to ask," Syros admitted shamefacedly.

"I will find out soon enough," Andros said. "Chief Petty-Captain Gycules, front and center." Gycules appeared almost instantly. "We are on training detail. Gather your men and let us start sorting out these pathetic recruits. Have anyone with military training form a platoon over there. The rest will go over there."

"Yes, sir." Gycules pounded a fist to his armored chest then extended the arm, fist still closed, straight out at Andros in what passed for a salute here-and-now, then vanished as quickly as he had appeared.

Andros turned back to Ranthar and Uncle Wolf Syros. "What do I do with the truly uncooperative ones, My Lord?"

Ranthar looked to Syros who said, "You have a free hand unless Ranthar says otherwise. Hard labor, flogging—execution if you deem it necessary." Syros waved an arm in the direction of the newcomers. "Every last one of these men is a convicted criminal. Oh, except for Zentros and his gang of sharps. Mythros had them captured from another realm for questioning and they were languishing in his dungeon until the tribunal could get to them."

"Sharpers, eh? What game were they running?"

"The Orphan Prince, which is why Mythros wanted to talk with them." Syros pointed to Zentros and his troupe. "He was looking for a line on Democriphon and this bunch got caught in the middle."

"Really…" Ranthar looked over at Zentros. "Captain Andros, have Zentros and his minions sent over to the Town Hall. I want to speak with them. While Captain Andros is trying to turn straw into gold, we need to start hitting Styphon's temples again. What we need are fireseed, gold and to kill as many of Styphon's Own Guard as possible, and not necessarily in that order."

"That could prove difficult, First Captain," Uncle Wolf Syros replied. "The very men we need to lead any attacks are busy training the new recruits—if you can call them that."

"You bring up a very good point, Uncle Wolf. I'll give Captain Andros and Gycules a quarter-moon to start whipping these whoresons into shape, before I sent them out in the field."

"Do you think that wise?" Syros asked.

"I've got to run Mallegast Village while Democriphon is busy building a working relationship with Prince Mythros. Plus, we have several Bands of Styphon's Guardsmen and a few thousand Royal Cavalry looking for us. So what are my choices? If we don't attack some of the temples, we'll have to face not only the Royal Army of Hos-Bletha, but the might of Styphon's Red Hand. Plus, we need the fireseed. I know Democriphon is working with Prince Mythros to build a fireseed works in Pytha, but that's a start-up. It's going to take a moon or two before there's any significant fireseed production. Meanwhile, we have hundreds of new recruits who need training with their new weapons as well as bamboo bombs to build."

Syros shrugged. "When you put it that way...."

# FIFTY-NINE

## I

Chancellor Archimanes calmly waited outside the presence chamber until he was noticed by his king. The wait proved to be a long one. Great King Niclophon sat, as if in a daze, staring at a document sent to him by Prince Mythros and countersigned by Princes Kosklos, Vythron and Xandros. The so-called Edict of Pytha called into question the legitimacy of his position and demanded that he stand before the Council of Princes to determine if he was to retain the Silver Throne as Great King of Hos-Bletha.

The document presented proof of the assassination of Great King Marocles and Great Queen Delra and the suspected involvement, and even collusion, of Styphon's House Upon Earth and Prince Niclophon. If Niclophon were found guilty of regicide, he would be executed. If he refused to face the council, the undersigned princes would declare him a usurper and declare his occupation of the Silver Throne null and void. Moreover, they were prepared to go to war to enforce their edict.

While the preamble and body of the message were appalling enough, the statement that Prince Mythros had found the true Prince in Exile, Valthros, was beyond endurance. It was horrific that the rot which infested Hos-Harphax had spread to Hos-Bletha, promoting the idea of removing rightful rulers from their territories, and even thrones. However, the discovery of the Orphan Prince was ten times worse. The Council of Princes could easily dispatch Niclophon and replace him with Marocles' son. Hereditary lines were important in Hos-Bletha; if the council so decreed, Valthros would be hailed as king by one and all.

Niclophon considered the possibility that this new Valthros could be yet another imposter, and almost as quickly dismissed it. In the entire kingdom no one was more skeptical than Mythros when it came to the Orphan Prince scam. The Prince of Pytha executed every sharper and pretender he caught running the Prince in Exile game. For Mythros, above all else, to declare that Valthros had been found, it had to be true.

He felt himself start to shudder and willed his body still. This was not the time to show weakness and fear. "Archimanes!"

"Yes, Your Majesty."

Niclophon almost jumped at the sound of his Chancellor's voice. "Have Highpriest Sangar brought before me at once. Styphon's House must be consulted."

"At once, Your Majesty."

## II

"I am afraid that I do not see the wisdom of declaring war on both princedoms at once, Valthros," Prince Mythros said.

Democriphon fought to keep from rolling his eyes. Prince Mythros was clever enough, to be sure, and on par with Duke Skranga in matters of intelligence, but he had never fought a war, let alone participated in battle. "Prince Mythros, the idea is to defeat both principalities as quickly as possible before the other princes get themselves organized."

"The only other prince not aligned with our cause is Phaedron, and he is likely to remain neutral as long as possible. Mythros said. "Valthros, how do you intend to march through Bletha to get to them?"

"That is the easy part," Valthros replied. "We simply declare war on Prince Carthames and Prince Basilron, then we wait for them to come to us," He pointed to the map with his dagger. "To attack us, they have to move east. Both armies will have to swarm over the Princedom of Bletha to get to us and Niclophon will certainly allow them passage, since they are fighting for his throne. That means they will be tearing up his lands, annoying his subjects, eating his food and likely committing all of the usual atrocities normally reserved for the enemy. Secondly, we will know where they are coming from and where they are likely to stage their attacks. As long as Prince Phaedron maintains the neutrality that you anticipate, we will only have one front to defend."

"That assumes that they will come to us rather than wait for us to attack them."

"Oh, they will come, all right. Your Great King Niclophon will see to it. To do anything else would make him look weak."

Mythros did not look convinced. "Valthros, individually, neither Carthames nor Basilron have sufficient might to challenge me, but together…?"

"They still fall well short of the combined power of Pytha and Artigos. Add Zynophon and the battle will be rather one-sided, I should think. I also think their recent history of border wars will keep them from working well together. By inviting them both to war, they will be tripping all over each other to get to us. That too will work for our benefit."

Prince Mythros shook his head. "You forget about the Royal Army. It is larger than my own, and Niclophon will surely aid Basilron and Carthames."

"I should hope so. First, over half the Royal Army left a moon ago to join the Grand Host. Niclophon will be lucky to field ten thousand men. We could settle the matter once and for all if we eliminate all of our enemies together. That is where Prince Kosklos comes in. He is an experienced captain-general and with the army of Artigos the war of numbers is on our side. I almost wish we had additional enemies to make it more interesting."

"Are you insane?"

"Why do people keep asking me that?" Democriphon jested. "Mythros, even in an equal battle of numbers we will have the advantage of home ground. Never underestimate that."

"I fear I lack your confidence on that score."

"Good. Overconfidence will get a soldier killed very quickly. However, I am bringing some of Great King Kalvan's innovations to the battle: superior fireseed, close order drills, hit-and-run tactics, the element of surprise… I still don't understand why your people here in Hos-Bletha failed to use King Kalvan's formula. I imagine by the time Niclophon's allies came calling we will have some lethal surprises for them."

"Yes, the fireseed sample you provided is certainly superior to that which Styphon's House produces. Niclophon has made the production of your, uh, Kalvan's fireseed...illegal. Thus, allowing Styphon's House to provide all the fireseed for Hos-Bletha. You say we might be able to improve on the existing stores?"

Democriphon nodded. "I can personally attest to that. Still, it would be better if you started more of your own fireseed works. We can use the one you've already started as the training center. I have two fireseed makers who can oversee the process until you've trained enough artificers in its production. Now, I think you might consider having rapiers made and issued to the men as well. I have no suggestions for altering the pikes."

"I will put my best men on fireseed production; it's essential to the war effort. There won't be time to get those specialized boots made and issued. But I'll put my shoemakers to work on them." Mythros no longer looked like a drowning man looking for reeds to clutch. He was beginning to show more enthusiasm for Democriphon's plan. "I do not suppose you have any other ideas to aid us in our upcoming battle."

Democriphon smiled and used a quill pen to draw something on a piece of sheepskin. "These are called gun carriages. They will allow you to move the guns far faster than the carts typically used in this kingdom. We will mount the cannons on the carriages and secure sturdy wheels on the sides. The limber will attach the horses to the gun carriage. Unfortunately, we won't have time to cast very many new cannons with trunnions, but my artificers will work out a way to keep them on the gun carriages. A team of horses can pull a four- or six-pound gun faster than anything the enemy will have. Imagine all of your cannon moving into position after position almost as fast as your cavalry does."

Though not a soldier like many princes, Mythros could grasp the significance of what Democriphon was saying. "It would almost be magic. I'm beginning to understand how Hos-Hostigos has held out so long against such overwhelming odds. Wait! How do you keep the cannon from flying backwards on those wheels?"

"We use wheel chocks to stay the wheels. The spade"—he paused to point to the trail at the back of the carriage drawing—"digs into the ground and keeps the gun carriage from moving too far back. We will also use ropes and chains on the carriage to stake it to the ground before touching off the powder. If we need to move fast, we simply remove the chock blocks and release the chains. We can recover the stakes later if needed."

Mythros looked over the sketch, then nodded. "I will have my best blacksmiths and carriage builders put to work immediately. You may have to explain some of the details to them."

Democriphon shrugged.

"Is there any way you can help us make those…*rifles*?...before hostilities take place?"

Democriphon sighed. "I only wish I could. I know very little about gunsmithing, and even less about how to make rifles."

Mythros could not keep the disappointment from his voice. "Well, maybe after Great King Niclophon has been removed from his throne, I might speak with King Kalvan about acquiring some. Do you have any other innovations?"

"Indeed. Next we have earthworks for the castles."

Mythros raised an eyebrow rather than admit his ignorance.

Democriphon continued. "Kalvan showed our castellans how to fortify the walls against cannon balls with a sloping gradient of soft earth. The earth absorbs cannon fire and reduces most of the damage to the underlying stone walls."

Mythros looked at the rough sketch Democriphon made on a sheepskin. "What is to stop the cavalry from climbing up the embankment and going over the town walls?"

Democriphon reminded himself that Mythros had never been in a real battle, and probably never worn armor outside of standing at a military parade. "Have you ever tried to climb a hill in full armor, Your Highness? I doubt ten men in all of Hos-Bletha could do so and still have strength to fight." He idly wondered if his Chief Petty-Captain might be capable of such a feat, then set the thought aside. "However, we can pour water over the top when we see them coming. Climbing up over mud is impossible, with or without armor. If it rains, all the better for us."

The Prince nodded. "I see. Plus, hot oil and stones could be dropped on the cavalry as they rode up the incline."

"Exactly," Democriphon said with growing enthusiasm. "Next, we slow their gun transports by digging trenches all around the town walls just out of cannon range. We dig them two rods down and three rods across. That will stop their gun carts dead in their tracks until they either fill the gap or bridge it."

"Will that not also prevent us from chasing them with our own cannon?"

"Not at all, sire. We know what to expect and can have sturdy planks made for bridging. Next, we dig a second wider, deeper gap and fill it with water. This will be our moat and will slow the foot soldiers and horses."

Mythros looked over the drawing critically. "This will take a lot of work. I can have a nearby stream diverted to fill the moat, but the digging will take at least a moon. But only if we use the army itself."

"I believe we have that much time," Democriphon said. "Armies are not gathered and equipped overnight. It will take at least a moon-half for Carthames and Basilron to call up their levy and irregulars, I should think. We do not have time to cast more than a few new guns, unfortunately. But we will have to proof those you do have with the improved fireseed. It was wise of you to import guns from Hos-Zygros. You have the best cannon in Hos-Bletha."

"Not even Niclophon has as many cast guns as we do," Mythros replied.

*That's very good news*, Democriphon decided. "I am certain we can get better range with Hostigos fireseed; however, I am not so sure if your current designs will survive sustained usage."

"I will consult with my smiths. I believe something can be arranged. Do you have any other ideas?"

Democriphon smiled like a cat that had gotten the better of a particularly meaty pigeon. "Actually, I do, and this comes from my own camp. It will take a lot of bamboo, fireseed and men to bury it. I call it a bomb field, and you will love it. Now, first let us discuss mercenary recruitment. We want to start recruiting them before our declaration of war is issued."

# SIXTY

## I

First Captain Ranthar looked over the scraggly band of conmen and flim-flammers, wondering just what he had gotten himself into with this bunch. A moon of imprisonment in Prince Mythros' dungeons had done little to improve their appearance. It was base metal, but all he had to work with. Like Gypsies, who were spread out over almost all the Europo-American Subsector, the local sharpers were everywhere in the Six Kingdoms there was a copper phennig to be bent.

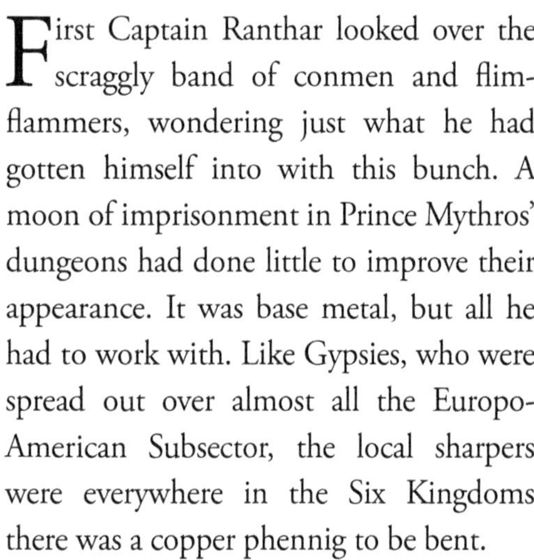

Their leader was a bandy-legged fellow with a curly-brown beard named Zentros. Ranthar decided to talk at him and study his reactions. It was probably the best way to gauge the reaction of the rest of the sharper band to his words. "Prince Mythros released all of you from his dungeons and into my hands for a specific reason. You are to work with the real Prince in Exile to get the word out that Prince Valthros has returned and is forming an army to remove the Regicide Niclophon and destroy the false temple of Styphon."

The last words got the best reaction.

All of the sharpers flinched at the name Styphon, like dogs that'd been whipped one too many times.

"You will spread the word far and near, mostly far, that the true Prince in Exile has been found and needs men to help him." Captain Ranthar turned to the map he had pinned to the wall. "Concentrate on Drathor, Syragon, Bletha and Eythros. The other princedoms are covered." *At least according to Uncle Wolf Syros.* "Let me make one thing very, very clear; you are to spread the information exactly as my officers give it to you—with no embellishments. We want men of fighting age, not their silver and gold. Should I learn that any of you have accepted more than food or lodging, I will have the offender skinned alive and staked out naked as the day he was born over an ant hill. Understood?"

Several of the sharpers turned white as a bedsheet.

Petty-Captain Gycules, who was standing to one side, pulled a mace out of his belt and whacked it a few times against his open hand. It made a meaty thud.

Every man in the room shouted a resounding "*yes, sir.*"

"You will be paid for your efforts by me, and only me," Ranthar added for emphasis. "You will each be given a horse and a purse with enough money to get by on until you finish your mission. When you return, you will each be given ten ounces of gold."

Ranthar could feel the breath go out of the room. Ten ounces of gold was more than many of them had ever seen at one time, and could carry a man for the better part of a year. "Now, I realize some of you will find the urge to run away almost too much to resist. Resist you shall!" Ranthar plunged a dagger into a table for effect. He then took out a rolled sheepskin and unfurled it. On it was a charcoal sketch of their leader Zentros' face, front and side, much like a Wanted poster. It was an excellent likeness made by one of Vanir's men.

"Each of you will sit and have your likenesses copied onto parchment. Should any decide to run off, these parchments shall be circulated throughout the Six Kingdoms. You will never be able to run a game on anybody ever again, and will likely be killed if you try."

Ranthar dropped the sketch on the table. "Before you go, you will be trained as soldiers. This is as much for your protection as our own. You will be sent into various provinces in pairs. This is also for your own protection. Should you meet other sharpers, you will not tell them where you came from, what you are doing or why. Just spread the word in your assigned areas then return for payment and possibly a new assignment. Any questions?"

Nobody spoke.

"Very well. Report to your petty-captains for training. When he determines that you're ready, I will arrange for your equipment and assignments. Dismissed."

It took some of them a few moments to realize they were expected to depart and see their petty-officer until they noticed some of their brethren, who had served as soldiers or mercenaries, getting up and leaving.

Uncle Wolf Syros entered as the last of the sharpers exited. "Fomenting rebellion amongst the enemy, Ranthar?"

"As much as possible, Uncle Wolf."

"Good." Syros nodded. "You should also have them remind everybody that shortly Styphon's House will be under the Ban of Galzar and any princedom that works with Styphon's Own Guard will also be under the ban."

Ranthar's brow went up. "Let us know when the conclave in Agrys City puts Styphon's House under the ban. That would be useful in keeping the manure eaters out of it. Of course, the Styphoni have enough on their plate with Kalvan in the north. However, we'll have to deal with the two Bands of Styphon's Own Guard first."

"Why first?"

"What?"

"Why do you have to deal with Styphon's Own Guard first?" the Uncle Wolf repeated. "They do not know who or where you are. What is more, should they learn of temple raids in other princedoms, they will certainly go there in search of you and your fellow bandits."

Ranthar thought on it. Luring the enemy away from the village certainly had a lot of merit to it, and after a couple raids—provided they were successful—they would have more fireseed to meet the enemy with.

Unfortunately, it also meant they might not be able to choose the time and place of the encounter. After some thought, Ranthar decided to go with Uncle Wolf Syros' suggestion.

"By leading the Styphoni away, we protect Mallegast and its people. I cannot say no to that. It also gives us a chance to acquire some much needed fireseed, even if it is the poorer quality stuff. As soon as the new recruits are trained, we make for Drathor."

"I will be with you," Syros said, "even though I cannot join in on the fighting. Oh, that reminds me, have you seen Gasphros? I have been all over the village and can find no sign of him anywhere."

Ranthar searched his eidetic memory and recalled that he saw the bard leave on horseback a few days ago. He said as much.

"I just wanted his help in working with the sharpers," Syros said. "I hope he is staying out of trouble and returns soon."

## II

The shadows had grown long by the time Baron Althaphon returned to his keep. It had been a long journey from Tarr-Beshta and he had hated every moment of it. War was coming, and while it had yet to be declared, The King was preparing his army. Part of that preparation was summoning the levies of men from his vassals, like Baron Althaphon. His biggest concern was about who would lead his men. Kythar his oldest son was seventeen winters old and now a grown man.

*I'm getting too fat and comfortable to ride into battle*, he decided. *Let it be Kythar's turn in the saddle. I will pray to Galzar that he lives to bring home the spoils of battle.*

The Baron poured some wine then settled into his favorite chair. He was about to drink when it occurred to him that he might not be alone. "You can come out, now, Gasphros. I have been expecting you."

He waited a moment. When nothing happened he sighed and took a drink only to spit it out violently. "What in Hadron's Name?!"

"That was some very expensive brandy you just sprayed on the floor,

Your Grace."

"*Brandy?* Damn my eyes, what is that? And why didn't you step out when I called?"

Gasphros stepped out of the shadows. "I wanted to be certain as to whether you really knew I was here, or were simply guessing. And that brandy was brought here from Hos-Hostigos at no small expense. It is called Ermut's Best and if you give it a chance I think you will find it very good. However, I advise that you sip rather than gulp it."

The bard helped himself to a silver goblet and poured a brandy for himself. "To your health, Your Grace."

Althaphon watched as Gasphros gingerly took a swallow. Satisfied that the draught was not poisoned, he followed the bard's example. "It burns as it goes down. Oh! It does have a kick. I could grow to like this very quickly."

Gasphros nodded. "I could arrange for another bottle or two, I think, but our supply is low."

"So you want my help in bringing more in?"

Gasphros started at the thought. "Sadly, it is too late for that at the moment. One would have to infiltrate the Grand Host of Styphon to reach Hostigos. It would be a long and dangerous trek. It does strike me that you have the resources to make it here at your winery. Just keep that besotted brother of yours well away from it."

"So you are here on business?"

"Well, yes, but not for brandy production. That is simply an enticement for your aid," the bard admitted.

Althaphon tried to take another drink only to find his chalice empty. He poured another draught. "You hardly need to entice me, Gasphros. I owe you a favor and I am a man of my word, at least when it is not given under duress. You helped me out of a rather tight spot and I am ready to return the favor. What would you have of me?"

Gasphros had expected no less and was pleased that his assessment of the Baron was not in error. "Tell me, have you restarted your fireseed works?"

"I have, and in a more remote location to avoid further interference from Styphon's own fools. They could come and search until the Golden Temple in Balph falls into ruins, and still find nothing." Althaphon held up his drink in a mock salute to the bard before downing it.

"Excellent. I am in a position to acquire as much as you can provide. Moreover, as speed is essential, I can pay for it with gold. I would also like to buy whatever grain, meat, fruit and animal feed you can sell me."

Althaphon put his chalice down. He was starting to feel the effects and wanted to keep his head clear. One did not discuss business while besotted. "This is not a favor; this is simply good business for me. How much do you want and how soon do you need it?"

"All you can provide. Immediately would not be too soon. And this is where the favor comes in; I need you to transport the barrels to the Blethan/Pythan border. There, my confederates will take charge of the shipment."

"Hmm…that sounds accep— But…wait! You want me to supply fireseed to Prince Mythros! I am sorry, Gasphros, but my oath of fealty prohibits such an action."

Gasphros nodded. "I understand, and want to assure you that your oath will remain unbroken. My confederates will not be taking a direct hand in the coming war. Yes, I know about that. The fireseed will not go to Prince Mythros or any in his employ."

"No?" Althaphon looked puzzled. He knew Gasphros well enough to know that he was not a liar. "Then why do you even need it?"

"I cannot give you specifics; however, I can say that this fireseed will be used against Styphon's House in the most direct manner possible."

The baron mulled the statement over in his mind. Was Gasphros going to give the fireseed to the Hostigi? It would have to travel a long way, first through the Princedoms of Taurnos, Artigos, then through Hos-Ktemnos. Besides, Kalvan had disclosed the fireseed secret in the first place. No, that didn't make sense. Kalvan should be sitting on tons of it. Then again, the Hostigi had been at almost constant war for the last several winters. Their supplies of fireseed could easily be running low. "If you cannot tell me where the fireseed is going, what can you tell me?"

Gasphros paused as he considered the matter. "I can only say that the fireseed is earmarked for those who hate the Styphoni, and will be used in a manner consistent with that. I will swear an oath that it will not be willingly turned over to Prince Mythros, although some may end up with him."

"I have no problem with that," the Baron said, nodding.

"Moreover, I will vow that none shall know the source of the fireseed; not even my confederates. That way if anybody is captured and tortured, they cannot give you up."

"And if you are captured?"

Gasphros laughed. "Come now, who can capture a bard?"

"My men did, once," Althaphon pointed out.

"No," Gasphros shook his head. "They found your daughter after she ignored my warnings to avoid the dress shop. I allowed myself to be caught rather than let her be taken alone."

The Baron recalled that Marisol had been found in a dress shop and Gasphros was caught while trying to free her. Or was he…? "Hmm. Oh, what the Styphon. May I have your oath on this?"

Gasphros said, "I swear to these terms, by the Twelve True Gods. If my word be false, let me be cast into the darkest Cavern in Regwarn."

"Very well. I can easily arrange for what you ask. But mark this well, if I find you have lied to me and broken your oath, there is no place in the Five…make that Six Kingdoms where you can escape my wrath."

Gasphros smiled wide. "Good. Then I have nothing to fear, for my word is as good as yours in this and all things. Shall we drink to our agreement?"

"Right after I put this to parchment," the Baron said. "I do not trust my memory with this brandy of yours."

# SIXTY-ONE

"Your Highness, before the strategy session begins, please tell me everything you know about the Kingdom's princes?" Democriphon asked.

Prince Mythros nodded and took a seat across from Democriphon. "Certainly. It is good to know one's enemy. Carthames is one prince I thought we could have won to our side. He hates the Styphoni almost as much as we do; not for religious reasons, but because Prince Basilron took a large loan from them during the border dispute between Drathor and Syragon some years ago. Carthames was close to victory when Styphon's House supplied Basilron with fireseed, weapons and enough mercenaries to bring the war to a standstill. Carthames petitioned Styphon's House for additional fireseed only to be denied. There was a sulfur spring in Syragon that the Styphoni want and could not allow Basilron to lose it.

"However, as much as Carthames hates the Styphoni, he is even more loyal to King Niclophon. The Prince takes his oath of fealty very seriously and refuses to break it. I had hoped that after showing him Valthros, the true great king, he would accept that his oath was given to the wrong man. Sadly, that was not to be."

Democriphon nodded. "This is just as well. When we defeat him in battle, we can trust any oaths he makes to us. An honorable enemy is preferable to a dishonorable friend. You always know exactly where you stand with them."

"Wise words," Mythros agreed. "Now, Basilron is a different story. He started the border war with Carthames out of simple avarice. He thinks only to increase his own holdings and is not concerned with the rightful holdings of his neighbors. Fortunately, he's also a poor tactician and is slow to follow the advice of his captain-generals. When Carthames proved to be a more powerful adversary than he had originally believed, Basilron nearly bankrupted himself fighting battles from which he should have withdrawn. If not for Styphon's House's intervention, Carthames might well have defeated him and taken over his realm.

"That war, even with Styphon's House's help, has left Syragon financially strapped. No doubt Prince Basilron thinks he can recoup his losses by joining with Carthames and sacking the other princedoms, all in the name of defending the kingdom. One other thing; Basilron's word is not to be trusted. He will seek out any excuse to ignore his obligations and will twist the wording of any accord if he feels it is to his advantage."

"Then Prince Basilron must not be allowed to survive the war," Democriphon said. "Styphoni sympathizers and self-aggrandizing fools are a liability to the realm."

Mythros nodded morosely. "I should not wish for the death of a fellow prince, but Basilron brings shame to the title."

Democriphon thought about some of the princes he had known back in Hos-Hostigos. Some, even as enemies, were good men who could be trusted. Even Gormoth of Nostor was as good as his word. He paid the ransoms of his captured underlings even when the realm's stocks of gold and silver were low. Sarrask of Sask, once a vicious enemy, became a great friend and ally to Hostigos. Hopefully, the same could be said of some of the princes here in Hos-Bletha after the dust settled.

Democriphon knew that no war was completely certain. Kalvan said many times: "No battle plan ever survived first contact with the enemy." For that reason, Democriphon wanted to keep Mallegast out of the firing line, leaving their headquarters free to bedevil Styphon's House. At best, it might force them to use some of their troops to guard the Blethan temples.

"Tell me about Prince Phaedron."

Mythros considered his words carefully. "Phaedron is ambivalent where Styphon's House is concerned. To be fair, the Styphoni have yet to step on his toes, nor he on theirs. His subjects are permitted to worship as they like, which is mostly Dralm, Galzar and Styphon. Dralm worship has been waning throughout Hos-Bletha, but Yirtta Allmother, the Fertility Goddess, is still highly favored and respected. The great storms that bedevil the coast have done much to keep the worship of Lytris, the Weather Goddess, important to sailors and fishermen.

"Phaedron dislikes Great King Niclophon for personal reasons, though he never confided in me what they are. He is a somewhat prudish man with little patience for certain behavior. He can be very prickly where court etiquette is concerned. Somehow, he obtained proof that Niclophon dallies with other men and used that knowledge to secure a high position for his son, Theodoros, in the Royal Army. For this reason alone, he may feel bound to join hostilities against us, although he might simply have Theodoros recalled in order to keep him safe."

Democriphon made a mental note to capture all enemy captain-generals alive, if possible, until they found this Theodoros. He could be used as leverage against his father.

"In terms of sheer numbers, I command the greatest army, next to the Royal Army, of course. Prince Phaedron's army is mostly tied down to watchtowers and selected forts because of the tremendous amount of shoreline he needs to defend against the Caribi barbarians. Caribi prefer to attack from the sea and do so often. Phaedron maintains a garrison near every town and village within ten marches of the shore. Like the rest of the kingdom, Phaedron has to purchase fireseed from Styphon's House in order to keep his garrisons at full readiness. Unlike most of the principalities, he strictly adheres to Niclophon's command that fireseed shall not be brought in from outside of Hos-Bletha, nor made by anyone other than Styphon's House.

"Most of us simply buy enough fireseed to satisfy the Styphoni, then make our own in secret. The border war between Syragon and Drathor occurred before Great King Kalvan's arrival and the dissemination of the Fireseed Mystery. Prince Basilron is the only Prince I know of, other than Prince Phaedron, who doesn't make his own fireseed."

"It could go badly for us if Phaedron threw in with Niclophon with his full might," Democriphon noted.

"I doubt that will happen," Mythros countered. "In order to do that, he would have to leave all of his shoreline undefended. By war's end, Prince Phaedron might well return home only to find out that Caribi and Swamp Ruthani had raided and sacked most of his princedom's towns and villages. Phaedron is no stranger to fighting, but I do not see him aiding Niclophon at the cost of his own realm. At most, he could field a third of his military forces under Niclophon's banner. A sizeable number, but far short of what I can bring to bear even without our allies."

"What about the island of Lydros? Does he have a large army there?"

Mythros shook his head. "Lydros is a rich land, but a poor holding. It is home to many Ruthani, many of whom give succor to the Caribi. It is barely tamed and mostly occupied by second sons and mercenaries, who have no troops to spare for their prince."

"Good. Now it is our allies I want to learn more about. Tell me first about Prince Kosklos of Artigos."

Mythros chuckled. "Kosklos is a warrior born and bred. There are stories that claim he killed two water snakes while still in his crib. He is a fierce fighter, a strong tactician, and less interested in treasure than glory."

"Glory?" Democriphon felt a chill go down his back. He had heard the same said of him back in Hostigos.

"Yes. He does not go looking for battles to fight, but when one finds him, he is all in and to Regwarn with any that ask for quarter. He leads his men from the front and often draws first blood. His men love him like a brother for it. He also never leaves a man behind if he can do anything to prevent it. No prince ever gained more loyalty from his men, soldiers and mercenaries alike, than Kosklos. However, you do not want him at your back in a battle."

"No?"

The Prince laughed heartily. "No. For he's likely to trample over you to get at the enemy. I have heard that he wanted to join in the northern wars when your Lord Kalvan first appeared there. After the Battle of Fyk, he wanted to meet this upstart Lord Kalvan whom everyone was talking about. King Niclophon had to practically sit on him to keep him from leaving Hos-Bletha."

"Oh? Did he want to join the Hostigi?"

"No, at that time he wanted to meet and defeat them."

"What?"

"Do understand, Kosklos cares nothing about politics outside of his own realm. However, he does like a challenge, and at that time, your Great King was the biggest challenge around. He took a single upstart princedom low on fireseed and defeated Nostor and Sask in a single season. Kosklos admires and respects Kalvan. That is why he wanted to beat him in battle. Since then he has found two others he considers to be worthy opponents; Grand Master Soton and some upstart captain-general named Phidestros. He does like a challenge."

"Indeed! I will have to devise a plan that uses Kosklos' talents without having them trip us up. Now what about Prince Vythron?"

"Vythron cares not who is king as long as it is the right king."

"Excuse me?"

"Prince Vythron voted Niclophon onto the throne when there were no other apparent heirs. Niclophon had the correct lineage, so he was acceptable. Vythron is a traditionalist. Now, however, he has been given proof that there is an heir, so Niclophon's title is illegal in his eyes. He has no love of war, but will fight one to see that you are seated on the Silver Throne as custom and tradition demand. He is a solid supporter of what is proper, at least in his eyes, and will stand side by side with us to the end.

"Unfortunately, he is not a warrior like you and Kosklos. He suffers from the Bleeders Disease, so even a shallow cut could kill him. His carriage is lined with silken pillows to keep him from bruising, and his private chambers are specially constructed to have naught but rounded edges and cushioned surfaces anywhere he might fall or injure himself. His mother's uncle, elder brother and younger sister also suffered from this malady and died because of it. Having no other siblings or heirs, every care is taken by his retainers regarding their prince's health and safety."

*Which is probably why he wore full armor in the meeting*, Democriphon surmised. "What about the rumors I've heard that he was in league with the Caribi?"

"Nonsense," Mythros snarled. "They don't attack his lands because they rarely travel that far north on their raiding expeditions. Styphon's House's galleys also patrol that area."

"Now for Prince Xandros."

A look of disgust twisted Mythros' face. "I shouldn't speak thus about a fellow prince and ally, but the man is a swine. He cares far more for his personal indulgences than the people he rules. His army is the smallest of all the princes in Hos-Bletha, yet he takes the panther's share of the crops produced by his subjects as taxes, takes the comeliest wenches from the towns and villages to fill his harem and even instituted The Lord's Privilege."

"Lord's Privilege? I have not heard of this before."

Mythros grimaced and said, "It means that he or any other noble in his realm may take the bride of any of his subjects to his bed on her wedding night. None below the rank of baron may refuse their Lord this right."

He was shocked. "Niclophon permits this?"

"The Great King cares little what a prince does within their own realm, provided tribute is paid and levies are met."

Democriphon's lack of respect for Niclophon was growing. The Great King provided few benefits for his princes, and even less for his common subjects. It brought home something that Kalvan had once said, when discussing former Great King Kaiphranos, about negligent rulers being nearly as detrimental as bad ones. "I see. What else can you tell me about Xandros."

"Do not trust him. Though he controls the smallest lands and fewest subjects, still, his wealth is great. Partly from over-taxation, but mostly from the secret deals he makes. During the Drathor/Syragon war, Prince Xandros made hundreds of thousands of ounces in silver and gold by supplying victuals to both Carthames and Basilron. He also provided information to both sides. Had he chosen one side or the other the war would have ended in a few moons. Instead, they battled for two winters, partly due to Xandros facilitating the pact between Styphon's House and Basilron. He even trades with the Ruthani and the Urgothi barbarians for animal hides, paying them in food and weapons that allow them to continue their raids against the rest of us."

"I don't understand," Democriphon said. "If you know all of this, why haven't the rest of the princes put an end to Xandros' rule? Surely, all of the princes of Hos-Bletha in common purpose could force even a do-nothing like Great King Niclophon to get off his arse."

"Actually, only I know the full extent of Xandros' perfidy, and only because I have an intelligencer planted in his castle. I cannot tell the others without their wondering if I have similar agents in their own castles."

Democriphon refrained from asking if he did.

"Another reason is that Xandros gives extravagant gifts to Niclophon to ensure his continuing favor."

Democriphon digested this disturbing piece of information, deciding he would be making special plans to guard against Xandros' potential betrayal.

# SIXTY-TWO

## I

Skranga reread the parchment before him over and over. It was a message from one of Chancellor Archimanes' informants offering information on an upcoming war. The sender wanted gold, fireseed and slaves, mostly female, for the information he would provide. Skranga rolled it back up and set it down having decided to send it off to Ranthar. It was too dangerous to send Calthros to Pytha Town now and Ranthar would know what to do. There was a polite knock at the door before Calthros poked his head inside.

"Your Worship, are you prepared to accept guests?"

Calthros blinked rapidly suggesting that it would be advisable to accept the guests. Skranga nodded and Calthros escorted several men dressed in the yellow robes of highpriests. It appeared that most of the temple masters within a hundred marches had arrived together. The highpriests all bowed at the waist and said, "Your Worship."

"Please be seated," Skranga said. He wanted to keep formalities at a minimum to avoid any mistakes in protocol. "Your Worships, how may I be of service?"

The priests looked confused until Calthros spoke up. "His Worship Sangar would prefer to keep things informal. Please speak your needs plainly."

One undernourished looking specimen spoke up. "Your Worship, we have learned that several princes are calling for the removal of Niclophon, and are preparing for war."

"Your name?"

The priest looked worried. "Highpriest Kyllos, Your Worship."

"Yes, Kyllos, I am not unaware of this development," Skranga said. "War is good for business, as long as we are not directly involved in it. Our fireseed sales will grow and I expect that we will be called upon to make loans to the various factions."

"This is so, and it is good, Your Worship," he replied. "However, Styphon's Own Guard has requested to join in the battles to come."

"Indeed?"

"Yes, Your Worship. They believe that the coming war could be the beginning of a Daemon Kalvan inspired revolution."

*Interesting*, thought Skranga as he tried to think of how to capitalize on it. "The Daemon Kalvan has transgressed against Styphon's House as no man before has ever done. He has dealt the Temple the worst blow possible by revealing the Fireseed Mystery. In response, the Temple is assembling the greatest army in the memory of man to bring the Daemon to bay and destroy him and his kind. The Usurper will soon be brought to justice: so what further harm could he do to us?"

"None, we are sure, Highpriest Sangar," admitted another temple master. "Still, our guardsmen have been disturbed by how the rebels have been beheading our priests and sacking our temples."

He addressed the highpriest directly. "The bulk of our military might labors in the north. Here in Hos-Bletha Styphon's Own Guard are few and widely scattered. If I were to allow you, each of you and more, to send your squads of Styphon's Own Guard to fight in the coming war, what might happen to your temples?" The priests looked back and forth at each other as if this was an event they had not considered.

"Exactly," Skranga continued. "The raiders could learn of it and see it as an invitation." *A damned good one, too!* "Our first duty is to the One God, Styphon, and our second is to Styphon's House Upon Earth."

"Your Worship, Sangar," spoke a third priest, "I am Highpriest Tyros. What if Hos-Bletha becomes divided, as happened in Hos-Harphax, or worse, is conquered by the rebels?"

Skranga raised his eyes to the ceiling as if he were seeking answers from the Skypalace of Styphon Himself. "Then, after we have removed the head of the Daemon Kalvan, we shall retake Hos-Bletha and restore the natural order of things."

The highpriests looked unconvinced.

Skranga had a flash of inspiration. "However, we can still work to help Great King Niclophon. I want each of you to prepare several wagons of victuals, gold, silver and fireseed. Especially fireseed. I will have my personal guardsmen take them to where they will do the most good."

"Your Worship, you will be left unprotected!" Highpriest Kyllos cried out.

"Nonsense, my child," Skranga said softly. "As a guest of Great King Niclophon, I could not be safer."

"What if some harm befalls your guardsmen, Your Worship?" asked another priest who had not yet given his name.

"There are several Bands of Styphon's Own Guard coming from the Holy City to deal with the bandits and raiders," Skranga replied. "When their mission has been concluded, the uprising and attacks against our temples will be over."

"Is this true, Your Worship?"

"Yes, Kyllos. I was ordered to keep that information private, however, I can see that all of you need to know it as well. See to it that no one speaks of this after you leave." Skranga looked balefully at the priests until they all averted their gaze. "Now, have your wagons filled and prepared for transport by, hmm, within the moon-quarter. Send your wagons and transports to Bletha Town where my men will take charge of them."

"Yes, Your Worship!" the priests spoke as one.

"Oh, and it might go better for our interests if the other temples in this region also contribute. Say nothing to any save yourselves and the other temple masters. For I fear the wagging of tongues will be our death."

Calthros served wine to the priests and they spoke casually for a candle, then they left for their temples to prepare the wagons.

"Your Worship?"

"Yes, Calthros?" Skranga said as he put quill to parchment.

"I am in awe of you, right now, Your Worship."

"As all men should be, my child," Skranga chuckled. He fanned the document until the ink dried, then he rolled up the parchment and handed it to Calthros. "You should take this to Ranthar immediately. He has much to prepare for."

## II

"Prince Xandros, once the enemy is on the move your forces will engage the enemy from the north. This is called a 'pincer movement.'" Democriphon looked around the room. Everybody looked tired except for Prince Kosklos. "I think that will do for the day."

Everybody sighed in relief and started out of the room. Democriphon placed a restraining hand on Kosklos' chest.

"Is there something you need from me, Prince Valthros?"

"Indeed I do, and I believe you will enjoy it," Democriphon said. "You may have noticed that I left you little to do in the upcoming battles."

"I did, but thought it best not to question you in front of the others."

Democriphon's respect for the young warrior raised another notch. "Actually, I encourage questions, but in this instance you acted correctly. I want you to ready your troops for a three-sided strategy."

"Your Majesty?"

"You will divide your army into three divisions. One quarter of your army is to remain in Artigos to guard against possible attacks."

Kosklos nodded.

"A second quarter is to assist myself and Prince Mythros here in Tarr-Pytha."

"Are you certain the enemy will obligingly come to us, Your Highness?" Kosklos asked hesitantly, as if he didn't want to criticize his strategy.

"Indeed I am. We are seceding from Hos-Bletha. We do not need to go anywhere to do that. However, to stop us from breaking away, King Niclophon's loyalists will have to come to us. So, yes, I am very confident that they will come here."

Kosklos' face went blank as he considered his new king's logic. "I have to concur, Your Majesty."

"Good. Now comes the most important part; I want you to take the remaining half of your army into Drathor and conquer it while Prince Carthames and Basilron are here attacking us in Tarr-Pytha."

"That is an excellent plan." Kosklos looked at the map, then his king. "However, my division will be a rather large fighting force, Your Majesty. We can hardly travel from one end of Hos-Bletha to the other without being noticed."

"Of course not. But you only have to move your troops from Artigos to Drathor; all the other princedoms you pass through belong to our allies. They will be forewarned that your troops will be on the move. Lead this division yourself. March only at night, keep swords and armor covered, hide in the forests and marshes during the day when you sleep. Divide the army into small units that will draw less attention. Disguise some as Styphoni. None will question you. You can disguise others as slave caravans. People actually pretend not to see them. You will have to leave soon to be in place when the battle starts."

Once again, Prince Kosklos' face went blank. Democriphon knew that the warrior prince did that to keep others from guessing what he was thinking; he did the same.

Finally, he broke into a smile. "By Galzar's Bloody Mace, this is a plan I can sink my teeth into, Your Majesty. By my sworn word, I will keep your plans in confidence."

"Excellent. Now let us join the others before they finish off the last of the winter wine."

## III

Ranthar couldn't wait any longer. Gasphros would have to be found, and quickly. The bard might have been captured and was being tortured for information. Ranthar wrote down his choice for a search party. He had just finished when he heard a commotion outside of the Town Hall. *Now what?* He stood up from his desk, little more than a table with a chest of drawers at the end, and went to the front entrance of the hall.

Coming through the main gate was Gasphros on a big bay horse that was blowing hard, its flanks lathered. The bard fairly leaped from his mount and ran to the Town Hall. He did not stop until he almost collided with Ranthar.

"Captain, I need some men to assist me in transporting some goods… and a fresh horse!"

"What goods?" Ranthar had been prepared to vent his spleen on the errant troubadour. Now, curiosity took the forefront in his mind. "And where have you been?"

"Out securing fireseed, victuals and supplies," Gasphros explained. "Oh, I will need gold enough to pay for it all." The bard pulled a scroll from his tunic and held it out to Ranthar. "This is an accounting of the costs, including the wagons and animals as we will not be likely to return them soon."

Ranthar took the scroll and read it. Grain, meat, wagons, horses, and best of all—fireseed! "I'll be slobber-knackered!" he exclaimed, hugging the troubadour and dancing a jig. "This couldn't have come at a better time."

The price was somewhat high, but easily manageable. The expedition's pay-chests were bulging from their temple takings. "I should have you flogged for being absent without my leave. Instead, I will pour you some Ermut's Best and recommend you for a medal. How soon must you leave to receive these goods?"

"Two candles ago," Gasphros said. "But I'll need some wagoners, too."

"Where are all these goods and fireseed coming from?" he asked.

Gasphros shrugged. "It's a long story, Captain. Let's just say that a Blethan Baron has been making his own fireseed on the sly. When I chanced upon Baron Althaphon's operation, he decided that it would be preferable to sell it to us at a profit, rather than face Styphon's House's wrath."

"A wise decision. And good timing since Democ—, I mean Prince Valthros has need of large quantities of fireseed at the moment." He turned to his manservant who had followed him to the gate. "See that our intrepid wanderer has a tankard of ale while I gather my list."

Ranthar ran back into the Town Hall, then returned with the parchment he had been working on. "Gather these men together, and whatever else you need. I will get your money from the paymaster."

*Great leaders are made by even better followers, Uncle Wolf Syros always said. Well, in that case, I think I'm looking fairly good just now.*

## IV

Prince Xandros, having returned to Tarr-Zynophon, considered his options. He had already sent his offer of services to the Inner Circle of Styphon's House and was awaiting his response. He considered sending a similar letter to Great King Niclophon in the hopes of gaining even more treasure, then thought better of it. Great Kings and Archpriests of Styphon's House possessed very little patience for those that double dealt with them. For now, he would simply play along with Mythros and Valthros—if indeed he were the true Orphan Prince—and wait for Styphon's House to respond.

The battle plan seemed vague to him, but that was in part because no one knew how much weight Styphon's House—now preparing to invade Hos-Hostigos—would bring to the table. Tarr-Syklos, the Zarthani Knights' southernmost fortress, was not open for inspection, but reports from Drathor suggested that the Sixteenth and Twenty-Third Lances had departed and only the Thirty-First Lance remained. From all reports, the Order's contribution to the Grand Host of Styphon's House had left their great border fortress with minimal reserves.

He understood that the declaration of war was made in Prince Mythros' and the Pretender Valthros names. This was to make Tarr-Pytha the focus of the war effort. That left the other princedoms able to work on other strategies.

Prince Kosklos was tasked with doing some sort of troop movement designed to take the attackers by surprise. That made no sense to him as Kosklos' army would be marching though Zynophon instead of the southern edge of Pytha, using that pincer movement that Valthros seemed so proud of.

He possessed some martial training, and to his nose the plan smelled wrong. He considered the possibility that Valthros knew nothing of how to make war. Prince Mythros had never taken part in a battle, so he was little wiser. However boorish the barbarian Kosklos was, he was a born warrior who knew how to fight a war. *How did he get sucked into a battle plan that seemed to all but eliminate him from the battle?*

Xandros poured a stein of Ermut's Best that he had snuck out of Mythros' stores. Instead of sipping, he took great swallows, enjoying the burning sensation that ran down his throat and into his gullet. By the bottom of the third goblet he realized what Valthros was really up to. *The jumped-up cockerel is sending Kosklos on a separate mission, and leaving me out of his plans! He suspects treachery, possibly from me, and keeps his true battle plans hidden from those that are not a part of them.*

He struggled to stand only to be overcome by his indulgence, falling back in his seat he lapsed into unconsciousness. When Xandros awoke the next morning, all thought of Valthros' treachery was lost in the blur of his burning throat and throbbing head.

## V

Calthros narrowly avoided being trampled as Gasphros and several mounted men raced out of the gates of Mallegast. *What in Styphon's black heart was that all about?* Dusting himself off, he turned back to the gates and waited for the challenge. Formalities settled, Calthros was escorted in to see Captain Ranthar at the Town Hall.

The former underpriest took in everything as he walked through the village. The buildings were mostly completed, people filled the streets and in the hos-plazos a company of freemen trained with pike, sword and arquebus. It would be idyllic were it not for the danger it masked.

He found Ranthar at his makeshift desk scribbling away at some parchment with a feather quill. When Ranthar failed to notice him, he cleared his throat politely. Ranthar looked up and smiled.

"Calthros, this is a good day for unexpected visitors. I hope things are going well for Skranga and Eldra," Ranthar said. Then he took a more serious tone. "Has Skranga managed to find some fireseed for us? Gasphros managed to arrange for some, but I fear it will not be enough."

"I daresay he has, sir," Calthros said lightly. "And more."

"More?"

"A Temple Band of Styphon's Own Guard—our pseudo-guard, that is—is escorting several hundred casks of fireseed, victuals and treasure and will be here in about ten candles. I rode ahead to insure you would not be surprised and react badly."

Ranthar motioned Calthros to a chair. "Several hundred casks! Where did he get it?"

Calthros explained about Skranga's meeting the temple masters.

"So 'where they will do the most good' is what he told them—ha! Kalvan chose his people well for this mission. We shall indeed see to it that these supplies are very well used. Why bother with the treasure, though? We already have enough gold to buy a principality."

"His Worship, the divine Sangar said, and I quote, 'anything we can take away from the Styphoni, even if we do not need it, can only be to our advantage.' Oh, and a third of the treasure is to be kept separate for His Worship's expenses."

"Expenses!" Ranthar laughed. "That old horse thief hasn't had to spend a pfennig since he put on those robes. He is creating a nest egg for the duchy he plans to run when this is all over. Well, so what? He's more than earned it. I am only surprised that he only wants to hold back a third." Ranthar dismissed the subject, and switched to another topic. "How long before we send 'Styphon's Own Guard' back to Bletha Town?"

Calthros pulled out a scroll. "This is from Skranga. In short, you have command of the Temple Band until your raids are completed."

"Really?" Ranthar felt like he was a kid at Year-End Day. *The equivalent of three full companies of trained mercenaries on top of a thousand freemen volunteers and my bandit crew. Oh, yes, and the criminals sent down by Democriphon.* "If the real Styphon's Own Guard from Balph catches up with us—well, now we can give them a real fight!"

"His Worship rather thought you would appreciate the help," Calthros said. "It also solves the problem he has been having with the men. We were not able to stage the false battle that the two of you had discussed about rotating the men between our camps. Now all the pseudo-guardsmen under our command can join you and take part in the next conflict. And get their share of the battle spoils."

"I suspect there will be plenty of that," Ranthar said in a low voice. "We leave tomorrow for Drathor."

# SPRING

# SIXTY-THREE

## I

The lands around Pytha Town, once green and verdant, were now ravaged beyond recognition. All the trees within eight marches had been chopped down. Democriphon looked out from the battlements of Tarr-Pytha and nodded with satisfaction. The clear cutting and brush removal they had done would prevent far worse from happening later.

Unlike the northern kingdoms which had killed all the local Ruthani, the Hos-Blethans were still subjected to attacks by the native inhabitants, both Ruthani and Caribi—and occasionally by invading nomads from the Sea of Grass, a generational event that had most recently occurred the previous summer. Huge stone walls and battlements were a necessity for any major town or population center that didn't want to be robbed of its possessions or find its inhabitants carted off into slavery.

The walls surrounding Pytha Town were now fortified with uncounted tons of earth, which would be able to absorb cannon fire with minimal damage. A moat, preceding the earthworks, would slow any foot soldiers attempting to scale the dirt, which would be practically impossible in full armor. There was always the possibility that some brave souls might shed their armor plate and attempt the climb, or use Ruthani irregulars who wore very little in the way of armor. For them, with the stroke of a sword, logs fastened with ropes were ready to roll down and crush any oncoming foe.

At just beyond cannon range a trench two lances wide and a lance deep would keep the gun carts from approaching the castle without great effort on the part of the attackers. Either the gap would have to be filled in with earth and stone or heavy planks would have to be brought in to bridge the gap. Such planks were not part of the standard equipment carried by armies in Hos-Bletha.

Between the trench and the moat, Democriphon arranged for a special surprise. A foot beneath the ground resided an interlocking network of bamboo. Bamboo packed to capacity with the last of Kalvan's fireseed, which yielded a third more explosive power than Styphon's Best.

Democriphon wanted to keep the bomb field in reserve. Secret weapons worked best by remaining secret as long as possible. Besides, there was the possibility that somebody could make the connection between what happened at 'Highpriest Sangar's' ransoming and a similar conflagration at Tarr-Pytha.

"Admiring your handiwork, Valthros?" Prince Mythros asked.

Democriphon turned to the voice. "Inspecting them would be more accurate. We will not have a second chance to address any faults when Princes Carthames and Basilron arrive."

Mythros nodded. "True. I have just received a report from one of my intelligencers. Carthames and his army are on the move. We expect that he will meet up with Basilron's forces in a moon-quarter, then they will all proceed here en masse."

"As we expected." Democriphon looked back out over the surrounding grounds. It was still late winter and the fields were bare. "Do we have enough victuals to feed the townspeople for at least a moon?"

"Yes. And that's not counting all the livestock we have been able to put in the stables. The dungeons you obligingly emptied are now used to house those subjects whose homes were in harm's way."

"That is good. Too often, it's the farmers and villagers that pay for the follies of their rulers."

"I suspect you and the other Hostigi had some personal knowledge of such follies and their effects on the peasant class."

"I have," Democriphon replied curtly. In the last two winters, he had seen more than his share of battlefield dead and destroyed towns and hamlets. "Next I will inspect the fireseed works. All will be for naught if we don't have fireseed enough to see us through the war."

"Valthros, we should also be seeing to the men. They will need words of inspiration to fire them for the coming battle."

Democriphon chuckled. "You do not have to call me that when we are alone, you know."

"It is best that you get used to it. It will be your name for a long time, if all goes as planned." Mythros looked out past the earthworks. "I hope I can restore these lands after this battle."

"I wouldn't bother right away, uh, Uncle Mythros. There may be several battles before Niclophon is deposed, and it never hurts to keep your defenses strong."

The Prince sighed. "No, I suppose it doesn't. Speaking of defenses, have Kosklos' men been briefed? We do not want them to do anything rash."

"They have. Prince Kosklos assured me that his men are well trained and will not exceed their orders. I only hope Vythron's forces are half as good as his captain-general claims."

"I can well believe it. The prince of Artigos has the best-trained army in all of Hos-Bletha, with the possible exception of Phaedron's men. Vythron is a stern ruler who maintains a competent army. Shortly, we will have a basis for comparison, I believe."

"So will Carthames and Basilron," Democriphon said with a grim smile.

## II

Chief Petty-Captain Gycules was careful to stay out of sight as the men in his command marched up to the temple. While the giant had no reason to believe his face would be recognized from his activities in Bletha as a bandit, he knew that because of his large stature he would stand out. That might make the Styphoni nervous, and nervous people often did foolish things.

The plan was simple enough; with the word out that raiders had struck temples throughout Hos-Bletha, every temple in the kingdom would be wary of strangers. The old dodge of pretending to have been attacked was unlikely to work anymore. Instead, First Captain Ranthar came up with another plan.

Vanir, dressed in the black robes of an underpriest, called up to the temple guard. "Open the gates. We are here on Styphon's House's business."

The guard did not look convinced. He shouted down from his watch-tower, "Maybe you are and maybe you are not. How do I know that you are not the raiders who struck Styphon's temples in Bletha?"

Ranthar had anticipated the challenge and made provisions for it. Vanir held up a scroll for the guard to see, then unrolled it.

"By order of Highpriest Sangar, Chief Highpriest of Styphon's House in Hos-Bletha, two squads of Styphon's Own Guard are hereby attached to each temple in the Princedom of Drathor for the protection of the One God's true believers on earth. All temple masters are hereby ordered forthwith to provide lodging and sacraments for this holy order until the threat has been ended. Signed, His Worship Sangar, Chief Highpriest of Hos-Bletha. In the service of Styphon, the One True God. All blessings in his name!"

Vanir rerolled the scroll. "You will open the gates and allow us to enter, or you will be in violation of His Worship's Edict."

The guard did not know what to do. His orders had been do not allow more than three visitors at a time. Before him now, he estimated no less than a hundred and fifty armed men. He looked over the phalanx of Styphon's Own Guard stretched before him. Every last one looked almost parade perfect. The dust of travel did little to detract from the gleam of their silvered armor and the sharp heads of their polearms. Every man in each squad stood stock still in perfect rows and files.

Lacking any better idea, he summoned the commander of the relief. The captain ascended to the parapet and listened to Vanir reread Sangar's edict. After looking over the assembled guard, he decided that they looked like true soldiers of the One God and ordered the gates opened. Less than a hundred heartbeats after the two companies of Styphon's Own Guard entered the gates, the screaming began.

## III

Petty-Captain Nolos could not restrain his enthusiasm. After moons of pretending to be one of Styphon's Own Dung Eaters, he was free to do what he came to Hos-Bletha to do; kill Styphoni. The Petty-Captain went at it with all the gusto he could summon, which was considerable. He hued a bloody swath through priest and warrior alike. When his right arm grew tired, he shifted his sword to the left and continued.

Inspired by their leader, his men worked to follow his example. Experienced mercenary and freeman alike fought like Regwarn's own demons. The battle was not without cost; men were wounded or killed only to be replaced by another only too happy to vent his spleen on the Styphoni.

When the battle was over, Nolos was almost disappointed. That lasted until his heartbeat returned to normal and he could feel the soreness in his arms, the burning in his chest and the multitude of cuts, bruises and abrasions in all the places his armor was not.

"I want the freemen to release the slaves while the mercenaries go over this temple joint by joint," Nolos ordered. "Make certain there are no priests or guards hiding. All treasure will be loaded onto the wagons. That goes double for fireseed, poor as it is. Strip the corpses of armor, weapons and treasure. All booty from the dead will be divided evenly after we are well away from here! Anybody trying to take more than his fair share will not like what happens next. Move!"

## IV

First Captain Ranthar sat in the Temple Master's chair with a leg hung over the arm as the novices were forced to their knees before him. The idea was to look as though sacking a temple of Styphon's House was the easiest thing in the world. Behind them were a score of hardened mercenaries with swords drawn.

"I suppose you are all wondering why I ordered you into my presence?" Ranthar asked.

The dozen or so white-robed novices stared blankly at him. "Your masters are dead. Those who were here to defend you, Styphon's Own Guard, are dead. The only question that remains is whether you follow them to Regwarn, or renounce your allegiance to the false god Styphon. What say you?"

As one, every white-robed novitiate screamed his devotion to Styphon. Ranthar wondered if they thought his troops had been sent by Investigator Roxthar to determine their beliefs, or if he had found an unusually devout group of novices. He knew that the black-robed underpriests would have tried to out-yell each other in order to be the first to recant their belief in Styphon's divinity.

Ranthar nodded and the mercenaries behind them struck off their heads. The corpses were quickly dragged away, save for their heads. The heads were lined-up in a row in front of Andros where their dead eyes would face the next group of novices. The next round of white-robed priests were brought in and forced to their knees in the pooling blood.

"Let us try this again," he said. He gestured toward the heads before him. "You may want to give more thought to your answer than the previous group."

## V

Ranthar nodded with satisfaction as the gold tiles were quickly and efficiently stripped from the temple dome. His men had had a great deal of practice. The battle had gone well and casualties were much lighter than anticipated. The freemen had performed better than Ranthar had hoped, and the former mercenaries fought as if they had a personal grudge to settle. It had been a good day.

He watched as Gasphros settled down on a bench breathing heavily. Ranthar suspected it had been a long time since the troubadour had taken such an active part in a battle and his muscles were reminding him of that fact.

Ranthar took a seat next to the bard. "How are you holding up?"

"I think…I will…live," Gasphros said between breaths.

Ranthar smiled. "I think so too. I hope the others did as well as we did, today. Did you enjoy yourself?"

Gasphros fought to control his breathing, then replied, "I do not… recall it…being so…much work."

"I saw you out of the corner of my eye. You slipped between foes like a shadow. Where did you learn how to move like that?"

The Bard smiled. "In a traveling…show. I trained with the…acrobats and cut-purses. Those…cut-purses went through…crowds like a…gentle rain."

"I will be more careful of my own purse henceforth."

Gasphros chuckled. "No need for that, my friend. It would violate the…thieves code for me to rob another…thief."

Ranthar did a double take. "Thief? Me?"

"Yes, you. What did you think you were doing when you put on that wolf-helm and held up those caravans? By the way, do not forget to send a cut of your take to the Thieves Guild. They can be quite unpleasant when they do not receive their dues."

Gasphros stood up and joined the search for hiding priests while Ranthar watched him go.

*Is he serious?*

# SIXTY-FOUR

## I

Ranthar, Gycules, Andros, Uncle Wolf Syros and Gasphros met up at the Boar's Head Inn in Syragon Town. All but Syros and Gasphros were dressed as peasants. Each time the door opened, the group looked to see who entered, only to turn back to their watered-down drinks.

"Zentros may have run off," Andros surmised. "You should have let Gycules talk to him before he was released. Our Chief Petty-Captain here could frighten a Styphon's Archpriest into converting to Dralm worship. Uh, that was meant as a compliment."

The giant chuckled. "I have been scaring the Regwarn out of people for years, Captain, whether I wanted to or not. I think my talking to him would have spurred him on to greater speed…away from us!" Everyone chuckled politely.

"We cannot remain here too much longer," Ranthar said. "We have over twelve hundred men scattered around the town. Sooner or later, somebody will notice and sound the alarm, or press gangs will start seizing our people to fight for

Basilron in the coming war."

"We should have let them hide out in the forest," Gasphros grumbled.

Captain Andros shook his head. "Among other people they will go unnoticed for a time. Outside the town they would stand out like a river dragon in a rabbit hutch."

Gycules nodded. "Indeed. I know something about hiding anything too big…wait, is that Zentros?"

All eyes went to the entrance and fell upon the man who had just entered. Ranthar nodded and gestured to the bard sitting at their table. Syros smiled as Gasphros cursed and handed over three gold coins to the Uncle Wolf.

"You are late," Ranthar accused the man. "Take a seat."

"I think you will forgive me when I give you my news. Two Temple Bands of Styphon's Own Guard and the Royal Blethan Cavalry are headed our way."

"What?" Ranthar almost forgot to keep his voice down. "How far away?"

"They are stopping at each temple along the main road to be sure they haven't been attacked. As if the missing gold from the temple domes could not tell them that much!"

"Well done, Zentros," Ranthar said. "Where are they likely to go next?"

"The temple in Lorax would be my guess. It is a straight shot from where I saw them last. They will be there the day after tomorrow at the latest."

"Very good, lad," Uncle Wolf said. "What of that other matter?"

Zentros smiled with evil glee. "The word has been put out that the Grand Host is coming to aid Basilron in the coming war, and will press any mercenary they find into service. By tomorrow, there won't be a free company within twenty marches of Syragon Town."

Gycules shook his ponderous head. "Tis a shame that people know not the difference between Styphon's Own Guard and the Grand Host. My heart goes out to poor Basilron."

Everybody laughed.

"You have done well, Zentros," Ranthar said. "I have another task for you, and the bonus you receive will make it worth your while. I will tell you what it is outside after I pay the bar tab."

## II

Jorand Rarth, under his outtime disguise as Archpriest Prythos, wasn't surprised at how happy he was to get back to Balph, the Holy City of Styphon's House. After spending an entire year traveling overland from the east coast to the west coast to recruit ten thousand Ros-Zarthani soldiers, and then back again to join the Grand Host of Styphon's House.

He had ridden six or seven horses into the ground and walked more miles than he could count; the only benefit was that he lost his big belly. Still, all in all, it had been a trial. This from a man who'd worked his way up the prole rackets on one of the anonymous Serv Sector Prole Fifth Level time-lines as a head-buster right up to the top of the Home Time Line rackets.

Somehow he had got caught up in another one of Hadron Tharn's schemes to rule the First Level underworld. Then, to make matters worse, he almost got caught in one of Dhergabar Metropolitan Police Chief Vothan Raldor sweeps of Old Dhergabar, the ancient heart of the city. He turned to Tharn for help and ended up on Kalvan's Time-Line helping to bring a bunch of mercenary barbarians across the continent. Although he had to admit, those Ros-Zarthani soldiers were one of the toughest outfits he ever had to ramrod.

All this to help Styphon's House win their war against Great King Kalvan. Since Tharn's brother-in-law, Verkan Vall the Paratime Police Chief, was one of Kalvan's biggest supporters, Tharn had figured giving Kalvan more trouble than he could handle might hand Chief Verkan a black-eye, as well.

Now that dirty job was done and Jorand was back in Balph where the living was good, at least for the elite few who ruled Styphon's House. As part of his cover, he had his own fortified manor with hot and cold running slaves. He had hoped that once the mission was over he would be able to escape into relative anonymity, managing his household and counting his gold crowns. Only occasionally having to attend boring councils of the Inner Circle.

He still had dreams of returning to Home Time Line but—until Management Party was voted out of office—he was reconciled to living in exile on Aryan-Transpacific. Here on Kalvan's Time-Line he was a member of the ruling elite in one of the most powerful and wealthy theocracies on the Fourth Level.

At the moment, he was stuck in an anteroom awaiting the pleasure of the man behind Styphon's Voice, Speaker Anaxthenes. With Sesklos on his deathbed, Anaxthenes was the most powerful man in Balph, now that Archpriest Roxthar was thankfully out of town. Roxthar was absolutely bugshit and scared him almost as much as Hadron Tharn!

One of the ubiquitous black-robed underpriests led Jorand into Anaxthenes' private audience chamber. It wasn't as opulent as Supreme Priest Sesklos' digs, but it was full of beautiful marble statuary and gold castings, mostly of Styphon. The Speaker was seated on a long divan and smoking a long clay pipe. Also in attendance were half a dozen archpriests, all of them Anaxthenes' cronies. Jorand knew a crime syndicate get-together when he saw one; after all, he had been one of the top bosses in Dhergabar for over half a century.

"Your Eminence, to what do I owe the honor of your summons?"

Anaxthenes nodded, as though recognizing him were a gift. "Archpriest Prythos, it has been brought to my attention that you just returned from a visit to the Old Lands."

"Yes, Your Eminence, I helped lead Archstratagos Zarphu and his men across the Great Mountains and over the Sea of Grass. I believe, despite their barbaric weapons, their fighting prowess will add much to the Grand Host. In battle against the Greffans they were victorious despite the appearance of calivers and some antiquated guns."

"Yes, I've heard all of that," Anaxthenes replied. "What I'm interested in is the potential for Styphon's House in the Old Lands."

"Obviously, there is a need for fireseed and arquebuses. But they are not receptive, I believe, to new gods."

Anaxthenes smiled like a wolf eyeing a pasture full of sheep. "Yes, but what did they think of our fireseed?"

"The Prince of Antiphon was most interested in obtaining fireseed and promised large sums of gold in exchange for fireseed and the weapons to use it with."

Archpriest Neamenestros said, "This war with the Usurper Kalvan is costing us far too much gold and silver. The Temple could use more gold in case the war against the False Kingdom of Hos-Hostigos goes on for another winter or two."

"I think it would be wise to spread our influence and temples into these lands," Anaxthenes continued. "While I would never say this in public, it is not out of the realm of possibility that this devil-sent Daemon Kalvan might actually win the war."

Several of the archpriests drew back in horror.

*They must be thinking of how Kalvan likes to blow upperpriests out of cannons*, Jorand decided. *I wonder what's in it for me?*

"The Daemon Kalvan has killed Prince Philesteus, pushed King Kaiphranos to suicide and won every battle he's fought."

"But what about the Grand Host?" an archpriest interjected.

Anaxthenes shrugged. "With an untested mercenary captain-general in charge, anything is possible. I would like to believe they'll succeed, but I will not wager my future and Styphon's House upon it. We need to establish a colony on the opposite side of the world."

"You make a good point," Archpriest Neamenestros said. "If things go badly, the Usurper will bring his army to Balph and none of us will be safe. It is only prudent to prepare for every eventuality."

All the archpriests shuddered in agreement.

*They may be outtimers, but they're not stupid*, Jorand thought. *This Styphon's House gang has a good racket and they know it. One with unlimited possibilities.*

"Now," Anaxthenes continued, "we have with us a man who knows the Old Lands and its rulers. I would like for Archpriest Prythos to head up an expedition there. We will put him in charge of the entire operation."

Jorand's stomach dropped. *I just got back! Not another transcontinental journey....*

"We will send along a hundred underpriests, two score highpriests, three Temple Bands of Styphon's Own Guard, five hundred mercenary cavalry, ten wagons of fireseed and twenty wagonloads of outdated calivers and arquebuses."

"They'll want big guns, too." one of the archpriests pointed out.

"Yes, we'll give them four or five of the old iron-hooped guns," Anaxthenes announced, with a smile on his face. "For gold."

"But there are five different city-states that follow the Western Ocean," Jorand told them. "All of them will want the guns for themselves."

Anaxthenes smiled. "Yes, and each one will want a temple of its own. We should be able to sell lots of fireseed and firearms to each of them."

*That sounds a lot easier than it's going to turn out to be*, Jorand thought. *Those Ros-Zarthani are a tough bunch of bastards and they don't take dishonor lightly. On the other hand, there'll be ample bribes and gifts to the man making those decisions. While this may be a primitive world, there are still a lot of perks for a man in the know.*

# SIXTY-FIVE

## I

Marshal Vuklos of Styphon's Own Guard raised his arm and called for a halt. They were only half a march from the Styphon's Temple in Lorax Town and Vuklos wanted to assess the situation before proceeding. Two marches back while resting and watering the horses, a peasant had approached and warned him that raiders had attacked the temple. Vuklos had received that same warning twice before. This time, however, there was a twist; the raiders had taken residence in the temple and disguised themselves as priests and guards. From what he had heard, the raiders were smart, brave and ruthless. But for all that, they had to be insane to challenge the might of Styphon's House Upon Earth.

From his vantage point atop a rise, Marshal Vuklos could see the golden light of the sun reflecting off the golden dome of the temple. Every temple dome that he had passed had been stripped of its of gold tiles. However, if the intruders wanted to pass themselves off as Styphoni, they would need to keep this dome intact.

Unlike the High Temple in Bletha Town, this was a primary temple for the separation of saltpeter from manure. The saltpeter would then be sent by wagon to the High Temple in Bletha Town to be combined with sulfur and charcoal to make fireseed.

"Grand-Captain Rolos!" he ordered. "Take a squad and investigate the temple. Look for signs of recent conflict and report back to me."

"Yes, sir!"

Rolos selected twenty men he knew he could count on and led them to the temple. Marshal Vuklos watched with keen interest as the grand-captain went up to the front gate. He was unable to hear what was being said, or even see clearly the interaction between Rolos and the gatekeepers, but he could see that the gate was not opening. Moments later, he heard the sharp reports of arquebus fire. He watched in surprise as the captain and his men of the advance party were cut down like grass before the scythe.

There could be no doubt; the temple had been seized and was now occupied by the enemy. "Form ranks!" Vuklos yelled.

The men dismounted and unleashed glaives which were kept next to the saddle. The front ranks took out their musketoons.

"Form on me. Arms at the ready. Forward!"

The Ruthani and irregular cavalry took the lead and only reined in when artillery fire brought down a dozen or so horsemen. The foot soldiers continued forward, spreading out a lance length from each other. Normally, this tactic was used to minimize injury and death from cannon fire. It also served to make harder targets for small arms fire.

Behind Styphon's Own Guard, Niclophon's Royal Army held firm. Their Captain-General, Theodoros, had been ordered to assist the Styphoni in rooting out and destroying the raiders and bandits that had been plaguing Bletha. Now, here he was in Drathor watching Styphon's Own Guard attack one of its own temples.

Captain-General Theodoros considered the situation. Each temple lodged one or two squads of Styphon's Own Guard, between twenty to forty men, plus twenty irregular cavalry, thirty to forty priests and initiates, plus forty to sixty slaves. The slaves were unlikely to assist in the defense of their slavers, so, at most, there would be one hundred and sixty temple defenders against twelve companies of Styphon's Own Guard. Theodoros felt no need to join in the slaughter to come. What he did not know was why Marshal Vuklos was killing his own people.

Since joining the Styphoni with his cavalry, Vuklos had been rude and dismissive toward the Blethans. He refused to discuss strategy, would not share information, and generally acted like the Blethan soldiers were not worth having along. Theodoros suspected that Vuklos wanted to be part of the Grand Host and join the hunt for the Daemon Kalvan. Now he was taking his ill-temper over his transfer to Hos-Bletha out on Theodoros and his men.

*So be it,* Theodoros thought, *I was ordered to assist with the capture and destruction of bandits, not Styphoni priests.* "Captain Wythos, have the men rest until we are given orders."

"Sir?"

"Marshal Vuklos of the much vaunted Styphon's Own Guard has chosen not to invite us on this little skirmish, so we will remain here. No point in exhausting the men pointlessly, so let them relax until they are needed. Mind you, they are to stay in armor and keep their weapons at the ready."

"Yes, sir!" Captain Wythos pounded his chest over his heart and extended his fist toward his captain-general. Theodoros returned the salute and the petty-captain hustled off to carry out his orders.

Theodoros watched Styphon's Own Guard with keen interest as they swarmed around the walls of the temple and traded fire. While a part of him wanted to join in the battle, the rest of him felt there was something very wrong going on and wanted no part of it.

## II

Marshal Vuklos' men forced the gate open with concentrated gunfire and brute force, losing close to a hundred men in the process. The raiders above threw everything they had at his soldiers. Return fire had little effect against the cover provided by the stone walls on the parapets.

Vuklos wondered how the raiders got in. *Probably disguised themselves as priests or even Styphon's Own Guard.* However they had done it, he intended to make certain they did not leave alive. Once the gate was down, his men surged forward with reckless abandon. Dozens were cut down by gunfire before the defenders on the walls were shot down.

More defenders swarmed into the courtyard from the temple. Every last one of them wearing the armor and red cloaks of Styphon's Own Guard. *Blasphemy!* The matching armor caused confusion among Vuklos' men; it was impossible to tell friend from foe. Anyone not immediately recognized as a personal friend was viciously attacked. This worked to the advantage of the imposters. Their smaller numbers allowed them to recognize their friends with ease, while the hundreds of Vuklos' men could not be expected to know every last face in their own garrison, let alone the two separate Temple Bands of Styphon's Own Guard. Even Vuklos was unable to tell if any two men fighting each other were friends or foes.

His error quickly became obvious; knowing that the temple raiders were disguised as Styphoni, he should have ordered the Blethans to move in. The Blethan armor, while far less impressive than that of the Guard, would have made it easy to separate between friend and foe. Vuklos looked back to see Theodoros' men waiting half a march back. He first cursed Theodoros for a coward, and then himself for a fool. His own disdain for the Blethans had caused his current predicament. The Blethans could hardly be faulted for not attacking a Styphon's House temple.

The battle continued into the temple. There, the priests had armed themselves with swords, spears and knives. Vuklos' men only hesitated for a moment; they had been trained to protect the priests, not attack them. When they started, nothing could hold them back. They mauled the priests like a pack of wolves in a sheep pen. Unlike the imposters outside who wore the holy armor, these false priests were easy to tell from the Guard. In a few heartbeats, every last one of them had been cut down.

"You damned fools!" shouted a voice from above. In a balcony stood a yellow-robed highpriest. "Styphon's House Upon Earth will send legions of its holy warriors to destroy you! Mark my words, infidels, you are doomed."

One of his guardsmen shot the man before Vuklos could stop him. "Hold your fire!" he shouted, running up the stairs to the priest. He recognized the priest. "Highpriest Marthos! What are you doing here?"

"Vuklos? You fool…I am…Temple Master here."

"Temple Master! Then, why did your men fire at us?"

"We were warned…that bandits disguised…as Styphon's Own Guard…were coming to destroy us." Highpriest Marthos coughed up some blood, then quietly expired.

Vuklos blood ran cold. He and the temple master had been tricked into fighting each other. The Marshal saw his future evaporate into nothingness. Grand Marshal Xenophes would have him stripped of command, excommunicated, possibly even turned over to Investigator Roxthar. He had to act quickly if he were to avoid such a fate.

He quickly ran back down the stairs shouting orders. "Take the bodies of the false guard and their accomplices and burn them. Quickly! We have destroyed one faction of the raiders, but none survived for questioning. Strip the bodies of armor and treasure and pile it before the altar. Then I want everyone out. Move!"

The men, confused and battle-worn, scrambled to obey. While they were distracted with their work, Vuklos slipped away unnoticed to the slave pens. There, he found men and women chained by work stations and on sleeping pallets. His first thought was to slay them all. He had little sentiment regarding the fate of slaves; unfortunately, the raiders always freed the slaves. Vuklos found the keys to the shackles and released the nearest man.

"Take these keys and free your brothers. My men have freed you from…the evil Styphoni. You will find treasure in the worship hall. Take everything you can carry, and flee after I have taken my men from this place. Spread the word that the raiders have struck here and killed all of Styphon's worshippers in this temple. Be careful not to tell anyone that you were a slave, or you may find yourself again in chains. Wait five candles before you leave this chamber. Understood?"

The man nodded vigorously. "Kill all of Styphon's curs!"

Vuklos, sick to his stomach, left the slave chambers and returned to his men. By this time they had most of the bodies piled onto a pyre and the flames growing quickly.

The Grand-Captain Rolos approached and saluted. "Sir, we doused the bodies with turpentine to speed things along. What are your orders, sir?"

"We are done here. We move on to the next temple in case there are more raiders to deal with."

"More, sir?"

"Of course. These bandits take the slaves from every temple they sack and make them part of their gangs. By now, there could be over a thousand of these bandits. We scarcely destroyed a hundred in this temple. We have much more to do. Rally the men outside and prepare to march."

"What about battle spoils, sir?"

*Damn!* Even Styphon's Own Guard were allowed to loot the bodies of the dead. "The spoils here were taken from our own people, Grand-Captain. To take such booty would be no different than robbing our own. We leave this tainted treasure here. Let the next temple master determine what to do with it. Styphon's Will be done!"

"Styphon's Will, will be done, sir!"

The Grand-Captain turned and ran out to the men. Vuklos could hear him barking orders to the men. The Marshal turned to the altar and kneeled. "Forgive me, Lord Styphon, for my transgression."

After a short prayer, Vuklos rose and marched out of the hall. He could feel the eyes of his god bore into his soul as he left.

## III

Captain-General Theodoros watched with interest as several pyres were lit, each comprised of over a dozen naked corpses. At least he hoped they were corpses; word of Investigator Roxthar's activities did not reassure him that this would be the case.

Theodoros ordered the captain to call the men to readiness as Marshal Vuklos returned ahead of his men.

"Why did you stay behind?" Vuklos demanded.

"I was tasked to work with you in ridding Hos-Bletha of bandits, not attacking Styphoni temples. Moreover, you did not inform me that you were going to attack and kill everybody there. What in the name of Styphon did you do that for?"

Vuklos struggled to keep his expression neutral, though Theodoros noticed it took some effort. *Something went very wrong down there in that temple*, he decided.

"The raiders had taken control of the temple. You may have noticed that they fired on us first. I lost over a hundred men taking that temple."

"Why are you burning the corpses?"

"I have no time to waste burying them, and I cannot leave them in the temple to rot. New priests and guardsmen will be sent to restaff the temple and would not appreciate it if I left a mess for them to clean up."

"Commendable." Theodoros pulled his gaze from the burning bodies back to Vuklos. "Marshal, I have been ordered to work with you, not play at being your cat's-paw. I suspect something more happened in that temple you are not telling me. If so, it matters not to me. I'm done accepting your disdain and condescension. From here, you march alone. I am taking my people back to Bletha Town to prepare them for war. You may not have heard, but four principalities have seceded from Hos-Bletha. My men and I are needed there. Good hunting." Theodoros turned and started walking away.

"Hold on, Captain-General. We were sent here because you could not deal with these bandits without our help."

Theodoros stopped and turned. “Marshal, you were sent to rid yourselves of them. The bandits seem to have a particular loathing for Styphon’s House and its priests. I suspect that if Styphon’s House withdrew from Hos-Bletha, so too would the bandits. Again, good hunting.”

Theodoros resumed his trek back to his men ignoring all further entreaties from the Styphoni Marshal. In less than a candle, the Blethan army had moved beyond earshot.

Marshal Vuklos, anxious to be away from the temple, ordered his men to move on to the next as soon as the wounded were attended to. Next time, he vowed, they would be more careful about who they were fighting.

## IV

From the tree line near the Styphoni temple of Lorax, several dozen pairs of eyes watched with great interest as the Styphoni and Blethan armies moved away. Gasphros and Uncle Wolf Syros let out a long sigh of relief.

“That went well, I think,” Uncle Wolf Syros observed.

“I had hoped more of the Styphoni would have died in the fighting,” Gasphros said. “The more of their solders who are killed now, the less we have to deal with later.”

“‘No war goes as planned,’” Syros quoted from the Book of Galzar. “We should wait at least four candles before entering the temple and stripping it.”

“Agreed.” Gasphros looked over his shoulder at the freemen assigned to him and the Uncle Wolf. “This mob has had quite a bit of practice. Three ounces of gold says they can have the gold tile stripped from the dome in under eight candles.”

“Ha! I would wager on seven candles.”

“Six, and I double the bet.”

“By Galzar, you have a wager! Plus the next bar tab?”

“Done and done! We light the first candle when they ascend the ladders.”

Syros considered that, decided it was not booby-trapped, and agreed.

"I'll have the freemen ready the wagons," Gasphros said as he stood up. "Care to make a second wager that we will be done here before nightfall?"

# SIXTY-SIX

## I

After two days of forced riding, Marshal Vuklos was in a foul mood. The dead in the temple near Lorax Town weighed heavily on his mind and soul. Killing infidels never bothered him. Why should they, they were unbelievers, after all. However, having already been tricked into killing fellow worshippers of the One God played havoc with his digestive system.

Thus far, he had lost over a hundred men, plus the support of the Blethan Royal Army, or rather twelve companies of horse. Vuklos considered filing a complaint against Theodoros, then dismissed it. The Blethan was young for a captain-general, so either he was very competent, or had very high connections that would shield him from his king's wrath. Either way, Vuklos would come off looking foolish, and he was done playing the fool for anybody.

Half a march ahead was Lynd Village. It was actually much larger than a simple village, but occasionally names stuck well beyond their accurate usage. Typical of this blasted place, the houses were primarily made of wood, many not much more than mere huts, with palm leaves as thatch. Here, the Styphon's House temple would be situated in the hos-plazos as was customary. That meant any attack on the temple would have been noticed by the locals.

"Grand-Captain Rolos!"

"Yes, sir!"

"Take three men into the village and question anybody around the hos-plazos," Marshal Vuklos ordered. "I want to know if anything unusual occurred around the temple. Report to me within two candles."

"Yes, sir!" The captain saluted, then selected his three men and raced off toward the town.

It was a long wait for Marshal Vuklos. He hoped that this temple, at least, had been spared any visit from the raiders. Since leaving Lorax he had prayed over and over that he would meet the villains in the open, away from any temples or towns, where he and his men could destroy the threat once and for all. Thus far, Styphon—possibly annoyed at him after what happened in Lorax—had turned a deaf ear to Vuklos' pleas.

When Grand-Captain Rolos returned, bearing a wide smile.

"Well?

"The raiders have been here, and still are, sir," Rolos reported.

"What? Then why are you smiling like that?"

"Because they are all dead. The temple set a trap of their own and wiped out every single one of them and burned their corpses. The temple master is waiting to meet with you."

*Perhaps Styphon has answered my prayers after all. If the raiders are all dead, then I can return to Balph and forget this god-forsaken realm.* "We should not keep our hosts waiting."

Rolos nodded once, then rode to join his Band. Half a candle later, Vuklos stood before the temple gates. Before he could even announce himself, the gates opened wide to reveal a black-robed priest.

"Welcome, Marshal Vuklos. I am Vanir, first assistant to His Worship Morthar. Your men can make themselves at home in the courtyard while you meet with His Worship. He is very anxious to speak with you."

Vuklos nodded and gestured to Rolos, then he followed the black-robed priest through the gates. In the courtyard he could smell the lingering aroma of seared flesh, voided bowels and burnt turpentine. He did not like the memories the odors evoked.

"How did you manage to destroy the raiders when every other temple had failed?"

Underpriest Vanir smiled knowingly. "I would not presume to speak for the Temple Master, Marshal. Please, be patient and all will be revealed." He escorted Vuklos through the narthex, up a staircase and down a wide hallway to a massive oak door. There, Vanir knocked three times, then twice again.

A voice from the other side said, "You may enter, my child."

Vanir opened the door, then stepped out of the way allowing Marshal Vuklos access. Inside, standing next to an open window, stood a hooded figure in yellow.

"Marshall…Vuklos, yes? To what do I owe the honor of this visit?"

"Your Worship, I have been ordered by the Inner Circle to track down the bandits and raiders…I believe them to be one and the same…and put them to the sword." Vuklos looked around the chamber suspiciously. "I understand you have already met these raiders and sent them to Regwarn. I admit to being amazed that a few squads of even Styphon's Own Guard and a couple score of underpriests could manage such a feat."

"Oh, it was nothing. One of the guardsmen developed a strategy for dealing with those infidels." The Temple Master never turned his gaze from the window. "Come over here and I will show you how it was done."

Vuklos crossed over to the window. He tried to get a look at the Temple Master's face, but the hood defied his efforts. Instead, he watched where the he pointed.

"If you look down there, you can see that your men, many more than those we destroyed, fill the courtyard near to overflowing. I allowed the raiders to enter as your men have. When all had entered, the gates were secured, from the outside, like so."

Vuklos watched as two underpriests forced the outer gates shut. "I see. No doubt you had the temple door closed and barricaded from within, too. The invaders would have been trapped with nowhere to go and no room to move. It would be simple indeed to destroy them all by firing down at them from the walls and windows of the temple."

"You have an excellent grasp of the situation, Marshal Vuklos." The Temple Master raised his hand, then brought it down quickly.

The courtyard suddenly filled with the sound of gunfire. Vuklos was shocked into immobility for several heartbeats as his men were cut down in a deadly crossfire. The soldiers tried to bring their weapons to bear only to be riddled with gunshot wounds from scores of arquebuses in every direction.

"Blasphemers!" Vuklos cried, as he reached for his sword. His hand halted when he felt the point of a dagger at his throat.

"One moment, Marshal, while I ready myself for your challenge." Morthar shed the yellow robes of the temple master to stand revealed in his armor. He pulled his sword as he stepped away from the window. "Vanir, wait outside while Vuklos and I talk things over. I don't think we shall be long."

Vanir stepped out of the chamber and closed the door behind him. From the other side of the door he could hear shouting, mostly by Vuklos, and the clash of steel. There was the crashing of furniture, the clang of a sword striking armor, and more clashing of steel as sword struck sword repeatedly.

It was a quarter-candle before the door opened. Vanir leaped back and raised his horse-pistol, then lowered it in relief. "That took longer than you said it would," Vanir accused.

The former mercenary was winded. He paused to gulp some water from his bottle, then said, "The Marshal was a damned sight better with his sword than I expected for an old man. Styphon's Own Guard deserves their reputation if Vuklos is any example of what they can turn out."

"You are bleeding."

"And bruised and sore," admitted the petty-captain, "and grateful for the long hours of practice time babysitting Sangar provided me with. When we torch these bodies, have Vuklos put on a high platform and burned with honors. I think he deserves it, even if he is a worshipper of a false god."

II

"Pay up, Gasphros. He made it."

The bard grumbled as he passed three gold coins to the Uncle Wolf. First Captain Ranthar watched the transaction with some small amusement. *Gasphros will be bankrupt by the end of this mission if he keeps betting like this.*

The group met up at the Black Ox Inn, a place Gasphros knew well, to compare notes. The reports were uniformly positive save for Captain Andros' report. In Carphax Town, Styphon's Own Guard had rushed out of the temple gates the second Andros' men appeared in the hos-plazos. There was no demand for identification and the fact that they were all disguised as guardsmen themselves mattered not at all. The battle was long and bloody. Though Andros had won out, the butcher bill was a high one costing him almost half his men. As a result, the captain was especially brutal when he finally took the temple.

Zentros took a seat next to Captain Andros. "Word is going around that Styphon's House is about to unleash the Grand Host on Hos-Hostigos. It's unfortunate that we cannot help from here."

Ranthar and Gasphros fought to keep their faces neutral. It would not do at all for the former sharper to know Great King Kalvan's actual orders.

"Much of that is already known to us," Ranthar said. "Do you have anything new to report?"

"Well, several of the smaller Styphoni temples have been abandoned," Zentros reported. "The priests take whatever they can carry and run to the larger temples for protection."

"Those are the token temples Styphon's House keeps in the less inhabited areas for appearance sake," observed Uncle Wolf Syros. "They don't even bother with guards and golden domes. If they even have domes, they're covered in copper or brass. And just a few slaves for donkey work."

"The slaves are often used as pack animals to carry the priests' goods,"

Zentros added. “Anything the priests left behind has already been scavenged to the floorboards by the locals. There is no point in even bothering with them.”

“How many important Styphoni temples are left in Syragon?” Ranthar asked.

“There are three of them that we haven’t hit, besides the main temple in Syragon Town,” Gasphros supplied.

“That’s the one all the priests from the small temples will be headed for, I’ll warrant,” Uncle Wolf Syros added. “There will be at least half a Temple Band of Styphon’s Own Guard stationed there. It will also have the highest number of slaves and priests, not to mention the highest walls. Plus, Prince Basilron’s own guard.”

“The temple dome on the Syragon Temple is twice as large as the smaller ones,” Gasphros said with a wink.

“And has at least twice as much gold on it, as well,” Zentros added, with an eager smile. “Say Captain, what have you been doing with all of the treasure you have taken from the other temples?”

*Actually, the larger temple has four times as much gold covering its dome*, Ranthar thought. He didn’t know whether or not the Zarthani had discovered solid geometry; if they hadn’t, it wasn’t his job to teach them. That would be Paratime Contamination.

“To answer your question, we buried the precious metals in several locations along the way,” Ranthar said. He still didn’t trust Zentros completely. In truth, everything was piled into wagons, disguised as merchant caravans and sent back to Mallegast along with the new freemen and some trusted soldiers via different routes. Later it would be transported to the treasury depot.

The mayor of Mallegast would have a lot to contend with for a while. Only the fireseed, weapons and armor stayed with Ranthar’s men, but Zentros did not need to know that—once a sharper, always a conman.

“Wait…it was my understanding that Styphon worship was popular in Hos-Bletha. Who is scavenging the temples, then?” Ranthar asked.

“Styphon is more popular with the noble class who benefit from Styphoni gold and fireseed,” Uncle Wolf Syros explained. “The underclasses suffer the most under the Styphoni. Few can afford the Temple tithes. A farmer could lose his lands if Styphon's House deems there is something desirable on his property."

"As happened to my father," Captain Andros said.

"Most people fear the Temple's power and try to stay out of their way," Syros said. "Now, however, Styphon's House has been challenged; first by Great King Kalvan, and now by mysterious raiders who are killing the priests and guardsmen in every temple they sack. Add to that, the Temple Band of Styphon's Own Guard that seemed to vanish not so long ago; suddenly people are beginning to think maybe the Styphoni are not so powerful after all."

"You left something out," Zentros said. "It is said that Galzar has had enough of Styphon's House and sent his own minions down from heaven to harry them."

"Galzar's minions?" Gycules blurted out.

"Indeed. One was shot in the head and barely twitched a whisker. Another is so big and strong that some think it may be Galzar in earthly guise amusing himself at Styphon's expense."

Ranthar noticed Gycules blushing while Uncle Wolf Syros looked scandalized. Zentros had not yet been initiated into the inner council and told about the wolf-helmed bandits. "That is very interesting, Zentros. I suppose Galzar worship is on the rise, then?"

"Indeed! Mercenaries, afraid of being pressed into service by the Grand Host, are flocking east to join with the Orphan Prince. It is well that Prince Mythros captured me before the true prince was revealed or I might have been stoned to death by angry villagers, although—truth be told—I did not enjoy spending time in his dungeon."

"That is good," Andros said, "but why there?"

"Oh, you have not heard." Zentros smiled slyly. "Mythros, Kosklos and Vythron have had the Styphoni temples in their realms sacked and the priests hanged."

"What?" Ranthar was surprised; it was news to him. That hadn't been part of their plan; it seemed a bold measure to take. "Why risk Styphon's House sending men to assist Niclophon in the coming war?"

Zentros shrugged. "Who knows? Maybe they just don't want anybody they don't trust around when all Regwarn breaks loose. Or maybe they didn't like the thought of all that gold going into someone else's purse."

*Or maybe Democriphon is following Kalvan's script a little too closely.* "Well, that means fewer temples for us," Ranthar said lightly. "Let us worry about the remaining temples in Syragon, then worry about what comes next."

"Agreed. All of Balph will be outraged when they get the latest news from Hos-Bletha," Zentros noted.

"Not to mention Prince Basilron," Gasphros added.

## III

"I don't have time for your Dralm-damned problems!" Basilron, Prince of Syragon, shouted at the yellow-robed highpriest before him. "I have a war to fight in the name of my Great King."

"You should remember that Styphon's House…"

"I remember Styphon's House aided my enemy, Prince Carthames, during our border war. Were it not King Niclophon's direct order to leave your temples unmolested, I might have raided them myself!"

Harmoth, temple master of Styphon's House in Drathor Town, could scarcely credit his ears. A mere prince was sneering at the power and might of Styphon's House. "Prince Basilron, it was you we aided with gold and fireseed—"

"So you claim," he snarled, "especially since I think this stinking war has everything to do with you and your kind. I do not know how or why, but I suspect if Styphon's House had never entered Hos-Bletha, we would not be facing civil war. But that's where the Kingdom is at. Tomorrow, I will take my army and join forces with Carthames, fool that he is, and then march into Pytha to battle the only Prince I fear in all of Hos-Bletha. If you need protection, I suggest you send word to Balph, and pray to your god that they send Grand Master Soton and the Grand Host. Oh, wait; they're not going to come. They're too busy trying to seize control of another great kingdom, are they not? The one ruled by Great King Kalvan."

"You mean the *Daemon Ka—*"

"I said Great King and meant it. Anybody who can stand up to the Grand Host, the army of Hos-Harphax and whatever else your temples have sent his way deserves the title. Now leave my chamber before I have you thrown out."

Highpriest Harmoth considered trying again, then gave it up as a useless proposition. Prince Basilron wanted nothing to do with Styphon's House, and there was nothing he could do about it—for now. The temple master gathered what dignity he could and withdrew.

Outside of the prince's private audience chamber, he met up with his four guardsmen. Prior to the advent of the Daemon Kalvan he wouldn't have needed any guards at all. After the Hostigi rebellion, the temple masters had been ordered to take two guards everywhere they went. He doubled that number after the raiders sacked their first temple in Syragon. Harmoth considered getting more guards as the raids continued, then elected against it. It would not do to look frightened.

During the carriage ride to the temple, he watched the reactions of the townsfolk. Where once the people on the street would avert their gaze lest they anger the One God, now they openly watched him pass. One townsman even sneered at him. Harmoth told himself everything would return to normal once the Daemon Kalvan and the infidel raiders were brought to heel.

# SIXTY-SEVEN

Democriphon inspected the soldiers standing in formation outside the palisades as he had seen Kalvan do many times before. Back when he had stood parade with his men in Hostigos he had thought it was a ridiculous thing to do. Now, as he walked before the men, occasionally stopping to correct some minor flaw in the uniform or to advise somebody to do a better job of cleaning his weapon, he noticed that many of the men swelled with pride as he approached. To be seen, and even addressed, by the king, or prince in this case, inspired the men. They were not just fighting for some faceless ruler; they were fighting for *their* prince! Even the mercenaries seemed to be inspired.

After the inspection came the speech. Mythros had prepared something for him to say before the men that would raise their spirits. They needed to be highly motivated if they were to survive the next moon. Democriphon took his place on the podium and paused to look over the assembled soldiers before him. Every eye was on him. Democriphon set his jaw, took a deep breath, and started:

"I am well aware, soldiers, that words alone cannot inspire courage. Whatever courage is in your heart, whether from nature or from habit, it will be displayed on the battlefield. For those, whom neither glory nor danger can move, exhortation is bestowed in vain; for the terror in his breast stops his ears.

"Therefore I call on you to maintain a brave and resolute spirit. And, remember, when you advance into battle, victory is in your hands and your hands alone. If we prevail, as we shall, great honors will be won. But if we lose through want of courage, there will be no place where we will be welcomed, save in Regwarn's Caverns were the faint of heart dwell forever.

"When I look out upon you, a strong belief in our coming victory lifts my spirts. Your courage and valor give me great confidence. I stand here today with pride. Pride in all of you. Never have I seen a better, more disciplined army than those who stand here before me now."

He paused to smile and scan the entire assembly. "My intelligencers tell me that the combined might of Drathor and Syragon will fall upon us within the next two or three days. And I feel pity for them! They know not the courage and determination they will face. They have no idea of the spirit of the men I see before me. When we have finished with them, even Galzar will weep for their poor souls!"

Several heads started nodding in the formed companies. It was time for the finish.

"For Prince Mythros! For Galzar! For the Kingdom of Hos-Bletha!"

Democriphon took another deep breath and stepped back as the soldiers and mercenaries cheered. He could hear "Down Carthames!" and "Down Basilron!" in the din that assailed his ears, as well as "Long Live Valthros!" After the noise died down, Uncle Wolf Karthros stepped forward to impart his blessings on the troops. He would be doing a lot of that over the next few days. When the Uncle Wolf had finished, Prince Mythros went to the podium and made a short speech condemning Niclophon the Pretender and his allies. When he was finished, the petty-captains then took over and marched the men off the newly christened parade ground.

Once the companies had left the field, Mythros walked back over to Democriphon.

"You were supposed to add, 'For the Orphan Prince,' Valthros, not 'For Prince Mythros.'"

"It felt wrong. Most of those men do not know me from Dralm. They can identify with you."

"Perhaps. Would you care to join me for some winter wine?"

Democriphon shook his head. "I have fortifications to inspect. Men to speak with and, hopefully, inspire. Back in…my previous life, I would drink with my men the night before a battle. Here, I do not have that luxury. Still, I will walk among them and hope they gain strength from it."

Mythros nodded. "You are far more versed in the ways of war than I. I trust that you know best."

*I hope I do, too*, Democriphon thought.

## II

"…and that is when I decided it was time to bring my men back to Bletha Town, Your Majesty."

Great King Niclophon mentally reviewed the report Captain-General Theodoros provided. The most shocking part, Styphon's Own Guard attacking its own temple, made him feel ill.

"You say that the temple had not been seized by the raiders," Niclophon repeated. "What did you see that drove you to that conclusion?"

"It's what I did not see, sire," Theodoros said, "that bothers me still. Even from half a march away, there should have been signs of a battle. I will grant that the raiders could have entered the temple wall through guile, but then what happened to the bodies of the dead? I cannot believe either the raiders or the temple priests would waste time burying the corpses, and there was no evidence of recent pyres having been set to destroy them. Not even so much as a whiff of turpentine or the stench of burning flesh."

Niclophon nodded absently. "Why did you not relay your suspicions to Marshal Vuklos?"

"As I mentioned earlier, Your Majesty, Vuklos showed no interest in my words. He sent a team to investigate the temple. Styphon's Own Guard shot the men inside, then Vuklos ordered his men into the temple without a word to me."

"Don't you believe that because his men were fired upon was proof that the temple had been taken over by the bandits?"

Theodoros shook his head. "Sire, I have investigated some of the temples that were attacked. As near as I could tell, everything had been done with military precision. Had I been leading the raiders, and had just seized a temple, I would set a trap for whoever came next. Maybe invite them into the courtyard where I could control the battle. I would not have tipped my hand by shooting at cavalrymen, and then wait for the main body to bring me to account. I believe that the priests and guards slaughtered in that temple were actual Styphoni. At that point, I feared for my men's safety. I foresaw that when Marshal Vuklos realized his mistake, he might decide to rid himself of any who witnessed his folly. I wanted my soldiers well away from Styphon's Own Guard before he reached that decision."

Niclophon, never having been a soldier himself, had to rely more heavily on the counsel of his captain-generals than his brother, Marocles, had before his death. Nonetheless, Theodoros made sense. Perhaps Prince Phaedron had done him a favor when he forced his son upon him. Unfortunately, his oldest and most experienced commander, Captain-General Lykron, had led his military contribution to the Grand Host of Styphon's House and was unavailable.

"You did the correct thing, Theodoros, though I fear I will hear different from Highpriest Sangar. Indeed, your return is well-timed; war is coming and I have a special mission for you. Styphon's House provided me with a special gift some moons ago, and I want you to transport it to the Pythan border. If you get there in time to meet up with Carthames and Basilron, join their march into Pytha. If not, go to Pytha with all possible speed. They will need your help.

"I am placing you in command of the Royal Army and such mercenaries and irregulars as are available when you go. Take all but a garrison sufficient to ensure Our security and such captains as you see fit. When you win out against the forces of this false Prince Valthros, I will elevate you to Grand Marshal of Hos-Bletha."

"Thank you, Your Majesty," Theodoros bowed, and started to back out then remembered something. "Ah, sire, what is this gift you spoke of?"

Niclophon smiled widely. "It is something I think you will like."

# SIXTY-EIGHT

## I

Prince Carthames and the army of Drathor, consisting of five thousand cavalry and two thousand infantry, were the first to reach the outskirts of Pytha Town at midday. The Drathor cavalry, resplendent in their polished-steel breastplates and orange and black plumes, were a sight calculated to strike fear into their enemy's heart. Most carried lances and swords, although there were a few squads, influenced by the northern wars, of cuirassiers which had abandoned the traditional lances for horse pistols and swords. The irregulars were mostly Ruthani from down south and some Sastragathi nomads from the lower Mother River area. Many of the Ruthani wore their traditional headbands with feathers, while the Sastragathi were dressed in leathers and skullcap helmets.

The Army of Syragon arrived at dusk, some three thousand cavalry and an equal amount of foot soldiers, most of them pikemen, arquebusiers and crossbowmen. Together their combined force was a third larger than anything Prince Mythros could put together.

Of the combined cavalry, over three thousand of them were irregulars. The princes gave them permission to loot the nearby farms and outbuildings outside the city walls. "Any farm animals or livestock, bring back to camp," Carthames ordered, knowing full well that his orders would be more disobeyed in the doing than obeyed. One of the problems with irregulars, besides the fact they would desert at the first sign of a bad omen, was that they viewed everything that wasn't nailed down as their personal property.

Soon the blue sky was filled with funnels of black smoke and billowing gray clouds. Carthames knew that this kind of damage was little more than vandalism, but it would hurt the enemy's morale. He wanted the townspeople worried about the sacking of their farms and villages that was as inevitable as nightfall.

The next morning the combined army advanced upon Pytha Town until they reached the first trench that encircled the entire settlement. It was far deeper and wider than the initial scouting reports had indicated and beyond were the town walls. The two armies milled about the edge of the first trench in confusion. The trench was two-men deep and twice as wide. Beyond the trench lay their target, Pytha Town, yet, until they bridged the trench, they might as well be a hundred marches away. Both Prince Carthames and Prince Basilron looked over the barrier to their progress with annoyance and consternation.

"We will have to fill this trench before we can proceed," Basilron observed.

"How?" Carthames waved a hand back at the assembled soldiers and mercenaries behind them. "We came equipped for battle, not ditch digging. I doubt there is more than a few score of spades in our combined armies."

"We passed by many farms," Basilron countered. "We can send back men to search for shovels and wheelbarrows."

*Most of which we've had burned*, he thought unhappily. Still, Carthames was surprised at Basilron's suggestion. In the five winters he had warred with his neighbor, he had never credited the man with any real intelligence. "That is a good idea," he admitted. "If our light cavalry haven't burned all the farms within fifty marches of here."

Then another thought struck him. "Or, if Prince Mythros anticipated our doing just that, then ordered every shovel, rake and wheelbarrow in the princedom to be taken into Pytha Town."

Basilron nodded. "It would be very shortsighted to create such a barrier only to leave the means to defeat it readily at hand. Still, it costs us nothing to look. Even a few rusty spades with broken handles could be made to work."

"That will take time," Carthames growled. "We need to get the trenches bridged before Mythros opens fire with his guns." He looked again at the outer trench. It was too deep for a man in armor to climb out of once he descended. Even a man with no armor would be hard-pressed to scale the sides of a hole over a lance deep.

Carthames had already considered that idea and discarded it. "Blunting swords to dig in dirt will not work. It would take days to bridge one section of the gap, and the earth will not support the weight of the cannon until it has been well packed and shored up at the sides."

Prince Basilron asked irritably, "Then what do you think we should do? Call it a day and return to our castles in disgrace?"

Carthames thought quickly. He looked again at the trench, then at his men. "There will be spades in the baggage train that can be used. And no lack of bodies we can press into service."

"That will work," Basilron said. He called over one of his captains, asking him when the baggage train was to arrive. They had pressed forward without much thought about their camp followers.

"They won't arrive until evening, Your Highness," the captain replied.

"We can't afford to wait until tomorrow," Carthames offered. "We'll send some men into the trench. They can help others climb up the other side. When enough have crossed over, they can be pulled out with ropes on the other side."

"And what will Prince Mythros' soldiers be doing while we are clawing our way to the other side?" Basilron asked.

"The same thing he would be doing if we were dumping earth into his little ditch here: firing at us with their cannon. At least here we are out of arquebus range."

Basilron looked to the walls of Tarr-Pytha. "Wait, if the walls are out of our cannon range, might we not be out of their range as well?"

Carthames was again surprised at Basilron's insight. In all of Hos-Bletha there were no cast guns larger than eighteen-pounders. There were still lots of old bombards around, some that could shoot hundred-pound stones and bigger, but they were highly inaccurate. Even if Mythros had imported founders who knew how to make larger cannons, it took time to cast guns. "You make a good point. Therefore, all Mythros and Kosklos can do is send their armies out to meet us. That is what we expected to deal with all along."

Carthames looked about and saw Captain-General Phyblos standing a polite distance from the princes. "Phyblos, send some musketeers to cover us while we send men to the other side of this trench. We need to provide as much protection as possible for the men crossing over."

Phyblos saluted, then called over his captains and petty-captains to relay the orders. Carthames turned to the men closest to them. "You lot, remove your armor and jump down into the trench. You will be the ladders the others will use to climb up the other side..."

## II

From the castle walls, Democriphon and Mythros watched as men jumped into the trench. With difficulty, they clawed their way up the other side and then assisted those that followed out of the trench.

"It looks like they didn't need the ladders I left behind in the farms," Democriphon observed. "This will work just as well."

Mythros looked at Democriphon with a shocked expression. "What? You wanted them to get past the first barrier? Why?"

"Because a prolonged siege is bad for us and good for them. In Hos-Hostigos I would be content to wait out a siege until winter came and forced the enemy to retreat. However, in this land where winter barely nods in your direction, Carthames and Basilron have plenty of time to wait us out. Sooner or later our foodstuffs would be gone and we would have to emerge weakened to meet them in battle. It's much better for them to come to us. The trench is there to slow them down and keep their guns out of range."

"I...see your point. Do you have any other strategies I should be made aware of?"

"Well...you know how Kalvan's fireseed tends to rupture cannon designed for Styphon's Best?"

Prince Mythros looked uneasy. "Yes, some hands and lives were lost when we first tested it out with handguns and the barrels exploded."

"Then you understand. Were your metal workers able to reinforce your eighteen-pounders?"

It took Mythros a moment to make the necessary mental connections. "Oh! Yes, they reinforced them with steel rings. How soon do we demonstrate this to the enemy?"

Democriphon pointed to the trench where soldiers still struggled to get out of and recover their armor. "When at least half of those soldiers have crossed the ditch. We shouldn't deprive our own men of the opportunity to fight for their new king."

## III

Prince Basilron struggled to make his way up the dirt wall. He had refused to remove his armor, making it that much harder for men—already exhausted from pushing and lifting man after man up the earthen wall—to get their prince up and over the embankment. When he finally achieved the summit, he raised himself with as much dignity as the situation afforded him.

It had taken half a day to get enough men over the trench to make Basilron comfortable with crossing over. He had not wanted to be the first commander over the trench, but had lost the coin toss with Carthames. Somebody had to oversee the battle from the other side; unfortunately, that someone had to be him.

Looking back, he saw several men approaching the gap with wooden planks, likely torn from some farmhouse or barn. Basilron swore with anger and chagrin. *Why hadn't those idiots brought the planks forward before I debased myself by climbing up the dirt? Carthames must have ordered them to bring them after I jumped in the trench. Curse and blast him! When this is over there will be a reckoning for my humiliation.*

On the other side of the trench, Prince Carthames was surprised to see the men arriving with the planks. *Now why did I not think of that? Somebody is due a promotion.* The Prince looked over at Basilron and saw the anger on his face. *Oh, by Styphon's brass bollocks! He thinks I am responsible for this. Well, let him. He needs to be taken down a few pegs.*

The planks went down across the gap and soldiers quickly made good use of the makeshift bridge. Carthames watched the boards bend and wobble under the weight of so many men trudging across. "Phyblos, order them to go over in pairs! We need to find something to shore up the planks from underneath. Send a squad to bring more timbers from that inn we passed a few marches back. This bridge will need a lot more support before it's strong enough to bring guns across."

## IV

Prince Mythros watched with some concern as more boards and timbers were placed over the ditch. He no longer feared the men crossing over it; the enemy cannon were another matter. He did not have the same confidence in the earthworks that fortified the walls as Democriphon.

"I think it is time we joined this war. Do you not think so, uncle?" Democriphon said in a voice that contained a barely suppressed chuckle.

"Yes, Valthros, I think the time has come," Mythros replied

"Would you care to give the command to your men to open fire? Mind you, they should not waste fireseed until the enemy is within range."

Mythros gave his command to his artillery commander who in turn relayed them to all the battery captains. "Remind me, Valthros, when are

Kosklos' forces supposed to take part in this?"

"After the other surprise I arranged."

"Another one? Why was I not informed of this?"

"While you have my trust and respect, I do not know all of your staff. There is another Kalvan saying about loose lips. I decided the fewer people in on my plans the better." Democriphon noticed the look on Mythros' face. "Fear not, uncle, this will be the last time I leave you out of my plans. By the end of this battle I expect to know who can be trusted and who cannot be. Your loyalty was never in doubt."

Mythros accepted Democriphon's explanation with some reservations, but decided to let it rest. He was about to ask another question when gunfire erupted from all sides, shaking the walls from the ground up to the parapets.

"Now would be a good time to retire, Mythros. I will stay to supervise the battle while you take cover."

"I see no reason to cower in my chamber while you risk your life."

"I do. I have learned many things from King Kalvan, and while he often uses confusing terminology, the wisdom of his words comes through very clear. In this case it is something he calls the 'Too Many Eggs in One Basket Rule.' The short of it is that you and I are the most important men on this wall, as far as our army and the enemy are concerned. We cannot afford to risk the both of us. If I fall, then you must stay alive to take my place. And, likewise for me, if you should fall in battle. If we both fall at once, the heart might well go out of our defenders."

Mythros agreed, reluctantly. On his way down to his throne room, he decided he had to meet this Great King Kalvan.

# SIXTY-NINE

## I

The eight-pounder gun, the largest Prince Carthames dared to test on the makeshift bridge, moved slowly over the planks as the boards creaked and squealed. The wood bowed ominously as the full weight of big gun, platform and oxen neared the center. Carthames, who knew little of architecture or bridge building, had simply ordered plank upon plank fitted over the trench without thinking to add supports underneath. To get the wheels over the ends of the makeshift bridge, smaller boards had been used to dig up enough earth to create a ramp at each side of the gap.

More planks were laid at other positions bridging the trench. No longer an obstacle to foot and horse, the armies swarmed over the gap energetically. The combined armies of Carthames and Basilron raced forward only to be caught short when they came to a wide moat. One soldier failed to stop in time and plunged into the chilly waters. Unable to tread water or swim and wearing heavy armor, he quickly sank from sight and all that was left behind was an explosion of bubbles.

Prince Basilron, who had been swept up in the rush, stood at the edge of the moat and silently stared. He wanted to swear but could not think of anything vile enough to cover the situation.

"Get more planks, Dralm-damnit," the Prince yelled. "Longer ones. This moat is almost two lances across."

Basilron stomped and raged until a lead ball grazed the steel pauldron that covered his shoulders. He sprang back, cursing. "You weasel-fornicating whoresons!"

Until that moment, he had not realized he was within musket range of the walls. Trying to look stoic, he moved back from the moat.

## II

Grand-Captain Delamos grimaced as he reloaded his musket. "I thought I had him."

Democriphon could not keep the amazement from his face. "That was a damned good shot from this distance. If not for his armor, Basilron would be either dead or gravely wounded." He reloaded his own musket and aimed at the prince. *What fool wears armor that ornate in a battle?* Democriphon fired, missed and cursed under his breath. "Where did you learn to shoot like that?"

"I was a mercenary captain," Delamos said. "Until several years ago when I took a wound to my leg, I decided to find less hazardous employment. I started as a master-at-arms in Mythros' court and worked my way up to captain of his guard. The prince has a keen eye for talent," he added matter-of-factly. The grand-captain took another shot, dropping a soldier.

"Have you been in any battles I would have heard of?"

"The battle of Fyk, maybe." Another shot. This time he put the lead ball through a man's head.

"Fyk? You were there?"

"Yes, but you would not have liked seeing me there." Delamos reloaded and took aim.

Democriphon, remembering he was in a battle, also took aim. "Why not?"

"My company had been hired by Prince Sarrask of Sask. That is also where I took my career-ending wound."

Democriphon started to question him further when a lead ball grazed his chest plate. "That's enough of that for now. Sound the first horn!"

A long blast from a great horn bellowed, followed by a second, shorter blast. Below, thousands of men bearing Vythron's colors of white and blue stood up from behind the concealing earthen berm and opened fire on the attackers. With only a small portion of their bodies visible, the defenders could fire at will with less risk to themselves. They also gained the advantage of resting their elbows on the ground before them and steadying their aim.

His men cut down the enemy in droves.

Prince Vythron, behind the earthen berm with his men, found he was enjoying himself immensely. It was a rare opportunity for him to participate directly in a battle. Through the dust and smoke, he spotted a set of ridiculously ornate black armor, chased in gold, and took aim.

The armored man succeeded in taking nine steps after he was struck in the helmet and fell to the ground.

## III

Prince Carthames watched intently as the bombard inched ever so slowly over the gap. The planks creaked but held. Once across, Carthames followed behind. The fighting was still well away from his position.

"Get it into range of the tarr walls and commence firing," Carthames ordered. He was about to give additional orders when his Captain-General rode up.

"Sire, we brought six more bombards and three cannon over the trench," Captain-General Phyblos reported. "Several guns fell into the trench. I have a crew of wainwrights and teamsters from the baggage train working on winching them back out…"

"Good. We can't spare any soldiers just now." *Mythros, or more likely that man who claims to be the Orphan Prince, expects me to waste men and horses pulling those cannons out. That was likely part of his plan.* "We're running out of time. Have the ten guns we got across the trench put into range. Let's put them to work and get those walls down."

The Captain-General saluted and rode away. Carthames looked over the battlefield trying to find Basilron in vain. He noticed men were falling everywhere he looked, as was to be expected, but he could not see any of Mythros' or Kosklos' colors on any of them. Somebody was killing his and Basilron's men, yet he could not see whom. It could not all be fire from the walls.

Two mercenaries carrying a wounded third came towards the plank bridge. Carthames braced them and demanded they tell him where the enemy was.

"The gods have deserted us!" one cried out.

The other said, "The enemy fire from above and below. There is another trench close to the dirt wall that surrounds the town. Men armed with arquebuses shoot at us from there. It is almost impossible to hit them with return fire. Most of the rounds strike the dirt instead. They present a very small target, My Lord."

Prince Carthames ignored the incorrect title. A common mercenary could hardly be expected to recognize him, and it was better that he did not. He had seen all the fire directed at Prince Basilron who was wearing his gold-chased parade armor.

He called out to a nearby petty-captain "Tell Captain-General Phyblos that I personally order him to pull his men back from the wall. I am going to start firing our guns. The advance is stalled and there's no point in losing any more of our men."

"Yes, sir!"

Carthames turned back to the bombard crew. "Let us prepare a little gift for our friends in Tarr-Pytha, shall we?"

## IV

The first volley of bombard shot was easily absorbed by the earthworks around the walls. Democriphon could only see three guns from his position though he could hear the others from around the castle. From the sound, he estimated Carthames and Basilron were using rock instead of iron balls. The stones were swallowed up by the wet earth and made little impact on the walls behind. He doubted, from his own experience, that the enemy would have had much better luck with iron cannonballs.

One bombard fired within his vision. The stone came out in fragments, carving up the artillerymen and any nearby soldiers. That happened when the loading crew used too much fireseed or there were cracks in the stone cannonball—or both. Too much of that would ruin the bombard, even cause it to rupture. Just one of many reasons Kalvan had started decommissioning bombards in Hostigos even before he became great king.

Prince Vythron and his men were still fighting, but the enemy had overrun a portion of the berm and they were beginning to take serious casualties. It was time to pull them back to safety. Looking around he spotted a petty-captain reloading his musket.

"Petty-Captain, go down and ready the hidden entrance." The man nodded once and ran off. Democriphon turned to the horn blower. "Sound the recall signal for Prince Vythron."

Down in the trench Vythron almost missed hearing the signal to withdraw due to the gunfire. When he finally did hear it, he signaled his men to the hidden tunnel that went beneath the walls. It chafed his sense of honor to pull out of an active battle, and he would not have if Valthros had not made it very clear that it was a part of his strategy. The prince had also explained that fighting to the last man over one's sense of honor just got good men killed, and often for nothing.

Vythron arrived at the tunnel opening where his men were waiting for him to go through first. "You waited for me? Dralm-damnit, while I am honored by your loyalty, I have to question if any of you have brains. Get your sorry arses in there now!"

In the face of their prince's command, none dared hesitate. The petty-captains ordered the lower ranks in first. The captains, not to be out-done by the petty-captains, ordered them in next. When finally everyone had gone through, Vythron deigned to enter. "I wonder if even Kosklos would have the stomach to get to safety after his men had done so?"

Inside the tunnel, Vythron and one of the petty-captains who had remained near the entrance shoved the heavy oak door closed, then backed away. Five lances back, the petty-captain put down a large pot filled with fireseed, lit a slowmatch, shoved a support beam away, and then hustled his prince out with all speed. The pair left the tunnel scant heartbeats before the rumble of a cave-in issued from the opening.

"I would like to see them try to follow us through that," Vythron laughed. "You, petty-captain, why did you wait?"

"My first duty is to my prince, Sire. You told us to enter, not how far to go. Besides, the support timber was very heavy and I feared you might tire yourself trying to move it, leaving you too slow to win your way free."

"You vex me, petty-captain…?"

"Gryog, sire."

"Gryog. I do not know whether to have you flogged for disobedience or rewarded for your forward-thinking. To Regwarn with it! I'll not waste a perfectly good whip on a hide as thick as yours must be," Vythron finished with a laugh. "To the walls! We have more killing to be done this day, by Galzar!"

## V

Captain-General Phyblos looked down upon the oncoming soldiers. Running as they did, even straight at the walls of Tarr-Pytha, made them difficult targets for arquebuses and muskets. The Captain-General had never held one of the *rifles* used by Kalvan's army, though he had heard stories enough about their greater range and accuracy. A few dozen of those *rifles* would have made short work of the attackers below.

Next to him, the newly arrived Prince Vythron loaded and fired his arquebus with a gleeful expression. It was Phyblos' understanding that the prince rarely took part in battle, yet here he stood side by side with his men risking his life instead of taking cover with Prince Mythros like any ruler with good sense.

Valthros, Phyblos had to admit, was a different case. He had to prove himself worthy of the people's loyalty and the quickest path to that was to show courage and acumen in war.

Something whizzed past his ear. "Sirs, might I suggest you retire to a safer vantage point where you can direct the battle and not fall victim to it?"

Democriphon and Vythron both looked at the Captain-General, then at each other, shrugged, and went back to shooting at the enemy. Phyblos stared at them for a moment, then shrugged and reloaded his musket.

# SEVENTY

## I

Around every temple to Styphon's House was a wall three rods in height. Originally, the Styphoni erected the walls not for protection, but to keep prying eyes out. Styphon's House, almost from its inception, took every precaution to guard its secrecy. It never occurred to the priests that they would need them for physical protection. Until Lord Kalvan appeared, seemingly out of thin air.

Since the advent of Lord Kalvan, Styphoni temples had been raided, their priests slain, their temple domes stripped of gold, along with the vaults, slaves freed and the buildings razed. Overnight, walls previously considered useless around the temples they protected were now deemed necessary and even insufficient by the Styphoni who lived within them. Fortifications were added to the walls, even in areas far from Hos-Hostigos.

Looking up at the west wall of the Drathor Town temple, Ranthar smiled wryly at the thought that Kalvan's actions in the past were making his job that much more difficult in the present. Their former tactic of entering the temple through guile could no longer be trusted. Something different would have to done. Gycules came up with the idea of using grappling hooks on ropes to ascend the walls. Ranthar thought it was a good idea until Uncle Wolf Syros suggested using ladders instead.

"Ladders!?" Ranthar kicked himself for not thinking of it sooner. Climbing a rope in full armor and weaponry would leave even the strongest fighters too weak to do battle. Even Gycules admitted he would need some time afterwards to recover from such an effort. Ladders, easily acquired, took far less effort to climb, and would not make any noise when affixed to the side of the wall, unlike a grappling hook.

"They will likely have doubled the guard," Petty-Captain Morthar observed. "We will need a distraction near the gates to divert their attention."

"I could lead a company to attack the front gate," Captain Andros offered. "While all eyes are on us, you can scale the walls and attack from within."

"All gunsights will be on you as well," Ranthar said. "There is no cover in the hos-plazos like there was in Spartos Town and Marthrax. You and your men would be cut down before we could mount an assault from the rear."

"What we need is a full army to come marching through Drathor Town," Gycules said.

"No, not a real army, we just need to make them think there is," Uncle Wolf Syros said. "We can use the bamboo bombs to duplicate the sound of cannon and bombard fire. With Prince Carthames' army away in Pytha, we will not have to worry about the prince's guard coming to investigate."

"But Styphon's Own Guard might," Ranthar said. "It could draw the Styphoni out. Unfortunately, it would also put the locals in harm's way. Captain-General Democriphon was very clear about avoiding that. It would also put our own people setting the charges at risk."

"This place is like a ghost town," Andros argued. "With the bulk of the army, the camp followers, artisans, ironmongers, bone-shakers, sharpers and whores away, there are few in the way to be harmed."

Ranthar doubted the town was as empty as all that, though he had to admit he had not seen many people on the streets since arriving in Drathor Town. "All right, I have no better idea. We set off the charges close enough to be heard and as out of sight as we can make them. Once Styphon's Own Guard comes out to investigate, we attack."

"If they do not come out?" Gycules asked.

It was a good question. Ranthar thought for a moment, then said, "Then we hope they at least get curious enough to leave their posts to see what is happening outside."

"And if…?" Morthar started.

"Then we try to take them out as quietly as we can," Ranthar finished. "Tonight we gather supplies, and observe the guard movements. Tomorrow we take the temple."

Everybody nodded and moved off to perform their duties. Most of the men were still on the outskirts of the town to avoid rousing suspicion. Ranthar watched everybody go until he spotted the Uncle Wolf and recalled there was something he wanted to ask him.

"Ah, Syros…"

"Yes, Captain Ranthar?"

"Have you ever heard of something called the Thieves Guild?"

## II

Drathor Town lay before him like a jewel waiting to be plucked. Grand Captain-General Kosklos, Prince of Artigos, stood at the forefront of his army taking in the scene before him. He looked the town over with a critical eye. There was no sign of any military activity. That was to be expected since Carthames had taken the better part of his army to attack Tarr-Pytha. The question was: how many men did he leave behind to safeguard his Tarr and town?

"Captain-General Nikocles!"

"Yes, Your Highness."

"Have the scouts reported back yet?"

"No, sir. Only the one sent to inspect the surrounding area."

*By the Twelve True Gods, I should already be speaking to that man.* "Have him sent to me at once."

"Yes, sir!" Nikocles thumped his chest in a salute and trotted off.

Kosklos shook his head. That was the problem with a prince who was also a field commander; the rest of the captain-generals acted like simple captains, with the accent on simple. Everyone was afraid of saying or doing anything without consulting the prince first. *What I really need are some men with brains enough to make their own decisions.*

The scout ran up with Nikocles, then seemed confused as to whether he should bow low or salute.

"Just salute, man!" Kosklos shouted. "This is not the throne room. Oh, bugger the niceties; just tell me what you found."

The man took his prince at his word. "There are at least eight hundred men hiding in the tree line, sir. They do not wear the colors of Drathor or any other princedom with which I am familiar. I managed to get close enough to observe them and even overheard some talk. I believe they are waiting for the command to enter the city and attack the Styphon's House temple."

Kosklos' eyes widened. "Attack Styphon's House!" News of the attacks on Styphoni temples in Taurnos and Bletha had reached even Artigos which had its own temple raids. Kosklos did not care about Styphon's House one way or the other; he never borrowed any gold from them and they had the good grace not to come to him and ask for any. It would be different if Soton had come with the Grand Host; that was a battle he would very much enjoy.

"That must be the bandits we've heard so much about."

"Shall we eliminate the bandits, sir?" Nikocles asked.

Kosklos thought it over then decided against it. "No, we have our mission. If these raiders stay out of our way, we will stay out of theirs. We are here to seize Tarr-Drathor, not defend Styphon's House. In fact, if the Styphoni want my aid, they can pay for it!"

The men all laughed with their prince. "Now, as soon as the rest of the scouts return, we can devise our strategy."

## III

"Whose army?"

Ranthar, normally difficult to put off his game, felt more than a little overwhelmed. If Carthames had returned so soon, it could mean that Tarr-Pytha had fallen and Democriphon was either captured or dead.

"From the colors, green on red, it has to be Kosklos' army," Uncle Wolf Syros said. "Technically, that makes them our allies. However, Captain-General Democriphon elected not to bring the other princes in on our special mission, so they will not be aware that we are their friends."

"Well, what in the Regwarn are they doing here," Ranthar demanded, "when they should be helping back at Tarr-Pytha?"

"Maybe Prince Kosklos decided to split-off on his own and loot Drathor Town while Prince Carthames and his army are away," Gycules suggested.

"Or he has switched sides and is now working with Carthames?" Morthar ventured.

"If that were the case, he would be at Tarr-Pytha, not here," Ranthar argued.

"I think he is here to seize Drathor for Prince Valthros," Uncle Wolf Syros said. "If things go well in Pytha, then Carthames has no place to retreat to. If it goes badly in Pytha, then they have lost one principality only to gain another."

"Uncle Wolf, you know more about the princes than any of us," Ranthar said, "what do you think of Kosklos?"

"Ha! Of all the princes, he has the greatest reputation as a warrior. I have heard he is honorable, treats his men well, and keeps his agreements. I have no doubt that he is here at Democriphon's behest."

"Good. Now, will he bother with us?"

Uncle Wolf Syros had to give the matter some thought. "No. I don't think he will. I suspect he will stick to his mission objective and nothing else. That is, as long as we do not interfere with his men."

Ranthar nodded. "We will need to send an envoy and let him know that we have no interest in getting in his way."

"I will go…"

"I am sorry, Syros, but bandits do not have Uncle Wolfs to speak for them," Ranthar said.

"Then it should fall to me," Chief Petty-Captain Gycules' voice boomed.

Ranthar thought it over. He hated to risk the big man. Of course, he hated to risk any of them. "Are you certain, Gycules? It could be dangerous."

The giant laughed. "And raiding Styphoni temples is not?"

*Good point!* "Okay, it is up to you. Take as much gold as you can carry and give it to the Prince as a token of respect. On second thought, take only half of what you can carry. You might leave us bankrupt with a full load!"

Everyone joined in on the laughter, even Gycules.

## IV

"…and the last bombard here." Prince Kosklos thrust a meaty finger at the map of Drathor Town indicating the front gates of Tarr-Drathor. "After we send soldiers to clear the town of the non-hostiles, we will commence bombardment of the gates." Kosklos stood straight and looked at each captain-general with a meaningful glare. "There will be no looting, raping or killing of the town's folk or the trees here will bend with the weight of the violators. Understood?"

Every head nodded. Kosklos was less concerned about the townsfolk's welfare than maintaining discipline in the ranks. The prince was not afraid to hang a few men to make his point. Besides, a town treated with respect was far less likely to join the fight against the invaders.

"Grand Captain-General."

Kosklos turned to the sound of the voice and spotted a petty-captain standing at attention. Whatever the man wanted, it had to be very important to interrupt his strategy session.

"Yes, Petty-Captain?"

"There…there is a man…I think it is a man…outside. He has requested an audience with the commanding captain-general, sir."

Petty-captains tended to be a stoic bunch, which is how they got to be petty-captains in the first place, at least in Kosklos' army. This man was pale and trying not to shake. The prince's curiosity was piqued.

"Take me to him."

Kosklos followed the petty-captain to the edge of the camp. There, a giant of a man stood holding a large sack on one shoulder and an impressive mace in the other. The most incredible thing was the man's head; it was the head of a great wolf!

On either side of Kosklos several men stood ready with their arquebuses. "Okay, I am here. What do you want of me?"

The giant threw down the heavy sack before the prince. "I bring you a token of my esteem, Captain-General."

The petty-captain inspected the bag. "Prince Kosklos…I mean… Grand Captain-General, this bag is filled with gold!"

"Indeed? Take it to my tent." The petty-captain tried, but could not get the bag onto his shoulder. To save face, he ordered two men to carry it for him while he remained with his prince. "Now, to what do I owe such generosity?"

The wolf-headed giant went down on one knee and placed his mace on the ground before him. "Sire, there is to be a reckoning with the House of Styphon here in Drathor Town. I come to ask only that you do not involve yourself in such a trifling matter."

Kosklos half-believed that the giant was one of Galzar's Minions until he went down on his knee. No avatar of a god would ever kneel before a mortal, even a king, let alone a prince.

"Stand, giant. I do not intend to interfere with your work, provided you do me the same courtesy."

Gycules stood back up with mace in hand. "I am pleased, Your Highness. I believe we will meet again, and it will be as friends."

As the giant turned to leave, one soldier ran foreword and seized a massive arm. "His Highness has not given you leave to depart!"

Gycules seized the man by the throat with his free hand and lifted him high above the ground. "The loyalty of your men do you credit, Your Highness. I ask your leave to depart."

Kosklos was torn between amusement and fear. Amusement won out. "You have my leave, provided you release my man."

Gycules turned his head to the dangling soldier. "Oh, yes. Of course." He released his hold and the soldier landed with a satisfying thud. This time when he turned none tried to stop him.

Prince Kosklos, holding in a chuckle, stepped over to the fallen soldier and helped him to his feet. "What is your name, soldier?"

"Tyrl, Your Highness."

"Son, I think Galzar gave you twice the allotment of courage any man is due. Sadly, I think he withheld some of the brains."

# SEVENTY-ONE

## I

It took three solid hits from the eighteen-pounder to bring down the gates of Tarr-Drathor. Kosklos stood well back of the big gun, as any intelligent man would do, and watched as Tarr-Drathor's defenders raced out with their helmets on their swords screaming "Oath to Galzar!"

Kosklos shook his head in disappointment. He had hoped that the defenders would make a better fight of it. He did not blame them for giving in so quickly, though. With their prince away, along with the bulk of his army, there was little chance they could have even held Kosklos' army for a day, let alone until their prince returned.

"Tyrl, inform the captains that I want them to empty three quarters of Carthames' treasury. Disarm the castellans and lock them in the dungeons with plenty of victuals. No looting! No molesting the women! There are tree branches and rope enough for any who disobey. Whoever becomes prince of this realm, be it Carthames, won over to our side, or some appointee of the Orphan Prince, we do not need to make things difficult for him. This is now a part of his patrimony!"

"Yes, sir!" Trooper Tyrl waited for leave to depart, then ran off to relay the orders.

Kosklos watched as his new aide departed. "I may have underestimated that boy's intelligence."

The battle over, Kosklos found himself becoming bored. He had hoped the fighting would have lasted a bit longer though he was pleased with the low casualties his men suffered. By the time Tyrl returned, Kosklos had decided to find a diversion to pass the time while his men settled accounts in the castle.

"Tyrl, what do you think about going to visit our giant wolf-headed friend?"

His hand went to his throat where he was still tender from being hoisted into the air. "I…I would not presume to advise Your Highness, but did you not agree to not interfere with his…uh…activities?"

*Brave and tactful*, thought Kosklos. "Indeed I did, and you are within your duties as my aide to remind me of such. However, I do not intend to interfere with anything…well, besides the castle, of course. No, lad, I just want a little entertainment."

## II

Ranthar could not believe his luck. Kosklos, the Prince of Artigos himself, provided all the distraction he needed by attacking the castle. Every one of Styphon's Own Guard ran to the front wall to see what was happening. *Styphon's Own Guard must be slipping to leave the rear unguarded like this*, Ranthar thought.

The ladders went up the back wall and in seconds the raiders were over the wall. At Gycules suggestion, they donned the wolf-helms that had brought such terror to the caravans in Bletha and Syragon. By the time the Styphoni knew they were being attacked, over two hundred wolf-muzzled raiders were among them.

Gycules led a platoon of men to open the gates, thus allowing more attackers to join the fray. The Styphoni defenders fought well, but against superior numbers they had no chance. Gycules pulled the gates open and allowed the wave of attackers to run past him. Before he turned to rejoin the battle, he spotted Prince Kosklos sitting on a barrel with several of his men around him. The prince did nothing but watch. Gycules shrugged and returned to his duties.

Ranthar hacked his way through the narthex and up the stairs, silently giving thanks that almost every Styphoni temple used the same floor plan. When he reached the temple master's chamber, he gave it a powerful kick intending to smash it open. Instead, he nearly broke his leg. He swore prolifically as he hopped on one foot and waited for feeling to return to his injured limb.

From down the hall, Petty-Captain Morthar ran to Ranthar's aid. "Are you wounded, sir?"

"I'll be fine, but this door is determined to remain shut," Ranthar grunted.

Petty-Captain Morthar knocked on the door to test the wood. "Solid oak. I'll wager he has a crossbar holding it closed. Should I get the chief?"

"And have him break something other than the door? He is strong, but Gycules is not almighty Galzar. We need something heavy to smash it open."

"I have another idea."

Ranthar and Morthar turned to see Gasphros approaching.

"This is my kind of play," Gasphros added with a smile. "Temple Master," he called out, "you must leave! The infidels have set the temple on fire."

## III

Temple Master Halzar and an underpriest cowered behind a wardrobe as the sounds of fighting came closer. Halzar held his horse pistol close while the underpriest had only his knife. The sound of fierce battle kept their attention on the door, even more than the fighting outside the window. When the noise outside the door ceased, neither knew what to do.

"Temple Master, I fear the temple has been overrun," The underpriest whispered. "We need to leave before the fire arrives. We must hurry."

Halzar looked over at the underpriest, undecided what to do. The underpriest was not as indecisive.

Ranthar stood ready as the door opened. Before the underpriest on the other side could look though the slight opening, Petty-Captain Morthar kicked the door open, knocking him teapot over kettle onto the floor. Ranthar rushed in only to be shot in the chest by the temple master. He fell back into Gasphros' arms as Morthar rushed past.

Highpriest Halzar fumbled with his pistol as Petty-Captain Morthar approached. Not having time to reload, he swung the pistol in Morthar's direction hoping to bluff him back.

He failed, and was run through.

Morthar cleaned his blade on the temple master's vestments then turned to help Ranthar and Gasphros. The bard had already dealt with the underpriest and was inspecting Ranthar's wound, only to find he didn't have one. He searched the impact site carefully; there was some powder residue, but no dent in the breastplate.

Ranthar saw the look on Gasphros face and thought quickly. He could not chance Gasphros becoming too curious about his armor. "Does it look bad?"

"Actually, I see no blood at all. Your breastplate stopped the ball completely." The bard sounded amazed.

"Are you sure, Gasphros? I suspect the priest forgot to ram a bullet into the barrel."

"Does it hurt?"

"No," Ranthar said, "just a slight bruise. I'm lucky that highpriests don't know how to load pistols."

Gasphros looked thoughtful and then sniffed the air. Shrugging his shoulders, he said, "He won't have the opportunity to learn from his mistake, at least."

Ranthar was relieved. Outtime contamination avoided.

"Galzar or Allfather Dralm, or somebody was looking after you, First Captain," Gasphros added as he helped Ranthar up.

## IV

Once the fighting over, Gycules decided it was time to see what Prince Kosklos wanted. Still wearing his wolf-helm, he strode across the hos-plazos.

Prince Kosklos stood up and stepped out to meet the giant. "Ho, my friend! A wonderful display!" The prince started clapping. "I have been enjoying the show."

Gycules stopped in front of Kosklos. Normally, he towered over almost every man he met. Kosklos, while not as tall as Gycules, still cut an imposing figure. He had not noticed the prince's stature the night before due to the distance between them.

"How may I assist you, Your Highness?"

Kosklos chuckled. "You have already done so, my friend. My siege of Tarr-Drathor proved unsatisfactory. Oh, my army took it with ease. If ever they tell the tale, this battle would take naught but a passing mention. But this," Kosklos gestured to the temple, "is worth a song or two. If you or your fellows ever have need of a war to fight, I shall be happy to accommodate you."

Gycules was processing that offer trying to determine if it was as ominous as it sounded while Kosklos turned and picked up a cask next to the barrel he had been sitting on.

"This is for you," the prince said as he hoisted the small cask to the giant. "Call it a token of *my* esteem! Compliments of Carthames' treasury."

Gycules was knocked back a step as he took hold of the cask. It was easily as heavy as the bag of gold he had carried the night before. "My thanks, Your Highness."

"Bah! Call me Kosklos." He extended his hand.

Under the helm, Gycules smiled as he accepted the hand. Kosklos had an incredibly strong grip. "Call me Gycules, Si…Kosklos."

"Until we meet again!" Kosklos turned and walked away in the direction of the castle.

Gycules watched as the prince strode off, then set down the cask and opened the top. Gold rakmars. A man's weight worth. Still smiling, he hefted the cask up on one shoulder and returned to the temple.

# SEVENTY-TWO

## I

The defenders watched as Prince Carthames' men laid ladders on the dirt earthworks and started climbing. Democriphon watched dispassionately as thousands of the enemy approached. The earthworks, while excellent at blunting cannon fire, did little to prevent this sort of attack. On wet earth the climb was nearly impossible, but the ladders supplied purchase where none had been before.

Democriphon felt saddened as he watched the men climb. They were brave to attempt such a thing unencumbered with armor. Only the sheer numbers of men making the climb offered any hope of success. Or rather, it would have had Democriphon not planned for such an assault.

"Now!" Democriphon shouted.

All along the wall, soldiers brought out axes. With a single swing, each man severed a rope. Logs that were secured to the top of the walls rolled downward. The climbers, having no place to go, could only watch in horror as the heavy logs rained down upon them, smashing and crushing them by the hundreds. Democriphon felt a little sick as he observed the tableau of flattened and mutilated bodies below.

Those soldiers who had escaped the avalanche of logs scrambled down the earthworks, stumbling and running wildly. Most of them went down under the volleys of gunfire that accompanied the tumbling logs. A few made it to the forward shield wall, but he estimated that some two-thirds of the attackers were dead or severely wounded. They wouldn't try that tactic again.

"That is no way for a soldier, or even a mercenary, to die," Prince Vythron declared. "I think it is time we ended this. I do not know what you have planned, but I suspect it will be devastating. Why wait?"

"The final actor in this play has yet to enter the stage," Democriphon said.

"What? What does that mean?"

Democriphon smiled mirthlessly. "I have been spending far too much time in the company of performers, Vythron. It means I am waiting for at least one more enemy to arrive. Possibly two."

Realization struck the Prince of Taurnos. "You mean Niclophon's forces?"

Democriphon noted that Vythron no longer referred to his former liege by his title of Great King. "Possibly. Or Prince Xandros' army."

"Prince Xandros!"

"My Intelligencers intercepted a message from Xandros addressed to Styphon's House. He means to betray us to them. Fortunately, even if the message had gotten through, Styphon's House has little of their former military might in Hos-Bletha. What forces they do have are busy with bandits and raiders."

Vythron sniffed his disdain. "Knowing how Styphon's House may be involved in the death of your parents, I can understand your hatred of them. Be assured, I will support you in removing them from Hos-Bletha, Prince Valthros."

"My thanks, Vythron. I—"

Democriphon's sentence was cut short by a thunderous crash. Behind him in the town, he could see damage that could only have been caused by heavy cannon shot.

"That was a big gun!" Vythron said unnecessarily. "I've never heard such a loud blast."

"That had to be a fifty pound bombard, at least," Democriphon said. "As my bard would say: 'now it is a party.'"

## II

Captain-General Theodoros surveyed the landscape taking in everything; the dirt buttressed walls, the deep trench, the moat that came two hundred paces or so after that, and finally the carpet of corpses everywhere.

The first ranging shot had gone over the wall and hit somewhere inside the town. While it might lower the townspeople's morale, such shots had little effect upon the course of the battle.

"Lower your aim and blast the wall," the Captain-General ordered. "I want to test the power of the cannon against those earthworks. Do not even try to get near those trenches. I doubt all the planks in Pytha would hold this gun."

As soon as the barrel had been swabbed, the artillerymen crew reset the elevation of the cannon barrel with a quadrant and packed the cannon with a sack of twelve pounds of fireseed and an eighteen-pound cannon ball. Theodoros nodded and the torch man touched off the powder. The ball, moving faster than the eye could see, flew into the earthen barrier that covered the wall. Clumps of dirt and earth launched into the air and rained down on the embankment. There was no visible damage to the wall.

"That was rather impressive," Theodoros said.

"Impressive?" Prince Carthames looked at the wall and back to Theodoros. "The wall was not even damaged, let alone breached. What is so impressive about that?"

"I am not talking about the cannon shot," Theodoros said. "This is, perhaps, the most powerful gun in all of Hos-Bletha, yet it failed to do any significant damage to the earthworks. That is truly impressive, sire."

Carthames considered the Captain-General's words. "Why bother with the walls at all? This cannon can shoot iron balls over the walls and pummel the castle directly."

Theodoros grimaced. "Tarr-Pytha is out of this gun's range. Every time we bring it closer to the walls, the enemy fires all their guns at us. We can damage buildings inside the town, but destroying it will not gain us access to the people within. We need to enter those walls if we are to attain victory."

A sly look crossed Carthames' face. "No, we don't. We can wait them out. Pytha Town only has so much room within its walls. Right now, those walls are packed with the townsfolk, farmers from many marches, victuals and even livestock. It will take moons, perhaps four or five, but eventually the food and water will be gone. The confined quarters will breed disease and fester devils. When all that has happened, we will be able to just walk in and take the tarr."

Theodoros shook his head. "That leaves us open to attack from Prince Mythros' allies. Haven't you noticed that Prince Kosklos' green and red colors are not in evidence anywhere? Yet he signed the same declaration as Mythros, Vythron and Xandros. Where is he?"

Prince Carthames forced himself to keep his eyes on Theodoros rather than look about for colors he knew were not in evidence. "You…make a good point. In fact, I have yet to see Xandros' colors either. Might they not still be in their own castles? Or even within Tarr-Pytha?"

The Captain-General shook his head. "As you mentioned earlier, the town is full to bursting with Mythros' and Vythron's men, the Prince's subjects and supplies. I hardly think even Bletha Town could hold all of that and two more armies."

"Then, where are they?"

"Indeed."

## III

The carriage bounced and jostled the occupants so badly even the thick down cushions failed to comfort them. Xandros and his Captain-General, unable to use their maps in the shaky conveyance, filled their time looking out at the landscape and discussing war in broader terms.

All around the carriage marched or rode on horseback half of the army of Zynophon. The rest of the armed guard remained at Tarr-Zynophon to protect it from attack by the Sastragathi.

"Sire, you already signed the declaration issued by Prince Mythros," Captain-General Pluthos, a short muscular man with skin ruddy from too much sun over many years, said. "As far as Great King Niclophon will be concerned, you have already chosen your side in this battle."

"I can always tell the king that I was playing along in order to win him some advantage in the fight," Xandros said. "Niclophon is not a warrior; he is a statesman. He understands political subterfuge."

"And if you find that this Valthros is winning out over the king's army?"

"Then we join in with him."

Pluthos refrained from rolling his eyes. It would not do to be seen as disrespectful of his prince. "Sire, any officer can tell you that no battle is certain until the last shot has been fired. Even then, one is well advised to be wary. We may arrive at Tarr-Pytha to find Mythros seemingly about to seize the victory only to have it snatched away by some clever stratagem on the part of…who is commanding King Niclophon's forces?"

"I believe it will be Captain-General Theodoros. Captain-General Lykron was sent off with the King's contribution to the Grand Host in Hos-Harphax. Prince Phaedron forced His Majesty to take his eldest son on as a captain-general. King Niclophon may be trying to get him killed just to be rid of him. This would be a good opportunity, I believe."

"Very well. Captain-General Theodoros could counter Mythros' stratagems and take Tarr-Pytha even when everything seems to be going the other way. As your commanding Captain-General, I advise that you pick the side you most agree with and stick with it."

"Really?" Xandros looked Pluthos in the eyes. "Why?"

"Because win or lose, you will still have your honor. Even your enemies will respect you for it."

"My honor will do little good for the treasury or my neck if I am on the losing side," the Prince countered. "We shall take the measure of the battle we find and pick our side by that and nothing more. I imagine your men will appreciate that even if you do not."

"The mercenaries certainly, as they owe no allegiance beyond what has been bought and paid for, and only for a time," Pluthos said. "The regulars owe their allegiance to Zynophon and their prince, in that order. They need to know that their prince is worthy of their allegiance."

"Zynophon before me?" Outrage colored Xandros' words. "I am Zynophon made flesh!"

"Sire, your forgiveness, but princes come and go, as did your father, your grandfather, and his father before him. One day you, too, will leave this mortal realm and be replaced by either a son, whom you have yet to sire, or whomever the Council of Nobles selects if you die without issue. But Zynophon remains, always."

Xandros mulled over the Captain-General's words. Much of what he considered boded poorly for Pluthos' future.

# SEVENTY-THREE

## I

"Just drink this and lay back, Tulog. This will help you sleep while you heal."

"What is it?"

"A combination of wild black cherry root bark and dried wild lettuce leaves made into a tea," Uncle Wolf Syros explained. "This is an especially potent recipe to help you sleep while I treat your wounds. Now mind me and drink or I will use less pleasant methods to make you sleep." Tulog did as he was ordered and drank. "Good. I will be back to change your bandages and clean your wounds better after you doze off."

Syros moved to the next man. The soldier, already unconscious, was missing his left hand and had severe slashes up and down both arms.

"May Galzar help you through this time of need," Syros said as he removed the tourniquet and inspected the stump. Somebody had applied a torch to the wound, cauterizing it before the man could bleed out. The tourniquet was no longer needed. Unfortunately, that made the man susceptible to other problems.

The fester devils would make short work of him if Syros failed to properly treat his arms.

The big troubadour had told him that Great King Kalvan had his healers wash their hands in lye soap every time each treated a new casualty. That was why their tent was next to a stream, although he was just about out of soap. He also suggested pouring Ermut's Best on the wounds, calling it a fester devil killer. Since Syros met the bard, the number of patients under his care who survived their battle wounds had doubled.

"Gasphros, bring me some of that Ermut's Best, vinegar, and clean wraps. While you are at it, pray that this man did not lose his sword hand."

The bard hastened to bring the requested items. "This is Tulog. He is left-handed but able to use the sword in either hand. He will adapt."

Syros examined the wound more closely. "Hmm...maybe we could have an iron hook or mace ball fitted over the stump when he heals." The Uncle Wolf poured the brandy onto the wound then soaked the wraps in vinegar before dressing the stump. "See if you can rig something to keep this arm elevated. It would be better if the blood didn't settle at the bottom of his arm."

Gasphros nodded, then ran off. Syros moved to the next wounded soldier. In the background he heard a noise that he did not bother to look at. After a moment, a heavy hand came down on his shoulder.

"Uncle Wolf, I am Kosklos, Prince of Artigos, and I beg your indulgence."

Syros turned to see a bear of a man nearly as large as Gycules. Among the Ruthani there was a legend of a wild beast that walked like a man but was covered in fur with gigantic feet; Prince Kosklos looked much like the descriptions of that beast.

"Your Highness, I do not wish to be insolent, but I have wounded men that need my care," Uncle Wolf Syros said.

"As do I, which is why I have come," Kosklos said. "My Uncle Wolf stayed with the men who guard my castle. He is ill and in no condition to travel, but he assured me he could address the hurts of the men that remained behind. My other Uncle Wolf is tending to my men back at

Tarr-Pytha. I was loath to come without either, however I had my mission. I ask that you tend my battle-injured men. In return, you and your fellows may take lodging in Tarr-Drathor with me. This will give you the chance to tend your fallen and rest before resuming you own mission."

"Mission? I do not understand what you mean," Syros said feigning ignorance.

"By Galzar, I almost believe you," Kosklos said with a smile. "Uncle Wolf, in all my years of fighting Ruthani and my own bandits, I never saw an Uncle Wolf tending to either." Kosklos lowered his voice. "I believe you are here at Prince Valthros' behest. I warrant your purpose is to attack every Styphoni temple in Drathor and Syragon until the Styphon's Own Guard detachments come to stop you. This would draw them out of Bletha, Pytha and every other princedom, thus getting them out of our way."

Uncle Wolf Syros measured his reply carefully. "I am certain I know not of what you speak. Nonetheless, you have wounded men in need of tending. I will convey your offer to my fellows."

"Good. We will eat, drink, dance and fight…ah…fight in the comradely sense, as we have no quarrel with you. Oh, and be sure to bring the big fellow with you; I would like to see how he fares at trading blows."

The prince tuned and walked away giving encouragement and praise to the wounded as he passed.

*I very much hope we are on the same side*, Syros thought.

## II

The blast kicked up dust and stone pebbles in every direction. A shard shot up over the wall and struck Prince Vythron on the cheek where his helm did not protect him.

"Great Galzar's Ghost!" The Prince ducked down behind the wall and removed his helmet. "This will take the better part of a day to stop bleeding."

Democriphon looked at the wound; it was shallow and fine. He had done more damage to himself while shaving. "Your Highness, you have the Bleeder's Disease. Is this a serious wound for you?"

Vythron grimaced. "Not as bad as my healers would have you think, but, yes, bad for me. Not the blood I will lose, though I could do better than to spare it. It is the treatment I will be taking for the next two days. Bloody rare meat to replace the lost blood, foul herbs, leafy vegetables… Ugh! I would rather bleed."

"Why do you fight instead of retire to a safe position?" Democriphon asked.

"Normally, I avoid fights such as this. However, as this is a fight against our Great King, I feel it my duty to put in an appearance with my men."

Vythron's character went up in a big way in Democriphon's estimation. "I think you have appeared enough this day. Please, retire and get that wound treated; for your men if not yourself."

Vythron sighed. "Very well. I will brief Mythros on how the battle progresses. At least, that is what you should tell any who ask."

"Agreed, now let us get you to…"

"Sire!"

Democriphon and Vythron both turned their heads in the direction of the voice. It was a petty-captain wearing a sash with the blue and gold colors of Pytha over his steel back-and-breast.

"What is it? Oh, stop bowing and speak, man!" Democriphon said irritably. *These Pythans need a few lessons on battlefield etiquette. I'll put Captain Andros on that first chance I get.*

"Another party has joined up with Niclophon's forces, sir. From the banner, I believe it is Xandros' army."

"Ha! So he shows his true colors at last." Democriphon turned to Vythron. "I warrant he took one look at that siege party and decided then and there which was the safer bet."

Prince Vythron agreed.

"Petty-Captain, escort Prince Vythron down to Prince Mythros. He has a report to make there. Oh, and see to it a healer gets a look at that cut."

The petty-captain saluted and went with Vythron. Democriphon turned his attention back to the battle. It was just about time to spring his little surprise.

## III

"Now this is a party!"

First Captain Ranthar nodded at Gasphros in agreement. As he looked out at the revelry all about him, he could not help thinking that the men needed this after months of almost constant danger. Prince Kosklos had brought his personal chef who supervised the buffet style meal laid out across several tables. Carthames, if ever he returned to his castle, would find his larder bare down to the stone slabs.

In the middle of the throne room which Kosklos had commandeered for the revelries, the prince and Gycules were locked in an arm wrestling match that had been going on for the last half-candle. Both men were red-faced and sweating and almost completely immobile. Neither could seem to move the other so much as a single joint in one direction or the other. The wagers grew in size as the battle continued.

"Who did you bet on, Captain Ranthar?"

He turned to Uncle Wolf Syros and smiled. "Honor demands that I support Gycules. We cannot have it get around that I do not support my men."

"Ha! Well said. Now, what do you really think?"

"I think one of them will blow out his heart before he gives in. I do not suppose you could go over there and declare a tie?"

Syros gave the matter some thought. "I suppose I'll have to. At this point it may be the only way for both of them to save face. To be honest, I had not believed there was a man in the Six Kingdoms that matched Gycules in strength, let alone could best it."

"No one's bested anyone, yet." Ranthar pulled out a flask of Ermut's Best he had been saving. "Here, split this between them. It might ease the disappointment."

The Uncle Wolf accepted the flask, then made his way over to the silent battle between the prince and the chief petty-captain. Ranthar did not wait to see how things would go. Instead, he walked out to inspect the men on guard.

Soldiers, wearing the green and red colors of Kosklos' army, walked back and forth on the parapets between the watchtowers. Ranthar walked up the stone stairs to tell them that they would soon be replaced and allowed to join the feast within Tarr-Drathor.

Captain Andros barely noticed that the first captain had joined him until Ranthar asked what had captured his attention.

"I noticed a cloud of dust off in the distance, sir," Andros explained. "I sent a scout to investigate and I am waiting for him to return."

Ranthar turned in the direction indicated by the Captain. There was the dust cloud and, closer, a man on horseback riding full out.

Andros did not wait for the scout's report. "Guards to position! We have trouble coming this way."

Even though he suspected the answer, Ranthar asked what Andros thought it was.

"Styphon's Own Guard would be my guess. Prince Valthros sent us out here to draw the Guard away from the temples in Basilron and Pytha; well, I guess we did our job."

"I think you are right. Our friend in Bletha Town will keep the guard from Bletha from joining in. Still, I think we are going to be outnumbered."

"Do you think Kosklos will join us in fending the Styphoni off?"

Ranthar turned in the direction of the stairs. "We'll soon find out."

## IV

Prince Kosklos looked out at the oncoming army. Even at their current distance he could make out the silver and red of their armor and capes.

"Styphon's Own Guard," he reported. "I did not think there were that many left in all of Hos-Bletha."

"There shouldn't be that many," Ranthar said. "Not after all the Temple Guards that we've killed!"

"They must have…wait…I can just make out…yes! Mercenaries." Kosklos became confused. "I thought Styphon's House was under the Ban of Galzar."

"No, that's just a rumor. A ban can only be brought by a conclave of highpriests at the High Temple of Galzar in Hos-Agrys," Uncle Wolf Syros said.

"Hmm. Judging by the number of guards, they must have emptied out every temple in all of Hos-Bletha unless Styphon's House sent reinforcements." Kosklos turned to Ranthar with a look of respect. "I can always judge a man by the quality of his enemies. This looks more like the fight I came here for. You may consider my men as your men. How do you wish to proceed?"

Ranthar breathed a mental sigh of relief. Without the aid of the Artigosi army, they wouldn't have stood a chance of surviving the upcoming battle.

"I have sent a few of my men to the temple to arrange for a little surprise," Ranthar said. "You should keep your men well away from there."

Kosklos' eyebrows went up then dropped back down. "I shall be certain to do so, Robinos." He looked back out at the oncoming guard. They were less than a tenth of a candle away. "May I suggest you have some of your, ah, wolf-men stand behind the wall? We want them to know we are here, yes?"

Ranthar thought it over. Better to meet Styphon's horde while protected by solid walls and aided by Kosklos' men than out in the open. "Agreed. What will we do about the gate you knocked down?"

"I have one cannon and two bombards loaded and ready to be touched off as soon as the enemy tries to breach the gate. Our guests may chance one attack, maybe even two if they are truly foolish, but I very much doubt they will try a third time."

Ranthar did not have as much faith in Kosklos' assessment. In his experience, fanatics did not always behave in a sane manner.

"We'll make our stand here, then." Ranthar looked over Prince

Kosklos and asked, “Are you certain you want to be a part of this?”

“Ha! I will have to sack all of the Styphon’s House temples in my realm when I return to Artigos as per my new great king’s command, so I might as well get started now.”

# SEVENTY-FOUR

## I

"Double-damn that treacherous bastard!" Prince Vythron roared. "I should have expected something like this."

Prince Mythros poured another goblet of wine and offered it to the outraged prince. The Uncle Wolf waved it away. "It will thin the blood, and he cannot afford that right now."

Mythros nodded and handed the chalice to the Uncle Wolf, instead. Vythron had already soaked several linen bandages and the blood still seeped from his cheek.

A big explosion sounded off from outside of the castle.

"How much longer is Valthros going to hold back?" Vythron grumbled.

Another, much larger explosion sounded off. Mythros and Vythron felt the reverberations through the floor.

"I think we have the answer to your query," Mythros said.

"Gods, demons, devils and monsters!" Captain-General Nikocles cursed as he regained his feet. "What in Galzar's Mace was that?"

Democriphon, also struggling to his

feet, brushed dust and dirt off himself. "That was the bomb field I had buried between the trench and the moat." He looked out through the haze of the settling dust. "I was not going to set it off until I found a way to coax Niclophon's forces to bring that cannon closer. It must have been hit by a misfire from one of the cannon's or bombards used by the enemy."

He shrugged. "Well, nothing to be done about it now. Blow the third signal!" The trumpeters let out three short blasts and one long one. Off in the distance they heard the same signal repeated.

The Pythan captain-general approached the wall and looked out at the devastation. Bodies, mostly pieces of bodies, littered the grounds in every direction. *By the Gods Mercy, this is no way to treat anyone, not even the enemy.* "Sire, may I be as bold as to inquire what that third trumpeting signaled?"

Democriphon smiled grimly. "Wait for the dust to clear and you'll soon see for yourself."

Armed and armored men wearing red and green Artigosi colors appeared as if they had sprung up out of the ground. In fact, they had been hiding in haylofts, attics, mews, root cellars and anywhere else they could stay undetected until called by the sound of the trumpeters. They came together under the command of Captain-General Soros, Kosklos' first cousin once removed.

Soros did not waste time with speeches. He seized the nearest horse and called for the attack. In seconds the men organized themselves and started for Tarr-Pytha.

## II

Captain-General Theodoros brushed himself off, then looked to his precious cannon. The blast had not been powerful enough to destroy it, but it had been thrown to one side on the ground, shorn of its moorings and mobility. It would take his artisans half a day to put it back in service.

*King Niclophon is not going to like this*, Theodoros sighed. Turning to the battlefield, he could see the bodies of his vanguard lying about like butcher's shop discards. All around him men were stumbling or down on the ground; he estimated about a third were down, either dead or stunned, but enough were up and alive to mount another offensive. He drew his sword and called out to his men. "An explosion such as that one can only be done once and no more. Come! It is time to dispatch this False Prince. For our Great King! For Hos-Bletha!"

"For Hos-Bletha!" his men shouted

Theodoros took great pride in his men as they girded themselves for the forthcoming battle. He turned to lead the charge towards the town walls. All around him, his men and Prince Carthames' troops rallied to his call. Only Xandros' men seemed to be holding back. *No matter*, he thought, *I shall settle with that double-crosser after this battle is done.*

Theodoros started running toward the walls when he heard gunshot from behind. *We are out of effective range for arquebus.* When he turned and looked, he saw several companies of new fighters, in red and green colors, had joined the fray. Unfortunately, they were not there to support him.

Prince Xandros saw the new combatants before Prince Carthames or Captain-General Theodoros and immediately realized what it meant. The Prince of Zynophon had chosen the wrong side. While he watched, Prince Kosklos' men slaughtered the pitiful remains of the Royal Army and its allies.

Xandros found a riderless horse and struggled to heft his considerable bulk onto the saddle. Once mounted, he gathered his remaining troops and spurred the beast forward, racing away from the battle as fast as the horse could carry him. It was not until he was well away from the fighting that he recalled the pay wagon had been left behind.

## III

Democriphon looked down at the battle still raging beyond the trench. "Captain-General Nikocles, I think now would be a good time for us to give Captain-General Soros our assistance, little though I think he needs it."

"Yes, sire!" Nikocles ran down the steps with more speed than was wise, shouting orders all the way. The soldiers quickly formed up in front of the main gate waiting to go forward. The first gate was pulled open to reveal the stone tunnel that led to the next gate. The second gate had to be cleared as it had been pulverized by Carthames' guns earlier.

"ALL RIGHT YOU SONS OF GALZAR!" Captain-General Nikocles shouted, "Let's send those bastards straight into Regwarn! Kill the wounded except for the mercenaries unless they want to fight. Go! Go! GO!"

The combined forces of Mythros and Vythron surged out of the tunnel. Two teams of engineers took the lead, placing planks over the moat to allow the fighting men to pass quickly over the obstacle. Several yelled out "Death to the regicide Niclophon!" while others started singing the ballad, "When the Orphan Prince Comes Marching Home."

Nikocles, normally a man to lead from the rear, ran as fast as he could to keep up with the front men. The battleground, covered in corpses and ravaged by the explosions, was unsafe for horses so no cavalry could join the main attack, just at the flanks.

"Niclophon's captain-general is mine!" Nikocles shouted as he approached the trench.

Again, Democriphon's engineers raced forward to allow passage over the second obstacle. To be able to move as quickly as they did, none of them could wear armor. Just a pistol and sword. Two were shot down before they reached their objective.

Nikocles raced straight toward the great brass cannon. There he saw Prince Carthames and a man wearing the regalia of a captain-general. The Pythan captain-general was forced to stop at the edge of the trench as he had out-raced the engineers.

## IV

Prince Carthames and Captain-General Theodoros tried to rally the men in vain; they were surrounded and outnumbered. Carthames fought two foes at once until he was disarmed and forced to his knees. He could see Theodoros still fighting like a madman. No, not a madman, but a very skilled swordsman fighting for his life. Carthames watched as the captain-general killed two opponents before the butt of an arquebus landed at the back of his helmet.

Across the trench, a captain-general in Pythan colors yelled in frustration, then ordered the prisoners taken to the castle. Carthames and Theodoros, stripped of arms and armor, were then bound with rope and marched off to the castle.

"Let Prince Valthros decide what to do with them," Nikocles muttered.

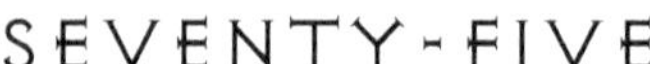

# SEVENTY-FIVE

## I

"Fire!" The cannon sent the eighteen-pound ball through more than twenty of Styphon's Own Guards as they tried to rush the gate. Dozens more swarmed through the gates over the bodies of the maimed and dead.

"Fire!" Prince Kosklos repeated, this time to the first bombard crew. The gunner touched the slowmatch to the fuse, then covered his ears. More Styphoni fell dead or dying, yet the survivors continued forward as fast as they could climb over the bodies of the fallen.

Prince Kosklos signaled to his firing line. A volley of arquebus fire rained down on Styphon's Own Guard.

"They must want your hide very badly, Robinos," Kosklos observed. "You must have seriously pissed-off somebody very high up."

"Good!" Ranthar shouted as he fired off a round. "That was the idea."

Kosklos laughed as he hefted a double-bladed battle-axe. It was the first such weapon Ranthar had seen on this time-line. "I think it is time to meet them up-close. I ordered my men to target the ones reloading, so we should be able to approach without getting shot too badly."

*Shot too badly?* Ranthar could not help wondering what the bear-like prince thought was "too badly."

Ranthar, Kosklos and their respective forces joined with the Styphoni, hacking and stabbing as they went. Ranthar noticed that none of the mercenaries were trying to force their way through the gates. Gunfire in the background suggested they were trading shots with the men on the walls. It made sense; mercenaries hired themselves out to risk their lives in battle, not throw them away in a suicidal rush on a fixed position.

Ranthar barely dodged a sword thrust to his face and stumbled over a body as he moved backwards. Unable to maintain his balance, he went down. His Styphoni opponent seized the advantage and moved in for the kill, only to find himself suddenly bereft of a head. Through the spray of blood that erupted from the man's neck, Ranthar could see Kosklos spare a glance back and wink at him.

*Oh, yes, I am so glad Kosklos is on my side!*

As Ranthar tried to get back up, he felt himself lifted up and returned to his feet. Behind him, Gycules had joined the battle. Moreover, he was wearing his wolf-helm and swinging his two-handed sword with one arm and a mace with the other. Ranthar almost laughed; the first petty-captain was competing with Kosklos! *No doubt they will compare body counts after the battle.*

Ranthar recovered in time to parry a thrust and skewer his attacker. He moved on to another foe when something struck his head. The last thing he remembered was Gycules leaping over his body.

## II

"Now, what are we to do with the both of you?"

Captain-General Theodoros and Prince Carthames stood before Democriphon as he sat on Mythros' chair-of-office. Prince Mythros stood to his right and Prince Vythron to his left.

"Prince Carthames, I could ransom you back to your princedom, but I fear by now Prince Kosklos has emptied out your treasury."

"What!" Carthames started forward only to be hustled back by two large men-at-arms. "What do you mean?"

"While you were here attacking me, I sent Kosklos to seize your castle. As of right now you have no home to return to," Democriphon said. "Now, I will offer you a choice. I have already decided to seize Basilron's lands as my own since he has no heirs to contest it. Shall I add your realm to my personal holdings as well, or will you accept me as the rightful heir of Marocles and swear an oath of fealty to me?"

Carthames thought it over. "No, an oath of fealty with a gun pointed at one's head is meaningless. I cannot swear an oath under these circumstances."

Democriphon considered Carthames' words. "Carthames, I like you. I am going to release you and ask Kosklos to return half your treasury. I will have you escorted out on the morrow. Tonight we shall feast as fellows."

Carthames was stunned. "Is this a bribe? My oath cannot be bought…"

"No bribe. You are free to go and your realm is your own."

Carthames stood staring for a moment. *What manner of man casually releases an enemy and returns treasure that is rightfully his as spoils of war?* "Sire? I have reconsidered. It would be an honor to serve you in Hos-Bletha. When next we meet in battle, it shall be as allies."

"Traitor!" Theodoros screamed. "How dare you betray your rightful king for this…this…pretender!"

"Theodoros," Democriphon's voice rang out like a shot. "You would be well-advised to look to your own interests right now."

Theodoros closed his mouth with an audible snap. In fact, he expected to be executed or enslaved, as often happened to enemy soldiers.

"Traditionally, there is no ransom for a captain-general, especially one who has been defeated in battle. I doubt Niclophon would welcome you with open arms." Democriphon stood up and approached the man. "I, however, do not kill without reason. I think you have potential and I would like to offer you a position in the new Kingdom."

Theodoros did not hesitate. "Nay. I have chosen my side and will stand by it. Take my head off if you wish, but I will not foreswear my oath to my king."

Democriphon nodded. Had he been made the same offer by King Kaiphranos, his answer would have been the same. "Very well. You are free to leave with the remainder of your army, less the mercenaries, if you will give me your Oath to Galzar that you will return home straight away and not attack Us or any of Our allies. I have a message for Uncle Niclophon, and I think it will come across better from you."

## III

Captain Ranthar woke up surprised to still be alive. He knew he was among the living by the throbbing in his head.

"Look who has decided to join us!"

Ranthar turned to see Uncle Wolf Syros sitting next to his cot. "Did somebody get the number of that cannon that shot me?"

Syros did not understand what Ranthar meant by 'number.' The Uncle Wolf assumed it was a practice to number or name the big guns in his homeland. "No cannon, Ra—Robinos. A rock. All that blasting so close to the gates dislodged some loose stones. Several men were stuck as the wall above the gates crumbled. You should have worn your helm, but I suppose your head is hard enough."

"How long was I out?"

"Half a day. I feared you might have a brain injury." Syros held up a fist with two fingers out. "How many fingers am I holding up?"

"On which hand?"

"The middle one," Syros said with chuckle.

"Two."

"You will be fine, I think, Robinos. No strong drink or vigorous activity for a few days and you will be back to robbing caravans in no time at all."

Ranthar shook his head then regretted the action. His head throbbed worse for a few minutes before returning to what currently passed for normal. "The Robinos' act is over. If Valthros has done as well I suspect, we have accomplished our mission. Niclophon will be so busy trying to sew his kingdom back together, there is no chance he will be sending any troops to aid the Grand Host any time soon."

Syros stroked his beard. "So that is it? Your mission is done and now you will return home?"

"Oh, that's not what I meant. No, I will be heading over to Pytha to see what Valthros' plans are. I am his second in command, so I imagine he will make me a captain-general or something. We didn't come here to start a civil war, but now that we have one, I will wager he will want to see it through to the end."

"Excellent! Then I will continue to be needed as well. By the way, you may want to make Gycules a captain before Prince Kosklos does. Those two have been getting on like brothers. You should have seen them trading blows after the battle. As Galzar is my witness, most men would have fallen dead from a single punch by either of them."

"Then I take it the battle was won despite my absence."

Syros laughed. "Indeed! Once the Styphoni were laid low the mercenaries quickly surrendered. There's no profit in fighting when the people paying you are dead. And, since they were hired by Styphon's House, they are only too happy to sign up with us against Niclophon."

Ranthar sat up quickly, which started his head pounding all over again. He looked at Syros, asking, "Are these mercenaries those Blethans with no loyalty to their king or foreigners to this kingdom?"

"Oh, they are loyal to the king, all right," Syros said solemnly. "However, there is a question as to whom their proper great king is. Prince Kosklos has been enlightening them on that point. We now have twenty-five hundred mercenaries for Valthros' army…as long as he doesn't pick any fights with Styphon's House—that is until the mercenaries' contracts have expired.

"So, what do we do now? More than half the temples in Hos-Bletha will soon be razed and their priests executed, assuming…Valthros' army has won in Pytha."

"We'll join up with Prince Kosklos and go to Pytha with his army. Wearing his colors we can travel unnoticed. I suppose we will have to give him a portion of the treasure from the temple we raided here."

"It would be a nice gesture," a voice boomed out from behind them.

Ranthar and Syros turned to find Kosklos and Gycules, arms around each other's shoulders, standing together. Both were bruised and bloody.

"Great Galzar!' Ranthar exclaimed. "Did you two take all that damage against Styphon's Own Guard?"

"Those weaklings? Hardly! Gycules and I were in a game of trading blows. It is rare I find a man that can hold his own with me, or even dares try!"

"I admitted he bettered me," Gycules added, "when one of my teeth became loose. I would much rather keep my teeth than win a simple game."

"Simple he calls it!" Kosklos laughed. "Anyway, I accept your offer of tribute and will happily escort you to Prince Valthros' enthronement. After a brief stop in Syragon."

"Syragon?" Ranthar said confused.

"Aye! Taking Drathor was only half my mission. Now we go to Syragon Town and take Tarr-Syragon from Basilron. With the extra twenty-five hundred mercenaries I just inherited from Styphon's House, we will make short work of the forces he left behind."

## IV

Before Captain-General Theodoros left with his remaining forces, minus the mercenaries, he braced Carthames in the courtyard of Tarr-Pytha. Carthames had decided to remain in Pytha until the coronation. This was on the advice of Vythron who reminded the Drathori prince that Kosklos held his Tarr and would not surrender it until so ordered by Valthros.

"Why have you foresworn your oath to Great King Niclophon?"

Carthames could see the fury in the younger man and understood it.

"When Valthros chose not to force my oath and even allowed that I could return to my homeland with half of my treasury intact, I was reminded of the kind of ruler Marocles was. At that moment, I truly believed this man to be the son of the greatest king Hos-Bletha ever knew. So, if Valthros is the son of Marocles, then he is the proper ruler of Hos-Bletha. As such, he is the only king I can support."

"And if he is a charlatan?"

"I very much doubt he could fool Mythros, but if he is, in fact, a fraud, I shall personally take his head off—and damned be the consequences!"

Theodoros nodded, then turned to go. Carthames was a man of honor, in his eyes, and underserving of the dagger the young captain-general had been prepared to thrust into the prince's throat.

# SEVENTY-SIX

## I

"The panther's share of my kingdom is now in the hands of this… this…imposter!" Skranga watched as Great King Niclophon raged and spat at Captain-General Theodoros. "He has five principalities under his thumb. One of them is Artigos. Artigos! Prince Kosklos is hailed as the mightiest warrior in all of Hos-Bletha, or what's left of my Kingdom."

"There is one other thing, Your Majesty. The imposter sends a message."

Niclophon drummed his fingers on the Silver Throne impatiently. "Well? Out with it."

"He says he knows not if you were involved in the death of his parents, but if you were not, then Styphon's House is, and any who stand with them will be brought down."

Skranga had intended to hold his tongue until Niclophon's rage passed. However, it was clear young Theodoros was about to be thrown to the panther's den. A captain-general who failed to defeat Democriphon was one he very much wanted to keep in charge of the Blethan army. And the comments about Styphon's House, while good for Democriphon, might place Eldra, Calthros and himself in danger.

"Sire, I should remind you that Prince Phaedron is every bit as good a strategist as Kosklos, and wields the second largest army in all of Hos-Bletha. I am quite certain you do not wish to antagonize such a man by harming his son. Besides, even Grand Marshal Soton has been momentarily foiled by the Daemon Kalvan."

Niclophon considered Sangar's words. "Yes, this is true. But…no… could Valthros be another Daemon like Kalvan?"

Skranga had not considered that. He decided to capitalize on it. "Indeed. Much of his strategies and actions have been similar to Kalvan's. I might even suggest that he is in league with this bandit Robinos. It would explain why the temples and caravans of Styphon's House have been his primary target."

"By Styphon's Beard! I think you are right, Your Worship." Niclophon returned his gaze to Theodoros. "You were ill-prepared for this kind of opponent and I cannot hold you at fault for it. I will send an envoy to Balph to demand the return of Captain-General Lykron and Our contribution to the Grand Host. When next we face this Daemon Valthros it will be with the full might of Hos-Bletha. I want every regular, irregular, mercenary and princely levy brought to bear when next we march on this imposter. If necessary, we will offer amnesty to the slaves and arm them for the fight. Go to your father and tell him he is to place his entire army under your command."

Skranga almost swallowed his tongue. He had overplayed his hand and now Democriphon would pay the price. As soon as he was dismissed from court he went back to his chambers before Niclophon requested that Styphon's House send the Grand Host to assist him in restoring his kingdom. He quickly explained to Eldra and Calthros what had happened.

## II

"Why would you tell him that about Robinos?" Lady Eldra demanded.

"Because he was a quarter-candle away from coming to that same conclusion. It doesn't matter, really. Ranthar's time as a bandit has served its purpose and he would be better used elsewhere. I think he would be more useful as an aide to Democriphon. Maybe he'll make him a baron and he can administer Mallegast. Whatever he does, banditry is no longer needed. Democriphon has his own power base from which he can raid Styphoni temples."

"What about the great murdering army they are about to face?"

"It will take at least two to three moons to gather that kind of force. Likely longer. It was bound to happen anyway. Remember what happened after Kalvan created Hos-Hostigos from the princes that seceded from Hos-Harphax. They are still warring over that! At least we know what is coming and from where far in advance. I suspect Niclophon's captain-generals will be just as reluctant to fight until the contribution to the Grand Host returns. That gives Democriphon a few more moons to prepare for the coming war."

Eldra sat on a padded bench. "What do we do until then?"

"The same thing we are doing now; feed disinformation to Great King Niclophon, while sending his plans to Democriphon. There's little else we can do."

## III

The Coronation went without incident. Mythros, Kosklos, Carthames and Vythron each gave their oath of fealty to Valthros, Great King of Hos-Bletha. As Basilron was dead, his dukes and barons were brought in to give their oaths of fealty and allegiance to Valthros, Prince of Syragon, Great King of Hos-Bletha. After the ceremony, Democriphon pulled Mythros off to the side.

"Why am I the Prince of Syragon? What difference does it make? I'm co-ruler of the entire kingdom, now."

"Tradition," Prince Mythros explained. "Niclophon is the Prince of Bletha, Great King of Hos-Bletha, and so it has always been. In your case this is doubly advantageous."

"It is? How so?"

"When you retire as king—assuming that the *real* Valthros ever has an issue—you will have a principality to sustain yourself in proper fashion. On the other hand, you may style yourself as an archduke as many kings who succeed have done in the past. Is this not better than a simple dukedom?"

"In truth, it is," Democriphon said as he rolled the term over in his mind. *Prince Valthros. Archduke Valthros. Archduke Democriphon…* "Do any of the retired kings ever change their names?"

"A king or prince may do as he pleases, Your Majesty. Oh, that reminds me: congratulations on your victory!"

"Thank you. I will strive to be worthy of the Silver Throne."

Both drank and watched as Prince Kosklos held a trio of women captivated with tales of his prowess in various battles that would have seemed fanciful, coming from anyone else, before Democriphon had heard of his game with Gycules.

"Ah, Uncle Mythros…" Democriphon started.

"Yes, Sire? And please, none of that, 'uncle,' we are family. What do you want to know?"

"Tell me, what are to be my first acts as Great King of Hos-Bletha?"

Mythros nodded. "First, there are the spoils of war to be divided out. At least a quarter of Carthames' treasury should be turned over to Kosklos, as he was acting upon your orders when he besieged Tarr-Drathor. Next, you are expected to appoint men from your war council to important positions and give out land grants, and such. You can promote those bandits of yours into positions of prestige. I advise you do so with great consideration, though. Those you appoint will be your representatives to the rest of the kingdom."

"Then, I can make Ranthar the Grand Captain-General of the Hos-Blethan army."

"If you think he is capable in that role."

"Very much so. Gycules should be the High Petty-Captain, then."

Mythros looked confused. "I have never heard of such a title."

"I think we expect too little of the petty-captains when in fact they can run a war without any officers. Gycules will be in charge of overseeing their training and organization. He did wonders in Mallegast. Andros will be a Captain-General under Ranthar. I think they will work well together."

"You know best in such matters, Your Highness. What titles will you bestow?"

"Titles? Hmm…I think Ranthar should be the Baron of Mallegast. I should give Gasphros a barony as well. I shall have to discuss this later. For now, I know exactly what we need."

Mythros waited patiently while Democriphon gathered the princes, Ranthar, Gasphros, Andros and Uncle Wolf Syros together.

"I do not think it will come as a surprise when I say war will be coming soon," Democriphon said.

Every head nodded.

"Moreover, Great King Niclophon will meet us with everything he has, including any help in men, gold and arms he can pry from Styphon's House. Therefore, I am going to send an envoy to Hos-Hostigos."

Ranthar and Gasphros nodded while the rest looked confused.

"I will offer to send gold and anything else that will aid Great King Kalvan. In return, we will ask for rifles, cannons, and artificers who will teach us to make these things ourselves."

Kosklos' face lit up like a panther that had gotten scent of meaty prey. "I have heard of the rifles, and cannon that can send shot farther than even the most powerful bombard. By the Wargod's Mace, I would be honored to lead the envoy!"

"I'm sorry, Prince Kosklos, but we will need you here. Niclophon the Usurper will be gathering forces to reassert his hegemony. There will be plenty of fighting, you can count on that."

Kosklos had a wolfish grin on his face.

*I wish I could find an excuse to join them*, Ranthar thought.

Democriphon said. “Gasphros, I want you to see whoever it was that was making that fireseed and provided us with victuals when we were still struggling in Mallegast.”

“Who?” Prince Mythros started to interject, then shut up. He was very curious as to which one of his underlings had been supplying fireseed to outsiders.

“…I believe now we could use his aid in a more expanded role. To help you deal with this person from a position of strength, I’ll make you a baron, with lands to be determined later in Syragon.”

“Your Majesty is most generous, and wise.” Gasphros gave a not quite mocking bow. “I will speak with my…friend…about the fireseed.”

“Excellent. We will have more to discuss later. For now, as you would say, it’s a party!”

# SEVENTY-SEVEN

## I

Captain-General Lykron was growing tired of endless war councils about strategy and how many horses and oxen would be needed to provide supplies for the largest army ever to see action in the history of the Five Kingdoms. But, mostly, he was tired of being ignored and dismissed by this upstart Grand Captain-General Phidestros. The former mercenary was ten years his junior and far less experienced at leading men. From what the Grand Master had told him, the mercenary had been jumped-up by Great King Lysandros who wanted someone in charge of the Grand Host of Styphon's House whom he could manage, rather than Grand Master Soton.

"But why?" he had asked. "Isn't Styphon's House paying all the bills?"

Soton had smiled wryly. "Yes, but we need to use Harphax City as the assembly point for the war against Hos-Hostigos. We also need the full cooperation and resources of Great King Lysandros. His troops and those of his liegemen number almost a quarter of our strength. The Usurper

Kalvan has proved himself, in battle after battle, to be a most sagacious commander. It will take our combined strength to put his rule to an end."

Lykron nodded in agreement; he understood the art of compromise. He had been after Great King Niclophon for a dozen winters to build a fleet of galleys to chase the Caribi to their home villages and burn them all out. Unfortunately, Niclophon was tight with his purse when it came to military matters, but opened it readily when it came to buying finery and jewelry for his latest conquests. If Niclophon had spent even half of all the gold he borrowed from Styphon's House on his army, they would have been able to end the Caribi menace and tame the Swamp Ruthani in the Lower Peninsula.

Fortunately, the meeting was starting to break up, except for Soton and Phidestros who were still conferring on the dais. Lykron was pulled from his musings when Captain-General Theodoros came into the council hall, striding determinedly toward him. He went to meet his junior officer before he attracted any attention.

"What are you doing here?" he whispered.

"Big problems at home, sir," Theodoros whispered hoarsely. "I've been riding non-stop for the better part of a moon-quarter to get here in time."

That got Lykron's full attention. "What's going on? I've heard lots about all the temple raids from the temple rats."

"That's not why I'm here," Theodoros said. "It's gotten far more serious. Several of the princes have broken their oaths and are supporting a Pretender."

"What!?"

"Several of your princes declared their support for this false prince."

"Not all of them! What about Prince Basilron—"

"Dead, his princedom forfeit."

"By all the gods, this is a disaster! Is Prince Carthames part of the conspiracy?" Lykron asked.

Theodoros dropped his eyes. "He was defeated in battle by the Pretender and his traitorous cohorts. He had no choice but to join their ranks."

"Yes, every man has a choice. Carthames just made the wrong one. I need to return to Bletha with the Royal Army. Or is it too late?"

Captain-General Theodoros shook his head.

"Good. Do we have any allies left?"

"Yes, Prince Phaedron is raising his levy to support Niclophon."

Lykron smiled. "Of course, he has always had my respect. What about Prince Kosklos?"

"In the enemy camp. What will you tell them, sir?"

"The truth is too dark. I will tell them that Bletha Town is under siege. That will get their attention."

"You will lie to the Grand Master! What will they say when they learn the truth?" Theodoros asked.

"Pshaw!" Lykron exclaimed. "By then the Grand Host will be a thousand marches away, too busy fighting the Hostigi to worry about anything I've said. My first duty is to my Great King and Commander, not Styphon's House. And don't you forget it.

"Wait here. I must address the Grand Master and Grand Captain-General Phidestros." He turned and marched to the dais.

## II

Grand Captain-General Phidestros gave only half an ear to what Grand Master Soton was saying. As the staff meeting broke up, a high-ranking officer wearing yellow and blue Blethan colors came into the room to confer with Captain-General Lykron, commander of the Hos-Bletha contingent. His main attention was on the young Blethan captain-general who accosted Lykron. A few moments later Lykron motioned for his attention. While it was hardly appropriate for a lower ranking officer to summon the commander of the Grand Host, Phidestros was curious and let the slight pass.

"Is there trouble, Captain-General Lykron?"

"Worse than you know, Grand Captain-General." He lowered his voice to a whisper. "There has been a revolt in Hos-Bletha. Bletha Town is under siege. Great King Niclophon has ordered me to return to Hos-Bletha at once!"

Phidestros first reaction was to cry "impossible," but he stilled his voice, and slowly took out his tobacco pouch to cover sudden silence.

There were less than twelve thousand regular Hos-Blethan troops under Lykron's command and, to tell the truth, they were over-armored and under-armed. They were certainly no match for Kalvan's regulars. In addition Lykron commanded a number of Sastragathi and Ruthani light cavalry companies that might be put to good use, especially if taken away from Blethan command and put under an officer who knew how to get some real use out of his auxiliaries.

"Captain-General Lykron, you know I have the authority to order you and your troops to remain with the Grand Host?"

"Yes, but—"

"No, I do not intend to force you to make such a choice. You have my permission to remove yourself and most of your men and return to Hos-Bletha."

Relief was openly visible on the Captain-General's face.

"I just have one request. I have need for some of your men."

The Captain-General's expression changed to that of a farmer about to make a deal with a shifty horse-trader.

"You are free to leave with all your regular troops, but I would like your light cavalry to stay with the Grand Host. I have something special in mind for them."

"You have my blessing, Captain-General Phidestros," Lykron said, looking visibly relieved. "I have many more back in Bletha. They are yours. Styphon be praised! I have preparations to make. May I leave now?"

"Of course, Lykron. You are dismissed."

Soton had drifted over to pick up the last part of the conversation. "Trouble in Hos-Bletha?"

"Yes, although this is one disaster that can't be laid at Kalvan's table. For too long, Great King Niclophon has more misruled, than ruled. Now it appears that even his long-suffering Blethans have grown weary of it."

"I owe him little good will," Soton said. "His weak hand has long made the Order's job of guarding the marches more difficult. But little good is to be gained by the loss of his troops from our Host."

"Maybe, maybe not. Do you have someone you trust who can speak both the Sastragathi and Ruthani tongues?"

Grand Master Soton nodded.

## III

In Balph, things were not so festive. Archpriest Anaxthenes presided over a very anxious Inner Circle. Everybody spoke about the events in Hos-Bletha and how it could affect Styphon's House's long-term plans and security.

"Every temple, priest and Temple Guardsman in this now divided Kingdom of Hos-Bletha has been razed, beheaded or slain in battle," announced Cimon unnecessarily. It was common knowledge. "Highpriest Sangar is advising us to stay away until the dust has settled there."

Anaxthenes struggled to recall just who Sangar was and failed. That was the problem with an organization as large as Styphon's House; too many people to keep track of. He did recall something about a Highpriest being sent to Hos-Bletha on an inspection tour or some such. Danthor had showed him the document a couple moons back.

"Sangar has the advantage of being in the middle of what is going on," Danthor said. "We have enough to deal with as it is. I say we wait and see if Great King Niclophon can regain his lost territories before we get involved. At worst, we can go in after the fighting is over and mop up the survivors."

"There is something to what Danthor says," Knight Commander Aristocles said. He had just arrived from Tarr-Ceros to act in absentia for Grand Master Soton, who had his hands full with the Grand Host of Styphon's House. "If we spread our forces too thin, we risk being overwhelmed. I counsel against fighting a war on too many fronts. As it stands we have yet to take down Kalvan and our recent forays into seizing the rest of the Five Kingdoms is draining us of fighting men. Let us pick a war and win it before moving on to the next."

Anaxthenes watched the Knight Commander warily. Of late he had acted more cautiously in military matters. It could be the toll of being second in command of the Order or he was losing faith in Styphon's House. Either way, he bore watching.

"I agree," Archpriest Neamenestros added. "Hos-Bletha is of minor concern to us just now. They are backward enough that when we have finished with Kalvan, we will have no trouble rolling over them."

Anaxthenes stifled his surprise. Even his staunchest ally in the Inner Circle was against taking action in Hos-Bletha. *He did not even wait for me to voice my opinion on the matter.*

Styphon's Voice weakly held up a hand and everybody became quiet. He had been brought in by four highpriests on a litter. "I agree," Sesklos said, his voice barely above a whisper. "We do not need to send Styphon's Own Guard or the Grand Host to address the ills of Hos-Bletha at this time. Instead, we will send cannon, arquebuses, fireseed and gold and hope Niclophon can extricate himself from the privy pit into which he has fallen. When we have finished our holy work with Kalvan, we will again look to the south and seize it as we will do in the rest of the Five Kingdoms."

## IV

The pair were in the loft of a farmer's barn, snuggling and squishing down as far as possible into the hay. The floor boards of the old loft groaned, but neither of the lovers heard nor cared.

Sitting up carefully, so that the parchment was beneath the light of a candle placed carefully on a nearby joist, he pointed to three choices sketched on the sheepskin map of southern Drathor. "Which do you like for my barony, my love?"

"Barony, zarony," the small woman said, tickling his ribs. "What do I know of such things? They are for men to decide. I just want to know... to know that I am...."

"That you are what?"

"That I...that I am the mighty Gycules' woman!" Tylla stopped the teasing and sat up suddenly with a deadly serious look on her face. She absently brushed pieces of straw from her bare skin as she studied Gycules' face.

Gycules rolled on his back, arms thrown wide, with a grand smile on his face. "I am to be a baron, and you already are Gycules' woman; for me that shall always be…"—he enjoyed seeing her face light up—"and that means you shall be a baroness!"

"Oh, no!"

"Oh, yes!" Gycules countered. "And you shall have gowns and jewels and servants, and my strong arms around you while I rely on your wisdom and kindly heart to rule as best we can."

"Oh, no...I mean, yes!" Tylla giggled, and tried to catch her breath. "Will your strong arms always be there?" she asked, barely whispering.

"As always as it is possible for a baron who has the trust of his lords," Gycules pledged.

Tylla stiffened for a moment. The memory of what had happened to Myklon was still fresh in her mind, and she asked, "Will you still be out fighting."

"As much as my king requires, Tylla," he said in a somber voice. Then he smiled. "But I will take great care not to leave you without a husband. I will keep vinegar and Ermut's Best with me at all times to wash my wounds and chase away the fester devils. In fact, all of my men will be ordered to do the same. I cannot promise to never die—no man can do that. But I will always fight to return to your side."

Tylla knew she had to accept his words if she wanted to be with the giant warrior. "And...and can we...this may sound so silly...but can we go before Uncle Wolf Syros, for our vows?" she asked.

"Of course. I was counting on it. 'Tis a pity Gasphros cannot assist in the ceremony, since he is returning to Mallegast. He gave a beautiful service at that wedding we raided. Ah, well. Just remember one thing—*I am not ticklish!*"

"Really? We'll see, My Lord," Tylla said, once again snuggling down against her mighty Gycules. "And no fooling around before the ceremony. I want to be able to walk straight when I go to give my vows."

*The End*

www.ingramcontent.com/pod-product-compliance
Lightning Source LLC
Chambersburg PA
CBHW070834020826
48982CB00019B/1099/J

* 9 7 8 0 9 3 7 9 1 2 6 3 8 *